Apache, My Son

Apache, My Son

by *George L. Walsh*

Deerfield Publishing
3626 E. Hiawatha Dr.
Okemos, MI 48864-4040
517-349-8676

Manufactured in the United States
First Printing
Printing and binding by Bookcrafters of Chelsea, MI
Cover design by Robert Brent of East Lansing, MI

Typesetting by Infinity Graphics of Okemos, MI

Acknowledgements

My deep and heartfelt thanks must go to Robert L. Fenton, entertainment lawyer and literary agent, who with great patience and understanding has guided and directed me on, around and through the perilous seas of the publishing business. This was my first journey through these waters that for me were uncharted, and his encouragement and assistance were essential to my survival.

A special thanks, too, goes to Kathy Mullins, Pamela Shores and Denise Quaderer for their typing skills, their word processors and their printers, without which there would have been no manuscript.

I am also indebted to those family members and friends who took the time to read portions of the manuscript and provide me with the comments and constructive criticism that helped me immensely. These kind people were Nola Deal, Kent Thibaudeau, Alan Sliker, Robert Dornbos, Penny Dornbos, Sara Kearsley, Marjorie Mitchell, Lois King and Betty Downs. In addition, I was the beneficiary of technical assistance provided by editorial consultant Boyd Miller, free-lance editor Janet Prescott and Dr. Harry C. George.

I am especially indebted to two people who also were kind enough to read portions of the manuscript and provide me with some much needed historical information. First, Mr. Dale C. Miles, tribal historian at the San Carlos Reservation, who spent a good deal of time with me describing Apache traditions and customs. In addition, he provided me with an excellent list of references for more detailed study. Second, Mrs. Lois Jordan of Straughn, Indiana, did the same for her Quaker heritage and also sent me a copy of the 1864 Discipline of the Society of Friends for the Indiana Yearly Meeting. I was astonished to find out that Lois's great, great uncle was Lawrie Tatum and, therefore, she was well acquainted with that family's history. It is indeed a small world that we live in.

During the late 1950s, I had the good fortune to meet and work with the Reverend Walter Price, who was then the executive director of the Berrien County, Michigan, Council of Churches. Walter's dedication to and enthusiasm for his ecumenical work, combined with an unfailing good humor, was contagious and inspiring to those who knew him, and I was no exception. A few years after we both left the area and went our separate ways, I lost track of the man. However, when I needed a name for the pastor of my fictional Cravenville Community Church, it could be none other than Walter

Price. Walter, wherever you are, I hope this brought a pleased smile to your lips.

And last but certainly not least, a big thank you goes to my wife, Patricia, for her help and encouragement throughout the whole process.

****

A historical novel must, by definition, refer to real people doing real things in real places. Although all of the actual people referred to in this novel passed away decades ago, I have researched their actions in specific locations as best I could and believe I have portrayed them accurately and honestly. What little dialogue I have assigned to these individuals represents my best guess as to what they might have said at that point in time or in the fictional settings I have created for them.

All of the other characters in this book are fictional – a product of my imagination. Any resemblance to specific individuals, living or dead, is purely coincidental, except for the Reverend Walter Price. Likewise, some of the communities mentioned and described in the book in relation to these fictional characters are also a figment of my imagination. I had no intention of misrepresenting any communities or individuals located in Idaho, Colorado, Arizona or Ohio. If I have done so, I wish, here and now, to apologize – openly and sincerely.

My only desire was to provide the reader with an exciting adventure story of the old west, based on historical fact.

Enjoy.

George L. Walsh
October 1997

Contents

THE MEN OF THE RAMBLING R

Raymond "Slim" Evers, Owner
Tex Riley, Foreman

Bronc Evans, Trig Mansfield, Curley Chance, Lefty White, Charley Landers, Kansas, Blackie Smith, Laredo Lee, Reno Lang, Red Rollins, Rusty Meyers, Cavalry, Reb Stuart, Denver Pike, Cheyenne Walters, Dusty Rhodes, Woody Meadows, Jud Ramsey, Ty Matthews, Cliff Reynolds, Sandy McAllister

Book 1
Tomad, Paul and Apache

To Robert D. Walsh, my little brother.

Prologue

In the early Spring of 1868, an Oglala Sioux war chief, Red Cloud, signed a peace treaty with a group of commissioners representing the United States Government, one of whom was General William Tecumseh Sherman. The ceremony took place at Fort Laramie in the Wyoming Territory, and the treaty ended a period of hostilities known as the Red Cloud War.

The trouble started several years earlier when immigrants, miners, and prospectors began using a road known as the Bozeman Trail as a short cut to the gold mining fields located near Virginia City in the southwest corner of the Montana Territory. While the trail did reduce the trip to the mines by several hundred miles, it also ran straight through Red Cloud's Teton domain. In June, 1866, Red Cloud and his followers rode into Fort Laramie to discuss the situation with government commissioners.

The commissioners hoped to negotiate a treaty whereby Red Cloud would allow the government to construct three forts along the trail to provide security for the travelers. In the midst of the discussions, however, Red Cloud was stunned to find out that a column of soldiers was already enroute to begin construction of the forts. Furious, he stormed out of the meeting and vowed that the trail would be soaked with blood.

Red Cloud kept his word. Even though the forts were constructed, they and their garrisons provided precious little protection for travelers. Indeed, the troops had great difficulty in venturing very far from their own walled protection and generally suffered casualties whenever they did so. Civilian casualties mounted even faster. The climax came on December 21, 1866, when Captain William Fetterman and a troop of 80 men galloped out of one of the forts, chased a Sioux decoy party for three miles, was ambushed, and annihilated.

The public outcry stemming from this debacle was loud and long. The Society of Friends, known as the Quakers, led the hue and cry and demanded an investigation. Other religious organizations and a large segment of the general public supported such a probe, and on February 18, 1867, President Andrew Johnson appointed the Sanborn Commission to look into the matter. By June of that year, the Commission issued a report stating the obvious—that the primary cause of the hostility was the military occupation of the Bozeman Trail, the building of the forts on Sioux land, and the deceitful manner in which all of this had occurred. It also recommended that the Army's warfare against the wronged Indians be terminated and a settlement be negotiated.

These negotiations were concluded with the signing of the treaty in the Spring of 1868: The forts were abandoned, and an uneasy peace was restored to the area. About a year later, however, General Sherman issued a general order to his military commanders in the west which unilaterally nullified all of the concessions that had been given to the Sioux and set the stage for the Great Sioux War. This conflict included the Battle of The Little Big Horn seven years later.

Nevertheless, the Sanborn Peace Commission had generated a public awareness about the Indian problem, and on April 10, 1869, Congress further strengthened the peace policy by authorizing the appointment of prominent and public-spirited citizens to a new Board of Indian Commissioners to advise and oversee the Indian bureau. This Board quickly recommended a new policy whereby local Indian agencies would be assigned to various Christian religious organizations and that these organizations be responsible for selecting honest agents from their own membership in order to foster the continuation of the peace process and, at the same time, begin a system of religious education for the inhabitants of the various reservations. This unusual policy was quickly approved, and the newly elected president, Ulysses S. Grant, enthusiastically supported the concept. Grant then contacted the Quakers, outlined the plan, and sought their support.

The Society of Friends immediately seized upon the opportunity, volunteered a number of its members for the agent positions, and labelled the idea a "Holy Experiment." One of the names they provided was that of Lawrie Tatum of Springdale, Iowa. In May, 1869, he was assigned the Fort Sill Reservation in the Oklahoma Territory, home for over 6,000 Indians, primarily Kiowas and Comanches.

This policy of pacification and containment was an immense undertaking. Later Tatum would write: "I was living on a farm in Iowa and knew nothing about being nominated for an Indian Agent until I saw my name in a newspaper with others who had been appointed Indian Agents and con-firmed by the Senate . . . . I knew little of the duties and responsibilities devolving upon an Indian Agent." Nevertheless, he accepted the assign-ment, left his Iowa home, and wended his way west to his agency. His family followed him to the reservation shortly thereafter.

Tatum's four year tenure as Indian Agent was a bittersweet experience. A man of high principles and with the utmost faith in his Quaker heritage, he was, at the same time, highly disciplined and stubborn. While these characteristics generated a certain amount of respect and admiration from his charges, the Indians never did acquire any real affection for the man.

On the one hand, he had remarkable success in negotiating the release of American and Mexican hostages captured by Indians who were under his supervision, 26 in all, over the four years. But the pacification program proved to be a dismal failure. Tatum soon found that he was receiving too little and too poor food for his charges. What meat he received was old and musty and made the Indians sick. Moreover, coffee and sugar—especially prized by the Indians—was soon stricken from the rations. In response, the Indians did what they naturally had to do—raid homes and ranches spread over a huge area, including Texas, to get the food they needed.

Tatum and his fellow Quakers also made a number of strategic errors. Primarily farmers themselves, they assumed the road to peace would best be accomplished by converting the Indians to their religious beliefs and to an agricultural economy. They never understood that the Indian male was a horseman, a hunter, and a warrior. Nomadic in nature, the Indian survived on meat, not vegetables. Farming, or a more apt description might be gar-dening, in his mind was women's work and below his dignity. Moreover, the pacifistic views of his supervisor were, for the most part, completely foreign to his heritage.

General Sherman's unilateral nullification of the concessions contained in the treaty of 1868 added an additional problem to the situation. Tatum was frequently forced to call on the military to respond to the Indian forays and civil disobedience and this, in turn, infuriated his Quaker superiors. They reminded Tatum that if he went among the Indians lovingly, sincerely, patiently, and trusting in the goodness and wisdom of God, the pacification process could not fail. Tatum did all that and more; and still the raids con-tinued, civilian casualties increased, and the military became even more involved, precisely what General Sherman had in mind all along.

Finally, frustrated and bitter, Tatum resigned on March 31, 1873, and he and his family returned to their Iowa home.

Chapter 1

Ruth Tatum was a vivacious and energetic young lady who grew into womanhood in her rural Iowa community. The skinny frame of a young girl was replaced by a slender, full-breasted figure of a teenager and topped by a mass of auburn hair. She was not beautiful, but her warm smile and unfailing energy attracted people to her. She was just pleasant to be around.

Ruth was also a Quaker, as were most of the neighbors who lived within a few miles of the Tatum home. She firmly believed in the pacifistic policies of her family and neighbors. At the same time she had a vivid imagination and an inquisitive mind. As she matured, she insisted on being a participant in theoretical discussions about her faith and frequently asked questions or made comments that both startled and amused her father. Noting her "show me" attitude, he once asked her if she thought she had been born in Missouri instead of Iowa.

Ruth was also a tomboy. She didn't neglect her domestic chores and responsibilities, of course, and soon was an excellent cook and seamstress. But whenever she could find the time, she loved to run deeply into the nearby woodlands, visit her animal friends, and enjoy the beauty of her God's creation—the great outdoors. She soon discovered that dresses and skirts were not designed for such activities. Her solution, therefore, was to "borrow" a pair of her brother's trousers whenever the opportunity presented itself. Reprimands and brotherly protests followed, of course, but she again found a solution by making herself a pair of deerskin leggings, much to the consternation of friends and family alike. Her father shook his head in resignation but smiled and said, "Ruth will be Ruth."

However, Ruth persisted in her tomboy ways and her father could restrain himself no longer. One afternoon, after Ruth returned from a two hour romp in her special world, her faced flushed with the excitement and the exercise inherent in the experience, Thomas Tatum motioned for her to follow him into the parlor. Closing the parlor doors, Tatum turned and looked at his offspring, a stern expression on his face.

"Daughter," he began, "Canst thee understand that thou art a woman, not a man? It is not becoming for thee to wear pants in public. It does not bring respect to our family and this household."

"But, father, I do not appear in public in my leggings," replied Ruth. "I go to the woodlands, almost a mile away. There I run and play and witness the beauty of God's handiwork—the trees, the flowers, and, best of all, the birds and the animals. They are my friends, we live on this land together, and I love them, just as I love thee, mother, and brother James.

"When I did this in the past," she continued. "My billowy dresses and skirts would always catch on vines, briars, and branches and would soon tear and rip. It seems like I was always mending them. My leggings allow me to move about without worrying about them. Is this wrong?"

"No, daughter," sighed Thomas. "That which thee has said is not wrong. But thy leggings are not proper attire for a young lady neither. Our neighbors have seen thee go and come from the woods."

"Let them look the other way!" cried Ruth with fervor. "Father, art thou telling me I *must* do as thou sayest?"

Tatum sighed again in resignation. "No, daughter, I have always tried to teach thee and James to think for thyselves. Thou knowest the teachings of the Friends. Thou art now old enough to assume the responsibility for and consequences of thy decisions. I cannot take that right from thee."

"Thank you, father!" exclaimed a pleased Ruth as she hugged her father and planted a kiss on his left cheek. "I will try to make thee proud of me."

Ruth was a good student, enjoyed going to school, and her favorite subject was history. She was particularly interested in learning about how the Society of Friends was so involved in trying to bring peace between the white man and the various Indian tribes in the western Great Plains of the United States. She devoured all of the written materials she could get her hands on regarding this involvement, and as she got a little older was fascinated by the stories about her Uncle Lawrie's participation in this peace effort.

Ruth felt almost like she had received a physical blow when she read about her uncle's apparent failure. She resolved to expand her knowledge about the various Indian tribes and the vast territory within which they lived. She decided she had found her life's work. She, too, would be a missionary, continue the Holy Experiment and bring peace, tranquility, and God's word to those people in that part of the world.

This resolve was strengthened when she unexpectedly had a chance to meet her Uncle Lawrie at a rare family reunion. For two hours she patiently waited for him to break loose from a crowd of family admirers. Finally, he did so, and she shyly approached him and introduced herself. He greeted her warmly and began to edge away. Quickly Ruth pleaded for a minute of his time and outlined her interest in his career as an Indian Agent. She requested his permission to ask one question. He smiled his agreement and waited expectantly.

"Uncle Lawrie," Ruth began, "As thee looks back on those events, what would thee have done differently had thee be given a second opportunity?"

The nature and depth of the question surprised him, and he pondered for several moments before answering.

"Ruth, the Indian people do not have the same hierarchy of authority and responsibility that the white society does. Therefore, before we try to convert them to our kind of culture, we must first educate them about what it is and how it works. That will take a long time. Our intentions were good, and the idea of a Holy Experiment is right, but we put the cart before the horse. Somehow we must find a way to educate these people first. Does that answer thy question?"

Ruth silently nodded in response, her mind working feverishly. Lawrie tipped his hat and headed for another group of family members.

This conversation confirmed a notion that Ruth's mind had been debating for some time. It was now quite obvious that the best way to accomplish her goal would be to function as a teacher. She loved being around children and decided that educating Indian young people in the beauty of peace, as well as the basic educational skills, would be a perfect response to her Uncle Lawrie's challenge. The only decision that now remained was how could she best prepare herself to attain this goal? The answer to this question was also quite obvious.

Therefore, after completing all of the educational experiences available to her in her small community, she decided to spend a year at William Penn College in Oskaloosa, Iowa. She worked on a nearby farm to support herself, studied long and hard, and was awarded the title of "Certified Teacher."

Prior to leaving for college, Ruth discussed her career aspirations with her family. Due to the very unusual nature of this vocational decision, the family, in turn, asked her to consult with the local congregation of Friends, or "Meeting" as it is called. A "Clearness Committee" was appointed by the meeting and this group had a number of discussions with her. They talked with Ruth, asked her questions, heard her responses, and prayed with her to make sure her call (leading) was from God and not a whim or misguided notion. These sessions, however, served to increase the clearness of purpose in Ruth's mind, and when she left for William Penn, she carried a letter of recommendation from her local meeting to the Iowa Yearly Meeting, whose center was also in Oskaloosa.

During her year at William Penn, Ruth was also interviewed several times by Representatives of the Iowa Yearly Meeting. These interviews followed the same format as had her local sessions. Again she impressed everyone with her dedication, enthusiasm, and desire, and as before, she received a letter of recommendation from this group.

As soon as she returned home from college, Ruth wrote to the Executive Committee on Indian Affairs, a special missionary arm created by a combination of several State Yearly Meetings, including Iowa. She outlined her goals and educational background, asked for a missionary assignment somewhere in the west, and included her two letters of recommendation. Impatiently she waited for a reply, but several months went by before the long awaited letter finally came. She was disappointed to learn that the Executive Committee had no place to send her at that time. However, they did know that an Indian Agent had need of a teacher at the Apache San Carlos Agency in the Arizona Territory. Although the committee indicated it was reluctant to inform her about this position, since there were no Friends in the immediate area to support her, Ruth was eager to pursue the matter further. A number of letters were exchanged, arrangements were finally made, and in the Summer of 1881, Ruth arrived at San Carlos. Agent J.C. Tiffany welcomed her with open arms.

****

The San Carlos Reservation was authorized in late 1872 and became operational in early 1873. It stretched 100 miles north to south and 70 east to west. It covered a total of 7,000 square miles, well over two million acres of land, and was larger than the State of Rhode Island. While the San Carlos, Black, Salt, and Gila Rivers provided an adequate water supply for some portions of the reservation and the Pinal and White Mountain Ranges provided some high country, the reservation had vast expanses of arid desert. Living conditions on the reservation, as a result, were extremely primitive.

As soon as the Apache Nation heard about the reservation, a number of hardy souls drifted in, surrendered their weapons, and tried to establish a living environment. One of the first to arrive was Eskiminzin and about 400 of his Arivaipa Apaches. The Arivaipa was the most peaceful and pacifistic tribe within the Apache Nation, and therefore, it was logical that it would be the first group to try this new way of life. Small bands from some of the other Apache tribes—Coyoteros, Pinals, Yumas, Tontos, and Chiricahuas—followed the Arivaipas example and by the Summer of 1873, about 700 Apaches were living on the reservation.

Unfortunately, the Bureau of Indian Affairs had not given adequate thought to the organization and administration of the reservation, and trouble began almost immediately. The Apaches were baffled by inconsistent policies. Acting Agents came and went, four within the first 18 months. Rules were either non-existent or were not enforced. Worse than that, there was no control over the use of alcoholic beverages, primarily "tizwin," which the Apaches produced themselves.

In January, 1874, four Chiricahuas got high on tizwin, went on a rampage, and killed two white men. All of the other Apaches, fearing a reprisal from the Army, promptly abandoned San Carlos and scattered to the four winds. But, with no weapons and little food, they soon began to trickle back to the reservation, fearing the worst. In April, 1874, the last of the escapees, including Eskiminzin, returned. Furious over the incident, the Army decided to make an example out of Eskiminzin and his Arivaipas. Eskiminzin and five sub-chiefs were arrested, put in chains, shipped to New Camp Grant, about 80 miles away, and were forced to work as a chain-gang making adobe bricks, all without benefit of a hearing or a trial. Further migration of Apaches onto the reservation ceased immediately. Troops of cavalry were stationed on the reservation, and it became, in effect, a prisoner of war camp.

The Bureau of Indian Affairs received a good deal of criticism over the San Carlos debacle and desperately tried to find a remedy to the situation. A possible solution came to them in a most unusual way and in the form of a most unusual young man.

✳✳✳✳✳✳✳✳✳✳✳✳

John Philip Clum was born on September 1, 1851, and grew up in the Hudson Valley, in upstate New York. He was of Holland-Dutch ancestry and was one of nine children. At the age of 16, he entered the Hudson River Institute at Claverack and spent two years as a military cadet. At the age of 18, in 1869, he entered Rutgers College, intending to spend four years at that institution. The lack of financial support from his family made it mandatory that he work on a near-by farm to pay for his education. Two years later, he was forced to leave Rutgers following a long sickness. The illness prevented him from attending classes, and at the same time he was unable to work to provide the necessary finances to continue his education.

In 1871, Clum saw a story in a newspaper that indicated that the War Department was organizing a meteorological service throughout the United States and was seeking applicants for this effort. Clum promptly traveled to Washington, D.C., applied for a job, took and passed the necessary examinations, was assigned to the United States Signal Corps., and was sent to Santa Fe, in the New Mexico Territory, to begin his new career.

For two years Clum performed his meteorological duties well. In addition, he joined the local social structure and enjoyed the relationship immensely. One of the few white men in the territory, Clum was also appointed to function as the Acting Governor of the Territory for a brief time. In November, 1873, Clum was astonished to receive a letter from the Bureau of Indian Affairs asking him to be their Agent at the San Carlos Reservation in Arizona. Intrigued by the proposal, Clum returned to Washington to ascertain what the position involved and how he been selected for it.

When President Grant had approached the Quakers in 1868, he had contacted other religious denominations with the same proposal. The Dutch Reformed Church had responded to this call in a manner similar to that of the Friends. For some reason, this church was assigned the San Carlos Reservation as its sphere of responsibility, and in 1873 one of Clum's classmates at Rutgers, responding to the need for an appropriate Agent, submitted John's name to the Bureau of Indian Affairs. He did so primarily because Clum was already in that area, at Santa Fe. When Clum discerned these facts, his interest in the position increased dramatically. He remained in the nation's capital for almost three months, asking questions and reading reports on the conditions at San Carlos and the events that had already taken place there. On February 27, 1874, John P. Clum was appointed as Indian Agent at San Carlos. Thus began a four year period that would include some of the most unusual events that ever would be recorded in the annals of the Bureau of Indian Affairs.

As Clum studied the various historical documents prior to his appointment, he came to the conclusion that the basic problem was not the Apaches but, instead, was the two-faced policies of his own government. The Bureau of Indian Affairs, on the one hand, had assumed that its job was to protect and pacify the Apaches and had functioned on that basis. The War Department, on the other hand, had decided that its job was to exterminate the Apaches and all other Indians as well. It was obvious to Clum that these two philosophies were incompatible, and, therefore, he made two demands as conditions for accepting his appointment. First, since the Bureau of Indian Affairs had the responsibility for the care of the Apaches, he, as the representative of that Bureau, must, at the same time, have *all* of the related authority, and not share this authority with the military. Secondly, he must receive the full and complete support from the Bureau of Indian Affairs in the use of that authority in carrying out his responsibilities. One can only imagine what the initial response was to these demands, especially since they came from a 22 year old.

Evidently the situation at San Carlos had deteriorated to the point where it was well beyond what Washington could tolerate. Clum's demands were eventually agreed to, and his appointment was confirmed.

Clum tarried in Washington for another month and continued his research about San Carlos. In late March or early April, he began an arduous four month journey to his new assignment. Starting in Washington, Clum traveled by train to St. Louis and then San Francisco, by steamer to San Diego, and used a stagecoach for the 500 miles to Tucson. The final 200 exhausting miles to San Carlos were covered with a freight wagon. He had lots of time to read and think during this trip and arrived at one unshakable conclusion that became the foundation for all his subsequent decisions and actions. The conclusion was simple: He would treat the Apaches as human beings, and he would give them a square deal. Simple, yes. Commonplace, no.

The freight wagon portion of his long journey involved a stopover at New Camp Grant, and Clum's attention was immediately drawn to a group of chained Indians. He insisted on talking to these men, secured the services of an interpreter, and the first Apache he spoke to was Eskiminzin. The chief, using his native tongue as well as broken English, described what had taken place and, the more he listened to Eskiminzin, the more angry Clum became.

As soon as he arrived at San Carlos, on August 1, 1874, Clum fired off a letter to his superiors in Washington, reminded them of the two conditions of his appointment, and demanded the release of Eskiminzin and his companions.

The tone of the letter must have shocked a few Washingtonians, but in October Clum's demand was met. Eskiminzin and his companions were released and returned to San Carlos. Clum's initial official act had produced an extraordinary result. First, he showed everyone, especially the Apaches, that someone was really in charge of the reservation. At the same time, Eskiminzin became his life-long friend and the staunch supporter of Clum's dealings with the entire Apache Nation.

Clum immediately embarked on a whirlwind of activities and organizational moves, using Eskiminzin as his advisor. Four Arivaipa braves were appointed as policemen. A court system was established with Apache chiefs acting as judges. A guardhouse was built and functioned as a jail and the living quarters for the policemen. The use and sale of intoxicants, including the Apache moonshine, was banned, and the police force actively enforced this rule. All residents of the reservation, save the policemen, were disarmed. If an Apache wanted to hunt, he was supplied with a pass covering a specific period of time, a rifle, and a sufficient amount of ammunition. Upon his return, he surrendered his rifle and unused ammunition. Clum also insisted that the Apaches keep their living quarters and villages clean and, surprisingly, the Apache's complied with this demand.

The results from all this were astonishing.

The court system worked extremely well. Under Clum's system, all Apache offenders were arrested by Apache police, were brought before an Apache court, with Apaches as witnesses, and, if convicted, were sentenced by Apache Judges. Finally they were delivered into the custody of Apache guards.

The whole concept was a novel proposition to these simple red men, but it appealed to them strongly. They soon realized that they were now a part of a system of self-determination, of self-government. Furthermore, they now knew, from a legal standpoint, what was being done, and, more importantly, why. By taking the Apaches into his confidence, Clum, in turn, secured their confidence and loyalty.

Clum's insistence on cleanliness also paid dividends. Sanitation improved significantly, the frequency and duration of sickness declined, and the birth rate began to improve.

Clum also began a building program. He used Apache labor, organized a six day work week, and paid his workers in scrip, which they could exchange for goods. Within a year, in addition to the guardhouse, the reservation had a main agency building, living quarters for the Agent and his staff, office, dispensary and small hospital, dining room, kitchen, storeroom, corrals, blacksmith and carpenter shops, tool rooms, and a wagon shed.

In subsequent years, the Apaches, with Clum's encouragement, developed an interest in agriculture and ranching. They constructed huge irrigation ditches, using picks, shovels, and their bare hands. Clum purchased herds of sheep, goats, and burros, as well.

It was unbelievable. Here, the members of one of the fiercest and most feared fighting societies in the west were learning how to be farmers and ranchers as well as the art of self governing, all at the same time. Clum, a non-Quaker, was, in fact, implementing the Holy Experiment concept.

Clum's reputation for understanding and fairness began to spread to many parts of the Apache Nation. In December, 1874, 1,400 Rio Verde Apaches arrived at San Carlos, and in January, 1875, 1,800 Coyoteros came in. Suddenly Clum had more than 4,000 Apaches under his supervision.

Eskiminzin and his Arivaipas now became invaluable as they assumed a public relations role. They circulated among the newcomers, explained to them the rules and system of this new government, and persuaded them to give up their weapons and trust their Agent. Clum promptly responded by adding a proportional number of these new residents to his police force and to the court system.

The success of Clum's efforts can best be judged by the fact that in October, 1875, all the cavalry troops were ordered away from San Carlos, and for the first time the reservation was completely supervised and controlled by a civilian and his native government.

For the Apaches, this was the dawn of a new era. They had acquired a better understanding of their own responsibilities. They were truly now self-governing and had the responsibility for maintaining order and enforcing discipline on their reservation. The Apaches were quick to appreciate the advantages of this change in their lives and the administration of their affairs. They also knew that Clum had been their champion, and, at this point in time, were fully prepared to fight alongside their white Agent and for him. This loyalty would soon be tested to the extreme.

Clum was now at the zenith of his popularity and influence. Even the Territorial Governor, Safford, had become John's friend and supporter. But, events began to take place which would result in Clum reaching the epitome of success, and also would produce his downfall.

In April, 1876, a group of Chiricahau Apaches, led by Geronimo, went on a rampage in southern Arizona. The residents of Arizona were fearful that the Apaches at San Carlos would join their brethren in an all-out war. Clum consulted with his Apache chiefs and was both pleased and surprised at their response. Eskiminzin and the other chiefs not only pledged to remain peaceful but offered to supply 500 men *to find and fight Geronimo*! This offer was relayed to Safford, who turned it down. However, two months later, when the United States Cavalry was unable to catch up with Geronimo, Safford reversed himself and asked Clum for help.

Clum's Apaches knew where Geronimo probably was hiding. Clum selected a force of 100 Arivaipa and Coyotero policemen and made a forced march, on foot, of 400 miles, all the way into the New Mexico Territory.

Unerringly, his Apaches located Geronimo and his renegades. Clum and his policemen, using a ploy, not only captured Geronimo but did so without blood being shed.

Clum had barely finished the task of putting Geronimo and six of his sub-chiefs in chains when another war chief, Victorio, and almost 400 additional renegades galloped into the camp. Clum faced a crisis of immense propor-tions but decided to try a bluff. Clum showed Victorio the shackled Geronimo and told him that this was what happened to bad Apaches! A stunned Victorio instantly surrendered, and his men threw down their weapons.

The next day, three troops of United States Cavalry arrived on the scene, just in time to see a long column of almost 500 docile Apaches begin their 400 mile trek to San Carlos, Geronimo in chains, and escorted by John Clum and his 100 policemen. The astonished cavalrymen could not believe their eyes!

Clum intended to turn his prisoners over to the civil authorities in Tuc-son. He assumed that Geronimo would be found guilty of murder and ex-ecuted. His Apaches agreed with Clum's plan, but, to everyone's dismay, the military insisted on taking control of the prisoners as soon as the column reached the San Carlos Reservation. Clum reluctantly agreed, primarily to avoid a confrontation with the Army. He was even more disturbed when the Bureau of Indian Affairs supported the Army, but the crowning blow came when the civil court only gave Geronimo a slap on the wrist and paroled the contrite war chief back to the San Carlos Reservation, where he could recu-perate and plan his next escapade. Even worse, from Clum's point of view, cavalry troops were again stationed on his reservation.

A furious Clum fired off a telegram to Commissioner Smith of the Bu-reau of Indian Affairs. Clum demanded that the troops be withdrawn from the reservation, that his salary be increased (he had not received a raise since his arrival), and that he be authorized to add two more companies to his Apache police force. In return, Clum would assume responsibility for supervising and controlling the *entire Apache Nation*. Shortly thereafter, Clum also warned his superiors that the failure to execute Geronimo would prove to be bloody and costly.

Commissioner Smith rejected Clum's demands, released his letter to the press, and publicly criticized his employee. The media followed his lead and described Clum as being arrogant, brassy, and impudent. An angry John P. Clum resigned on July 31, 1877, and left his beloved reservation, much to the consternation of his Apache friends.

The legacy Clum left behind was monumental. No renegade Indians ever found a haven at San Carlos. No Indians had left his reservation to raid and kill. No stolen stock was brought in to his reservation. The use of intoxicating beverages had been effectively prohibited. Clum's court system had worked exceedingly well. Victorio, himself, became a judge and was soon known for his fair and wise decisions. Most importantly, the Apaches had gained a new outlook on life; they had found a place, a plan, and a protector, which permitted them to live as human beings, unhunted and unafraid.

Unfortunately, Clum's successors were unable to use this legacy effectively. Agents and Acting Agents came and went with disturbing frequency. Graft and corruption began to creep into the day-to-day administration of the reservation, and the Apaches, of course, became the innocent victims of these practices. In addition, these Agents and Acting Agents were afraid to challenge their superiors or the military, given Clum's fate, and they did not have his vision, his personality, nor the trust he had won from his Apaches. Geronimo would escape and go on the warpath many more times, just as Clum had predicted, and death and destruction would follow him. Even Victorio, disgusted with the turn of events at San Carlos, would ultimately give up his judgeship and return to the warpath. It would be 10 more years before the bloody fighting would finally cease.

John P. Clum left San Carlos, but he did not leave Arizona. He bought "The Arizona Citizen" newspaper and continued to fight for his Apaches, using an editor's pen. He then moved to Tombstone, started "The Tombstone Epitaph" and became that city's first mayor. But, most of all, he was a living example of how the Holy Experiment was intended to function.

****

Turango was a member of the Arivaipa band of the Apache Nation. He had acquired an undying love of the great outdoors and enjoyed the frequent moves of his family and band since those moves gave him an opportunity to see new country at every stop. As he got older, he accompanied his father in forays against the white man in Arizona and the Mexicans across the border. His role was that of an errand boy, horse holder, food and firewood gatherer, and any other odd jobs his father found for him to do.

The death of his father while on a raid, when Turango was only 14, had a profound effect on the boy. Instead of the usual fiery demand for retribution and revenge, however, Turango felt only a sense of hopelessness at this sudden termination of his father's life. He had been vaguely aware that such a tragic event could happen, of course, but once it had taken place, Turango thought it was such a waste of a good life. He could not shake the belief that war did not produce a desirable outcome, save survival, for either side. He was surprised to learn that other Arivaipas shared his view. Although small in number, these men believed that fighting the white man was a useless and forlorn process, doomed to failure. Furthermore, this group believed that the real answer was to learn the white man's ways and, thereby, learn to live in the white man's world. They called themselves the Apache equivalent of "Moderates" or "Progressives" but other Apaches had more derisive names for them. Nevertheless, Turango gravitated toward this group and eventually became one of its leading spokesmen.

Other events helped Turango and his friends attain some credibility with their peers. General Crook conducted a vicious and brilliant campaign between November, 1872, and March, 1873, and as a result, a number of demoralized and stunned Apaches soon began to arrive at the newly established reservation at San Carlos. Included in the early arrivals was Eskiminzin and his 400 Arivaipa followers. However, Turango's group did not follow Eskiminzin's example, and when they learned about Eskiminzin's imprisonment, they were pleased they had not done so. However, when the Rio Verde and Coyotero Apaches also moved onto the reservation, the views expressed by Turango and his small group of moderates were suddenly more acceptable to the others.

In 1877, John P. Clum further shocked the Apache Nation by capturing Geronimo with his Apache Police Force and sending the chief to San Carlos in chains. However, Geronimo's escape in 1878 to Mexico raised the morale of the rest of the Apache Nation, and when word got out that Clum was no longer the Agent at San Carlos, few additional Apaches chose to surrender and go there. However, these Apaches also realized that the white soldiers had become more numerous than ever and at the same time there were fewer and fewer Apache braves to continue the fight.

Turango and his fellow moderates remained steadfast in their belief that continuing the war was useless but at the same time they insisted on retaining their nomadic life style and refused to surrender. They didn't want to fight, but they also wanted to keep their way of life as long as possible, especially after hearing about Clum's departure from San Carlos.

Fortunately for Turango, he had a special friend during this time. Mourning Dove and he had grown up together, shared each other's secrets, and she had become the love of his life. At first a gangly and awkward girl, she had grown into a slender, lithe young woman with sparkling dark eyes and long, shiny black hair. Best of all she shared his beliefs and supported him with her love. In 1876 Turango began his courtship in earnest. This effort was primarily directed toward Mourning Dove's father, as was Apache custom. He was successful, in that he was able to win Mourning Dove's hand at a bargain price. In 1877 she became his wife and, in 1878 a son was born. But their joy was short-lived. Mourning Dove had hemorrhaged profusely during the birth, her strength ebbed quickly, and she died with her head in Turango's lap. Turango was crushed. His world was shattered! Had his God, Usen, deserted him? But wait, there was the boy! His boy would live. His name will be Tomad, and he will grow up to be a credit to his Apache heritage. And, more than anything else, Tomad will not die fighting the white man. This would be Turango's promise to the memory of Mourning Dove and the faith they had shared.

In the meantime, the war between the white man and groups of Apaches continued unabated. However, by 1880 two great war chiefs, Cochise and Victorio, had been killed and Geronimo dutifully returned to San Carlos. The end of the Apache Nation as an independent society was now in sight. The White Mountain Apaches would go on the warpath in 1881, and Geronimo would again escape and cause trouble in both 1881 and 1882. But in 1883, General Crook would return, conduct another brilliant campaign, aided by the White Mountain Apaches, and the war would now be virtually over. In August, 1883, Turango and five-year-old Tomad arrived at the San Carlos Reservation and sought refuge there.

Chapter 2

Two years had passed quickly for Ruth Tatum. The first school year had been extremely difficult. In addition to adjusting to a new and primitive way of life, she had been forced to use an interpreter to do her teaching. She was frustrated with this arrangement for two reasons: First, it displayed her own weakness, and, second, it wasted too much time. The solution was obvious. With the help of her interpreter and other Apaches, she spent an exhausting Summer in an intensive effort to learn as much of the native language as she could. At the end of this time she was proficient enough to be able to do her teaching in Apache, even though she could not converse fluently. As the second school year progressed, however, she continued her private study, but less intensively. Nevertheless, her conversational skills improved markedly and, by the end of her second year of teaching, she was very comfortable with her ability in this regard.

In addition, Ruth had also used these two years to research the history of the San Carlos Reservation and, in so doing, had learned about Clum's success in pacifying the Apaches under his supervision. This knowledge reinforced her belief that the Holy Experiment concept was a valid one and made Ruth all the more determined to do her part in helping to make this concept become a reality.

****

Strangely enough, it was one of Turango's former detractors who informed a new Agent, Charles D. Ford, about Turango's pacifistic views and his desire to learn how to live in the white man's world. Ford immediately seized on this information, sought out Turango, and was pleased with the man's philosophy and attitude. An appropriate arrangement was quickly agreed to. Ford and his white assistants would teach Turango the basic skills of carpentry, masonry, and farming. In return, Turango would attend a tutorial program supervised by Ruth Tatum. Turango would use most of each day learning his vocational skills but would also spend the late afternoons and/ or early evenings in Ruth's classroom learning the three R's.

At first Ruth was not especially pleased with this additional workload, but Turango's work ethic and his rapid progress impressed her greatly, and she was soon totally immersed in the program. It was obvious that Turango had above average intelligence, and soon they began to have conversations, first in Apache, and later in English, that were very stimulating to her. The fact that his pacifistic views were so close to her own amazed her, and her respect for the man deepened.

Little Tomad apparently had inherited his father's intelligence, for he, too, took to his schooling with dedication and enthusiasm. Eventually she and Turango would include Tomad in some very elementary discussions, much to the delight of all three participants.

Thus, the third year of Ruth's teaching career became an especially satisfying one. She knew she had become a better teacher to the Apache children in general, and her special sessions with Turango had become extremely refreshing. As her fourth year of teaching progressed, Ruth knew what was beginning to happen and, try as she might, she could not block it out of her mind.

Turango, too, knew what was taking place. The intense feelings he had for Mourning Dove had returned, much to his surprise and with some consternation. He, too, fought these feelings for a number of months, but the respect and admiration he had for Ruth deepened with each passing day. Finally he could contain himself no longer.

One night he raised the concept of courtship and romance with Ruth and explained that this was a part of the white man's culture he felt he should know about. Ruth blushed, instinctively knowing what was on his mind, but explained the whole process in great detail. Turango listened intently and asked several questions. The concept of an equal partnership puzzled him greatly, and it took a great deal of discussion before he seemed to understand it completely. Ruth decided to test both his understanding and his intentions with an example. "Turango," she murmured, "let us assume that you and I wanted to get married. Because we come from different cultures, each of us might have to make concessions or sacrifices for the good of our partnership. For example, I might have to insist that you and Tomad take Christian first names so that you would both be part of my faith. At the same time, however, I might have to accept an Indian last name out of respect for your heritage. Both of us would sacrifice something old, and both of us would acquire something new as evidence of our love for each other. Do you understand what I am saying?"

Turango hesitated for several moments, continued to look deeply into Ruth's eyes, and slowly nodded his head yes. He grasped Ruth's hands and rose to his feet, pulling Ruth up with him. He learned forward and gently pressed his lips against hers. Ruth did not resist and squeezed his hand in response. Turango pulled back, and Ruth thought she saw a twinkle in his jet black eyes.

"I must speak with Tomad about this," he said simply, as he released her hands. "He must be part of any decision that we make."

"Yes, by all means," Ruth agreed. "His feelings must be considered."

Two days later Turango received permission from Agent Ford to be excused from his work assignments, and neither father nor son attended school that day. Ruth was somewhat fearful until she was told that the two had gone on an all day outing in the desert. It was almost dusk when they returned. After the evening meal, they located Ruth and suggested that they go to the schoolhouse.

It was an amusing scene. Ruth sat behind her desk while Turango and Tomad occupied small, first row chairs directly in front of the desk.

"Tomad and I have spent the day together," Turango informed Ruth with a very solemn look on his face. "I have told Tomad what we talked about, and we agree that all should sacrifice toward a common good. Tomad has never known the love a mother can give. I have tried to be both father and mother to him, but that is not possible. I know I have failed him."

Turango and Tomad rose from their chairs, Tomad's left hand was held in Turango's right hand. "If you are willing, we can become one family."

Ruth stood up and swept around her desk, tears in her eyes. She put her arms tightly around both Turango and Tomad and pulled the three of them closely together. She exchanged a kiss with Turango and then bent down to hug and kiss Tomad. Brushing back her tears, she gave Tomad a stern look that was hard to maintain. "This will not give you special privileges with the teacher during school hours, young man." But, as a big smile spread across her face, she continued, "You might get some extra help with your homework! I'll do all I can to be a good mother to you, Tomad, and a good wife to you, Turango. Come, let us tell Mr. Ford our wonderful news!"

****

As soon as Ruth agreed to marry Turango, she knew she had violated the marriage tenets contained in the Quakers Discipline. First, she had not followed the notification, review, and certification process prescribed in the Discipline. Secondly, and even more importantly, she was marrying outside the society of Friends. While this practice was not specifically prohibited by the Discipline, it was definitely frowned upon and at a minimum required a far more intensive notification, review, and certification process. But Ruth was not only marrying outside her society; she was also marrying outside her race. Ruth decided, therefore, that adhering to the Friends tenets would be virtually impossible, given the geographical problems, and almost surely an exercise in futility, given the racial situation.

Nevertheless, Ruth knew she had to notify her family about this development. She composed a long letter outlining what had happened, how it had happened, and why she had made this momentous decision. She concluded her letter by pointing out that she felt this was a logical and appropriate outcome from the Holy Experiment concept and invited her family to witness the marriage.

Six weeks later she received the reply. Her father described his shock and disappointment, outlined the tenets of Discipline she had seemingly scorned, and, as Ruth had expected, respectfully declined to allow any family members to attend the event. However, he ended the letter with words that made Ruth smile through her tears.

"Ruth," he wrote, "I have known for a long time that you have marched to a different drummer than the rest of us. Therefore, this decision probably should not have surprised me. But you are of age, and you have a good head on your shoulders. I assume you have thought this through very carefully and prayerfully and that this is what you want to do. Please be assured that my love for you, and that of the whole family, is steadfast and unyielding. Your happiness and good health will always be in our prayers, and you will always be welcome in our home. May God be with you!"

❉❉❉❉❉❉❉❉❉❉❉❉

Turango and Ruth were married on August 1, 1885, almost two years to the day of his arrival at San Carlos. The event took place in the schoolhouse, and by mid-morning the room was filled. Ruth was pleased to see that most of her school children and their parents were present. In the front row, as honored guests, were Agent Ford and Eskiminzin, head chief of the Arivaipa Apaches.

Ruth had given a great deal of thought to how the marriage ceremony should take place and had discussed it with Turango. She was pleased to find out that the usual Apache ritual was carried out using much of the same simplicity that was inherent in Quaker marriages. Therefore, it was relatively easy to make it a joint ceremony, and she made her preparations on that basis.

At the appointed hour Ruth, Turango, and Tomad stood facing their audience, and Ruth began to recite what she had prepared, uttering each sentence first in English and repeating it in Apache.

"Today Turango, Tomad, and I stand before you and want to tell you about our desire to become one family. Four years ago I came here as a representative of my faith and my God to teach your children the white man's language, the white man's numbers, and how to live in the white man's world. At the same time I have learned your language and have acquired a deep affection for the Apache Nation and the heritage that Turango and Tomad have taught me.

"I hope I have shown you that my God loves all people, red man and white man alike, and that he wants all of us to live together in peace and harmony.

"Today, it is our desire and goal to show you, and all others, that it is possible for two people, one red and one white, to join together and become a symbol of that peace and harmony. It is our wish that Tomad, and any other children that may follow, will see the beauty of this union and the glory of God's love that we share.

"Turango, Tomad, and I realize that we are trying to create something new. To do this we believe each of us, at the same time, must give up something old as a way of showing our love for each other. Turango has agreed to accept the name Jacob, and Tomad has agreed to accept the name Paul, out of respect for my faith. I have agreed to accept the family name of Redstone to show my respect for Turango's and Tomad's Apache heritage. We will now make our pledge, one to another."

Turango and Ruth now joined hands and faced one another with Tomad between them. Turango spoke first as Tomad looked up at him.

"Before God and this assembly, I, Jacob, take Ruth as my wife and, with divine assistance, promise to be a loving and faithful husband for as long as we both shall live."

Tomad turned and gazed up at Ruth.

"Before God and this assembly, I, Ruth, take Jacob as my husband and, with divine assistance, promise to be a loving and faithful wife for as long as we both shall live."

Tomad made a half turn and faced the audience as did Jacob and Ruth.

"I, Paul, take Jacob and Ruth as my father and mother and promise to love them and to honor them for as long as they both shall live."

"Will Agent Ford and Eskiminzin please now join us?" asked Ruth. The two men quickly responded. The five people formed a circle with Paul at the top and Ruth, Eskiminzin, Ford, and Jacob following, in clockwise order. The five completed the circle by clasping hands as Ruth spoke again to the audience.

"Would each of you bow your heads, or raise your eyes toward the heavens, whichever you wish, and silently ask your God to bless this marriage and give us a life together full of love and happiness."

A minute later Jacob and Ruth said a loud "Amen," and the ceremony was over.

The Holy Experiment now had taken on a new and very different perspective.

****

Jacob had prepared for his marriage to Ruth by building them a two room adobe cottage. While Jacob made a few pieces of furniture, Ford and his associates were able to obtain a number of second hand items from the nearby community of San Carlos, including a dresser, a few chairs, and an army cot for Paul. Ruth's bed, of course, was already available.

The big room, shaped like an L, contained a small fireplace and was their living quarters, although the very top of the L was reserved for Paul's cot. A few pegs, inserted into the back wall, were available for Paul to hang his clothes. The upper right quarter of the building was Jacob's and Ruth's bedroom and contained the only dresser. The cottage was snug but cozy, warm in Winter and cool in Summer, and Ruth was pleased with what they had. Ford and his staff collaborated on preparing community meals, so there was little need for each adobe to have cooking facilities.

Ruth, at the same time, had prepared for the wedding by making herself a new cotton dress. Quaker custom did not dictate the use of special wedding attire, and she needed the dress for her teaching duties anyway.

Soon after they occupied their new quarters, Jacob and Ruth had a strategy conference.

"Ruth, I agree that Paul and I must learn as much as we can about the white man's way of life so that we may become part of it," Jacob began. "But it is equally important for Paul to retain as much of his Apache heritage as possible, particularly in the art of survival in the desert. He is seven years old now, and I must do with him what my father did with me. His ability to exist in this land could very well mean the difference between life and death for him and even for you and me."

Jacob went on to describe briefly what would be involved, and Ruth had to catch her breath. Yes, there would be some danger as time went on, but Jacob could, and would, minimize the risk as much as possible. But complete safety could not be guaranteed. "You must trust me," concluded Jacob.

Reluctantly, and not without a pang of fear, Ruth acquiesced, and Paul's training began immediately. For the first several months it consisted of walks in the desert, short at first but more extended as time went on. Every kind of vegetation was identified, described, and categorized as being edible or not. All of the desert animals were covered in the same manner. Lastly, every possible and probable location for water or substitute liquids was ascertained and described geographically. Paul was quizzed repeatedly in all of these matters.

Now Paul was ready for phase two of his training. It was a huge and potentially deadly game of hide and seek. At first he was shown how to make and follow a trail, using physical clues. Jacob then began to test Paul's knowledge and skill by stationing him in one location and then walking out into the desert. After a specified time interval, Jacob would suddenly drop from sight, and Paul's job was to find him. The intervals were short at first, usually only a few minutes, but were slowly extended—to 10 minutes, 20 minutes, 30 minutes and so on. Finally, after more than a year of such exercises, it was time for a major test. Jacob left Paul for a full hour before the game could begin. This was the dangerous part, since Jacob had to leave a variety of clues in his wake and could not keep Paul in sight while he was doing so. The first test went reasonably well, although Paul did make a few mistakes. The game, therefore, was repeated several more times.

Paul improved his skills rapidly, and Jacob's eyes glowed with pride. The ultimate test came when the two of them played a massive series of games just prior to Paul's tenth birthday. The exercise was extended over three days and two nights and included a period of 24 hours when Paul did not have access to a ready supply of water. Paul passed this grueling and very dangerous trial with flying colors, much to Ruth's relief and with extreme satisfaction for Jacob. Best of all, this training had been so intense and had covered such a long period of time that the bonding between father and son had progressed to a point where it was better than anything Jacob had experienced with his own father and significantly better than most Apache boys would ever experience. Jacob was extremely proud and happy, and Ruth was pleased to be a part of this beautiful and satisfying relationship.

Soon after this extraordinary experience, Agent Ford asked Jacob and Ruth to meet with him. He greeted both of them warmly and waved to a couple of nearby chairs. "Please sit down," he said. "I have some news for you."

"More'n a year ago," he continued, "you both came to me and told me about your dream of having a place of your own and your desire to live in the white man's world. You told me that this would be living proof of the validity of the Holy Experiment. I told you then, and I'll say it again now, that while your dream is a beautiful one, I don't think it is a realistic one. You both are ready and able to make such a move, but I seriously doubt if the white man's society is ready for you. There will be great risk for you. It is highly unlikely that you and your marriage will be accepted by the people in the community where you settle. Since you first saw me, you have twice told me that this is your desire. I must ask you one more time. Is that still what you wish to do?"

Jacob looked at Ruth, and Ruth looked at Jacob. Their hands were entwined in a firm clasp. Both looked back at Agent Ford, and Jacob nodded his head in the affirmative. "Yes," Jacob said, "that is still our dream, and it is still our wish."

Agent Ford sighed in resignation.

"I must admit that if anyone can make this work, you two are the most likely to succeed. Both of you have worked long and hard here at San Carlos, and everyone here has great respect for you. Both of you have skills that will fit the white man's world well. All of us here at San Carlos will miss you terribly."

Ford's words caught Jacob and Ruth by surprise, and they glanced at one another, wondering what was coming next. Agent Ford picked up some papers from his desk.

"I wrote the Friends at their Philadelphia Headquarters some time ago and told them of your desire. I have here some information they have sent me, which I reluctantly now give to you.

"They have located a small homestead, complete with grazing land, near Hawthorne, Colorado. It is Government land, but the Friends will be allowed to lease it for a period of five years. The Friends convinced the Government that this is a social experiment with the hope that, if successful, it can serve as an example for others, an alternative to reservation life."

A look of sadness swept across Ford's face, and he sighed again with resignation.

"Jacob, I still don't think the time is right for you and Ruth to make this kind of decision and take this kind of chance. Furthermore, there may not be any Friends in that region to support you in time of need.

"There is a small log house on the property. How and why it got there I do not know, but I understand it is in a bad state of disrepair. However, that shouldn't present much of a problem for you, Jacob. We will let you take as many tools with you as you want.

"One more thing. The Friends are grateful for the years of service and dedication you have given to the reservation. We have paid both of you very little, especially Ruth. Therefore, should you decide to go ahead with this idea, the Friends will give you $ 600 to help you get started. It isn't much, but it is all they can do. It should allow you to buy some cattle and still have some money to live on until you can sell some beef. I will provide you with a quantity of seeds for corn, pumpkin, and other vegetables. You have two horses and should be able to hunt and fish. But, even with all that, you still will have a very small margin for error. I must tell you that, in my opinion, the odds are against you. I don't think you should take the risk, especially with Paul involved."

Jacob and Ruth squeezed their hands and rose from their chairs.

"We appreciate all you and the Friends have done for us here at San Carlos and for giving us this opportunity," said Jacob. "We must discuss this with Paul and pray about it. We will give you our answer tomorrow."

****

Jacob, Ruth, and Paul returned the following morning and, as Agent Ford suspected, all three voted in favor of the move. After that events moved swiftly. Agent Ford notified the Friends of the Redstone decision. As soon as a confirming reply was received, a large freight wagon was leased for a month and loaded with all the personal belongings and equipment that the family possessed. Finally, tearful goodbyes were exchanged, and late in the Summer of 1888 the family began the long trek to Hawthorne, Colorado. Agent Ford sent along four Apache policemen as an escort and to bring back the wagon. A representative of the Friends had agreed to meet them in Dundee, about 50 miles southwest of Hawthorne, and guide the group to the homestead.

Everything went as planned, and two weeks later their destination was reached. The roof of the log house needed some repairs to make it liveable, so Jacob began that task immediately while the others unloaded the wagon. By nightfall the wagon was empty, the possessions were all safely housed, and the roof repairs had progressed to the point where a suitable amount of protection was provided. Some additional materials and another day's work would complete the project. Ruth, Paul, and the Friends representative, James McComb, slept in the house that night, while Jacob and the Apache policemen slept under the wagon. The weatherman cooperated nicely as no rain fell and, better yet, a clear, sunny day followed.

The log house contained a heavy iron stove, much to Ruth's delight. She used up most of their remaining food supplies, feeding her men a hearty breakfast. As soon as that meal was over, one Apache policeman tied his horse to the back of the wagon, climbed up into the driver's seat, urged the team of harnessed horses into action, and began the trip back to San Carlos, his three companions following in his wake.

Soon thereafter, McComb, Ruth, and Jacob, with Paul riding double, walked their horses in the direction of Hawthorne and reached the community by late morning.

"Ruth, head for the general store and buy what we need," said Jacob. "Mr. McComb, Paul, and I have to go to the bank and take care of some matters. We'll meet you at the store in a little while and help you get everything packed on the horses."

Since it was now about noon, and the hot sun was rapidly approaching its zenith, only a handful of people were out on the streets of Hawthorne. Most of them barely glanced at the trio of riders and took no special note of them, particularly since McComb rode in the middle. However, two citizens walking the sidewalk nearest Jacob paused to take a second look, and startled expressions spread across their faces. They continued to stare at the backs of the trio as they moved down the street.

Ruth pulled her horse to the right as she drew even with Arnold's General Store, and her companions continued to walk their horses until they reached the bank. Jacob let Paul slide off the horse before he, himself, dismounted. Jacob tied his reins and joined Mr. McComb as they entered the bank. The two men and the boy walked through the lobby and continued on until they reached a gated area, outside a private office. A clerk rose from his desk, off to one side of the enclosure, and met the trio at the gate, his eyebrows raised.

"Mr. McComb and Mr. Redstone are here to see Mr. Quigley," McComb informed the clerk.

The clerk didn't respond immediately as he stared at Jacob and Paul.

"Mr. McComb and Mr. Redstone are here to see Mr. Quigley," McComb repeated in a louder voice.

"Ah . . . oh yes," stammered the clerk, trying to cover his embarrassment. "I . . . I'll tell him you are here."

The clerk turned abruptly, took three quick steps, and knocked on the glass door.

"What is it?" a voice from within the room demanded.

"Mr. McComb to see you, sir," announced the clerk as he glanced back at the visitors.

The sound of a moving chair was heard through the door, a softer sound of footsteps quickly followed, the door was flung open, and David Quigley plunged through the opening, brushed past his clerk, and reached the gated area, his hand outstretched, a big smile on his face.

"Glad to see you again, Jim," he boomed. "What can I do for you this fine day?"

McComb motioned toward Jacob and Paul.

"This is Mr. Redstone, David, and his son, Paul. He is the man who is moving into the Russell Place."

Quigley turned toward the two and, for the first time, looked directly at these new people. The outstretched hand dropped suddenly, before Jacob could grasp it, and the smile vanished from the banker's face.

"This is an Indian," he whispered to McComb, astonishment in his voice. "You never said anything about an Indian being part of this deal."

"Let's go into your office," suggested McComb in a calm voice. "We can talk better there."

"Yes . . . yes, of course," replied a nonplussed Quigley. "Yes, that would be better." He waved in the direction of his office and stared at the backs of the two men and the boy before following them in and closing the door. He found his chair, sat down heavily, and looked at his three visitors, McComb sitting, Jacob and Paul standing. He directed his attention to McComb.

"You never said anything about an Indian being a part of this arrangement," he repeated. "What do you think you're doing?"

"Mr. Quigley, the Friends feel very strongly that peace must come to the plains and, at the same time, be fair to both the white man and the red man. Sooner or later, these cultures must come together and find a way to live in harmony. We call it our Holy Experiment, and we are determined to make it succeed. Jacob, his wife, and his son want to lead the way in trying to make this come about. They are extremely well qualified to try this. Jacob and Paul, who are Apaches, joined his wife in being part of our faith."

"His wife?" muttered Quigley, in a barely audible voice. "You mean his squaw, don't you?"

"No, I do not," replied McComb in a calm, even voice. "Ruth Redstone is white and from Iowa. She has spent the past seven years teaching school at the San Carlos Apache Reservation in Arizona. She has been one of the most dedicated and devoted representatives of our faith that we have ever had. She is Paul's stepmother, of course."

Quigley slumped back in his chair, pulled a big handkerchief from an inner pocket, and wiped his brow, his mind still in turmoil. Finally, he turned toward Jacob and, in a weak voice, said, "Can you speak English?"

"Yes, I can, Mr. Quigley," replied Jacob in a strong voice," and so can Paul. Ruth has taught us both very well. All we want to do is live among you and be a credit to your community."

Quigley was surprised at the preciseness and the variety of the words he had just heard. They were better than what he was used to hearing from most of his customers. His mind continued its whirl of puzzlement.

Mr. McComb pulled a wallet from an inner coat pocket, withdrew a slip of paper, handed it to Quigley, and broke the silence.

"This is a bank draft for $ 600 and is drawn on our bank in Philadelphia. It is to be deposited in an account for Jacob and Ruth Redstone. The Friends assume you will help them make the best use of this money. I left you my card the last time we spoke. If there are any problems with this account, I shall expect to hear from you immediately. Now I would appreciate it if you would have the proper forms prepared for this account so that Jacob and Ruth can provide you with the appropriate signatures."

The mention of some normal banking procedures finally managed to penetrate the fog encompassing Quigley's mind. He shook his head, as if to eliminate the cobwebs, moved to the office door, opened it part way, and spoke to the clerk outside. "Willoughby, make out the forms for a new account. The account will be in the names of Jacob and Ruth Redstone. Bring the forms to me as soon as they are completed." He closed the door, returned to his chair, and focused a worried look at McComb.

"I hope you understand that this won't set well with the folks hereabouts. It's really going to take some getting used to. I'll do what I can, but I have to live with these people, too."

Quigley turned his attention to Jacob and Paul.

"Do *you* understand what you probably are letting yourself in for? We have lots of good people here, but I doubt if any of them have faced a situation like this before. You're going to have to be very patient and understanding with all of us, and I'm not sure even that will be enough. Like I said, I'll do what I can."

Jacob smiled and put his arm around Paul.

"We understand, don't we son? We'll pray for guidance and, with God's help, two years from now we'll gather together again and find out your fears were groundless."

Quigley was again struck with the richness of the words he was hearing and again shook his head, still with some disbelief. His brief reverie was broken, however, as his office door opened and Willoughby slipped into the room, handed Quigley two forms, and quickly made his exit.

Quigley handed Jacob a pen and showed him where to sign both forms. Jacob did so, the preciseness and readability of the writing again surprising the banker.

"I will keep the first form on file until Ruth signs the second one, and you return it to me. As soon as I get it back, we will throw the first one away, and the second one will be our official record. I'm only doing this to protect you and your account until we get both signatures on file."

"Ruth is in town, and I will get her to sign this form as soon as possible," responded Jacob as he nodded his head in understanding. "I should have it back to you later this afternoon." He extended his hand to Quigley and this time the banker grasped it firmly.

Chapter 3

Ruth dismounted and entered Arnold's General Store. She decided to browse before making any purchases. As she moved about the store, she was conscious that several pairs of eyes followed her every move. She finished her inspection and moved toward a counter where a man and two women were conversing. The talking ceased as Ruth approached the group.

"My name is Ruth Redstone," she announced brightly and with a big smile, "and I need to buy a number of things. Could either of you help me?"

"I'm Martha Arnold," said the woman behind the counter, "and this is my husband, Otis. We own this store. You must be a stranger in town. Arrive recently?"

"Yes, as a matter of fact we arrived only yesterday," Ruth explained. "We are living in the log house about five miles west of here."

"We?" asked Martha, curiosity in her voice. "Land's sake, that's the old Russell place. It ain't been lived in for three-four years now. Must be in pretty bad shape, I reckon."

"Here, now," interrupted Otis. "Tell me what you want and I'll go gather 'em while you folks get acquainted."

Ruth handed him a list and asked him to add several additional items she had spotted during her trip through the store. Arnold grabbed the list and began to collect an armload of items as Ruth turned her attention back to Martha and the other woman, who had remained silent.

"Yes, the house will need a good deal of work," Ruth admitted. "My husband and my son will have lots of things to do, but we are so happy to have a home of our own, I'm sure we'll all enjoy the work." Ruth looked at the other woman as she spoke.

"Land's sake, I've plumb forgot my manners," Martha exclaimed. "This here is Sally Quigley. Her husband is the banker in town."

"I'm pleased to meet you," smiled Ruth. "I believe Jacob and Paul are with your husband at the bank right now."

"I'm happy to meet you, too," replied Sally as she returned the smile. "David did mention he was expecting some new folks soon. You must be them."

"Guess so," said Ruth as she watched Otis pile another arm load of goods on the counter. "Don't forget the lamp oil," she reminded him.

"Seems like David said you folks were living south of here," Sally probed. "You come a long way?"

"About 200 miles," responded Ruth carefully. "All the way from deep in the Arizona Territory. It was a long, hot trip. It seems much cooler up here. How much do I owe you, Mr. Arnold?"

Otis was busy adding up a group of figures on a piece of paper, frequently wetting the tip of his pencil as he did so. He checked the figures a second time and finally looked up at Ruth, a pained expression on his face. "Twenty-one dollars and seventeen cents, it comes to. That seems like a lot, but I checked it twice. Them trousers and shirts and the cotton material you wanted took up quite a bit of it."

"Well, my men need shirts and pants," laughed Ruth, although she, too, was a little surprised at the total. She opened a well worn purse, extracted three $ 10 gold eagles and handed them to Otis.

"I'll take them," snapped Martha, as she grabbed the coins out of Otis' hand. "Everyone knows I handle the money in this here family."

Before Ruth could think of anything appropriate to say, the store's main door opened. Jacob and Paul appeared and headed directly for the group standing at the counter.

"Injuns," gasped Martha. Her hands flew to her breast, but she didn't let go of the three coins. Sally Quigley also drew back, fear on her face. Otis just stared at the twosome, too dumbfounded to do anything but look.

"No, not Indians," responded Ruth in an calm, even voice. "Apaches. Jacob, Paul, these are some new friends. This is Otis and Martha Arnold, who own the store here, and this is Sally Quigley. I think you have already met her husband, the banker. Otis, Martha, Sally, may I present my husband Jacob and my stepson, Paul."

Jacob removed his hat and smiled at the stunned trio of Hawthorne citizens.

"Take off your hat, son," he directed Paul. "Show these nice people we know how to be polite. Paul and I are happy to make your acquaintance," he continued as he eyed the three people who were having a great deal of trouble getting their faces to assume normal expressions.

Ruth broke the deafening silence by pointing at Martha's hands.

"I believe I have some change coming, Mrs. Arnold. Jacob, you and Paul pack these things in the burlap bags we brought along and take them to the horses. I'll be along directly." Ruth gazed at Martha Arnold. "My change please," she reminded the woman.

Still dumbfounded, Martha mechanically opened her cash box, counted out the change, and handed it to Ruth.

Ruth dropped the money into her purse, snapped it shut, gathered the remaining items into her arms, and strode, calmly and deliberately, out of the store.

Martha Arnold finally found her voice.

"Land O'Goshen, I never thought I'd see something like this. A white woman and married to an Apache no less. Married? I don't believe it."

"I've got to talk to David about this," said Sally Quigley, a grim look on her face as she hurried out of the store. "How could he know about this and not tell me about it?"

Martha watched Sally disappear out of the store before turning to Otis. "I don't want to see that Redstone woman in this store again," she admonished her husband angerly.

"Just a minute, Martha," protested Otis, who finally had found his voice. "Ain't that good money you were so quick to grab from me? Since when are we so rich we can afford to not sell things to folks who can pay for 'em? If they can't pay, that's different. But as long as they have legal tender in their pockets, we'll sell 'em what they need. Now settle down."

"Huh," sniveled Martha. "Spoken like a man. We'll see about that!"

****

That night, after Paul went to bed, Jacob and Ruth held each other tightly as they reviewed the day's events. Mr. McComb had left on the afternoon stage, and they were now on their own in a world that was obviously going to be hostile, at least for the present.

"Maybe it was a mistake to come here, Ruth," whispered Jacob. "Perhaps Agent Ford was right."

"No," cried Ruth resolutely. "We must continue our Holy Experiment. We must give these people some time to get used to us. Come pray with me. We must ask God for guidance and strength to help us do what we know is right."

****

The news about the arrival of the Redstone family had swept through Hawthorne, and by the following Sunday the town was abuzz with gossip about this event. Reverend Abner Meeker held his usual Sunday service at the Hawthorne Community Church and was about to recite the benediction when he was interrupted by a member of his congregation.

"Hold it a minute, Brother Meeker," came a voice. "I have things to say that need saying."

The speaker was Andrew Tuttle, who had risen to his feet. Tuttle was a thin, bony man with jet black hair and an oversized Adam's apple that bobbed up and down when he talked.

"This town got some visitors this past week," he began, "and damned if it wasn't a stinkin' Injun and his white squaw."

"Please, Brother Tuttle, this is God's house," interrupted Meeker. "Kindly choose your words better."

"Shut up, preacher," Tuttle responded irritably. "We got a problem here, and I'll call it what it is. Not only that, but they're squattin' on good grazin' land. Just like the Russells did 'til I chased them off."

"That isn't true, Andy," countered David Quigley, as he, too, got to his feet. "The Redstones have a valid lease on the property, tendered them by the United States Government. And I'll remind you, Andy, that it *is* Government land and not part of the Tuttle Ranch. You had no right to force the Russells to leave. That was the Government's job if it didn't want them there."

Tuttle gave Quigley a withering stare.

"It looks like we got an Injun lover right here in town," he snarled. "I've always grazed my cattle on that land, and I aim to keep on doin' it. Besides, no one in this town is goin' to be safe with Injuns around. How do we know how many more Apaches are hid out somewhere?"

A woman screamed in terror, other voices expressed fear, and Tuttle knew he had made a significant impact on his audience.

"That isn't true either, Andy," countered Quigley a second time. "I have it on good authority that the Redstones are Quakers and don't believe in fighting and such."

"Huh," snorted Tuttle. "Have any of you ever heard of Apaches that didn't fight? And don't tell me about the Quakers. Them's the Injun lovers that said Injuns would be peaceful and make good farmers. And what happened? General Custer and almost 300 brave men were massacred at the Little Big Horn. Have all of you forgot about that?"

A chorus of no's followed that statement, and the din in the room grew louder.

Lem Tuttle jumped to his feet.

"Paw's right," he shouted. "We got to get rid of these Redstones afore any real trouble starts."

Sheriff Turk Edwards had listened to the words and had carefully watched the faces of the congregation. The tone of the meeting now had reached a level that disturbed him. As soon as Lem Tuttle had shouted his words, the sheriff jumped to his feet and yelled for silence. The babble had risen to too high a pitch, however, for him to be heard. Sensing that the situation had almost reached a crisis state, he pulled his gun and fired a shot into the floor. Talk and movement suddenly stopped, and everyone's eyes were cast in the sheriff's direction.

"That's better," he muttered as he sheathed his weapon.

"Seems to me you all are about to run off half cocked," he said in a loud voice. "What do you think you're doin'? All that has happened is that a Apache man, a Apache boy, and a white woman have come to live in our community. To hear Andy talk, you'd think they was about to start a war. What have they done wrong? They put money in the bank and bought supplies at Arnold's store. Ain't that what the rest of us do all the time?"

"They're Injuns," snapped Andy, anger in his voice. "Leastways, two of 'em are," he added in a little calmer voice.

"They shore are," admitted Edwards, "but since when is that a crime? Seems to me all of you are forgettin' one important fact. Supposin' Andy is right, and they're here scoutin' us out. If you hurt or kill them, wouldn't you be making it plumb shore that a whole passel of Apaches would be down on our necks and we might have a massacre like Andy was talking about? I know for a fact that four Apaches brought them here in a wagon. That means the whole Apache Nation knows they're here. Why don't you all lay low for a spell and see what they do. I'll keep an eye on 'em. Why spark trouble when mebby there ain't none?"

Edwards' words reduced the tension in the room significantly, and Turk saw several heads nod affirmatively as their owners looked in his direction.

Andy Tuttle was smart enough to sense that the mood of the room had changed dramatically and that the fire he had wanted to start was now virtually put out. He slammed his hat on his head and headed for the front door of the church, his wife and three sons following him.

Edwards caught up with Tuttle as the man had just reached his horse. He pressed Andy's right shoulder, and Tuttle turned to look at him, his face florid with anger. Edwards spoke quietly but firmly.

"Andy, I weren't here when you chased off the Russells. Don't try it with the Redstones. Quigley was right. They got a legal right to live where they are. You leave 'em alone and keep your cattle on your own range land. I don't like them being here neither, but the law is on their side. I'll enforce it if I have to."

Tuttle was surprised at the sheriff's words and examined Edwards' face closely. The determination in the voice was matched by the expression on Turk's face. Tuttle pulled himself up into his saddle and looked down at Edwards. The message in Edwards' eyes had not changed, and Tuttle scowled in frustration.

"All right, sheriff, you win this round. But you better keep an eagle eye on them folks." He spurred his horse and quickly caught up with the rest of his family.

✳✳✳✳✳✳✳✳✳✳✳✳

The next morning Edwards arrived at this office later than usual. He went over the day's schedule with his two deputies, finished some paperwork, and wandered around Hawthorne for an hour gauging the mood of the populace. Satisfied with what he could see and hear, he made his way to "Pop" Dawson's Livery Stable, saddled his horse, and headed out of town in a westward direction. He was in no hurry and carried on an intermittent conversation with himself about how he would handle things when he reached his destination. It was almost noon when the Redstone homestead came into view. He walked his horse into the courtyard, reined it to a stop, and examined his surroundings. Finally, he cupped his mouth with his left hand and shouted, "Hello the house; anyone home?"

Ruth immediately emerged from the house, wiping her hands on her apron, and Jacob and Paul came into view from behind the building. The father and the son were stripped to the waist, and both of their bronze torsos glistened with perspiration. Jacob and Ruth both had a puzzled look on their faces.

"Mornin' folks," smiled Edwards as he touched the brim of his hat. "I'm Sheriff Edwards, and I thought I'd stop by and say howdy. Mind if I step down?"

"Please do," responded Ruth. "Would you or your horse like a drink of water?"

"Why, yes, we would," acknowledged the sheriff. "It's a hot day, and Peso here shore would like to wet his whistle, and I reckon I would, too. Here, let me help you with that bucket."

Edwards swung himself out of his saddle and grabbed the water bucket from Ruth's hand as Jacob and Paul joined them. The sheriff poured a generous quantity of water into his hat and held it in place as the horse eagerly gulped down its contents. Edwards dropped the nearly empty bucket into the well, heard the splash, and waited a few moments before cranking it back up to the top of the well. He picked up a nearby ladle, dipped it into the bucket, and drained its contents. He returned the ladle to its resting place, wiped his mouth with the left sleeve of his shirt, and smiled.

"That tasted mighty good, nice and cold. You got a good well here."

"You didn't come all the way out here to test our well," stated Jacob, suspicion in his voice.

"Well, no I didn't," admitted Edwards, as he looked around. "Is there someplace we can talk?"

"Oh, please excuse me," replied a flustered Ruth. "Come inside out of the sun. We aren't really settled in yet, but I think we can find enough space for all of us. I'm washing the inside from top to bottom, but the kitchen area is done, and we can sit there."

The sheriff tied Peso to a post and followed his hosts into the little ranch house.

The kitchen area contained a small table and three chairs. The three adults occupied the chairs, while Paul sat on the floor. Edwards removed his hat, placed it in his lap, and cleared his throat.

"We sorta had a town meeting at the church yesterday," he began, "and, as you might expect, you folks were the topic under discussion. Some folks are afraid you might go on the warpath, Jacob, and wipe out the town. Do they have any reason to feel that way?"

"No," answered Jacob, unable to keep his face straight at such a thought. "We don't even own a gun, and you can search the house if you want to. I do have a bow and a quiver of arrows, though. Paul and I plan on doing some hunting and fishing in the mountains further west of here. Do I have to surrender my arsenal to you?"

"No," laughed the sheriff, "and I'll take your word about the gun. I couldn't find it if you didn't want me to anyhow."

Edwards paused for a moment to let his words sink in.

"Jacob, when you came here, you had four other Apaches with you," he continued. "Are they still around?"

"No, by now they should almost be back at the San Carlos Reservation. They had to take the wagon back, and since it was empty, they should have made the trip back a lot quicker than when they came with us."

Edwards nodded. "That's what I figgered. There weren't no reason for them to stay if you were what you claimed to be. You see, the sheriff in Dundee wired me about you folks and told me McComb was with you. I talked to banker Quigley, put two and two together, and figgered out what was happening. I was here when you arrived, but you didn't see me. I didn't tell Quigley what I knew. I figgered that was McComb's job."

Edwards paused again, sighed, and toyed with his hat.

"I talked with Quigley after you was in town the other day. He told me about yore dream, and while I can't argue against the idear, I shore don't think this is the right time or the right place to try it. On the other hand, mebby there ain't a right place or a right time. I dunno.

"But I am sheriff of Hawthorne, and I shore don't want any trouble. Yesterday there was some talk of them coming out here and running you off or worse. I managed to defuse that idear by telling 'em the whole Apache Nation might come down on 'em. I think things have quieted down, at least for now. I'll try to keep it that way, but I can't be too obvious about it. These folks are my friends, too, and I have to live here."

"We appreciate what you did, sheriff," Jacob quickly broke in. Jacob put his arm around Ruth. "We don't want trouble either. All we want to do is live in peace and try to fit in. What can we do to help you and help ourselves at the same time?"

"Well, there are a couple of things you can do," drawled Edwards carefully. "Stay out of town as much as you can for the time being." He looked at Ruth. "We do have a school in town, but I don't think it would be a good idear to send Paul there, leastways not right away."

"I agree, sheriff," said Ruth. "I am a school teacher and can give Paul all the education he needs right here at home. I'll have to buy some slate and chalk, of course, and I'll do that the next time we have to go to town."

"I have a question, sheriff," said Jacob in a low voice. "I will have to buy a small amount of cattle to get a herd started. How should I go about that?"

"A good question," mused Edwards thoughtfully. "Yore big problem in Hawthorne is gonna be Andy Tuttle. He lost a cousin or somethin' at the Little Big Horn, and he hates Indians somethin' fierce. His three boys are no different, and they are powerful people around Hawthorne. We can't let you have a run-in with him. More'n that, he'll try to keep you from buyin' anythin' in and around Hawthorne. I'll have to give that some thought. Mebby I could get one of the other ranchers to sell you some of his calf crop on the sly to get you started. Better'n that, mebby some one around Dundee would do it. Give me a little time to think about it. It looks like you got a lot to keep you busy for a spell anyhow."

Edwards slipped his hat back on and rose from his chair.

"Reckon I better head back to Hawthorne and tell folks there ain't no massacre comin'! They should be right glad to hear that," Edwards observed, a twinkle in his eyes.

Jacob and Ruth also had gotten to their feet and before Edwards could move away from the table, Ruth reached out and pulled at his arm.

"Sheriff, it's past the noon hour! I have a pot of stew cooking. Won't you please stay for lunch?"

Edwards hesitated and scratched his jaw reflectively. "I couldn't help smelling it," he observed, with a grin. "Are you shore it won't be too much trouble?"

"Of course not," replied Ruth emphatically. "We insist. You men folk clear out of here for a little while and get washed up. I'll set the table. Lunch should be ready in about half an hour. Paul can help me."

Edwards and Jacob walked outdoors and after they had washed, Jacob showed the sheriff the repairs he was working on and described his plans for the ranch. The sheriff listened carefully and then shook his head.

"I don't know about havin' a vegetable garden. We can go for a long time without rain around here, and then we can get a gully washer. Your well could run dry, too. I think that's one reason the Russells had such a hard time of it. Course Andy Tuttle didn't like them neither, and he helped push them out of here. Reckon you'll just have to try it and see what happens."

Ruth called them back to the house. Once the adults were seated at the table, Paul again occupying the floor, Edwards was surprised to have Jacob say grace before beginning the meal.

The smell of the cooking stew had not deceived the sheriff. The stew was as good as he could ever remember tasting, and he couldn't help eating more than he had intended to. He thanked Ruth profusely.

After the meal he went outside, untied Peso, and shook hands with Jacob before swinging into the saddle.

Bracing himself with his right hand on Peso's rump, he looked down at the Redstones.

"If you all play straight with me, I'll do what I can to help you. But, as I told you, I can't be too obvious about it. You'll just have to trust me. Hopefully this will work out good for everyone." With that he nudged Peso into motion and departed at a much faster gait than when he had arrived.

Jacob encircled Ruth's waist with one arm and engulfed Paul with the other as all three watched the horseman fade into the distance.

"I like him," murmured Jacob softly. "Like he says, we'll just have to trust him. Perhaps things aren't as bad as we thought the other night."

Chapter 4

The single file column of four riders and their pack horse had spent most of the afternoon slowly wending their way down, around, and through the lower foothills of the mountain range. They were following a very faint and rock-strewn trail and letting their horses carefully pick their way through the debris. On several occasions the men had been barely able to squeeze between boulders on both sides of the trail, their stirrups scraping these obstacles as they went by.

At long last they spotted a level piece of land which even contained a small amount of grass. The first man in the tiny column, a short and stocky individual, pulled his horse to the right, stopped, and watched his three companions move up alongside him. He half turned in his saddle and scowled at the tall, lanky man next in line.

"Curley, you said this would be a shortcut to Hawthorne, and we ain't hardly gotten anywhere for the past three hours. Are you shore this is the right way?"

Curley Chance took off his hat, scratched his head vigorously, and looked around at his surroundings. "It were five years ago that I come this way, Slim. I spotted a lot of things up above that looks familiar, but the landscape down here is shore different. For certain they've had a rock slide, probably more'n one, and it shore changed things. I gotta believe we're almost out of this stuff though 'cause that tree line ahead looks some familiar."

Slim Evers leaned back a little further in his saddle and spoke to the remaining two men, "Trig, pass the reins of that pack horse on to Bronc and move up behind Curley. Your arm must be plumb wore out by now from pulling that cayuse through this rock garden. Let's all take a minute and check the horses' hooves. Don't want none of the them to go lame on us."

Each man dismounted and carefully examined his horse, and Bronc did the same with the pack horse. No problems were evident, and after a few more minutes of rest Slim pulled himself back into his saddle, and the other three men did likewise. Slim waved his arm, urged his horse forward, and the tiny column continued their meticulous movement downward.

Curley's prediction proved to be correct, and about a half hour later, the quantity of rocks and boulders decreased significantly and, soon thereafter, disappeared completely, being replaced with good grass and sod. The trail they had been following became more distinct and led them in an eastwardly direction.

A grove of oak trees a short distance to their left caught Slim's attention, and he motioned in that direction. "It looks like a good spot for a campsite," he observed, "and I think the horses have come far enough for one day. It'll have to be a dry camp, though, as I don't see any water hereabouts. We'll have to water the horses with our canteens."

It didn't take long for the four experienced men to put a campsite in order, and soon the smell of frying bacon and perking coffee brought smiles to the faces of the hungry group.

Supper finished, the eating utensils were washed and dried, and the men then fashioned cigarettes or filled their pipes as they watched the sun disappear over the horizon in a blaze of red and pink. Darkness quickly followed.

"If'n my memory serves me right," began Curley with a sheepish smile on his face, "we should be about 10 or 12 miles from Hawthorne, due east from here. It's a fair-sized town, and we won't have no trouble gettin' the vittles we need."

"I expect you're right," agreed Slim. "We'll get our supplies and then swing south ag'in. We should be back at the Rambling R in a week or so. It shore will feel good to get home ag'in. This trip took a lot longer than I thought it would, and I didn't find what I was after. We shore could use a good range to get closer to the Denver beef market up north, but I didn't see anythin' that was available and within the price range I had in mind. So we did a lot of ridin' for nothin'! What do you know about this Hawthorne area, Curley?"

"Well, not a whole lot," replied Curley. "I drifted south after helping drive a herd to Montana. I was purty well broke when I hit the town. Had to look for work if I wanted to keep eatin'! The biggest ranch in the area is run by the Tuttle family. The old man's name is Andy, and he has three sons. Mean dudes they are, too. I worked for them for almost a month, but I had words with one of the boys, Lem I think it was, and was told to pack my

things and git. It weren't the same as working for the Rambling R," concluded Curley as he gave Slim an appreciative look.

"Maybe I'm too soft with ornery cusses like you," grinned Slim. "Why
do you think I'm getting gray hair already."

"Its cause you got such sweet, innocent lambs like me and Trig to boss
around that keeps the scales even," interjected Bronc Evans. "See how lucky
you've been. Two more Curley's, and this expedition would have been a
total loss for you," he continued and ducked as Curley flipped a boot in his
direction.

Curley got up, retrieved his boot, and looked down at the laughing Evans.
"You've been shore happy to eat my cookin'," he observed. "Mebby I should
let you do that job for the rest of the trip."

"No, I must admit you do have some uses," smiled Bronc. "I can cook,
but you do it a lot better. I'll just wash and wipe afterward and be right
content."

"Well, enough talking for now," said Slim as he spread his bedroll. "I'm
turning in and if you boys are smart you'll shut up and let me sleep."

The others followed his example, and in a surprisingly short time only
the snores of the sleeping men disturbed the tranquility of the scene.

****

Trig Mansfield yawned, stretched, pulled back his blanket, opened his
eyes, and was startled as he looked right into a sun that was well above the
eastern horizon.

"Musta overslept," he muttered. He sat up and looked around with an
embarrassed expression on his face, but relaxed and grunted with satisfaction as he saw that his three companions were still rolled in their blankets.
His movements broke the sleep of his nearest companion, however, and
Slim Evers raised himself up on one elbow and looked around, a puzzled
look on his face as well.

"Reckon we all were plumb tuckered from yesterday," he whispered. "Let
the boys sleep a little more. We ain't in no hurry, and the horses could use a
little more rest anyhow. I'll gather some firewood, and you mix up some
flapjack batter for us."

A half hour later, the smell of the cooking roused the remaining two
sleepyheads. They, too, were surprised at the lateness of the hour and were
quickly the target of some needling and caustic words. "Why, Trig and I
have spent the past hour taking turns shaking you hombres," concluded Slim

with a grin, "and we couldn't make the slightest change in yore snoring. We oughta have enough wood sawed to last us a year."

Bronc and Curley took the good natured kidding silently until Slim admitted that he and Trig had been late in rising, too.

"Reckon yesterday's ride did us all in," Bronc observed. "I must admit that the blankets felt right good." He reached for the tin plate Trig had filled with food and grabbed a fork as well. Bronc sighed with satisfaction, learned back against the trunk of an oak tree, and attacked his food with vigor. The others did likewise, and all talk ceased until the inner man was satisfied.

By the time breakfast was finished and the utensils had been washed, dried, and packed away, the sun had moved well up into the sky. The horses were again watered, although the amount was very limited, given the depleted condition of their canteens, particularly the two gallon containers carried by the pack horse.

"Time to move on, boys," Slim announced. "Curley, you lead the pack horse for a spell." He mounted his horse, and the others quickly followed suit. Slim led the way and was followed by Bronc, Trig, and Curley with the pack horse. The trail soon widened a bit and Bronc pulled even with Slim as Curley moved up beside Trig. They maintained a leisurely pace and enjoyed the warmth of the sun.

A short time later the group emerged from a tree lined slope and began to cross a mesa of excellent grazing land. A mile or so further on Bronc touched Slim's left arm and signalled a halt.

"Why are we stoppin'?" asked a surprised Evers.

"I don't rightly know," replied Bronc softly. He raised himself in his saddle and looked around. "Somethin' ain't right here. Look at all this fine grass, and we ain't seen but a handful of cows and steers. Kinda strange we ain't come across more cattle than that. It don't feel right to me."

"Huh," grunted Slim. "I've been sorta day dreamin' and wasn't payin' much attention, but you're shore right. This range could handle a big bunch without no trouble a'tall. Curley, are we on the Tuttle Ranch?"

"Not as I remember it, Slim," replied Curley. The Tuttle ranch is north and east of Hawthorne. I don't rightly remember anybody owning this here ground. In fact, now that I think about it, I do believe this were Government land when I was here five years ago."

Bronc stood up in his stirrups and, using his hat to shield his eyes, examined the entire landscape, starting with the northern extreme and moving slowly south. The movement of his head stopped suddenly, and he grunted in surprise.

"There's somethin' on the ground off there to the southeast," he declared. "Can't rightly make out what it is. Let's take a look."

Bronc and Slim kicked their horses into action and raced in that direction, while Trig, Curley and the pack horse followed at a much slower pace.

The object of their attention quickly came into view and turned out to be the bloated carcass of a dead steer. Bronc swung from the saddle, approached the body, and tried to shoo the swarm of flies away with his hat without much success. He walked around the carcass and then stopped short.

"Why, this critter's been shot," he exclaimed. "Right between the eyes, too. "Why would anybody do a fool thing like that?"

"Mebby it stepped in a hole and busted a leg," offered Slim as Trig, Curley, and the pack horse arrived. Curley kept the pack horse a short distance away from the steer's body.

"Shore, that would make sense," agreed Bronc slowly. "But if'n that's true, why lose all the meat by lettin' it rot? This don't smell right to me—in more ways than one." Bronc motioned for Trig to join him as he marched toward the back quarters of the animal. "The brand, if there is one, must be on his off quarter," Bronc murmured. "Help me hoist his rear and see if we can find one."

The two men grunted and strained and lifted the hind quarter about a foot, before letting go and having it plop back to the turf.

"It has a JR brand," announced Bronc. "Mean anythin' to you, Curley?"

Curley shook his head in the negative. "Don't recall anythin' like that from when I was around here before," he said. "Remember, I thought this was Government range. Anybody could be using it for grazin' purposes."

Bronc and Trig remounted, and the foursome continued their slow trek in an easterly direction and, presumably, toward the town of Hawthorne, if Curley's recollection were correct. About a mile and a half later, however, they noticed a small log house off to their right and Slim motioned for the group to move in that direction.

Ruth Redstone had just finished wheeling in a bucket of water from her well when the nickers from several horses reached her ear and, as she looked over her left shoulder, four riders and a pack horse stood high against the horizon. She caught her breath and glanced at the doorway to the little ranch house in order to gauge the distance she would have to run. If these men were punchers from the dreaded Tuttle Ranch . . . . But she examined the four riders again. Now they were very close, and she found that she did not recognize any of them. She lost some of her fear and remained stationary as the riders stopped a few yards away.

"Good morning, ma'am," said Slim pleasantly as he removed his hat. "Our horses smelled your water and are right thirsty. Would you be willing to share some with us?"

"Of course," answered Ruth warily. "Use this full bucket here. I can draw some more if you need it."

"Why, thank you, ma'am. That's right kind of you," murmured Slim, as he dismounted. "But I'll do the cranking if'n we need more. Fill your canteens, boys, and give the horses as much as they want," continued Slim as he turned toward his men.

He turned back to Ruth.

"My name is Slim Evers, ma'am, and that lanky fellar there is Curley. The other two galoots are Bronc and Trig, Trig being the bearded one."

Each man had dismounted and tipped his hat as he was introduced. They quickly filled their canteens and emptied the bucket in the process.

"Drop that bucket down ag'in, ma'am," directed Slim, "and I'll crank her up for you."

Ruth dropped the bucket back into the well, heard the expected splash, and stepped back to examine her visitors more closely. A second appraisal confirmed her first impression. She hadn't seen any of these men before. Slim's voice broke into her thoughts.

"I've got a full bucket, ma'am. You lead the way, and I'll lug it for you."

Ruth moved toward her house, Slim following in her wake. She glanced at the other three men again and noticed that the two men named Bronc and Trig each wore two guns, both of which were tied down. Her fears moved up several degrees in intensity, but she walked through the open doorway and pointed to a little kitchen area. Slim put the water on the floor near the stove and examined his surroundings.

In addition to the kitchen area, which had an iron stove, small table, and three chairs, the cabin contained a main room with a sofa and rocking chair. Two closed doors indicated the probable location of bedrooms. Reexamining the kitchen area, Slim could not help noticing the almost complete absence of food supplies. This fact disturbed him greatly.

Slim exited the house, and Ruth followed him but stopped just outside the doorway and examined her visitors anew.

Curley was watering the pack horse, using his hat as a container, while the other two men had lit cigarettes and were standing by the well, looking at her and Slim.

Slim took a few steps and then turned and faced Ruth.

"Ma'am, I do want to thank you for the water. Is this a ranch, and, if so, do you own much of the land hereabouts?"

"Yes, to both of your questions, Mr. Evers," replied Ruth. "This is the Redstone Ranch, and we own the land for about three miles in each direction. We leased it from the Government almost two years ago."

"We, ma'am?" inquired Slim cautiously.

"Yes, we!" answered Ruth quickly. "My husband, my son, and I own this ranch. Both of my men went to ride our eastern range this morning, and then they expected to go to Hawthorne after that. They should be back sometime this afternoon."

Slim paused for a moment and then made a silent decision. He took a long look at Ruth and asked, "Ma'am, are you a good cook?"

Despite her fears, Ruth couldn't resist smiling at this strange question.

"Yes, as a matter of fact I consider myself to be a rather good cook," she assured him in a firm confident voice. "At least Jacob and Paul haven't had cause to complain."

"That's what I figgered," grinned Slim. "Now I have a favor to ask of you. Me and my boys have been on the trail for more'n two weeks, and we got another week to go. We all are plumb tired of our own cookin'. If'n we were to supply the grub, would you be willin' to give us a home cooked supper for a change?"

The absurdity of the request tickled Ruth's fancy, and she couldn't resist the challenge. "I would be happy to do that, Mr. Evers," she grinned. I haven't fed this large a group in a long, long time. However, if that's what we are going to do, you're going to have to quit calling me ma'am. It makes me feel old. The name is Ruth; my husband is Jacob, and my son is Paul."

"Very good, ma'am . . . I mean Ruth," agreed Slim. "You make out a list of what you need for this feed, and I'll send two of my boys into town to get it. Get that list started, and I'll be back in a minute."

Ruth disappeared into the house as Slim walked over to the well where Curley had joined Bronc and Trig. All three were chewing on some beef jerky.

"Boys," Slim began, "we're goin' to stay here the rest of the day. We're in luck. Mrs. Redstone has agreed to fix us a home cooked meal for tonight. Trouble is their pantry is almost empty. Bronc, you and Trig head for town and buy the supplies we need. But buy half ag'in more'n what we want. Mrs. Redstone is making up a list of what she needs." Our big breakfast and that jerky you're chewing will have to hold us 'til tonight."

"What for we staying," asked a surprised Bronc. "I thought you was in a hurry to get back to the Rambling R."

"I was, but I changed my mind," replied Slim. "This here is the JR Ranch, and it's bein' run by this woman, her man, and her boy. I ain't told her about the steer we found yet, but I'm thinkin' you had the right idear. Somethin' ain't right about this whole setup, and I aim to get to the bottom of it. But I need some time to figger it out. Shut up now, here she comes. Just do what I say."

Ruth joined the group and handed a slip of paper to Slim, who promptly passed it on to Bronc.

"Get goin', boys," he directed. "Don't waste time goin' or comin' and build up a good appetite. Ruth don't know it, but she's got a tall job ahead of her, and she needs all the fixin's right quick. Point them in the right direction, Ruth."

"Oh, I have plenty of time," responded Ruth brightly as she pointed in a northeasterly direction. Her fears had by now become dissipated, and she was beginning to like these strangers, especially Slim, the older man. Probably old enough to be her father, she thought to herself.

Bronc, Trig, and Curley quickly stripped the bags and packages from the pack horse. Curley held its reins until Bronc and Trig were mounted, and then he handed them up to Bronc. The two men and the three horses immediately headed in the direction Ruth had indicated.

Slim pointed to his left as he nudged Curley, "That wood pile needs to be whittled down in size. There should be an axe around here somewhere. Why don't you get at it. I want to talk to Ruth some more."

Ruth smiled. "The axe is over by the overhang," she informed Curley. "That's where we corral our two horses."

As Curley trudged in the direction of the corral, Slim followed Ruth back into the log house.

Chapter 5

Ruth entered the house, pulled an apron from a peg on the door, and headed for the kitchen area. "I'll bake some biscuits for tonight and have that over with when your men return," she said in a sparkling tone, but Slim's voice stopped her movement.

"Ruth, ma'am, please come over here and set a spell. I have somethin' I want to talk to you about."

Ruth turned and slowly moved to the sofa and sat down, her apprehensions returning in a rush. Slim remained standing until she had settled in the sofa, and then he sat down in the nearby rocking chair.

"Is . . . is there something wrong?" Ruth murmured, fear in her voice.

"Well, yes, there is, sorta," responded Slim. "Me and the boys came in over your western range this morning. About a mile and a half from here we found one of your steers. It was dead, shot through the head."

"Oh no," gasped Ruth as her hands flew to her breast. "Not another one." Tears of frustration began to emerge and flow down her cheeks.

Slim paused for a few moments in sympathy and then leaned forward in the chair, a grim look on his face.

"You said another one. Has this happened before?" he probed.

Ruth dabbed at her eyes with her apron, took a deep breath, and replied in a calm voice, "Yes, this is the third one in the past month." The tears began to flow again.

Slim swore under his breath, but spoke calmly, "Who would do a fool thing like that and why?"

Ruth again used the apron to dry her face. After putting it in her lap and smoothing it out, she took another deep breath, and looked Slim straight in the face.

"I know the answers to both of your questions, Mr. Evers," she sighed. "One of the Tuttles shot the steer or had one of their men do it. They want to force us to leave our ranch, and I guess they'll do anything to accomplish that objective."

"But why?" asked a puzzled Slim.

"A relative of Mr. Tuttle's was killed in the battle of the Little Big Horn, up in Montana," answered Ruth.

"But what does that have to do with you folks?," persisted Slim.

Ruth sighed again and continued to look Slim straight in the eye as she spoke in a defiant tone of voice.

"I'm afraid I haven't been completely honest with you, Mr. Evers, and you and your men may not want to stay for supper. The truth is that my husband is a full-blooded Apache and so is my son. I should say my stepson. I married Jacob when Paul was seven years old. That was five years ago. I think Mr. Tuttle hates Indians in general and us in particular."

Slim slumped back in the rocking chair and thought for a moment before speaking again.

"That don't make no difference to me or my men, Ruth. We still would like to have a home cooked meal. But are you shore of what you are saying?"

"Yes, I'm sure, Mr. Evers," Ruth slowly replied. "Mr. Tuttle had made no attempt to conceal his feelings on that subject. My goodness, that battle involved the Sioux Nation and took place over 14 years ago. We are Apaches and aren't even related to the Sioux. Furthermore, Custer and his men attacked the Sioux on *their* land, in *their* village, with *their* families in the same camp. All the Friends and I detest fighting and killing, but even animals will fight to protect their mates and their young. Why would anyone expect the Sioux to do otherwise? I don't pretend to have a military mind, nor do I want one, but it seems to me that campaign was full of mistakes. And isn't it strange - whenever the Army wins a fight, it's a battle; but if the Indians win a fight, it's a massacre. I have never understood the difference."

"I must say, you shore surprise me," said a startled Slim Evers. "You seem to be right well informed. May I ask how come you're married to an Apache named Jacob and how come you own a ranch in this section of the country?"

"Well, it's a long story, Mr. Evers." Ruth couldn't hold back a thin smile. "Are you sure you want to hear all of it?"

Slim slumped back further in the rocking chair, crossed his right leg over his left knee, and plopped his big hat on the floor next to the rocker.

"Ruth, I've got more time than money; I ain't in any hurry to go no place; and I don't have anythin' else that has to be done." Slim smiled inwardly at the last part of his comment as the sound of Curley's axe drifted through the open front doorway. "But, you gotta start calling me Slim, not Mr. Evers. Now you're making *me* feel old, and I'm too old as it is."

Ruth's smile widened a bit further as she gazed at stockily build man in the rocker. The nickname certainly didn't fit the individual, she mused silently.

"Well, all right . . ., Slim," she began. "You asked for it, so here goes. I am a Quaker, and my church, the Friends, became very concerned about the treatment received by the Plains Indians from our Government, the treaty violations by our Government, and the resulting bloodshed, especially along the Bozeman Trail in the middle 1860's. At our behest, Congress empowered President Andrew Johnson to appoint a commission to investigate the causes of that trouble. He did so—it was called the Sanborn Commission. The commission determined that most of the hostility was caused by the military occupation of the Bozeman Trail across Indian country and the forts the Army had built to carry out that occupation."

Ruth paused to get up and get herself a drink of water. She returned to the sofa and continued her narration.

"In view of these findings, President Johnson appointed a peace commission, negotiations with the Sioux began, and finally resulted in the Peace Treaty of 1868."

"I remember reading about that," interrupted Slim. "Wasn't that the treaty that Red Cloud and a lot of other chiefs signed?"

"Yes, that is correct. After that treaty was signed, President Grant asked the Friends and other religious groups to lead an effort to maintain the peace and work with the Indians to help them adjust to life with the white man. Our leaders decided this called for a special missionary effort and asked a number of our people to participate. They called it a Holy Experiment. My Uncle, Lawrie Tatum, was one of the first people the Friends called on to carry out this mission. He became the Indian Agent at Fort Sill, in the Oklahoma Territory, in 1869.

"I was too young to participate at that time, so I continued my schooling and became a Certified Teacher. I also used that extra year to study the whole history of the Indian problem since I expected I would be sent to some reservation to teach Indian children about our culture, our God, and the beauty of peace. My first task in that additional year of study was to examine and try to understand that Treaty of 1868.

"That treaty, Mr. Evers . . . I mean Slim, is one of the worst documents I have ever read. There are so many contradictions in that treaty it would drive a Supreme Court Justice to tears. I have read those six pages I don't know how many times, and I still don't really know what they say. I don't see how anyone could have translated those words into something an Indian could remotely understand. It calls the same land ceded and unceded at the same time. It also tells the Indians they are confined to a reservation but are also free to roam at will! And on and on."

The disgust in Ruth's voice was obvious, and she was forced to again pause and get another drink of water before continuing.

"The treaty did force the Army to abandon those forts along the Bozeman Trail, and I suspect that's about all Red Cloud was told or wanted to hear. So he signed. Still it really didn't make much difference what the treaty said because, about a year later, General Sherman, who was one of its signers, suddenly nullified all of the concessions made to the Indians by a simple stroke of a military pen. And the fighting began again.

"Uncle Lawrie immediately began to have trouble with the Kiowas and Comanches on his reservation at Fort Sill and had to make periodic appeals to the Army to help him keep order. The Friends disapproved of his actions and began to criticize him and his policies. Finally he resigned in 1873 and went back to his home in Iowa.

"John P. Clum, a missionary from a different faith, assumed the responsibility for managing the San Carlos Reservation in Arizona, in 1874. He had much more success than Uncle Lawrie. Mr. Clum organized an Apache Police Force to help him control the reservation and even captured Geronimo in 1877. Although Mr. Clum left the reservation later that year, other missionaries continued his work. The Friends sent me to teach at the reservation in 1881. That's where I met Jacob and Paul.

"Jacob was a member of the Arivaipas band of the Apache Nation. He and a small number of other Apaches thought it was useless to continue to fight the white man and that they should learn to live in harmony with him but as an independent society. Jacob and his friends became known as moderates or progressives and were not looked upon very favorably by Geronimo, Victorio, Chato, and the other Chiefs. Jacob married his childhood sweetheart, Mourning Dove. Unfortunately she died when Paul was born in 1878. Overcome with grief, Jacob vowed that his son would not die in battle with the white man. In many ways Jacob was almost a Quaker within the Apache community.

"By 1883 it was obvious that the white man's might and power was going to prevail over the Apache Nation and that continuing on as an independent society was no longer possible. Jacob decided the time had come for him to learn the white man's ways and join the white man's world. So he, Paul, and their few belongings arrived at the San Carlos Reservation during the Summer of 1883.

"Jacob insisted that Paul go to school and learn English. The Agent reminded Jacob that he, too, needed to learn English if he really wanted to adapt to the white man's world. So both of them came to my school. Paul would study with the other children, but I would tutor Jacob late in the afternoon or early in the evening. Jacob is very intelligent, and it was so gratifying to see him make such rapid progress in learning to read and write. I tutored him for two years and . . . well, I admired his dedication and his love for Paul so much that I couldn't help falling in love with him myself.

"The Agent's staff taught Jacob all they knew about carpentry, masonry, and farming and found that Jacob was very good with his hands. Before we were married, Jacob built us a small adobe house and made some of the furniture we had in our little home. After Jacob and I were married, Jacob continued to work on the reservation—repairing buildings and building new ones, while I continued to teach school. But both of us had a dream about having a home of our own in the white man's world, and we believed that this would be a natural extension of the Holy Experiment concept. In addition, Jacob felt he had to use his new skills and education to make his way in the white man's world. We kept the Agent and the Friends informed about our dream and two years ago the Friends agreed to lease this land for a homestead as a reward for our years of service. No one had much in the way of resources to pay us for our work, of course, while we were at the reservation.

"So we came here with high hopes of living our dream, but it seems we dreamed too high. I guess we should have expected some opposition to our being here, but the hatred seems to be so deep. It's almost unbearable." The tears began to flow again, and Slim watched Ruth in thoughtful silence as an idea started to formulate in his brain. He finally rose from the rocker, moved close to Ruth, and put his hand on her shoulder.

"Go ahead and cry, Ruth," he said softly. "It'll do you good to get it out of your system. We've talked enough for now. I'm goin' out to check on how Curley is gettin' along. Come out and join us when you feel up to it." He squeezed her shoulder, turned, and quietly left the room.

Slim slowly walked over to the wood pile as Curley stopped swinging the axe and wiped the perspiration off his face. He had already removed his shirt, and his upper body was covered with perspiration.

"Set down and rest a spell," directed Slim as he threw off his vest and started to unbutton his shirt.

"Oh hell, it ain't too bad," objected Curley. "I'll rest for a couple of minutes and then get right back at it."

"No, you take a long rest," drawled Slim as he continued to unbutton his shirt. He pulled it off and handed it to Curley. "I need to work somethin' off," he continued, "and this is the best way I know how to do it. Besides Mrs. Redstone will be out in a bit, and I don't want her to think I'm too old to do a man's job. Now hand me that axe and give me a chaw of that jerky."

"You kinda like her, don't you?" grinned Curley. "Trying to show off, too!"

"Oh, shut up!" snapped Slim. "You'd better set down over there, out of the sun, afore it bakes any more stupid idears in your head. G'wan, get going. I can handle this axe just as good as you can."

****

Jacob and Paul had spent the morning and a part of the afternoon riding over the eastern half of their little ranch. A late lunch consisted of a few pieces of beef jerky as they sat on a small section of grass within a grove of cottonwood trees. Their horses were picketed nearby.

"Son, I have to go into town and talk to Mr. Quigley, the banker. I want you to come with me, but you'll have to wander around for a little while when I see him. Think you can do that and not get into trouble?"

Paul smiled knowingly. Both his father and mother had stressed the need for his excellent behavior ever since their arrival in Hawthorne two years ago, and they had been extremely firm in their admonitions. He had never disappointed them, and he had no intention of starting now.

The father and son mounted their horses, headed in an easternly direction, and soon arrived in Hawthorne. They walked their horses down the main street, crossed an intersection and, halfway down the second block, turned to their left and stopped at the hitch rail in front of the Continental Bank Building. Jacob dismounted, tied his horse, and reached into one pocket as Paul completed the tying of his horse.

"Here is two cents, son. Go over to Mr. Arnold's General Store and pick out some candy. Stay in this section of town so I can find you easy. I won't be with Mr. Quigley for very long."

Paul palmed the two pennies and headed across the street, maintaining a watchful eye for horses and wagons as he did so. Jacob watched him disappear inside the General Store and then turned and entered the bank building.

He walked through the lobby area and approached the far end of the room, where Quigley had an office. The office door was closed, and he could hear voices on the other side. A teller informed Jacob that Mr. Quigley was in conference but should be available in a few minutes.

Jacob found a chair and sat down. The few minutes dragged into almost a quarter of an hour, and he was becoming concerned about Paul when the door opened and Andy Tuttle emerged from the room. Tuttle glanced in Jacob's direction but brushed passed him without speaking.

Quigley ushered Jacob into his office, motioned for him to sit down in a nearby chair, moved swiftly around his desk, sat down in a beautiful leather upholstered lounge chair, and reached for a piece of paper lying on his desk. He cleared his throat before speaking. "I've been expecting you, Jacob. I've looked over your loan application and . . . well, I don't see how I can approve your request."

"But, Mr. Quigley, I'm only asking for $ 50," interjected a surprised Jacob. "Surely my ranch is security enough for that small amount. It's true that cattle prices were down last Fall, and we didn't get enough money to carry us through this year. But Fall is only two months away, and I'll sell more cattle at that time."

Quigley shifted his weight in the mammoth chair to get more comfortable and cleared his throat again.

"But that's the problem, Jacob," he droned. "Cattle prices aren't any better now than they were last Fall. In fact they seem to be drifting downward, not upward. You don't have many head to sell, and if you keep selling them at lower prices, you'll end up with no herd and no money."

Quigley paused and pulled a document from a pile of papers on his desk.

"Here's your lease back, Jacob. I don't really know how good your ranch would be as far as security for a loan. There is a provision in your lease that, should you and Ruth ever abandon the property, possession of the homestead would revert back to the Friends. The Friends, in turn, might be forced to give it back to the Government if you aren't here to manage it. No, Jacob, you are a poor risk and, as a prudent banker, I can't approve this loan."

Jacob sat stunned for a moment. He hadn't anticipated any difficulty in getting the loan, and his disappointment was great. Also he couldn't help wondering if Quigley's conversation with Andy Tuttle had anything to do with the banker's decision.

He finally broke the silence by pushing back his chair and getting to his feet.

"Are you sure you won't change your mind?" he inquired as he examined the banker's face.

"I'm quite sure, Jacob," answered Quigley, as he avoided Jacob's eyes.

"Good day, Mr. Quigley," Jacob murmured. "Thank you for your time." He turned on his heel, opened the office door, and left it ajar as he walked back through the bank lobby and out the front door.

Chapter 6

Bronc Evans and Trig Mansfield had kept their horses at a quick trot all the way to Hawthorne. They continued down the main street and stopped at a sign identifying Arnold's General Store about half-way down the second block. They turned to the right and pulled up at the hitch rail, the pack horse between them.

Bronc, who was nearest the three steps leading up from the street level to the wooden sidewalk, swung from the saddle, turned, and collided with a young boy who had just run down the steps, two sticks of licorice held in his right hand.

Paul went tumbling, and the two sticks of licorice flew from his hand and landed in the dusty street. He immediately bounced to his feet, took three quick steps over to Bronc, and looked up into his face, fear in his voice.

"Oh, I'm so sorry, sir. I was running when I shouldn't have. Did I hurt you in some way?"

Bronc looked at his adversary. The lad was obviously about ten or twelve years old, had a slight frame, and could not weigh more than one hundred pounds, dripping wet. Bronc, on the other hand, was just an inch or so under six feet and carried almost two hundred pounds of work-toned brawn and muscle. The boy's inquiry and the fear shown in his voice almost caused Bronc to laugh out loud. He barely caught himself in time and decided to make a joke out of it.

"Well, now, I don't rightly know, son," he said in a low, calm voice. "I'll have to try things out to make shore." Slowly and cautiously he used his right hand to slide over his left hand and up his left arm. Then he continued the meticulous examination over his rib, chest, and stomach areas. The boy's eyes were riveted on his right hand and followed its movement every inch of the way. Finally the hand stopped moving, and Bronc heaved a deep sigh.

"Outside of a busted arm and two or three cracked ribs, I seem to be in one piece," he reported in a casual voice. Instantly, he realized he had carried his little joke too far.

A wave of horror swept across Paul's face, and he shrank back a full step. "Mister, I'm so sorry," he gasped. "I'll never run in town like that again. Jacob will fix me good for this. What can I do for you?"

Bronc reached out with both hands and grasped both of Paul's shoulders. "Son, don't you fret none. I'm the one who should be saying I'm sorry. I was only funnin' you. I'm fine, but are you hurt some? You took quite a tumble there."

A tremendous look of relief replaced the fear on Paul's bronze face, and as Bronc's words sank in, he couldn't repress a little smile.

"I'm all right, too," he said. "But you sure scared me. I really thought I had hurt you." Suddenly he looked around. "Oh, what happened to my licorice?" he exclaimed.

"Yore what?" asked a puzzled Bronc.

"My candy, my licorice sticks," explained Paul as he continued to look down at the street. "There they are," he said excitedly as he took a couple of steps and picked up his treats with his right hand. He walked over to a nearby watering trough and plunged his hand and its treasure into the water, held them under for a few seconds, pulled them back out of the water, shook the hand vigorously, and took a deep bite out of both sticks. They must have tasted all right because the smile expanded into a large grin.

Bronc and Trig, who had joined him, watched this sequence of activity with no little amusement. Finally Trig nudged Bronc and pointed toward the store. Bronc nodded in agreement, ascended the steps, and looked back over his left shoulder just before entering the store. The boy had crossed the street and was slowly moving down the sidewalk staring at the displays in the windows of the various businesses located in that area.

Bronc and Trig had carried the first two bags of supplies out of the store and were in the process of securing these bags on their pack horse when Bronc glanced across the street, hoping to see the boy again. Instead he was a witness to an incident that made his eyes flash and his blood boil.

****

Lem and Sam Tuttle had accompanied their father into Hawthorne after having lunch at their ranch. Lem wasn't eager to make the trip as he had other things he really wanted to do. However, his father's requests were, in reality, orders, and he decided not to make an issue of it. Nonetheless, he wasn't in the best of moods when they arrived in Hawthorne.

"I've got to see Quigley at the bank and then do a few other things," Andy informed his two sons. I'll meet you both at the Palace in a couple of hours.

Lem and Sam had nothing special to do, so they headed for the Palace Saloon immediately after their father entered the bank. Three drinks did not mellow Lem one bit, but, instead, made him more angry and belligerent. "Let's go take a walk around town," he finally suggested with disgust in his voice.

Sam nodded agreement, and the two men walked out of the saloon, turned right, and took half a dozen steps when Lem suddenly stopped short and pointed at Paul, a few feet ahead of them, who was staring at a store window displaying the latest in women's dress fashions.

"Damnation," Lem bellowed. "A white man can't walk down the sidewalk in his own town without running into a stinkin' Injun. Look at him Sam. He looks like he owns the place."

Paul was so engrossed with the gaudy and fancy dresses displayed in the window that he barely heard the sound of Lem's voice and, therefore, the words didn't register with him, either.

The lack of response only served to enrage Lem more. He took two quick steps, grabbed Paul by the collar of his shirt, and yanked him halfway across the sidewalk.

"So you think you can ignore me," he snarled, "and me being a Tuttle, too!"

Completely surprised by the sudden yank, Paul was speechless even though his mouth was open. He finally started to say something, but his response hadn't been fast enough for Lem.

"He's a stinkin Injun and don't even know it," snarled Lem again. "I'll teach you to parade around in a white man's town." With that he hit Paul in the face with the back of his left hand. The blow knocked Paul off the sidewalk and onto the street.

Half dazed, the boy struggled to get to his feet. Lem, followed by Sam, stepped off the sidewalk, the flat of Lem's right hand caught Paul on the side of his face, and the boy went sprawling again.

Bronc yanked the knots on his tie rope in anger and took a step toward the altercation, only to have Trig's arm restrain him.

"'Tain't our affair," rasped the bearded one. "Slim said to get back pronto."

"Mebby we should make it our affair," responded Bronc heatedly.

Before their conversation could proceed any further, however, a running man came into their view. The man launched himself in a flying leap over the hitch rail and landed on Lem's back, driving him face first into the dust of the street. Sam quickly responded to this unexpected assault by grabbing Jacob, pulling him off of Lem, and pining his arms to his side.

A furious Lem picked himself up and faced Jacob. Lem's right fist landed on Jacob's unprotected face as he tried to extricate himself from Sam's enveloping arms. Jacob got one hand loose and quickly raised it in front of his face, trying to ward off another blow. But Sam's hand again locked the arm in a firm grip. Lem sneered, moved closer to Jacob, and landed two monstrous blows as Jacob was unable to defend himself. Jacob slumped forward, and only Sam's tight hold on one arm kept him from falling all the way to the street.

Paul had regained his senses, saw his father was in trouble, and went into action. He raced over to Sam and, without slowing down, swung his right leg as hard as he could. The toe of his boot caught Sam in his left shin and even the protection of his boot didn't spare Sam from feeling the effect of the impact.

"Yow!" Sam yelled as he hopped up and down on one leg and released his hold on Jacob, who promptly fell to his knees.

Paul's success was short lived, however. Lem yanked him back and swung at him again, only this time it was with his fist, and not the flat of his hand. Fortunately his aim did not keep pace with his moving target, and Paul did not receive the full impact of the blow. But it was enough. Head spinning and sick with pain, Paul fell in the street and groaned.

Jacob tried to regain an erect position, but as he struggled to rise Sam moved close to him and landed a short chopping punch. Jacob settled back in the dust, completely unconscious.

By the time this last blow had landed, a small crowd of people had gathered to watch the melee. Bronc and Trig had remained with their horses across the street.

Sheriff Turk Edwards pushed his way through the rapidly expanding crowd and surveyed the battleground. Both Jacob and Paul were still lying prone in the dust of the street. Edwards shook his head in dismay.

"Well, what was this all about?" Edwards inquired as he looked at Lem and Sam Tuttle, his eyes glinting.

"Why this damn Injun jumped us from the sidewalk," snapped Lem, "and then that kid of his tried to help him. It's a damn shame when a white man can't walk down the street of his own town without being attacked by savages. Ain't that so, Sam!"

"That's shore true," agreed Sam. "We were just minding our own business, Turk, when he came at us from the sidewalk. He's lucky we only beat him up and didn't kill him. Mebby we shoulda."

"Anybody see it any different?" inquired Edwards as he looked around at the assembled citizenry. Getting no response, he pointed to the figures in the street. "Some of you help them two get over to the jail. I'll have Judge Pardee set up Court and see if we can get this all settled this afternoon." Edwards again shook his head in disbelief.

A few of the citizens half carried and half dragged Jacob and Paul to the nearby jail. Most of the others either returned to their places of business or headed for a small courthouse down the street, where, apparently, a hearing or a trial would soon take place.

✳✳✳✳✳✳✳✳✳✳✳✳

Bronc and Trig finished securing the supplies they had purchased. Not only was the pack horse fully loaded, but additional packages had been tied together and slung over the necks of the two riding horses.

Trig started to untie the reins of his horse when Bronc's voice stopped him.

"We ain't going back to the ranch just yet," he growled. "Ever since we found that dead steer, I've been having a bad feeling about this whole range. And that feeling ain't gettin' any better. Let's you and I mosey down to that courtroom and see how things come out."

"Slim ain't goin' to be happy on two counts, if'n we do that," Trig rasped. "First, we're goin' to be late gittin' back to the ranch, and second, we're butt'n in somethin' that ain't none of our concern."

"Ain't the first time we been guilty of both them sins," replied Bronc. "And I'm goin' to follow my instincts. Something smells here, and it ain't us, even if'n we ain't taken a bath for a spell. No, I gotta see what kind of law they got around this here town. C'mon, let's follow our noses."

Bronc and Trig retied their reins and slowly moved down the street until they reached the building which housed the local courtroom. The small crowd that had gathered was split into groups of twos and threes. Obviously the earlier confrontation was the topic of discussion. Bronc and Trig slipped into the courtroom and sat in the back row of chairs. The local citizens drifted in, a few at a time, and about fifteen minutes later the Sheriff arrived with his two beaten, bedraggled, and dust-covered prisoners in tow. Lem and Sam Tuttle followed close behind.

The Sheriff pointed to two chairs, and Jacob and Paul were barely seated when a side door opened and Judge Joseph Pardee entered his courtroom. He gaveled the room to order and turned to Edwards, "What do we have in the way of a problem, Sheriff?" he asked.

"The defendants are Jacob and Paul Redstone, your honor. They are accused of disturbing the peace and assaulting Lem and Sam Tuttle."

One or two snickers were heard from among the assembled citizenry, and Edwards turned and glared at the audience. The judge rapped his gavel again.

"Quiet in the courtroom," intoned the judge. "You have witnesses to these acts, Sheriff?"

"Yes, your Honor, I shore do. Both Lem and Sam are here."

"Very well, call your witnesses, Sheriff."

In turn, Lem and Sam were called, sworn in, and repeated the story they had told Edwards earlier.

"Any other witnesses, Sheriff," the judge inquired.

"None that I know of," answered Edwards.

Judge Pardee looked over the assembled populace and addressed the group. "Did any of our other citizens witness this incident and, if so, can anyone supply any additional testimony?"

Pardee waited expectantly for a few moments and, when no response was forthcoming, he rapped his gavel and spoke. "Very well, I find the defendants . . . ."

"Hold it," came from a voice in the back of the room. "I ain't one of your citizens, but I shore enough saw what happened."

Necks turned and eyes stared at the stranger standing at the far edge of the back row of chairs.

"Judge Pardee slammed his gavel with more than the usual impetus and glared at the stranger."

"Who might you be?" he snapped. "And what do you have to add to what we already know?"

"The name's Bronc Evans," came the reply. "Me and my pardner had bought some supplies at Arnold's store and were packing 'em on our horses. I saw the whole thing, and it weren't quite the way it's been told here."

"Are you saying these two defendants didn't attack Lem and Sam?" asked the judge incredulously.

"Well, the father jumped the Tuttles right enough, but why don't you ask Lem and Sam *why* he done it?"

"We were minding our own business and he had no reason," piped up Lem before the judge could ask him.

"Shore enough," chimed in Sam. "He was just lookin' for a fight, and we gave it to him." Sam laughed uproariously at his own comment and many of the attendees joined in.

Pardee gaveled the room to silence, and Bronc patiently waited for the crowd to quiet down.

"Then you got two liars in this courtroom," he announced calmly. "That ain't the way it were at all."

Lem and Sam rose from their chairs and glared at Bronc as expressions of astonishment erupted from the rest of the audience.

Pardee again banged his gavel several times before the room quieted down.

"All right, mister, you seem to know so much," jeered the judge. "Why did Jacob attack Lem and Sam?"

"I'll tell you why," snapped Bronc, his anger starting to show. He pointed at the Tuttles, who were still standing. "Those two yellow coyotes were beatin' up his boy! Ain't that somethin'! Two growed men beatin' up a 10 year old boy!"

"I'm 12 years old," mumbled Paul through swollen lips.

"Twelve years old," echoed Bronc, having all he could do to avoid smiling at the interruption. "Now, that shore makes him full growed, don't it. That must have made them pore old Tuttles shake in their boots.

"The father came to help his son," Bronc continued. "Somethin' any paw would do. Them Tuttles are nothin' but two bit liars."

"Are you goin' to believe the word of one stranger against the two of us?" yelled Lem at the judge, his face turning a deep red under his tan.

A bearded man got up and stood alongside Bronc. "My name is Trig Mansfield," he said in a raspy voice. "Bronc and me are pardners, and I was across the street loading the supplies, too. I saw the same thing Bronc did. Them two cusses pushed the boy off the sidewalk and then slapped him. His paw tried to help the boy, but it was one ag'in two, and he never had a chance."

The room was stunned into silence and Lem and Sam slumped into their chairs.

Judge Pardee stared at Bronc and Trig for a moment before looking at Edwards.

"Well, Sheriff, it appears we have two witnesses on each side of the issue. I don't see how I can rule either way."

Pardee paused and looked around the room. Finally he slammed the gavel down one more time.

"Case dismissed. All charges are dropped. Court adjourned."

The attendees jumped to their feet, and many rushed out to tell their friends about this unusual court day while a few remained to discuss the situation.

Lem and Sam hurriedly left the courtroom, their faces dark with anger. They took long looks at Bronc and Trig as they reached the doorway and then disappeared outside.

Jacob and Paul slowly and painfully trudged their way across the room to where Bronc and Trig had remained standing.

"I don't know how to thank you," mumbled Jacob, despite his sore jaw and swollen face, as he shook hands with both men. "I'm afraid you have made some enemies in the Tuttle family." Jacob put one arm around his son's shoulders. "I told you, Paul, there's a lot of good people in this world."

The four of them had moved to the doorway as Jacob spoke. They passed through the entrance only to find Lem and Sam Tuttle standing on the sidewalk.

Lem moved close to Bronc and pointed a finger at his chest.

"I don't know who you are, stranger, but you shore bought yourself a heap of trouble. I ought to teach you a good lesson about sticking your nose in where it don't belong."

Bronc brushed the finger aside and moved his jaw to about an inch from Lem's face. "I followed my nose cause I can smell you Tuttles a mile downwind. You want to teach me a lesson? You want to do it right now? Step out in the street, and we'll have it out with guns. If you can't stomach that, take off your gun belt, and we'll have it out with our fists. And I'm tellin' you - *I ain't 12 years old!*"

Bronc's words had dripped with vehemence, and Lem shrank back with an involuntary movement. Sam gripped his arm and pulled him back further.

"He's crazy," whispered Sam. "Don't let him rile you. He ain't goin' to stay around long, but if he does we can find a better time and place."

Lem shrugged his shoulders and reluctantly followed his brother down the street in the direction of the Palace Saloon, Bronc's eyes boring into his back.

"You weren't afraid of him at all, were you," asked Paul as he stared at Bronc, awe in his voice.

"No, not one bit," answered Bronc in a matter-of-fact voice, a thin smile on his lips. "What are you two goin' to do now," he asked as he looked at Jacob.

"Well, Paul and I have had a hard day," Jacob again mumbled painfully. "It's time we went home. We have a small ranch west of here," he explained but did not see Bronc and Trig exchange glances.

"Well, ain't that funny," drawled Bronc. "We're headed in that direction, too. Why don't we ride along together?"

"You would be very welcome," replied Jacob, again with some difficulty. "Come on, son, let's get our horses. Maybe we can show these gentlemen our ranch before they leave the country."

Jacob and Paul located their horses and, slowly and cautiously, pulled themselves up into their saddles, reined their horses to the left, and urged them into motion. They passed their two new friends as Bronc and Trig pulled away from Arnold's General Store. The two Rambling R men, and their heavily loaded pack horse, followed Jacob and Paul out of town.

Chapter 7

What had been planned as a joyous and bountiful banquet occasion immediately changed to a solemn and fretful situation when the four riders arrived at the JR Ranch.

Ruth took one look at her injured menfolk, screamed in anguish, and helped Jacob and Paul shuffle into their home. Once the shock had worn off, she was all business, however. Ruth had already heated water in preparation for cooking. She poured some into a large bowl, appropriated some towels from a small closet, and began to bathe the faces of Jacob and Paul as they leaned back into the sofa.

Slim and his men did not intrude but stayed outside and unloaded the horses. Bronc described the events in town as the work progressed.

"I had no idear they were who they were until after the trial," he explained as he motioned toward the house. "I don't like havin' to leave here after all this hullabaloo. Mebby I made Lem and Sam so mad at me they'll forget about the Redstones."

"Well, you did the right thing," sighed Slim. "These people have no business bein' treated like that. But I don't know what to do neither. We can't stay, and I don't like leavin' neither. Curley, you and Trig take those extra supplies and begin storin' 'em in the pantry area. It's time I went in to see how they all are doin'."

Slim entered the house and remained standing while Ruth finished the bathing.

"How are yore patients doin'?" he finally inquired.

"Well, they look a lot better now that I've gotten them cleaned up," she murmured. "Oh, my," she continued, "in all the excitement I forgot to introduce you. Jacob, Paul, this is Mr. Evers. He and his men stopped here for water this morning and . . . well, one thing led to another, and I promised them a home cooked meal after Mr. Evers said he would supply the food."

"The name is Slim, and I'm right glad to meet you," said Slim as he shook hands with both Jacob and Paul. "Me and my boys have been on the trail for more'n two weeks with another week to go. A well cooked meal sounded real good to us, and so we made a bargain. But mebby you'd like us to move on now since you're not feeling so good."

Curley and Trig had entered the room as Slim spoke and were loaded down with bags and packages.

"Oh, no," exclaimed Ruth. "We owe you much more than that now. Jacob has explained to me what happened in town." Ruth eyed the pile of supplies in the kitchen. She got up and moved to that area for a closer inspection.

"I agree with my wife, Mr. Evers . . . I mean Slim," chimed in Jacob. "You must stay now and give us a chance to do something for you. Please sit down so we can get better acquainted." He turned to his son. "Don't you agree, Paul?"

Paul nodded his head vigorously in the affirmative but didn't know what to say and, therefore, said nothing.

Slim had barely settled himself in the rocking chair when Ruth walked over to his side and looked down at him.

"Mr. Evers . . . ah, Slim," she began in as stern a voice as she could muster, "there seems to be far more food here than I can cook in one week, let alone one night." She had to stop and turn around to watch as Curley and Trig delivered a second load. She turned back to stare at Slim as tears began to slide down her face.

"Well, now, I guess that may be true, ma'am," admitted Slim, feeling a little uncomfortable and becoming flushed in embarrassment. "Bronc did a fool thing in town and bought a lot more stuff than we can rightly use," he explained, feigning exasperation. "That pore pack horse won't last five miles if'n we make him carry all this weight. I figger you folks can put it to better use than we can." He had a hard time maintaining his look into Ruth's eyes as he spoke.

Ruth started to say something but stopped and turned toward to the kitchen, her apron again raised to her face as she walked back to the pile of goods.

Jacob watched her for a few moments and then focused his attention on the man sitting across from him.

"I guess we have more to thank you for," he said softly. "Isn't there something we can do for you?"

"Don't thank me for nothin'," snorted Slim. "What I'm afraid of is that me and my boys may have brought you more trouble than anythin' else."

"The trouble was already here, Slim," sighed Jacob. "Ruth and I thought we could make a place for ourselves in the white man's world. We had a dream, but maybe it wasn't a realistic one." Jacob looked up as Ruth returned to his end of the sofa and put a hand on his shoulder.

"I've told Mr. Evers . . . Slim, about our dream, my dear. We had a lot of time to talk today. Slim and his men found another one of our cattle shot and killed on our western range, and I had to talk to someone."

Jacob stiffened and closed his eyes for a few moments. His face looked grim where it wasn't swollen.

"This *has* been a bad day for the Redstone family. You might as well hear the rest of it. Mr. Quigley has rejected our request for a loan. We're going to have to sell more cattle to get by, and prices aren't very good right now." Jacob looked up at Ruth, "It doesn't seem to get any easier, does it? Our luck seems to be getting worse, not better."

Slim looked at his two hosts and made a silent decision.

"I figger you're due for a change in yore luck, and mebby my coming here is a start in that direction. Jacob, I've got a proposition for you and Ruth to think about.

"Jacob, you got a lot of good range land hereabouts. How many head do you think it could feed on a regular basis, and how many head do you have now?"

"We had 78 animals at last count," replied Jacob.

"Minus one," Ruth corrected him.

"Yes, 77 then," mused Jacob. "As best I can tell this range should be able to handle 600 or so. Does that make sense to you?"

"At least that many," agreed Slim.

"Jacob, I own a cattle ranch about a week's ride southwest of here," Slim went on. "I cut back on the cattle I sold last year cause prices weren't good. I plan on doing the same this year for the same reason, but that means I'm also getting overstocked. It ain't been a big problem yet, but I'm startin' to get a mite nervous about it. If'n I was to have some of my boys drive a herd of 300 or 400 critters up here, would you lease yore grazin' land to me? I'll pay you a dollar a head each year for as long as we do it. We'll divide up any calf crop based on the size of our two herds, if'n the markings and colors don't tell us who they belong to. Would you be willin' to do that for a year or two? After that we can kinda sort out where we are and what we do next."

Jacob exchanged looks with Ruth and saw her nod her head yes. He cleared his throat and stared at Slim appreciatively.

"My wife says yes, and so do I," he said softly. "We'll have to go to town and get the papers made up and signed, but I don't think I'm up to doing that today."

"No need for that," Slim corrected him. "Yore hand will be good enough for me. In order to seal the bargain, though, I'm going to give you $ 100 as a deposit, and I do want a written receipt for that." Slim dug into a vest pocket and produced five golden double eagles. Rising from his rocker, he bent over and shook hands with Jacob and then handed him the money.

"Reckon I'd better check on my men," he drawled. "You all have a lot to talk about. Make shore this is what you want to do. We'll be leavin' after supper, so you got time to change yore minds if'n you want to."

Slim, Bronc, Trig, and Curley spent the rest of the afternoon doing a few odd jobs with the horses and their gear but mostly just lounging. Slim told the others about the proposition he had made to the Redstones.

"I'm right glad you did that," approved Bronc. "It kinda kills three birds with one stone. Our range gets some relief, this range gets used proper, and the Redstones get the money they need to boot. I had the feelin' you were gettin' some thoughts like that when we saw all that unused grass."

Late in the day Paul came out to join them.

"Ruth says supper will be ready in a little while," he informed them. "She sure sounds happier than she was a couple hours ago."

"Well, I'm shore buildin' up a big appetite," grinned Bronc. Then his hands gripped both of Paul's shoulders, and he looked over the boy with a critical eye.

"You shore were a good Apache brave today," he informed the lad, admiration in his voice. "Them Tuttles were some surprised when they took you on. As soon as you get some meat on your bones and someone shows you how to use your fists, them Tuttles will shore run for cover."

Paul looked down and blushed through his tan. Then he murmured, "Ruth says we're Quakers and should not have to fight. I think she's angry with me and Jacob."

"Yore maw is plumb right," interjected Slim as he flashed a hard look at Bronc. "We oughta be able to settle things without fighting. It's just that most folks weren't raised the way yore maw was. She's got the right idear. It just ain't caught on yet."

"What Slim says is true enough," agreed Bronc, who also was determined to get in the last word. "But it ain't wrong to know how to defend yourself. Besides, you was born Apache, and that's the heritage you should be proud of, too. Apaches is fighters, and you couldn't help yoreself today. Yore Uncle Bronc was proud of you. All of us kids had to have special names where I grew up and, by gum, you need one too. From now on I'm calling you 'Apache,' and I hope you ain't ashamed to hear it."

"I . . . don't know," stammered a slightly bewildered boy. "I'll go see if Ruth says it's all right." He turned and dashed back into the house.

"You may have just lost your supper invitation," grinned Curley as he watched Paul disappear into the house. "But I kinda like the name you gave him. Let's wash up and get ready to eat. I'm gettin' hungrier by the minute."

✳✳✳✳✳✳✳✳✳✳✳✳

The supper was as delicious and enjoyable as Slim had hoped. And Bronc had not been excluded. The Redstones surprised the Rambling R men by bowing their heads and Ruth giving thanks before passing the food.

The lack of furniture presented a small problem, but Slim was told to occupy the rocker while his three companions used the floor to sit on and leaned against a wall as support for their backs. They held their plates in their laps, and their coffee cups were on the floor beside them.

"Ma'am, you shore are a good cook," opined Bronc. "This is the best meal I've et in a long time. I know I've had two cups of coffee already, but I shore could use a third."

Ruth rose from her chair, moved to the stove, and picked up the big coffee pot.

"Don't get up, Bronc, I'll bring it to you," she told him with a smile. "I can't help wondering, though, if you are trying to get on my good side, Mr. Evans, after what you told my son."

Bronc shifted his weight a little uncomfortably before handing up his cup to Ruth and responding.

"Ma'am, I ain't gonna lie to you. That's how I feel. That boy is a good lad, and he shore enough is Apache to me. Yore way is right, I won't argue with you on that. But my way is real, and I'm right sorry to say it. There are too many Tuttles in this world, and they got to be stood up to. Me and Trig have done it for a long time. I hope you don't think ill of me for doin' it in town today."

Ruth had filled his cup and those of his two friends as he spoke. She returned to look down at him.

"No, Bronc, I don't think ill of you," she said softly. "How can I? You saved my husband and son from some unfair charges. And it was very wrong for those men to pick on Paul. I don't know what to think anymore." She turned around and returned the coffee pot to the stove, her personal distress very evident.

Jacob came to her rescue.

"I came from a small group of Apaches who believed war and fighting really accomplished nothing. Ruth and I agreed we would try to live our lives that way. But I, too, have Apache blood in me, and I could not allow the Tuttles to hurt my son that way. I failed you, Ruth, and I'm sorry. At the same time, I don't mind you calling Paul Apache," he added with a smile, looking at Bronc.

"I don't think you failed Ruth a'tall," retorted Slim. "Ruth, today you told me that the Sioux had to protect their women and children at the Little Big Horn. Ain't that true of Apaches, too?"

Ruth nodded her head yes but with an air of helplessness as she looked down for a moment. "I don't know what to think," she repeated. "I just wish the Tuttles and everyone else in town could accept us as human beings and let us live our lives in peace. I don't know why that is so hard to do."

"Well, we won't solve that problem tonight," said Jacob as he rose from the table. "Slim and his men want to get started for Dundee, and it's time they were on their way. They should be able to make the foothills by nightfall."

"The foothills?" questioned Slim.

"Yes, there is a much easier way to get to Dundee than following the stage road. It can't be done by wagons and buggies, but men on horseback can make it easy, and it will save you about five miles. Come outside, and I'll point it out to you."

"Curley, help Ruth and Apache with the dishes. Bronc, you and Trig saddle our horses and load up the pack horse. Show me that short cut, Jacob."

Slim and Jacob accompanied Bronc and Trig outside. Jacob pointed out the route he wanted Slim to take and told them which landmarks to look for. His comments were more than sufficient for experienced plainsmen.

"Ruth and I talked more about your proposal," Jacob added, "and we want to go along with it. I don't like taking your money this early, but you know we need it badly, and I'll have to swallow my pride—for Ruth's and Paul's sake. I'll do everything I can to justify your trust in me."

Slim shook hands with Jacob again and slapped him on a shoulder.

"A deal that's good for both parties is a good deal, Jacob. I'll have a herd here by the middle of September, and I aim to come along with it. Take care of yourself, and I'll see you then."

A mounted Curley brought Slim his saddled horse, and Evers quickly pulled himself up into the saddle. He touched his hat in a salute as he looked at Jacob, Ruth, and Paul, waved his arm, and the little group trotted off in a southwesterly direction.

****

Dusk had settled in, and Ruth helped Paul get ready for bed. She had bathed his face and upper body again and had put some salve on his cuts and bruises.

Both Paul and Jacob had had some difficulty eating because of Paul's swollen lips and Jacob's very painful jaw.

Paul climbed into bed, and Ruth was refilling the bowl with more hot water for Jacob when the sound of hoofbeats came to them through the open windows.

Six horsemen pulled their galloping horses to a stop in the courtyard outside the JR log house. As a cloud of dust drifted toward the building, one rider pulled his horse a few paces in front of the others and raised himself up from the saddle.

"This is Lem Tuttle," he yelled at the house. "Our business today ain't over yet, Redstone. I aim to finish it right here and now. Come out where I can see you, or do I have to come in and git you?"

Ruth's hands flew to her throat, and she looked at her husband, fear in her face.

****

Lem and Sam left the scene outside the courthouse and stamped their way back to the Palace Saloon. Lem slammed his hat down on a table as the bartender brought a bottle and glasses.

"I shouldn't have let that stranger buffalo me," he growled heatedly. "It ain't right for a Tuttle to back off like I did."

Sam rubbed his jaw reflectively.

"I dunno Lem. Both of them hombres wore two guns. They shore knew who we were, and they didn't hesitate a'tall. I wonder who they is."

Their conversation stopped instantly as Andy Tuttle entered the saloon and moved purposefully in their direction. A deep scowl had spread across his face and remained there as he approached his two sons. He yanked a chair away from the table, sat down heavily, and slammed his hat down on the table.

"I just heard tell of some trouble you boys got into while I was busy," he began. "Can't you two behave yourselves without me bein' around? What happened this time?"

Sam explained the events of the afternoon, while Lem stared at his drink.

"Lord, gawd, what is the matter with you boys," Andy snorted in disgust. "Shore I hate that Injun and his white squaw, and I got most of the folks hereabouts feeling the same way. But tryin' to beat up his 12 year old kid ain't goin' to set well with a lot of 'em. I've heard that a'ready. Why can't you two use yore heads a little bit?"

"But, paw . . .," Lem began, but Andy cut him off.

"Don't paw me," he snapped. "What you did was dumb. I ought to whip the tar out of both of you!"

Andy paused, and the ensuing silence was deep and profound.

"Any idea who those strangers were?" he finally asked.

"No," admitted Sam. "They said they was in town for supplies, and I did see a loaded pack horse outside of Arnold's. Reckon they musta headed outta town by now."

"Finish your drinks and head back to the ranch with me," directed Andy. "You've had enough fun for one day."

The ride back to their ranch was made in silence, for the most part. Lem resented his father's words, and the tone of voice Andy had used only made Lem more angry and sullen. The evening meal did not improve his mood one bit. He located a hidden bottle of liquor and headed for the cook's shack where Sam, his brother, Tim, and three ranch hands were starting a game of poker.

Lem's bottle was passed around, and the card game was stopped as Lem began to verbalize his anger and frustration with the day's events. Sam produced a second bottle, and supporting comments began to come from all around the table.

Moe Bascomb, Irish McLean, and Fargo Hines had worked for the Tuttles for several years and had become good friends with the three brothers. While they didn't share the intense Tuttle hatred against Indians in general, and the Redstones in particular, their dislike was strong enough to make them sympathize with the Tuttles.

An unsteady Lem rose to his feet and threw the two empty bottles across the room, where they splattered into a thousand pieces.

"I ain't gonna take no more guff from a stinkin' Injun," he declared loudly. "It's time us Tuttles showed people hereabouts we mean what we say. C'mon, guys, let's ride out there and show them Redstones how we handle Injuns with squaws and brat kids in these parts."

The others shouted words of agreement, and the six men filed out of the shack and headed for the corral at an unsteady gait.

****

Jacob pulled Ruth into his arms and hugged her. Still holding her, he yelled back through the window.

"We have no business that needs finishing, Tuttle. What happened today is done and over. I don't hold grudges. Now go away and leave us alone!"

"Haw, haw, haw," sneered Lem as the others joined him in sarcastic laughter. "You don't hold grudges, huh. Well, I do, and you and I are goin' to have it out right here and now. Now come out of there, or we'll come in and git yuh."

Jacob carefully released Ruth, only to have Paul come racing across the room and fly into his arms. He hugged his son, too, and gently pushed him alongside Ruth.

"I'll have to go outside and talk to them, Ruth. Otherwise I think they'll come in here, and you and Paul won't be safe."

"I won't let you go out alone," said Ruth firmly. In her heart she felt Jacob would be safer with her by his side than if he were alone.

"I'm waiting," came the voice from outside. "I'll give you one minute to come out, or we're comin' in."

Ruth looked at her husband again, saw the pain on his face, and made a quick decision.

"Paul," she said with as stern a voice as she could command, "your father and I are going out to talk to those men. If anything bad should happen, no matter what it is, I want you to slip out a back window and run as far and as fast as you can. Find Mr. Evers and ask him to take care of you!"

"But I won't go," cried Paul, tears in his eyes. His stomach tensed as his Apache instincts told him danger was round and about him. He felt a sense of fear but did not know why.

"Your minute is about up," again came the voice from outside. "What will it be?"

"I'm coming out," shouted Jacob. "Just give me a minute." He then pulled Paul to his bosom and hugged his son tightly. Releasing him, he looked Paul straight in the eyes.

"Bronc said you were an Apache brave. He even called you Apache. An Apache son obeys his father without question. Do you understand that?"

Paul nodded his head slowly in the affirmative.

"Very good. You do what Ruth has told you to do. If anything bad happens, anything bad at all, you run and find Mr. Evers. You know about where he should be. Ruth and I will take care of ourselves."

"Time's up," yelled Lem. "C'mon out, or we're comin' in."

"I'm coming," shouted Jacob. Grasping Ruth's hand, he opened the door, and the two of them stepped out into the moonlight. Jacob closed the door firmly behind them.

Jacob and Ruth, hand in hand, walked a few paces and looked up at their visitors.

"So you finally came out," sneered Lem. I was hoping we'd have to come in and git you. I see you decided to hide behind your squaw's skirts, though."

"My husband doesn't need to hide behind anything," stated Ruth defiantly. "This is our home. Say what you want to say, and then go away and leave us alone."

Jacob released Ruth's hand and raised his arms.

"I'm not armed, Mr. Tuttle," he stated flatly. "We're not looking for trouble. All we want to do is live in peace."

"You want to live in peace," jeered Lem, "I'll show you how to live in peace." He suddenly drew his Colt and pulled the trigger, firing at point-blank range.

Jacob staggered back, his hands flying to his throat where blood was gushing out. His knees buckled, and he fell forward.

Ruth screamed in horror, dropped to her knees, and tried to cradle the head of her dead husband in her lap.

Sam Tuttle quickly dismounted, drew his gun, and moved to Ruth's side. She looked up to him, tears flowing down her face.

"Why did you kill him?" she cried. "We haven't done anything to you people. Why do you act like animals?"

"Animals!" yelled Sam, in a furious voice. "You, a white squaw, calling us animals?" He swung his gun barrel at her head.

Ruth saw the missile coming and tried to duck. She received a glancing blow, screamed in pain, and fell sideways. The last thing she saw was Sam's face and the barrel heading her way again.

Sam's gun slammed into her face—again, again, and again. The first of these blows elicited a slight groan. After that there was nothing but silence, except for the thud of the gun hitting bone and skin.

Sam rose to his feet, wiped his gun barrel along the side of his trousers, and threw Lem an evil grin.

"I reckon they're both enjoying some peace now," he declared. "I don't hear a word from either of 'em."

The shock of the brutal violence had stunned the four remaining riders, and even Lem suddenly realized things had somehow gotten out of hand. That thought instantly sobered him and brought him back to reality.

"The kid!" he screamed. "That kid saw and heard everythin'. We got to find him." He motioned to Sam. "The house. He must be in the house. C'mon, we gotta git him."

Three quick strides brought both men to the doorway. They pushed the door open and rushed inside with guns drawn. It only took moments to search the house. No boy was found, but an open bedroom window told a silent tale. The two men dashed back outside.

"The kid's got away," Lem shouted. "Spread out and hunt him down. We can't let him git away, he knows too much. Irish, Fargo, rope them two horses. He won't git far without a horse."

✳✳✳✳✳✳✳✳✳✳✳✳

The Rambling R men followed Jacob's directions, located the landmarks he had described, and found a well-worn trail through the foothills. Since almost an hour of daylight still remained and there was no need to cook a night meal, they pushed on until they located a good campsite, a slight distance to the right of the trail.

With no food to cook they decided not to light a fire. A day ending cigarette or pipe was smoked before bedrolls were spread, and the men soon became cocoons in their blankets.

It was well past midnight when the lithe figure of a boy slipped into camp. He quickly examined the shapes of the four sleeping men and then boldly moved to the side of one of them and shook Slim's shoulder.

"Mr. Evers, Mr. Evers," he whispered. "This is Paul. I need your help."

"What?" muttered Slim, still half asleep. Suddenly he sat up. "Paul? What are you doin' here? What's wrong?"

"The Tuttles came to our house. They killed Jacob and I think Ruth, too." The shock of the event could no longer be contained. Paul's shoulders began to shake, and deep sobs racked his chest.

Instinctively, Slim reached out and gathered the boy in his arms and drew him close to his chest.

"Bronc, Trig, Curley. Wake up! We got trouble!"

The three men threw off their blankets, reached for their guns, stood up, and looked around. Curley was the first to find his voice.

"Trouble, what kind of trouble?" he asked.

Slim didn't answer, but three pairs of eyes were drawn to the figure sobbing in Slim's arms. Three men moved in unison and surrounded the two forms.

"It's Paul," said Slim as he looked up. "He says the Tuttles came to the ranch and killed his maw and paw."

Paul stopped crying and turned his face away from Slim's chest. "It's true," he said in a subdued voice. "Lem shot Jacob, and Sam beat Ruth something fierce. He used his gun on her. They been chasing me all night, but they couldn't catch me. Ruth and Jacob told me to run and find you. I didn't know what else to do."

"You mean the Tuttles are out there right now, looking for you?" snapped Bronc, his eyes flashing.

"I'm not sure," answered Paul. "I lost them about an hour ago. I heard someone say something about holing up and tracking me in the morning."

"How many were there?" asked Slim.

"Besides Lem and Sam, they had their brother, Tim, and three more, six in all."

"I'm staying up and taking the first watch," stated Bronc matter of factly. "Apache can have my blanket. Trig can relieve me in a couple of hours, and I'll use his blanket. I'll shore hear 'em long before they can get here, if'n they're still lookin' for him. I'll get you all awake if'n I need to."

Slim nodded his agreement and motioned for Bronc to hand over his blanket. Gently he pulled Paul down close to him and spread the blanket over the boy. Slim put his arm around the youngster, and Paul rested his head on Slim's right shoulder. Paul stared up at the stars in the heavens as Slim watched him closely.

After a long silence the boy's chest started to heave again, and the tears began to flow. Slim's strong arms drew the boy closer to his chest and held him tight.

"It's all right, son," he murmured. "Let it come out. Let it all come out. There's no shame in lovin' your maw and paw. You're with friends now, and nothin's goin' to happen to you."

A strange warmth began to permeate Slim's whole being as he held the boy close. Slim couldn't remember a feeling like that ever before. Yet it felt so good. Was this something that had been missing in his life? Slim looked into the night sky as he gently rocked the boy back and forth. This had become a night he would never forget.

Chapter 8

The first rays of a new day's sun had just begun to peek over the eastern horizon when Trig gently shook Slim. Slim carefully slid his aching arm and shoulder from under Paul's body and lowered the sleeping boy's head onto part of his blanket.

Slim got up and noticed Bronc had gathered a good supply of wood and was busy getting a fire started.

Bronc noticed the puzzled look on Slim's face.

"Me and Trig been talkin'. We reckon we outta let them skunks find Apache. We gotta go back to the JR now, and I'd druther face them on our ground than wonder where they are and when they're goin' to hit us. They can't let the boy live to tell the tale on what they done."

Slim nodded his approval of the plan.

"I can't agree more, Bronc, but let's copper our bet a mite. Curley, Ruth gave us a bunch of biscuits for breakfast today. Take a few, grab a rifle, and plant yourself up there by that brush off to the left. Anythin' we say down here will drift up to you, and you'll know what to do."

Curley did as he was told and, as he left the campsite, Paul stirred and sat up.

"C'mon over by the fire and get ready for some grub," Slim calmly instructed him. "I want you to tell us all about last night—everythin' you can remember."

Paul did as he was told and as he finished his tale Bronc handed him a tin plate filed with biscuits and bacon, a grim expression on his face.

Paul consumed a mouthful or two, and then his eyes widened in fear.

"The fire!" he exclaimed. "They'll see the fire! Quick, put it out!" He dropped his plate and reached for some dirt.

Bronc reached out and held the boy's arm.

"Don't worry none, Apache," he said in a calm and smooth voice. "Didn't yore paw say to trust us? We know what we're doin'." He filled Paul's plate again and handed it to him. "Eat it all," he commanded. "You had a bad night and need all the strength you can get. Don't worry none," Bronc repeated.

Breakfast was finished, but the fire was fed more wood and continued to burn brightly. Paul rotated his gaze among the three men and was amazed. Each man was calm and relaxed. Bronc was smoking a cigarette, and Slim had his pipe going. Trig fed the fire a few sticks from time to time and then returned to sit by his blanket, seemingly without a care in the world.

An hour passed, and finally hoofbeats were heard in the distance. Bronc flipped the remains of his cigarette into the fire, and Slim knocked the ashes out of his pipe. He turned to Paul.

"Son, I want you to move back a bit and sit alongside my saddle and blankets. Now, you stay right there and don't move. We're goin' to be busy in a little bit and don't want to worry about where you are. Do you understand?"

Paul really didn't understand what was happening but did as he was told. He took up his assigned position as the hoofbeats drew closer.

Bronc, Trig, and Slim all rose to their feet, and Bronc and Trig shook their holsters to make sure everything was free and clear.

The six riders rounded a slight bend in the trail and pulled to a surprised stop when they spotted the fire and the standing threesome.

Lem raised his hand, moved his arm, and the six men slowly walked their horses toward the camp. Tim, Lem, and Sam Tuttle were in the lead while Moe, Irish, and Fargo followed close behind. Lem raised his arm a second time, and the men reined their horses to a stop, about 10 yards short of the fire.

Lem stood up in his stirrups, looked around, and saw Paul sitting at the back of the campsite. He pointed his hand at Paul. "We've come for the boy," he announced.

"That so?" inquired Slim politely. "How come? He ain't yourn."

Lem eyed the speaker suspiciously.

"I don't know who you are mister, but we come for the boy. Why we come ain't none of yore business."

"That so?" again inquired Slim politely. "How come you want the boy? What has he done?"

"He's a witness to a killing," snarled Lem. "We're takin' him back to Hawthorne so he can testify to it."

"That so?" repeated Slim. "You boys a posse? Funny thing, but I don't see any badges. How come he was a witness to a killing?"

"That ain't none of your business," again snarled Lem, his anger rising. "We're Tuttles, and we don't need any badges. Now hand him over, pronto!"

"Of course you can have the boy," interrupted Bronc in an oily voice. "Step down and go get him."

Paul was startled at this comment but, remembering his instructions, did not move.

"Now you're talkin' sense," said a pleased Lem. "Step down, Sam, and help me corral the kid."

Both men dismounted and took two steps forward when Bronc's voice stopped them.

"Course you got one little problem in gettin' to the boy," he drawled. "You're gonna have to go through me first."

"And me," came a raspy second from the bearded man standing a few feet away.

"You buttin' in ag'in?" demanded Lem, his voice again rising. "You did too much of that yesterday. I don't know who you think you are, but this is the last time yore goin' to git away with it. Take the bearded one, Sam," he whispered. "Tim can handle the old man."

"You're goin' to be dead right about that," observed Bronc. "I don't figger I'm goin' to have to butt in ag'in. Now why don't you teach me that lesson you been so het up about."

Lem's eyes widened in surprise and fury, and his right hand went into motion. Sam's hand, too, was moving.

Bronc and Trig's Colts roared in unison.

Lem's face was a fixture in amazement as he slowly slid to his knees and then fell forward. Sam's gun fell from its owner's frozen right hand as the left hand reached for his stomach, just above the belt buckle. Sam's eyes dropped down to the same area, and the last view he had in this world was the sight of blood oozing out through his fingers. He turned sideways and collapsed.

The sounds of the two explosions were still reverberating through the foothills when the crack of rifle was heard. Tim Tuttle stood up in his stirrups and stiffened, his finger spasmodically pulled the trigger of his drawn gun, and then he pitched from his saddle.

Bronc's left hand swept across his body, trying to brush aside the gun smoke as he eyed the remaining three riders. His Colt was pointing in their direction as were Colts in the hands of Trig and Slim.

"Any of you want to teach me a lesson?" he inquired innocently as the stunned men tried to control their nervous horses.

"Either reach for those guns or unbuckle 'em and drop 'em on the ground," Slim then commanded.

Their horses now under control, the three men quickly unbuckled their belts and dropped them as instructed.

Trig gathered the discarded weapons, including those of the dead Tuttle brothers, while Bronc and Slim continued to cover the men with their Colts.

"You men can step down now," Slim informed them. "Use yore lariats to lash those bodies to their horses. Then we're goin' to take a little ride back to the JR Ranch and Hawthorne."

Curley came down from his outpost and joined his friends while the bodies of the Tuttle brothers were tied onto their horses. The fire was extinguished, the pack horse was loaded, and the other horses were saddled and mounted. Slim pulled Paul up to ride with him. He led the group back down the trail with Moe, Irish and Fargo each leading a horse carrying its grim cargo. Bronc and Trig followed with Curley bringing up the rear with the pack horse.

It was almost noon when the little cavalcade reached its first destination. Slim held Paul tight and motioned to Bronc. Bronc dismounted and examined Jacob first. Then he walked over and looked down at the bloody pulp that had once been the face of a kind and caring woman. He felt for any vital signs.

His face turned dark with rage. He slowly turned and, with measured steps, walked over to the nearest Tuttle puncher. Suddenly he reached up and yanked Moe out of his saddle. Moe started to scramble to his feet when a fist caught him full in the face. A second blow sent him sprawling.

"Stop it, Bronc!" shouted Slim. "That's enough!"

Bronc ignored Moe's groans and unloosened the blanket from his own bedroll. He walked over and covered Ruth's body.

"Bronc, use my blanket for Jacob," Slim directed while holding Paul tightly. Paul's head was down, but no tears were flowing.

Moe had regained his feet and was trying to stem the flow of blood from his nose. He moved to his horse and was just putting his foot in his stirrup when Bronc's voice reached him.

"You listen to me real good," Bronc growled and then raised his voice so that the other two men could hear him, too. "When we reach town you all are goin' to tell the truth on what happened out here and at our camp. If'n you don't, I swear to gawd I'll kill each of you with my bare hands. You won't be able to run far enough or long enough. I'll get you!"

"And he won't be alone," echoed Trig. "I'll be right along with him. You lie in town, and you'll curse the day you was born. That's a promise!"

Paul raised his head and looked back at Slim. "Let's go now, Slim, please. I don't want to stay here any longer."

Slim squeezed the boy with his big hands, nudged his horse, and led the group toward Hawthorne.

****

The arrival of Slim and his entourage created an immediate sensation in Hawthorne. Eyes of the local citizenry were drawn to the three body-draped horses, and as the bare heads of the victims bobbed up and down with the movements of their steeds, they were soon recognized as being Tuttles.

Slim and his group walked their horses through the center of main street, the size of the gathering crowd increasing with every step. They crossed the intersection at the end of the first block and continued on until they came abreast of the sheriff's office, whereupon Slim turned his horse to the right and approached the tie rail. He remained mounted.

Deputy Lester Dickson had been lounging outside the sheriff's office, but as the horsemen proceeded down main street he got up and dashed inside. He reappeared with Sheriff Turk Edwards at his heels.

Edwards stepped off the sidewalk and on to the street. He examined each of the corpses carefully, trying desperately to keep his facial expression under control. Finally, he looked up at Slim.

"These are all three of the Tuttle boys," he said, stating the obvious. "They're all dead. You know how come they got that way?"

"Yes," replied Slim calmly. "Me and my boys killed them. You got a coroner or undertaker in this town?"

Edwards couldn't hide his astonishment at this admission. He finally got his face under control.

"You have a good reason to kill these boys?" he asked in as calm a voice as he could muster.

"The best damn reason in the world," snapped Slim. "They're murderers! Now do you have a coroner or undertaker in this town?"

"Yes," answered a perplexed Edwards. "Harvey Breen answers to both them titles. His place is down the street a ways."

"Good! Have someone take these three Tuttles down to him. Tell him to park them someplace and come up here with a wagon. We got to go get some more bodies."

"More bodies!" Edwards exploded. "How many more, and who are they?"

"Two more," replied Slim. "Jacob and Ruth Redstone. Them's the two these varmints murdered. Help the boy down, and he'll tell you all about it.

"These three Tuttle men are witnesses and were part of it. They got a story to tell, too. Now take these dead ones off our hands and get the undertaker up here, pronto. Those other bodies have been laying outside for a long time and won't keep long in this heat. Sheriff, you and I are goin' with yore coroner to the Redstone Ranch so you can see for yourself what happened."

With these words Slim helped Paul slide down the side of his horse toward the sheriff. Instinctively Edwards reached to steady the boy. Slim dismounted, and all three moved toward the sheriff's office as Edwards spoke to Dickson, "Lester, have some folks help you get those bodies down to Harvey and tell him to get up here with his wagon, right quick."

Moe, Irish, and Fargo had dismounted, too, and now handed three sets of reins to Lester. They tied their own horses and watched Bronc, Trig, and Curley do the same. Bronc and Trig shoved the three men in the direction of the sheriff's office as Bronc spoke to them from behind.

"Remember what I said out on the trail," he warned them. "I'll be listenin' to every word."

Edwards and another deputy rearranged the desk and chairs in the main room of the office so that when Edwards sat behind the desk, Paul and the three Tuttle men sat in chairs facing Edwards, and the others stood.

Slim put his hand on Paul's right shoulder and spoke softly. "Son, tell these folks what happened last night. Take yore time and don't be afraid to stop if'n you have to."

Slim flashed a look at Edwards.

"This ain't goin' to be easy for the boy. Give him time and hear him out."

Paul began his tale and managed to complete it without breaking down, although his voice quivered a couple of times. Edwards was shocked, and his face showed it. Paul completed this portion of his narrative by describing his arrival at Slim's campsite.

"Before he goes any further, mebby the sheriff has some questions for these brave men," Slim drawled, his voice dripping with sarcasm.

"I only have one for the moment," snarled Edwards. He looked at each of the three men in turn. "Is the kid telling it as it was?" he demanded to know.

Moe looked around and saw Bronc's eyes boring into him. Irish and Fargo could only look down. Moe nodded helplessly. "He's giving you the straight of it." Moe described what had taken place at the Tuttle Ranch and concluded, "We didn't have any idea it would turn out that way."

"Six of you went out there, half drunk, and you didn't think it would turn out that way?" asked an incredulous Edwards. "What did you expect?" he went on, disgust in his voice.

"Paul, tell the sheriff what happened this morning," interrupted Slim.

Paul again did as he was told, and now his voice took on a stronger, more vibrant tone. Excitedly he described the shootout and the devastating results. His voice reflected his wonderment as admiration for Slim glowed in his face.

Edwards got up, his face red with anger. He pulled off his hat, slammed it down on the desk, and stared up at the ceiling.

Finally getting his emotions under control, he took a long look at each of the three men sitting in front of him. He motioned to the deputy standing nearby, who also was having trouble masking his disgust.

"Jerry, throw these skunks in the last cell. I want them as far away from me as I can get them. Then you'd better ride out to the Tuttle Ranch and tell Andy about his boys. Tell Andy he can come into town to take care of his boys, but he's to come alone. I mean that! Tell him if he brings any of his ranch hands with him he'll get thrown in jail!"

Jerry nodded his understanding and herded his three prisoners to the cell block.

Edwards reclaimed his hat and headed for the doorway to the street with Slim, Paul, Bronc, and Trig at his heels. He found Harvey Breen sitting in a wagon waiting for him.

Lester had saddled the sheriff's horse and handed him the reins. Edwards swung into the saddle and waited for Slim to join him.

"Bronc, you stay here with Paul in the sheriff's office," instructed Slim. "Trig, you and Curley take care of the horses and get some rooms at the hotel. Then join up with Bronc here. I'll be back as soon as I can." With that Slim swung into his saddle, pulled his horse away from the tie rail, and soon caught up with the sheriff and wagon, already moving down the street.

****

As soon as they arrived at the JR Ranch, Slim let the sheriff examine the crime scene with the undertaker while he entered the little ranch house that had been the scene of a savory banquet less than 24 hours earlier. He quickly searched the house, located the papers he was seeking, and then joined the two Hawthorne officials outside the house. Both of the blanket covered bodies were now in the wagon.

"Well, robbery shore wasn't a motive," sighed Edwards. "I found these in Jacob's pocket." He showed Slim five gold double eagles.

"Yes, I gave them to him yesterday," Slim told him. "It was good faith money to complete a deal we had made."

"What kind of a deal?" asked Edwards.

"It don't matter none now," replied Slim with an effort. "If'n you have no objection, I would like to use that money for a funeral for the two of them."

"Don't see nothing wrong with that," admitted the sheriff as he dropped the coins into Slim's hands. "But don't expect many folks from around here to attend it."

"That don't matter none, neither," growled Slim. "We'll take our chances on that. You find anything to dispute what Paul said?"

"No," sighed Edwards. "I figgered he was telling the truth. The faces of them other three told me that. Killing an unarmed man is bad enough, but what they did to the woman made my stomach turn. I knew the Tuttles hated these folks, but this . . . ." Edwards shook his head in disbelief.

The undertaker had already started back to Hawthorne when Slim and the sheriff pulled themselves back into their saddles. The sheriff urged his mount forward, but Slim paused for a moment and took a long look at the little log house. He, too, shook his head in disbelief before kicking his horse into movement.

****

On the way back to Hawthorne, Slim told the Sheriff about searching the house, what he had found, and what he intended to do.

The sheriff gave his approval but again warned about expecting much in the way of attendance at the funeral.

****

As soon as Slim reached town he located the Western Union office and sent two telegrams, as he told the sheriff he would do. The first was directed to Mr. James McComb, the representative of the Friends who was located in Kansas City, Kansas. Slim had found the name on papers he had located at the JR Ranch. The telegram was straightforward, simply notifying the man of Jacob's and Ruth's deaths and asking for advice on what to do about the property.

The second telegram was common enough but puzzled the telegraph operator somewhat. It read as follows:

Mr. Tex Riley,
General Delivery
Cravenville, Arizona

Will be delayed for two weeks due to messy situation in Hawthorne, Colorado. Regret missing my quartet. Advise them as soon as possible.

Slim

As soon as the telegram reached Cravenville, the operator there, Nate Green, rose from his key and moved to the doorway of his office. Spotting his son across the street, he yelled and motioned for the lad to come to him. Toby Green, age 15, responded to the wave and ran to his father's side.

"Toby, check the livery stable, the general store, and any saloons you come to. See if any Rambling R men are in town. If you see any, bring them right here. Tell 'em I got a telegram for Tex."

Toby dashed off and returned five minutes later, accompanied by Reno Lang and Laredo Lee.

"Found them at the general store, paw," he stated proudly. "Gave 'em your message and here they are."

Laredo flipped the lad a quarter and looked at Nate. "Heard tell you got a telegram for Tex. Where is it?"

Nate handed him the message, and Laredo read it, with Reno looking over his right shoulder. Laredo snapped the paper with his fingers and then read it a second time.

"Don't like the sound of it," he mused out loud. "Funny thing that Slim used General Delivery and not the ranch proper. Let's get our horses and head back to the ranch. We can stay in town another night. I think Tex needs to get this right soon."

They made excellent time getting back to the Rambling R and quickly located Tex, who was working on some ledgers in the den of the main ranch house.

The foreman looked up as the two men entered the room, a surprised expression on his face.

"We decided not to stay in town" explained Laredo. "Slim sent you a wire, and I don't like the sound of it. Thought you'd better get it, right quick." He handed the telegram to Tex as he spoke.

Tex read the message, thought for a moment, read it again, and then turned toward Reno.

"Lefty was in the bunkhouse a little while ago. Should be there now or close by. Go fetch him for me."

Tex leaned back in his chair and was deep in thought when the sound of boots and jingling spurs announced the return of Reno with Lefty White at his side. Silently Tex handed the wire to the little left-hander and leaned back in his chair again, his eyes on his second-in-command.

Lefty read the message and frowned. "He's shore askin' for help but only wants the four of us. We'll start in the mornin' and push it hard."

Tex nodded his agreement. "I reckon you're right. Get there as fast as you can."

The next morning at the crack of dawn, Lefty, Charley Landers, Kansas, Blackie Smith, and a heavily loaded pack horse left the Rambling R at a fast lope and headed in a northeasternly direction.

Chapter 9

Deputy Jerry Hastings slowed his horse to a walk as he approached the courtyard of the Tuttle Ranch. He noticed a Tuttle puncher, Jim Sloan, saddling a horse inside a nearby corral and turned his own mount in that direction.

Sloan led his horse out of the corral, replaced the entrance bars, and looked up as Hastings approached him.

"Howdy, Jerry, what brings you out our way?" Sloan said, in a friendly voice.

"Andy around?" asked Jerry quietly.

"Why no, he's out on the north range, about a mile or so away. I was about to join up with him," replied Sloan. "You want to come along?"

"No, I'll wait for him here. You ride out to Andy and tell him there's been trouble in town involving his boys. The sheriff wants Andy to come to town right quick."

Sloan swung into his saddle. "I'll git the message to him as fast as I can. We should be back directly." Sloan spurred his horse and was gone in a cloud of dust.

Hastings dismounted and led his horse to a watering trough a short distance away. He rolled a cigarette and mentally tried to prepare himself for the storm he knew was coming.

Hastings was just finishing his cigarette when two figures topped a low lying distant ridge and galloped in his direction, a thin line of dust trailing in their wake. The two riders pounded into the courtyard, reined their horses to a skidding stop, and Andy Tuttle threw himself from the saddle, handing his reins to Sloan in the process.

"Jim tells me my boys are in some kind of trouble in Hawthorne," he began. "Is that true?"

"Yes," answered Hastings in a non-committal tone.

"Well, what kind of trouble?" Tuttle demanded to know.

"Big trouble, Andy," answered Hastings calmly.

"What kind of trouble?" Tuttle again demanded to know. "Are they in jail?"

"No, they ain't in jail," replied Jerry, trying to steel himself for what was to follow.

"If they ain't in jail, it can't be big trouble," declared a slightly relieved Andy Tuttle. "What they gone and done?"

Hastings realized he couldn't drag it out any longer.

"They murdered Jacob and Ruth Redstone, Andy," Hastings informed him, again using as level a tone as he could maintain.

"They killed the Redstones?" cried an astonished Tuttle. "Are you shore?"

"Yes, we're shore. But that ain't the worst of it. They tried to kill the Redstones boy, too, but they got caught at it." Hastings' voice rose a notch, and his eyes glinted. "Four strangers caught 'em at it."

"Four strangers? Were two of them those guys who helped Redstone yesterday at the courthouse?"

"Yeah, they were two of 'em," agreed Hastings.

"You say they was caught at it, but they ain't in jail. Where are my boys"

"At the undertakers, Andy. Lem, Sam, and Tim are all dead."

A shocked Andy Tuttle stepped back a full pace in utter amazement. His Adam's apple bobbed up and down, but no sound was heard. Jim Sloan, too, was speechless.

"Lem . . . Sam . . . Tim . . . all dead," gasped Andy as he finally got his vocal chords working again. "And four strangers done it?"

Hastings nodded and remained silent, not knowing what else to do.

"Jim, round up the men," exclaimed Tuttle savagely. "I'll get my Colt, and then we're headin' for town!"

Sloan dropped the reins he had been holding and started to wheel his horse when Hastings' loud voice stopped him.

"Hold it, Jim, stay put. You ain't goin' anywhere." Hastings unconsciously let his right hand drop to the butt of his Colt.

Tuttle, who taken a step or two in the direction of his ranch house, spun around and looked at Hastings, surprise on his face.

"Sheriff Edwards says you are to come alone," Jerry explained, "and I'll ask you to leave your Colt to home." Hastings paused a second as Tuttle stared at him in amazement. "In fact, on second thought, I won't be askin' you to keep yore Colt here; I'll be tellin' you! We've had enough trouble in town for one day, and Turk don't want no more. You climb aboard your horse, and we'll go to town, but the Colt stays here!"

Andy Tuttle didn't believe his own ears. He couldn't remember the last time someone told him he couldn't do something he wanted to. He looked at Hastings, his face a thundercloud.

"You're tellin' me I can't take my Colt and my men to town if I want to? You think you can stop me?"

"I can, and I will," stated Hastings, his voice again on the rise. "Sheriff Edwards says you're to come alone, and that's the way you're comin'!"

A slight movement by Sloan caught Jerry's eyes.

"Don't you touch hardware, Jim." he snapped. "I'm faster'n you, and I shore would hate to put a hole in you!"

Sloan stopped his movement and returned his hand to the horn on his saddle as Hastings turned his attention back to Tuttle.

"Climb aboard your horse, Andy. We're headin' for town—you first and me right behind. Git goin'; I ain't got all day."

Tuttle climbed back up into his saddle, settled in, and gave Hastings another angry look. "I'll tend to you later, Jerry. You've gotten too big for your britches."

Hastings also mounted his horse and kept a keen eye on Sloan at the same time.

Tuttle turned to his puncher. "Jim, round up all the men and have 'em here at the ranch when I get back." He spurred his horse into motion, and Hastings did the same.

****

Bronc, Paul, Trig, and Curley were lounging outside the sheriff's office when Deputy Hastings and Andy Tuttle pounded into town. Tuttle viciously pulled his horse to a skidding halt, flung himself out of the saddle, and stepped from the street to the sidewalk. He paused to glance at the three strangers before plunging inside the building.

Bronc motioned to Trig, got up, and bent down in front of Paul. "Apache, you stay outside here with Curley. Slim had some telegrams to send and should be back soon. Me and Trig will be inside if'n you need anythin'." He and Trig then slowly moved through the doorway into the office proper, following in the footsteps of Jerry Hastings.

Although the door to a side office was closed, the sound of loud voices easily sifted through the enclosure. Hastings rolled a cigarette and smiled grimly as Bronc and Trig leaned against a wall, both of their hands hooked inside their gun belts.

Another volley of words was heard, this time primarily coming from the sheriff. The door opened, and Andy Tuttle stamped out and paused to stare at Bronc and Trig. Tuttle pointed at the two men.

"Them's two of the strangers that done in my boys?" he thundered.

Bronc and Trig straightened up and tensed their bodies.

"Yeah, that's two of 'em," acknowledged Edwards.

Tuttle took a step forward and stared at the two men, his face dark with rage.

"You butted in yesterday, and today you killed my boys. You should be real proud of yourselves. You got anythin' to say to me?"

"Not much," drawled Bronc as he tensed for action. "I'm right sorry we couldn't kill 'em twice!"

Tuttle's eyes opened wide in amazement. He was about to leap at Bronc when Edwards restrained him.

"That's enough," he growled. "Jerry, take Andy back to the cell block. He wants to talk to his three punchers."

"Me and Trig will go along with him," announced Bronc in a matter-of-fact voice. "I'm right curious to hear what them boys have to say."

It was all Andy could do to control himself. He gave Edwards a withering look. "I want to talk to my men, and I don't need these strangers to nursemaid me. They ain't yore deputies. Tell them to stay here and keep out of my way."

"Ordinarily I would agree with you, Andy," said Edwards. "But this time it's different. Bronc and Trig will go with you, and if you want me to deputize them, I will."

Tuttle stared at Edwards, unable to again believe his own ears. He opened his mouth to say something, stopped and closed it, opened it again, threw up his hands in frustration, and silently followed Hastings through the open doorway to the cell block. A grim faced Bronc Evans and Trig Mansfield kept pace right behind him.

The four men reached the end of the cell block, and Tuttle looked in at his three riders. Hastings, Bronc, and Trig stopped a few paces short of the last cell and waited.

Tuttle glanced back at the threesome before addressing his men.

"Lem, Sam, and Tim are dead. The sheriff tells me you boys were part of it and saw the whole thing. Tell me what happened!"

Moe did most of the talking, with Irish and Fargo adding brief comments. All three glanced periodically at the three men standing behind Tuttle. A deadly silence followed the completion of their story. Tuttle's shoulders sagged, and he shuffled out of the cell block, head down, and without a glance at the others standing in the area. Hastings and Trig followed Tuttle, but Bronc slid over to the bars and looked at the three cell mates.

"I'm right glad you told the truth," he informed them. You all got a chance to live to a ripe old age after all."

****

Slim had sent his telegrams and had done a few more administrative chores before he returned to the sheriff's office and his friends. He learned about Andy Tuttle's visit and also found out that Tuttle had visited the undertaker. Tuttle demanded that his sons be handled ahead of the Redstones and informed the undertaker that he would return on the morrow with a wagon and take his sons home. He had made no arrangements for their funerals, sensing that the community was in no mood for such an event. But, before leaving town, he had made his thoughts known regarding the burial of the Redstones. Despite the brutal acts of his sons, those wishes did fall on some sympathetic ears.

After supper at the hotel, Slim and his men had a meeting with Paul in the room Slim and Paul were sharing. Slim put his arm around Paul as they sat on the bed and, again, found that the special warm glow he had experienced at the camp site had returned anew.

"Son," Slim began, "when white folks die, we have what we call a funeral. This is our way of honoring these folks and paying our last respects to them. I've arranged to have a funeral service for Jacob and Ruth. It's set for the day after tomorrow. It will be short, and I'll say a few words, but I expect only a few folks will be there. That's all right. It's more important who is there, not how many.

"But I got a couple of problems, and I need yore help. Some folks hereabouts have a strange idear on who should be buried in their cemetery. It don't make no sense to me—the dead are beyond caring, anyhow. However, I don't want to get into a fight over the matter. It ain't worth it. Besides, I got a better idear.

"Is there a place on your ranch that yore folks liked a heap? Mebby there's a spot in the foothills west of yore ranch house that the warm sun hits and is real pretty. Is there a place yore paw took you that he liked real well?"

Paul cogitated for a few minutes and then smiled brightly.

"Jacob and Ruth did have a place they went to a few times. There is a little stream and lots of wildflowers. Ruth would pack a little food, and we would eat out there. Then she would pick some flowers to take home with her."

"Sounds like just the right place," Bronc allowed, trying to maintain a stern look on his face and not doing very well.

"That's good, Paul," Slim went on. "But yore father was an Apache, too, and we can't forget that. Don't the Apaches have a ceremony for someone who dies? Do you know what it is?"

Paul thought carefully again before speaking.

"I barely remember something like that when I lived in the hills with Jacob. I don't think Apaches do much when that happens, but I'm not sure. That's one thing my father never taught me. I think only the chiefs and the medicine men did that sort of thing."

"Well, that's all right, Paul," sighed Slim, "we'll do the best we can. Why don't you write down a few things you would like to say, and we'll let you do that right after we bury them in the hills."

****

The next morning after breakfast, Slim, Bronc, and Paul paid a visit to Otis Arnold's General Store. First, Slim selected a pick and two short-handled spades and handed them to Bronc. Then he pushed Paul toward Arnold and gave the man a hard look.

"Paul has to go to a funeral tomorrow and needs some nice clean duds. You know what he needs. Measure him up and pick out the right stuff. We'll be back this afternoon to pick 'em up."

Arnold hesitated a moment, but Slim's look was unwavering. Arnold sighed and called to his wife. "Martha, we got a customer here. Help me measure him, and you can pick out what he needs."

Martha Arnold did as she was told. She selected a number of items and looked at Slim for approval. Slim nodded his head in the affirmative.

"It won't take much sewing to get these ready for the boy," she said. "Come back just afore closing, and he can have 'em then."

Slim paid the bill, and he and Paul marched out of the store. However, Bronc tarried a bit and had a short conversation with the Arnolds. Then he joined Slim and Paul on the sidewalk, outside the store. He handed the pick and one shovel to Slim and the other shovel to Paul.

"Have to stop at the bank for a minute," he announced. "Trig and Curley have the horses ready outside the sheriff's office. I'll meet you there."

Bronc went to the bank, insisted on seeing Mr. Quigley immediately, and had a brief but spirited conversation with the man. A few minutes later he joined his friends outside the sheriff's office.

Sheriff Edwards had insisted on supplying a horse for Paul. Jerry Hastings found a suitable animal and had it saddled and ready when Slim and Paul arrived.

Trig and Curley secured the pick and shovels, Bronc arrived, and the group was mounted and was ready to move out when Hastings swung into his saddle and pulled his horse even with Slim's.

"I know what you're goin' to do. Edwards gave me the day off, and I'm comin' along. Don't try to stop me. Don't expect no trouble, but havin' the law along with you won't do no harm."

Slim smiled his approval and waved his little troop into motion.

Paul guided them to the spot he had selected for the graves, and Slim was pleased with the beauty of the location. Furthermore, there was level ground virtually all the way to the site. They would have to carry the pine boxes only a very short distance.

Bronc began the work with his pick, while Curley and Trig handled the shoveling. The six men spelled off each other, as Paul insisted on helping, too.

Slim suggested they dig one combined grave rather than two separate ones, and the others agreed. Paul gave Slim a pleased look, but made no comment.

Rapid progress was made, and the job was completed in about an hour. The perspiring men drank from the tiny stream and took a long rest, lounging on the grass a short distance from the grave. Their hands were not used to this kind of work, but they all had gloves, and only a few blisters were in evidence.

"Paul, it's almost noon," announced Slim. "There's lots of grub at the ranch. Would you mind if'n we stopped there and used some of it up? No sense in havin' it go to waste."

"Yes, let's do that," agreed Paul. "That's what Ruth would want us to do. I'll be all right. I just couldn't bear to see Jacob and Ruth there, on the ground, looking like they did yesterday."

The men rose and were surprised at their stiffness and the sore and aching muscles that suddenly made their presence known.

"Guess we set too long," complained Bronc. "I'm sore in places I didn't know about."

"That's what you get from spendin' all yore time in the saddle," laughed Hastings, trying to conceal his own problem. "Reckon it's the right kind of soreness, though."

The group reached the JR Ranch, had a leisurely lunch, and arrived in Hawthorne by mid-afternoon.

Trig, Curley, and Hastings took possession of all the horses and headed for the livery stable as Slim, Paul, and Bronc had a short conversation on the sidewalk outside the sheriff's office.

"I have one more job to do," stated Slim. "Bronc, you and Paul stay here for about an hour, and if'n I'm not back by then, take Paul down to Arnold's and pick up his clothes. If'n I miss you here, I'll meet up with you at the hotel."

Slim proceeded down the street until he came to the offices of Judge Joseph Pardee. He found the judge reading a law book.

"Judge, my name is Slim Evers. I've got a matter I need to talk to you about."

"I know *who* you are," admitted the judge as he shook hands. "But I don't know where you're from nor how come you ended up here in Hawthorne."

"Well, I didn't end up here," smiled Slim. "Me and my boys needed supplies and were just pass'n through when all the trouble started." His eyes narrowed. "I'm right glad we were here, though. It seems to me you folks had a problem here what needed attention, but you all looked the other way."

The judge coughed and cleared his throat, trying to cover his uneasiness.

"I suppose one could look at it that way, but human attitudes are easy to come by and hard to change. I'm not proud of what we have done, but the Tuttles have been here for a long time and have a lot of influence. Most people aren't strong enough to stand up to folks like that, even if they are wrong. And, remember, an awful lot of folks didn't think Andy was wrong. Is that what you come to see me about?"

"No, it ain't," Slim allowed. "Judge, I need yore advice on somethin'. It's got to do with Redstone's boy, Paul. He can't stay here now, and I'm not shore he can or should go back to his reservation."

Slim paused and took a deep breath.

"I have an idear, but I haven't talked to Paul about it yet. Wanted to see how it would set with you first.

"I own a big cattle ranch in Arizona. A lot of good men work for me. You've seen three of them here in Hawthorne. It would be a good place to bring up a lad like Paul. My ranch is not far from Cravenville. They have a good school and a church there, and it ain't so far from the San Carlos Reservation that he can't go back to visit now and ag'in.

"Judge, I like the boy. This has been a terrible blow to him, and it ain't fair. I could give the boy a good home. Is there some way I could do that if'n Paul favors the idear?"

"Well now, that's an interesting thought," mused the judge. "You say you own a ranch in Arizona. What do you call it? Maybe I would recognize it."

"I call it the Rambling R," replied Slim, watching Pardee's face carefully.

"Thunderation!" exclaimed the judge, sitting upright in his chair. "I've heard about *that* ranch for sure. Now I understand more about what has happened around here the past couple of days. Your ranch does not have the most reassuring reputation, Mr. Evers," he added in a stern voice.

"If'n you mean I hire men who don't back away from a fight, yore dead right," replied Slim in a hard voice. "Folks have found it's plumb fatal to steal from us or try to push us around. We've had more'n our share of trouble over the years, and I've lost some good men. But things are better now, and I still think it would be a good place for Paul to grow up on."

Pardee paused to digest this information.

"Are you married, Mr. Evers?" he finally asked.

"No, I ain't," admitted Slim. "Never have been, neither. Does that make a difference?"

"I'm afraid it does. If you were married, you and your wife could adopt the boy. Courts like to have a woman involved in the upbringing of children, preferably one who had kids of her own. Course, Paul is almost a man now, and that would help some."

Pardee paused again and stroked his jaw.

"Let me ponder your idea, Evers. I must admit it has some merit, and you are obviously concerned for the welfare of the boy. By the way, Slim can't be your real name. What name would I use, should I need to prepare any papers?"

"My Christian name is Raymond," smiled Slim. "But I've been known as Slim ever since I was a kid. I think you can see why."

Pardee chuckled, rose, and stretched out his hand.

"I'll think about what you have suggested," he assured Slim as he shook hands. "Come back tomorrow, and we can talk again."

Slim rose, too, and took a step toward the door before stopping and looking back at Pardee.

"I think you ought to plan on being at the funeral tomorrow, judge. It might make a good impression on folks around here." Without waiting for a reply, Slim walked out of the office and onto the sidewalk.

Chapter 10

The funeral was scheduled for ten o'clock in the morning at Breen's Funeral Parlor. Hawthorne had a community church, and Harvey Breen had approached its pastor, the Reverend Abner Meeker, about handling the religious portion of the service. The good Reverend demurred at first, but Breen had made his arguments loud and strong, and when he added a golden double eagle as an exclamation point, Pastor Meeker could not resist the call.

Shortly before the appointed hour, Slim, Bronc, Trig, Curley, and Paul arrived, the latter attired in his brand new clothes. Slim was surprised to find Breen's parlor almost full. In addition to Sheriff Edwards and Deputy Hastings, Otis and Martha Arnold, Judge and Mrs. Pardee, Donald and Sally Quigley, and three other couples were present.

At Slim's request, the bodies of the victims were not shown; Paul having indicated that he wanted to remember them as they were when they were alive.

The Reverend Meeker began the service by reading several Bible passages, principally from the Book of John. He offered a short prayer and then recited the Twenty-third Psalm. Pausing, he looked around the room and then announced, "Mr. Evers would like to say some words in behalf of the deceased."

Slim stepped to the little podium, and he, too, looked over the assembled gathering.

"I want to thank you all for comin' this morning," he began. "I think Jacob and Ruth would be pleased. I know Paul is.

"I met Ruth Redstone for the first time three days ago, and I only knew her for one day. Me and my men stopped by the JR Ranch to water our horses. We had been on the trail for over two weeks, and when Ruth told me she was a good cook, I made a deal with her: If we supplied the grub, she would make us a home cooked meal. We found out she *was* a good cook. I think me and the boys can still taste that meal.

"I spent a good part of the day talking to her while two of my men came to Hawthorne for supplies. I found out some things about her, and I want to tell you folks what I learned just in case you didn't know or had forgot.

"Ruth told me she was a Quaker. As far as I can tell, her church was started back east a long time ago, and the folks who belong to her church think about things a heap different than you and I do. Mostly they don't believe in fightin' and killin'. They figger there must be a better way than that to settle things. They even went so far as to try to bring peace between the Indians and the white man all over the plains west of the Mississippi. Some of them became what they called missionaries and took on the job of bein' Indian Agents and such. They tried to figger out a way to have the white man and the red man live together in a way that was fair to both sides. That sorta makes some sense, don't it?

"Jacob, as you all know, was an Apache. Accordin' to Ruth, though, he never fought ag'in white men cause he belonged to a small group of Apaches that didn't think that fightin' the white man was a good idear. Don't that beat all! They came from two different ways of life. Yet, Jacob and Ruth both had the same idear on how folks should treat one another.

"Jacob and Ruth met at the San Carlos Reservation in Arizony. Jacob worked on the reservation, buildin' and fixin' things, and Ruth was a school teacher. Her job was to teach them Apache young'uns how to write the white man's letters, read the white man's words, and use the white man's numbers.

"Jacob and Ruth got married and kept on working on the reservation. Paul was Jacob's son, but Ruth loved him like he was her own.

"Jacob and Ruth had a dream. They wanted to do somethin' better than livin' on a reservation. More'n that, they wanted to show folks that the two of them, one red and one white, could live together and be a family, just like most of you.

"So they got a stake together and come to Hawthorne. Their church leased the land for 'em and helped give 'em a start. All they wanted was a place where they could live in peace, have a little ranch, and raise their boy. Is that so awful wrong? Is that so awful bad? Ain't that what most of us folks want to do with our lives?

"Jacob didn't carry a gun. Some folks think that makes a man a coward. Apaches may be a lot of things, but they shore ain't cowards. To my way of thinkin', it may take more courage not to carry a gun. But it didn't do him no good. He got killed anyhow. And Ruth, too.

"Like I have said, I only knew these two folks for one day. But that was long enough for me to find out they was good people. They would have helped make Hawthorne a better town. Ruth told me she thought that most people hereabouts hated them, and she couldn't figger out why. What had they done to cause that? What did they do that caused them to die like they did? I can't figger it out, neither."

Slim paused, looked at the two pine boxes, and shook his head in disbelief.

"I guess that's all I have to say," he muttered.

Slim moved away from the podium and took a step toward his chair when a voice stopped him.

"I have something that needs said," announced a burly man standing near the back of the room.

"I'm Ezra Poe, and I know all of you, except'n them strangers. More'n a year ago I was in Otis' store and allowed to the fact that I needed to add a room to my house cause my kids was gettin' bigger and needed more space. Jacob musta been in the store cause next day he shows up at my place with a tool box and asks if he can be of help. Now, I never heard tell of an Injun that could do that sorta thing, and I weren't easy about havin' him around. But I don't look a gift horse in the mouth, neither. I figgered I'd try him for one day, and then I'd soon be shut of him.

"Now, I gotta tell you I know my way around a axe, saw, bit, and auger, but I shore had to step lively to keep up with him! He knew right well what he was doin'. At mid-day he dug in his pocket for some bread and corn and set himself under a tree while I went inside and et. He was back at work afore I got back outside ag'in.

"The next day he comes back, and this time he brung his boy with him. I'll bet the lad remembers it."

Slim looked down at Paul, who nodded yes.

"Well, I figgered the boy would set around and watch us work," Poe went on. "Nosiree! He worked right alongside his paw and did right well, too. Come mid-day and Emma come out to me. "Ezra," she says, "it ain't fittin' that these folks do all this work and us not feedin' 'em. Invite them into the house."

"Well, I shore had to think on that. But she was right, and I invited them in to eat with us. I nearly fell off my chair when Jacob asked if we said grace. That comin' from some Injun!

"Jacob and Paul spent three more days helpin' me, and Jacob even went around our house and found a couple of places that needed fixin'. We did that, too. I never told anyone about this cause I figgered most folks wouldn't understand why we done it. Besides I was skeered at what Andy Tuttle and his boys would say and do. I ain't afeered no more, and I'm right glad to git this off my chest!" Ezra quickly sat down.

Slim was speechless with surprise at the interruption. Before he could get his voice going again, a second man rose from his chair.

"I'm Luther Bennett, as you all know, except'n you strangers. About eight months ago Rachel here got real sick with the fever. Mrs. Redstone somehow heard about it and come over to my place. For three days and nights she nursed Rachel, washed our clothes, and fed me and the young'uns. I never reckoned I'd see an angel here on earth, but I shore enough did. I never told folks about this, neither, for the same reasons Ezra didn't."

As soon as Luther sat down, the third man rose.

"I'm Ned Stark. I don't have any stories to tell, like Ezra and Luther here, but I got to ask a question. Preacher, all of us are members of your flock. Did anyone in town extend a hand in welcome to the Redstones when they got here?"

Pastor Meeker lowered his eyes and slowly shook his head no.

"Not even me, as far as I know, Brother Ned," he muttered. "And since it seems like it's time for confessions, I have one to make, too. I didn't want to take part in this service. Me, a man of the cloth, and I didn't want to share my faith with these folks! Harvey even had to bribe me."

Meeker dug into his pocket and produced a gold coin. He stepped around the podium, bent down in front of Paul, and handed him the double eagle.

"Paul, I want you to have this coin, and I want you to keep it as long as you can. Look at it often and try to remember that some of us in Hawthorne are sorry for the way we acted and how we treated your folks. Try to forgive us for being what we were."

"Preacher," interrupted Stark. "It's my understandin' that the Redstones won't be buried in our cemetery. I ain't proud of that, but I reckon it's too late to do anythin' about it. But next Sunday I think all of Hawthorne needs to hear somethin' from you on brotherly love and bein' good neighbors. Maybe Ezra and Luther should tell their stories ag'in, too. Does that sound right to you?"

"It certainly does, Ned," acknowledged Meeker. "And I'll do it. But right now I'm going to bring this service to a close with a prayer. Will you all rise and please hold hands."

It was a good prayer, warm and vibrant, with a little fire and brimstone at the end. The assembled group responded with a loud "Amen," and the service was over.

****

It took a while for the attendees to depart. Slim had shaken hands with each of the Hawthorne residents and exchanged conversation with several of them. Finally, all were gone save Turk Edwards and Jerry Hastings. The six men loaded the coffins on Breen's wagon, and soon the entire group walked their horses down the main street behind Breen in his wagon.

By noon they reached the burial site and hauled the coffins over to the gaping hole in the ground. The coffins were lowered into the grave, side by side, and then the men stepped back a few paces as Paul moved to the side of the grave. Paul had searched the recesses of his memory and had a vague idea of what he should do. He knelt on his knees. Four times he picked up a double handful of dirt and let it sift through his hands as he softly intoned what he wanted to say in his native tongue as he looked skyward. Finally he filled each hand with dirt, rose, walked to the very edge of the grave, and dropped one handful on each box. Then he turned around, walked to the edge of the little stream, sat down, and stared into the water.

Slim joined him as the other men began to fill the grave, the sound of dirt hitting the boxes painfully loud. Slim put an arm around Paul's shoulder and remained silent. Paul looked up at him, tears in his eyes.

"You said your service in English," he said softly. "I thought this one should be in Apache. I hope the others understand."

"I'm shore they do," answered Slim as he squeezed the boy. "You did right. That's the way it shoulda been done. I'm right proud of you."

The trip back to town was again interrupted by a stop at the JR Ranch and the consumption of food. They were surprised to find that the Redstones two horses had returned, none the worse for apparently roaming wild for several days.

"We'll take them horses into town until we figger out what to do with 'em," decided Slim. "And we'll take along the saddles and trappings, too." The horses were roped and saddled in short order, and soon the group headed for town, reaching Hawthorne by mid-afternoon.

Leaving his men and Paul at the hotel, Slim revisited judge Pardee in his office.

"It was a nice service," admitted the judge, "and your words sure bore some fruit. Hawthorne won't be the same for quite a spell, I do believe. It's strange, perhaps in death Jacob and Ruth may have done more good in getting people to live together better than if they had stayed alive. And, in a perverse way, maybe Andy Tuttle and his boys did more than anyone to bring it about. But, enough of that. I know what brings you here, of course.

"Mr. Evers, as I told you yesterday, you cannot adopt Paul since you aren't married. But this court could make the boy a ward of the court and place Paul in your custody. Furthermore, I know you have a judge in Cravenville, and I could transfer jurisdiction over this matter to his court. That way you could take Paul home with you and report to that court instead of mine. Do you like that idea?"

"Yes, of course," said Slim, greatly relieved. "That would be fine."

"How does the boy feel about it?" asked Pardee.

"I honestly don't know, judge," answered Slim. "I ain't talked to him about it. Didn't want to 'til I knew what was possible. How soon must we settle this?"

"Well, I'll need a couple of days to do the papers," responded Pardee, "and I'll want to question the boy before I can make it official. Let me know when you want me to get started. Also, I should have at least one witness that will testify that this is what the boy wants to do."

"Thank you a heap, judge!" Slim exclaimed, as he rose from his chair and shook hands with Pardee. "I'll get back to you as soon as I can."

That night after supper Slim had Bronc, Trig, and Curley come to the room he shared with Paul. As all the men squeezed into the room, Slim explained to Paul what he wanted to do and what was involved.

"You can go back to the reservation if'n you want to, Paul," he concluded, "and that must be yore own decision. I'll agree with whatever you want. But if'n you do that, it means yore paw and yore maw's dream of livin' in the white man's world will die. You're all that's left of that dream. I think it was a good dream, and I'd like to try and make it work out right. You'll have to go to school and work hard at the ranch, of course. Now, I ain't aimin' to replace Jacob as your paw. I can't do that, and I don't want to. If'n you don't like it with us'ns, you can go back to San Carlos anytime you want to. I know this is a big thing to spring on you so soon after what happened. Right now I just want you to think about it."

Bronc Evans squeezed past Trig and looked down at Paul sitting on the bed. "Apache, I would be plumb happy if'n you came and stayed at the Rambling R with us'ns. You got good stuff in you, and I would be proud to have you as a pardner!"

Not to be outdone, Trig and Curley echoed Bronc's words, and Paul couldn't help smiling at these expressions of encouragement. Further, he had acquired a special warm feeling toward these kind but violent men and remembered how they had risked their lives to save his own. He looked around the room and saw four intense and deeply tanned faces.

"I don't need to think very long, Slim," he said simply. "Let's go to the Rambling R."

Grins of pleasure filled the room, and Slim gave Paul a big hug while the others slapped him on his back or shook his hand.

****

Andy Tuttle had buried his three sons in a shaded area near his ranch house and then buried his sorrow in a bottle of whiskey. Sarah Tuttle, equally distraught over the death of her sons, left him alone and mechanically did her housework. Periodically she brought Andy food, but he only picked at it. Tuttle's hatred for the Redstones had collided with the realization that his sons had committed two despicable acts as a result of that hatred. The resulting mental battle in his mind went on, and his drinking continued.

****

The next day was a busy one for Slim. At mid-morning, the Friends representative from Kansas City, Mr. McComb, arrived by stagecoach. Slim and Bronc took the man on a tour of the JR Ranch, while Paul remained in town with Trig and Curley. As the latter three wandered the streets and shops of Hawthorne, they were pleased with the warm greetings they received. Many people expressed their sympathy to Paul, much to his surprise. It was obvious that news of what had taken place at the funeral had spread throughout the community.

Late in the afternoon, Slim, Paul, and the rest of Rambling R men visited the offices of Judge Pardee.

Pardee questioned the boy and was satisfied with the answers he received. The three witnesses signed sworn statements, and the judge began to prepare the necessary legal papers.

****

Shortly before dusk, four dusty and weary riders and their much lighter pack horse reached Hawthorne. Leaving their animals at the nearby livery stable, the four men checked into the hotel and headed for its dining room. Slim's reinforcements had arrived.

****

Andy Tuttle's anguish remained with him for another day. His emotional battle continued on, unabated. Moreover, the vacuum created by inaction added a third dimension to the conflict. He slept little that night, spending most of the time pacing the floor of the main room in his ranch house.

A breakfast that seemed tasteless added to his discomfort. Finally he could contain himself no more. Slapping his cloth napkin down on the breakfast table, he pushed back his chair, rose, and strode purposefully toward a peg on the front wall, over which his gun belt and holstered Colt were hung.

"What are you going to do, Andrew?" asked a concerned Sarah Tuttle.

"I'm goin' to town, get my men out of jail, and find those hombres what shot my boys. I'm goin' to settle up with 'em!"

"Oh, Andrew, don't do it! They were my boys, too, and killing someone else won't bring them back." Sarah stopped for a moment and wiped her tears before continuing her plea.

"Andrew, I might be able to forgive the boys for killing that Indian, but what they did to that woman weren't right. How would you feel if someone did that to me?"

Andy paused as he held the gun belt and looked down. He raised his head again and slowly buckled on the belt.

"The Indian was unarmed," Sarah reminded Andy, "and so was the woman. Besides, they tried to kill the boy. That's terrible, Andy. What kind of sons did we raise?"

"I don't know if Moe and the men could talk plain when they told me that," answered Andy gruffly. "Two of them strangers was standin' right there listen'n to everythin' they said."

"But you said Jerry Hastings was standing there, too. Why wouldn't they tell the truth? The sheriff and Jerry would have stopped anything from happening to them."

"I don't know, Sarah!" replied Andy viciously. "I just know I got to get to town." He walked over to his wife, held her by both shoulders, and kissed her. "Wish me well, Sarah."

She returned the kiss, but the tears wouldn't stop coming. Gently Andy pushed her aside, walked to the front door, and disappeared from view.

Jim Sloan was standing on the front porch, waiting for instructions.

"Have all the men saddle their horses, Jim," Andy muttered. "We're headin' for town."

Sloan hesitated and examined Tuttle closely.

"What for we goin' there, boss?" he asked softly.

"We're goin' to get Moe, Irish, and Fargo out of jail!" snapped Tuttle savagely. "Then we're goin' to look up them strangers and settle the score for my boys. Now get the rest of the men."

Sloan again hesitated.

"Andy, me and the boys like our jobs, and we like workin' for you. But we're ranch hands, not gunmen. If those strangers were good enough to take Lem and Sam, they're too good for us. Most of us don't fancy gettin' killed, too."

Tuttle stared at Sloan, disgust showing on his face.

"Well, you shore fancy them jobs you mentioned and the pay that comes with 'em," he growled. "Seems like some fighting might come with the territory. Now, if you wanta keep those jobs, you'll be riding with me to town!"

Sloan stared at Tuttle, a pained expression on his face. Shrugging his shoulders, he turned and headed for the bunkhouse. Tuttle strolled out to the corral, selected a horse, and roped and saddled the animal. He was just finishing the saddling when Sloan emerged from the bunkhouse and led a small group of men in Andy's direction.

Sloan approached Tuttle as the other men entered the corral and began to select their mounts.

"I hope you understand there's only goin' to be seven of us, Andy. That ain't very many."

"Edwards only has a couple of deputies, and they won't fire on us," responded Tuttle. "And Moe, Irish, and Fargo will give us 10. Them strangers won't dare take on that many. Quit your worry'n. Things are goin' to be just fine."

The men finished saddling. One led a saddled horse to Sloan and handed him the reins. As soon as Sloan eased himself into the saddle, Tuttle mounted his horse, raised his arm, and waved the group into motion.

Chapter 11

The residents of Hawthorne were greeted by a bright red dawn that same morning, an indication that a significant change in the weather was coming their way.

Sheriff Edwards found Deputy Jerry Hastings waiting for him when he arrived at his office. "Good morning, Jerry," Edwards greeted Hastings. "I got a feeling we might be in for a big blow 'afore the day is over."

"Yes," agreed Hastings, "it shore looks and feels that way. But we may have another problem. Like you told me to do, I been checkin' the livery stables right regular. 'Pop' Dawson told me four strangers left their horses and a pack horse at his place last night and registered at the hotel."

"What names did they use?" asked Edwards, raising his eyebrows.

Hastings couldn't help smiling. "Real interestin' ones," he replied. "L. White, C. Green, K. Jones, and B. Smith. Kinda original, don't you think? What's more interestin', though, is their horses have the same brands on 'em as those rode by Evers and his men."

"Evers sent two telegrams the other day," mused Edwards thoughtfully. "I thought they was plain enough, but mebby I was wrong. Evers is around town somewhere, probably still at the hotel. Go fetch him. It's time him and me had a parley."

Hastings quickly left the office, and it wasn't long before he returned with Slim Evers and Bronc Evans.

"You wanted to see me?" Slim inquired in a calm, polite voice.

"Yes, I did," acknowledged Edwards and waved his hand in the direction of a couple of chairs. "Set a spell. I need some questions answered."

Slim did as he was asked to do, but Bronc opted to lean against a nearby wall, his hands hooked inside his gun belt. Hastings did the same but stationed himself slightly behind Bronc.

"I'll get right at it, Evers. Four strangers rode into town last night and put up at the hotel. Their horses have the same brand as yores do. Are they yore men and, if so, what are they doin' in Hawthorne? And what are you up to?"

"They are my men," admitted Slim with a grin. "I must compliment you on yore sheriffin'. My boys are here for two reasons. First, I weren't shore how you and yore town would feel about us'ns helpin' the Redstones, especially if'n Andy Tuttle took it on himself to go on the warpath. Secondly, I'm planin' on buyin' the Redstone herd, and I needed some men to drive them critters south, seein' as how I 'spect to be tied up in these parts for a spell. Are them good enough reasons for you?"

Edwards nodded his head. "I reckon I can understand yore thinkin'. But you can rest easy. I enforce the law in this here town, and no one, not even Andy Tuttle, is goin' to get away with takin' the law into his own hands, leastways not as long as I can draw a breath and pull a trigger. But I'm some curious. Your brand is an <RRR>. That brand ain't used anywhere around here, and yet I got a feelin' I've seen it 'afore. Enlighten me."

"It stands for the Rambling R Ranch," explained Slim, again with a grin. "It's in the Arizony territory, less'n 200 miles southwest of here, near Cravenville. I own it."

Edwards pushed back his chair and stared at Slim again with raised eyebrows. "I shore enough have heard some tales about *that* ranch and some of the men who work for it. Funny, yore name shoulda rung some bells with me, but I guess I was too occupied with our troubles to give it the right amount of attention. If the stories I've heard are true, I'm right glad to make yore acquaintance."

He rose to shake Slim's hand but was stopped by the pounding of hoof-beats just outside his office, the sound of boots hitting the board sidewalk, and the sudden appearance of dust-covered Deputy Lester Dickson.

"I done what you told me to do," he began breathlessly. "I set myself up within eye sight of the Tuttle Ranch. Andy and his whole crew saddled up and headed for Hawthorne a while ago. They oughta be about 10 minutes behind me!"

"You see, me and you had the same idear, Evers," smiled Edwards grimly. "I'm some surprised Andy took this long to get goin'. How many of 'em are there, Lester?"

"I was set far off, and they was bobbin' up and down as they rode. I would have to say six or seven," answered Dickson.

"How many deputies do you have, sheriff?" asked Slim carefully.

"Well, there's Lester, Jerry, and me," began Edwards.

"Hold on, Turk," protested Dickson. "I worked for Tuttle for quite a spell, and I like the man. And I ain't ashamed to say his views on Injuns ain't much different than mine."

"You swore to uphold the law," Edwards reminded him.

"Mebby so," whined Dickson, "But I never thought I'd have to take on Tuttle and his crew as part of that."

"How about you, Jerry?" asked Edwards wearily.

"I swore to uphold the law, too," snapped Hastings. "I never figgered I could pick and choose when I done it." Hastings shot a hard look at Dickson. "You can count me in, Turk!"

Edwards gave Hastings an appreciative glance but turned his attention to his immediate problem.

"If I know Andy, and I do, he'll try to bust his guys out of jail first, then look for you, Evers, and yore men."

"Lester, you grab a shotgun from the rack and go back in the cell block. Set yourself up, and if Andy and his boys get by me and Jerry, you'll have to decide right quick if you're a deputy or not."

"Anybody else in town who could help you?" interrupted Slim.

"I reckon most everyone feels like Lester. You've started some people thinkin', Evers, but I doubt if they've got to the point yet where they would be willin' to fight for the idear. No, I reckon it's up to Jerry and me."

"Mebby not, sheriff," countered Slim. "I reckon both you and I would like to avoid further bloodshed. Bronc, here, and Trig, too, wore badges at one time. They was Texas Rangers. Deputize them, me, and all my men. A show of force might keep Tuttle from tryin' anythin'. What do you say?"

Edwards' hesitation was brief. He nodded his assent and reached for a desk drawer where he kept his spare badges. "Don't know if I got enough to go around," he muttered.

Slim jerked his thumb at Bronc, who was already on the move. Evans disappeared out the doorway and quickly returned, a number of men in his wake. "The boys were just outside waitin'," he explained, a sheepish look on his face.

"Bronc, I'll go out on the sidewalk with Sheriff Edwards and Deputy Hastings. You take Trig and Curley one way, and Lefty, you take yore men t'other way. Keep us covered from both sides. Tell Apache to stay out of sight." Slim couldn't help smiling at his use of Paul's new nickname.

Edwards paused in the distribution of his spare deputy badges and stared at Slim, a quizzical look on his face.

Despite his tan, Slim blushed his embarrassment.

"I'm right sorry, sheriff," stammered Evers. "I'm so used to give'n my men orders, I plumb forgot where I was."

Edwards waved off the apology.

"Everyone raise yore hands. Okay, you're all deputies. Do what Evers told you to. I can't think of a better plan, and we ain't got much time anyhow."

Edwards paused for a moment and watched his new deputies disappear out the door. He hitched up his gun belt a trifle and motioned for Slim and Jerry to follow him. As soon as the threesome walked out on the sidewalk, Jerry moved to the right and Slim to the left. Edwards glanced around, noted the positions his new deputies had assumed, and looked up the street where a group of horsemen was just coming into view.

Andy Tuttle led his riders down the street and into the second block of the town. He wheeled his horse to the right, walked it a few steps, and pulled it to a stop. His six men clustered about behind him. All of the group remained mounted.

"I've come for my men," he announced loudly as he eyed Edwards and his two companions. "I don't want to hurt you and Jerry, sheriff, so just stand aside, and there won't be no trouble. I don't know who this other hombre is, but tell him to stand aside, too."

"He's a new deputy, Andy," Edwards explained. "I'm shore you can see his badge. His name's Evers. Hold it!" Edwards snarled as Tuttle drew back in surprise. "I'll drill the first man who makes a quick move. Sloan, you and you other men, look around you. I've got me a whole passel of deputies. Them three on my left are the ones that done in Lem, Sam, and Tim. You know they got to be good to do that. Them four on my right are friends of theirs, and I would guess that they're just as good with their guns. Now unless you all want to have a blood bath and end up joining the Tuttle boys, I suggest you put yore hands on yore saddle pommels and keep 'em there. This is between me and Andy!"

Tuttle, Sloan, and the other men looked around, and Tuttle's mouth sagged open in surprise. Sloan took one look at the grim-faced circle of men and nodded knowingly. "I didn't want any part of this," he muttered. Placing his hands on his saddle horn, he turned and spoke in a louder voice. "Do what the man says, boys. I don't aim to die for nothin'." The other men quickly followed suit.

Tuttle looked at Sloan, shock in his eyes. He turned back to Edwards, only to find the sheriff's stare boring in on him.

"This is between you and me," repeated Edwards. "What you want to do is ag'in the law. More'n that, yore reason for doin' it is plumb wrong, too.

Moe, Irish, and Fargo will have a hearing in Judge Pardee's court in a day or two. 'Till then they stay in jail. As far as yore boys are concerned, they got just what they deserved. Mebby it kept them from gettin' hung. Anyway, you got any complaints, you take 'em up with me. What are you goin' to do now?"

Andrew Tuttle stared at Edwards, his mouth open in complete amazement. The verbal lashing he had gotten from Hastings was nothing compared to this. He could not comprehend what was happening. He only knew that the world he had known had suddenly changed and, from his point of view, not for the better. Tears of frustration came to his eyes, and he lost all control of himself. He screamed in anguish and reached for his gun.

A roar and a cloud of smoke erupted from just above Edwards' right hip. Tuttle again screamed, but this time in agony, and sagged in his saddle, his right arm dangling and a stream of blood slowly moving down the arm and over his hand.

Edwards slowly sheathed his weapon as Jim Sloan reached out to steady Tuttle.

"I coulda killed you, Andy," Edwards informed him, "but I didn't want to make Sarah a widder, too. She's had enough grief to hold her for a spell. Sloan, take Andy down to Doc Bridges and get him patched up. The rest of you men go back to the ranch and stay there. Don't come back to town until you can behave yourselves. Now git!"

Sloan dismounted, took control of Andy's reins, and led both horses as he walked down the street toward the doctor's office. The other Tuttle men turned and headed back out of town.

Edwards watched them leave, paused, and reloaded his gun.

"You handled that right well," said Slim in admiration. "I'm glad you didn't kill him. It weren't necessary. Reckon I won't need this anymore," he continued as he handed his deputy badge back to Edwards. Hastings was collecting similar items from the other Rambling R men.

"Got to thank you for the idear," Edwards responded. "Andy won't be usin' that gun hand ag'in for a long time. Mebby it will give him enough time to think things out and get over some of his grief and anger."

Edwards paused for a breath and looked intently at Slim.

"You and yore men made it all work out right," he observed. "Me and Jerry are real grateful. Anything we can do for you while you stay here, just ask."

Edwards turned and entered his office, while Slim and his men headed for the hotel.

****

Early that morning Slim had privately briefed the four newcomers on what had happened in and around Hawthorne over the past week. He then brought Paul into the meeting room, and the boy soon found out he had acquired four new friends.

Paul had witnessed the confrontation in front of the sheriff's office but from a safe distance. Again he was impressed by the calmness and self assurance exhibited by the Rambling R men regardless of the obvious danger. They seemed to take everything in stride, as if it was just a normal day's work. It was strange and puzzling to his young mind.

Slim called his men together and outlined his plans.

"Curley, show Lefty, Charley, Kansas, and Blackie where the JR Ranch house is and then help them round up the JR cattle. Hold them close to the ranch house." He turned to Paul. "Son, if'n you don't object, I want to make yore folks' home our headquarters for a day or so. There's plenty of food out there, and it should be et up. Lefty and the boys can sleep there, too. I'm goin' to meet with Mr. McComb, the man from Kansas City, later today and make the arrangements to buy them critters. Once we get that all done and the herd rounded up, Lefty and some of the boys will drive 'em to the Rambling R."

"That makes sense to me," agreed Paul. "I'm sure Jacob and Ruth would want you to use our home. However, I do have one suggestion. There's a storm coming; I can smell it. I don't think you will have time to gather them in before the storm gets here. Won't that just scatter them again?"

Slim smiled and gave Paul an approving look.

"Boys, I think we got ourselves a good young cattleman. That shore enough is good thinking. Curley, you and the boys stay put for the rest of the day here in town. We'll start the roundup in the morning. Besides, the horses you all brought in yesterday could use a day's rest and good feed."

By noon a number of black clouds began to gather, and two hours later a steady rain began to fall. The rain continued all afternoon and into the early evening hours before finally coming to a halt.

The Rambling R men amused themselves by playing cards and drinking sparingly in the hotel bar. Bronc was surprised when Paul told them he didn't know any card games.

"Apache, yore maw shore made shore you got some book learnin'," he observed. "But yore Uncle Bronc will have to pervide you with some special learnin'. Now, take these pasteboards here. There's lots of games you can play with 'em, but the best one of all is a game we call poker. Now that's a game you gotta learn if'n you're comin' to work on the Rambling R. Pull up a chair, son. I'll show you how we play the game."

Paul learned to shuffle the cards, and then the teaching began. The pupil was clumsy and confused at first but soon began to make some sense of what he should do. His eyes brightened with excitement, and he responded to Bronc's booming laughter and good natured kidding with smiles and laughter of his own. Slim left the group several times for brief intervals, taking Curley with him on one occasion. But whenever he was in the room, he sent Bronc a look of gratitude and smiled approvingly. The healing process had begun, and Bronc was just the man to help it along.

One of Slim's errands involved meeting with David Quigley. Financial arrangements were discussed, and the proper papers were signed.

Later Slim met with McComb in the hotel and arranged for the purchase of the tiny JR herd. A bill of sale was signed, copies were filed in Judge Pardee's court, and a bank draft changed hands.

Slim also paid a visit to Sheriff Edwards. Slim informed him of what he was doing and what would happen on the morrow.

Finally, Slim and Curley had a meeting with Judge Pardee. Slim explained that Curley would soon leave with the trail herd. Pardee arranged for Curley to prepare a written deposition on the events that had taken place earlier at the Rambling R campsite.

Slim and Curley returned to the hotel bar, joined their friends, and enjoyed a restful and relaxing evening.

The coldness of the rain outside the building was more than offset by the warmth of fun and companionship in the room. Slim sighed his contentment—this is what living was all about.

****

Up at dawn and fortified with a hearty breakfast, Curley, Lefty, and their three companions paid their hotel bill, saddled their horses, paid their livery stable fees, and headed for the JR Ranch.

At mid-morning, Bronc and Trig took the two pack horses, loaded them with supplies from Arnold's Store, and joined their friends at the JR.

The five Rambling R men had made short work of their little roundup. They had herded the few animals they found on the eastern range as they came from town. Then they swept the northern half of the range as well as the western quarter. It was early afternoon when a quick count indicated they were short about a dozen animals.

"I saw a small bunch south of here," Curley told the others. "We'll pick them up as we head out. Let's grab a quick bite and then git goin'. We oughta be able to do six or eight miles by nightfall."

The group consumed most of what remained in the way of food at the ranch. Goodbyes and handshakes were exchanged, the cattle were started, and Bronc and Trig watched their friends slowly move south before turning their own horses and heading back to Hawthorne.

Slim and Paul had spent the day in a leisurely fashion, wandering around town, visiting with Reverend Meeker, and sitting on the hotel veranda. Sheriff Edwards found them at the latter location and told them that Judge Pardee had scheduled a hearing for Moe, Irish, and Fargo for the next morning at ten o'clock. Slim, Paul, Bronc, and Trig were all expected to attend and Slim assured the sheriff that they would be present.

Shortly after lunch, Paul shyly asked Slim if he would play poker with him, much to Slim's delight. Bronc and Trig returned and found the two having a fine time. The game was expanded to four, and the rest of the afternoon passed quickly. The healing process had moved another step forward.

The next morning Judge Pardee held a hearing for Moe, Irish, and Fargo in front of a filled courtroom. Paul, Slim, Bronc, and Trig testified, and Curley's deposition was read. Sheriff Edwards and Deputy Hastings also testified. When Pardee turned to the three defendants and asked them if they wanted to say anything, all three shook their heads and remained silent.

"Very well, then. May I assume that the statements you made to Sheriff Edwards and Deputy Hastings, to which they have testified, are correct and that you do not want to change them in any way?"

The three men exchanged looks, and Moe glanced at Bronc Evans.

"That's the truth, judge," said Moe wearily. "And we ain't proud of it. I didn't figger it would go that far, but all at once we was in too deep to git out. And Lem and Sam weren't ones you dare argue with. We're ready to take our punishment."

Judge Pardee laid down his gavel, folded his hands, and eyed the three men from his elevated perch.

"This court is disturbed by the fact that you three actively participated in the lengthy search for Paul but is also mindful you did so at the insistence of the Tuttle boys. This court is also aware that none of you fired your weapons nor did you engage in any of the physical abuse imposed on Mrs. Redstone. Furthermore, this court acknowledges the fact that your attitude toward the Redstones differed little from that of most of us here in Hawthorne. This court, therefore, does not believe it should punish you for the sins of all of us and as a result has decided to be lenient. Will the defendants please rise."

The three men rose and faced the judge.

"It is the decision of this court to put each of you on three years probation and as the one and only condition of that probation that you leave this community immediately and not come back. This court will instruct Andrew Tuttle to pay you all the wages due you as of today. You have until tomorrow morning to leave this area, or you will be in violation of the terms of your probation and be subject to a jail term of the same period of time. Court adjourned!"

Slim and his men waited for the courtroom to clear before approaching the judge.

Slim shook hands with Pardee and complimented him. "I think that was a good and fair decision, judge."

"Thank you, Mr. Evers," replied Pardee. "I have to spend the rest of the morning doing the paper work on this hearing, but if you will come back around three o'clock, I'll have your papers ready for the boy."

"We'll be back," said Slim with a grin as he looked at Paul. "Won't we, son?"

Paul nodded his approval.

Chapter 12

After an early morning rise and a hearty breakfast, Slim was ready to begin what he would always remember as being a special day in his life. He and Paul had obtained the finished papers from Judge Pardee the previous afternoon, so this day would now be the first official day that Paul would be in his custody.

At the conclusion of breakfast, Slim issued his instructions. "Bronc, you, Trig, and Paul mosey down to the livery stable and get our horses saddled and ready. Paul, show them which of yore horses you generally ride. We'll have to use Jacob's horse as a pack horse. Trig, take Paul's horse out and ride him for a spell. I don't want him too rambunctious for Paul to handle. After all, he ain't been rid for several days. Bronc, you and Paul take Jacob's horse up to Arnold's store and get what supplies we need. I'll pay our bill here at the hotel, and then I got to see the judge for a minute. I'll pick up Trig at the livery stable, and we'll join you at the store. I guess that about covers things. Let's get movin'."

Bronc, Trig, and Paul headed for the livery stable, where Paul identified his horse, his saddle, and the trappings that went with it. Trig quickly saddled the animal, swung himself astride, and guided the horse out of the stable and down the street. Bronc saddled his own horse and then turned his attention to Jacob's animal.

"We'll use Jacob's saddle 'cause we don't want to throw it away," he informed Paul. "Besides, we don't have the usual layout for a pack horse, so we'll have to do the best we can."

Bronc finished his work and led the two horses out of stable and down the street with Paul at his side. They stopped at Arnold's store, made their purchases, and Bronc began to secure the sacks and packages on the back of Jacob's horse. Part way through the process, Bronc glanced at Paul and found the lad's eyes riveted on his hands, watching in rapt attention. Bronc paused, and Paul immediately looked into Bronc's face.

"How do you do that?" he asked, wonderment in his voice.

"Do what?" replied Bronc. "Oh, you mean these knots. These here are square knots. We ain't got the right rig, or I'd be usin' half hitches."

"Square knots? Half hitches? I don't understand," Paul admitted.

"Well, now, I'll tell you what, Apache. Tonight I'll let you untie these knots and let you see how they is done. But I got to admit somethin'. I'm purty good at doin' this, but Curley is a lot better. As soon as we catch up with him, he can learn you real good. And we got two more back at the ranch, Reno and Laredo, who are right good, too. Between 'em they can learn you things yore maw never thought about."

As soon as he uttered the words, Bronc swore under his breath.

"I didn't mean it the way it come out, Apache," he apologized. "Yore maw shore knew how to book learn you, and she did a right good job, too. It's just that me and the boys know about other things that don't come in books."

"Oh, I understand what you said, Bronc," smiled Paul. "Jacob told me the same thing. He spent many hours and days with me showing me how to live in the desert, how to follow a trail, and how not to leave a trail. I'm Apache, remember? Jacob wanted me to keep that heritage with me always."

"Say, you two hombres are holding up the parade," a cheerful voice boomed out at them. Bronc and Paul looked around and saw Slim and Trig looking down at them, a big grin showing on Slim's face.

"I got two more sacks to get and tie on, and then we'll be ready," replied Bronc. He entered the store and quickly returned with his two parcels. He tied the two sacks together and flipped one sack and a portion of the tie line over the pack horse's neck, directly in front of the saddle. He untied the horse's reins from the tie rail, shifted the reins to his left hand, and eased into his own saddle. Paul had also mounted, and as soon as Bronc pulled away from the tie rail, Slim waved the group into motion.

A mounted Sheriff Edwards caught up with the little cavalcade as the group reached the western edge of Hawthorne.

"Thought I'd ride along as far as the JR," he explained. "I decided it weren't right for you all to leave town without a proper escort."

A somewhat surprised Evers nodded his approval and motioned for Edwards to move up alongside him. Trig dropped back and joined Bronc and Paul.

"We're goin' to stop at the JR and pick up what's left in the way of food," Slim informed the sheriff. "No sense in letting it rot. We purty well cleaned it out the other day, though."

"That's what I figgered," said Edwards. "I'll nail the door and windy's shut to keep the wolves and coyotes out; and I'll check on the place now and ag'in. Seems like it's somethin' that ought to be done, at least for a spell."

The remainder of the ride to the little homestead was made in silence. As soon as they arrived, all dismounted, and Slim, Paul, and Bronc entered the house. Bronc went through the pantry area, assembled a small quantity of cans, filled a couple of sacks, and carried his booty out to the pack horse. Slim and Paul went through the rest of the house. Slim watched the boy carefully.

"Paul," he said, "I saw a family Bible you shore should take along. Grab all your clothes, too, but I think you should leave Jacob's and Ruth's clothes behind. What else you want, I don't know. The sheriff said he'd watch over the place for a spell. Mebby after you get settled, you'll want some more things. If'n that's so, we can send a wagon up here with a few of the boys and get what you want. No need to make a final decision right now. We can't carry a whole lot anyhow."

Paul flashed Slim a look of gratitude and nodded his understanding. He found a few trinkets and a blanket he wanted. Paul carefully folded the few pieces of clothing he possessed, picked up the Bible, and headed for the doorway. Paul paused as he reached the entranceway and looked back into the room. Jacob's bow and quiver of arrows, hanging on a far wall, caught his eye. He stared at these objects for a few moments and couldn't help recalling a number of hunting and fishing trips he had taken with Jacob and how much fun they had been. These thoughts brought a thin smile to his sad face. Paul marched purposely over to the wall, strapped on the quiver, hung the bow around his neck, and then returned to the doorway. He again paused for a moment, looked back into the house, brushed away a few tears, and then moved out into the courtyard and headed for his horse. Bronc met him, helped Paul fill two saddlebags with his clothes and trinkets, carefully tied the blanket behind Paul's saddle, and showed Paul how to secure the bow and arrows on the pack horse.

Sheriff Edwards watched the group mount and then he walked over to Slim, reached up, and exchanged a strong grip with the man. He did the same with Bronc and Trig, who now had the pack horse in tow, before moving beside Paul and looking up at the boy.

"Son, I'm shore sorry about how things turned out. It ain't fair, and it shouldn't have happened. But it did, and we can't change that. Yore paw and maw were good folks, and you can't ever forget that. But Slim, Bronc, and Trig here are good people, too, and they want to give you a new life. I'm right glad they were here when they were. So go with them and start that new life. Someday, mebby, you can come back here and give us folks another chance to do right by you. Go now, and good luck to you!"

Edwards squeezed Paul's hand, then waved the group forward and watched them head for the foothills.

The Rambling R group made a brief stop at the gravesite before swinging south. They followed the trail Jacob had pointed out to Slim, passed their earlier campsite, and were more than halfway to Dundee when nightfall came. Later Paul made up his bedroll next to Slim, crawled under his blanket, and looked up into a star-filled sky. The first day of his new life had come to an end.

✳✳✳✳✳✳✳✳✳✳✳✳

Two days later Slim and his companions caught up with the trail herd. During those two days, Slim spent most of his time describing for Paul the history of the Rambling R Ranch: How it began; the trials and torment of its initial years; the successes and failures in its recent years; and his hopes and plans for its future. He talked about some of the men who had come to him, those who had died fighting for him, those who had moved on to other locations, and those who had remained and had become part of what he considered to be his family. Paul was fascinated by this information and responded by asking questions and making comments that gave Slim a chance to share even more specific experiences and decisions. Paul was astonished to learn that Bronc and Trig were former Texas Rangers, and he tried to learn all there was to know about his "Uncle Bronc".

At night Paul helped set up the campsite, gathered firewood, watered the horses, and otherwise made himself useful. Most importantly, he helped Bronc untie the bags and packages carried by the pack horse and began to learn how to secure them the following morning. In short, Slim and the Rambling R men kept him physically busy, his mind active, and made him feel he was important to them. The healing process continued.

As soon as they joined the trail herd, Paul found that he had entered another new world. He continued to ride alongside Slim, but now his education covered a new subject: Managing a trail herd. Slim explained to him the role each puncher had in this process, and then, together, they would actually perform these tasks. Slim also told Paul that what was happening was minuscule in relation to what would take place if they were driving

1,000 to 5,000 head of cattle. Such an effort would require one or two full-time cooks and one or two chuck wagons for food supplies, depending on the size of the herd they were moving. In addition, they would also have an extensive remuda to support the drovers.

"In fact," Slim went on, "we don't have enough horses for what we're doin' now, even though this is a tiny herd. We have to night ride this bunch, and so at least two horses don't get enough rest each night. That means that each fourth day we'll stop and graze the herd. That way our horses will rest, too, and graze so that they can keep their strength. We ain't in no hurry, and we gotta take care of our horseflesh. I reckon I don't need to tell any Apache about how important that is.

"You'll be some surprised to know that this drive is a lot longer than we usually do," Slim continued on. "Years ago we sometimes had to push cattle more'n a thousand miles to get 'em to market. But the railroads have come along, and now all we have to do is meet up with 'em, load the critters on cars, and the railroad does the rest. I hear tell that they're goin' to build a siding, or spur as they call it, that will pass close by Cravenville. If'n that comes about, our longest drive will be less'n 50 miles. The old cattle drives are shore a thing of the past, just a memory for an old goat like me. Kinda miss it, though. These past few days have been fun."

Paul listened carefully and drank it all in. At night, too, Curley would seek him out and help him with his knot tying skills. This was great fun for Paul, and he caught on very fast. Soon he was helping Curley re-secure the bags and packages. This was a big job as they now had three pack horses to contend with. Curley would inspect Paul's work and have him redo the ropes and knots when necessary. As the days passed, however, these adjustments rapidly decreased in number, and Curley was hard pressed to find anything to complain about. Nonetheless, Slim told him to keep after Paul, and Curley had to swear under his breath when, toward the end of the drive, he told Paul to keep practicing when he knew virtual perfection had been achieved. Still, Reno and Laredo were going to be plumb surprised when Paul showed them how much he had already learned, Curley mused, and couldn't help smiling at the thought.

Slim and Paul also assumed their share of night riding, and here the pupil turned on the teacher. Jacob had taught Paul well on how to read the stars, how to deal with changing landscapes, and how to maintain control over the various points of the compass. Slim was amazed at the lad's knowledge about nature and his environment.

"Paul," Slim exclaimed one night, "we shore are goin' to take some camping trips together. It's important you know all you can about the territory around the ranch, but I do believe I can learn a heap from you on how to stay alive and comfortable in rough country. Yesiree, we shore enough are goin' to do that! And I'll bet you ol' Tex will want to do the same thing. We got some good times comin' our way, son!"

Two nights later Paul was arranging his bedroll when Bronc mentioned, "It felt good to be back on Rambling R land ag'in." Paul looked up in surprise.

"Are we on Rambling R ground?" he blurted out. "Why didn't we keep going and sleep at the ranch tonight?" His remark brought chuckles from all around the campfire, and he looked at Slim with a mystified expression on his face.

Slim motioned for him to settle under his blanket before responding.

"Son, we've got a good day's ride ahead of us before we get to the ranch house. If'n we didn't have the cattle, it would be some quicker, but I want to take them critters almost all the way in. We gotta brand them ag'in before we cut 'em loose."

Paul was dumbfounded by Slim's statement. "You mean we have that far to go, and you own all this land?"

"That's about the size of it," acknowledged Slim as he smiled at the pun.

"Shucks, Apache, if'n we cut back east and went about seven miles we would end up at one of our line camps," added Bronc. "Each of our line camps has bunks for four men, and we keep at least two men at each of 'em most of the time. I'm shore Slim plans on havin' you pay 'em a visit afore too long so you can see how we do things around here."

"Bronc's right, son," agreed Slim. "Them ain't the campin' trips I had in mind, though, but we'll get to them, too. However, that's enough talk for now. Settle down now and get some shuteye. Tomorrow you're goin' to see yore new home."

Paul had difficulty sleeping that night. He started to review all the things he had learned during the trail drive over the past two weeks, and these thoughts, combined with the idea of a new and different kind of home, kept his mind working at top speed for a long time. Even when he finally drifted off to sleep, he was restless and frequently switched from one position to another under his blanket. Slim woke once during the night and spent a half hour looking at his ward and noting the restlessness. Slim was sure he understood what was happening, sighed with contentment, and again felt that warm sensation he had experienced earlier. He finally closed his eyes, and soon he was in a deep and contented sleep.

****

Paul was the first one awake and up the next morning. He had gathered an armload of firewood and was stacking it near the coals left from the night before, when his fellow travelers began to stir.

Lefty White, the night rider, rode in and joined the group for breakfast. Tin plates and utensils were washed, the food was packed away, the fire was extinguished, the horses were saddled and mounted, and finally they all moved out to begin the last leg of their long journey.

For Paul, that day's ride moved him into a world that was beyond anything he had ever imagined. Soon he began to see cattle grazing; a few at first but increasing in numbers as they covered each mile until, finally, there were cattle as far as his eyes could see to his right and to his left. They cropped the grass in groups of 10, 20, or 50. There were large open spaces between groups, of course, but, to Paul, it seemed like it was one huge mass. His eyes widened in amazement, and his mouth fell open. A hand rested on his right shoulder as Slim moved in close.

"A right pretty sight, ain't it, son?" he said softly. "Think of all the people that beef will feed some day. It ain't an easy life, Paul, bein' a cattle rancher, but it can be a good life. That's what Jacob had in mind—not this big, of course, but somethin' he could call his own. It was a good dream, son, 'cause I had the same dream myself. I'm right proud of what I've managed to do, and I'm right proud to have you now be a part of it, too. Someday I hope you'll feel the same way."

Paul didn't reply as he still was completely overwhelmed by what he was seeing. Nevertheless, the boy was beginning to accept the fact that despite the tragedy he had experienced so recently, perhaps he was also a very lucky person at the same time. Sheriff Edwards' parting words came back to him, and he really began to believe that his new life might, indeed, be a very good life. Slim's voice broke into his thoughts.

"Two riders are headin' this way," Slim informed him and pointed off to their left. "You're about to meet someone I also think of as being a son to me, Paul. But he's full growed already and has been for quite a spell. I'll be some surprised if'n you don't end up thinkin' he's yore big brother, but we'll see about that."

Paul watched the two men approach and wondered which one was the man Slim was referring to. He soon found out. The man to his left waved a greeting to Slim and then swung his horse and headed toward Curley. The second man came on steadily, guided his horse around the tail end of the little herd, and swung in beside Slim, a big grin on his face.

"Shore glad to see you," he began as he shook hands with Slim. "I was beginnin' to get a little worried about you. Say, who have we got here? Seems like you picked up somethin' new along the trail!"

"I shore did," laughed Slim. "Tex, I want you to meet young Paul Redstone. Bronc has already saddled him with the name 'Apache', and I reckon it's gonna stick. Paul has come to live with us for a spell. I'll tell you all about it later."

Tex Riley reined in his horse and let Slim and Paul pass by him. Then he swung his cayuse to the right, passed behind Slim and Paul, urged his horse forward, and moved up beside Paul on his right side.

"Welcome to the Rambling R, Apache," he boomed and stretched out his right hand. Paul met his grasp and winced as his hand was squeezed. "I can see why Bronc put the handle on you," Tex continued with a smile. "Are you a full-blooded Apache?"

"Yes, I am," answered Paul in a firm voice, "and I'm proud of it, too."

"Good for you, son, I would be, too," Tex informed him with a laugh. "Say, Slim, it looks like you picked up a lot of new critters along the way," Tex continued as he rose in his saddle and looked over Paul's head at Evers. "These belong to Apache?"

"Well sort of," responded Slim. "I bought 'em from his folks. That's part of what I'll tell you about. Paul, I think we've eaten enough dust for one day. Lefty and the boys can handle this herd without our help now. Let's head for the ranch so you can see yore new home. Tex, lead the way."

Tex urged his horse into a faster gait, and his two companions did the same. A little more than an hour later the ranch buildings came into view, and Paul was again overcome with awe. A mammoth, two story, white building was obviously a ranch house, but many other smaller buildings dotted the landscape in several directions. There was a huge corral, although only a small number of horses could be seen within the enclosure. A blacksmith area, a storage warehouse, and a large bunkhouse, complete with a good-sized adjacent cooking facility, accounted for some of the smaller buildings. A number of men were engaged in a variety of tasks but stopped their work and waved friendly greetings as the three riders passed them enroute to the big house. Slim, Tex, and Paul had dismounted and were tying their horses when two figures burst out of the house, swept down five steps, and rapidly approached them.

Maria Martinez squealed with delight at the sight of Slim, and her husband, Antonio, grinned his pleasure. Maria, who was heavyset and plump, almost knocked Slim over as she reached him and clasped him with a big hug.

"It is so good to have you back, Señor Slim," she chortled and then poked him in the ribs. "Have you been eating right? I will have to prepare a banquet for you tonight to celebrate your safe return. What do we have here?" she continued as she looked at Paul.

"Maria, we have an addition to our family," answered Slim as he shook hands with Antonio, a tall gangly man. "His name is Paul Redstone, but Bronc calls him Apache, and I reckon that's probably how it will be. His paw and maw are dead, Maria, and I told him he could come live with us. I didn't think you'd mind."

"Mind! You know better than that, Slim Evers," responded Maria, who now gave her full attention to Paul. She engulfed him with a bear hug and lifted him off his feet, much to his consternation. He looked at Slim, alarm on his face.

"Don't break him in two," laughed Slim. "He doesn't have too much meat on his bones yet, but I reckon you can do something about that."

Maria released the boy and eyed him carefully.

"Yes, I can take care of that. His father and mother dead? Mary, Mother of God," she cried, as she crossed herself. "How can that be? Well, you will be safe here, my son. Señor Slim will surely see to that."

"Antonio," interrupted Tex, "take my things and put them in the den. I'll sleep there for now until I can get set up in the bunkhouse. Give Apache my room and help him get settled in."

Slim flashed Tex a look of gratitude, as Tex had read his mind. Maria was already heading back to the ranch house with Paul in tow, one of her arms around his shoulder.

"Antonio, what few clothes Paul has are in his saddle bags, and the blanket is his, too," explained Slim. "He also has a Bible and a few trinkets with him. Take all of it up to his room and help him all you can. He's had a bad time of it."

"It will be done, Señor Slim," murmured Antonio, a sad expression on his face. "We will think of him as your son."

Slim was startled at these words. Did it show that plainly? he wondered. He glanced at Tex and blushed through his tan. Tex's smile expanded to a full grin as he watched Slim's discomfort grow.

Chapter 13

The evening meal had been a bountiful repast. Maria had asked Paul what he liked to eat. When he responded by telling her what Ruth had been able to cook, given her very limited resources, Maria was aghast. No wonder he doesn't have much meat on his bones, she mused silently, although she was aware that short height and slim builds were common in the Apache world.

So she prepared thick steaks and backed them up with fried potatoes and two Mexican dishes. Although Paul approached the Mexican food with a good deal of caution, he soon realized he had eaten similar food at the San Carlos Reservation, although it wasn't nearly as tasty as what he now had before him. He apologized to Maria for forgetting to give her that information, but she just laughed and said she was glad she now had more ideas to work with.

The big meal, combined with the excitement of their arrival and the lack of sleep during the previous night, quickly caught up with Paul. His head began to droop soon after the meal was over, and, finally, Antonio tapped him on the shoulder and motioned for Paul to follow him upstairs. Five minutes later Slim went up to the bedroom to say good-night but found the boy already sound asleep.

Slim returned to the downstairs, filled two mugs with hot, steaming coffee, and motioned for Tex to follow him into the den.

Tex's eyes glinted in anger as he sipped his coffee and listened as Slim described the events that had taken place in and around Hawthorne.

"Do you think Tuttle will trail the lad here?" he asked as Slim paused to drink some coffee.

"Damn!" exclaimed Slim in disgust. "I never gave that any thought," he explained, "especially after he was shot up like he was. I wonder if'n I got somethin' to worry about."

"I doubt it," replied Tex thoughtfully. "I'm shore Bronc, Trig, and Curley have told the men about what happened. I'll tell the boys to keep their eyes peeled for any strangers who come around. If'n he does try somethin', Tuttle won't get off so easy ag'in. I won't be as forgivin' as that sheriff was."

"And I thought I had gotten rid of those bloodthirsty genes in yore system!" grunted Slim, feigning concern.

"Huh," snorted Tex in return. "I can remember a few times when you were plumb glad them genes were alive and kicking and not too long ago, neither!"

Both men laughed, and then Slim sobered.

"Tex, you know I've always thought of you as being a son I never had. You and I look at life a bit differently, but that don't make no never mind. Our goals are the same, and, as far as the ranch is concerned, we think alike. But you were near full growed when we came together. Havin' Paul come along now, like he has, won't change our situation one little bit. But havin' him here will shore change what I do, when I do it, and how I do it. I ain't saying it right well, but do you understand what I'm tryin' to tell you?"

Tex nodded, downed the remainder of his coffee, and looked at his friend and mentor.

"Slim, for the past year you've talked about gettin' old so much, I was afraid you were startin' to believe it yourself. You kinda had me worried. Havin' the lad come along now is the best thing I coulda hoped for. Why, you look 10 years younger now than you did when you left more'n a month ago!"

"You never were a good liar," smiled a relieved Evers. "But I hope you're right. I must admit I do feel younger. However, I ain't shore how the folks around here are goin' to take all this. The people around Hawthorne didn't like the idear none. Maybe the folks in Cravenville will feel the same."

"That'll be their problem," growled Tex. "If'n you say he's yore son, he shore enough is yore son. And that should be the end of it."

"I shore hope so," said Slim wearily. But the sparkle quickly returned to his eyes as he looked at the man across from him. "Thank you for understandin' me, Tex," he said simply. The two men rose to their feet and their hands met in a firm grasp. Nothing more needed to be said.

****

The next day began an exciting four weeks for Paul. He and Slim spent a number of days riding and exploring a portion of the Rambling R Ranch. However, Slim was too wise to completely monopolize Paul's time. Once Tex took Paul with him to a distant line camp and spent five days with him there. Tex showed Paul how the ranch operation was organized and let him work his way through the process by actually doing some range and fence riding near that location.

On another occasion, Bronc and Trig took Paul on a four day exploration trip in an area well north of the Rambling R's boundary line. The three of them camped out for three nights and lived off the land even though they had brought along adequate food supplies.

In preparation for this trip, Paul had spent a good deal of time practicing his use of Jacob's bow and arrows. Twice during the trip he stalked deer in an attempt to obtain fresh meat. The first time he fired an arrow too soon and missed his target by a wide margin, much to his chagrin, and the deer easily escaped. Paul decided to be more careful and patient with his second opportunity and was rewarded with a hit. The wounded deer dashed off but left a trail of blood. Paul, on foot, and Bronc, mounted, doggedly tracked the deer for more than an hour before catching up with the dead animal. Paul cleaned and dressed the carcass, as Jacob had taught him and with Bronc's help returned to their campsite with the meat, justifiably proud of his accomplishment.

On two occasions the threesome located clear, sparkling, mountain streams in their wanderings. They easily fashioned crude fishing poles from small saplings, added some string and hooks that they had included in their supplies, dug up a few worms, and soon had a plentiful number of trout for their next meal.

Late in the third day they made a curve to the southeast and began the return trip to the Rambling R. Paul sniffed the air and shook his head.

"I think a storm is brewing, and there is no way we can get back to the Ranch before nightfall," he muttered. "Looks like we're going to have a wet night in front of us, Bronc."

Bronc nodded his agreement and pulled his horse to a stop, deep in thought. Suddenly a bright smile spread across his face.

"Mebby not, Apache. I got me an idear. If'n that storm will just hold off for a couple of hours, we may stay dry at that. C'mon, follow me."

Bronc led the way at an increased rate of speed, turned further south about an hour later, and glanced back at the darkening horizon.

"It's goin' to be close, Apache, but I think we can make it. Trig knows what I got in mind. If'n it's still standin', we got a nice surprise for you."

Bronc continued to lead and maintained a steady gait. The wind began to pick up and soon growls of thunder could be heard far off in the distance. The rain was just beginning to fall when they emerged from a shallow pass, and Paul saw a small glen with a dilapidated shack standing at its far end, outlined by a flash of lightning.

The three explorers swung from their saddles and tied their horses to posts that were part of the remains of what had been a corral adjacent to the shack. Saddlebags, bedrolls, and rifles were pulled from their mounts, and they all dashed for the entrance to the shack as the rain began to come down in sheets. Bronc tried the door and found it stuck tight. Bronc motioned to Trig. Both men lowered their shoulders, paused for a moment, and then together banged into the door and drove it open, knocking it off one hinge in the process. A quick inspection disclosed a few leaky holes in the roof, but enough dry spots were available for the three new occupants. Bronc found one such location, stacked his belongings, sat on the floor and grinned his pleasure.

"It ain't perfect, Apache, but it'll do. We even got us a couple of double bunks, but I ain't shore how sturdy they are. I reckon we better sleep on the floor tonight."

Paul looked at his surroundings with more than a little interest. It was obvious the shack was old and had not been used for some time. It had been crudely constructed, and Paul couldn't help wondering what was holding it up. Nevertheless, it was shelter, and it was possible to stay relatively dry.

The rain eased up after an hour or so and stopped a short time later. They found a small stove in one corner of the shack together with an adequate supply of dry wood. Trig started a fire, a supper of venison and trout was consumed, and even Paul had to admit that the world looked pretty good to him.

The next morning the threesome spent an hour replenishing the cache of firewood and making some makeshift repairs to the hinge on the front door before starting back to the Rambling R. "We may have need of this old place ag'in someday, Apache," Bronc explained as they packed up to leave.

They reached the Rambling R by nightfall. It had been a satisfying and fun-filled trip, and Paul already was looking forward to the next one.

In the meantime, Maria Martinez accompanied the weekly supply wagon into Cravenville and purchased new work clothes for Paul as well as a second suit to go with the one he had worn at the funeral. Ollie and Elsa Woods, owners of the general store, were surprised by these purchases, but Maria gave no explanation, and the Woods's curiosity remained unsatisfied.

At the same time, Laredo and Reno used their store of knowledge in the task of training Paul in his rope and knot skills and, as Curley expected, were pleasantly surprised at how far he already had progressed. The boy had a natural affinity toward this kind of activity and enjoyed it very much. During his four day outing with Bronc and Trig, Bronc let Paul do all the securing of their supplies on the pack horse and found that the lad had learned his lessons well.

All good times must come to an end, however, at least temporarily. One night after supper, Slim asked Paul to join him in the big den. They discussed the events of the past month, and Slim indicated he was very pleased with how things had gone. Paul agreed with that assessment.

"However, young man, while you've learned a lot about the Rambling R, we ain't been able to give you any book learnin' time," Slim pointed out. Evers reached out and picked up the latest issue of the weekly "Cravenville Clarion." "This paper says that school begins next week, and we gotta enroll you. So you put on one of yore new suits tomorrow mornin', and then we're goin' into town to take care of that little matter. What do you have to say about that?"

"I wasn't allowed to go to school in Hawthorne," Paul reminded him. "Jacob and Ruth thought it would be better if I didn't try to do that. So Ruth was my teacher right at home. She bought me a slate and some chalk, and she worked me hard. In fact, I sometimes thought I would have been better off in school," laughed Paul.

"Well, you won't have no trouble on that score here," Slim assured him. "And you should be in school with other kids—you'll have a better idear on how you're doin'. Tex and I have some other things to do in town tomorrow anyhow, so the three of us will ride in and get you all squared away. So get ready for bed, and I'll be up in a few minutes to say good night."

* * * * * * * * * * * *

After an early rise and a hearty breakfast, the three riders made the eight mile trip to Cravenville. The schoolhouse was located on the ranch side of the community and was set back from the main north and south street. A few children were clustered around the front door waiting to enroll, so Slim and his two companions tied their horses to a tie rail at the end of the street and sat down on a nearby bench. They watched as each child entered the school and emerged in a minute or two. As soon as the last child, a girl, disappeared into the school, Slim motioned to Paul, and the three of them strolled in that direction, arriving just as the last child came dancing out of the door. A tall, full-bodied woman with long, light-brown hair followed the girl out the door and looked around before settling her gaze on her three visitors.

"Is there something I can help you with?" she asked in a soft but clear, melodic voice.

Slim removed his hat, and Tex and Paul quickly followed his example.

"Well, yes, you can," acknowledged Slim. "My name is Slim Evers, and I've brought you a new pupil. His name is Paul Redstone, and we need to get him enrolled in yore school." Slim put his arm around Paul's shoulder as he talked.

"Why, Mr. Evers, I should have recognized you. I've heard about you and your Rambling R Ranch, of course, and I've seen you once or twice from afar, but this is the first time I've really met you. I'm Catherine Cornell, and is this Paul?"

As she spoke Catherine had centered her attention on Slim, but as soon as she said Paul's name, her gaze was transferred to the boy. His features and bronze complexion now became obvious, and she gasped, unable to conceal her surprise.

"Is this Paul?" she repeated in a faltering voice. "And who is this?" she continued as she glanced at Tex.

"Yes, the boy *is* Paul," replied Slim, watching her closely. "That's Tex Riley, my foreman, right behind him. Shouldn't we go inside and get this all taken care of?"

"Oh . . . yes, of course," Catherine sputtered, still surprised and confused. "Please follow me."

Catherine turned, pushed the door open wide, and held it that way as her three visitors brushed past her and entered the room.

"Please sit down," she told them as she hurried toward her desk. "I think you'll find some bigger chairs for you and Mr. Riley over there, Mr. Evers," she said as she pointed to the opposite side of the room. "Bring them over near the desk and tell Paul to sit here." She pointed to a chair directly in front of the desk.

"Tell Paul yourself," smiled Slim.

"Mr. Evers . . . I'm sorry, but I don't speak . . . ."

"Apache," supplied Slim. "Yes, Paul is a full-blooded Apache. But why don't you just tell him what to do in our words. He'll be able to understand."

"Well . . . all right," came the slow answer. "Paul . . . please . . . sit . . . in . . . this . . . chair. Catherine had carefully and slowly enunciated each word and watched closely to see if Paul displayed any degree of comprehension.

"I'll be happy to do so, Miss Cornell," said Paul with a smile, enjoying the joke. "Would you prefer to have me face you directly or sit off to one side?"

Catherine's surprise was complete, and her face showed it. Her eyes widened in astonishment, and she stared at the boy for a few moments before looking at the two men, both displaying big grins.

The humor in the situation finally registered with her, and she couldn't resist a burst of laughter.

"I guess I walked into that one," she admitted after she got herself under control. "But I had no way of knowing."

"Of course not," agreed Slim. "I didn't intend to play a joke on you. It just sorta happened. Paul's maw was a school teacher just like you. Paul ain't been in a real school for a couple of years, though, and I promised myself I would get that changed."

"His mother *was* a school teacher?" asked a puzzled Catherine. "Where is she now? May I talk to her?"

"Well, his real maw was Apache, but she died when Paul was born. His stepmaw was his school teacher, but she's dead, too."

"Oh, my goodness!" exclaimed Catherine as her hands rose to her face. "How terrible—losing two mothers. How nice of you, Mr. Evers, to want to help the boy. I'll be happy to do all I can for him, too!"

Catherine paused for a moment and drummed her fingers on her desk as she planned a course of action. She stopped the movement in her fingers and looked at Slim.

"Mr. Evers, do you and Mr. Riley have something to do for a half an hour or a little more? I would like to talk to Paul and give him a little test."

"A test already?" asked a startled Slim. "He ain't been in school for two years, you know."

"I know," laughed Catherine. "That's the point. I know where all my students from last year are as far as what grade they should be in. I want to get an idea of where Paul is so I can get him started right and not embarrass him in front of the other students."

"I reckon that sounds fair enough," admitted Slim, somewhat relieved. "Tex and I will clear out and leave you and Paul alone. Paul, you do what Miss Cornell asks you to do. We'll be back in about an hour."

****

Slim and Tex did their errands and an hour later returned to the schoolhouse and found Paul and his new teacher waiting for them. They stood in the entrance to the school, her hand on his shoulder.

"Go get your horse, Paul," she murmured softly. "I want to talk to Mr. Evers for a minute."

Paul bounced down the school steps and jogged his way toward his horse, which was still tied to the rail at the end of the street.

"Paul's school teacher mother did a fine job with the boy," Catherine informed Slim with a big smile. "He is very bright and will be a lot of fun to work with. I'm looking forward to it. School will begin on Monday morning at nine o'clock. I usually let the children out about four o'clock. Do you have any questions for me?"

"No, I reckon not," Slim replied. "But if'n you have any trouble with Paul, I want to know about it right quick. It's mighty important to me that this work out right for the lad. So don't you hesitate none if'n you need me."

"I'm sure I won't have any trouble with Paul," Catherine assured Slim. "During the course of the school year I always have two or three conferences with the parents of the children. I assume you want me to think of him as being your son and that I should hold these conferences with you."

"Yes, that would be good," agreed Slim. Suddenly a frown swept across his face, only to quickly disappear. "Ma'am, I do travel some, and sometimes I'm out on our range for days at a time. If'n you need to see me, and I ain't right there, Tex here can come in my place. He's sorta like a son to me, too, and I'm shore he'll do anything that you think needs done."

"Very well, Mr. Evers, I'll remember that. Now if you'll excuse me, I have a lot to do to get ready for the opening day of school. Good day, gentlemen."

Both Slim and Tex tipped their hats and watched the woman disappear back into the schoolhouse. The two men turned and walked toward their horses, where Paul was waiting for them.

****

Melvin Stewart had been a resident of Cravenville for almost 20 years. Born and raised in Missouri, he had drifted west at an early age and found that his soft hands and long, thin fingers didn't particularly take to manual work of any kind. On the other hand, he soon discovered that these same hands and fingers were extremely well suited for handling playing cards. He also discovered he had an excellent memory and a mind that handled with ease mathematical problems, such as figuring odds. The combination of these attributes, together with the will power to spend hours in practice, pushed him into a career of being a professional gambler. He spent several years roaming the west with only a moderate degree of success. But then his luck changed for the better. Perhaps the experience gained from hundreds of poker games generated the change, or perhaps his mind just began to function better. In any event, he ran into an extended hot streak and built himself a financial stake large enough for him to enter a high stakes game of freeze-out in Denver, Colorado. His good luck and/or good playing continued, and he found himself in the finals with two other players, the survivors from a field of ten.

The final hand was one Stewart would never forget. It was a game of seven card stud, and when the fifth card was dealt, he had a jack of hearts in the hole and the jack of diamonds and two sevens showing. He looked at the cards showing for both of his opponents and, based on the betting so far, figured the man on his left was pushing for a straight while the man on his right, like himself, had hopes for a full house. But since the highest card showing for the latter player was only a 10, Stewart felt he had the man beat as of the moment.

The sixth card fell face up, and the betting began anew. Stewart had gotten no help, but the nature of the betting convinced him that the man on his left had hit his straight and that the 10 that appeared for the man on his right had, indeed, filled in his full house. Stewart, therefore, now had only the third best hand at the table with one down card to go.

All of his experience told Stewart it was now time to fold, but his instincts told him otherwise. He decided to go with his instincts and do it with a theatrical flair. When the betting was completed, he pointed his finger at the dealer and announced, "All I need is a black jack. Hit me!"

The dealer grinned and slid the card to him. The other two players got their cards, and the betting began again.

Stewart decided to carry his theatrics one step further. Without looking at the last card, he met each bet and each raise without hesitation. Finally, he called the final bet and sat back in his chair while the other two players turned over their cards. The man to his left had his king high straight, and the man on his right showed his full house, 10s over fives. Both pairs of eyes turned to Stewart's cards. Stewart straightened up and slowly turned over his first two hole cards. He paused and stared at the final hole card. Slowly his right hand moved to the card, his first and second fingers gripped the corner of the card, and after another brief pause, he flipped it over. A jack of clubs stared at him, and the room erupted in a huge roar. Stewart became an instant celebrity, and the media bestowed upon him the sobriquet of "Black Jack".

****

Stewart banked his winnings in Denver and drifted south, eventually arriving in Cravenville. He found a saloon and gambling house up for sale and decided, right there on the spot, to settle down and change his life style. He didn't see how he could ever again top, or even equal, his performance in Denver, and his instincts told him not to try.

He changed the name to the "Black Jack Saloon" and began to invest his time and money in his newly found community. And at the same time Stewart made two very smart decisions.

First, he ran nothing but honest games at his establishment, figuring that the house percentages were good enough for him. Anyone caught cheating was immediately ejected from the premises, much to the chagrin of several itinerant gamblers.

Secondly, and perhaps most importantly, he organized a Friday night poker game and invited most of the important town fathers to participate. What was different about this game, however, was that he allowed only a minimum amount of drinking, and he insisted that the stakes be very small. The purposes of the game, he explained, were entertainment and comraderie. Seldom did more than $ 20 change hands, and over a period of time gains and losses tended to offset one another. Once in a while one of the players would grouse about the low stakes rule, particularly if that someone was having an especially good night, but Stewart remained adamant, and the wives loved him for it. There was little bluffing, the pots were hard-fought, and Stewart enjoyed these nights as much as, or more than, he did any of his professional games.

Two years after his arrival in Cravenville he married a local girl, and this union was blessed with the birth of two sons—Seth, now 13, and Sid, now 11. Stewart, despite his unusual occupation, had become a pillar of the community and greatly respected by everyone.

This respect was all-important for Stewart. This was something he had dreamed about his entire life. Why was this so important? It was because Stewart had a secret, a secret he did not share even with his wife. Sometime, much earlier, someone in his family had made a "mistake", a dreadful mistake. The Stewart family was not purely of the white race. In fact, Stewart had Indian blood in him, Cherokee blood, to be exact. He was never told which side of his family had made this terrible mistake, only that he was one-eighth Cherokee. This knowledge disturbed him greatly but at the same time drove him toward his goal of respectability as a way of making up for this awful mistake. He would not lose what had taken him so many years to obtain. And this thought, more than any other, governed everything he did and everything he thought about.

✳✳✳✳✳✳✳✳✳✳✳✳

A very pleased Slim Evers and his two companions made the return trip to the Rambling R in high spirits. Slim spoke to Paul as they rode. "Miss Cornell seems like a right nice teacher, son. Our little joke didn't seem to upset her none, and she sounded like she really wants to help you learn all you can. I liked her a heap, didn't you?"

"Yes," agreed Paul, smiling at Slim's enthusiasm. "She was very kind and patient with me. I did make a few mistakes in the test she gave me." Then Paul's expression took on a more somber look. "In some ways, she reminded me of Ruth."

Slim quickly glanced at Paul and reached out to squeeze the boy's arm. "Ain't nothin' wrong with that," he assured the boy. "It makes sense, too, since they are both school teachers. Didn't you like her, too, Tex?" asked Slim, as he looked past Paul at his foreman.

"Yeah, I shore did," responded Tex calmly. "It looks like Apache's got himself a good teacher."

Slim rambled on, reviewing the interview and continuing to express his pleasure about the tone and scope of the meeting. It was on this high note that they arrived back at the Rambling R.

Later that evening, after supper and after Paul had gone to bed, Slim and Tex were back drinking coffee in the den. Slim again reviewed the pleasurable events of the day. Tex remained silent and let Slim ramble on.

Tex's silence finally registered with Slim. He paused and gazed at his foreman, a puzzled look on his face.

"You were awful quiet during the ride from town, and you ain't sayin' anythin' now, Tex. Is somethin' botherin' you?"

"I don't rightly know," sighed Tex. "I'm just wonderin' if'n we missed a bet. We gave Apache plenty to do here at the ranch over the past month, but we never took him to town. We're sorta springin' him on folks without no warnin', like we did to Miss Cornell today. She was some surprised, and it sorta threw her off balance at first. I just hope we ain't made a problem for Apache."

"Oh, you are a worrywart," exclaimed Slim, a little irked at what he had just heard. "There won't be no trouble, and if'n there is a little, I'm shore Miss Cornell can handle it. Sometimes I think you worry too much, Tex!"

Tex did not respond to this rebuke and decided to change the subject. "Get out the checkerboard, and I'll shore give *you* somethin' to worry about."

"Huh," snorted Slim. "I been gone more'n month, but I shore ain't lost my touch. Set 'em up. You're due for a lickin'!"

****

Mondays were always slow at the Black Jack, and this one was particularly slow. Stewart, as was his custom, arrived at his establishment late in the morning. He spent the remainder of the morning counting his weekend receipts, entering the data in his account ledger, and preparing the deposit he would soon take to the bank. He prepared an order for liquor, another order for packs of playing cards, wrote the appropriate checks, addressed and sealed two envelopes, and locked his safe.

He picked up his deposit and two letters, briefly inspected the almost vacant saloon, and waved to the bartender.

"I'm going to do a few errands and take the afternoon off, Clancy," he announced. "When Jocko comes in, tell him I'll be back about eight tonight."

Clancy, the bartender, waved back and continued to wash and dry the glassware left over from Saturday night.

Stewart walked to the bank, made his deposit, reminded Bert Milner about Friday's poker game, mailed his letters at Nate Green's combination post office and Western Union establishment, and sighed with pleasure. He glanced at the clear, blue sky and nodded his satisfaction. Now his pace quickened as he marched toward Clem Duffield's livery stable. Clem had Stewart's horse all saddled and ready for the usual Monday ride. Stewart slipped the old man his usual dollar tip, mounted his horse, and walked it down main street until he reached the south end of town, whereupon he kicked his horse into motion and raced out into the prairie.

Stewart enjoyed these Monday rides, but he also had another purpose in mind. Every once in a great while someone would ask him how he managed to keep so deep a tan while spending so much time indoors. Stewart would laugh at the remark and point out that he had always tanned very easily and retained it for long periods of time. Of course, he knew what the real reason was and, therefore, it was mandatory that he spend as much time out-of-doors as possible if he wanted to maintain the facade. He must be doing something right, he mused, as he had not heard the comment for several years.

An hour and a half later he returned to Cravenville, turned his horse over to Duffield, and headed for his home on the eastern edge of town. Since he always had a very late breakfast on Mondays, he generally skipped lunch and told his wife to plan an early supper. This allowed him to take a two hour nap after his ride, especially on those Mondays when the two boys were in school and the house was quiet.

This was the first day of school, and he looked forward to getting the most out of his routine. He enjoyed a nice nap, as expected, and was just washing his face when the two boys came bounding into the house.

"Hey, paw," shouted Seth, "you'll never guess who we had in school today."

"No, I can't," smiled Stewart as his wife came out of her sewing room, a puzzled look on her face.

"An Injun, paw. A real live Injun."

"An Indian?" asked Stewart, his eye brows raised in surprise. "Did Miss Cornell use this Indian as part of her lesson today?"

"No, paw!" both boys spoke in unison. "Hush up, Sid," snapped Seth. "No, paw, he's one of us. He's 12 years old and is goin' to school with us!"

"An Indian going to school here in Cravenville," interrupted Louise Stewart, fear in her voice. "Well, I declare, what are we coming to?"

"Wait a minute," declared Stewart, a rise in his voice. "Let's start over. Calm down, Seth, and both you and Sid sit down and go over this with me again. You say you have an Indian as a classmate? Where did he come from? Where does he live?"

"Don't know where he come from," replied Seth, "But Miss Cornell said he's livin' out at the Rambling R."

"Out at the Rambling R?" questioned an unbelieving Stewart. "They ain't got any Indians livin' out there. They've had a Mexican man and woman out there for years, but they don't have any kids. No, you must be mistaken. They don't have any Indians living out there."

"Paw, his name is Paul Redstone, and Miss Cornell said he lives out at the Rambling R," countered Seth, with some exasperation.

"Does he speak English?" inquired Stewart, who was at a loss on what else to say.

"Yeah, he sure does," replied Seth, as his hands flew open. "He talks as good as you and me, and he's good with numbers, too. Better'n than most of the rest of us, as a matter of fact. His clothes were neat and clean, too. I can't figger it."

"I can't either," agreed Stewart as he sank back in his chair. "I'll have to talk to the other school board members. Maybe someone knows something I don't know."

"Well, get out of your school clothes and get ready for supper, both of you," directed Louise Stewart. "Then you can do your chores. Supper will be ready in half an hour." Louise gazed at her husband, who appeared to be deep in thought.

Chapter 14

Three days later Paul arrived home from school and immediately tried to locate Slim. Maria told him Slim and Tex were out on the range and would be back for supper. Paul changed his clothes, went into the den, and patiently waited until he heard the sound of footsteps in the main room and the exchange of talk between Maria and Slim. Slim's face, wearing a big grin, quickly appeared in the doorway of the den, and he boomed an appropriate greeting as he entered the room, with Tex following in his footsteps.

"Howdy, son. How was school today? Did you pass yore numbers test?"

"Yes," smiled Paul. "I made one mistake on the test while one of the girls had all the right answers. So I finished second."

"Well that's right good," acknowledged Slim, and Tex nodded his approval. "Girls is tough competition in school. It seem like I always had two or three ahead of me when I went to school. I reckon they like to study better'n boys."

Paul handed Slim an envelope.

"Miss Cornell told me to give this to you," he explained.

"A note from the teacher already?" asked a surprised Evers. "Did you do somethin' wrong I should know about?"

"Not that I'm aware of," replied Paul. "Miss Cornell said she was sure you would know what to do."

Slim sat down at his desk and, using a knife, slit open the sealed envelope. He read the message, frowned, and read it a second time. He then handed it to Tex as he slid back in his chair and stared at the ceiling. Tex scanned the note which read:

Dear Mr. Evers:

A special school board meeting has been called for next Monday night at seven o'clock. I understand the topic for the meeting is going to be Paul and how he became enrolled at our school.

You told me that if I needed you, you would help me. I'm sorry to have to call on you so soon, but I think it is very important for you to be at that meeting.

Sincerely yours,

Catherine M. Cornell

"What a fool I've been," sighed Slim. "You were right, Tex. I shoulda done things differently. Of course I'll go to that meetin'."

"No, *we* will go to the meeting," Tex corrected him as he stood behind Paul and put both of his hands on the boy's shoulders. "We'll meet Apache after school, and the three of us will wander around town until it's time for supper. Then we'll go to The Steak House, have a big meal, and let everyone take a good look at us. After we eat, you'll go to the meeting, and I'll stay with Apache. That's what we shoulda done a long time ago, and that's what we're goin' to do now."

Slim's eyes were focused on Tex as his foreman spoke, and Evers nodded his approval of the plan. "Yore plumb right, Tex," Slim agreed. "We'll let every one get a good look at us. Is that all right with you, Paul?"

"I guess so," answered Paul, puzzlement in his voice. "What is the problem?"

"It ain't a real problem, exactly," replied Slim slowly. "I just didn't let the folks around here meet you proper like. People are a mite confused about all this, and I'll just have to straighten things out Monday night. Don't worry none. Everythin' is goin' to be just fine. Now run along. Curley has a new knot he wants to show you. He's out at the corral, and I told him you'd be out there directly."

✸✸✸✸✸✸✸✸✸✸✸

The following Monday afternoon, Slim and Tex, as planned, met Paul as he left the schoolhouse. The three of them strolled through town, stopping at most of the business establishments, where Slim introduced Paul to one and all. Most of the time Paul received a cool reception, at best, but, in a few instances, the greetings were warm and friendly. One of the latter involved Ollie and Elsa Woods, who laughingly told Slim he had finally satisfied their curiosity.

Slim was a little irked by the fact that the cool responses had greatly outnumbered the warm ones until Tex reminded him that it was to be expected and to give the people time to get used to the idea. Furthermore, Tex told Slim that Paul's precise English and natural politeness would favorably impress people once they thought about it and got over shock of the initial encounter.

Meal time arrived, and the trio made their way to The Steak House. Tex insisted on a table nearest the window looking out onto the street, and they enjoyed a leisurely supper. A few eyebrows were raised when they entered the restaurant, but Tex's presence, his reputation, and his twin Colts negated any possibility of a scene, as Tex had anticipated.

Supper finished, Slim and his companions strolled outside. Slim pulled an old gold time piece from his vest pocket, glanced at it, and grunted his satisfaction. "I'm goin' to mosey up the street and wait for the board members to arrive before goin' in. Where will I find you two when this is all over?"

"Apache and I will be in the hotel lobby," Tex informed him.

Slim shook his head in mock dismay, grinned, and began walking down the street.

Tex guided Paul to the hotel and led the way across the lobby to the reservation counter. "Somewhere around here you got a checkerboard and a box of checkers," he informed the astonished night clerk. "Go find 'em. Me and Apache got some time to kill."

✳✳✳✳✳✳✳✳✳✳✳✳

Slim waited patiently in the gathering dusk until the fifth and final board member arrived and entered the schoolhouse. He had deliberately selected a sidewalk chair about a half block from the school, had slid it away from any store lights or kerosene lamps, and had buried himself in the shadows cast by the buildings. He watched the five board members arrive and was sure that none had noticed him.

He sauntered up to the schoolhouse, climbed the three steps to the front door, pushed it open, and entered the room. Six heads turned in his direction, and six pairs of eyes bore into him. Four pairs of eyes registered surprise and some consternation. A fifth pair, those belonging to Ollie Woods, twinkled with delight, and the last pair, those belonging to Catherine Cornell, showed a great deal of relief.

"What are you doing here?" Carl Crane, president of the board and owner of a feed and grain store, demanded to know.

"Well, now, I find I've picked up a lot of interest in our school system recently, and I thought I'd come by and see how it works," answered Slim. He walked around the meeting table and shook hands with each of the five men: Crane; Black Jack Stewart; Ollie Woods; Leo Leslie, owner and editor of the Cravenville Clarion; and Tom Fleming, owner of the Regal Hotel. Slim stopped in front of Catherine and bowed slightly. "Mighty nice to see you again, Miss Cornell. Paul tells me he likes school a heap."

Catherine murmured a soft "thank you" before Crane broke in.

"As long as you are here, pull up a chair, Slim," intoned Crane. "I find it hard to believe you're here by accident, seeing as how your Paul is going to be the topic of discussion." He fixed his gaze on Catherine as he finished speaking.

"If'n that's true, I'm right glad I came," observed Slim, wearing his poker face. "Why is Paul goin' to be the topic of conversation?"

"Miss Cornell had no business enrolling him in our school," interrupted Stewart, angrily. "Indians don't belong in our school. Miss Cornell should have known better."

"I don't agree with you, Mr. Stewart," Catherine responded. "My contract calls for me to teach the children of this community. It doesn't say anything about whether they have to be white, black, brown, or red. It also doesn't say how tall they should be or how much they should weigh."

Crane's fist hit the table. "Don't get sarcastic with us, Miss Cornell," he snapped. "You're in enough trouble as it is."

"Why is Miss Cornell in trouble, Carl?" inquired Slim in a cold voice. "I brought Paul to the school and asked her to enroll him. What else could she do?"

"She could have refused!" shouted Stewart.

"For what reason?" Slim shot back.

"The boy ain't a resident of the community, that's why," sneered Stewart.

"Ain't the Rambling R Ranch a part of the community?" retorted Slim, his eyes now fixed on Stewart. Without waiting for an answer, he went on, "And that's where Paul lives."

"For how long?" sneered Stewart again.

"For the rest of his life, I hope," responded Slim with fervor. Then he leaned forward in his chair. "Let's quit playing games and quit wasting everybody's time," he growled. "Now you folks listen, and listen real good, especially you, Stewart. Paul was made a ward of the court in Hawthorne, Colorado. Judge Pardee, up there, placed Paul in my custody. Judge Pardee then sent all the legal papers to our Judge Parks and transferred jurisdiction over Paul to him. Them papers are now in Parks's hands. Paul will remain in my custody until he is 21 years old or until I do somethin' the court don't like. That makes him a resident of this community, just like you and me. And it also means that Miss Cornell was dead right when she enrolled him in school."

Slim sank back in his chair and looked around the room at each person, one at a time. Catherine's eyes glistened with relief and admiration.

Crane coughed to break the silence.

"Does anyone else have anything to say," he inquired plaintively.

"Yeah," smirked Ollie Woods, "Let's vote."

"All right," agreed Crane. "All those in favor of letting Paul Redstone remain in school, raise your hands."

Fleming, Leslie, and Woods immediately shot their hands upward, and Crane, seeing how the vote was going, slowly raised his hand as well.

"All opposed, raise their hands," he droned and watched Stewart's arm shoot into the air.

"The vote is four to one. Paul Redstone stays in school."

Slim rose, pushed back his chair, and faced the table and its occupants, a grim expression on his face.

"One more thing you all should know," he drawled. "As far as anyone hereabouts is concerned, Paul Redstone is *my son*! I'll say it ag'in, Paul Redstone is *my son*!" Slim turned, strode to the door, flung it open, and disappeared into the night.

Slim found Paul and Tex in the hotel lobby as he had been told he would. He motioned for them to follow him up the street. They found their horses, pulled themselves into their saddles, and urged their steeds into motion.

Later that evening, as Slim and Tex sipped their final coffee of the day, Slim told Tex what had taken place at the meeting and concluded, "I reckon I got everythin' straightened out. There won't be any more trouble."

✳✳✳✳✳✳✳✳✳✳✳✳

Black Jack Stewart arrived home that night in a foul mood. Evers showing up had surprised him, and he was sure that Catherine Cornell was the cause of that event. Further, the meeting had not gone the way he wanted it to, and it was obvious that the Indian boy was going to be a permanent fixture at the school. He had cornered Crane after the meeting and had criticized the man for changing his vote at the last moment.

"What difference did it make?" Crane had countered. "You saw the same thing I did. We had three votes against us. Besides, if what Evers said is true, we didn't have a leg to stand on anyhow. I'll stop by to see Parks tomorrow, and if he has the papers Evers says he does, we can't legally keep the boy out of our school. I can't believe Evers would try to bluff us on that score. It's over, Mel. Go home and forget about it. There ain't nothing more we can do."

Stewart had a hard time sleeping that night and finally woke up more angry than ever.

Everything was fine at breakfast until Seth spoke up.

"Did yuh get rid of that Apache last night, paw? I'm shore gettin' tired of seein' him around. He's too smart for his own good. He makes me and Sid look bad."

"No, I didn't," snarled Black Jack. "He is living at the Rambling R, like you said, and has a legal right to go to school at our expense. It ain't right, but it looks like we can't do anything about it. As long as he wants to come to school, he can come."

Seth pondered this last statement for a little while before he spoke again.

"Supposin' he didn't want to come to school," Seth suggested cautiously. "Wouldn't that take care of things?"

"Well, yes, I guess it would," answered Stewart slowly. But you said he's a good student. Why wouldn't he want to come to school?"

"I dunno, paw," answered Seth, slyly. "Maybe, me and Sid and Danny Crane could show him it ain't no fun comin' to school. He might even decide it would be healthier if he stayed home at the ranch. Wouldn't that take care of things?" Seth repeated.

"Of course it would," replied Stewart, the light of understanding slowly moving across his dark countenance. He was silent for a few minutes as he considered his son's suggestion. "All right, have your 'talk' with him. Wait a week or so before you do it, though, and make sure no else is around. Okay?"

Seth grinned his agreement and dashed out of the house with Sid following in his footsteps.

✴✴✴✴✴✴✴✴✴✴✴✴

About 10 days later, Catherine asked Paul to stay after school and help her tidy up the school room. She liked to rotate this task among her students as a way to get them to appreciate what it took to provide the facilities for their education. These were light tasks—washing the slates, dusting the chairs, and, in the Winter, bringing in firewood. She was reluctant to ask Paul to stay late since he had such a long ride back to the Rambling R. But at the same time she did not want to exclude him from these duties, as that would appear to be favoritism. Besides, she had to admit that he already was her favorite student, and she could not let that show.

Paul accomplished his tasks with his usual dedication and enthusiasm. He found his jacket, as the air was now getting nippy as soon as the sun went down, walked to the school door, and turned, expecting Catherine to be right behind him. However, she had remained at her desk and looked up when Paul hesitated at the door.

"Thank you, Paul, you did a good job," she smiled. "You can go now."

"Aren't you coming?" asked Paul.

"No, I have to prepare some papers for tomorrow's lessons. Run along, I shan't be long."

Paul closed the door carefully, hopped down the three steps, and had walked about a dozen paces when a voice stopped him.

"Hey, red boy, come over here. We got somethin' to show you."

Seth Stewart waved to him and motioned for Paul to come. Sid Stewart and Danny Crane, also age 13, were crouched on the ground and staring at something that Paul could not make out. The threesome was about 30 feet away, off to one side from the schoolhouse, and partially out of sight from the end of Cravenville's main street.

Paul hesitated but changed direction as Seth's wave became more emphatic.

"What's the matter?" asked Paul as he drew close to Seth.

"We found a snake over here," answered Seth as he pointed toward Sid and Danny. "We don't know if it's dangerous or not. Can't you tell about such things?"

"Well, my father taught me a lot about snakes," acknowledged Paul. "I can probably help you. Where is it?"

"Over by Sid and Danny," replied Seth as he again pointed.

Paul brushed past Seth and bent over to see what Sid and Danny were looking at when Seth suddenly shoved him in the back and Paul went sprawling. He bounced to his feet and found himself looking at three figures that blocked his route to his horse.

Seth was a head taller than Paul and was at least 25 pounds heavier. Danny Crane was only slightly smaller than Seth, while Sid was about Paul's size.

"Why'd you do that?" asked Paul calmly. "What do you want?"

"We want you, red boy," sneered Seth. "You're too smart for your own good. Why don't you go back to the Rambling R and stay there? We don't need you around here."

Visions of his altercation with Lem and Sam Tuttle in Hawthorne tore through Paul's mind. In addition, all the stories Ruth had told him about her faith and how fighting was evil also returned, as did the stories of his Apache heritage that Jacob had told him. He was an Apache and, therefore, could not run. But, at the same time, he was also a Quaker and, therefore, could not fight, even if he knew how, which he did not.

Paul decided to try to bluff his way out of the situation.

"I'm going home," he announced as he brushed himself off, hitched up his trousers, and moved forward.

The bluff didn't work.

"You're going nowhere," snarled Seth as he gave Paul another hard push, this time using the boy's chest as his target. Paul staggered back but retained his footing. Seth moved forward and reached out to clutch Paul's jacket. Instinctively Paul remembered a wrestling move that Jacob had showed him one day when they had been playing. He grabbed Seth's arms with both hands, fell backwards, pulling Seth with him, and, using his feet, flipped Seth over his head, and then bounced to his feet.

Seth landed with a thud that knocked his wind out, temporily stunning him, and he lay motionless for a few moments. Paul, in the meantime, was transfixed by his unexpected success and couldn't stop staring at his fallen opponent. A heavyweight banged into him from behind and quickly brought him back to reality. The force of the blow drove him into the ground alongside Seth. A third figure landed on his back and began to hit him.

Paul pushed Sid aside and tried to get to his feet, only to have Danny smash into him from behind a second time. He again struggled to get to his feet, but by this time an enraged Seth had recovered his breath and waded in, fists flying. No matter which way Paul would turn, a fist would find him. He tried to use his hands and arms to protect his face and head and received blows to his stomach and rib cage instead. He sank to his knees and felt a hand pull his hair back and his face upward. Out of a corner of one rapidly swelling eye, he saw Seth poised to deliver a crushing blow.

"What's going on here?" a loud voice inquired. "What do you boys think you're doing?"

Seth glanced over his right shoulder and saw Catherine Cornell standing, hands on hips, her face flushed with anger.

"Let him go, Danny," Seth yelled. "Let's get out of here."

Crane released his grip on Paul's hair, kneed him in the back, and pushed him forward before racing off in pursuit of his two companions, who already were running toward town.

Catherine reached Paul's side as he once again attempted to get to his feet. She held his arm and helped steady him. Paul's nose was bleeding, one eye was almost swollen shut, and his face was covered with bruises.

"Oh, Paul, I'm so sorry," cried Catherine in dismay. "How badly are you hurt?"

Paul steadied himself and slowly started to limp in the direction of his horse. "I'm all right," he assured the teacher. "I'll be able to get back to the ranch, if I take it easy."

"Let's go see Doctor Hodges," suggested Catherine. "You may be hurt more than you think."

"No," retorted Paul, in a stronger voice. "Just help me get up in the saddle. Once I get started, I'll get along all right. I have to get back to the ranch. Slim will wonder why I am so late."

With Catherine's help, he gritted his teeth and pulled himself up into the saddle. Catherine untied his horse and handed him his reins. "I don't like you going without seeing Doctor Hodges," she repeated, with concern.

"I'll be all right," Paul again assured her. He pulled the horse away from her and weakly kneed his horse into motion. Catherine watched him disappear around the schoolhouse and bit her lip in vexation and concern.

※※※※※※※※※※※※

Red Rollins and Rusty Meyers were returning from the eastern line camp after spending a week patrolling that portion of the Rambling R's range and inspecting fences. They were in a jovial mood and looking forward to a couple of days of relaxation and good food, perhaps even an outing to Cravenville. They were jogging along when Red raised himself in his saddle and pointed off to their left where a horse slowly plodded along, its rider bent over in his saddle.

"Hey, that looks like Apache's horse over there," observed Red. "He must be comin' home from school. Kinda late, though. Maybe the kid was bad and had to stay after school." Red couldn't help laughing at the thought. "C'mon let's catch up with him and give him some company."

The two men spurred their horses and rapidly closed in on their objective. Red greeted the boy as he pulled in abreast of Paul.

"Hi, Apache. How come you're so late from school?"

Paul raised his head and looked at Red with one eye swollen shut, one glazed eye and a face filled with pain.

"What the hell!" exclaimed Red, an unbelieving look on his face. He reached out, pulled the reins from Paul's hands, and stopped the horse.

"Damn it, Rusty. You fork that bronc of yourn and make tracks for Cravenville. Get Doc Hodges and don't take no for an answer. Get him out to the ranch right quick. Now git!"

Rusty wheeled his horse and was gone in a cloud of dust as Red spoke to Paul.

"Hang on to your saddle horn, kid. I'm takin' your reins, and I'll lead your horse. If'n I go too fast, you yell right off. I'm takin' you to the ranch as quick as I can. You understand?"

Paul nodded his agreement and gripped the pommel with both hands.

Despite his words Red did not move as fast as he would have liked, as he was afraid Paul might fall out of the saddle. Still, it wasn't long before the ranch buildings came into view, and soon he was moving down the ranch's courtyard, the horse in tow and Paul still slumped in the saddle.

Several men looked in his direction from a variety of vantage points as Red slowly approached the main building. One of them, Curley Chance, stared at the twosome for a moment and then ran up the steps of the ranch house and disappeared inside. Almost immediately, Slim, Tex, Curley, and Maria Martinez emerged from the house, quickly descended the steps, and ran out to the tie rail, which Red had now reached.

"What happened, Red?" barked Tex, who was the first to arrive.

"I don't know, Tex," replied Red. "Me and Rusty found him like this out on the trail from town. I told Rusty to hightail it to Cravenville and get Doc Hodges."

Tex Riley's strong arms gently lifted Paul out of the saddle and, as he lowered Paul, he carefully shifted the boy's weight toward his chest in order to obtain a more secure hold. Try as he might, Paul was unable to stifle a soft groan. Tex instantly froze and took a deep breath.

"Where do you hurt, son?" he whispered. "I have to know."

"My left side is real sore," mumbled Paul through swollen lips, "and that's where your arm is."

"All right, then," murmured Tex, "Put both your arms around my neck, hold tight, and pull yourself up a bit. Then I'll shift my arm a mite and get a better hold. Ready? Good. Pull yourself up."

Paul did as he was told, and Tex made a quick adjustment. Bronc Evans, who had just arrived on the scene, reached out with his arms to help Tex, but Tex shook his head.

"Don't touch him, Bronc," Tex muttered. "I ain't shore where he hurts and how much. I've got a good hold. Lead the way, and let's get him up to bed."

Slim and Bronc held the door open and then stuck close to Tex, matching him step by step, as a precaution against Paul slipping out of Tex's arms. Tex entered the house, marched up the staircase, found the bedroom, and gently lowered Paul down on the bed. He unbuttoned Paul's shirt, spread both sides open and began a meticulous examination of Paul's stomach and rib cage areas.

Despite the boy's bronze coloring, a deeper dark blotch was clearly evident far down on his left side.

Maria rushed into the room carrying a bowl of hot water, a hand towel, bandages, and some salve. She slid past the men and took her position at the side of the bed. Tex reached out to restrain her.

"Maria, I don't think we should undress him any further cause I don't want to make him move, at least not 'til the doctor gets here and we find out what we can do. Bathe his face and wash his front as best you can, but watch out for that bad bruise down on his left side. Then bundle him up with blankets so he can keep warm. The rest of us will clear out and give you room."

"I'm staying here," Slim informed them in a firm tone, and Tex nodded his approval.

****

Three hours later Slim, Tex, and Bronc were in the den discussing what had taken place. Doctor Fred Hodges had arrived and was still with Paul. He had shooed Slim out of the room but had retained Maria as his nurse.

Slim had paced the den for over half an hour while Tex and Bronc silently sat and watched him, both with their own private thoughts. Finally Slim stopped and stared down at Tex.

"Damn it, Tex, it's Hawthorne all over ag'in. I brought Paul here, told him he was safe, that there wouldn't be any trouble, and he gets beat up ag'in. Who would do a thing like that?"

"From what you told me a week or so ago, I can just about guess, but guessin' ain't good enough," growled a grim Tex. "I aim to do better'n that. Slim, we've tried handlin' this situation yore way, but it ain't worked. From now on, we're doin' it my way. Tell me I've got a free hand and then stay out of the way."

"You've got it, of course," quickly answered Slim as he looked at his foreman, gratitude in his eyes. "Do what you have to do, and do it right!"

"Me and Trig have cards in this game, too," interrupted Bronc, his eyes flashing, "and don't you forget it, Tex Riley. This ain't a lone hand play. Me and Trig are his uncles, and we shore enough are goin' to be part of any showdown. What do we do first?"

"*We* don't do nothin' right now," replied Tex. "I'm goin' to town in the mornin' to see Miss Cornell and find out what I can. Then I'll talk to Apache. Once I get the lay of the land, we'll figger out what to do next. Bronc, you and Trig tell the boys to cover for you. I want one of you in the ranch house and near Paul every minute. I don't figger anyone will try to get at him ag'in, but we ain't gonna take any chances."

"I'll get my bedroll and sleep in his room," agreed Bronc. "I'll move in just as soon as the doc let's me."

A short time later Hodges entered the room, sat down, and looked around. He saw three intense faces.

"I gave the boy a sedative, and he's sleeping now. He's been beaten pretty badly, but I don't think anything is broken. He probably has a cracked rib, though, which will be painful, so we need to keep him quiet for a couple of days." He paused and looked around the room again.

"I can't be certain, of course, but the size of the cuts and bruises tells me he wasn't hit by an adult. Kids, most likely, and more'n one. I've told Maria what to do, so there's no need for me to stay the night. Paul will probably sleep all night anyway. I'll come back tomorrow afternoon, after office hours, and look in on the lad. I'm sorry this had to happen, Slim."

"So am I, Fred, and I'm right glad the news ain't too bad. Thank you for comin' out."

"Well, Rusty was pretty insistent," smiled Hodges. "I'll find my way out. Good night gentlemen." Hodges looked around again and was surprised to see that he was talking to only two men, Bronc Evans having disappeared.

Chapter 15

A distraught and worried Catherine Cornell did not sleep well that night. Arising early, she prepared and ate a meager breakfast, dressed herself, and arrived at the school much earlier than usual. She was surprised and pleased to find Tex Riley waiting for her.

Catherine rushed forward and, instinctively, threw her arms around his neck as tears ran down her face. His arms, also instinctively, enveloped her and pulled her close to his chest.

"Oh, Mr. Riley, I'm so sorry about Paul," she sobbed. Then she jerked her head back and looked into Tex's face. "How is Paul? I tried to get him to go see Doctor Hodges, but he insisted on going back to the ranch. How badly was he hurt?"

Tex gazed into the brown eyes and the concerned face so close to his own and couldn't resist a thin smile. "We think Apache will be all right. He's sore and probably will be in bed for a couple of days. One of the boys fetched Doc Hodges, and Doc says he don't think anythin' was broken. I reckon Apache was luckier than he looked."

Catherine drew back, her arms dropped away from around Tex's neck, and she breathed a deep sigh of relief, as Tex let her slip from his grasp.

"Oh, I am so thankful, Mr. Riley. That really is good news. Thank you for coming to tell me. This will make my day a lot easier to live through. What can I do for you?"

"Well, you can start by not calling me Mr. Riley," replied Tex. "The name to my friends is Tex, and I would shore enough like to think of you as a friend."

"All right, Tex," smiled Catherine, still overjoyed at the news about Paul. "You had better start calling me Catherine then. But why do you call Paul, 'Apache'?"

"That's a handle that Bronc gave him, and me and the boys kinda like it. And he shore enough is Apache. But I think you should call him Paul in school. I don't reckon the other kids would cotton to 'Apache'.

"The other reason I come to see you is to find out if'n you saw where the fight took place. If'n you did, would you show it to me?"

"Why, yes, I did, Mr. . . . I mean, Tex. It was over here to your right." Catherine pointed in that direction and took a step before Tex restrained her with his left arm. She looked at him in surprise.

"Walk slowly, Catherine," Tex told her, "and tell me when we get close to the spot. Then stop right quick."

Catherine did as she was told and then stopped, her curiosity now aroused. Tex stopped walking at the same time.

"Please stay put for a few minutes," he requested and then he began to move forward, very slowly and very gingerly, his eyes riveted to the ground. Tex crouched and extended the first finger on his right hand as if to measure something. He moved forward again, changed direction a little bit to his left, and then crouched and repeated the use of his finger. A short grunt reached Catherine's ears, and then Tex rose and moved forward again. He continued his inspection, moving forward or sideways and, as Catherine quickly noticed, was most careful where he stepped, placing one boot in a particular spot, shifting his weight very slowly, and then locating a spot for his other boot. Catherine's curiosity was now fully aroused, and she watched him closely, bewilderment on her face.

Finally Tex moved to his left, turned, and took long, purposeful steps in her direction. He touched her arm and motioned toward the schoolhouse.

"Let's go inside where we can talk," he suggested, and Catherine concurred by simply keeping pace with him.

She unlocked the door, went inside, and moved toward a nearby window, intending to raise the blinds, only to have Tex's voice stop her.

"Leave the blinds down," Tex directed. "I don't want any of yore kids to see me here. I picketed my horse a ways up the hill and out of sight. Lock the door from the inside."

Catherine glanced at Tex, more puzzled than ever, but did as she was told and then walked behind her desk and sat down in her chair. Tex followed, faced her across the desk, leaned forward, and gripped the edge of the desk with both hands.

"Catherine, you showed me where the fight took place. I gotta believe you also saw who beat up Paul. There were three of 'em, weren't there? And all of them come to your school."

Catherine's mouth fell open.

"Three of them and all from my school? How did you know that?"

"That don't matter none," said Tex calmly. "What are their names, Catherine?"

Catherine's shoulders sagged, and she had to hold her face in her hands for several moments before replying.

"Tex, I detest violence, and I hate what happened to Paul. But I am a teacher, and my students must trust me in order for me to do my job. I can't take sides in disputes between students, and I can't disclose any secrets they choose to tell me. I don't see how I can tell you those names. It will just cause more trouble."

"Catherine, there is more trouble comin' no matter what you do. The only question is what kind of trouble. This weren't a kid's fight, not with three ag'in one. Slim told you that Apache's second maw, Ruth, died, but he didn't tell you all of it. Apache's maw, Ruth, and his paw, Jacob, didn't just die—they was murdered! They was murdered by white folks who didn't want an Indian family livin' in their town. But it didn't stop there. Them same folks tried to kill Apache, too. Slim, and a few of the boys, just happened to be around and put a stop to it. I don't aim to have that kind of trouble here in Cravenville. I aim to put a stop to it, right here and now. Now, I'll ask you ag'in. What are the names of them three kids?"

Catherine's hands had flown to her breast as Tex spoke, and horror had replaced the concern in her face.

"I didn't have any idea," she murmured softly as tears slowly slid down her face. "Poor Paul, he must think this is a terrible world he's living in. And to think we call Indians savages."

Catherine paused, sighed, and took a deep breath.

"It was Seth and Sid Stewart," she said softly, "and Danny Crane."

"What do they look like?" probed Tex. "How big are they?"

Catherine described the three boys, and Tex snorted in disgust.

"Three to one ag'in him," he muttered, "and two of 'em bigger'n him. No, that shore weren't no kid's fight. Some folks don't want Apache around to dirty up the landscape, and I figger I know who two of 'em are.

"Catherine, if'n this was just a kid's fight, I might not butt in like I'm doin'. But Apache is different. We all know Apaches, generally speakin', don't grow up very big. Most kids anywhere near Apache's age will be bigger'n him. Now Apaches are damn good fighters. Just ask anyone in the Army about that. But this Apache is different. He ain't been taught how to fight. Why? Cause Jacob and Ruth were Quakers, and Quakers, like you, don't like fightin' as a way of settlin' things. So Tex Riley is goin' to butt in and with both feet.

"Thank you, Catherine, for givin' me those names. I woulda got them anyhow, but this way was much easier. Now I better light out of here. It's almost time for yore kids to get here. Unlock yore back door, go outside, and look around. Let me know if'n anyone is in sight."

Catherine did as she was told and walked to both ends of the building before signalling Tex to come ahead. Tex slipped out the back door, paused as he reached Catherine's side, and squeezed her outstretched hands before hurrying up the hill and disappearing out of sight among the trees. Catherine closed the door, walked to the front of the building and unlocked the front door, a smile on her face. The day had suddenly become much more brighter than it had been a scant half hour earlier.

****

Tex used the ride back to the Rambling R as an opportunity to formulate the plan he would employ in the coming days. Bronc was waiting for him as he swung from the saddle and tied his horse, outside the main ranch house.

"How's Apache?" Tex asked.

"His face is a bit better, but his side is still real sore. And he don't like the nursemaids you put on him," grinned Bronc. "I told him as soon as he could throw me down and pin me, I'd go away. He said that would have to wait for a day or two. You find out anythin' useful?"

"Enough," came the short reply. "You and Trig keep on what yore doin'. We'll have plenty to do in a few days. I'll go see the kid now."

Tex's visit with Paul did not last long. It was obvious the boy still had a lot of pain, and, as Tex expected, he refused to name his attackers. The subject of nursemaids came up, but Tex waved him off and refused to debate the issue.

Tex's meeting with Slim was even shorter. He told Slim he had found out what he wanted to know and that the appropriate response would come later. In the meantime he had duties to perform out on the range and would be back for supper. Slim's job was to supervise Paul's care and be there when Doctor Hodges returned later in the day. End of meeting.

Two days later, Paul announced he was ready to go back to school, but Tex, after conferring with Doctor Hodges, insisted that Paul wait two more days before doing so.

****

Seth Stewart informed his father that Paul had been absent from school for several days and was rewarded with lavish praise and an increase in his allowance. Seth neglected to tell Black Jack about having been seen by the teacher and made his two conspirators swear to maintain the secret. The three boys were extremely nervous about how Miss Cornell would treat them in school the day after the fight, but when nothing out of the ordinary took place, Seth was elated. The teacher would not dare tell on them, he allowed to his two friends, because she had to be afraid of what they might do to her. The three of them were in complete control, Seth exalted, and good times were sure to follow.

∗∗∗∗∗∗∗∗∗∗∗∗

That afternoon Tex rode into Cravenville after school was out, found Catherine in the schoolhouse, and invited her to dinner at The Steak House. She promptly accepted the invitation and found that she enjoyed the meal and conversation very much. It wasn't until the two were walking toward her little bungalow that she realized she had done most of the talking and that she really hadn't learned very much about her tall and strongly built companion. I'll have to learn more about him the next time, she promised herself.

Catherine was somewhat surprised when her cheerful escort suddenly took on a serious countenance when they reached her gate.

"Catherine, this has been a very pleasant evening and one I'll remember for a long time," Tex began. "I'm hopin' we can do this agin' right soon. But, right now I gotta ask you to do me a favor. It'll be mighty important that you do exactly what I want you to and, at the same time, not ask me any questions. You'll just have to trust me! Can you do that?"

Catherine hesitated for a moment and then nodded her head in the affirmative.

"Yes, Tex, this has been a most enjoyable evening, and I do trust you. What do you want me to do?"

Tex carefully gave her his instructions. Catherine caught her breath in dismay.

"There's going to be trouble, isn't there?" she asked plaintively.

"Most likely," responded Tex. "But remember why we're doin' this. Do you still want to do it? Do you still trust me?"

Catherine sighed in resignation, and again she slowly nodded her head in the affirmative.

"Thank you, Catherine," murmured Tex softly. "I thought I could count on you." Tex smiled and, suddenly, the warmth of the evening's earlier relationship returned with renewed vigor.

Tex's hands found hers, and he gently drew her close to him. He bent down, and his lips met hers. Her response to this first kiss was almost completely passive. But when he released her hands and surrounded her waist with his strong arms, she responded by putting her arms around his neck and by meeting his second kiss with all the intensity she could summon.

Tex gently released her and again smiled.

"Trust me, Catherine," he repeated in a hoarse voice. And then he was gone.

Catherine turned away and slowly walked the few yards to her door. Despite the great joy now contained in her heart, she could not dismiss a sense of foreboding. She realized that she had agreed to be a willing participant in what, she knew, could be a very troublesome event.

****

Seth Stewart was astonished when Paul walked into the classroom two days later shortly after nine o'clock. Paul was warmly greeted by Catherine Cornell. Several other students, taking their cue from the teacher, made him feel welcome as well.

As far as Seth was concerned, the hands of the big grandfather's clock, standing in one corner of the schoolroom, seemed to be eternally slow that morning. As the time for the noon lunch recess finally arrived, he dashed outside and anxiously waited for his two confederates to join him on the walk home. All but Paul and one other student went home for lunch each day. Paul generally ate the lunch Maria had prepared for him and talked with his classmate in and around the schoolhouse. Catherine, on this particular day, however, had brought her own lunch and in accordance with Tex's instructions, spent the entire hour talking and laughing with Paul and the other student.

Seth, Sid, and Danny walked down the main street until they came to an alley between the bank and Wood's General Store. They looked around, didn't notice anybody paying attention to them, dashed down the alley, and ducked in behind some big boxes behind the general store.

"I never figgered on that dumb Injun coming back to school," whispered Seth, a worried look on his face. "I already told paw we had taken care of his problem. Now it's back, and we gotta do somethin' fast."

"I'm scared," whined Sid. "Why'd Paul come back? We beat him up bad."

"Shut up, Sid," growled Seth. "I dunno why he came back neither. We gotta give him another lesson and make it stick this time."

"What about Miss Cornell?" asked Danny.

"She saw us and didn't say nothin' before," retorted Seth. "I'm shore she's so scared of us she won't say nothin' ag'in."

"I don't like it, Seth," said Danny. "Two times is real risky."

"You got a better idea?" Seth snapped back.

"No."

"All right, we wait for him after school and give him another good lickin'. One more time should convince him good. Let's get home afore someone starts wonderin' why we're late." With these words, Seth got up and sauntered back up the alley, his two companions following close behind.

****

The hands of the clock again moved far too slowly, as far as Seth was concerned, as the afternoon wore on. He was eagerly awaiting the confrontation with Paul that he had determined would occur. Unknown to Seth, the hands of the clock also moved far too slowly in the mind of his teacher as well, and her concern increased proportionately.

Finally, at long last she tapped the top of her desk and was the target of all the eyes in the room.

"Children, it is almost four o'clock," she announced in as calm a voice as she could muster. "You can put away your slates and be ready to leave in a minute or two. Paul, I want you to stay for a while. I want to go over what we have done while you have been gone and show you how you can catch up."

Paul was both surprised and irked at the announcement. While most of his cuts and bruises had pretty well healed, the deep bruise on his side was still painful. Sitting at his desk for six hours had proven to be more uncomfortable than he had anticipated. Why hadn't the teacher talked about this with him at noon? Paul asked himself. But, true to his Apache heritage, he said nothing.

Seth Stewart, on the other hand, had been hard pressed to conceal a gleeful chuckle at the announcement. The teacher had played right into their hands. Now no one, save the teacher, would be anywhere near the school when the attack would occur. He exchanged smiles with Sid and Danny.

Catherine spent a long half hour in her discussion with Paul, much to the latter's disgust. Finally she said he could go, and he hurried to the door and left the building. Catherine followed him to the door and pulled it almost shut, leaving an opening of a few inches, and stepped back two paces. She could now see out without being seen. She immediately caught her breath and barely suppressed a scream.

Three boys rose from the ground and blocked Paul's route to his horse.

"What's the matter, red boy? Can't you take a hint?" snarled Seth. "You were told you ain't wanted around here. I reckon we're just goin' to have to tell you ag'in."

During his confinement, Paul had reviewed the sequence of events that had taken place during the previous confrontation. It was obvious that his attempt to bluff his way out of the situation had been a total failure. Therefore, a new strategy had to be employed should the situation arise again.

Paul had thought long and hard and finally concluded that maybe a successful defense began with a good offense. Unfortunately, he didn't have a clue as to what would constitute a good offense, nor did he have either the skills or the tools to carry it out. So, despite many hours of thought, he still had no real concept of what he should do.

Still, one fact returned to his mind over and over again. The action before had begun by his moving backwards. Perhaps he should reverse the process and move forward.

Therefore, as soon as Seth had made his statement, Paul lowered his head and dashed straight at the bigger boy. Paul didn't make a direct hit, but his left shoulder caught Seth right in the pit of his stomach and, for the second time in a week, Seth found himself flat on his back and out of breath.

However, as Seth went down, his feet and Paul's feet became entangled, and Paul fell to the ground as well. Danny and Sid were on him in a flash, and the flailing of fists began. Seth gulped in a new quantity of oxygen and got to his feet.

"Grab both his arms!" he screamed in a fit of rage. "I want all of him."

Danny and Sid did as they were told, and despite all Paul could do, he was dragged to his feet, tightly held by the two boys, and totally helpless.

"Knock me down twice, will yuh?" Seth screamed, now beside himself. "I'm goin' to enjoy this!"

Seth wound up and was ready to deliver a crushing blow when he suddenly paused, wonderment and then consternation spreading across his face. A figure of a man, rapidly closing in on his two friends, had come into view. Mesmerized, he was unable to speak for a moment and failed to see the look of horror and astonishment on the faces of his confederates.

The sound of footsteps behind him finally penetrated his brain. He turned toward the sound, just in time to receive the full impact of the back of Tex's right fist, as it swung left to right.

The blow knocked Seth clear off his feet, and he went sprawling in the dirt, tears of pain oozing from his eyes.

Danny and Sid released Paul's arms, turned, and found themselves enveloped by Bronc's brawny arms. Bronc yanked the two boys together, the backs of their heads met with a loud crack, and both boys slumped to the ground.

Seth, in the meantime, tried to get to his feet and had partially succeeded when a firm hand gripped the front of his shirt, yanked him upward, and he looked directly into Tex's blazing eyes. A fist delivered a short vicious blow, flush into the center of Seth's face. Bells rang, stars suddenly appeared, blood spurted from his nose, and he yelled at the sudden increase in the level of his pain. Another blow followed. Again it was short, and again the center of his face was the target.

The hand released him, and Seth fell to his knees, sobbing, and sick to his stomach.

Tex ignored his victim and strode to Paul's side, where Bronc and Trig had already congregated. Catherine also breathlessly arrived on the scene.

"Apache, I'm sorry I had to use you as bait," said Tex. "But you gave me no choice. How bad are you hurt?"

Paul admitted he had a few more cuts and bruises but in the main hadn't fared badly. His side pained him, but he indicated that this had been true before the fight, and he flashed Catherine a vexed look, not realizing that Catherine had done only what Tex had told her to do.

Tex exhaled a big sigh of relief and turned to the teacher.

"Catherine, take Paul in the schoolhouse, clean him up, and watch him for a spell. Me and Bronc and Trig have some jobs to do. We'll be back as soon as we can."

"Are those 'jobs' really necessary?" asked Catherine, anxiously.

"Yes, Catherine, they are," answered Tex firmly. "We're goin' to make damn shore this doesn't happen ag'in."

Tex walked back to Seth, gripped the collar of the boy's shirt, yanked him to his feet, and half pulled and half dragged him in the direction of Cravenville's main street.

Bronc and Trig followed him, Danny and Sid in their grasp. The two men ignored the moans and groans emanating from their partially recovered charges.

Several Cravenville citizens, including Tom Fleming and Ollie Woods, were sitting at a big table in the Black Jack enjoying a cup of coffee and conversation with its proprietor when the front swinging doors were pushed open and Tex surged into the room, still dragging and pulling Seth. Bronc and Trig were right behind him with their two captives.

Tex pulled Seth to his full height and turned him so that the lad's face was in full view. The men at the table gasped, almost in unison, and Stewart's face turned white.

"I caught yore boy tryin' to beat up Apache ag'in," declared Tex as his eyes bored in on Stewart. "I'm bringin' him to you, and here he is." With that Tex retained his hold on the boy's collar with his right hand, gripped the back portion of the boy's trouser belt with his left hand, picked Seth up, and tossed him onto the table.

Seth landed face down. The table shook and tilted from the impact, cups and saucers flew in every direction, and the men shielded themselves to avoid being hit by Seth's arms and legs.

"What have you done with my son?" Stewart demanded to know, his face still white with dismay.

"I just gave him a sample of what I'm goin' to give you, Stewart," came the grim reply, as Tex began to untie the rawhide thongs holding down his Colts.

"Clancy, you keep your hands on top of the bar," warned Bronc. "This ain't none of yore affair."

Tex unbuckled his gun belt and handed it to Trig.

"Stewart, I don't know what you got ag'in Apache," continued Tex, "and I don't care. Apache is one of us, and when someone tangles with him, they shore enough are tangling with the Rambling R. You're about to find out what that means, and it's goin' to be somethin' you ain't never goin' to forget."

Tex advanced in Stewart's direction as he spoke. Black Jack backpedalled, trying to figure out what else he could do.

Stewart had experienced a few situations in his life where apprehension, even grave concern, had been a factor. But, never before, had the word fear really entered his mind. That is, until now. Over the years he had been a witness to a number of altercations involving Rambling R men, including one that included the man now standing before him. None of those confrontations had been pretty to behold. Moreover, he knew that Tex's reputation had been acquired through his involvement in many more incidents than the one Stewart had witnessed.

These thoughts flowed through Stewart's mind as he again backpedalled, dodged, and weaved. Each time he changed his direction, Tex moved with him and continued his slow and deliberate stalking. Stewart glanced over his shoulder and saw that he was rapidly running out of room within which to maneuver. Desperation now began to set in. Stewart gripped a chair and rolled it at Tex, as he tried to change direction again. Tex stopped the chair, picked it up, and hurled it halfway across the room. Stewart's fear now turned into stark terror. He changed direction again, but this time Tex cut him off and lunged for him.

Stewart fought in desperation and terror but to no avail. Tex's blows were hard, frequent, and very painful. The Cravenville citizens were awed by what they were witnessing. This was a Tex Riley they couldn't remember seeing before—cold, heartless, and brutal.

Tex landed another strong punch that drove Stewart back against his bar. Slowly, the half-conscious man slid to his knees and stared up at Tex with glazed and pain-filled eyes, virtually helpless.

Tex moved toward Stewart again.

"No, Tex," cried Tom Fleming. "For God's sake, not any more. He's hurt bad."

"Yeah, he's hurt bad," Tex agreed. "But not bad enough."

Tex reached down and grabbed Stewart's coat with both hands. He yanked the gambler to his feet and then slammed him against the bar. Holding Stewart with his left hand to steady the man, Tex's right arm moved and the flat of his open hand caught the left side of Stewart's face with a loud whack! Stewart's head snapped back and then fell forward just in time to meet the back side of Tex's right hand, now a clenched fist. The sound of this impact was duller than the first, but the effect was the same. The arm made a second trip, again with the flat of the hand and then returned with the same clenched fist. Then Tex released his grip on the coat, and as Stewart started to slide down, the right fist returned again, this time with all the power Tex could muster. The blow almost lifted Stewart off his feet, and the unconscious man made a nose dive to the floor.

"Now he hurts enough," stated Tex simply, breathing heavily.

Tex moved over to the table and leaned over it, using both hands to steady himself. Slowly Tex looked each man in the face.

"You all know Slim took me in and has treated me like a son. Two weeks ago he told you, Tom, and you, Ollie, that Apache was also a son to him. If'n that is true, and it is, that makes me Apache's big brother. And big brothers take care of little brothers. So pass the word, boys. If'n anyone so much as lays a hand on Apache ag'in, they're gonna have to deal with me.

And if'n they have to deal with me . . . ." Tex pulled himself up to his full height and pointed to the huddled figure on the floor, "They're gonna look like that, or worse."

"Listen well, boys," added Bronc. "Me and Trig are Apache's uncles and whatever Tex don't get around to doin', we will. Like Tex says, you pass the word and make shore everybody hears it."

Tex motioned for Trig to come to him. Trig responded, dragged Sid with him, and handed Tex his gun belt. Tex threw the gun belt over one shoulder, grabbed a handful of Sid's hair, and pulled him close.

"Did you hear what I said, Sid?" he asked.

Sid nodded his head vigorously in the affirmative and immediately wished he had not, his headache now more intense than before.

Tex's eyes then bored into Seth.

"Did you hear what I said Seth?" he again asked.

Seth mumbled a weak "yes" and looked down.

"Look at me!" snapped Tex, and Seth quickly responded, fear and pain still showing on his face.

"There's one more thing you boys better remember," Tex growled. "Miss Cornell is a special friend of mine, and what I said about Apache goes for her, too. Don't ever forget it! Do you understand me?"

Both boys again shook their heads in the affirmative. As Tex released Sid, he again addressed the boy.

"You'd better go get Doc Hodges. Both yore brother and yore paw need his attention. Now git!"

Sid wasted no time in disappearing out the door despite his headache.

Tex buckled his gun belt, retied the rawhide thongs, and motioned to Bronc.

"You and Trig take Danny down to his paw. I reckon you ought to have a meetin' with Carl and explain to him how things are goin' to be done around here from now on."

Bronc grinned and nodded his understanding. He and Trig headed for the door, Danny Crane still in tow.

As Tex slowly backed out of the saloon, he kept everyone in the room in his sight, especially Clancy, the bartender.

Once the doors swung shut behind Tex, everyone in the room let out a collective sigh of relief.

"I've known Tex for a long time," mused Fleming. "But I've never seen him like that. We're mighty lucky nobody got killed around here today."

Ollie Woods glanced over to the huddled shape on the floor. "I'm not sure Black Jack would agree with you on that, Tom," he observed dryly.

Chapter 16

Tex entered the schoolhouse and found both of his friends in a better mood than when he had left them. Catherine insisted on washing the bruises on Tex's face and hands but at the same time couldn't shake the sadness she was feeling over what had happened. The conversation she had with Tex, therefore, was cool and reserved.

A short time later Bronc and Trig appeared at the schoolhouse, and Bronc carried marks on his face and hands that were suspiciously similar to those exhibited by Tex. Catherine sighed in resignation and insisted on washing Bronc's injuries, too.

Bronc grinned his thanks but didn't add sparkle to the atmosphere when he allowed, "Old Doc Hodges ought to be right pleased with the Rambling R 'cause of us bringin' him so much business in one day."

Tex gave Bronc a hard look and glanced at Catherine. It was obvious that the teacher wasn't happy with the remark, but Tex only shrugged his shoulders and changed the subject.

"Bronc, you, Trig, and Paul start back to the ranch. I'll walk Catherine home and then catch up with you."

"I'll be all right, Tex," protested Catherine. "Go with your friends."

"No, Catherine, I'll walk you home. We should be seen together, especially right now. Later on . . . well, we'll talk about that."

Tex and Catherine strolled through town, Tex insisting that they walk the full length of the main street before backtracking to her bungalow. For the most part the walk was made in silence. Yet when Catherine glanced at her companion from time to time, she couldn't resist feeling admiration for the man. He walked tall, with his head held high, and he seemed to be completely oblivious to the stares that came in his direction. He acted as if nothing unusual had happened in the past hour or so. They reached her gate, and Tex suggested that they meet again for supper the following Saturday night. She nodded her approval, and Tex touched his hat, turned, and walked away.

****

Tex met Catherine as planned, and they again had supper at The Steak House. However, the conversation was strained, and Catherine only picked at her food. As they were sipping their coffee, Tex decided to address the situation head on.

"Catherine, somethin' has been botherin' you all evening. Wouldn't you feel better if'n you got it out so we both can look at it?"

Catherine put down her cup and sighed.

"Tex, did Seth tell you his father was behind the attacks on Paul?"

"No, I didn't ask him."

"You didn't ask *him*!" gasped Catherine. "You beat up his father without knowing whether he was involved or not?"

"Catherine, I could not, and would not, force a boy to tell on his father. When I brung Seth to the Black Jack and saw Stewart's face, I knew. But it really didn't matter. Three to one, with two of 'em bigger'n Apache, is not a kid's fight. And when they tried it a second time, I knew it was more'n that. The fact that both of Stewart's boys took part made it easy for me. I was goin' to make an example out of Stewart, no matter what."

Catherine stared at Tex, too shocked to talk.

"Catherine," Tex went on, "I told you before that Apaches ain't big people as a general rule. Almost all the boys Apache's age will be bigger'n him. Now, we have lots of folks out at the ranch that can teach him how to fight, if'n he wants to learn. But, even if'n he wants to learn how to fight, I'm not shore he will ever have the will to fight. You forget how he's been brought up. Bronc told me he sorta hinted that Apache should learn how to protect himself when they met him up there in Hawthorne. Bronc says Ruth gave him a look that almost burned him to a crisp. If and when Apache wants to learn about that, me and the boys will shore show him how. But that will be his decision, not our'n. At some point in time he will have to fight his battles in his own way. But until we get to that point, I'm his big brother, and I decided to make damn shore nothin' like this happened to him ag'in."

Catherine again sipped her coffee, now deep in thought.

"Tex, I like you very much, you know that. And I agree that something had to be done about Paul. But I am having a great deal of difficulty trying to live with your brutality. It's almost like I know two Tex Rileys, but I don't know which one is the real you. I think I understand what you have told me, but did it have to be that vicious? Seth has a broken nose and isn't back to school yet. And I've heard that Mr. Stewart is in real bad shape, too. They say he has a broken jaw and his face is a terrible mess. I've heard he can't eat very well. Was all that necessary, Tex?"

"I thought so," replied Tex simply.

Catherine frowned and finished her coffee.

"Please take me home, Tex," she said softly. "I have a great deal to think about."

Tex walked her home, and she permitted one goodnight kiss before turning and walking quickly to her door, tears in her eyes.

✳✳✳✳✳✳✳✳✳✳✳✳

Seven months passed rapidly. Paul continued to do well in school, and Catherine noticed that Seth, Sid, and Danny did everything possible to keep out of Paul's way. She couldn't help smiling inwardly as she realized that Tex's message had certainly been heard and taken to heart.

She and Tex had continued to see each other but at less frequent intervals. She knew he was her friend, but at the same time she still could not fully accept his violent methods. Furthermore, she had heard bits and pieces about his past and found that there, too, violence was a common denominator. This, in turn, only added to her distress.

One day, however, Catherine was in Wood's General Store having a pleasant conversation with Elsa Woods when Stewart's name fell into the conversation quite by accident. This prompted them to the recall Stewart's fight with Tex and the seriousness of the injuries he had received.

"I just can't get over how brutal Tex was at that time," commented Catherine, her distress showing. "It seems Tex went out of his way to hurt the man."

"Of course he did!" exclaimed Elsa in surprise. "Land's sake, child, haven't you figured out why?"

"Well, yes," replied Catherine slowly. "He felt he had to protect Paul from more beatings. But I think he just went too far."

"And?" asked Elsa as she raised her eyebrows.

"And what?" asked a puzzled Catherine.

"Land's sake, girl," retorted Elsa. "Tex shore did a heap more'n that!"

"What are you talking about?" Catherine inquired, even more perplexed.

"Tex knows this town," replied Elsa. "More'n that, he knows what teenaged boys can do, him being one himself some time back. Me and Ollie didn't figure it out at first, neither, but then it came to us right after Ollie remembered what it was that Tex said to the boys after Tex was done with Black Jack. Tex wanted to protect someone else, too. Someone very special to him. Someone that had to be part of the ambush he used to get to the bottom of things. Someone who could be a target for revenge. Now, who do *you* suppose that someone was?"

Catherine stared at Elsa, at first unable to comprehend what she was hearing. Suddenly the light broke through, and she remembered some of the conversations she had had with Tex and how he had insisted that they be seen together. Tears came to her eyes, and she gasped for breath.

"I never knew," she whispered. "I never even suspected anything like that. Oh, my poor Tex. I didn't understand, and I didn't trust him like he asked me to. I have wronged him so." Catherine's eyes filled with tears.

"Thank you, Elsa," she finally said after dabbing at her eyes with a handkerchief. "I wish I had talked to you a long time ago!"

✳✳✳✳✳✳✳✳✳✳✳✳

The chase had been long and exhausting. Shag Norton and his gang had held up a bank in the northern portion of the Utah territory, and just about anything that could go wrong with the caper did.

First, they bungled the job and had to shoot their way out of the town, killing a bank teller and two citizens in the process.

Secondly, gunfire from residents of the community had downed Swede Hanson's horse as they left the town, and he had either been killed or captured. A goodly portion of their loot had been in Swede's saddlebags.

Lastly, they had barely eluded the relentless pursuit by the posses on several occasions and during the last encounter had been forced to split up and scatter, agreeing to meet at a designated spot as soon as possible. When the gang reassembled, one member, Ed Smiley, did not appear. And Smiley had the rest of the loot in his saddlebags.

Norton swore in disgust and waited an extra six hours for his man to appear. Smiley didn't show up. But a posse did, and another chase began.

Norton and his three remaining men finally crossed the border into Arizona and sought refuge in an abandoned shack, about 50 miles north of Cravenville. The wornout men and jaded horses could finally rest and relax. But the frustration resulting from the nerveracking chase, combined with the lack of any tangible gain, remained with a bitter Norton.

The first order of business had to be to supplement their dwindling food supplies. After a day's rest for the horses, Shag and Zeb Butler headed for

Cravenville, while Slick Sawtell and Linc Carter did what they could to make the shack rainproof and make the ramshackle corral more secure.

It took Shag and Zeb two days to do their grocery shopping, and Shag returned with renewed enthusiasm.

"Boys," he declared, "Cravenville has a bank that's just made for the takin'. What with that skunk Smiley runnin' out on us and Swede not makin' it, we got to git ourselves some cash right soon. We'll hole up here for a few days and then hit that bank. Then we can go huntin' for Smiley. No one double crosses Shag Norton and gits away with it."

"We're short two men," Sawtell reminded Shag. "Can four do the job?"

"Shore we can!" retorted Norton. "And it means bigger shares for all of us. I never did like splittin' things six ways nohow. Me and Zeb looked over the town, and it should be as smooth as bull butter."

"That's what you said about the last job," commented Carter dryly.

"We just hit some bad luck," snapped Norton in return, his eyes flashing. "You got a problem with yore nerves?"

Carter shrugged his shoulders but didn't respond to the challenge.

"I agree with Shag," broke in Butler. "It ain't a big town—only has two or three ranches near it. We shouldn't have any trouble if we do things right."

"I'm still the leader of this here gang," Shag pointed out, "and I say we go with it. We'll give the horses three more days to build up their strength. After pulling the job we'll head east, double back, stop here to pick up the rest of our grub, and then head north to look for Smiley. Any questions?"

Hearing none, he grinned with satisfaction and began to ponder how he could refine the operation and make it a sure-fire success.

****

It was the last day of school, and Catherine had decided to release the children at noon rather than keeping them confined all day. It was highly unlikely anything useful could be accomplished in the afternoon anyway.

Earlier Catherine had sent a note to Tex, by way of Paul, asking him to come to see her this day, telling him that she wanted to have lunch with him and that she had something important to talk to him about. Tex had sent a note back, accepting the invitation.

That morning Tex told Paul to wait at the school until he got there, thinking Paul could join Catherine and him for lunch. In addition, Tex mentioned to Slim that it was almost the right day for the weekly trip into Cravenville for supplies and the mail and suggested that this could be done at the same time. In that way, Paul could ride back on the ranch wagon and have some company. Slim readily agreed, and the arrangements were made.

It was Red Rollins' turn to drive the wagon into Cravenville, and so at mid-morning he hitched up the team, climbed up into the driver's seat, and carefully deposited his Winchester on the seat alongside him. Tex shook his head in amusement as he swung into his own saddle. It was a longstanding tradition on the ranch that wherever Red and Charley Landers went, their Winchesters went with them. They were kidded about this a lot, but both men grinned and suffered in silence. They were the two best riflemen on the ranch and had explained many times that they felt naked without their favorite weapons.

Red cracked the team into motion, and Tex moved along beside him. They had a leisurely journey, arrived at the schoolhouse a little after noon, and found Paul sitting on the front steps waiting for them. Paul explained that Catherine had gone to the bank and would be back in a few minutes.

Tex tied his horse to the wagon and sat down beside Paul, while Red remained in the wagon. Paul began to talk about all he had learned during the past school year when a burst of gunfire stopped his narrative in mid-sentence.

✲✲✲✲✲✲✲✲✲✲✲✲

Toby Green was a scavenger. As soon as school let out, he decided it was a good day for his weekly exploration trip down the alleys between and behind the bank and Wood's General Store. He usually found one or more items that Ollie Woods, or Bert Milner had discarded that he could play with or use around his house. He had even been able to build himself a tree house, using leftover slats from crates and cartons, and was very proud of this achievement.

On this particular day he decided to approach his objective by the back way instead of proceeding up main street as was his custom. He figured there would be more people out and about around noon as compared to late afternoon, when he usually did his survey, and he didn't want to be seen if he could avoid it.

He slipped behind the buildings facing main street and was about to step out into the alley when he heard the soft sound of slowly moving horses. Toby ducked behind a group of barrels and carefully peeked out. Four mounted men turned into the alley, just in front of the boy, and walked their mounts to the back of the bank. Two men dismounted, handed their reins to their two companions, pulled some gunny sacks from their saddlebags, and moved up the alley toward main street. Toby couldn't check a soft gasp when the two remaining riders pulled their neckerchieves up over their noses.

Silently Toby moved back from the barrels, and as soon as he moved around the edge of the nearest building, he raced toward main street. He stopped and peered around the front of the building just in time to see both of the strangers disappear into the bank.

Toby dashed up the street and burst into the sheriff's office, out of breath. Sheriff Buck Buchanan and two deputies looked at him in surprise.

"What are you up to, Toby?" drawled Buchanan. "You sure look like you are hell bent for an election."

Toby's chest heaved as he tried to catch his breath. He pointed behind him and gulped for more air.

"Sheriff, I just seen four strangers ride into town," the boy gasped between deep breaths. "They parked their horses behind the bank, and two of 'em circled around and went in. The other two are sittin' there with neckerchieves over their faces."

Buchanan sprang into action. He turned to his two deputies, "Chuck, you and Joe go down and cover the front of the bank. Shoo as many people off the street as you can. I'll go up the back way and cover the alley. Get goin'. Toby, you stay here and don't go outside for any reason."

All three men were out the door in a flash. Buchanan followed his two men for a few steps and then turned off down a side street. He quickly reached the alley entrance. He stopped and peeked around the back of a building.

The two men were about 50 yards away with their backs to him. Cautiously he edged forward, cut the distance in half, and slid behind a stack of crates, his gun drawn.

"Throw up your hands," he yelled. "This is the sheriff speakin'."

Linc Carter and Zeb Butler spun in their saddles, astonished at the sound of the voice. Both of them dropped the reins they were holding, their hands moved, and the alley reverberated with the sounds of their shots. Two bullets thudded into the crates sheltering the sheriff. Buchanan leveled his gun and pulled the trigger as two loose horses galloped down the alley.

Carter's body sagged and slowly slid out of his saddle as Butler again fired at the sheriff.

The back door of the bank flew open, and Norton's covered face peered out, anger in his eyes.

Butler swung out of his saddle, paused to fire again at the sheriff and shouted at Norton, "Linc's hit, we're cornered out here, and I'm comin' in."

He bulled his way into Norton, knocking him back a couple of steps. Zeb reached for the door and slammed it shut.

"What the hell happened?" screamed Norton. "And where are the horses?"

"I don't know," yelled Butler. "Someone threw down on us, said he was the sheriff, and plugged Linc. The horses got away."

Norton issued a stream of curses but was cut short by the sound of shots from the front of the bank. Norton and Butler raced back to the bank lobby area and found Sawtell crouched below a broken window, his gun trained on Milner, a bank teller, and Catherine Cornell, as the three lay on the floor.

"As soon as the shooting started out back, two hombres started to cross the street with their guns out," reported Slick. "I drilled one of 'em and drove 'em back. What happened out back?"

"Sheriff showed up and got Linc," explained Butler as he, too, moved to the front of the bank and peered out a window. "There's a bunch of people out there, Shag, and they all got guns," he announced.

Norton was thinking fast, and Swede's fate gave him an idea. Quickly Shag moved to Catherine's side, yanked her to her feet, dragged her to the front door, and pushed her out on the sidewalk, his left arm around her waist and his right hand holding a Colt to her head.

"Stand back, all of you," he shouted. "We're comin' out. One shot from any of you, and this lady dies."

"Hold your fire," a voice called out. "It's Miss Cornell."

Norton pushed Catherine ahead of him as Slick and Zeb dashed around him, untied the three nearest horses, quickly mounted, and handed one set of reins to Shag.

"Missy, I'm goin' to step into this stirrup," Norton told her. "As soon as I do, you step on my boot and pull yourself up into the saddle. I'll be right behind you, so don't make no mistakes. One false move, and you're dead."

Catherine did as she was told, and as soon as she had settled her weight in the saddle, Norton grabbed the pommel and pulled himself up right behind her, his gun boring into her right side. The three men kicked their horses into action and raced down the street in the direction of the schoolhouse.

✳✳✳✳✳✳✳✳✳✳✳✳

Tex rose at the sound of the gunfire and stiffened. Two more shots were heard, and then there was total silence. Tex continued to stare in the direction of Cravenville, vexed and uneasy.

"Whatever it was, it must be all over," volunteered Red, holding the reins of his team in one hand and clutching his Winchester with the other.

"Maybe somebody was celebrating the end of school," added Paul with a smile. "Is that what white folks do?"

"Not as a rule," replied Tex, still worried. "We generally save that for the Fourth of July."

No additional shots were heard, however, and Tex relaxed a little. "Catherine should be along in a few minutes. Mebby she can tell us what was going on," he muttered as he motioned for Paul to sit down. Tex lowered himself beside the boy, still not completely satisfied with the situation.

A couple of minutes passed, and suddenly three galloping horses swept around the corner of the nearest building and headed their way. The third horse carried two riders, one with flowing long brown hair and wearing a bright yellow dress. All three outlaws saw Tex, Red, Paul, and the wagon, immediately swerved their horses, and the first two men each fired a shot in the general direction of this new threat.

Tex dove for cover behind the wagon, pulling Paul with him. Red, who had stood up, simply fell back over the seat and landed in the box of the wagon. One slug shattered a front window in the schoolhouse, and the second ricocheted off a wagon wheel. The team of horses reared and pulled but did not run.

Red jumped out of the wagon, knelt, and raised the Winchester to his shoulder.

"Don't shoot," yelled Tex "That's Catherine with 'em."

Red paused, took a deep breath, and pulled the trigger.

Zeb Butler threw up his hands, and his gun went flying. Butler pitched from the saddle, hit the ground, rolled over twice, and lay still.

Tex, gun in hand, dashed around Red and stared at the backs of fast moving riders. They were rapidly moving out of rifle range.

"I won't fire ag'in," Red announced, "It's too far and too dangerous. But I did have a clear shot at one of 'em, and I took it."

Tex heard the sound of hooves and made a quick decision. "Apache, go over there and study them tracks. I'll stop people from blottin' 'em out."

A swarm of riders turned the corner and raced toward them. Tex fired two quick shots in the air and held up his hands. The riders reined in their horses and watched as Tex jogged toward them, shouting as he moved.

"Stay where you are," he yelled. "Don't move. What happened?"

Buck Buchanan held up his hand and waited for Tex to reach him before speaking.

"Four men tried to rob the bank, Tex. I got one of 'em, but they took Miss Cornell as a hostage, and we didn't dare fire at 'em. Chuck Corwin took a slug and is hurt bad."

"You did right, Buck. Red downed another one—he's out checkin' on him now. Buck, tell these folks to turn around, go back to town, and settle down. We'll form a posse, shore enough, but let's take our time and do it right. We got Catherine to worry about."

Buchanan immediately saw the wisdom of Tex's suggestion and responded accordingly.

"All right, folks, turn around and go back to town. Tex is right. We got to get ourselves organized afore we do anythin'. Tom, you and Carl stay here 'til I sort out what we do."

A chorus of protests rose, but Buchanan was firm. Still grumbling, most of the people turned and drifted back toward Cravenville with only Tom Fleming and Carl Crane remaining with Buchanan.

Red arrived and made a terse report. "The fellar out there is dead. I hit him plumb center. Apache wants to see you, Tex."

Tex looked at the sheriff.

"Buck, this could be a long, hard ride. We're goin' to need good men and plenty of provisions. I'll get the men, you get the vittles. Tell Ollie to pack some riding clothes for Catherine. She'll need them when they let her go. Buck, Catherine is special to me, and I aim to run this show. Make me a deputy, and I'll get on with it."

"You beat me to it, Tex. You've been a deputy ever since I got here. What do you want us to do?"

"Red, hightail it back to the ranch and send me the first two or three men you see. Tell the rest of the boys to stay put and take care of the ranch. Buck, get us a pack horse and all the supplies it can hold. Tom, you and Carl pack that body on one of your horses and one of you take him back to town. The other one of you move out a mile or two and point people in the right direction. Apache and I will start trailin' these coyotes right now. Buck, follow our trail as soon as you can."

"You takin' the boy with you?" asked Buchanan incredulously as he tried to avoid the dust floating back from Red's rapid departure."

"He's Apache, Buck, and he says he knows how to track. We're goin' to need all the help we can get. Besides, she's his teacher, and I probably couldn't stop him from comin' along even if'n I wanted to."

The three men did as they were told, and Tex walked over to Apache. Tex listened as Paul described a distinguishing characteristic for each of the three tracks and the man's eyes glowed with pleasure and admiration.

"Tex, get my horse and follow me," directed the boy. "I will remain on foot for the time being."

Tex mounted his own horse, galloped to the edge of town, untied Paul's horse, and led it back past the schoolhouse, past Tom and Carl as they were tying Butler's body on Carl's horse, and caught up with Paul about a quarter of a mile farther on. A few minutes later they came upon Butler's stolen horse. Tex dismounted, handed Paul both reins, and carefully approached the animal. Big brown eyes watched Tex close in but did not exhibit fear. Perhaps it felt like it had done enough running for the moment. At any rate, Tex took control of the dangling reins and watched as Paul carefully examined all four hooves. The boy nodded in satisfaction, rose, mounted his own horse, and watched as Tex remounted and turned his horse back toward Cravenville.

"I'll take this cayuse back to Tom and catch up with you, Apache. We can't have him running loose and messing up our tracks. I'll be back right quick."

Paul guided his horse alongside the two sets of tracks, and Tex caught up with him about five minutes later.

"All they're worryin' about right now is speed," observed Tex, "and one horse is carrying double. It won't be long before they'll have to slow down and try to hide their trail. That's when the fun will begin, Apache. Do you think you can handle that?"

"I will do my best, Tex," the boy declared. "Jacob taught me well, but this is not the desert. Jacob and I did a lot of exploring in the mountains around Hawthorne, though, and that will help. But I'm going to need your help, too. Both of us have a special reason not to fail. Let us pray for dry weather. Any rain now would be very bad."

****

Shag Norton and Slick Sawtell kept their horses at top speed for over half an hour before reining in their mounts and continuing at a fast trot. As soon as they reached some high ground, the two men pulled their horses to a complete stop and carefully examined their back trail. They could see for quite a distance and were pleased to note the absence of any pursuit. Better yet, no telltale cloud of dust was visible farther down the horizon.

"It looks like we got a good head start," reflected Sawtell. "I'm some surprised they're so slow in trailin' us, though. No matter. Get rid of the gal, and let's git goin'."

Norton was about to let Catherine slide off his mount when he abruptly changed his mind.

"No, I aim to keep her with us, at least for a spell," he informed Slick.

"What the hell for?" thundered Sawtell. "She'll only slow us down, and we can't afford that. Let her go!"

"No," repeated Norton. "I don't know why we ain't being pushed harder, neither. And she's still our ace in the hole. If someone is pullin' a fast one on us, we may need her yet. We'll keep goin' east for a little while and look for a chance to swing north and hide our trail. C'mon, let's go."

Sawtell swore under his breath, spurred his horse into motion, and followed his leader.

About a half an hour later they came upon some hard ground, which stretched out in a northeasterly direction. Norton grinned his satisfaction and led the way on to the hard soil. Well over an hour later they came upon a tiny stream only two or three inches deep and pulled their horses to stop. The men dismounted, and Norton let Catherine do the same. Both horses and humans drank deeply, and the two men topped off the water levels in the canteens they had acquired along with the stolen horses.

After a short rest, they all remounted and guided their mounts into the water and followed the bed of the little stream in a northwesterly direction, back toward the shack and their spare food. An hour later the stream disappeared under some rocks, and they were forced to emerge and travel by land again. The horses, especially Norton's, were now close to exhaustion, and progress was very slow. Reluctantly Norton finally called a halt, and the two men quickly put together a makeshift camp. Catherine found a soft area of sod and collapsed. Not only was she stiff and sore from the long ride, but the tension and mental strain resulting from the bank holdup and the danger inherent in her present circumstances had exhausted her. She closed her eyes, tried to get her nerves under control, and thought of Tex. Today was the day she was going to tell him how sorry she was for not understanding him better and was going to ask for his forgiveness. Her chances of being able to do that now seemed remote, and tears of frustration and fear filled her eyes.

Norton pulled the saddlebags from the two animals, slung them over one arm, and looked around. Spotting a large log, he walked over to it, sat down, and began to fish through the bags. The more he searched, the more irritated he became. Finally he threw the bags halfway across the little clearing and glared at his companion.

"All right, Sawtell, where is the money?"

"What money?" responded Slick in surprise.

"The money from the bank, of course, you fool," snapped Shag. "What other money do you think I'd be talkin' about?"

"Who you callin' a fool?" retorted Sawtell, his voice rising. "You had the bag when you went to the back of the bank. What'd you do with it?"

Norton stared at Sawtell with unbelieving eyes. Suddenly he jumped to his feet, pulled off his hat, slammed it to the ground, and jumped on it with both feet as he shouted a long string of curses. Sawtell stared at him, amazement on his face, and Catherine sat up, shocked at what she was hearing.

Ultimately Norton ran out of breath, stopped jumping up and down on his hat, and looked down at the ground, hands on his hips.

"The damn bag's still in the bank," he groaned and launched another string of expletives. He ran out of breath a second time, and a sheepish look spread across his face.

"I just got to the back door when the shootin' started," he began to explain. "I had my gun in my right hand and had to put the bag down to open the damn door so's I could find out what was goin' on. Zeb came runnin' in and almost knocked me flat. Then the shootin' started out front, and me and Zeb ran back there to see what you were doin'. That damn bag is still asettin' by that door." And for a third time he emitted a tirade of profanities.

Sawtell shook his head in disgust.

"We shore are a great gang of bank robbers," he allowed. "Swede get's himself caught or killed, and we lose half of the loot from the last job. Then Smiley walks out on us, and we lose the other half. We try it ag'in, lose two more men, and don't get nothin' to show for it."

"And no grub, neither," added Norton with a deep frown.

Catherine's hands flew to her mouth, and try though she might, could not completely suppress a laugh. It came out as a soft gurgle, but Norton heard it.

He stamped his way to her side, glared at her, and swung his fist, hitting her on the side of the face. She rolled over from the force of the blow and screamed in pain.

"Think it's funny, don't you?" Shag snarled. "I don't see you laughin' now." He looked down at his victim, his eyes glowing with anger. "We didn't get any money," he continued, "but I shore enough got you. Laugh at Shag Norton, will you? Nobody gets away with that, and I'm goin' to show you what happens when they try." He reached down and tore at her dress.

Catherine fought back as hard as she could, her fingernails leaving a bloody trail down one of Norton's cheeks. This only enraged the man further, and now he was uncontrollable. He hit her several more times and continued to tear at her clothing. Half unconscious and exhausted, Catherine ceased to struggle. Norton continued his assault on her, an evil grin on his face.

Chapter 17

Tex and Paul continued to follow the trail of the outlaws. Periodically, Paul would dismount and examine the tracks of the two horses, grunt his satisfaction, and remount. The twosome reached some high ground, and Paul quickly raised his arm and reined his horse to a stop. He handed his reins to Tex, slid off his horse, and carefully examined the ground as he circled the area.

"They stopped here, Tex, rested a bit, and then went on," Paul reported to his mounted companion.

"Stopped to check their back trail," agreed Tex. "Did anyone dismount, Apache?"

Paul shook his head in the negative, and Tex swore.

"It looks like I made a big mistake, Apache. I figgered if'n they saw there wasn't a posse right behind them, they'd relax and let Catherine go. She's only goin' to slow 'em down and ain't no good to 'em now. Right here is where they should have done it. Are you shore no one dismounted?" asked Tex again, although his own eyes could see no evidence to support his hope.

"It was a good gamble," Paul assured him. "If the posse was hot on their trail, they would either use her or kill her in order to make better speed. This way we at least know she's still alive. I'll proceed on foot and see if I can pick up any sign that they have dropped her along the way. Lead my horse and follow me."

Paul trotted along for almost a mile before pausing and waving for Tex to join him. Tex handed him his reins, and Paul leaped into the saddle.

"No one dismounted, Tex. I'm sorry."

"I don't like it, Apache. They should have let her go by now. I don't understand it. It don't make no sense." Tex scowled in vexation.

Tex stood up in his stirrups and peered off in the distance.

"One more thing, Apache. Them fellars might get it in their heads to back track to see who's follerin' them. We got to keep our eyes peeled for an ambush, seein' as how there's only two of us."

"More are coming," Paul reminded him.

"Yes, but that don't do us no good right now," warned Tex. "Let's keep goin', but we gotta be careful."

They urged their horses forward and continued to follow the trail before them. Paul dismounted periodically to verify that they were following the right tracks.

It was almost dusk when they arrived at the hard ground that had pleased Norton so much.

"Well, Apache, here's where the fun begins," Tex growled, a deep scowl spreading across his face. "This is where it's goin' to get tough."

"Yes, but I think our desperate friends have made their first mistake," observed Paul quietly.

"Why do you say that?" asked a perplexed Riley. "This hard ground will make trackin' almost impossible."

"Well, yes and no," answered Paul thoughtfully. "It will be more difficult, but remember one horse is carrying double. Perhaps keeping Catherine with them will now be their undoing. That horse will have to make deeper marks than it usually would. There will also be waste at some point in time, and I can smell real good.

"Tex, there is still some light. You stay here, start to set up a camp, and wait for the others. I'll go ahead on foot and see what I can find."

"Wait a minute, Apache," cried Tex, in alarm. "That's too risky. They could be out there waitin' for us."

"I don't think so, Tex," responded Paul carefully. "If they wanted to ambush us, they'd have done it before now. They certainly wouldn't be trying to hide their trail if they wanted us to catch up with them. I'll be careful, and I bet I can see better and farther than they can."

Tex hesitated, but Paul's logic made sense, he admitted to himself.

"All right, Apache. I don't like it, but I think you're right. Go ahead, but be right careful." Tex squeezed the boy's shoulder and watched him move out on foot.

Tex did what he could to get an area ready for a campsite, but he frequently glanced up the trail to where he had last seen Paul. His nervousness and concern increased with each passing minute.

The sound of hoofbeats reached his ears, and he turned toward the sound, poised for a quick draw with both hands.

Sheriff Buchanan came into view and was quickly followed by Red Rollins, Bronc Evans, and Trig Mansfield, the latter leading a heavily loaded pack horse.

Tex relaxed and shot a curious look at Red as the group pulled their horses to a stop and swung from the saddle.

"How come you're here?" asked Tex as he continued to stare at Red.

"Met Bronc, Trig, and Rusty half way to the ranch," grinned Red. "Told Rusty to lend me his horse and gave him the wagon in return. Figgered you might have better use for my Winchester than Rusty's six gun, seein' as how Bronc and Trig were comin' along. Where's Apache?"

"He went on ahead, alone and on foot, to see if he can pick up some signs before it got dark. I'm startin' to get worried about him." Tex again glanced up the trail, but now the settling dusk had reduced the range of his vision by a considerable distance.

"You boys unload the pack horse," Buchanan interrupted. "I want to bring Tex up to date on the news." He motioned toward a fallen tree and moved in that direction. Tex followed him and sat down beside the sheriff.

"What's up?" asked Tex as soon as he was settled on the log.

"Well, first off, I don't think them varmints got away with a dime," responded Buchanan with a grin. "We found a bag of money settin' by the back door of the bank nice as you please. I reckon I ruined the whole game by jumpin' those jaspers in the alley. Not only that, but the two dead ones didn't have enough cash on 'em to say so. The other two were so busy tryin' to get away, I just don't think they took nothin' with them. Bert was countin' it when I left, but he didn't think anythin' was missin' either."

"I'm right glad to hear that Buck. Anythin' else?"

"Yes, and it gets better, Tex. The two horses in the alley stayed put, and the other two didn't run off far. We got all four, and I went through the saddlebags. Tex, there weren't enough grub in those bags to last four growed men more'n a day at the most!"

"That means they got more grub cached not far away," breathed Tex.

"That's the way I figger it," agreed the sheriff. "I've sent wires to all our nearby towns to be on the lookout for 'em. Have you found out anythin' about Miss Cornell?"

"No, and I'm real worried, Buck. They should have let her go when they reached that high ground back aways. I don't know why they didn't do it."

"Yeah, I saw that too," frowned Buchanan. "It don't make sense a'tall. She's only goin' to slow 'em down, 'specially since they only got two horses. If they had three horses, I could understand it."

A soft whistle penetrated the dusk and interrupted their conversation.

Tex bounced up and ran to the edge of the clearing, as the other men joined him, guns in their hands.

"Apache?" Tex whispered hoarsely.

"Yes, don't shoot, I'm coming in."

"Spread out and cover him," snapped Tex to his companions. "He might not be alone. Hold it! Red, you and Trig cover the horses," added Tex, as he swiftly made a change in his thinking. Then he went into a slight crouch, both hands poised to make a snap draw as he tried to pierce the dusk and see Paul.

A figure emerged out of the darkness and moved rapidly in their direction. Tex breathed a deep sigh of relief as soon as it became evident Paul was alone.

Paul received warm greetings from everyone and smiled his acknowledgements in return.

"I was able to track them for over a mile," he announced. "They didn't waver in one direction or the other. The horse carrying double is giving them away. It's getting real tired and can't hold a straight trail."

"Good for you, Apache," responded Tex. "I'm shore glad you're along. Bronc, get a fire goin', but put it in the lee of that rock over there. Dig out a hole for the coals. Red, you help him. We'll eat, bed down early, and be ready to go at dawn."

"I'll take the first watch," Bronc informed him. "Trig can relieve me in about four hours."

Despite the hot meal and a camp full of friends, Tex could not get to sleep. His concern about Catherine was now profound, and sleep would not come. Finally he threw off his blanket, poured a cup of coffee, and joined Bronc.

"Roll in yore blankets, Bronc," Tex murmured. "I'll stand yore watch."

"Aw, I ain't sleepy," Bronc replied. "Asides, I think you can use some company." Bronc eyed his companion. "She's goin' to be all right, Tex. You gotta believe that. It shore was bad luck to have her get mixed up in this, though."

"She wanted to see me about somethin', Bronc. Didn't say what for. Even sent me a special invitation. I just can't figger why they didn't let her go. She can't help them now."

"Well, she still would have value, if'n we caught up with 'em," Bronc reminded him. "At least we know she's still alive," he added, echoing Paul's earlier comment.

✳✳✳✳✳✳✳✳✳✳✳

Catherine's night had been much worse than Tex's. In addition to the stiffness and soreness she had sustained from the long ride, the blows to her face and the violation of her body had added to her pain and suffering. She crawled behind some trees for privacy and wrapped herself, as best she could, with her torn clothing.

Unfortunately, not only did the saddlebags lack any food, but the stolen horses did not have bedrolls tied behind the saddles, either. By midnight, the night air had become down-right chilly, and Catherine was beginning to shiver.

Unable to sleep, Sawtell finally got up and began to collect firewood.

"What do you think you're doin'?" grunted Norton.

"I'm collectin' wood for a fire," replied Slick, disgust in his voice. "I'll be damned if I'm gonna freeze. That posse has to be holed up somewhere and is gettin' a good night's sleep. We covered our tracks well, and they can't be anywhere near, what with the head start we got. Asides, this is a low spot, and the trees are thick. Nobody will be able to see a fire more'n a hundred yards from here."

"They can smell it," Shag reminded him.

"They won't be close enough to do that," retorted Slick, "and I'm goin' to take the chance regardless."

Norton started to protest further, but he, too, was getting cold and the thought of a warm fire was too strong to ignore. He helped gather a good quantity of twigs and branches, and soon the two men had a small fire going.

Sawtell walked over to where Catherine was huddled.

"Ma'am, we got a fire goin'. You'll freeze if you stay out here. Come along and set by the fire. I'll give you a hand."

Sawtell helped Catherine to her feet and guided her as she staggered in the direction of the fire. Norton's lips curled in contempt as he watched the twosome approach the fire.

"What's the idea, Slick?" Shag sneered. "You gettin' sweet on the gal? You must like used merchandise."

Sawtell flashed Norton a hard look but did not respond to the taunt. He helped Catherine get settled by the fire, and she gave him an appreciative glance.

"Now that I think about it, you might have a good idear at that," growled Norton. "Get her nice and warm. I may want to have another go with her afore mornin'. I need to get warm, too."

An hour later Norton was good as his word. Catherine did not resist but closed her eyes, refusing to look at the leering face so close to her own. Sawtell watched but did not interfere.

At long last dawn arrived, and Catherine again crawled behind some trees for privacy.

The horses were quickly saddled, and Norton started to walk toward Catherine's location when Sawtell's voice stopped him.

"Where you goin', Shag?" he inquired.

"To get the gal," replied Norton as he looked back at Sawtell.

"She stays here," Slick informed him. "You damned near killed that horse of yourn yesterday ridin' double. We got a good head start, and I aim to keep it that way. She'll just slow us down, and I don't want no posse to catch up with us. Now mount up, and let's get out of here."

"You tellin' me what to do?" asked Norton in an icy voice. "You think you're good enough to do that?"

"Yeah, I do," retorted Sawtell, "But that ain't the point. We ain't in the clear yet, Shag, and we need each other whether we like it or not. We gotta make tracks and get outta this neck of the woods right quick. Keepin' her with us could mean the rope. Is she worth that?"

Norton stared angerly at Sawtell for several moments. Then he relaxed and nodded his agreement.

"Reckon you're right," Norton admitted. He pulled his gun and spun the cylinder and again took a step in Catherine's direction.

"Now what?" snapped Sawtell, in exasperation.

"I'm goin' to put her out of her misery," sneered Norton. "You're plumb right. We don't need her no more."

"You damn fool!" exploded Sawtell. "Last night you were afraid of a fire. Now you want to fire a shot and tell the whole world where we are? Leave her behind. She don't know where she is and has nowhere to go. If the posse finds her, they shore will have to take care of her, and that means fewer men chasin' us. Mount up, and let's get goin'. Times awastin'."

"Reckon you're right," Norton again admitted. He raised his voice so Catherine could hear him. "We're goin', missy. Hope you enjoyed yore little stay with us. I shore did."

Catherine heard the horses move away. Finally she could hear them no more. Her head slumped, and she began to sob uncontrollably.

****

Tex remained with Bronc until it was time to wake Trig. Then Tex sought his own blankets and tried to sleep again. It seemed like he had just closed his eyes when Trig shook his shoulder.

"It's almost dawn, Tex," he rasped. "Everybody else is up. We thought we'd let you sleep a few extra minutes. We figgered a cold breakfast would be best. Here's a can of beans."

Tex quickly rose, strapped on his gun belt, and grabbed the can that had been offered him. "Saddle up, boys. We'll eat on the way," he told his friends.

Paul led them as far as he had gone, then dismounted and proceeded on foot, his dark eyes bright and eager. Several times he crouched close to the ground, studied it carefully, straightened up, and waved the rest on. In less than two hours they reached the tiny stream.

"Upstream or downstream?" growled Tex after they examined the far bank and found no tracks.

"Bronc, you, Trig, and Red head downstream. Buck, Apache, and I will go upstream. Three shots will be the signal if'n anyone finds some sign."

"Wait a minute, Tex," objected Paul. "Which way would be your best guess? Maybe I can save us some time."

Tex thought for a moment and then pointed upstream.

Paul dismounted and handed Tex his reins.

"Remember, one horse is carrying double and was real tired. He won't be able to go in a straight line, and this steam doesn't have a very wide bed. If they went this way, I'll bet I'll see some sign within a quarter of a mile. Follow me."

Paul began to slowly wade in the stream, his eyes darting from one bank to the other. He had gone about a hundred yards when he quickly bent down and examined the edge of the right bank. He raised up and waved his companions onward. Another hundred yards, and the procedure was repeated. Several more hundred yard intervals were covered, and Tex began to think Paul had been tricked when the boy bent down again. He waved his arm, and now he advanced faster in the water. After another quarter of a mile he slowed down and began another detailed search. He quickly raised himself up and waved for the others to join him.

"The horse is almost exhausted," Paul informed the group, "and he is wandering back and forth, no matter how hard they try to stop him. They will have to stop not much farther ahead."

"All right boys, we gotta be ready for an ambush," Tex announced. "Everybody dismount. Bronc, you and Trig give yore reins to Red. Bronc, you take the right bank and Trig, you take the left one. Buck, take my reins, and

Apache, give him yourn. Buck, you and Red hold back until Apache and me get about 20 yards or so out in front, then keep pace with us. Everyone ready? Let's go."

Slowly the entire group moved forward, step in step, Tex and Paul still walking in the stream. Paul's eyes continued to dart back and forth, from one bank to the other, while Tex's gaze was directed straight ahead. As before, Tex was prepared to make a snap draw.

One hundred yards. Two hundred yards. A quarter mile. Still the group moved forward. A large boulder loomed ahead, and suddenly the stream dropped from sight. Paul pointed.

"There's where they left the water, Tex. Look at the deep hole the one horse made. He's almost finished."

A minute later the group was reunited, and all the horses were out of the water.

"We'll go on foot," said Tex. "Spread out and be ready for anythin'!"

Again the progress was slow. Paul led and followed an obvious trail, at least obvious to him. Now Paul concentrated his attention on their front. Suddenly he whistled and sank to his knees.

"I can see a small clearing ahead, Tex," he whispered. "That's where I would stop."

Tex motioned to his men and pointed ahead. Bronc and Trig moved further to their right as Buck and Red did the same on the left. When all were in place, Tex waved them forward.

"Get behind me, Apache," he told the boy. "You've done yore job. Now I'll do mine."

Slightly bent over, Tex edged forward step by step. The clearing became more visible, but there was no activity. Tex stopped for a moment, handed his reins to Paul, drew both guns, then charged. He burst into the clearing and quickly looked around as the other men arrived, leading their horses.

"Tex!" yelled Bronc. "Over here. It's Catherine."

Tex jammed both Colts into his holsters and ran to Bronc's side. As he got close he saw a huddled figure, wrapped in a torn yellow dress, her back against a tree, and her eyes closed.

Tex dropped to his knees, fearing the worst. But the head moved, the eyes opened, and tears flowed down the bruised and battered cheeks.

"Tex!" was all she could say.

His arms swept around her, and he pulled her to his chest. Now Catherine's sobs were uncontrollable. Gently Tex rocked her and stroked her head with his right hand, the left arm holding her tight.

Tex looked up, tears in his own eyes.

"Get a fire going, Bronc," he cried hoarsely. "She needs hot food and coffee. Tell Red and Trig to act as lookouts. We'll stay here for a spell."

****

An hour later Catherine, her hunger gone and wrapped in a blanket, related her ordeal, sparing no details. Tex was at her side, his arm around her, and, whenever she faltered, he took her into his arms and comforted her.

"Slick insisted that Shag leave me behind," Catherine concluded. "I thought they were going to fight about it, but Slick convinced him the horse couldn't keep on carrying both of us and that they had to leave this area as soon as possible. Norton was going to shoot me, but Slick talked him out of doing that, too. Tex, I'm sure Slick is an outlaw, but I really think I owe him my life."

"I'll remember that, Catherine, if'n I get the chance," Tex assured her. "I reckon he must be purty good with a gun, though, or Norton wouldn't have backed down. We'll have to remember that, too. But Norton is the man I want." Tex's eyes glinted as he looked at the bruises on Catherine's face and knew what else had happened to her.

"Shag Norton and Slick Sawtell," muttered Buchanan. "Heard tell of Norton. He's been operatin' in Utah and Wyoming up to now. This is the first time he's been in these parts as far as I know."

"The way they talked, I got the impression they had been chased a long distance recently," said Catherine. "Apparently they had tried to rob a bank somewhere, and it didn't go well. Someone named Swede was killed, and someone named Smiley ran off with some of the money."

"Smiley!" Bronc and Trig exclaimed in unison.

"You know him?" asked a startled Catherine.

"We shore do," acknowledged Bronc. "Tex does, too. He rode with Cleveringer and his bunch a few years back. Ain't seen him since. Remember him, Tex?"

"Yes, as soon as you said Cleveringer, it came back to me."

Bronc and Tex locked eyes.

"Tex, are you thinkin' the same thing I am?" Bronc inquired, a grin spreading across his face.

"I shore am!" answered Tex, the glint still in his eyes.

"Am I missing somethin'?" asked a perplexed sheriff. "What are you boys talkin' about?"

Bronc's grin remained as he turned to Paul.

"Apache, remember that trip you and me and Trig took last Summer? Where did we go to get us out of that rainstorm?"

Paul thought for a moment before answering. "Well, you led us to that old abandoned shack back in the hills. It hadn't been used for a long time, though. It was almost ready to fall down."

"Shore enough," agreed Bronc. "That shack was used by Cleveringer, and Smiley was with him when he did. I'll bet Smiley told Norton about it, and that's where their spare grub is. That's why he swung west ag'in."

"Catherine, I'm proud of you," said Tex, so relieved now. "You've been a big help to us. Red, you stay here and let Catherine rest a little longer. Give her those riding clothes Buck brung along. Then take her to town and let Doc Hodges take care of her."

"You still might have need for my Winchester," Red reminded Tex.

"Red's right, Tex," Catherine said fiercely. "The doctor can't do much for me now. What's done is done. You can't lose a man just to take care of me. And you would be a horse short, too."

"Catherine can ride with me," interjected Paul. "Together she and I can't weigh much more than a good sized man. We can't outrun the pack horse anyway, and we will have need of him in case your guess is wrong."

Tex threw up his hands in resignation.

"All right, all right," he sighed. "We'll let Catherine rest a spell and then head for that shack."

"I'm ready to go now," said Catherine firmly. "Give me a minute to get into those clothes, and I'll be ready."

Tex looked at her, admiringly. This lady was a thoroughbred, no doubt about it!

Chapter 18

Three bareheaded men, flat on their stomachs, inched their way to the top of the ridge, slowly raised their heads, and peered over the crest of the hill. The shack they were seeking was below them and slightly to their left. Two horses were confined in a small corral, a few yards from one side of the building. Tex smiled his satisfaction and took several minutes to examine the surrounding landscape. Then he half slid, half crawled back down the slope, the sheriff and Bronc following his example. Ten yards back were the remaining members of the posse, all their horses tethered a full 100 yards further in their rear.

"They're there, just like we figgered," whispered Tex. "There's less'n an hour of day light left, so what we have to do has to be did quick. I don't want to spend all night here and have any of 'em get away in the dark."

"Buck, you circle around to the left and cover the front door. Bronc, you and Trig swing right and cover the back and far side. Red, slide up to where I was and cover me with yore rifle. If'n either one of them gets by me, you bring 'em down."

"What are you going to do?" asked Catherine, fear in her heart.

"I'm goin' to slide down near the corral and see if'n I can spook the horses," replied Tex. "Mebby I can draw one of 'em out of the shack. It'll be a lot easier if'n only one man is holed up inside instead of two. He can't watch three windys all at the same time. Apache, you stay with Catherine. C'mon, Red, we'll crawl back up to the top ag'in."

Tex and Red began to crawl forward, and the other three men started for their assigned locations. Tex and Red had only covered a few yards when noises behind them brought the two men to a quick halt. Tex glanced back and saw Paul and Catherine crawling, too.

"Damn it, Apache, I told you to stay with Catherine," whispered an irritated Tex.

"You said for us to stay together, but you didn't say where," came the defiant response from Paul. "I want to see what's going on."

"So do I," echoed Catherine.

Tex swore under his breath and closed his eyes in frustration. For a few moments he was utterly speechless. He finally regained control of himself and examined the area in front of them. He pointed to several bushes off to their left.

"Slide over there, Apache, and use those bushes as cover. And for gawd's sake keep yore heads down and don't get spotted. If'n there's any shootin', duck down and stay flat!"

"You are talking to an Apache," replied Paul in as loud a whisper as he dared, "and Apaches know what to do. Catherine and I will be fine."

Tex banged his head into the ground but was also hard pressed to keep his face straight. The boy was something else and was becoming very special to him.

Tex resumed his crawling and joined Red at the top of the ridge. He glanced to his left and saw that Paul and Catherine had reached their destination and were well hidden.

"I'll give Buck, Bronc, and Trig a few more minutes to get in place," he whispered in Red's right ear. "Then I'll move in."

Red nodded in agreement, slid his rifle forward, lined up his sights, and continued to watch the shack, particularly the window on their side of the building. He turned his head for a moment to speak to Tex, only to find his companion gone. He sighed and concentrated his attention on the window.

Tex had moved a few paces to his right before beginning his descent, trying to avoid the possible field of vision from the window on his side of the building. His progress was slow as he took advantage of any and all cover the landscape provided him, pausing at each location to determine the next leg of his advance. At the third such location, he noticed a thin wisp of smoke emerging from a small chimney and smiled with satisfaction. One of the men was evidently beginning to cook supper and, therefore, was not apt to be peering out a window.

Tex reached the last location that provided him some cover and paused again. He searched the area around him and spied a section that contained a number of small pebbles. He reached out, gathered in half a dozen, aimed carefully, and threw two of them at the horse nearest him.

****

Slick Sawtell was slicing bacon and heating a skillet in preparation for the night meal while Shag Norton was filling two burlap bags with canned goods.

"We got enough grub for about a week," he muttered to himself as he worked. "What the hell is wrong with them horses," he grumbled in a louder voice as a whinny and some snorts reached his ears. A short period of silence followed, but then more whinnies and snorts were heard, and he dropped one bag in disgust.

"May be a coyote or mountain lion around," observed Slick as he dropped some slices of bacon in the skillet. "I'm busy, Shag. Go outside and calm 'em down. We can't afford to have 'em get riled up and leave us here on foot."

Norton put down the bag he was filling, shoved the other bag to one side, got to his feet, and walked out the open doorway. He turned to his left, hopped down one step off the porch, sauntered over to the corral, bent over, and slid between two rails. Just as he straightened up, he was shocked to hear a loud voice.

"Norton!"

Shag spun on his heel, amazement on his face, and clawed for his gun as he spotted the figure of a man standing just outside the corral.

Tex's twin Colts roared in unison. Again they roared. The two messengers of death spoke for a third time.

The first two slugs caught Norton in the chest and drove him back against the corral railings, his gun dropping to the ground. Mortally wounded, he gripped the end of a corral railing with his right hand and, for a brief moment, steadied himself. Norton's body shuddered from the impact of two more bullets, which drove him back against the railings a second time. His knees could no longer hold him erect, and the dead man started to slump to the ground just as the third set of bullets tore into him. He fell forward, face first into the dirt.

The sounds of Tex's third shots were still reverberating around the little glen when a loud voice was heard.

"You in the shack! This is Sheriff Buchanan from Cravenville. I've got this place surrounded. Come out with your hands up!"

Sawtell dashed to the front door and slammed it shut. He ducked, moved to the nearest window, and opened it.

"You're funnin' me, sheriff," he shouted. "You ain't got no posse here. You're goin' to have to come in an git me!"

"Posse members," Buchanan yelled. "Show Mr. Sawtell how wrong he is."

A burst of gunfire erupted. The deep throated sound of six guns was augmented by the crack of a rifle.

Window panes exploded into a thousand pieces, and the whine of ricocheting bullets filled the little shack. Then there was silence.

"Okay, you win," shouted a white-faced Sawtell. "I'm comin' out." He sheathed his weapon, opened the door, and walked out, his hands high in the air. He no sooner left the confines of the shack when he froze at the sound of a voice just to his immediate left.

"I don't want to kill you, Slick," said the voice. "But you make one quick move, and I'll blow you apart."

Sawtell raised his hands a bit higher and watched as three more men arrived, each with a gun in his hand. One of the men had a sheriff's badge pinned to his vest.

****

Catherine took over the meal preparations. Paul carefully tied up Sawtell with Tex, arms across his chest, an interested spectator. Sheriff Buchanan was busy searching the shack for any possible holdup money. Bronc, Trig, and Red had left to get the horses.

"I know what you did for Miss Cornell," Tex told Slick, "and I'll put in a good word for you at the right time."

"Yeah, well thanks," responded Sawtell as he managed a thin smile. "What I can't figger out is how you caught up with us so fast. I thought we hid our tracks real well."

"You're lookin' at the reason," Tex informed him.

"Huh? What do you mean?" asked a puzzled Sawtell.

"The boy, Slick. He's a full-blooded Apache, and he shore knows how to track. His paw learned him right good. And you fellars made some mistakes, but I ain't goin' to tell you what they was."

Sawtell stared at Paul, unable to believe what he had just heard. Then he looked down at his bonds.

"I reckon the kid knows somethin' about trussin' a fellar up, too," he finally admitted. "How am I suppose to eat?"

"You'll get help," laughed Tex.

Bronc, Trig, and Red returned with the horses, and now both the shack and corral were filled to overflowing.

The meal had to be served and eaten in two shifts, the stove not having enough cooking space to accommodate this many diners. Bronc and Trig ate in the first shift and then buried Norton while the second shift consumed their food.

Paul fed Sawtell, and the outlaw still found it hard to believe that the lad had tracked them so well. Tex had deliberately not told Slick about Smiley's connection in the chase and had warned his friends to remain silent on this matter as well.

After the meal Buchanan prodded Sawtell into telling them a little of the history of the Norton gang. Even Sawtell joined in the laughter when the money bag in Cravenville was discussed.

Bed-time arrived, and Catherine was given the privacy of the shack. The men slept outside, the prisoner being tied securely. Nevertheless, Tex insisted on two night shifts of two sentries each as an added precaution.

After an early rise and a hearty breakfast, the posse headed for Cravenville. They arrived at mid-afternoon amid great joy when those citizens saw that Catherine was alive and well, at least as far as they could tell.

****

Several days later Tex and Catherine met for their long delayed luncheon. Following the meal, they walked about the town until Catherine suggested they head for the schoolhouse. Upon reaching their destination, they sat down on the school steps, and Catherine reached for Tex's hand.

"Tex," she murmured. "I have so much to talk to you about, I don't know where to start."

"Why not try the beginnin'," he replied, a quizzical smile on his face. "You sent me an invitation, remember?"

"Yes, I remember. I wanted to tell you how sorry I was about not understanding you better and trusting you more. Mrs. Woods and I had a talk some time ago, and I had my eyes opened. I didn't even suspect that Stewart or his boys would try to get back at me and that you were trying to prevent that from happening. You asked me to trust you, and I did but not enough."

"You come from a different kind of upbringing than me, Catherine," responded Tex, a pleased look on his face. "You trusted me enough to help me take care of Apache's problem. That was as much as I dared hope for. That was trust enough for me, and I know it was shore hard for you to do." He squeezed her hand in an attempt to emphasize his feelings.

Catherine squeezed back, her eyes conveyed her thanks, and then she took a deep breath.

"You're right, Tex. I do come from a different culture than you do and that, I'm afraid, is the problem. I look at you, and I'm very sure that I love

Tex Riley, the man. But at the same time, I find it very difficult trying to find a way to love Tex Riley, the gunman.

"I just can't get used to the violent world you live in. Your motives are good, and I respect you for them. But how you implement those motives disturbs me greatly. Maybe it's because I'm a woman, but even when I now know why you did it, what you did to Stewart still frightens me. And how you killed Norton does, too. One or two bullets would have been sufficient. You used six. I just can't get used to that kind of violence. Tex, was that really necessary?"

"I thought it was," came the simple and short reply.

Catherine paused, her eyes now filled with tears, and she squeezed his hands even harder.

"Darling, I know that what I'm about to say to you is going to hurt you terribly, and I'm very sorry," she went on, her voice strained. "I'm going back East to my parents' home in Ohio. I need time to think. I guess I never realized how violent this part of the country was when I came here. Maybe I thought my being a school teacher would keep me from becoming part of that violence. Obviously I was wrong."

"Is what Norton did to you worryin' you, Catherine?" asked Tex softly. "If'n that's so, you must know it makes no difference to me. You couldn't help that."

Catherine squeezed his hand again and smiled through her tears.

"Thank you, Tex. I knew you would say that. Oh, that's part of it, of course. I won't know for a while if even more will come from it. If so, I'll just have to find a way to live with it."

"In that case you'll need someone to help you," Tex reminded her. "Someone who loves you a heap."

"Well, I'll assume, for the moment, that all that won't be necessary. But it still leaves the basic problem. Tex, I won't ask you to come East with me. Your world is here, on the Rambling R, helping Slim, and being a big brother to Paul. Unfortunately, I think my world is back East and not here in Cravenville."

"It sounds like your decision is final," observed Tex, again softly.

"Yes, Tex. I'll be leaving tomorrow on the afternoon stage. Please don't come to see me go. I want to say goodbye now. Just kiss me, my love, and tell me you understand me and forgive me."

It was a long kiss that eliminated the need for any verbal assurances. Afterward the two strolled hand in hand back to her bungalow. Tex pulled her into his arms and gave her a back breaking hug. Catherine reluctantly pushed herself back, turned, and fled into the house.

The next day Tex was not at the stage office, as she requested.

But as the stagecoach reached the outskirts of Cravenville, and Catherine began her long journey to the east, she saw him in the distance, sitting on his horse, large against the horizon. That vision was something that time would never erase.

****

The Summer passed rapidly for Paul. His classroom world of book learning was now replaced by the classroom of the real world. He spent a week at each of the Rambling R's four line camps and assumed a full share of the work load at each location. Twice Slim and Tex took him on extended camping trips. Tex followed in the footsteps of Jacob and created some difficult hide and seek games so that Paul could practice his tracking skills. These games were much less dangerous than those Jacob had arranged, however, as Slim stayed with Paul during the entire exercise. Nevertheless, they were strenuous games and had an added benefit as Paul became familiar with a large part of the countryside surrounding the ranch.

Bronc and Trig also took him on what would be their annual exploration trip, living off the land. They again visited the old Cleveringer shack before proceeding further north.

As for Tex, the reverse was true, He buried himself with the work that had to be done, driving the men hard but himself harder. Still the days seemed to move very slowly, and he often wondered if he had given Catherine up too easily. Should he have argued and pleaded with her to stay? But in the end he would shake his head no. That was not the way it should be. It was her decision, he understood it, and, in a strange way, he admired her for having the strength to abide by her convictions. But that didn't make his day-to-day living any easier.

About mid-August, Tex was surprised to receive a letter. Although the envelope showed no return address, the precise and beautiful penmanship used in writing his name and address instantly told him who it was from. Eagerly but carefully, he tore open the envelope and read its contents. He read it a second time, rubbed his jaw reflectively, and stared at the horizon from his seat on the veranda of the ranch house.

My dearest Tex:

I had to send you a note to let you know I arrived home safe and sound after the long journey from Cravenville. Somehow I had forgotten how far Ohio is from Arizona, and the trip took longer than I expected.

I spent two months with my parents whom I had not seen for over three years. I will be leaving again, however, as I have secured a teaching position in a rural school in another part of Ohio. I love working with children, and I am sure you wish me success as I begin a new life.

You will be pleased to know that I had no after-effects from my encounter with Mr. Norton. The anguish of the event still remains with me, of course, but time is a great healer and I believe I can cope with it, now that the other possibility is no longer in the picture.

Tex, I saw you as we left Cravenville, and I will retain that picture as long as I live. I think of you often, and my prayer is that both you and Paul will have a safe and bountiful life in far away Arizona. I miss you both.

Love,

Catherine

I really don't know much more than I knew already, Tex mused to himself. Would she tell me she had a problem, if'n she had one? I kinda don't think so, because she must know I'd go to her, if'n I knew where to go. It might take me a spell to find her, but I would. So, I reckon, I got no choice but to believe her. I wish I could be shore.

****

It was a bright, sunshine-filled late August day when a galloping rider approached the Rambling R's main courtyard. Curley Chance reined in his foam-flecked mount, threw himself from the saddle, quickly secured his horse, and raced up the pathway and steps to the ranch house. He burst into the front room, paused for a moment to let his eyes adjust to change in light, saw no one was in the room, and stamped his way to the big den. Slim was seated at his desk, working on some ledgers.

"We may be gettin' trouble, Slim," he announced, somewhat breathlessly. "Six Injuns rode past Number One in broad daylight about three hours ago. They was movin' slow, had their lances upside down, and were showin' their hands up and open."

"Peace signals," observed Slim thoughtfully. "But we better not take any chances. Reno and Laredo are in the bunkhouse. Send one of them south—

the quartet is breakin' in some horses out thataway. Send the other one to fetch Tex and Apache. They're out west a few miles checkin' out the range. You grab a rifle and set yourself up somewhere close by. I'll tell Antonio and Marie to stay inside and under cover."

Curley turned on his heel and raced to the bunkhouse. Reno and Laredo immediately emerged, hurried to a nearby corral, caught and saddled their horses, and were gone in a cloud of dust.

Reb Stuart and Cavalry rode in from another section of the ranch a short time later. Curley quickly told them what was going on, and they, too, found their rifles and positioned themselves in concealed locations. A half hour later, Lefty White, Charley Landers, Blackie Smith, and Kansas galloped in and corralled their horses. Charley and Kansas sought cover while Lefty and Blackie joined Slim on the veranda. Tex and Paul rode in a few minutes later, and they, too, joined the group on the front porch. Both Lefty and Tex told Slim they had sent their messengers on to other ranch locations to warn anyone they came upon in order to prevent any unnecessary bloodshed if, in fact, their visitors were on a peaceful mission.

An anxious hour passed tediously until six figures were seen slowly approaching the ranch buildings. Their lances were still pointed downward, and their open palms were clearly visible.

Slim led Paul and his men from the veranda and met the Indians at the hitch rail, his open hand raised in greeting. The six red men remained mounted.

A grizzled, older man in the center of the first row urged his pony ahead a step or two and spoke.

"I am Eskiminzin, chief of the Arivaipa Apaches, and I speak your tongue. Beside me is Casadora, chief of the Coyoteros, and Sagully, chief of the Yumas. We have come in peace. Our only wish is to see Tomad, Turango's son, and a son of the Apache Nation. We have come from the San Carlos Reservation."

"We of the Rambling R welcome you and your companions, Eskiminzin," responded Slim, a smile on his face. "You must be thirsty and hungry from your long journey. Please step down and join us for some refreshments."

Slim turned to Tex, as the six Apaches slid off their ponies.

"Have Antonio and Maria prepare all the Mexican food they can put their hands on. Bring back some pitchers of water and all the cups you can carry. Blackie, give him a hand."

Slim pulled Paul to his side and put his arm around the boy's shoulder as Eskiminzin and his companions bunched up in front of Slim.

"Eskiminzin, this is Tomad. We call him Paul because that is the name Jacob and Ruth wanted him to have. My men like to call him Apache cause we all want him to remember his Apache heritage. Come, there is a large table on the porch, big enough for all of us. You can tell us why you are here. Water will be here in a minute, and food is being prepared."

Eskiminzin examined Paul from top to bottom and then grinned. The chief moved toward the porch area, and everyone followed him. Soon all were seated, some in chairs and some on the top railing of the veranda fencing. Water cups were filled, and Eskiminzin looked Paul over once again.

"Tomad looks well," observed Eskiminzin. "Perhaps the white man's world agrees with him."

"He's a good lad," responded Slim, pride in his voice. "I only wish Jacob and Ruth could be here and see him, too."

The old chief shook his head sadly.

"You speak well, Mr. Evers," he said slowly. "And we know you have done well for Tomad. Let me tell you why we are here." Eskiminzin drank deeply, wiped his mouth with the back of one sleeve, and began to speak, somewhat haltingly but well enough for all to hear and understand.

"Four of our Apache police force at San Carlos helped Turango, Tomad, and Ruth move to Hawthorne. Each year they returned to see how our brother and his family were getting along. The last time they were surprised to see the house nailed shut, no horses, and no cattle. They returned to San Carlos and told our white Agent what they had found. Our Agent promised to find out what had happened and why. His efforts took many moons, but the trail led here. We are here to ask Tomad to come back to us and be a son of the Apache Nation again." The chief looked at Paul as he concluded his story.

"Does our chief know the whole story about Hawthorne?" asked Paul quietly.

"I don't know," replied Eskiminzin, his face a blank. "I will ask Tomad to tell me what he knows."

Slowly and carefully Paul described all the events that had taken place a little more than a year earlier. As he concluded his story, Paul got up, moved behind Slim, and put his arms around the man's neck.

"Eskiminzin must understand I would not be alive today if it were not for this man and the men who rode with him. He tried to help Jacob and Ruth, too, and was kind to both of them as well as to me. He wants me to be his son and wants me to live in his world. How would Eskiminzin answer that?"

Before Eskiminzin could respond, Antonio and Maria arrived with plates heaped with food. All conversation ended until everyone's hunger was satisfied.

Eskiminzin and his companions belched their approval of the meal, and the chief resumed the discussion.

"Tomad speaks the truth," Eskiminzin declared, a solemn expression on his face. "Our people returned to Hawthorne and found the graves of Turango and Ruth. We knew most of the story. Tomad has now given us the missing pieces. Mr. Evers is a friend of the Apaches, and I will do what I can to prevent any harm from coming to him from the Apache Nation. But the dream that Turango and Ruth had died when they did and is now buried with their bones. Tomad should return to San Carlos and regain his Apache heritage."

"I don't agree with you, Eskiminzin," said Slim quietly. "Jacob's and Ruth's dream lives on, and it is right here. Paul is the living evidence of that dream and, with my help, I hope he can make that dream a reality. But it is not for me to say. I told Paul he is free to go to San Carlos any time he chooses—today, tomorrow, 10 years from now. He will always have that choice. That decision is his and his alone."

Eskiminzin looked at Evers and smiled his pleasure.

"Mr. Evers speaks well, and he speaks the truth. What does Tomad say?"

"I will ponder what has been said here," answered Paul. "I will give you my answer when the sun rises again."

Slim rose to his feet, as did the others, and he looked at the old chief.

"Eskiminzin, you and your Apaches will be our guests for the night." Slim pointed to a nearby small grove of trees. "I think the Apaches will find that a suitable place to camp. My men will bring you meat and water and wood for your fires. Does Eskiminzin have anything more he would like me to do?"

A pleased Eskiminzin shook his head no and led his people to the designated location. They took their ponies with them.

More Rambling R men drifted in and were informed as to what was happening. Even though he trusted the Apaches, Slim told Tex to arrange for two shifts of sentries, four men each, on the presumption that all of his men would sleep easier if they knew that some form of security was in place.

About an hour before daylight, a small, lithe figure slipped out of the ranch house, easily avoided the sentries, and made his way to the Apache camp.

An hour later six mounted Apaches turned their horses to the southeast and slowly disappeared in that direction.

Slim and Tex, roused by the sentries, hurried to the campsite and found Paul, his back against a tree, watching the six figures get smaller in the distance.

"Eskiminzin said to thank you for your welcome and the food you gave them," Paul told Slim. "He says you are a great chief."

"You didn't go with them." Slim made it a comment, not a question.

"No. I told Eskiminzin that you spoke the truth. Jacob's and Ruth's dream is not dead. It lives on in me, and I must give it every chance to become a reality. My place is here, on the Rambling R, if you will have me." Paul smiled as he looked at Slim.

Slim reached out, put one arm around Paul's shoulder and drew the boy in close to him as Tex watched.

"Have you!" answered Slim, tears in his eyes. "Of course I'll have you. But you gotta remember two things, always. You are *Apache*, and you are *my son!*"

Book 2
Tex

*In memory of my father, L.V. (Mickey) Walsh,
who stimulated my interest in western novels
through his favorite western author,
Ernest Haycox.*

PROLOGUE

The brief, but violent thunderstorm during the night had temporarily the oppressive Idaho weather conditions that had prevailed for the past several days. Unfortunately, the bright and cloudless dawn of a new July day only brought back the heat and humidity with renewed vigor. Despite the heat, however, the two riders kept their horses at a fast lope, anxious to reach their destination. There was much work to be done and not much time to do it. Their friends were already at the site and hard at work, wondering at the delay in the arrival of these horsemen.

The two men were traveling over the southwest section of the range belonging to the MJ Ranch. The bigger man had a scowl on his face, the result of a difficult question and answer period he had experienced at the ranch before leaving. This accounted for the delay in their start that morning.

Art French was the foreman of the MJ Ranch, and his companion, a leaner, shorter man, was Stan Cook, a ranch hand especially hired by French because of his past. The man had been in and out of jail repeatedly and, therefore, was well qualified to assist French in the plans he had regarding the future of the ranch.

"That Evers fellar shore knows somethin' about cattle ranchin'," French growled out loud. "I figgered he was just a dude friend of Johnson's when he got here, but his questions had me sweatin' for an answer, and I don't know if I've got him convinced yet. Evers could be a problem, Stan."

"Well we got a good setup here," replied Cook. "We ship one more herd, and Johnson's goin' to have a tough time stayin' in business for another year. Kip wants to make this drive the biggest yet, and that should do the trick."

"Kip don't have to answer questions like I do," growled French again. "Johnson is a greenhorn, but he ain't stupid. We've pushed things too hard to my way of thinkin', and havin' Evers show up here like he's done makes me nervous."

"That kid of hisn is a strange one," commented Cook, hoping to change the subject. He knew French was edgy about Kip throwing his weight around like he had been doing lately.

"They call him Apache," Cook went on. "He shore enough is an Indian. Wonder how he and Evers got tied in together. I heard Johnson say that Evers had never married. The kid's eyes get to me sometimes. It's almost like he's lookin' right through you."

"Yeah, and havin' him around makes me nervous, too," retorted French. "Mebby we should lay low for a spell, at least until Evers leaves. I think I'll send word to Kip to do just that. Why take chances when we don't have to?"

During their ride the two men examined whatever groups of cattle they came upon as a matter of habit. Spotting a group of 20 or so head grazing off to their right, they changed direction, slowed down and walked their way past the cattle.

Suddenly French swore and urged his horse toward several cows grazing off to one side.

"Mavericks," he said disgustedly. "I thought you had swept this section clean!"

"I did," replied a peevish Cook. "They musta hid out in the brush somewhere. Bud and Wes wouldn't have drifted them this far south. No matter. We can push them along with us. It'll slow us down some, but we ain't got far to go, and three more is money in the bank."

French started to object, but what Cook had said was true. It was money in the bank, and they might as well cash it in.

Confident that they were alone and preoccupied with their thoughts and now the cattle they had found, neither man had given any thought to checking their back trail. Had they done so, both men would have been startled and dismayed.

Far in their rear, barely within eyesight, rode a lone man. Short and stocky, with graying hair, he was an excellent horseman and used every grove of trees, brush and other forms of concealment as well as avoiding high ground of any kind to keep the twosome in sight except for brief intervals. He wasn't really worried about losing them. He could follow their tracks if necessary. But if he kept them in sight, it was all to the better.

French and Cook drove the mavericks for about a mile, then made an abrupt right turn. They followed a shallow draw for about half a mile, turned right again, went up a low slope and emerged onto a beautiful meadow, thick with grass. A sizable herd of cattle was busy grazing, although they had been divided into two distinct groups.

Two men were busy working on the makings of a fire, their horses tied to a fallen tree stump a few yards behind them. They looked up at the sound of the two riders and their tiny herd and waved.

French and Cook returned the greeting, turned the three animals to their left, drove them a few more yards and then, leaving the cattle, joined their companions at the fire.

"Hi Salty, Hi Dan," greeted French as he dismounted. "Sorry we're late. Got held up at the ranch."

"Well, we got a little later start ourselves," responded the man called Dan. "Me and Salty got the branded critters separated from the unbranded ones. You're just in time to help us with the branding. The iron should be ready in a little while."

"Good," said French. "Gives us time to talk a bit."

Salty and Dan looked at him, puzzlement showing on their faces.

"I got a problem at the ranch," French explained. "A fellar named Evers has showed up and asked a lot of fool questions. He's a friend of Johnson and knows somethin' about the cattle ranchin' business. I'm havin' a hard time satisfyin' him. Tell Kip I want to lay low for a while, leastways 'til this hombre leaves. Stan agrees with me."

This last comment was news to Cook, but he remained silent.

"May be just as well," said Salty complacently. "It's gettin' harder for me and Dan to be gone for a couple days at a time. Kip covers for us, but some of the other hands have acted a little funny about it. Besides, we gotta figger out a way to get some more time in order to make the drive. We best not push our luck too hard."

"We'll tell Kip tonight," chimed in Dan. "He won't be none too pleased, but I think you're right. Everythin' has been goin' so good, there's no reason to spoil it."

French examined the heating branding iron.

"It's almost hot enough," he observed. "Let's get started. Cook and I will bring the cattle in. Dan, you rope and hog tie 'em. Salty can do the branding."

Cook and French took one step toward their horses and then froze at the sound of a voice.

"Don't no one move! I'll drill the first man who reaches for hardware," came the sound.

French and Cook turned, amazement written over their faces.

"Evers!" exclaimed French. "What are you doin' here?"

"Checkin' on a lyin' foreman," came the cold reply. "Now drop those gun belts. Use your left hands you fools! Any false moves, and I'll cut loose!"

Slowly and reluctantly, the four men did as they were told.

"Now move away from those belts," continued Evers and motioned to the left with his gun. He took a step toward the belts and then stopped short. French's eyes had opened wide, and his mouth started to twitch. Warned that something was amiss, Evers began to turn. A gun roared, and a bullet plowed into his back. He stiffened, his head snapped back and his gun hand rose. The thumb on the hammer of his gun jerked spasmodically and his gun answered the sound of the first shot. But this shot went straight up. Evers collapsed, dead before he hit the ground.

CHAPTER 1

It was another hot, sultry summer day in the little cattle town of Harding, Idaho. The sun was rapidly approaching the midday hour, but human activity in the community was still very minimal.

Harding was a typical small Western town with a one-block business district followed by a second block of residential homes, white picket fences, flower beds and scattered trees.

The south side of the business district was occupied by the general store, a two-story hotel, a lunch room, a bank and a sub-station of the County Sheriff's Office. The northern side had a livery stable, a freight office and small warehouse, a millinery shop, a barber shop, a land office and the always-present saloon. The general store and saloon faced each other and were adjacent to the tracks of the Northern Continental Railroad.

The town itself had two main functions. First, it was the commercial center for the three cattle ranches in its immediate area and, second, it was on the east-west route of the railroad. The Westbound passed through on Mondays and Thursdays, and the Eastbound returned on Tuesdays and Fridays. Except for the cattle shipping season, stops were limited to the exchange of mail, periodic freight deliveries and passengers that had business in Ridgeway, the County seat, 50 plus miles to the northeast. A local stage line connected the two communities on a three-times-a-week basis.

Amos Stone, owner of the general store, leaned back in his chair against the side of his building that faced the railroad tracks and the station agent's office, a small shanty 40 yards or so in the distance. Two men had joined him in this morning ritual: Dave Hawkins, the station agent, and Doc Raynor.

Emily Stone, Amos' wife, who had been making a half-hearted attempt to sweep the dust and dirt from the wooden deck in front of their store, paused and leaned on her big broom as the wail of a distant train whistle reached her ears.

"Well, old 27 is late ag'in," she allowed in a voice just loud enough for Hawkins to hear.

Dave laughed, took a watch from a shirt pocket, and then frowned. "Yeah, Flanagan *is* later than usual. Wonder what his excuse will be this time."

The train whistle wailed again, and Hawkins, shielding his eyes from the sun with his hand, peered down the track at the locomotive, which was just coming into view around a slight bend in the tracks.

Dave continued to stare and then grunted in surprise. "Huh, Flanagan's pulling more cars than usual," he commented. "A lot more than usual," he added. "No wonder he's so late. Funny, I wasn't told about this."

The front legs of his chair met the wood porch with a thud, and he got up and started to walk toward his little shack as the train approached the station, whitish smoke belching from its big stack.

In addition to the usual two smoking cars, mail car, and freight car, there were three cattle cars and two more smoking cars. The locomotive chugged down the track and kept going until the last car was well past the station. Finally it ground to a halt and exhaled a blast of steam. The brakeman jumped off the last car, laboriously turned the switch and waved to Flanagan in the engine cab.

Huffing and puffing, old 27 slowly backed up, turned into a siding and sputtered its way past the station again.

Doc Raynor and Amos had remained in their seats as all this activity continued. "Amos, there are men and horses in those cattle cars," Doc declared. "What the hell do you think is going on?"

Amos, too, was staring at the cars with a puzzled look on his face.

The train stopped, the brakeman unhooked the last five cars and again waved to the engine cab. Flanagan waited for the mail to be exchanged between the conductor and station agent, watched three passengers exit his train and head up the street toward the center of town and finally saw the hand signal from the conductor to proceed. Flanagan moved his controls into forward and slowly chugged his way back on to the main tracks, where he stopped and waited for the brakeman to again adjust the switch. Finally, tooting his horn, he picked up speed and continued his run westward.

As soon as the cars on the siding had been unhooked from the main train, doors on the cattle cars were slid open, wooden ramps were lowered and men began to lead saddled horses down the ramps. Other men began to exit the smoking cars.

Doc Raynor's jaw dropped. He paused to get his breath and then whispered to Amos, "My God, there are greasers in that crowd. Look at the big sombreros! Must be five or six of 'em."

Amos was also dumbfounded. "What are they doin' this far north?" he exclaimed. "And with a group of white men," he added.

One of the first men off the smoking cars caught their attention as he approached them. A little over six feet tall, strongly built through the shoulders and chest, he wore two guns, slung low and tied down. He approached Amos and Doc with a measured stride and with both hands brushing the butts of his Colts.

"I'm not sure I like the looks of this hombre," muttered Amos before the stranger was within hearing range.

"Good morning, gentlemen." The stranger smiled and touched his Stetson. "I'm lookin' for the proprietor of the general store. By any chance might one of you be he?"

"I'm the owner," said Amos, rising from his chair. "Stone is the name, Amos Stone. What can I do for you?"

The stranger again smiled, turned a bit, raised his arm and pointed in the direction of the toiling men behind him. "As you can plainly see, I have quite a crowd with me, and they do get hungry. I need all the flour, beans, bacon and coffee you can spare." He pulled a wad of bills from his shirt pocket and continued, "I'll be payin' cash and figger you should add an extry 10 percent to your prices to cover any trouble this might cause you with your friends and regular customers."

The sight of the cash and the words "10 percent" eliminated whatever doubt and fear Amos had begun to feel and galvanized him into action. A grin on his face, he grabbed the stranger's right hand and pumped it vigorously a number of times before he spoke. "Well now, I think I can take right good care of your needs. I can get new supplies in a week or two for my regular folks. Need cooking utensils?" he asked hopefully.

"No, we brought those along," replied the stranger. "Pile what you can on the porch, and I'll send a few of my boys over with the pack horses as soon as we get everythin' unloaded. By the way, didn't I see a lunch room sign as we came into town?"

"Yes, you did," affirmed Doc Raynor. "It's down the street just past the hotel. On the south side," he added as he motioned in that direction.

"Good," said the man. "How many can they feed at a time?"

Doc thought for a moment and then answered, "Well, I think Norm can squeeze 15 or 16 in if he has to."

The stranger turned and waved to one man who had mounted and was approaching the threesome. "Lefty," he said, "you and Blackie take half the men and fill your bellies at the eatery up the street. Take three of Sanchez' men with you, and if you have any trouble gettin' 'em fed, take care of it. I'll bring Sanchez and the rest of the boys up when you all are finished."

The horseman nodded, turned his horse and guided it back to the men and horses scattered along the tracks. Most of the horses were now out of the cars, and several more men were mounted and beginning to drift toward the tie rails located along the one block business district of Harding. All of the men were heavily armed, noted Raynor as he watched, including the group of Mexicans.

One of the Mexicans had also mounted, and he, too, slowly approached the twosome on the sidewalk, Amos and Emily Stone having already disappeared into the store.

The stranger turned and spoke. "Sanchez, send three of your men with Lefty and Blackie to get somethin' to eat." He eyed the men that had not, as yet, moved toward the town area. "Send Reno, Laredo, Curley and one of your men over here with the pack horses and help Mr. Stone get our supplies out of his store and loaded up."

"Si, Señor Tex," the man replied. "Eet weel be done pronto." He turned his horse and headed back to the men still working with the horses.

Tex glanced back to Doc Raynor. "I guess that other fellar is the station agent. If so, I need to talk to him."

"He is," replied Raynor. "Name's Dave Hawkins. Say, you don't need a doctor's services, too, do you?"

"No," Tex laughed. "I guess we can get along without that." He left Raynor and walked toward the agent's office.

By this time, several other townspeople had gathered and were silently watching the bustling activity and trying to avoid the resulting clouds of dust that were floating around.

The county sheriff maintained a sub-office in Harding, and the one deputy assigned there, Sam Owens, now arrived and joined Doc Raynor.

"Sure is a passel of men," Sam observed. "Must be over 20 of 'em. At first I thought it was a posse of some sort, but I don't see badges on any of 'em, and those Mex's shore look out of place. Wonder what's goin' on."

"Don't know," answered Doc. "That two-gun man over by Dave's appears to be the leader. He just bought all of Amos' spare food supplies and has four pack horses, so they seem to be getting ready for some sort of trip. Sure doesn't look like they are going to be around here for long."

"Several other of those guys also wear two guns," observed Owens. "But, all in all, they don't seem to be lookin' for trouble. I reckon I better notify the sheriff about this here bunch."

"Why don't you wait a spell, maybe talk to that leader and see where they head for. No sense in sparking trouble. One man can't do much ag'in a bunch this big, nohow," answered Doc. "Besides, that guy was real polite, offered to pay a premium price for his supplies to Amos. By the way, that Mexican over there called him Tex. That name mean anything to you?"

"No," mused Owens. "But I'll check my wanted posters in a bit to make sure. Haven't heard tell of a gang this large, though, and those greasers are a real puzzle. Guess I'll set a spell, think it over a bit and keep an eye on things."

Tex turned the corner of the tiny depot, put his arms on the sill of the open window and paused to watch Hawkins make the proper notations in his records regarding the arrival and departure of Flanagan and Twenty-Seven.

Dave looked up and asked, "Can I do something for you?"

"As a matter of fact, you can," answered Tex. "First, I want these cars left here on the siding until I come back with my men. Don't know whether it will be in a week or a month, but I want them here when I need 'em. Then I need all yore information on beef shipments out of here in the past three years. Need to know what ranchers shipped how many and when. Also the brands that were used if'n you know that."

"Now just wait a damn minute," sputtered Dave, "that there is confidential company information. I can't give it to you."

"Well, I'll tell you what you do," continued Tex. "You telegraph your regional superintendent and tell him Tex Riley is here askin' for confidential information and wait for his reply. I'll be back in an hour or so to go over it with you. Now, I came over here to tell you about the cars, which I have already arranged for, and so you can answer any questions your friends ask you with the truth. However, whatever information we exchange about the beef shipments is strictly between you and me. If'n I find out otherwise, I'm goin' to be real put out, and you'll be lookin' for another job. You hear me? Now, get that there wire goin' and I'll see you later."

Tex turned and walked away, leaving Dave with his mouth open but silent. Tex walked up the steps to the general store, noting the progress his men had made in loading the pack horses. He went inside, located Amos Stone and paid his bill, counting out the money as Amos and Emily watched closely.

"Nice doin' business with you, Mr. Stone," he drawled. "Maybe we'll get a chance to do it ag'in someday," he continued as he turned away and strode to the front door. He glanced down the street, located the sheriff's sub-office and marched down the sidewalk in that direction.

Owens noticed this movement, got up from his chair and hurried along Tex's path. They both arrived at the office door at the same time.

"I'm Deputy Sheriff Owens," he announced. "Are you looking for me?"

"Why, yes I am," replied Tex. "Can we talk inside?"

"Shore," answered Owens. "Come on in and set down." He waved to a nearby chair.

"I'll get right to the point, sheriff," stated Tex. "Do you have any kind of a county map? Me and my boys are goin' to need some campsites with water and good grass. I'm particularly interested in the northern half of the county, especially the northwest section."

"Well, I don't have any store-made maps," said Owens, "but I can draw you a rough outline of that area and lay out where your water and grass would be. What, exactly, is the reason you are here?" he asked with a touch of concern.

"You won't believe this," smiled Tex, "but we are combinin' business with a little pleasure. About a year ago, a couple of the boys spotted a herd of wild horses in that area. I've got men from three ranches, and we're goin' to try to locate this herd, break what we need to, mebby do a little prospectin' on the side and, if worse comes to worse, have a campin' trip as sort of a vacation."

"Well, I declare," exclaimed a surprised and somewhat relieved Owens. "I ain't heard tell of any wild horses up thataway."

Tex eyed Owens closely. "I understand that it's purty wild country up there, and mebby the herd has moved on. That's why I want to know where water and grass is. We may have to do a lot of ridin' and cover a lot of territory to find out for shore. Like I said, we may just end up with a long campin' trip."

The explanation seemed to satisfy the deputy as he searched through his desk, located a piece of paper and began to draw a crude map.

Tex remained silent and watched the man continue his outline. Finally he spoke. "Continue the route of those streams into the next county if'n you can, and give me an idea on how far the high country extends north and east of there."

Owens looked up, a sharp retort on his lips, but paused a moment and finally said, "Well, this is the best I can do. I don't do this for a livin', you know." Despite this comment, however, he did add a few more lines and descriptions to the sketch.

Tex examined the paper, asked a couple more questions, made a notation or two and smiled. "You did real good, and I shore appreciate it, Mr. Owens. I'm shore we'll get along just fine." He folded the paper, put it in his shirt pocket, shook hands with the deputy and walked out into the street.

Some of the men were already leaving the lunchroom. The man called Lefty met Tex in the street and fell in alongside him.

"Have any trouble over Sanchez' men?" asked Tex.

"No," replied Lefty. "The owner started to object, but I told him more men were comin' and he should tend to his cookin', or we would. I think he got the message right quick."

Tex grinned. "I knew you would handle it okay. Go on down and send Sanchez and the rest of the boys up. Have Cavalry and Reb finish loadin' the pack horses. The stuff is all paid for."

* * * * * * * * * * *

Tex put a toothpick in his mouth and pushed his chair back. He and Sanchez got to their feet and approached the counter where the owner stood waiting, a frown on his face.

Ignoring the frown, Tex complimented the owner on the quality of the food and continued, "Sure hope we didn't disrupt your local business much. Did my boys all pay their bills okay?" The owner nodded, and Tex went on, "Here's for our two meals and $ 10 more for any extry work we caused."

The owner accepted the money but remained silent.

Tex and Sanchez left the lunchroom and headed back down the street. "Get the men mounted," directed Tex. "I have one more stop at the agent's office, and then we'll be on our way."

Tex reached the station agent's shanty, bent over the window sill and had a brief conversation with Dave Hawkins regarding a piece of paper the agent had given him. Tex straightened up, carefully folded the paper and slid it into a shirt pocket. One of the mounted men led a horse to Tex, and he vaulted into the saddle, waved his arm and led the horsemen out of Harding in a column of twos.

Amos, Dave, Doc Raynor, Deputy Owens and several other local citizens watched the group head northwest alongside the railroad tracks.

CHAPTER 2

Tex and Sanchez led the way as the cavalcade followed the railroad tracks for over a mile. However, at that point the tracks began a curve to the left, or westward direction. The column of riders, instead, began a slight curve more to the north and soon located a narrow, shallow draw that they followed for about eight miles. Another curve to the right took them along the base of a long line of foothills and, more than two hours later, they came upon a tiny brook and a flat area of two or three acres of good grass, about 18 miles from Harding.

Tex signaled a halt, and the men quickly fell to the task of preparing a campsite, unloading the pack horses and letting all the horses drink and graze.

The night meal was prepared and consumed with little talking and noise. The tin plates and utensils were washed, and many of the men rolled cigarettes or filled pipes and exchanged conversation as the shadows lengthened into darkness.

Tex sat beside Sanchez, coffee cup in hand, studying the map Deputy Owens had scrawled.

Sanchez broke the silence and asked, "Do you theenk the gringo sheriffe beleef'd your wild horse tale, Señor Tex?"

Tex grimaced, then rubbed his jaw reflectively before answering, "I don't know, but it was the most logical story I could come up with. I'm not the best liar around, but we'll find out tomorrow if anyone is followin' us. If not, we'll simply drop outta sight for a spell, and it won't make any difference what anyone thinks. I plan to continue our curve to the north and then east," he added, using the light from the campfire to show Sanchez where he was pointing. "The deputy said there was water here and here," he added as his finger continued to move. "I figger Apache will meet us day after to-morrow, and he'll guide us to the MJ from there.

"Apache, you know, is Slim's adopted son, although he never made it legal, seein' as how Slim wasn't married. I'm proud of the lad 'cause he has kept his head through all of this. He rode way north, he did, before he wired me about Slim gettin' killed. His wire was right well thought out, a combination of English and Apache words that took me and Lefty quite a spell to figger out. Not only that, he sent it usin' his real name, Paul, and that told me right off that somethin' was bad wrong. Bronc saddled the lad with the name "Apache" when they was in Colorado, as a way of tellin' him to be proud of his heritage. Me and the boys picked up on it, and we ain't called him Paul hardly a'tall.

"The lad must have been real broke up, too, what with losing his maw and paw five years ago and now Slim. This was his first real long trip with Slim; Slim wantin' to get him acquainted with Marty Johnson and the MJ Ranch. They planned on doin' some huntin' and fishin' together, too. It's a real shame this had to happen."

Sanchez looked around at the others as they began spreading out their bedrolls and getting ready to turn in. "The men are ver' angri, Tex; weel you be able to control theem?"

"Yes, I think so," replied Tex. "As soon as we meet up with Apache I'll talk to all of 'em. Lefty and Blackie will back anythin' I say or do. It's Bronc and Trig I'm worried about. Trig never did talk much, but Bronc ain't said 10 words since we left the Rambling R. One or both of 'em usually went with Slim on his trips because he wanted the company and because both of them are first-class gunmen. They always thought of themselves as Slim's personal bodyguards. They both feel this wouldn't have happened if'n they had been along. Probably right, too."

"Señor Bronc and Señor Trig, they are ver' good, as you say, but as good as Señor Tex?" asked Sanchez, slyly.

"I don't know," grinned Tex. "But I shore wouldn't want to live on the difference. We'd probably kill each other in an even break. And don't forget Lefty and Blackie. The same goes for them. I'm just glad Slim got us all on the same side."

"By the way," continued Tex, "I shore want to thank you for the men you brought along. Being able to leave five of 'em on the Rambling R made my job a heap easier. Everyone wanted to come along, and I had to draw the line somewheres. Your five boys gave me some leeway, and them, along with the five men I left behind, should be enough to handle things 'til we get back. They'll be plumb busy, though, doing the work of 20 or more men."

Tex motioned in the direction of the other Mexicans.

"And, of course, the five you brought along with us will give me an ace in the hole which might prove plumb useful. Don't this make you awfully short handed at the 'Internationale' though?"

"Ah, but Señor Slim was my special fren' too!" answered Sanchez. "He giv' me mucho dinero to geet started, many year ago, an' I no' forget that! I borrow vaqueros from other ranchos, for I mus' ride weeth you. Eef you had not tol' me about theese, I would be mucho angri. We mus' ride together until we find who done theese terrible theeng."

Tex nodded. "Your story is very similar to Marty Johnson's. Marty's father and Slim were friends, and when Marty got tired of the big city life back east and wanted to try ranchin', his father contacted Slim for advice and help. Slim asked around, and about six months later heard about this little spread near Ridgeway. Marty didn't have a hull lot of money, but managed to beg and borrow enough to cover about 25 percent of the purchase price. Slim matched Marty's amount, and he and Marty's father cosigned a bank note for the rest. Still and all, that only bought the land and buildings and a couple of graded bulls. The previous owners had sold off all but a few cows. Even though Marty's name is on all the legal papers, Slim was to be an equal partner until Marty could buy him out."

Tex paused for a moment and then continued. "Slim had wanted to have some access to a northern range anyhow. So, first off we shipped Marty a mixed herd of one-, two-, and three-year olds, about 700 head in all. The next year we shipped 500 more, and Marty bought three more graded bulls. All these critters had a Rambling R brand on their hides, of course, so we road-branded them and transferred them to the MJ.

"Slim's deal with Marty was right well thought out," Tex continued on. "All the cash from the sale of our 1,200 head, over several years, was to stay with Marty so he could run the ranch. After deducting the cost of the hired hands and the interest on the note, anythin' left over was to be split three quarters for Slim and one quarter for Marty. This was our way of payin' Marty for the use of his land. Of course, there wasn't much left over each year at first, and what little there was was simply added to the total of Slim's original investment, but no money changed hands.

"Once our cattle was disposed of, they were to split the remainder from any more cattle sales on a 50-50 basis, and Marty was to use any extry money to begin payin' off the note. Ag'in, Slim's share was to be added to his account balance."

"Once the note was paid off, Marty was to get three quarters of the remainder each year, Slim one quarter, and Marty was to begin the actual buyout process with Slim. However, we ain't got to the point yet where the note has had much, if anythin', paid down on it, as far as I know."

Tex again paused for a few moments and then went on. "Marty's brand is the $\mathbf{M_J}$, a mighty tough brand to blot. I think that's why Slim suggested it. What sold Slim on the location is that it has unfailin' water and controls much of the water in the hull area. The big rancher in the valley is a fellar named Henderson, and he wanted Marty's ranch real bad. But there must have been bad blood between him and the previous owners 'cause they sold it without givin' Henderson a chance to bid on it. Was he plumb surprised when Marty showed up!

"The two ranches didn't get along too well at first, but a couple of summers later a bad drought came along. Most of Henderson's wells ran dry, but Marty was a good neighbor and supplied him with as much water as he could spare, although he did charge somethin' for helpin' to haul it. Since then, accordin' to Slim, the two ranches have tolerated each other fairly well, although I wouldn't go so far as to say they're friendly. I think Slim came up here to improve relations somewhat, but he also had some concern about how Marty was runnin' the ranch. Seems like the natural increase ain't what it should have been the past couple of years. He wasn't expectin' trouble, though, or he woulda taken Bronc and Trig with him."

Tex paused again and finished drinking his coffee.

"The natural increase problem is shore somethin' I'm going to look into as soon as we get there. That can kill a ranch real fast, especially one with a note outstandin'. If Slim stumbled on to somethin' and was killed because of it . . . ." Tex stopped for a minute, took a deep breath and went on, "Then there's going to be a hangin', maybe more'n one, before we go back to the Rambling R." His voice was icy cold.

"Well, I've done a heap of talkin'," he sighed, "and I'm right tired." He looked up and was a little surprised to see Lefty standing close by.

"I come to tell you I got Denver and Cheyenne to stand the first watch," Lefty said, "and Red and Curley to do the second. I didn't want to butt in while you was talkin', but I sure will go along with that hangin' idear. We ain't leavin' till we get that job done. You got anythin' else to say?" he asked Tex.

"No," answered Tex. "Let's all turn in and get some shuteye."

* * * * * * * * * * * *

The last two sentries awakened the sleeping men at dawn. A hasty breakfast was cooked and eaten, and the camp was rapidly dismantled.

As the men mounted, Tex motioned to three of them. "Bronc, you, Trig and Red hide your horses over there," he said, pointing to a ridge of trees several hundred yards in the distance. "Stay here for two, three hours and make shore no one is followin' our trail. If there is, turn 'em back and convince 'em it'll be right unhealthy for 'em to try it ag'in. Then join up with the rest of us. We're goin' to continue to curve north and east, and you shouldn't have any trouble findin' us. I expect to see y'all by noon."

He and Sanchez led the way as the horsemen moved out. They continued to follow along the base of the line of foothills, turning and weaving to make use of any accessible route and bearing to the northeast as much as possible.

They stopped at noon to rest the horses and cook the midday meal. There was no water available, but their canteens had been filled the night before, and there was plenty available for cooking and for the horses.

* * * * * * * * * * * *

Bronc, Trig and Red rode to the ridge of trees that Tex had pointed out to them. Pausing at the top of the ridge, they carefully examined their surroundings. Trig reached out, nudged Bronc's left shoulder and pointed to a densely wooded area off to their left. Bronc nodded his agreement as his eyes turned back to re-examine the terrain directly in front of them.

"Red," Bronc said as he pointed to a suitable location, "take the horses down there, picket 'em and stay with 'em. Trig and I are going to move over to the left here and get set up. Keep us in sight so if'n we need the horses in a hurry, you can bring 'em to us fast."

Bronc and Trig dismounted, handed their reins to Red and moved toward the wooded area as Red led their horses toward the spot Bronc had indicated.

Bronc and Trig reached their outpost location and were pleased to see that they had a good view of the abandoned campsite as well as portion of their group's back trail and yet had excellent concealment. Bronc waved to Red, received a salute in return, and both he and Trig settled down for a long wait.

"No sense both of us watchin' all the time," Bronc muttered to his companion. "Keep your eyes peeled. I'm going to try to catch a few winks. Wake me in a little while, and then you can do the same."

Bronc rolled over on his back, slid his hat down over his face and closed his eyes. Sleep did not come to him, however, but his drowsiness, enhanced by the warmth of the sun, soon placed him in a pensive state — half awake and half asleep. His mind continued to relax, and he began to daydream and drift back in time.

* * * * * * * * * * * *

Bronc and Trig became acquainted as teenagers when their families moved to the same town in eastern Texas during the late 1870s. If opposites are attracted to one another, Bronc and Trig were a perfect match. While Trig was an intovert — silent and reserved — Bronc, on the other hand, was extremely outgoing and verbose. Yet their friendship began as soon as they met and became more steadfast and deeper as time went on.

Both men had a natural ability in the use of a Colt with both hands. Their favorite sport and pastime was to practice their speed and accuracy with that weapon, using tin cans, fence posts and other suitable targets in the process. Their biggest problem was earning enough money to pay for the cartridges they consumed in these games.

For some unknown reason, both men took a special interest in law enforcement. The reputation and achievements of the Texas Rangers aroused their respect and interest and soon, after reaching their 20th birthdays, they joined this famous organization, but only after they were assured that they would be able to serve together.

For almost three years they served the Rangers well. Friends and foes alike soon discovered that the time and money they had spent in their youth had not been wasted. The speed and accuracy of their gunplay had been a significant element in their survival of several critical situations. They were good, they knew they were good and each man's confidence in his own skill, ability and courage, as well as that of his companion, had no limit.

About this time, however, their company commander had become embroiled in some organizational politics and ended up on the wrong side of the controversy. His replacement decided to ignore his predecessor's commitments and attempted to split up the work assignments for Bronc and Trig. The two men objected strenuously, refused to accept this change and eventually had charges of insubordination brought against them.

Extremely bitter about this matter, Bronc and Trig decided to leave the service and head farther west. Several months later, as they drifted about, they heard about an unusual ranch, the Rambling R, and its most unusual owner, one Slim Evers. Evers, they learned, took particular satisfaction in giving jobs to drifters, saddle tramps and men of questionable backgrounds. He seemed to have a special willingness to provide such individuals with an opportunity to become useful and contributing members of society. Sometimes he was successful, and sometimes he was not, but he never quit trying.

Bronc and Trig found the ranch, met Slim and found both very much to their liking. Slim taught them the cattle ranching business, and they, in turn, used their law enforcement knowledge and experience to become his traveling companions and his protectors. It was during these trips that their respect and admiration for the man virtually reached the level of adoration. The news of Slim's death, therefore, shocked them severely. Their rage and frustration were almost more than they could handle.

* * * * * * * * * * * *

Bronc groaned and quickly sat up, his pleasant reverie now completely shattered. Trig stared at him, a surprised look on his face.

"Had a bad dream," Bronc growled in a low voice. "You try sleepin'. Mebby you can do better'n me. I'll watch for a spell."

* * * * * * * * * * * *

Tex and his men had almost finished their noon meal when hoofbeats announced the arrival of Bronc, Trig and Red. All three filled their tin plates, and Bronc sat down beside Tex and Sanchez.

"Any trouble?" asked Tex.

"Well, yes and no," answered Bronc between mouthfuls. "We were about to leave when that sheriff's deputy showed up. Since he was alone, we didn't do nothin' but sit and watch. If he had started down yore trail, we would have stopped him, but he didn't. He just walked around, looked over the campsite, ate some cold food he had brung and then headed back the way he had come."

Bronc paused to drain his coffee cup before continuing his report.

"We waited a little while, but he didn't come back. I'm shore he didn't see or hear us, as Red had taken the horses even more past that ridge than you said to. And Trig and I had good cover."

Tex nodded. "Yeah, I don't think he would want to follow a crowd this size too far. I was followin' his map right to the letter, since it was what I wanted to do anyhow. Even if he tells the sheriff in Ridgeway about us now, they won't likely try to find us. I'll bet he notifies the sheriff in the next county, though, that we are around. By day after tomorrow we'll be at the MJ, and it won't matter none nohow. As soon as you fellars finish eatin', we'll be on our way."

* * * * * * * * * * * *

At mid afternoon, Tex sent four riders to locate a campsite for that night. Two returned a couple of hours later and guided the group to a fine location, complete with a tiny stream, grass and a grove of pine trees and firs.

As supper was being prepared, Sanchez approached Tex and announced, "I hav' tol' Juan and Luis to be the fir' watchers tonight. My men mus' share een thes' duties. Hokay?"

"Fine," agreed Tex. "Lefty and Kansas can handle the second shift."

* * * * * * * * * * * *

Up at dawn again and after a quick breakfast, the band of men continued their journey at its slow but methodical pace. Circling and reversing directions several times due to the rough terrain, they still were able to make considerable progress toward the northeasterly point of the compass.

A noon lunch stop, rest for the horses and they were on the trail again.

Late in the afternoon Tex raised his hand and stopped the column. Shielding his eyes from the sun, he spoke softly. "We've got company. Look over there," he said, pointing to a lone rider, sitting motionless at the crease of a chain of foothills. Finally, the rider waved and urged his horse forward.

"It's Apache," announced Tex. "I figgered we'd be runnin' into him sometime today."

As the rider approached the line of men, his dark hair and Indian features became apparent. He had a slender, lithe frame and wore plain clothes and worn boots. One white feather was stuck in his weather-beaten felt hat.

Despite his Indian stoicism, his dark, brooding eyes still contained a film of moisture as he heard the warm greetings from all along the column, and he returned the strong clasp of Tex's hand with all the strength he could muster.

"It's good to see you, Apache," Tex spoke softly. "All the boys feel the same." He turned in his saddle, "You know Sanchez. He wanted to come, too."

Again there was a strong clasping of hands, and Apache smiled a bit. "You brought just about everybody, I see. How did you manage that?" he asked.

"Well, it weren't easy," stated Tex. "Sanchez was good enough to bring along some extry men to help out at the ranch. So I was able to bring along most everyone who wanted to come."

Tex quickly changed the subject. "You have any idears for camp tonight?"

"Yes," answered Apache. "About a mile ahead is a perfect spot, and we can reach the MJ easily by late afternoon, tomorrow." He continued in his soft, precise English, "I have much to tell you."

"Good enough," said Tex. "Lead on, and we'll follow." He waved his arm, and the cavalcade of men moved forward.

* * * * * * * * * * * *

The setting up of a campsite was in full swing as the men unsaddled their horses, unloaded the pack horses, collected wood and filled their canteens at a nearby rivulet. A small group of men was not so engaged, however, as it gathered in a loose circle away from the bustling activity. Seated Indian style were Tex, Sanchez, Bronc, Trig, Lefty, Blackie and, of course, Apache.

All eyes were turned toward Apache, and he began to speak.

"Tex," he asked, "did you know Marty had to change his foreman a couple of years ago?"

Surprised, Tex thought for a moment and then said, "If Slim told me about that, I shore don't recollect it. Maybe it slipped his mind to tell me. What happened to John Mason? He was the one Marty and Slim hired when Marty first came out here."

"Yes, that's true," Apache agreed. "John had to go back East to take care of some family matters. But he wrote Marty and told him he would have to stay there and wouldn't be back. So Marty hired a new foreman, a fellow named Art French. Don't think Slim had anything to do with the hiring. Maybe he figgered Marty had to start making decisions on his own."

"What do you think of him?" asked Tex.

Apache paused and then went on. "I don't know why, Tex, but I don't feel easy with him. His story about Slim's killing doesn't set well with me, and I'll tell you why in a minute. Also, I think Marty is afraid of him. But let me go on.

"When Slim and I first got here, we spent a few days riding around the ranch with Marty and French. After that, Marty and Slim spent a lot of time going over some ledgers in Marty's den at the ranch."

"The tally books," interrupted Lefty.

"I knew it," breathed Tex audibly, "I knew it, I knew it. The natural increase figgers don't make sense!"

"Well, after that Slim talked to French," continued Apache, "and they had words, although Slim did most of the talking. I could tell Slim was angry about something. Then things sort of settled down, and it was peaceful for a spell."

Apache paused for a minute or two, took a deep breath and began talking again.

"The day Slim was killed Marty suggested that he and I ride into Ridgeway and said Slim wanted to stay at the ranch. Later, French said that he, Slim and a puncher named Cook rode out to the southwest range to look over the cattle down there. He said they split up to cover more ground and when he and Cook met later on, Slim didn't show up. They backtracked to where they had split up, followed his tracks and found his horse in about half a mile. His body was nearby, shot in the back. He said they looked around, couldn't find anything to tell them what happened and finally brought him back to the ranch."

"Funny thing, though," Apache continued after a period of silence, "I talked to Mary Johnson, and she said she heard a horse leave the ranch a while after French and Cook did and thought it had to be Slim. But she didn't go out of the house to look, and so she can't be sure it was him."

"I near went crazy when they brought Slim in. I wanted to go right back to where they found him and see if I could find tracks or a trail of some kind. It was near dark, though, and Marty wouldn't let me go by myself. We talked most of the night, and he convinced me that we needed help before we could do anything. He thought old man Henderson might be behind it, and, if so, I might be in danger, too."

"We worked on the wording of the wire," Apache went on, "and he told me to ride well out of the county to send it and then drop outta sight. I had packed several day's supply of grub and stayed near the telegraph office until I got your replies. I spent more'n a week scouting the Henderson ranch and the area around it but haven't found out anything. We had a big storm, with lots of wind and rain, while I went to send you the wire. So there wasn't any reason to go back to where Slim was killed, at least not alone. Any tracks or anything else would have been blown or washed out."

"Every three or four nights, I would slip back to the MJ for grub and to see Marty. We would figure on what I should do next. Three days ago I rode this way, figuring you should be getting here sometime soon."

"Well, you did right well, Apache, and I'm real proud of you," Tex said amid sounds of agreement from around the circle. "Anythin' else you should tell us?" Tex inquired.

"Yes, one more thing," replied Apache. "Four nights ago, three of Marty's punchers went into Ridgeway for supplies and a night on the town. They got into a fight with a bunch of Double H riders, Henderson men, and were pretty badly beat up. Next morning they drew their pay and left the ranch. I think that's what they were told to do. Tex, that only leaves Marty with

French and three men!", Apache exclaimed. "Not nearly enough for a ranch that size."

"Ah," sighed Tex, "only a foreman and three men left, huh! My, ain't that interestin'! Loyal to who, I wonder. Well, I can't say I'm surprised. Boys, let me tell you what I found out at Harding. I decided to come here by way of Harding to avoid runnin' into Ridgeway people, but I also wanted to play a hunch, and I think it paid off. The station agent there showed me his records, and the Henderson ranch has made one small shipment of beef each year for the past two years. Both shipments were for around 200 hundred head and took place in late August or early September. In other words, it's almost about that same time ag'in this year.

"Now, why would a big ranch like Henderson's make little shipments like that, especially in Harding, when their main railhead is at Canyon City, northeast of Ridgeway? And the cattle did have Double H brands 'cause the station agent remembers watchin' them load.

"And Slim was having trouble with the tally books," Tex reminded the group. "What does that tell us?" he asked no one in particular and everyone in general.

"Maverickin'!" snapped Lefty. "It fair yells at us. And if they are shipped with a Double H brand, it means that MJ men are in on it! Oh, I reckon we got a range to clean up as well as findin' a murderer," he went on.

Tex raised his hand. "Hold it," he said. "There is somethin' that don't read right. If'n the cattle have Double H brands, and MJ men are part of it, why ship the cattle out of Harding? The MJ men could drive the cattle over the MJ range and could mix them in with the regular Double H herd. Why go to Harding?"

The group was silent for a few moments. Then Bronc drawled, "If'n not all the MJ crew were in on it, it would be dangerous to drive Double H cows south to north over MJ range. It wouldn't be hard to spot that if you knew what you be doin'."

"Exactly," answered Tex. "And three men have been chased off the ranch. Boys, someone made a big mistake when they killed Slim, far bigger than they could possibly imagine. And somethin' tells me we may be gettin' here at just the right time, 'cause things may be movin' faster than some folks expected. In that case, we may play a few cards of our own and move things along even faster."

"Señor Tex," Sanchez interrupted, "I mus' speeck. I listen to wat you say, and I theenk you be forgetting one theeng. Wat eef Henderson does not know about Harding shipments? Ees that no' possible?"

"Huh," grunted Tex. "You shore got an idear there. That would shore put a different frame around the picture. And it gives me more to think about. Anybody else got somethin' to say?"

No response was forthcoming from the other men, so Tex turned to Apache.

"Clear some dirt here," he said, "and draw a layout of the MJ so we can all get an idear of what it looks like."

Apache did as he was asked, examined his work carefully, made a couple of adjustments and then stepped back.

"Where is Ridgeway?" asked Tex.

Apache added this location to his drawing and again stepped back as all the men leaned forward and studied it carefully.

Tex spoke again. "Show me where the main trail is from the MJ to Ridgeway; also where it forks off to the Double H."

Apache made the necessary lines and watched as the men further studied the sketch.

"Apache," mused Tex thoughtfully, "is there any high ground, heavily wooded, that's within eye sight of the ranch and near that main trail to town and the Double H?"

"Why, yes there is," answered Apache. "There is a line of hills that starts here," as he pointed, "and they run for several miles in this direction," his finger continuing on.

"Good, that's what I want to know," said Tex. "Okay, if no one has any other thoughts, let's eat and then let me be. I've got a lot of thinkin' to do. Don't no one rub out that map," he added.

CHAPTER 3

The sentries again woke the men at dawn, and camp activity commenced immediately thereafter with all the men engaged in a variety of tasks.

After breakfast, Tex waved his arms and called out, "Gather around men. I've got some things to tell you." He leaned back against a tree, bent his knee to steady himself and folded his arms as the men gathered around him.

"You all know why we came here," he began. "We aim to find the man who murdered Slim Evers. Most of you, like me, grew up on the wild side. Many of you, like me, had trouble with the law and didn't have much respect for it. Some of you, like me, have spent time behind bars. But Slim had faith in each of us regardless of what we were or what we had did, and he gave us a second or third chance to be part of his world. Therefore, whatever we do, it has to be did Slim's way, accordin' to the law!"

"What if that don't work?" asked Curley.

"Well, we'll cross that bridge when we come to it," answered Tex. "But I full intend to make it work or mebby die tryin'. And that reminds me. If'n somethin' happens to me, Sanchez will be in charge. If'n somethin' happens to him, Lefty will take over. After that, it won't matter much. You all can decide for yourself."

Tex paused for a moment and then went on. "But we may have two problems. I'm thinkin' that killin' Slim is only one part of a puzzle. I can't be shore, yet, but I have a strong feelin' that MJ cattle have been rustled for the past two years and mebby Slim found out somethin' and was killed for it."

Tex continued, "It seems Henderson, or Double H riders, may be involved. I'm guessin' that unbranded cows and steers have been set aside or missed during roundups. If so, then MJ riders have been part of the game, too. Apache tells me that three of Marty's men have been chased off the ranch, leavin' only the foreman and three men to watch the range. That smells funny and might mean that a bigger game has started. Also, the Double H is a big ranch and has a bunch of riders."

Tex went on, "It also means that we may have some fightin' to do. Now a man doesn't like to see his friends get killed, but I full intend to push things hard when we get there. We got a ranch to get back to, and I ain't goin' to waste a lot of time in these parts, if'n I can help it. There will be risk in what I do."

"Tex," interrupted Lefty, "every time we buckle these guns on we know we're takin' risks. You tell us what you want us to do, and if'n I get killed in the doin', just bury me next to Slim, and I'll be right happy."

Low growls and words of agreement spread around the half circle of men.

Tex smiled grimly. "Thanks, men. I knew I could count on all of you, but I wanted to give y'all the straight of it. And maybe understand why I'll be doin' some of the things I do. Any questions?"

Hearing none, Tex went on. "Lefty, Charley, Kansas, Blackie, I got a special job for you. I want you to swing east and circle around until you come to the road from Canyon City. Don't get spotted if you can help it. Apache can tell you the best way there. Ride into Ridgeway on that road. You'll be lookin' for work, and you heard that the MJ is lookin' for riders. I want to see how that idear sets with folks. Try to arrive at the MJ by late afternoon and make shore all the punchers are there before tellin' the rest of us to come in. Three shots will be the signal. Be shore your horses look tired when you get to Ridgeway.

"The rest of us are goin' to follow Apache to the high ground, east of the ranch house. Reb, I want you and Cavalry to set up a signal system, dawn to dusk, using mirrors, between that high ground and the ranch house. I want to know when we are goin' to have visitors and how many before they get to the ranch so we can get ready for 'em. We'll build a little lean-to as a shelter for you and the horses."

Tex turned to Sanchez. "Who's your best man with a rifle?" he asked.

"Juan," answered Sanchez.

"All right," responded Tex. "Juan, Red and Charley will protect whoever is the signal man out there. If'n we get visitors, and there's no sun, one of you will have to ride like hell to tell us. One more thing. If'n we have any kind of a shootin' fracas at the ranch, you boys have to make shore no one gets away. Bring down the horses! No one can get far without a horse."

Tex continued, "Using a rough map Apache sketched out last night, I have split up the MJ range into four sections. I'll sit down with Marty to get some real boundaries to follow, but we're goin' to fence ride each section.

"Now, I don't trust the foreman or any of Marty's remainin' men. I repeat, we do not trust anyone! But we got to keep 'em busy and out where we can see 'em.

"Here's what we're goin' to do. I'll have one of his men and one of you ride together in three of the sections. But I'll want some men to follow you, outta sight, to make shore you have help if you need it. Rusty, you get the northwest section. Denver, you and Cheyenne will ride shotgun for him. Curley, you have the west section, and Laredo and Reno will ride shotgun for you.

"Sanchez, which of your men is best with a short gun," asked Tex, "besides you?"

"Felipé," came the quick reply.

"Felipé gets the southwest section then," declared Tex. "However, I want you and all the rest of your men to cover him," said Tex as he looked at Sanchez. "Use both sides of his trail. Take plenty of grub, 'cause after he rides that section and heads back to the ranch, I want you to keep one man with you and stay put for a day or two and try to locate that maverick herd we think is out there.

"That leaves the northeast section. That's the section closest to the Henderson ranch," continued Tex, "and I don't want any of Marty's men in that section. It could be a trouble spot, and I want my best men there. Lefty, I figger that suits you to a T. Blackie, you and Kansas will ride shotgun for him. Each group of you better work out some sort of signal in case of trouble."

Tex looked around. "You boys ridin' shotgun have three jobs: Protect your friend, get to know the ranch and keep an eye out for unbranded cattle. If'n we see too many, we may have to have a fast roundup to get that problem under control.

"Dusty, you, Bronc and Trig will stay at the ranch and keep me out of trouble," continued Tex, ignoring the laughter of incredulity that followed. "Dusty will help Reb or Cavalry with the signals. Bronc, you and Trig get the foreman to keep an eye on. He doesn't know it yet, but he's bein' replaced, and I don't want him gettin' in the way. Don't let him out of your sight! Remember, once we get there, no one leaves that ranch unless I know where they're goin' and why. Apache, I want you on call for anythin' special I might need done.

"One more thing," Tex went on. "We'll have a lot of horses to watch over, and some of you will have to bunk outdoors. Switch around on that, but I want two night watches of three men each. Work that out among you, and Apache can be part of that, too."

Tex turned to Sanchez. "I think most of your men can understand English?" he asked.

"Si," replied Sanchez. "All can. I peek heem that way!"

"Good," laughed Tex. "But after we get to the ranch, only speak in Spanish to them. And them back to you, *comprende*?"

"Si," again replied Sanchez with a broad grin. "Eet will be a good treeck." He spoke rapidly in Spanish to his companions, and they nodded and smiled.

"I guess that covers everythin' for now," said Tex. "Okay boys, let's ride."

* * * * * * * * * * * *

It was late afternoon when four riders trotted into Ridgeway from the road to Canyon City. They moved down the main street until coming to the Sweetwater Saloon. They turned toward the tie rail in front of the saloon and dismounted.

"Might as well start here," muttered Lefty. "Besides, I'm thirsty."

The four men entered the saloon, paused for a moment to let their eyes get used to the change in brightness and moved to the bar. Only two lone drinkers stood before the long bar, but a poker game was in progress off to one side with five players.

"What'll it be, gents?" asked the bartender as he eyed the strangers carefully. After taking their orders and preparing the drinks, he continued, "You boys just passing through?"

"Don't rightly know," replied Lefty as he sipped his drink and slid a coin across the bar. "You might help us, though. How do we find the MJ Ranch from here?"

The startled bartender was slow to respond. Finally, he asked, "Why are you looking for that ranch?"

"Don't rightly know why that's any business of yourn," Lefty coolly answered. But, after a short pause, he went on. "Well, we're lookin' for jobs. Met three fellars in Canyon City who said the MJ was shorthanded, and so here we are. First-rate punchers we are, too!"

The bartender thought for a moment and then raised his voice. "Hey, Donie," he called. "These strangers are lookin' for the MJ. Said they ran into three guys in Canyon City who told them the MJ was shorthanded. What do you think of that?"

Laughter erupted from the card table, and the game stopped as the players turned to look at the four men at the bar. One put his cards down and peered at the strangers carefully. "You don't want to work for the MJ," he sneered. "Didn't those fellars tell you it wasn't healthy?" he asked.

Lefty looked at the speaker before answering. He didn't particularly like what he saw. The man appeared to be in his early twenties. He wore expensive clothes, beginning with a new Stetson with a bright band around the crown. A fancy white shirt was under a black vest, and both the vest and shirt had silver buttons. A pearl handled Colt was clearly visible in his holster. A real dude, mused Lefty.

Using the same haughty tone of voice as the card player, Lefty mimicked, "No, sonny, they didn't say nothin' like that a'tall."

The young man's face turned red, and he exclaimed, "Don't get smart with me, mister. You don't know who you are talking to."

"No, I don't," Lefty answered coolly. "Who might I be talkin' to?" Lefty sensed that his companions had moved slightly to give themselves elbow room and were ready for action.

"You're talking to Donie Henderson, that's who," the man said in the same loud, insolent voice, "and the Hendersons run this town and everything around it. You best move on and find a job somewhere else," he added.

"You run the MJ?" asked Lefty casually.

"No, leastways not yet," scowled Henderson, "but that ranch is shore dying, and whatever jobs they have won't last long. Like I said, you best move on."

Lefty finished his drink, turned his back to Henderson and looked at the bartender.

"I asked you for directions to the MJ," he said evenly. "Now, what are they?"

The bartender hesitated, looked at Donie Henderson, shrugged and said, "Go out of town west for a couple of miles, take the left fork and it will get you there."

"Thanks," Lefty muttered, and turned to leave, almost bumping into a man who had just entered the saloon.

"Watch where you're goin'," snapped the man.

A quick retort had almost reached his lips when Lefty saw the star on the vest of the newcomer.

Ben Hamilton was a big man, primarily around the middle. His girth was the subject of many snide comments, although none were made within earshot of him. He no longer did much riding, letting his deputies handle that end of his office's duties. He had been hand-picked by Henry Henderson, and everyone knew where his power came from.

Hamilton looked at the four men and asked, "Where did you boys ride in from?"

"Canyon City," lied Lefty, watching the face of the lawman. "Why do you ask?"

"See a big group of riders along the way?" continued Hamilton, ignoring the question. "Maybe some Mexicans included?" he probed.

"Nope," answered Lefty. "Didn't see nothin' like that a'tall." His companions nodded in agreement.

Donie Henderson spoke up. "Ben, these hombres are looking for jobs. Seems like they think the MJ may be looking for punchers. I told them they'd be better off moving on. Don't you agree?"

"Yes," concurred Hamilton. "The MJ has had a lot of trouble and probably won't be around long." He looked over the four men carefully, noting Blackie's two guns and the fact that his guns and Lefty's lone weapon were tied down. "You boys don't look like the average cow punchers to me," he drawled. "We don't cotton to strangers starting trouble in this county. We have ways of takin' care of it, and you best remember that. Like Donie said, I'd move on if I were you."

Lefty smiled. "Why, sheriff, everyone needs a job, and we're first-rate punchers. Come on boys, let's move on. This town is right unfriendly."

Hamilton watched the men exit the saloon and heard the sound of horses move away. He motioned to Donie, and the two of them went to a separate table. The sheriff looked at Henderson and asked, "You don't suppose Johnson has hired some gunmen to help him out, do you? Johnson was mighty angry when that Evers fellar was killed."

Donie pursed his lips and thought for a moment. "Oh, I don't think so, Ben. I reckon you're just jittery. Why did you ask them where they was from?"

"Well, my deputy in Harding wired me about a big crowd of men that went through there several days ago," replied Hamilton. "Headed west and north they were. Owens trailed them for a day and didn't find out anythin' unusual. I was just checkin'."

Donie thought for a few moments. "I'll tell dad about these riders," he said. "But I'll bet they'll ride on." He rose, walked to the card table and picked up his money and chips.

"Guess I'll cash these in," he said, handing the chips to the dealer. "Reckon I'll be heading back to the ranch."

* * * * * * * * * * * *

Lefty and his companions pulled their horses to a slow walk as they approached the end of the line of foothills, northeast of the MJ Ranch. They received the assurances they were expecting, from a hidden messenger, and moved forward at a trot as the ranch buildings came into view. They had discussed their plans; what they had to do and how they were going to do it as they made the trip from Ridgeway. They were now eager to accomplish their part of the operation.

After eating supper with his men in the bunkhouse, foreman Art French was heading for the main ranch house when he saw the four approaching riders. His three men were sitting on a bench outside the bunkhouse, smoking and talking. The conversation stopped as they watched the riders reach the porch where French was standing.

Lefty had Charley on his right; Blackie was behind Lefty with Kansas on his right and slightly behind him.

"Howdy," greeted Lefty. "Another hot day," he volunteered.

"And close," agreed French. "What do you fellars want?"

"We heard tell that the MJ was short of men, and we need jobs. So here we are!" smiled Lefty.

"Where did you hear that news?" countered French. "Anyone in Ridgeway tell you that?" he asked, his face a blank.

"Well, no," admitted Lefty. "We run into some fellars in Canyon City who told us, and since we need the jobs real bad, we came right along."

French studied them for a moment and shrugged his shoulders. "Sorry, boys, but I only hire men I know, not saddle tramps."

"Well now, my name is Lefty White," replied Lefty, ignoring the second half of the remark. He swung from the saddle, his right hand grasping the saddle pommel and his left hand only an inch or two from his gun. "Now you know me real well, and there ain't no reason a'tall why you can't hire me, is there?" he asked with a cold edge to his voice. "I'm right glad to receive such a warm welcome," he added. Lefty had taken a couple of steps toward French as he spoke and stretched out his right hand as a friendly gesture.

"Now, see here," began French, as he brushed aside the outstretched hand and reached for his gun, only to find the end of a Colt 45 barrel pressuring the center of his belly, just above the belt buckle.

"Now, tell your men to come over here with their hands up, or I'll blow you apart," snarled Lefty, even though he knew Blackie and Kansas had the three covered. "Any more in the bunkhouse?" he asked, poking French's stomach for emphasis.

"No, that's all there is," answered French slowly. He signaled his men to come toward the ranch house.

"Kansas," Lefty yelled, "check the bunkhouse; Charley, watch the ranch house. If'n Kansas runs into trouble at the bunkhouse, you're a dead man," Lefty warned French.

Kansas spurred his horse and reached the bunkhouse in a few strides. He dismounted and cautiously entered the building. In a moment he reappeared with a big grin on his face. "All clear," he said. "We got 'em all."

"Good," replied Lefty. "Send the signal."

Kansas raised his gun and fired three spaced shots into the air.

Lefty yelled again, "Marty, are you and Mary in the house? You can come out now. There ain't goin' to be no trouble."

Marty and Mary Johnson emerged from the house, smiles on their faces and joy in their hearts. "I can't tell you how happy I was to hear your name," Marty exclaimed. "I'm real glad to see you."

Lefty grinned. "I thought you might enjoy that. I figgered you'd stay inside and out of the line of fire 'til things got settled. The rest of the boys will be along directly."

Lefty's gun was still pressed against French's stomach. He relaxed a bit and pulled it back as the other three MJ men arrived with Kansas and the mounted Blackie trailing right behind. Charley had dismounted, and his gun, too, covered the foreman and his men.

Stunned and bewildered, French was slowly getting his bearings. Who were these men? he wondered. Where did they come from and why were they here? But his psyche received another rude shock as more men galloped into the ranch area, guns drawn and at the ready. As soon as it was evident everything was under control, the guns were holstered and the men dismounted.

Tex approached the group on the ranch porch and grinned as Marty and Mary greeted him warmly.

"Apache said you would be here soon," said Marty, "and by gum, he was right. It sure is good to see you. My God, did you bring everyone?"

"Almost," answered Tex, "and wait till you see who's with the pack horses. You're in for another pleasant surprise." Tex turned to Lefty. "Good job done, pardner, and not a shot fired."

Tex then turned back to French, who still had a look of amazement on his face.

"French," Tex began, "you might as well know why we're here. We're goin' to find out who murdered Slim Evers, and then we're to make shore that them that did it are hung, legal and proper."

"And," Tex went on, "while we're here, we're goin' to put this ranch back in tip-top shape. While we do that, you and your men will be our guests. I have some questions I want answered, and 'til I get those answers, no one leaves this ranch unless I say so! My boys have orders to shoot anyone who does, so don't make no false moves."

French remained silent, his mind racing. He looked past Tex and received another shock. More men had arrived with the pack horses, and included was a group of Mexicans and Apache, the boy who disappeared after Evers was killed! French found a chair, sat down and pondered all these new developments. Fear began to flow into his veins as he watched all the activity around him. His three punchers joined him, and they, too, were stunned and silent.

Sanchez cantered up to the porch group and dismounted.

Tex introduced Sanchez to Marty and Mary. Marty's eyes lit up as he shook hands. "Slim mentioned you several times, and I'm proud to meet you. You and your men are most welcome."

Sanchez turned to Mary and bowed. "I am mucho glad to meet you señora," he said, "but I do not like the reason. I theenk we will make some people ver' seeck about that, ver' queek," he added.

Marty nodded but did not speak.

Mary broke in. "Have you eaten? You must be starved," she went on as Tex shook his head no.

"We've brought along grub supplies," Tex told Marty, "and they should last for a spell. Several of the boys will help Mary with the cookin', but we are shore going to be squeezed for bunks."

Marty scratched his head and looked around his premises. "Well, we have eight spare bunks in the bunkhouse, and we can bed down a fair number here in the main house and on the porch."

Tex nodded his agreement. "I think it would be best if Sanchez and his men slept here in the main house or on the porch. Some of the boys will have to bed down outside and act as sentries. We'll figger it all out later. Let's eat, and then we'll get organized."

CHAPTER 4

Kip Kelso, resident gunman and policy enforcer for the Henderson Ranch, relaxed in a chair on the ranch veranda, his legs stretched out and crossed with one boot on top of the wood railing. It was late afternoon, and Kelso was deep in thought, reviewing the events of recent years, especially the past month, and vaguely aware of some disturbing thoughts that resulted therefrom.

Kelso had been big for his age, and although he didn't like school, he found he could tolerate the experience by bullying the other boys into doing errands for him and giving him answers to test questions. In addition, he found he could extort money from these boys even though the amounts were small.

Even these games eventually bored him, and at the age of 15 he quit school and found a job punching cattle. He would last a year or so at one ranch and then quit and move on to another. It was at his third such job that he ran into a puncher named Art French. The two hit it off well, and French began to show Kelso how to use a six-gun. Kip soon displayed a natural adeptness in handling the weapon, both in speed and accuracy.

Two years later Kelso showed up in the Ridgeway area. His first killing was a relatively easy one. The man was a buffalo hunter with limited skills with a revolver. The two had argued over a poker game with Kelso assuming the man had been cheating. He later found out he was wrong. It was soon evident that his skill with a Colt was largely offset by his lack of skill at playing cards in general and poker in particular.

The second killing was different, however, as this individual had some known ability with a gun. This altercation was over a dance hall girl and was witnessed by Henry Henderson.

Henderson had invited Kelso to the Double H Ranch and made him a proposition Kelso couldn't refuse. Henderson didn't want a loose cannon roaming around his town, and so he offered Kelso $ 100 a month to be his resident gunman as well as mentor and confidante to his son, Donie. That was twice the amount he had ever earned as a puncher, and Kelso jumped at it. Thinking back, Kelso ruefully reflected, maybe it wasn't such a good bargain after all.

Henry Henderson had married late in life and only had the one child. Mrs. Henderson, an Eastern girl, had never really taken to Western life and after the birth of Donie, her strength and whatever enthusiasm she had had never returned. She had died when Donie was five.

A series of housekeepers followed, but none were allowed to discipline the boy, who was the apple of his father's eye. Donie was only a year younger than Kelso, and that small age difference had made it difficult for Kip to assume a mentor's role.

At first Donie and Kelso got along well, primarily because Donie was awed by Kelso's dexterity with a gun. Kelso tried to teach the young man some basic points in the use of the weapon, but Donie's patience was short-lived, indeed, and he refused to practice much. Still, he fancied himself to be a gunfighter. Kelso knew better, that Donie had no nerve and that he was basically a coward. This latter character weakness had made him useful to Kelso, but Donie's increasingly quick temper had begun to try Kelso's patience. Only Kelso's presence had prevented two gunfights in recent months involving Donie and had, no doubt, saved his life.

Donie, of course, always had money to spend and had a weakness for fancy clothes and women. Kelso was Donie's frequent companion and felt the need to dress accordingly. But the cost of such clothes and entertainment, plus his poker losses, even in his bunkhouse games, consumed his monthly salary, and he had little to show for his station in life.

When Kelso heard that his old friend, Art French, had become foreman of the MJ Ranch, an idea began to form in Kip's brain. Kelso rekindled his friendship with French and after a few months, approached Art with his idea. Kelso was pleased to find out that French had a similar scheme in the back of his mind. French replaced several MJ hands with men he could trust, and operations began.

In order for the plan to work, however, French and Kelso needed a front man who could sell cattle with no questions asked. They also needed someone they could control. Donie Henderson fit that description perfectly, at least at first.

Donie could not understand why his father had not given him greater latitude in managing the Double H Ranch. Donie considered himself to be foreman but in reality made few decisions and only supervised a very limited number of working arrangements.

Kelso played on Donie's unhappiness and his inflated ego and convinced him that if the MJ would falter and go under, his father would surely let him run the ranch as his own. One thing led to another, and Donie was soon a full participant in the scheme.

Henry Henderson had inadvertently helped Kelso in his plan. Still unhappy about the MJ getting away from him, Henry knew that the local branch of the Cattlemen's and Merchant's Bank, where he was the largest stockholder, was the collection agent for the outstanding note against the MJ Ranch. If the ranch went under, he was prepared to step in and pay off the note at a large discount. Since the original of the note was held at the main bank office in Chicago, Henderson was not aware that the note was supported by two endorsers.

Donie knew of his father's plan, and this alone justified his participation in Kelso's scheme. He was helping his father acquire the ranch but using a faster method.

The first two years of the operation had turned out quite well. Kelso, in particular, was pleased with his extra income.

About a month ago, however, someone named Slim Evers had shown up at the MJ. He was obviously a good friend of Marty Johnson and, more to the point, apparently had extensive experience in the cattle ranching business. He had asked pointed questions, and French had been hard pressed to give satisfactory answers.

Worse than that, about a week later Evers had followed French and Stan Cook, one of the MJ men French had hired, and caught them and two Double H riders branding MJ mavericks with a Double H iron. Before he could take any significant action, however, Evers died from a bullet in the back. The killing of Evers had been a bad and unpredictable development. But in reality, no other alternative had been available, Kelso told himself.

Kelso hated loose ends, and he was disturbed that the Indian boy, who had come to the ranch with Evers, had disappeared right after the shooting. Probably so scared he ran all the way to his reservation, Kelso mused, smiling at the thought. But it was still a loose end.

The brawl in town, about a week ago, while appearing to be an accident, may actually have been set up by young Henderson and French, Kelso reflected. Donie had confronted the MJ men and had started the fight. Fortunately there were enough Double H men to overwhelm their opponents.

But Henry, of course, had heard about the fight in town and had told Kelso to get a handle on the situation. For his own part, Kelso was also upset because Donie had refused to confirm or deny he had arranged it with French, and Kip did not want these men doing things without his knowledge. The net result was good, however, as the last three uncooperative punchers were now gone from the MJ.

Kelso had taken Donie aside and worked on his ego again. It was almost time to drive another herd to Harding. Perhaps if they speeded up the branding process and added some more strays, it might be enough to do in the MJ.

Donie thought for a while and finally agreed. They would step up operations, drive the herd to Harding, hurt the MJ even more and have another cash payoff to boot. Donie would send Dan Sims and Salty Spencer, Double H riders, down to the MJ to assist in the branding operation as soon as their Double H duties could be reassigned. That would take a day or two.

This morning Kelso had met French in town, and French had agreed to the change in plans and would help in its implementation. French did not admit he had had a hand in the altercation in Ridgeway, however.

Kelso closed his eyes and sighed. While his main problem was keeping a tight rein on Donie's temper and keeping his mouth shut, French's attitude also was beginning to irritate him. Things weren't getting any easier.

* * * * * * * * * * *

Dusk was approaching on the MJ, and the two-shift dinner process was in full swing. Many of the Rambling R men had used this opportunity to visit Slim's gravesite, either individually or in groups of twos or threes. The Mexican contingent, except for Sanchez, stayed in the background out of respect for their comrades' grief and to keep an eye on French and the other three MJ punchers.

Marty and Mary Johnson accompanied Tex and Sanchez as they reached Evers' final resting place. Marty and Mary were bareheaded, but Tex and Sanchez removed their hats as they arrived at the tiny cemetery. After a couple of minutes of silence, each person with his or her own thoughts, Marty spoke. "I want to get a head stone for Slim, but strange as it may seem, I don't ever remember hearing his first name, and I don't know when he was born."

Tex smiled grimly. "I don't know when he was born either, but I do know his first name. When he arranged for me to get a parole, he and I had to sign some legal papers, since I was released into his custody. His first name is Raymond. That's where the Rambling R comes from. Rambling Raymond.

"As soon as we get things cleaned up around here," he went on, "a head stone will be the first order of business. That was a good thought, Marty."

The little group turned and headed back to the main house. Dusk had fallen, and Red Rollins, Charley Landers, Reb Stuart, and Juan rode in from their outpost. Dismounting, they turned their horses loose in a makeshift corral, adjacent to the main corral. Tex left his group, met briefly with Red and then retraced his steps.

"Everything is set for the signal crew," he said, primarily to himself. "Guess it's time we all had a council of war." Turning to Sanchez, he said, "Get Lefty and meet us in the den. I'll get Bronc and Trig."

In a few minutes the men had gathered in the big den, a coffee pot and cups nearby.

Lefty reported on his stop in Ridgeway. Marty sighed and responded, "Well, it's no secret we have had to struggle ever since we got here, but maybe Donie Henderson and the sheriff know more than they should about how we are getting along. However, losing those three punchers may have been the basis for their comments. Sometimes events like that tend to be overdone."

Tex nodded. "We can look into that later on. Right now I want to get the line ridin' jobs laid out and workin'. Marty, what are the names of your three punchers?"

"Stan Cook, Wes Adams and Bud Charles," replied Marty.

"All right," mused Tex. "Marty, I want you to sketch out the four sections of the ranch that need looked after. Apache gave us a purty good idea of what they look like, but I want you to give me somethin' each of the boys can take with them. Cook will go with Felipé, Adams will go with Rusty, and Charles will go with Curley. Tomorrow mornin', after breakfast, I'll bring the MJ men here and tell them about these arrangements. I don't expect them to be very happy about it.

"Sanchez, while I'm keepin' 'em busy, you take all the outriders and get set up to ride shotgun. Lefty, you, Blackie and Kansas can leave together but split up as soon as you get out of sight of the ranch. Red and his men can leave with Sanchez' gang."

"What about French?" asked Marty.

"He stays at the ranch," answered Tex. "I've got a good job for him, and Bronc or Trig will stay as close to him as a tick on a cow."

Tex looked around. "Any questions?" he asked.

Hearing none, he rose and said, "Meeting's over. Let's get some shuteye. Tomorrow's goin' to be a busy day. Marty, I want to go over the tally books with you as soon as things settle down in the mornin'."

* * * * * * * * * * * *

Art French and the three remaining MJ riders had been lounging outside the bunkhouse all evening, watching the activity going on around them. The significance of the numerous trips to the gravesite was not lost on them, since French had told them why Tex and his men were there.

When Red and his three companions rode in, Cook watched them dismount and exclaimed in disgust, "My God, four more of those hombres. They keep comin' in. I count 23 in all, and that doesn't include that Indian boy, Apache. I shore reckoned he had run and left these parts for good. Where'd he find all these fellars? And why the Mexicans? I don't like it!"

"I reckon this changes things considerable," Wes Adams agreed. "As soon as I git the chance, I'm goin' to hit the trail outta here."

"You're going nowhere," growled French. "Somehow, one of us has to get word to Kelso about this bunch. Kip was gonna send Salty and Dan to help us with the branding, and they may already be with the herd. We gotta get word to them, too."

"Gettin' away from here is goin' to take some doin'," interjected Cook. "There's so many of them and so few of us."

"Calm down," cautioned French. "We'll just have to wait for the right time or place and then make a move. Meantime, keep your eyes and ears open and your mouths shut. We'll see what happens tomorrow."

* * * * * * * * * * * *

Dawn, a hearty breakfast and a burst of activity began a new day on the MJ. French was mildly pleased when Sanchez led a large body of men away from the ranch. Fewer men to keep an eye on us, he reasoned.

Bronc Evans approached the MJ group as they sat outside the bunkhouse and announced, "Tex wants to see you boys in the ranch house. I reckon he has some jobs for your idle hands to do."

French did not deem that comment worthy of a reply but got to his feet and motioned for the other three to follow him.

Inside the house, Tex outlined what he wanted done and made the appropriate pairings. He turned to Cook and told him, "Felipé don't speak English, but he knows what to do. I reckon you two can get along okay." Tex smiled inwardly at the scowl that quickly appeared on Cook's face but just as quickly disappeared.

"What about me?" asked French.

"Oh, I have a good job for you," replied Tex. "That chuck wagon needs a lot of work to get it ready for a hard pull. Bronc will help you, but you leave your gun belt in the bunkhouse. I wouldn't want to have any accidents happen."

French turned red with an angry retort on the tip of his tongue. He controlled himself, however, but not without some effort. He turned and left the ranch house, Bronc Evans right behind him. Cook, Adams and Charles retained their sidearms, French noted, with a small degree of satisfaction.

The six section riders found their horses, saddled and were soon on their way, amply supplied with food.

Their dust had barely settled when Lefty, Blackie and Kansas saddled their horses and rode north.

The three rode together for more than a mile, checking the brands of the cattle they saw. Blackie and Kansas then veered to the left and disappeared among the trees and undergrowth that was thick in that area.

Lefty continued his solitary ride, riding back and forth to look over the cattle he saw as well as to get comfortable with the terrain and the visible check points from the sketch he carried.

About noon he came upon the first sizable herd he had seen, 50 to 60 head grazing in a lush meadow. His eyes narrowed, however, when he drew close to the animals and saw they all had Double H brands.

Lefty swore and yanked the sketch from his pocket. "If Marty is right," he muttered, "these damn cows are more'n a mile from the ranch boundary. Too far to wander. They had to be driven this far," he continued to himself. "Well, I'll just have to drive 'em back ag'in," he muttered again.

Suiting his actions to his thoughts, Lefty rode back and forth, yelling and gesturing. He had thoughts of firing his gun to speed the process along but rejected the idea and continued his efforts to get the herd moving. He finally registered his presence with the leaders of the animals, and they started to trot their way in the direction desired. The rest followed.

Lefty had just worked the herd up to a reasonable speed when he spotted four riders approaching about a quarter of a mile away. He pulled up his horse gently, removed his big hat, wiped the inside band with his kerchief, put it back on his head, crooked his right leg around the horn of his saddle and reached for tobacco and papers. He had passed the pre- arranged signal on to his friends, and now there was nothing to do but await developments.

Lefty had just lit his cigarette when the four riders cantered up. In the lead was the colorfully dressed Donie Henderson.

"What do you think you're doing with those cattle?" yelled Henderson. "Can't you read brands?"

"I'm sendin' them back to where they belong," replied Lefty calmly. "And, yeah, I can read brands. They're all Double H. Ain't you got nobody on your ranch who can line ride and know where your boundary is?"

"A real smart guy, aren't you," yelled Donie again. Then he recognized who he was talking to and continued. "You're the saddle tramp that had a lot to say in town yesterday. Didn't I tell you to ride on?"

"Yeah, you did," admitted Lefty, "but I like it here. Now, about these cows. It's right nice of you all to come by and take 'em off my hands. You can drive 'em back on their own range. I'll just ride along to make sure you don't get lost along the way."

"Why you . . . ," sputtered Donie. "Who do you think you are, telling me what to do!"

Suddenly he drew his Colt and pointed it at Lefty.

"Drop your gun and get off your horse!" he screamed. "I've got a good mind to teach you a lesson. Cover him for me, boys," he told his men. They responded, and Lefty found himself looking at three guns as Donie holstered his own weapon.

Lefty slowly pulled his gun from its holster and dropped it on the ground. He slid off his horse, took a couple of steps away from the animal and flipped his cigarette with the fingers on his right hand. His eyes were riveted on the dark face of Donie Henderson.

"Wait a minute, Donie," one of the other riders began. "He was only doin' his job."

"Shut up, Bo," Donie sneered. "This gent needs to be taught a lesson about how Hendersons run this range and that working for the MJ is real unhealthy."

With these words, Donie spurred his horse and raised the quirt that he always carried. Riding past Lefty, he slashed down at Lefty's face.

Lefty ducked and avoided any contact with his face, but his left shoulder caught the blow, cutting the shirt and drawing blood.

Donie turned his horse and again raced toward Lefty, swinging his quirt in circles. Lefty turned away and ducked again, avoiding the lash. But this time he stepped on a piece of wood and went sprawling.

Two of the three riders laughed and urged Donie on. "Ride 'em cowboy," one yelled. "Show him what Henderson law is, Donie."

Donie swept in again as Lefty regained his feet. Using his arms to protect his face, he took another slash on his right arm, which also drew blood.

Henderson pulled up, a wicked smile on his face.

"Hey, cowboy, the fun has just started. I'm going to cut you to pieces," he exclaimed. "Where do you want the next one?"

Henderson began to circle his quirt again and was about to charge when he froze at the sound of a rifle shot. Bits of wood exploded from a nearby stump. A second shot and more exploding chips drew four pairs of eyes to a nearby ridge where a wisp of smoke could be seen.

"Somebody is up there," Donie pointed.

"Holster your guns and raise your hands!" came from a loud voice behind them. Four necks turned, and the four Double H men saw Blackie slowly approaching, reins tied around his saddle pommel and a Colt in each hand.

"I'll drill anyone who makes a quick move," he snapped. "Now holster those guns — slow and deliberate!"

The three punchers complied with his order.

As soon as he heard Blackie's voice, Lefty leaped into action, driven by a cold fury. Three quick strides brought him to Donie's side. Lefty reached up and yanked Donie out of the saddle.

Henderson landed hard, knocking some wind out of him. Half dazed, he got one foot under himself and began to rise, only to be jolted with a vicious left fist to his face. The blow sent him rolling. Even more dazed now, he felt a heavy weight land on his upper legs. A hand grabbed his shirt at the neck and raised his face.

Lefty snarled, "You like to use a quirt? Let's see how you like a fist."

His left fist landed again, a second time, a third time. Finally, Lefty raised himself up and came down with a fourth blow, with everything he had behind it.

Donie found himself tasting blood, his own. Intense pain quickly followed. Then he saw stars. And finally sweet oblivion took over.

Lefty got to his feet and walked over to his gun. Blowing dirt off it, he sheathed the weapon and then stared up at the three riders whose hands were still in the air.

"You all were havin' a right good time a few minutes ago," he observed. "Any one of you want to try laughin' some more? Get off your horse and laugh in my face! Any takers?"

He waited for a few moments, but none of the three moved to take up the challenge.

"Nobody laughin', huh? One of you climb down, pick up that trash and sling him over his saddle," he continued, pointing at Donie's unconscious form. "The rest of you git those cattle movin' and don't stop 'till you git on your side of the line. Like I said, me and Blackie will follow along so you don't get lost."

By the time the riders and cattle had reached the ranch boundaries, Donie's groans indicated he had regained consciousness. Lefty pointed to the man named Bo and said, "Help him git set in the saddle. You other two keep those cattle movin'. I don't want them nowhere near the ranch line."

Bo dismounted and helped the unsteady Donie get up into his saddle. Donie started to slide off, but Bo grabbed and steadied him. Seeing that Donie appeared to be stable, at least temporarily, Bo vaulted onto his own horse and reached out to hold Donie's shoulder. He looked at Lefty and said, "Old Henry Henderson ain't goin' to like what you did to his boy."

"That depends on how you tell what happened," observed Lefty. "But you tell Henry and all your friends in yore bunkhouse that from now on you keep Double H cattle on your side of the line, and if'n I catch anyone drivin' Double H cattle on to MJ range, they'll shore enough have to walk home, if'n they can still walk. You tell 'em that. Now git!"

Lefty and Blackie watched the Double H riders drive the cattle a good quarter mile further and then head for their ranch house, Bo still helping Donie stay in the saddle.

Kansas left the cover of a grove of trees and joined the other two, a big grin on his face. "A right lovely day," he opined. Then he sobered and asked Lefty, "How bad are you hurt? I would have cut loose sooner, but I had to give Blackie time to get behind 'em."

"Not bad," Lefty replied. "I'll live. Let's eat, and then I want to ride around some before headin' back to the ranch. We might as well stay together now that they know there is at least three of us. Didn't I see a little brook a ways back? We'll go there, eat and rest the horses."

* * * * * * * * * * * *

Stan Cook spent most of the day mumbling to himself. After trying to engage Felipé in some sort of conversation and receiving a series of "No comprendes", he gave up in disgust.

Several ideas had come to Cook while he rode but were promptly rejected since their first day of riding would take them through an area farthest removed from the hidden herd of mavericks. There was nothing to fear at the moment.

He could always kill Felipé and get to the herd. But then what? If Felipé didn't return, that whole crowd would be down on him in a flash. It would be impossible for the three of them to move the herd fast enough and far enough to avoid capture. Besides, the branding wasn't completed, and they couldn't sell the herd without Donie anyway. No, they were boxed in and had to sit tight. Maybe French would come up with an idea that might work.

* * * * * * * * * * * *

Sanchez had led his three men south at a fast gait in order to locate positions from which they could observe Cook's and Felipé's arrival and begin their escort function. However, it soon became painfully obvious that Tex's plan to cover the twosome from both sides of the range was not going to work.

The eastern boundary of the MJ Ranch was marked by a long line of hills, heavily wooded and containing thick underbrush. While difficult to move through, it did provide excellent cover. On the other hand, the range itself was quite flat and except for a handful of arroyos and gullies, it contained few other undulations until it ran into another, higher line of hills, about five miles to the west, the western edge of the MJ property. Outside of some tiny groves of cottonwoods, scattered here and there, there was no protective cover at all.

Midway between the eastern and western line of hills ran a stream of slowly moving water. Originating high up in the Bitterroot Mountains north and a little west of the MJ Ranch, it emerged from the foothills and made its way southeast until it came to about two miles from the ranch buildings. Then it quickly turned straight south and effectively divided this fine range land into two, almost equal parts.

Sanchez motioned for his men to follow him, and the four horsemen climbed the nearest hill, found a narrow open route through the brush and meandered in, between and around trees for about a half mile before coming to a halt to discuss the situation. Finally, Sanchez left Luis and Federico to wait for Cook and Felipé to appear, after which they were to assume their escort and shotgun role. In the meantime Sanchez and José rode on ahead, staying within the woods for concealment and began the search for any pathway or trail that could lead to a glen, meadow or valley that could be the hiding place for the suspected herd of mavericks. Although they found two such possibilities and rode a considerable distance to check each out, their search proved fruitless.

Sanchez was not surprised at this lack of success. Both he and Tex were operating under the assumption that if the herd, in fact, did exist, it would be positioned as far south as possible, away from the main ranch buildings and as close to Harding as practical. This, in turn, would reduce the time needed to drive the cattle to Harding to a minimum and would get the gang members back to their usual jobs as quickly as possible. Both men reasoned that such a drive would consume about five days — three and a half days on the trail, a half day to load the cattle onto rail cars and one day to return to the Ridgeway area.

Cook and Felipé had followed the eastern boundary of the MJ Ranch, always staying at least a quarter to a half mile or so away from the line of hills. They did not ride in a straight line, of course, as they would change their route whenever they found cattle grazing. They would walk their horses close to the animals and check their brands, their overall condition and the quality of the grass. This south range contained the best grazing land on the whole ranch, but still the cattle had to be moved frequently to avoid overgrazing. The progress of the two riders was slow, therefore, and it was noon before they reached the southernmost boundary of the ranch.

After a cold lunch and rest for the horses, they moved slowly west for just over two miles, reaching the stream, which continued south and disappeared in rough terrain. At this point the two riders turned north and began their trek back to the ranch, using the bed of the stream as their left guide but again wandering here and there to check out the cattle they ran into. By the end of the day they would have covered about half of the southern and southwestern portion of the ranch property.

As soon as Cook and Felipé had turned north, the Mexicans faced a dilemma. Sanchez and José had joined Luis and Federico during the lunch hour, and the four men watched the duo change direction, Sanchez with a frown on his face. Now there would be no adequate cover for the escort riders, and Felipé was essentially on his own.

Sanchez directed Luis and Federico to follow the two riders at a very safe distance, out of sight but within hearing range of gunshots, if possible. He also told them to have Tex insist that Cook and Felipé follow the same route on the morrow, supposedly to give Felipé another day to familiarize himself with that section of the ranch. What Sanchez really wanted was a full day to search the southwestern section of this range without worrying about running into Cook and Felipé and/or leaving tracks that could be spotted.

As soon as Luis and Federico left, Sanchez and José continued down the southern boundary line, again searching for the hidden cattle but also looking for a trail that could be used to drive the herd to Harding. They soon discovered the latter and followed it for several miles. There was ample evidence it had been used by cattle but not recently.

Satisfied they had learned something significant, the two men returned to the MJ range and continued their slow search for the mavericks. Dusk found them at the southwestern corner of the range and farthest away from the ranch itself. Here the area adjacent to the range had turned considerably rougher and wilder and began a line of good-sized hills that continued on north. They finally found a small break in the foliage, followed it for about half a mile and dismounted. They made a makeshift camp and had a cold supper, not wishing to start a fire. Soon they spread their bedrolls and were sound asleep.

Dawn, a cold breakfast, and they were on their way again, continuing their slow, methodical search. Again, they were looking for anything that might lead them to the hidden cattle.

It was almost noon when José stood up in his stirrups, let loose with a shrill whistle and waved his big sombrero. Sanchez turned in his saddle, waved his hand in response and raced to join his countryman. José had dismounted and was carefully examining the ground around the entrance to a shallow but wide draw when Sanchez reached him. Sanchez dismounted, too, and also examined the ground.

"Cattle have turned in here recently," said José in Spanish. "Here are some faint tracks, and look at that bush there. Several of its branches have been chewed."

"Yes, you are right," breathed Sanchez, also in Spanish. "Maybe this is what we have been looking for." He glanced around and examined the higher ground to his right.

"Go up there, dismount and cover me from the trees," he said. "I will proceed on foot and see where this draw takes me. You keep pace with me from up there."

José did as he was told, and as soon as he was in position, Sanchez began walking down the shallow gully, reins in one hand, his horse in tow.

His progress was slow as more cattle tracks became obvious in softer areas of the ground, and he examined each area carefully. It took him almost a half hour to cover half a mile, when José's whistle caught his attention. José motioned for him to scale the right slope of the draw. There was good footing, and soon Sanchez and his horse reached the top and joined José. José took a few steps and parted the branches of a scrub pine and pointed. Sanchez looked and couldn't resist a big grin. There, in a grassy meadow with a small stream at the far end, was a good-sized herd of cattle, grazing contentedly.

Sanchez searched the landscape but could not see any human beings. Not satisfied, however, he told José to follow the line of pines and scout the area. He, Sanchez, would wait here and cover José should any trouble develop.

It was a long half hour before José returned and reported he saw no one about. Tying their horses, both men stepped out into the open, guns drawn and at the ready. The two men spread out and advanced slowly, ever alert for the sudden appearance of other men.

They approached a fallen tree stump and noted the ashes and other evidence of a recent fire and the presence of humans and horses. Finally satisfied that no others were about, both men sheathed their weapons and made a walking examination of the cattle nearest them. None had brands.

Sanchez proceeded farther down the meadow, and his eyes lit up when he saw the Double H brand on numerous animals, although a few had no brands at all.

He motioned for José to join him at the edge of the woods, where they had left their horses. Grabbing their reins, the two men led their horses deeper into the woods and back toward the main range.

After covering several hundred yards, Sanchez stopped and spoke to José in Spanish.

"We will watch over the herd together until it is dark. Then I will return to the hacienda and tell Señor Tex what we have found. You must remain here and keep watch over the herd until I return. We must not light a fire; cold food will have to do for now. I will return tomorrow with more men as soon as I can. We will hide our horses well and proceed on foot. Come, we will eat and then return to the herd. Señor Tex will be pleased at our success."

Sanchez and José spent the remainder of the day hidden in the woods adjacent to the meadow and grazing cattle. One would watch while the other catnapped, but nothing broke the serenity of the scene.

Dusk came, and the two returned to their campsite and horses. They ate another cold meal, which pretty much exhausted their supply of food, and Sanchez decided to sleep a few hours before returning to the MJ. Shortly after ten o'clock, José woke him, and he saddled his horse, silently shook hands with José and urged his mount forward as he began the trip back to the MJ. He rode slowly, not wishing to arrive before midnight, figuring that all but the sentries would be sound asleep by that time.

CHAPTER 5

It was late afternoon when Bo Franklin, Luke Turner, and Pete Harris arrived at the Henderson Ranch with Donie in tow. It had been a slow ride as they had had to stop several times to give Donie some rest and relief. Donie was a mess. His right eye was swollen shut tight and badly discolored. His nose was crooked, and there were splotches of dried blood on both his shirt and vest.

Henry Henderson and Kip Kelso had been discussing ranch affairs on the front veranda when the little cavalcade approached. Donie was bent over in the saddle. As the other two men dismounted Bo raised Donie up to help him out of the saddle and his face came into view.

Henry gasped and then roared, "What the hell happened?" Without waiting for an answer, he waved Luke and Pete over and said, "Help me get him into the house." Turning, he saw another ranch hand approaching and spoke to him. "Chick, fork a fresh bronc and ride like blazes to town and get Doc Conklin. It looks like Donie is hurt bad."

Chick waved and raced to the corral. He found a horse already saddled, mounted and had the horse in a full gallop as he passed the ranch house.

Henry led Pete and Luke as they assisted Donie into the house. But Kelso pulled Bo aside and asked what had happened.

Bo described the events and added, "Donie went too far ag'in. And we were dumb enough to go along with him."

Kelso thought for a moment and then looked Bo straight in the eye. "That ain't what you're goin' to tell the old man. You were mindin' your own business when four MJ riders jumped you. When Donie tried to tell them who you were, this one fellar, who Donie had words with in town yesterday, knocked him off his horse and beat him up."

"That's not how it was," protested Bo. "Donie got what he asked for."

"Now you listen to me," said Kelso coldly. "You want to work here and stay alive? You do as I tell you, or you and I are goin' to tangle. You savvy?"

Bo slowly nodded.

"Good," snapped Kelso. "Now go in there and tell the old man how it happened. And remember, I'll be listenin' to every word, so make it convincin'."

Bo entered the ranch house with Kelso at his heels. Henderson was trying to make Donie comfortable on a sofa while the two ranch hands stood off to one side. They glanced at Bo and Kelso as the two men entered the room, and Kelso motioned for them to leave. They responded immediately, anxious to get out of sight before their boss exploded.

Henry stepped back from the sofa, looked around and focused on Bo.

"All right, Bo, tell me what happened," he said with a surprisingly quiet voice.

Bo removed his hat, took a quick look at Kelso and then told the story Kelso had provided him.

"By thunder," exclaimed Henry. "Has Johnson gone loco? You say these men were in town yesterday?"

"Yes sir, that's what Donie said," answered Bo. "It looks like those four got jobs at the MJ after they left town."

"We can't let them get away with this, Mr. Henderson," broke in Kelso. "If Johnson has hired some tough guys to make trouble, and they get away with it, he'll probably hire more. We've got to put a stop to it right now." Kelso had glanced at Bo as he spoke and motioned for him to leave. Bo quickly strode to the doorway and disappeared.

Henderson paused for a moment as he continued to look at Donie with a puzzled expression on his face. "I guess you're right, Kip," he agreed, "but it's too late today. We'll wait for Doc Conklin to get here and look over Donie. Tomorrow morning you, me and a few of the boys will ride to the MJ and set Johnson straight on how we do things in these parts. If talking doesn't do any good, you'll have to convince him your way. You agree?"

Kelso smiled. "Yes sir, Mr. Henderson. Johnson has no right to push around the Double H. It's about time he found that out. I'll be ready if you need me."

Henry paced back and forth in the room, pausing frequently to look at Donie on the sofa. Donie had lapsed into a troubled sleep, punctuated by a groan now and then. Kelso remained in the room, silent and watchful.

Finally Henry stopped his pacing and looked at Kelso. "I've got to get out of here, get some fresh air and have a cigar," he announced. "Will you stay here and watch Donie while I'm gone?" he asked Kelso.

"Shore," answered Kelso. "Be glad to. Go outside and watch for the Doc. He should be along soon."

As soon as Henderson was out the front door, Kelso moved quickly to Donie's side and shook him, eliciting another groan.

"Donie, wake up," he hissed. "Can you hear me?"

Donie's one good eye opened, and he replied with a feeble "yes".

"Now, listen careful," Kelso went on. "We got a chance to make somethin' out of all this." He told Donie the story he had forced Bo to relate.

"Can you remember what I just said?" Kelso asked anxiously and received another weak "yes".

"All right," he said. "Your father and I are goin' to take a few of the boys and ride to the MJ tomorrow mornin'. If things work out right, you may be real close to havin' a ranch of your own. But you got to do what I say. Remember what I've told you when your father asks any questions. Savvy?"

Kelso received another "yes" and walked back to where he had been sitting.

Henry Henderson soon returned and began pacing again.

Henderson was a big man, heavy in the chest and shoulders. Over 60 years old now, he still carried himself well. He had a large head but was three quarters bald with a fringe of gray hair running from one ear around his head to the other ear. Jowls had replaced the firmness his face had once had, but his cold gray eyes still had a piercing look. Despite his years, his body was still hard as nails, and he could outride any man on the ranch. Resolute but stubborn, he had built a prosperous ranch and through it controlled the politics of his county.

While Donie was his pride and joy, even Henderson had to admit that the boy had not matured into the man Henry had hoped he would. Policies, procedures and processes related to the ranch operation didn't seem to stick with Donie, and Henry was forced to verbalize these principles to Donie too many times. Henry had hoped that Kelso would provide a stabilizing force for Donie, but he was beginning to feel a vague uneasiness that this wasn't working well either.

Now he had trouble with the MJ to contend with. Never happy about not getting a chance to buy the ranch, he had tolerated its presence and allowed a cool relationship to exist with its owner, Marty Johnson. Well, by damn, maybe that's all going to change, he reflected. This attack on Donie could not be tolerated.

* * * * * * * * * * * *

Doc Conklin finally arrived, shooed Henderson and Kelso out of the room and began his examination of Donie.

Kelso left Henderson on the front porch and continued on to the bunk-house, determined to get to Luke and Pete and reinforce their support of the story Bo had relayed to Henderson. He surmised that Bo had already talked to them, and he wanted to make sure no one would deviate from that tale. Their fear of Kelso and his gunplay would ensure their cooperation in this regard, he was certain.

Conklin presently stepped out of the house and joined Henry on the porch. He pulled a cigar from an inner pocket and lit it before leaning back in his chair.

"Well?" asked Henry impatiently.

"Someone sure gave Donie what for," replied Doc. "His nose is broken, I'm certain of that. I can't tell much about the eye 'cause it's still swollen. I'll be back tomorrow to check on that. He has a few bumps and bruises, mostly from the fall from his horse. Nothing serious though. I've given him a sedative, and he should sleep 'til morning. Like I said, I'll be back tomorrow afternoon to look him over again. Keep him quiet 'til then."

"Someone is shore going to pay for this," growled Henderson.

Conklin took a couple of puffs on his cigar and then looked at Henderson.

"Henry, we've been friends for a long time," he began. "I heard Donie's story, and it don't make no sense a'tall. Why would a complete stranger to these parts, only arrived yesterday, pick on Donie and beat him up without any reason?"

"I dunno," muttered Henry.

"Well, maybe you should know that Donie does not have a good reputation around town," continued Conklin. "He likes to bully people, he's obnoxious and in fact he's getting so most folks could do without him."

"I didn't know that," said Henry in surprise. "How come I haven't heard anything like that?"

"You haven't heard anything 'cause people are scared to say anything," replied Conklin. "First, he's your son, and I'm not sure you would hear it or believe it even if someone did tell you. Secondly, and maybe more importantly, he's usually with Kelso, and everyone is afraid of Kelso. You should know that. That's why you hired him," added Doc dryly.

Henderson remained silent, so Conklin continued.

"Kelso wasn't with Donie today," he pointed out, "and maybe Donie flew off the handle with this rider and got knocked around because of it."

"But there were three of my men there, too," exploded Henry angrily. "They wouldn't have stood around and let this happen."

"But Donie said there were four MJ riders involved," Doc reminded Henry. "Maybe your boys didn't have any choice in the matter. A week or so ago a bunch of your men beat up three MJ men in town. You weren't upset about that, and Donie was in the middle of that scrape, too. Maybe it was pay back time."

Henry thought for a moment and then spoke. "I don't like your words, Doc. Donie may be a little hard to handle, but he didn't do nothing that would call for this. I'm going to the MJ tomorrow morning and straighten it all out. I'll have some answers by the time you get here tomorrow."

"I knew you wouldn't listen to me," sighed Doc wearily. He rose from his chair, left the porch and approached his buggy. Henry followed him down the steps. Conklin paused before stepping up into the rig and turned to Henderson. "Think about what I said, Henry. You've got to put some tight reins on Donie. Try listening when you get to the MJ tomorrow. You might learn something useful."

Conklin pulled himself up into his rig, settled in his seat, waved and started his horse in motion. "See you tomorrow, Henry," he called over his shoulder.

Henderson watched Conklin depart. He turned and reentered the house, still disturbed at Doc's words. Yet he knew there was an element of truth in what the doctor had said, and the uneasy thoughts he had had earlier returned with renewed vigor. He shook his head and moved toward the stairs and his second story bedroom. He stopped, looked over at the sleeping Donie, again shook his head and continued his slow journey up the stairs.

* * * * * * * * * * * *

It was early evening when Lefty, Blackie and Kansas arrived at the MJ. All the other line riders had returned earlier. Within a few minutes all the other outriders and Red's outpost crew rode in as a group, minus Sanchez and one other Mexican.

Tex nodded his approval. Sanchez had anticipated a problem and had arranged for the outriders to meet at the outpost before coming in to the ranch.

French, too, watched the cavalcade arrive but was too tired, stiff and sore to note the shortage of two riders. That devil, Evans, had pushed the work hard all day and seemed to take particular delight in handing Art the hardest and dirtiest aspects of every task they attempted. Moreover, Bronc had seen fit to criticize the quality of much of Art's efforts. French almost challenged him a couple of times, but the glint in Bronc's eyes and the expression on his face instinctively told French that this wasn't the time nor the place to raise the issue. He failed to see the disappointment in Bronc's expression when he didn't rise to the bait.

Lefty, Blackie and Kansas met with Tex and Marty in the main room of the ranch house and described their altercation with Donie Henderson and the Double H punchers. None of the other line riders had run into trouble that day, Tex informed them.

Mary Johnson insisted on Lefty removing his shirt so she could put some salve on his cuts.

"You were lucky he didn't get to your face or eyes, Lefty," she observed.

"No," disagreed Lefty, "that brat is the lucky one. If'n he had done that, he'd have a lot more to worry about than just a busted face. I'm shore lookin' forward to tanglin' with him ag'in."

Tex laughed, although he, too, was relieved that Lefty had been spared any serious injuries.

"From what you have told me, I don't think he'll be sittin' a saddle for a day or two. And I'll bet my last dollar he doesn't go anywhere near that section of his range when he can ride again. Tomorrow, though, I think you, Blackie and Kansas should ride together and be prepared for anythin'. Stop any trouble before it starts."

Mary held up Lefty's shirt. "I'll try to mend it," she sighed ruefully, "but I'm not sure it will do much good. I hope you have another shirt in your saddle bags."

"Of course," Lefty grinned. "Do what you can with it, and mebby I can use it as a spare. Or I can use it as a cloth for cleanin' my gun," he commented as his eyes flashed.

"Well, I'll let you men talk," Mary said as she took the shirt and left the room.

"Not much more to talk about," observed Tex. "We play the same game tomorrow as we did today and have the boys get more familiar with the ranch. I'm hopin' Sanchez and José may come up with somethin' soon. Already I'm getting anxious about how things are goin' on the Rambling R."

"Oh, you are a worrywart," shrugged Lefty. "Nothin' is going wrong down there. And if'n there is, we can shore straighten it out as soon as we get back. I think this whole range needs a good cleanin' up, and we're just the ones to do it. Besides, I'm startin' to like it around here."

"You always did like trouble," countered Blackie. "If'n me, Kansas and Charley hadn't been nursemaids to you many a time, you would have been long ago dead."

"Nursemaid to me!" sniffed Lefty. "My God, look who's talkin'. Come on, let's get out of here. I've got to find me a shirt!"

The three left the room, and the verbal accusations and counter accusations drifted back to the house as they looked for Lefty's saddle bags.

"They're quite a foursome," stated Marty with a grin.

Tex nodded. "We call them The Quartet; and I can't think of four fellars I'd rather ride with. They're fightin' fools, and I'm shore glad they're on our side. Young Henderson has no idea who he's riled. If'n he did, he wouldn't sleep at all tonight."

Tex strolled outside and reached for tobacco and paper. Lighting his cigarette, he noticed Bronc and Trig sitting on a porch rail a little ways to his left. He walked over to join them.

"I see you kept French busy today," he said, looking at Bronc.

"Yeah," drawled Evans, "and he didn't like it a little bit. Thought he might take a swing at me a couple of times. Too bad he didn't have the nerve."

"Don't push things too hard," Tex cautioned. "I might have need of him, and I want him in one piece. Trig, tomorrow you keep Mr. French busy. Bronc, you didn't get much sleep last night. I'll have one of the boys cover your night shift."

Bronc started to protest.

"No," said Tex firmly. "You and Apache sleep in. I want you fresh and wide awake if'n I need you for anythin'. You and Apache sleep in the main house tonight. We have a couple of spare couches since Sanchez and José aren't here."

Bronc saw that Tex was both serious and firm, so he nodded and went searching for his bedroll.

A full moon shown brightly, and the sky was full of stars. It was a peaceful ending to a busy day on the MJ Ranch.

CHAPTER 6

The next morning found Donie much improved. He was still sore, but the swelling in the right eye had gone down some, and he could see a little bit with it. Nevertheless, after breakfast Henry told Donie to stay put until Doc Conklin could look him over again.

Henry strapped on his Colt and walked out on the front porch. His favorite horse was saddled and waiting for him, along with four riders.

Kelso had selected Bo Franklin to ride along, together with two other Double H hands, Jeff Holmes and Cole Southern. He had deliberately excluded Luke Turner and Pete Harris, figuring he could keep one man in line a lot easier than three.

Henry pulled himself into the saddle and with a wave of his arm led his little troop in the direction of the MJ. Kelso rode at his side.

* * * * * * * * * * * *

The morning activities at the MJ were a duplication of the previous day. The pairings of line riders remained the same, and the large group of men left the ranch in a body before the line riders had finished breakfast.

It was almost mid-morning, and Marty and Tex were discussing general ranch activities and strategy when Dusty Rhodes dashed in.

"We got a signal from Reb just a minute ago," he said. "We're gettin' visitors, five in all."

Tex and Marty rose from their chairs, and Tex gave his orders quickly.

"Dusty, you and Cavalry go get French and take him to the bunkhouse, tie him up and gag him. I don't want a peep out of him. If'n he objects, put him to sleep and don't be gentle about it. Then cover us from the bunk-house. Send Trig to me pronto."

Dusty turned and was gone.

"Marty," Tex continued, "wake up Bronc and Apache. Tell Apache to stay out of sight. Tell Bronc to join me at the front door."

Tex reached the front of the house just as Trig entered. Bronc and Marty joined him a minute later.

"Marty, go out on the porch in front of the door and tell me if you recognize any of 'em," ordered Tex.

Tex heard a movement behind and turned to see Mary coming out of the kitchen.

"Bronc, take Mary to where Apache is," snapped Tex, "and tell her to stay there until either Marty or I come for her."

"It's Henry Henderson," interrupted Marty from the porch, "and Kelso is with him."

"Who's Kelso?" asked Tex.

"Henderson's resident gunslinger and Donie's friend," replied Marty, still watching the riders as they drew near.

"Step out and greet them," said Tex, "and get me involved as soon as you can. Trig, you and Bronc cover me when I go out."

Both Trig and Bronc, who had returned, nodded.

Henderson, with Kelso on his left and the other three men behind him, reached the tie rail in front of the porch and pulled up.

Marty stepped to the edge of the porch and raised his hand in a greeting.

"Good morning, Henry," he said. "It's a nice day for a ride."

Henderson scowled and ignored the greeting.

"I'll get right to the point, Johnson," he thundered. "This ain't a social call. There was a problem at our boundary lines yesterday, and one of your riders beat up my son and without provocation, too. Donie was hurt bad, and I mean to find out why and then do something about it!"

"Your son got what he deserved, Henderson," replied Marty. "And there was provocation. However, my foreman gives the riding orders around here, and I'll let you talk to him about it."

Tex stepped out of the doorway and moved to Marty's right, placing himself on Henderson's left and directly in front of Kelso.

Henderson drew back in surprise with his mouth open.

"Who's this guy?" he asked. "And where is Art French?"

"The name is Riley," drawled Tex. "I'm the new foreman here. French is tied up on other matters," Tex continued, smiling inwardly at the joke. "What's your problem, Henderson?"

Henderson regained control of himself and told the story of the incident as it had been presented to him.

"That's a purty accurate story," agreed Tex, "except'n for the fact it's just the reverse of what really happened.

"One of my riders found a herd of your beef about a mile inside MJ range. He rounded 'em up and was drivin' 'em back when your son and three Double H punchers came up on him. He was ready to turn the beef over to your riders when Donie threw down on him. While your riders covered him, Donie tried to cut him to pieces with his quirt. Two of my men happened to be nearby, heard the fracas and put a stop to it. Lefty yanked Donie off his horse and gave him a good thrashin'. Just what he deserved, too."

While this exchange was going on, Kelso was regaining his senses. He had been dumbfounded when Tex appeared and announced he was the new foreman. Where was French? If he had been fired, why hadn't he shown up at the Henderson Ranch? Where were the other MJ men, and why didn't one of them get to him if French couldn't? Something was very wrong here. He, Kelso, had come here today to do a job on Johnson, but it was obvious this new meddler had to be taken care of first.

"Just what he deserved, too!" Riley had said.

Kelso plunged into the discussion.

"A likely cock and bull story, Mr. Henderson," he said, his voice rising. "All three of our riders said the same thing."

"Then you got three liars on your payroll," observed Tex calmly, his eyes on Kelso.

"Liars!" exclaimed Kelso, finding the excuse he needed. "Liars, huh! I've got a good mind to show you what happens when you cause trouble in Henderson country!"

"This ain't a shootin' affair, Henderson," warned Tex, "less'n you want it to be one. Tell your man to back off."

"I knew it," cried Kelso exultingly. "He's yellar. First they beat up Donie, then give us a cock and bull story to cover it up and then call us liars!"

Kelso stepped off his horse and moved away to give himself elbow room while still facing Tex.

"Hold it!" came a voice from the other side of the group. Bronc had spoken as both he and Trig had moved down the porch steps and onto level ground. Both men were in a slight crouch with their hands only an inch or so away from their guns.

"I don't like five-to-one odds," Bronc went on. "This looks like a set play to me with one of you fellars figgerin' on cuttin' in from the side. That ain't goin' to happen, and to make shore it don't happen, I want each of you to raise your hands and put them on your hats."

"Now see here . . . ," Henderson began as he turned in the saddle.

Bronc's right hand moved, and there was a roar at his hip. Henderson's big Stetson flew in the air and landed several yards away, a round hole in its crown.

"That was a warnin'," Bronc snarled. "Get those hands up, pronto!"

Henderson slowly raised his hands, an astonished look on his face. The other three riders followed suit.

Bronc smiled grimly. "All right, Tex," he announced. "No one is goin' to interfere. Big Mouth is all yourn."

Kelso had been surprised again at the interruption and the shot that was fired. He couldn't see who was talking or where he was because of the horses. By the same token, he reasoned, he or they couldn't see him nor could they stop him from his appointed task. This meddler had to be eliminated.

"You beat up Donie, dream up a phony story and call three men liars," he repeated.

"You must have made your reputation talkin' people to death," observed Tex calmly, knowing full well what would result from his statement.

Kelso's eyes widened and his hand went for his gun.

But Tex's hand was moving, too, and the report from his right hand gun was just reaching Kelso's ears when the bullet slammed into him. The force of the slug drove him back two quick steps, and he fell like a stone, flat on his back.

Bo Franklin quickly dismounted and checked the prone man for any vital signs. He looked up at Henderson and slowly shook his head sideways.

Bo again glanced down at Kelso, in amazement. He gulped and turned toward Tex, who had carefully dropped his deadly messenger back into its holster.

Bo finally found his voice. "Holy cow," he exclaimed. "Kelso barely got his gun out of his holster. And he was the fastest gun in these parts!" He continued to look at Tex in awe.

"Yeah, he was a mite slow," observed Tex dryly. Tex turned to Henderson, who also was shocked into silence as he looked at the body of his gunman. "I told you this weren't a shootin' affair, Henderson, but it looks like that's what you wanted. It got one man killed. I hope you're satisfied. Now you listen careful 'cause I'm goin' to tell you somethin' just once.

"The MJ is here to stay. Henderson law is now plumb out of style. The same law applies to everyone. The MJ ain't lookin' for a fight. There is no reason these two ranches can't get along fine, but if you force us to fight, fight we will. And if necessary, we will kill, just like today. And you other men take note of it. Tell your friends in the bunkhouse, 'don't make trouble for the MJ!'"

He turned back to Henderson.

"What I told you about yesterday is the truth. If'n you want to wait, I'll send for Lefty, and he can show you the cuts he got from your son's quirt. Your son is plumb lucky he didn't catch Lefty in the face, 'cause if'n he had, he'd more than likely be dead today."

Henderson had listened silently, still in a state of shock. Finally he shook his head, as if to clear it, and turned in his saddle.

"Bo," he said, "you were there yesterday. Is this man telling the truth?"

Bo looked down, wet his lips, glanced at Kelso's body and looked at Henderson.

"I'm sorry, Mr. Henderson," Bo murmured. "He's givin' you the straight of it. Kelso said he would kill me if I didn't tell you the story I did. He told Luke and Pete the same thing. I'm sorry, Mr. Henderson, but Luke, Pete and me, we're not gunmen, just ranch hands. You don't know what it is to be afraid of someone like Kelso." Bo stopped and hung his head.

Tex broke the ensuing silence by walking over and picking up Henderson's hat and handed it to him.

"I'm afraid it might be plumb ruined," he said. "Bronc always was a bit hasty. Of course, he might have aimed a few inches lower. Maybe the Henderson family has been lucky two days in a row," Tex added, wearing his poker face.

Henderson accepted the hat, looked at the hole in the crown, glanced at both Tex and Marty and finally slammed the hat on his head.

Tex continued, "You think on what I said. There is no reason we can't have two good ranches on this range. You think about it."

Henderson nodded slowly and then recovered a little energy. He faced his men and pointed, "Jeff, you and Cole pack Kelso on his horse. Bo, you ride with me. It's time we headed back to the ranch. He spurred his horse and pulled it around to head back up the trail, Bo following him. Jeff and Cole soon followed, leading Kelso's horse and the blanket-covered body slung over the saddle.

Marty, Tex, Bronc and Trig watched the group depart.

"Trig, you can release French now. Get him back to work. Marty, you'd better get to Mary. Those shots may have scared her. Bronc, you and Apache better get some breakfast." With these words, Tex paused to reload the spent chamber in his Colt and returned the gun to its resting place.

Tex had just reached the porch when Mary came out the front door. She hugged Tex and exclaimed, "I was so afraid for you. That man was really looking for a fight, wasn't he?"

Tex returned the hug and looked into her eyes. "I suppose so, Mary, but it's all over now. I 'speck Mr. Henderson has had quite a jolt today. Maybe it'll do him some good. We'll just have to wait and see." Tex turned and gently directed her toward Marty.

Marty nodded and took Mary's hand to lead her back into the ranch house. Suddenly she stopped and turned to Tex.

"Oh, Tex, I almost forgot what I wanted to see you about," she said. "We are running very low on food supplies. We can butcher some cows for meat, but we need lots of other fixings to go along with it."

"Yes," Tex agreed. "I thought it was about time we had that problem. Make a list, and I'll have some of the boys go to town tomorrow."

* * * * * * * * * * * *

The ride back to the Henderson Ranch was slow and, for the most part, in silence. Henry appeared to be in deep thought most of the time. Bo tried to interrupt once with another apology, but Henry waved him off.

Eventually, Henry did turn to Bo and spoke softly. "It's okay, Bo, I understand why you did it. Maybe I've created a devil here without knowing it. I just don't know. What do the other hands think of Donie, anyway?"

Bo hesitated and looked embarrassed. "Really, sir, I don't think I should say anythin'. I can't speak for the other men."

"Come, come," snorted Henry. "Surely you have an opinion. Speak up, man. Tell me the truth."

Again Bo hesitated. "Please, sir," he said softly. "He is *your* son, and I don't feel right in sayin' anythin'. I've already caused too much trouble today."

"Nonsense," snorted Henry again. "But I won't ask you a second time. Maybe what you ain't saying is more important anyhow."

As they approached the ranch, Henry turned in his saddle and spoke to Jeff and Cole behind him. "Find a couple of shovels and bury Kip in that grassy area behind the ranch house. I don't know of any kinfolk, so that will have to do."

"Bo, you've had a hard day. Take the rest of the day off and tell the rest of the men what happened as they come in. I'll be in the house with Donie."

Henry dismounted at the tie rail, noting that Doc Conklin's rig was parked nearby. Wearily he climbed the porch steps and entered the house.

Two faces turned toward him as he entered the room, undid his gun belt and hung it over a chair.

"How's Donie today, Doc?" he asked as he approached the sofa.

"Well, did you straighten them out at the MJ?" growled Donie eagerly before Conklin could answer.

"No," answered Henry, looking at Donie.

"What do you mean, no?" asked Donie pugnaciously. "Didn't you and Kip settle things with Johnson?"

"Kip's dead," Henry replied.

"What?" Donie's and Conklin's voices were in unison.

"Kip's dead," repeated Henry. "He started a fight at the MJ, and Johnson's foreman killed him."

"Art . . . French . . . killed . . . Kelso . . . !" gasped Donie, unable to believe his ears.

"No, Art French didn't kill Kelso," replied Henry. "Johnson's got himself a new foreman. A fellar named Riley. He killed Kelso. Kip never got his gun all the way out of his holster neither."

"You mean Johnson's hired himself a gunslinger!" gasped Donie again.

Henry rubbed his forehead.

"I don't know, Donie, but the man was shore fast with a gun. Fastest I've ever seen. But there's something about him that I liked. He didn't take any guff from me or Kip, none a'tall."

"A gunman," exploded Donie. "I never figured on Johnson doing something like that!"

"Maybe he decided to fight fire with fire," interjected Doc, trying desperately to keep a smile from spreading across his face. "You've been having your own way for a long time, Henry, what with Kelso around and all. Perhaps those times are coming to an end."

"Shut up, Doc," replied Henry crossly. "You've already told me what you think. I don't need to hear it ag'in. How's Donie doing, anyhow?"

"The patient is much better, thank you," answered Doc sweetly. "The swelling in the eye has gone down, and I don't believe there'll be any damage there. The nose will get better but won't be as straight as before. In other words, I think he'll live."

"Sometimes you get too smart for your own good," growled Henry. "Now go back to town and send me your bill. I want to talk to Donie."

Conklin picked up his bag, found his hat and left the ranch house, the smile finally erupting as he moved to his rig. It just might be that things are going to get much better around Ridgeway, he thought. Kelso's death was going to be an excellent start in that direction. Wonder who this Riley fellow was, he mused, and what Marty Johnson was up to at the MJ. It was going to be a lovely ride back to town.

Henry approached Donie, pulled up a chair and sat down facing his son. "Tell me ag'in what happened yesterday," he said evenly. "I want to get the whole of it."

Donie looked at his father closely, but found only a bland face that disclosed nothing. He began the narrative as Kelso had told him to say and, half way through the story, his father's hand flashed out and slapped him in the face with a loud whack. His head snapped back, and he raised his hand to his stinging left cheek in astonishment.

"You lie!" thundered Henry. "That weren't the way it was at all. In fact, it was just the other way around, weren't it?" he asked, peering intently at Donie.

Donie shrank back, fear in his eyes. The slap had surprised him more than hurt him, but the look on his father's face was more than he could stomach.

"I d — don't know wh — what you mean," he stammered.

"Four to one you were ag'in him and him on his land," thundered Henry again. "And he was doing what he should be doing, riding line the way it should be done. Don't you know nothing about ranching? And then trying to use your quirt on him! Ain't you got no guts at all? You're damn lucky, only you don't know it. If someone had tried that on me, I'd a killed him!"

Donie was speechless at the outburst.

"You'd better spend less time buying fancy duds," Henry continued, "and more time learning how to run a ranch. And you'd better control that temper of yourn 'cause Kelso ain't going to be around to protect you none."

Henry leaned down at Donie with a hard look on his face. "And don't you ever lie to me ag'in. If you do, I'll whip you worse than that MJ rider ever thought of doing. You understand, boy!"

All Donie could do was nod slowly. He had never seen his father like this. What had his world come to? Kelso was dead, his protector gone. The Double H ranch hands hated him, he knew, but had feared Kelso more. Now, Kelso was gone. What was he to do? He really had to think hard on this one. He closed his eyes, settled back and had some very troubled thoughts.

Henry rose from his chair, looked down at his son, snorted in disgust and left the room.

CHAPTER 7

Bright sunshine and a cloudless sky announced the arrival of a new day at the MJ Ranch, and the early morning activities of the previous days were repeated. The line riders had reported no unusual activities or problems during the previous days, and Tex, therefore, felt it was a good time to make some significant changes in the disposition of his forces.

Red, Rusty and Curley were told to stay put at the ranch as Tex had a special job for them. Only Charley and Reb would man the signal outpost. Instead of riding shotgun, Denver and Cheyenne would now ride the northwest range with Adams, and Laredo and Reno were to cover the west section with Charles. Lefty, Blackie and Kansas would again patrol the northeast section as a group, while Felipé was again paired with Cook. However, the shotgun procedures involving this latter twosome had been materially altered.

At about midnight the previous night, Sanchez had arrived after his slow ride. He found the sentinels and quietly walked his horse to the ranch house. He slipped into the house, located Tex and woke him.

He reported that he and José had located the herd of mavericks and the probable drive trail. It hadn't been too hard, which was a good indication that Cook, and probably French too, were in on the rustling. The gang had had little to fear if all the punchers loyal to Marty were gone or assigned other ranges to patrol. Sanchez had left José to keep an eye on the herd while he returned to the ranch for instructions and reinforcements.

On his way to the ranch Sanchez worked out a plan that he presented to Tex. Tex immediately objected, saying it was too dangerous for Felipé. But Sanchez was not to be denied. He pointed out that he, too, had a debt to pay to Slim, that his men wanted to do their share as far as risk taking was concerned and that they were eager for action. He further pointed out that only Tex's men had been engaged in any altercations so far and it was time his men got involved.

Tex saw that Sanchez was deadly serious. He finally threw up his hands and reluctantly agreed. A pleased Sanchez sought out Juan, Federico, Luis and Felipé, woke them and gave them their instructions in Spanish. Sanchez then slept for a few hours but slipped out of the house again just before dawn.

It was a small group of men that first departed the ranch that morning. It consisted of Charley and Reb for the outpost duty as well as Juan, Federico and Luis. The group found Sanchez waiting for them at the outpost, and he, Federico, Luis and Juan immediately headed southwest at a fast pace.

A half hour or so after the first group left the ranch, the line riders saddled their horses and were soon on their way.

Red, Rusty and Curley were lounging outside the bunkhouse when Tex caught up with them.

"Red," he said, "hitch up the ranch wagon and take it into town. Here is a list of supplies we need, and here is money to cover it," he continued, handing over a wad of bills. He went on, "Find out if Marty has any unpaid bills at the store and pay them, too."

He turned to Rusty and Curley. "You two follow Red into town. Stay back of him, but keep him in your sight. Slip into town and make shore he stays out of trouble. That town seems to be right unfriendly to the MJ, and I want to be ready for anythin'."

The three punchers grinned, and the trio moved toward the corral to find horses for themselves and the wagon.

French again watched the activity, but now he had much more on his mind. Kelso's death had stunned him. He had been impressed with Kip's natural skill with a Colt, but Riley had beaten him in the draw so easily, it was beyond belief. Without a doubt Riley was a top gunman, and French was thankful he had not yielded to certain temptations he had felt regarding taking on Mr. Riley.

French had other disturbing thoughts as well. He was aware that today's ride would take Cook and Felipé very close to the hidden herd of mavericks. He had had a whispered conversation with Cook the night before but could not come up with a definite plan of action. Kelso's death had removed a large portion of the thinking apparatus from the gang, and that, combined with Donie's incapacitation, had left them with no one to fill the void. At least not at the moment.

In addition, French was finding that his ability to think clearly was now becoming very difficult. Trig Mansfield had turned out to be just as much a devil as Bronc Evans. Trig had worked him unceasingly the whole day, and French was exhausted. These had been two of the hardest days of his life. And even worse, he felt a prickling on the back of his neck like there was a pair of eyes on him at all times. He had glanced around a number of times and saw nothing, but the feeling remained. It was very nerve-racking and bothered him to no end.

* * * * * * * * * * *

It also had been a nerve-racking night on the Double H for Donie Henderson. Although he now slept in his own bed, and not the sofa, sleep had not been that easy to come by. He had tossed and turned all night, and when he was awake one plan after another had come and gone. Finally, at daybreak, he could sleep no longer. And he concentrated his thoughts on what should be done next.

He had been a close companion of Kip Kelso over the past several years, and they had had many discussions together, especially after Donie had become involved in the rustling scheme that Kelso had presented to him. It was not surprising, therefore, that Donie's thoughts, like Kelso's, eventually centered on the presence of, and the interference created by, the new foreman of the MJ. Donie's thoughts continually returned to this theme and obsessed him. Something had to be done about this one man, and then everything would fall into place, Donie convinced himself.

Donie rose, dressed with some difficulty and swore at his soreness. He went to a small desk in his room, opened the bottom drawer, fished through a multitude of odds and ends and located what he was after, a checkbook. This book represented an account located in a bank in Canyon City that had no connection with the bank in Ridgeway. Further, the balance shown therein was, for the most part, his proceeds from the sale of the cattle shipped out of Harding. He paused, found ink and a pen and wrote out a check.

Much to his relief, Donie found that his father had already eaten breakfast and had departed the ranch house. The housekeeper served Donie and he ate his food leisurely, his thoughts still on his problems. Breakfast finished, he strolled out the front door and looked around the yard. Chick Snyder, the rider who had fetched Doc Conklin for him, was combing a horse near the corral. Nodding in satisfaction, Donie approached the man, and they exchanged greetings. After some small talk, Donie got around to the problem at hand.

"Chick," he said, "I've got a job for you. I want you to ride up to Canyon City and find a fellar there for me. His name is Ed Smiley, and he hangs around the Palace Saloon, at least he did when I was there last, about 10 days ago. Tell him I have a job for him that's worth a $ 1,000 to me; $ 500 now and $ 500 when it's done. If he says he's interested, take this check to the bank, use it to get the cash and give him the $ 500. Then bring him to Ridgeway and report back to me. Tell him I will meet with him as soon as I can get to town. Any questions?"

Chick looked at the check and then at Donie. Casually he asked, "Does your father know about this?"

Anger immediately crept into Donie's voice. "It's none of your business whether he does or not," snapped Donie. "You're paid to do what you're told. Now do it."

Chick shrugged his shoulders, turned on his heel and mounted his horse. Without a look back, he rode out of the yard, Donie's eyes following him all the way.

Donie finally ambled back to the house, his thought processes still working overtime.

* * * * * * * * * * * *

Red Rollins' journey to Ridgeway was slow but uneventful. Several times he glanced back over his shoulder, whenever the opportunity presented itself, and he could see Rusty and Curley well in his rear. Reaching town, he continued down the main street until he came to the general store. He pulled the wagon alongside the tie rail, set the brake, jumped down on the wooden sidewalk and entered the store, list in hand.

Deuce Lawson, Milt Haines and Joe Gilmore, three Double H riders, had ridden into Ridgeway from the opposite direction. They had spent the previous six days at a distant line camp of the Henderson Ranch, inspecting and repairing fences as needed. They had been participants in the week-ago altercation with the MJ punchers and had earned the praise and gratitude of one Donie Henderson. While they didn't have much use for Donie Henderson, praise from, and gratitude expressed by, the son of the owner was not to be taken lightly. They had been very pleased with themselves.

They had just been in the process of pulling into the tie rail in front of the Sweetwater Saloon when Red had driven by in the wagon.

Deuce turned in his saddle and looked at the wagon as the horses stopped at the tie rail.

"Hey, guys," he asked, "ain't that the MJ wagon that just went by?"

The other two riders took a long look as Red stopped the wagon in front of the general store.

"It's shore got an MJ painted on its side," observed Joe. "What about it?"

"I never saw the driver afore," replied Deuce. "Do you suppose Johnson has hired himself a new puncher? Maybe the warnin' he got last week ain't sunk in yet. I wonder if Donie knows this?"

The three men dismounted, and Deuce continued to stare as Red came out of the store with a bag over his shoulder. He dumped the bag in the back of the wagon and reentered the store.

"I wonder if Donie knows this," repeated Deuce with a funny look on his face. "Hey, fellars, maybe Donie don't know the MJ has a new rider. Maybe we should give him a Henderson welcome like we done last week. C'mon, let's have a little fun."

Deuce started to cross the street, Milt and Joe following close behind.

"I don't know," began Milt, but Deuce waved him off.

"We've been a hull week out in the sticks," he commented, "and we're due for a little fun and excitement. You guys follow my lead."

Red had deposited a second bag of supplies in the wagon and was back in the store getting a third load.

Deuce moved up two steps to the sidewalk and leaned against a support. The other two men positioned themselves together at the back of the wagon.

Red again came out of the store, a heavy sack of potatoes slung over his shoulders. Just as he began his short trip down the steps, Deuce stuck out his foot and tripped him.

Red and his bag of potatoes went sailing, the bag in one direction and Red in another, sprawling in the dust of the street.

Red rolled over, spit dust and looked around. The three Double H punchers were laughing, and Deuce was doubled over with delight.

"The MJ shore hires clumsy oxes," Deuce chortled. And he lost himself again in laughter.

Red sat up. "What for you do that?" he asked plaintively, although his eyes were flashing.

Deuce stopped laughing and moved down the steps.

"What for?" he asked. "I'll tell you what for. This is Henderson country, and we don't like the MJ. You'd be smart if you moved on and found a job elsewhere!"

While Deuce was speaking, Red had gotten to his feet and had taken two slow steps toward his bag of potatoes. He gripped both ends of the top of the bag, turned and suddenly with all his might slung the bag at the two Double H men a few feet away, and then he leaped at Deuce.

Red's aim had been good, and while Milt took the full brunt of the bag, he was pushed into Joe and both went down as their hats went flying. They shoved the bag away from themselves, rose to their feet and stepped back into the street to allow more room for Deuce and Red, who were rolling around in the dust, locked in each other's arms.

Milt had stepped back the farthest. He heard a voice behind him saying, "Hey you!"

Milt turned and promptly saw stars as Curley's gun barrel came crashing down on his forehead and nose. He slumped to the ground with blood spurting from his nose.

Joe was engrossed with the wrestling match between Deuce and Red and didn't hear the footsteps behind him.

Rusty's gun barrel came down on the back of his head, and he, too, crumpled to the street.

Red and Deuce had struggled to their feet. Red landed a good punch and drove Deuce back a step or two. Curley's arm rose again, and his gun barrel crashed against Deuce's bare head. Deuce fell forward, and the street received its third heap of humanity.

"Why'd you not let me finish my fight?" exclaimed Red angrily.

"Your job's to git supplies and not git into trouble," observed Curley dryly, "even if it ain't your fault. Rusty, help Red with the rest of the supplies, while I take care of these jaspers."

As Rusty hugged and pushed a reluctant Red back into the store, Curley strode to each of the three Double H riders. In turn, he yanked their guns from their holsters, unloaded the cartridges into the dust of the street, dropped the guns into a nearby watering trough and then dragged each unconscious man away from the street and deposited him alongside the trough. Sweating from his exertions, he pushed his hat back on his head and reached for tobacco and papers, a satisfied look on his face.

Several more trips by Red and Rusty had completed the loading of the wagon, when Sheriff Hamilton pushed his way through the crowd that had gathered. He was followed by one of his deputies.

"Who are you boys?" Hamilton demanded, "And what's goin' on here?"

Curley looked at the speaker, noted the star on his vest and blew a cloud of smoke.

"We're new punchers at the MJ," he answered calmly with arms across his chest. "We come here for ranch supplies, and these three rannies jumped Red and started a fight. We finished it," he added with a grin.

"New riders at the MJ?" asked Hamilton, his eyebrows rising. "How many new riders you got out there anyhow?" he continued.

"Don't rightly know," answered Curley. "We just signed on today and ain't met the rest of the crew. Mr. Johnson just sent us to town for supplies."

"Didn't French hire you?" asked Hamilton incredulously.

"Don't know about any French fellar," replied Curley. "We only met Mr. Johnson." Red and Rusty remained silent but nodded in agreement.

Groans were beginning to emanate from the sprawled punchers, and Doc Conklin, who had also arrived, bent down and began to examine the three men.

After a brief inspection of each man, he looked up at Hamilton and pointed to the other side of the street. "I was sitting over there and saw the whole thing, Ben. It was as this man said. Deuce and his boys started the fight, and these boys finished it. You got no reason to hold them for anything. Let them go back to the MJ."

As Hamilton silently considered this suggestion, Conklin bent down again and observed, "Broken noses are starting to be an epidemic out at the Double H. A couple of you guys help me get Milt over to my office, where I can work on him. Deuce and Joe should be okay, excepting for a couple of giant headaches. Let them rest for a spell."

Conklin looked up at Hamilton and asked, "Well, Ben?"

"Oh, all right," sighed Hamilton. "Reckon there's been no real harm done. You boys can go back to the MJ. It sure must be gettin' crowded out there though," he added as he examined the bland faces of Curley, Red and Rusty.

Curley threw away the remains of his cigarette.

"Don't know about that," he commented. "C'mon boys, let's head back to the ranch."

Rusty and Curley located their horses as Red climbed up into the wagon seat. The little caravan rolled out of town, each man with a grin on his face.

* * * * * * * * * * * *

Cook and Felipé had spent another quiet day in each other's company. Cook had given up trying to make conversation with Felipé and spent the riding time in silence or in muttering to himself. Felipé had smiled inwardly at the growing frustration in Cook's voice. But he also knew that there were other things on Cook's mind that had contributed to his agitation. As they rode south, they again used the bank of the stream as their left guide.

They stopped at noon, ate their lunch and rested their horses before swinging southwest to check the rest of that boundary line. Finally they turned north again and began the journey back to the ranch.

About mid-afternoon Felipé suddenly pulled up, began talking excitedly in Spanish and pointed to his left. Cook pulled his horse to a stop, too, looked to where Felipé was pointing and swore under his breath. There, beyond a shallow ridge covered with scrub pine trees, was a wisp of smoke. Cook knew what it meant. Dan and Salty had arrived from the Double H and had begun branding operations, pending the arrival of other members of the gang. They had assumed, of course, that the only other punchers in the area would be Cook or another member of their group.

Felipé spurred his horse in the direction of the smoke, and Cook followed quickly.

Felipé was exulting as he rode toward the smoke. The most dangerous part of the plan was for him to find a plausible excuse to leave the normal patroling and "stumble" on the concealed herd. His surprise, therefore, had not been faked. Now a logical reason had been dropped right into his lap and one that no range rider could possibly ignore.

As he reached the ridge of trees, Felipé slowed down and proceeded cautiously. Cook had caught up with him, and he, too, slowed to a walk and was just to Felipé's right and slightly behind him.

Carefully, the two riders reached the top of the ridge and began the slight descent, still pretty well concealed among the scrub pines.

Reaching the edge of the pines, Felipé leaned forward in his saddle, slowly pushed aside the last of the pine branches and peered out.

It was a long, narrow meadow, rich in grass with a small stream running north and south at the far end. Cattle were grazing contentedly in a variety of locations on the meadow. Off to his right, about 50 yards away, was the source of the smoke, a small fire. Two men were busily engaged in branding a roped and tied calf.

Felipé relaxed in his saddle and sat back down, releasing the branches as he did so. He had no sooner settled in his saddle when he felt a cold steel barrel pressed against his ribs.

"Enjoy what you saw, greaser?" growled Cook, his face red with anger. "Seen too much, you did," he went on, "and you're goin' to pay for it. I'll just relieve you of that hog leg. Then you'll have to meet the boys."

Felipé felt his gun leave its holster. Cook motioned for him to ride on, and he guided his horse through the last barrier of branches with Cook right behind.

The two men had finished their task, released the calf and stood up. The movement of the two riders caught their eye, but generated no reaction until Felipé's big sombrero registered with them.

"What the hell?" one sputtered as both of them reached for their guns.

"It's okay boys," Cook yelled. "I've got him covered."

The two men dropped their guns back into their holsters and waited silently as the two horsemen approached them, surprise still on their faces.

Cook and Felipé pulled up, and Cook motioned for Felipé to dismount.

"Salty," Cook said, "keep a gun on him while I dismount. Dan, search him careful-like. Look for a knife. Greasers always have at least one."

Cook dismounted as the search began. A knife was found, strapped to Felipé's right leg inside his pants. Cook tied his hands and motioned for him to sit by the fire.

"What's goin' on, Cook?" asked Salty Spencer. "And where did this Mex' come from?"

"He and a whole bunch of fellars showed up at the ranch three days ago, over 20 in all, including more Mexicans," replied Cook. "Don't know where they come from, but they've shore been raisin' hell since they got here. They've been ridin' all over MJ range lookin' for unbranded cattle and anythin' else they can find. I'm some surprised you two didn't run into any of 'em."

"We came late yesterday," explained Dan Sims. "We've been away from the ranch for two days. Kip told us to spend a day or so fence ridin' our western boundary and then swing down here and do some branding before going back to the ranch. Said he would cover for us."

"Kelso's dead," deadpanned Cook.

"What!", came from a startled Salty. "Who, how . . . ?"

"A guy named Riley is the head of this gang," explained Cook, "and made himself foreman of the MJ." He paused and waited for the response to this bit of news.

The surprised look on the two faces opposite him satisfied Cook's sadistic side, and he went on.

"Oh, French is still around. He's just been confined to the ranch proper. A couple of Riley's men have worked his laigs off the last couple of days." And Cook couldn't help smiling at the thought.

"What about Kelso?" Sims asked.

"Well, one of Riley's riders met up with Donie on the north range, and they had words. One thing led to another, and Donie was beat up real good. Bo Franklin and a couple of your boys had to cart Donie back to the Double H.

"Henry Henderson and Kelso rode down to the MJ the next mornin' to find out what was goin' on. Kelso picked a fight with Riley, and Riley killed him. French says Riley must be a first class gunman, maybe a professional.

"A professional gunfighter?" breathed Sims. "And a gang of more'n 20 to boot?"

"Well, it's kinda funny, but he don't act like no gunfighter," answered Cook. "Kelso picked the fight with him, not t'other way around. He does wear two guns, though, but so do several of his men. Boys, we got big trouble, and we got a heap of thinkin' to do. We can't count on French helpin' us 'cause I'm not sure anyone can get away from that ranch without being spotted."

Cook paused. "I can't go back to the ranch without Felipé, and I shore as hell can't go back with him. And if neither one of us goes back, Riley will have men swarmin' this whole area by mid mornin'. Whatever we do, we got to do it fast. I don't aim to swing or spend the rest of my life behind bars."

"We got about a hundred critters branded," suggested Sims. "We could drive 'em to Harding," he added hopefully.

"If that don't beat all," exclaimed Cook, with disgust. "How far do you think we'd get? Them riders can do six miles to our one. Besides, what would we do with 'em even if we got there? We can't sell 'em. Donie made all them arrangements. We don't even know who the buyer was!"

Cook again paused and looked around. "We've got only one witness to worry about, right now," he said, nodding at Felipé. "If we get rid of him, we can saddle up and ride out of here. We'll have almost a day's head start, and we can lose anybody followin' us when we get to the mountains west of Harding."

"What do you mean, we?" asked Salty, alarm in his voice. "I don't want any part of a killing. Rustling is one thing; killing is another."

"You yellow dog!" screamed Cook. "We've already got one killing hanging over our heads, you damn fool. Or did you forget that?"

"No, I ain't forgot that," Salty roared back. "But we didn't do that one."

Salty and Sims got to their feet and confronted Cook. All three began to yell and scream at each other, punctuated with profanities.

Felipé had been quietly listening to the conversation and at the same time had been examining his surroundings. He noted that all four horses had been tied to the broken branches extending from a good-sized section of a fallen tree only a few yards away. The section had obviously been dragged from the nearby woods and had acted as both a picket line for the horses and a place to sit for the men.

As soon as Spencer and Sims got up and blocked Cook's view of him, Felipé quickly got to his feet, took three big strides and dove for an area behind the log.

Cook's eyes caught Felipé's movement and, shoving Salty to one side, he drew and fired. His bullet thudded into the log.

"He's tryin' to get away!" Cook screamed. "Gun him down!"

Spencer and Sims instinctively drew their guns and turned toward Felipé. Before any further shots could be fired, however, all three men were startled to hear a yell behind them.

Three bodies reversed direction, and three pairs of eyes were astonished to see five men with big sombreros, standing in a line with guns drawn. Three gun hands swung in the direction of this new threat.

Five guns roared, almost as one. Cook threw up his hands, and his gun went flying. He stiffened and then pitched forward on his face. Sims staggered back and collapsed. Spencer simply folded up and slowly slid to his knees, groaning in pain.

Sanchez and his men slowly approached the fire, guns at the ready. Felipé peered over the log, grinned and rose to greet his countrymen.

CHAPTER 8

It was late afternoon when the three Double H punchers, Deuce, Milt, and Joe, reached the Henderson Ranch. The ride from town had not been pleasant. Two of the men had throbbing heads that the riding did not alleviate. The third man, Milt, also had a headache but, in addition, had had to stop twice to relieve the nausea that had overwhelmed him. His nose also pained him greatly, and much of his face had become discolored.

Henry and Donie Henderson had been sitting on the porch and watched the trio slowly approach the house. A couple of the Henderson ranch hands had been walking across the yard as the riders went by and stopped in surprise at what they saw. They followed the three men on foot as the punchers reached the house.

"What the hell happened to you guys?" demanded Henry.

Deuce and Joe slowly dismounted, and Deuce reached up to aid Milt. He spoke to the two ranch hands. "Help git Milt to the bunkhouse. He don't feel so good."

As Milt was assisted in his trip to the bunkhouse, Deuce removed his hat and faced the Hendersons with a sheepish look on his face. He wet his lips and mumbled, "We had a little trouble in town."

"What kind of trouble?" probed Henry.

"Well, sir," hesitated Deuce, looking from Henry to Donie and back again, "we saw the MJ ranch wagon in town, and it was driven by someone we didn't know, a new hand it looked like. We. . . , well, we knowed you and Donie want everyone hereabouts to know who runs things, so we sort of decided to have some fun with this hombre. He didn't take kindly to the funnin'."

"You mean you was three to his one, and he whipped you?" thundered Henry in disbelief.

"Well, no," Deuce shook his head. "He and I was rollin' around in the street, and Milt and Joe were sort of standin' around, ready to pitch in if I needed help. Two other MJ punchers came along and slugged Milt and Joe with their guns. I had just got to my feet when someone cold cocked me, too. When we come to, we was layin' in the street, Doc Conklin workin' on us and the MJ punchers were gone. Hamilton told us they said they was new hires at the MJ and had come to town for supplies. Me and the boys only saw one, though."

Henry waited expectantly and when nothing more was forthcoming waved his hand and said, "All right, go to the bunkhouse and get cleaned up. You look awful. I'll see you later if I have anything more to talk to you about."

Henry, Donie at his side, watched the two men slowly take their horses to the corral.

"What are we going to do, dad?" asked Donie. "How many men has Johnson hired? Were these boys the same ones I ran into, or are they differ- ent ones?"

"I don't know, Donie," sighed Henry. "That new foreman shore said not to fool with the MJ, and it looks like he meant it. You tell our boys to ease off and not start any trouble with the MJ or any of its riders. I've got to sort things out and try to figger out what's going on. You tell the men that."

Donie nodded and strode toward the bunkhouse where most of the men were gathered and talking to Deuce, Milt and Joe.

Reaching the bunkhouse, he stepped inside, whereupon the talk stopped. He relayed his father's message and asked if there were any questions. He paused but received no response. Turning on his heel, he retraced his step to the main house. The babble of sound behind him began again as soon as he had left the premises.

Deuce looked up from his bunk when a pause in the discussion took place. "Didn't see Kelso around," he observed. "Wonder what he thinks about all this? Donie looked like he's had some trouble, too."

"Kelso's dead," replied Bo Franklin, smiling at Deuce's startled look. "Reckon we better bring you up to date on the news around here."

* * * * * * * * * * * *

It was late afternoon when Sanchez, Felipé and José galloped up to the main house at the MJ. Sanchez and Felipé dismounted and handed their reins to José, who led the three foam- flecked horses to the corral.

Tex met Sanchez and Felipé on the porch but turned and retraced his steps as Sanchez motioned for him to follow the Mexicans inside.

"How'd things go?" asked Tex once they were inside, a worried look on his face.

"Ver' good!" answered a pleased Sanchez. He then related the events that had taken place. Felipé augmented the tale with comments of his own.

Tex listened carefully and frowned. "It sounds like none of them actually killed Slim," he mused. "But I'll bet they knew who did. And one is still alive!"

Turning to Marty, who had joined them, he asked, "Do you have anythin' that could cushion a ride in the ranch wagon? We've got to get that wounded man here so he can be doctored. We've got to keep him alive!"

"Why, yes," answered Marty. "We have an old set of bed springs that ought to do the job. And we got lots of blankets."

"Good," said Tex. "Get them. I'll get the wagon ready."

Tex left Marty to his tasks, and he, Sanchez and Felipé went out on the porch where his men had gathered.

"Red," Tex began, "hitch up the wagon ag'in and bring it here. We've got to fix it up to handle a wounded man. No, he's not ourn. José will go with you and show you the way.

"Bronc, you and Trig go get Mr. French. It's time me and him had a discussion about conditions on this here ranch."

In a few minutes the springs and blankets were loaded into the wagon, and Red and José were on their way.

Bronc and Trig had fetched French, and all three were standing in the yard.

Tex untied the rawhide thongs around his legs, unbuckled his gun belt and handed it to Marty.

"Hold this for a spell," he directed Marty.

Tex walked over to where French was standing.

"We found that herd of mavericks your friends hid away," he announced, "and we know yore part in it. You're shore goin' to get tried for rustlin'.

"French," he continued, "there is nothin' lower in cow country than havin' someone steal from the man who's payin' his wages. But that goes double for a foreman. I don't know what's goin' to happen to you in town, but you're goin' to find out right now what happens when you double cross the MJ. You've wanted a part of me ever since we got here, and this is goin' to be your one and only chance to get it. Stand back, boys, and give us room!"

French was uncertain as to how Tex knew for sure about his part in the rustling. Had Cook been captured and talked? He knew he could not escape from this group of men, and, yes, he did want a crack at Riley. Wetting his lips, he threw off his vest and began circling warily. Finally he rushed at Tex, arms swinging.

Tex ducked, deftly stepped aside, and the fight was on.

* * * * * * * * * * * *

Slim Evers, by nature, had not been a violent man. Yet, the world he knew and the occupation he had chosen had, by definition, placed him in a violent environment. Cattle ranching was dangerous in those days, and violence was a necessary evil. Success and survival had to be fought for, won and defended.

He knew Tex had had a very difficult childhood and had, by necessity, learned how to take care of himself. His uncanny skill with a gun had developed early, and that, combined with a nervy recklessness, had made him a very dangerous man. Scrapes with the law had been an inevitable result, the last one being very serious.

Yet, Slim Evers had somehow seen a lot of good possibilities in this man, as he had in others, and finally had Tex released from prison into his custody. From that point on, Slim had spent a great deal of time talking to Tex, maturing him and slowly bringing his mental attitude in tune with that of society. Slim soon found out that Tex was highly intelligent, and once the intellectual processes were channeled in the right direction, Tex's progress into manhood and responsibility had been rapid.

Slim became especially proud of his product, and after a lengthy period of learning the cattle business from beginning to end, Tex became his foreman. At the same time, Slim encouraged Tex to practice and hone his violent skills. As a result, Tex became the chief enforcer and defender of the Rambling R's policies and property. In reality, Tex Riley had become Slim Evers' alter ego.

Other men came to the Rambling R — Bronc Evans, Trig Mansfield, Lefty White and Blackie Smith, to name the most outstanding. But sooner or later, all acknowledged and bowed to Tex's superior skills.

* * * * * * * * * * * *

Art French, to his chagrin, soon discovered that while Tex was a first-class gunman, he was no amateur when it came to his fists, either. When French did land some strong punches, the responses shook him to his boots and were very painful. Twice he was sent sprawling into the dust. Twice he staggered to his feet and, half blind and bleeding profusely, he returned to the attack. Rustler or not, he did have courage, even though he now knew it was a hopeless cause.

His punches had lost much of their power, and he was breathing heavily. As he moved in one more time, Tex's form became blurred and out of focus.

Tex, on the other hand, had finally found a release for all the fury his mind had stored up over the death of Slim Evers. But it wasn't a hot, out of control, passionate fury that had resulted. Instead, it was a cold, controlled, deadly anger that governed every move he made. Before him, for all he knew, was the man who had pulled the trigger, and he must be dealt with.

Instead of dodging and weaving, as he had been doing, Tex met this latest rush straight up and planted two brutal punches just above French's belt buckle. French's forward progress was stopped in its tracks. His remaining breath wheezed out of his mouth, and his hands came down to protect his stomach. A right hand caught him on the jaw and straightened him up. He stood suspended for a moment or two, and a second right hand finished him off for good, his unconscious body landing face down in the dust.

At the sound of the last blow, everyone knew the fight was over.

Tex stepped back, also breathing heavily. Blood trickled from a badly cut lip and from a cut on his left cheek. Knuckles on both his hands were severely bruised, especially the right one.

"Bronc, you and Trig take French to the bunkhouse, clean him up and tie him in his bunk," Tex directed through battered lips.

Tex turned to Marty and retrieved his gun belt but did not put it on.

"Marty," he asked, "is there a doctor in town? One you can trust?"

"Yes to both questions," replied Marty. "Jim Conklin is one of the few people who has been friendly to us since we got here."

"All right, then," Tex went on. "I want you to ride into town for him. Don't hurry none. The ranch wagon won't be here for at least a couple of hours. Tell him on the quiet that a gunshot wound is the problem, and he'd better plan on stayin' here a day or so.

"Curley, you and Rusty ride along with Marty but stay out of town. Wait for him to come back with the Doc, and see if'n they get followed. Tell Charley and Reb to stay put at the outpost 'til you all get back. If'n Marty and the Doc are followed, it'll be up to all of you to stop anyone from gettin' back to town. Understand?"

Curley nodded and began to move toward the corral. Suddenly he stopped and looked back at Tex.

"Why don't you send Apache and Dusty to the outpost as well?" he inquired. "We might need Apache's trackin' skill in the dark, and Dusty would be handy if we have to spread out some."

"Good idear," Tex agreed. He motioned for Apache and Dusty to get moving.

Tex wearily mounted the veranda steps and slowly reentered the house. French had fought well, he mused, and the cuts and bruises Tex had sustained were making their presence acutely known.

He sank into a chair and closed his eyes for a minute. Hearing a noise, he opened his eyes and saw Mary standing in front of him, a pan of hot water in one hand and a cloth in the other.

"Sit back, Tex," she murmured softly. "Let me see what I can do about your face and hands."

She bathed his cuts and bruises for a bit and then continued speaking, conscious that Bronc and Trig had entered the room and were silently watching.

"I don't like fighting," she said, "but I'm glad you did what you did to him. Has he really been stealing from us all this time? Do you think he killed Slim, too?"

"Well, I know he was in on the rustlin' and he doctored the tally books to cover it. He made it look like the natural increase was only 30 percent when it was really probably about 40 percent. I'll know for shore after we do a roundup, which we'll get to right quick. Slim had to question him on this and likely didn't get a good answer.

"As far as killin' Slim, I don't know," Tex continued slowly. "A man who fought as well as he did, with no chance to escape, ain't likely to shoot someone in the back. It don't fit. I'll have to have another talk with Mr. French before we turn him over to the law."

Tex looked at Bronc and Trig and said, "Well, what do you boys want?"

"Our old jobs back," answered Bronc, and Trig nodded agreement.

"Your old jobs?" asked a puzzled Tex.

"Yeah," drawled Bronc, "our old jobs. Trig and I been talkin'. We were Slim's bodyguards, sort of, and since you're the new boss, we've decided to be your bodyguards, too."

"I don't need bodyguards," protested Tex. "I can take care of myself."

"Shore you can," agreed Bronc, "better'n we can, too. But look at your hands. They look plumb awful, and you ain't in any shape to make a fast, accurate draw if'n you have to. That's goin' to be our job. Besides, you been hoggin' all the fun in this here expedition, and now it's our turn. Where you go, we go. And six guns are always better'n two."

Despite the pain, Tex couldn't help laughing.

"All right, you old war horse," he agreed. "You go where I go. I couldn't lick either of you right now anyhow."

Tex grew serious. "I know what you are really sayin', and I thank you. I couldn't put myself in better hands."

* * * * * * * * * * * *

The sun was rapidly approaching the western horizon when the ranch wagon returned with its escort of Mexicans. Two of Sanchez' men pulled horses with blanket-draped bodies slung over the saddles and tied in.

All of the range riders were back from their daytime patrols and watched silently as the caravan slowly paraded by.

Wes Adams and Bud Charles had heard about the fight between Art French and Tex Riley as soon as they had returned from their range riding. Upon entering the bunkhouse they had found the battered French bound in his bunk and under the watchful eyes of Trig Mansfield.

As disturbing as this turn of events had been to them, they also were not prepared for the arrival of Sanchez' men and the two body-draped horses, and their distress increased accordingly.

Tex met the cavalcade as it reached the house. He sent for Adams and Charles, and as they approached, he cut the ropes holding the bodies and allowed the corpses to slide to the ground. The blankets flew open, and the first face they saw was that of Stan Cook.

The faces of both men reflected shock and surprise.

"We know who he is," Tex pointed out, "but we don't know the other man. Who is he?"

Adams gulped and wet his lips. "That's Dan Sims of the Double H," he said weakly, and looked away.

By this time Sanchez and his men had managed to lift the prone body of the wounded man out of the wagon and were prepared to carry him into the house.

"Look at him, Adams," snapped Tex. "Who is he?"

Wes wet his lips again and replied, "That's Salty Spencer. He works for Henderson, too."

* * * * * * * * * * * *

Marty Johnson reached Ridgeway and trotted his horse down its main street until he came to the office of Doctor James Conklin. Dismounting, he tied his reins to a building post and looked around. Seeing that no one had paid any attention to him in the gathering dusk, he walked to the door of the office and gently knocked. He heard the scrape of a chair and the sound of footsteps. The door opened, and Doc Conklin peered out.

"Why, hello there, Johnson," he said, with a smile on his face. "I haven't seen you in quite a spell. C'mon in. What can I do for you? And how's that wife of yours?" he continued.

"Mary's fine, Doc. Thank you for asking," replied Marty. "But we do have a problem at the ranch. One of the guys accidentally shot himself and needs some doctoring. Can you come out to the ranch?"

"One of your new hands?" asked Doc, eyebrows raised.

"Why, yes it was," lied Marty. "Seems like he was real careless."

"The boys I saw earlier today didn't seem like the careless type," observed Doc with a sly look in his eyes. "Real serious, was it?" he asked.

"I don't really know, Doc," answered Marty. "That's why I came for you. But I think we ought to get moving. You might want to plan on staying a day or so, though, just in case."

Doc had watched Marty's face closely during this exchange but could find nothing to justify a nagging suspicion. Finally, he sighed and grabbed his bag. He went to a cabinet, gathered some supplies, placed them in his bag and followed Marty out the door.

"Wait here, Mr. Johnson," he said. "My rig is at the livery stable. I'll only be a minute."

Conklin hurried down the sidewalk and turned into a doorway. In a surprisingly short time, he reappeared in his rig and started down the street. Marty had already mounted and pulled alongside the rig as it moved along slowly.

They made good time getting to the ranch. About halfway there, however, two more riders joined them, one riding alongside the rig opposite from Marty and one behind the rig. Doc recognized the man next to him as being one of the participants in the morning's altercation. He tipped his hat, and Curley returned the salute but said nothing. About a mile from the ranch, Doc glanced over his shoulder, only to find that the trailing rider was gone.

He was somewhat puzzled by these comings and goings, but this puzzlement was nothing to the astonishment that consumed him as he guided his rig into the ranch yard. There were men everywhere! There were groups of twos and threes, some smoking, others lounging and talking. Several men were in and around a corral jammed with horses. Other horses were in a temporary corral, and more men were there, too. Even more surprising, several dark complexioned men with big sombreros were evident. Mexicans, no less!

Tex saw the rig arrive, exited the house, stepped off the porch and raised a hand as a greeting.

"Doctor Conklin, I presume?" he asked. "I would like to shake hands with you, but right now mine are quite sore. My name is Riley, and the wounded man is inside. Please come this way."

Conklin glanced down and while dusk had set in, there was enough light from the house so that he could see Tex's cut and bruised knuckles.

"Looks like you've been in a fight," he observed. "By the way, are you the hombre that killed Kip Kelso?"

"Guilty on both counts," answered Tex. "After you're through with the wounded man, we have a patient down in the bunkhouse you'll need to look at. Seems like he ran into my fists a few times, and he seems sorta broken up about it. His name is French."

Conklin stopped and looked Tex over. "I'm glad you seem to have a sense of humor, young man," he said wryly. "You may need a lot of it to get along with the Hendersons, especially after what one of your men did to Donie the other day. And what your men did in town this morning."

"Maybe the Hendersons will need a sense of humor to get along with the MJ," Tex replied quietly. "But we can talk about that later. The wounded man is over here," he said, pointing to a couch.

Conklin moved over to the couch, looked down and was startled by what he saw. "This is Salty Spencer of the Double H!" he exclaimed.

"It shore enough is," agreed Tex. "But he still needs a doctor. I'll explain later. Mary Johnson has said she'll help you all she can. One of my men will stay here, but the rest of us will vamoose. And Doc, I really need to have this man stay alive, so do your damndest for him. Trig, here, will let us know if you need anyone or anythin'."

Doc nodded, bent down and began his examination. Mary Johnson and Trig Mansfield watched in silence.

* * * * * * * * * * * *

A small group of men had gathered on the porch outside the door of the main house of the MJ. Present were Marty, Tex, Sanchez, Bronc and Lefty. Pipes had been filled and lit, tobacco and papers had appeared and also been lit, and conversation had been at a minimum, each man with his own thoughts.

After a rather lengthy pause, Tex turned to Sanchez and spoke. "I want to begin a complete roundup tomorrow. We'll start with the southwest section and move north. We'll need to separate and brand those mavericks you found, but everythin' else should purty much be a countin' exercise and should move along fairly fast. How many men and how much time do you think you'll need for that section?"

Sanchez pondered for a few moments. "I theenk 12 men an' two days would be mucho plenty. The range is ver' open weeth no' too many draws and arroyos. Si, I theenk that many would do."

"That's about what I figgered," agreed Tex. "Lefty, from what you and the boys tell me, there are only a few unbranded cows in the other three sections. Either those ranges were stripped clean, or they have had good roundups."

"Yes, that's a fact," answered Lefty. "I've only seen two unbranded steers, and we all know it ain't hard to miss a few in every roundup. That northern section has a lot of rough ground, too."

"It's settled then. Tomorrow we begin, and it will be mainly a countin' exercise. I'll talk to the men in the mornin' and make the work assignments. Sanchez will be in charge, and I'll pull Juan from the outpost detail to help you out. The chuck wagon is all fixed up, and we have plenty of supplies. Two days for the south section and one day for each of the others should do the job. After all, we're only talkin' about a herd of no more than 1,800 head. It should be easy as pie," he finished with a grin.

The conversation stopped suddenly as footsteps were heard approaching the porch. Wes Adams and Bud Charles emerged from the darkness and faced the group, hats in hand.

Wes Adams shifted his weight from one side to the other and back again. He looked down for a moment, then raised his head and wet his lips.

"Me and Bud been talkin'," he began nervously, "and we'd like to make a deal. The rustlin' business is shore shot to hell, and you think, or know, we've been part of it. But we have some information that may be worth somethin' to you. We figger we could trade that for a break on the rustlin' business."

"I won't promise anythin' off hand," responded Tex, "but where we come from rustlin' is either the rope or a damn long prison term. Come clean with us now, and I'll see what it's worth. You really don't have a hull lot to lose."

Adams thought for a moment and looked at Charles, who nodded. Adams plunged ahead.

"We saw what you done to Kelso and Cook and Sims, and French, too. We don't want that done to us. You boys look real mean to us, and we figger you won't be leavin' 'til the job is done."

Adams paused, took a deep breath and went on.

"French told us what we were to do when he hired us. He knew us from another ranch we worked at together. Our main job was just to drift mavericks south into Cook's section, and he took it from there. We didn't do any branding! I swear that's the truth. We only got an extra $ 10 a month from French."

"Did you help drive the herd to Harding?" Tex asked casually.

"You already know about that?" asked Wes, with surprise. Obviously that was some of the information he had hoped to trade on.

"There's a lot of things I already know," snapped Tex. "You lie to me, and any chance you think you have will be long gone. Now, who drove the cattle to Harding?"

"I did once," replied Adams, fear in his voice. "Bud did it once, too. Kelso was always trail boss. Cook went along both times, and so did Dan and Salty. Five men were plenty for a herd that size. As far as we know, them's the only Double H riders in on the plan."

"The cattle all had Double H brands," Tex reminded the two. "Who made the shipping arrangements, and who sold the cattle?"

Adams nervously shifted his feet, and Charles, too, seemed to be very uncomfortable.

"Looky here, Riley," Adams began again, "me and Bud are only ranch hands, not gunmen. The Hendersons are right powerful people in these parts, and we might not live long or well if we talk ag'in them. The only reason me and Bud come here tonight is because you killed Kelso and you seem to have enough men to stand up to the Hendersons. If we were to testify ag'in one of them, would you perfect us?"

Tex thought for a moment and then agreed, "Yes, I will give you all the protection me and my men can provide as far as the rustlin' goes. Now, who shipped and sold that cattle?"

If Adams understood what Tex really had said, he gave no such indication. Wetting his lips again, he uttered two words. "Donie Henderson."

"And you are willin' to testify to that in court?" persisted Tex.

Adams looked down again and wearily said a weak, "Yes."

Tex looked at Bud Charles. "You, too?"

Bud answered in the affirmative.

"All right, then, I'm goin' to count on that," commented Tex. "But in the meantime, we're goin' to run a roundup on every section of this ranch. You boys better work your butts off, and if'n you know of any cattle hidden away anywhere, you'd better make shore we know it right quick. I'm goin' to give you some room to roam, and should you pull out on me, I'll hunt you down like dogs, and it *will* be the rope. You understand me?"

"Yes sir!" two frightened men replied in unison.

"You can count on us," added Adams.

Getting no further response, both men turned and hurried back to the bunkhouse.

"Well, it looks like you have a couple of more men for the roundup, Sanchez," Tex muttered grimly. "I'm shore you'll keep them busy. We'll make shore they leave their guns to home, however."

CHAPTER 9

A short time after Adams and Charles had left for the bunkhouse, Doc Conklin emerged from the ranch house and wiped the perspiration from his face with a big handkerchief. Bronc pushed a chair his way, and the good doctor sat down heavily.

"The patient is alive and doing reasonably well," he announced. "Whoever patched him up right off did a real good job. Probably saved his life, too," he added.

"You can thank Sanchez for that," Tex said, pointing to the Mexican. "He's had a lot of experience with bullet holes."

"Giving them or receiving them?" probed Conklin, glancing at Sanchez.

"Both," answered Tex.

"By the way," Tex went on, after a brief pause, "I'd better introduce the rest of our little group." And he promptly did so.

The doctor acknowledged each introduction and then turned back to Lefty.

"Reckon you're the one that gave Donie what for," he said. "That's a job that should have been done a long time ago. Probably won't do much good, though," he amended. "That boy sure is a problem."

"Maybe not much longer," interjected Tex. "But before you get too settled, you'd better see to our other invalid. Bronc, take the Doc down to the bunkhouse and have him look at French. On the way back, stop at the woodshed and have him meet our other two guests. You stayin' the night, Doc?"

"Yes," Conklin replied. "Mrs. Johnson is making me a bed next to the couch. My God, Sheriff Hamilton thought you might be a bit crowded out here, but he don't know the half of it! Where'd all you people come from, anyway?"

"More on that later, Doc," said Tex. "Get goin', Bronc."

* * * * * * * * * * *

A short time later Doc returned, his face flushed and a grinning Bronc right behind.

"Good Lord, man," Conklin exploded, "that's Stan Cook and Dan Sims you got back there in the shed, and they're both dead! What the hell is going on around here, and what am I into?"

"Sit down, Doc, and take it easy," Tex replied calmly. "We got a lot to talk about. Bronc, it's time you turned in. Bronc will relieve Trig at two o'clock and help you keep an eye on Spencer," Tex explained as he looked at Conklin.

"We caught Cook, Sims and Spencer rustlin' MJ cattle," Tex continued. "They have a herd of MJ beef with a Double H brand hid out on our south range nearest Harding. They've shipped out about 200 head of our beef from Harding in each of the past two years. French was in on it, too, and so was Kelso. We don't know who else . . . yet!"

"I can't believe Henry Henderson would lower himself to rustle cattle," said Conklin, aghast. "He has more cattle than he needs now. It doesn't sound like him a'tall."

"Don't he want this ranch real bad?" inquired Tex, wearing his poker face.

"Well, yes," replied Conklin, then remaining silent for several moments. "But rustling? That just ain't Henry's style."

"What about Donie?" asked Tex casually as he reached for tobacco and papers.

"Good Lord," breathed Conklin, a startled look on his face. "Donie! Of course he *could* do it, but he would never have the guts. Nor the brains to pull it off."

"What if he was pushed by Kelso?" asked Tex as he worked on forming his cigarette.

"My, oh my, you said a mouthful there," exclaimed Conklin. "Donie might do just about anything if Kelso handled him right."

Conklin stared at Tex for a long minute.

"Do *you* think Donie *is* involved?" he finally breathed, fear and concern becoming apparent, both in his voice and in his facial expression.

"Don't know yet," lied Tex, not willing to trust Conklin too much at this stage of the game. He decided to change the subject.

"Doc," he said in a serious tone, "you've seen a number of things tonight no one else has seen, especially how many of us are here. We're goin' to need your cooperation, and we're goin' to have to trust you in return."

Tex paused and then went on, "The rustlin' ain't the reason we're here. That came up as a surprise to us, too. A long ways south of here is the

Rambling R Ranch. All of us, except'n Sanchez and his men, work there. Some of us damn near grew up there. That ranch was started by a man named Raymond "Slim" Evers. That name mean anythin' to you?"

Doc thought for a moment and then his face lit up. "Of course, the man who was killed about a month ago. Mr. Johnson's friend."

"Partner," amended Tex. "A silent partner. We're here to find the man who did that killin'. And then we're going to hang him, all legal and proper. That's the way Slim would want it, at least the legal part."

Tex again paused a bit to let this information sink in.

"Now, Doc, tell us about the legal system in this here county. What can we expect in the way of law and order?" he asked.

Conklin rubbed his jaw and silently cogitated for a few moments. He looked around at the various faces of his audience and finally made his decision.

"Riley," he said, "I'm going to level with you. I kind of like your style, and I'll cooperate with you and, at the same time, hopefully I'll earn your trust, too. Maybe, together, we can make this area a better place in which to live.

"Henry Henderson and I go back a long ways and are good friends. But that doesn't mean I agree with everything he does. Henry is crude, rough and bullheaded. He's been a power in this county for a long time, probably too long. Too much power breeds arrogance. He tends to step on folks and look down on them, although I don't think he is really fully aware of how far he goes sometimes. Make no mistake about it, though, Henry controls the political structure of the county. You can't get elected to any office without his endorsement. Sheriff Hamilton is Henderson's man, top to bottom."

Conklin paused and took a deep breath before continuing.

"Ted Willis functions as prosecuting attorney but also practices on his own. Ain't enough court business to keep a person occupied as prosecutor full time.

"Judge Palmer splits his time between Ridgeway and Canyon City. He was appointed by the governor and hasn't had to run for re-election yet.

"I think both Willis and Palmer are honest and decent men. I think you'd get a square deal from both of them. Don't trust Hamilton, though."

Tex took off his hat, scratched his head and sighed. "Would Willis be willin' to take on the Hendersons?" he asked.

"Yes, I think he would," replied Doc after some hesitation. "But you'd better have a very strong case for him to use. He wouldn't dare incur Henry's wrath unless he had a damn good chance of winning. He's no fool!"

"Of course," agreed Tex thoughtfully. "If and when we have to do that, we shore will have a strong case."

Doc Conklin rose from his chair and stretched.

"Reckon I'd better get back to my patient," he observed. "I've enjoyed talking to you, Riley. We can talk again in the morning if you want to. Goodnight, gentlemen."

A chorus of goodnights followed him as he went back into the house. The little group soon broke up and sought their own bedrolls.

* * * * * * * * * * * *

Dawn arrived again, and the activity of the previous day was repeated at the MJ.

Conklin was satisfied with the progress of his patient and was prepared to return to town by mid-morning if conditions didn't change. Spencer's fever had broken, and he was taking liquid nourishment.

Fortified with a hearty breakfast and several cups of coffee, Conklin found a chair on the porch and watched all the activity with more than a little interest. For one thing, there seemed to be more men around than he had seen the night before, although he hadn't tried to count noses in the dusk and gloom of nightfall.

Tex had given some additional thought to the roundup plans and suggested a few refinements at breakfast with Sanchez. Sanchez agreed and after all had eaten, Tex called the men together. The only man missing was Apache, who was in the bunkhouse watching French.

"Some of you have complained about not havin' enough work to do," he began, "and so I've decided to correct that situation right now." He grinned at the moans and groans that followed.

"We're goin' to do a fast but complete roundup. Sanchez will be in charge of the range operations, while I'll stay here at the ranch with Bronc, Trig, Cavalry and Apache. Reb, Red and Charley will do their usual job. Dusty will drive the chuck wagon and do the cookin'. Denver and Cheyenne will be in charge of the extry horses and will go with the chuck wagon. Since we are short of horses, take all of the spare ones here at the ranch except Marty's and Apache's and leave Mary's mare here, too. Marty will join up with you tomorrow to count the main herd. I want him to stay around the ranch house as much as possible.

"Sanchez will take all of his men with him as well as Adams, Charles, Curley and Rusty," Tex went on. "Lefty, Blackie, Kansas, Reno and Laredo will sweep the north range and will drive their cattle toward the ranch. Cut out any unbranded animals and bring 'em in to the ranch proper.

"Dusty is takin' both brandin' irons with him 'cause we'll need to take care of that maverick herd first. Leave the Double H beef where they are, but bring out the MJ animals, merge them with the main herd and then sweep everythin' north toward the ranch. Any questions?"

Hearing none, he waved his arm, and the men scattered in all directions.

"You've got so many men here, you must feel like a general," observed Conklin wryly.

Tex laughed. "To tell the truth, it's easy to lose track of someone without half tryin'. But they're all good boys and know the cattle business. Some have more experience than I do and don't need to be told what to do. But they like to humor me!"

"Harrumph," snorted Conklin. "And the moon is made of green cheese, too! I have eyes, and I can see who the real boss is. The Hendersons have never seen an outfit like this one," he added thoughtfully.

"They shore ain't!" emphatically agreed Tex, "And unless you knew Slim Evers, you'd never understand why. And that debt is going to get paid! Make no mistake about it, these boys are fightin' men, too. We've had more'n our share of trouble over the years, but once we cured the problem, it never came back. And if Henderson's the problem here, it shore enough will get cured. You can bet on it!"

Tex paused for a moment, and then his tone was calmer, "You looked over French. Any special problems?"

"No," answered Doc. "He won't see too well for a day or two, and his sore jaw will restrict what he can eat for a spell. But he should be able to ride in a couple of days. You plan on taking him to town?"

"Not until the roundup is over," replied Tex, "and then I'm not sure I want him in Hamilton's jail. I'll have to think on that. Before I do anythin', I may want to talk to Willis. You suppose you could talk to him on the sly and let him know what's goin' on before I get to town?"

"Yes, I'll do that," said Conklin. "You willing to trust me that far?"

"I think so," Tex said with a blank face. "We could always find a rope for you, if'n we had to."

"Harrumph," snorted Doc again. "Don't get smart with me, young man. By the way, how do your hands feel? Your face don't look so good either."

"I'll live," growled Tex.

"Well, I'll check my patient one more time and then head for town. I'll plan on coming back out here tomorrow afternoon if nothing else comes up. Maybe I'll get a chance to talk to Willis before then."

* * * * * * * * * * * *

Tex watched his mass of riders leave the MJ, supervised the loading of the last items in the chuck wagon and made his way to the bunkhouse as the wagon rattled its way across the MJ courtyard.

Entering the bunkhouse, he motioned for Apache to leave and then stood at the end of the first bunk and looked down at the bound ex-foreman.

* * * * * * * * * * * *

Apache was walking his way to the main house when Doc Conklin came out of the house and moved down the steps to where his rig was parked. Preoccupied with his thoughts, he didn't see the Indian boy.

"Good morning, Doctor," Apache greeted the man.

An automatic response began as Doc turned his head at the sound of the voice.

"Good . . . ah, good morning," he stammered and stared after the young man as Apache mounted the steps and entered the house.

Conklin pulled himself up into his rig and settled back in his seat.

Good Lord, he thought, first a bunch of Mexicans and now an Indian. This Riley fellow was just full of surprises. Wonder what else he has up his sleeve? Doc pulled his horse away from the hitching post and began his trip back to town, his mind full of interesting thoughts, most of which were of the pleasant variety.

* * * * * * * * * * * *

French partly opened one eye and noticed Tex standing at the foot of his bunk.

"You feelin' better?" asked Tex pleasantly.

French nodded slightly.

"I'm gettin' along," he mumbled through swollen lips. "Ain't the first time I come out second best."

"You put up a good fight," Tex admitted. "Better'n I expected. You've got guts. Why'd you ever get yourself caught up in a rustlin' deal? You're a better man than that."

French shrugged and mumbled again, "It seemed like a good idea at the time. Kelso was a real convincin' hombre, and I wasn't hard to win over. It looked like easy money, what with Johnson bein' a sort of greenhorn."

"It was a losin' game, right from the start," stated Tex. "Slim made a big mistake. If'n he thought rustlin' was goin' on, he shoulda come back to the Rambling R and sent a bunch of us up here to straighten things out. We'd got things under control right quick."

"But the man who killed Slim made a bigger mistake," Tex went on, "and he sure enough is goin' to hang for it. Like I told you, I don't know what the penalty is for rustlin' up here, but that could be the rope, too."

"You can only hang a man once," French pointed out.

"That's true," admitted Tex. "But why hang once if you don't have to hang at all? I want the man who murdered Slim, and I could be up to makin' a deal on the rustlin' charges. You get my drift?"

French turned this thought over in his mind for a few moments.

"I could tell you Kelso did it," he offered.

"Then I'd have to call you a liar," replied Tex. "Kelso wasn't much good, but he fancied himself to be a gunfighter. If'n you want to build yourself a reputation, you don't do it shootin' people in the back. No, Kelso didn't do it, and I don't think you did either. But I think you know who did."

Tex took a step away from the bunk, then looked back.

"Think about what I told you, French. Me and my boys are goin' to stay here until we get the answers we want. You've made one mistake. Don't make a second one. It could be plumb fatal."

French didn't reply and watched Tex move away. He shut his one eye and became consumed with conflicting thoughts.

* * * * * * * * * * * *

It was mid afternoon when Cavalry entered the main house and found Tex taking a nap. Reluctantly he poked Tex a couple of times, and Tex responded by opening his eyes and stifling a big yawn.

"Sorry to wake you, Tex," Cavalry began, "but we got visitors comin', three in all. Thought you'd want to know."

Tex was instantly wide awake.

"Of course," he said simply. "Find Trig and get to the bunkhouse. Gag French and make shore he's tied down tight. Cover us from there."

Bronc and Apache had also been sleeping. Tex quickly roused both men and gave them their instructions.

"Apache, you'd better gag Spencer and stay with him. I don't want a peep out of him. Bronc, grab a rifle and set yourself up around the corral, but stay out of sight."

Both men did as they were told as Marty and Mary Johnson entered the room.

"Marty, go out on the porch and let me know who's comin' if'n you can," Tex continued. "I'll be just inside the door. Mary, stay with Apache and Spencer. Marty, we can't let anyone come in the house or go to the bunkhouse."

Marty nodded as he went out on the porch and looked at the approaching riders.

"It's Sheriff Hamilton," he declared, "and two deputies. Wonder what they want?"

"I can purty well guess what's on his mind," replied Tex. "I don't want to talk to him if I can avoid it right now. Think you can handle it, Marty?"

"Sure," replied Marty with a scowl. "I figure I know why he's here, too. Let's find out if we're right."

Marty stepped off the porch and reached the tie rail in front of the house at the same time Hamilton and his two deputies arrived. Hamilton started to dismount when Marty's voice stopped him.

"Don't bother stepping down," said Marty curtly. "You won't be staying that long."

"That's not bein' neighborly," protested Hamilton, a hurt look on his face. He pulled himself upright in his saddle.

"You stop by the Henderson Ranch for instructions?" Marty continued coldly.

"That's enough of that," snapped Hamilton, angrily. "You have no call to say that. I'm here on sheriff's business and you oughta show some respect for the law."

"You're a sheriff in name only," snapped Marty right back. "Everyone knows you're Henry's errand boy. What's he got you doing this time?"

"I didn't stop at the Henderson Ranch," retorted Hamilton, his voice rising. "I came here on sheriff's business, and I shore don't need to see Henry about that."

"Then why are you here?" asked Marty a bit calmer.

"Well, we had a fracas in town yesterday involvin' some of your men and a shootin' out here the day afore that. I want to know what you're up to and how many new men you've hired."

"Now, let me see if I'm getting this straight," replied Marty, his voice suddenly velvety. "Henry Henderson and a bunch of his men ride in on MJ property, threaten the MJ foreman on MJ land, in front of the MJ ranch house. Then three Henderson riders jump one of my men in town. And you got the gall to come out here to ask me what I'm up to? You say you didn't stop at the Henderson Ranch on the way out here? This is one time you damn well shoulda stopped there first. Now you listen to me, Hamilton. The MJ is fed up with being pushed around by the Henderson Ranch and anyone connected with it. The MJ is here to stay, and if we have to fight to stay here, that's exactly what we'll do."

"You're loco, Johnson," exclaimed Hamilton. "I don't know how many new men you've hired, but Henderson will still have twice as many riders as you. You'll never be able to stand up ag'in them."

"That's my problem," retorted Marty heatedly. "But you'd better find out where you stand in all this. Henderson law may soon be a thing of the past. If you ain't careful, you may be, too!"

"I don't like your talk, Johnson," snarled Hamilton, "but if that's the way you feel, so be it. I guess I made this ride today for nothin'."

"Yes, you did," answered Marty. "But that's because you rode to the wrong ranch. Tell Henderson to mind his own business, and there won't be any trouble."

Hamilton turned his horse with a disgusted yank and led his men on the trail back to town.

Marty Johnson, still seething over the purpose of the sheriff's visit on the one hand, was, at the same time pleased with his role in the verbal exchange. He leaned forward, gripped the tie rail with both hands and stared at the backs of the departing trio, a somewhat satisfied look on his face.

* * * * * * * * * * * *

The sun had almost reached the western horizon when a weary Chick Snyder loped into the courtyard of the Henderson Ranch. He pulled up by the corral and stiffly dismounted. Pushing open the corral gate, Chick led his tired horse into the corral, stripped off his saddle and blanket and set his horse off with a slap on its rump. He was hanging his gear on the corral fence when he noticed Bo Franklin leaning against a fence post nearby.

"Where you been, Chick?" inquired Bo. "I ain't seen you since breakfast yesterday."

"Been to Canyon City," replied Chick.

"What the hell for?" came from a surprised Bo.

"Did an errand for Donie," muttered Chick. He looked around and then whispered, "Bo, we gotta talk. I don't like what's goin' on at this here ranch, and it's goin' to get worse afore it gets any better. I can't talk now 'cause I gotta see Donie, and I'm starved. But we gotta talk."

"All right," said Bo thoughtfully. "Supposin' you wander out here, casual like, to look over your horse about an hour after you finish eatin'. I'll accidentally run into you. That okay?"

Chick nodded and headed for the ranch house.

Donie had seen Chick arrive and as soon as Chick headed his way, Donie stepped off the porch and met Chick halfway to the house. The two men veered off to Chick's left and ended up near the blacksmith area.

Donie looked at Chick and waited.

"Well, I did like you told me," Chick began. "Smiley took the money and said he would be in Ridgeway in a couple of days. Said he had some personal things to tend to."

"Did he remember me?" asked Donie.

"Sort of," responded Chick. "Said he was shore he would know you when he saw you."

"Very good, Chick. You must be tired," said Donie. "Go fill your belly and get a good night's sleep. Remember now, this is between you and me. I'll tell dad about it at the right time. You understand?"

Chick nodded but made no reply.

Donie, pleased with himself, turned and retraced his steps back to the main house. Chick's eyes followed him, a frown on his face.

A little more than an hour later Bo and Chick met behind the corral. Bo motioned Chick to follow, and they walked another 20 paces, reaching a small grove of trees well away from the other ranch buildings. The two men seated themselves but did not light any cigarettes.

"You wanted to talk?" began Bo in a low voice.

"Yeah," answered Chick. "Bo, Donie has hired himself a, for certain, professional gunfighter!"

"What?" exclaimed Bo. "How do you know that?"

"'Cause I did it for him," explained Chick. "He give me a check to take to Canyon City. For $ 500, it was."

"Five hundred dollars!" interrupted Bo. "Where did Donie git that kind of money?"

"Dunno about that," replied Chick. "I was to look up a fellar named Smiley and offer him $ 500 to do a job for Donie. If he said yes, I was to give him the money. It took me a while to find the guy, but I finally did. He said yes, and the bank cashed the check right off, and I gave him the money. What's more, he's to get another $ 500 when the job's over. Bo, I don't like it."

"A thousand dollars," breathed Bo. "Where in the world did Donie get that kind of money? Old Henry doesn't pay him that much, and he shore wouldn't give it to him. Does Henry know anythin' about this?"

"I don't think so," said Chick. "I asked Donie the same question and was told it weren't none of my business. Damn it, Bo, I figgered that after Kelso got himself killed, things would git better around here. Kelso was mean, but I never thought of him being a professional. I mean, he didn't go around the countryside sellin' his gun. If a professional comes here, we got worse trouble than we ever had."

"I don't understand it either, Chick," mused Bo. "It shore ain't good news. I wonder if Donie is after that MJ rider that thrashed him the other day?"

Chick had no answer, and both men remained silent for a few moments.

Finally Bo spoke up. "Let's keep this to ourselves right now. No sense in gettin' everybody riled. Time enough for that later. You head back to the bunkhouse while I lay low for a little while. Then I'll wander back. Let's sleep on it. Maybe somethin' will come to us."

* * * * * * * * * * * *

After Henry and Donie Henderson finished breakfast the next morning, they came out of the ranch house to find Bo Franklin, as expected, mounted and waiting for instructions.

"Bo," began Henry, "I want you to take five or six of the boys up to the north range and move that herd west to the grassy mesa area. That range has been grazed over purty hard, and we need to rest it for a spell. We shore could use a good rain."

"Yes sir," responded Bo. "But sir, we're going to be a little short-handed. I ain't seen Dan Sims and Salty Spencer for several days, and their bunks ain't been slept in. Do you know where they are and when they'll be back?"

"Why, no I don't," answered a puzzled Henry. "I didn't know they were gone." He turned to Donie. "Son, do you know where Dan and Salty are?"

"Yes I do, dad," replied Donie, who was well prepared for the question. "You said we wasn't to get into any more trouble with the MJ, and so I sent them to the southwest range to hunt for strays and drift them back from the boundary line so there wouldn't be any problems. I told them to stay out two or three days and do a good job of it. As a matter of fact, I was going to take Deuce, Joe and Chick with me and go do the same thing on our south section."

"That's a right good idear, son," responded Henry, beaming with pleasure. "That's the kind of thinking I want you to do."

"Beg pardon, sir," interrupted Bo, "but with Milt still not feeling well, Dan and Salty gone, and Luke and Pete riding fence out east, I shore could use Chick in helping me move that herd."

Henry thought for a moment and then nodded his approval. "Yes, that's what we should do. Donie, three of you should be enough to handle that south range. Bo, you take Chick with you, and thanks for the suggestion."

Henry turned away and headed for the corral, thereby missing the scowl that had appeared on Donie's face. Bo had glanced at Donie and smiled inwardly at the scowl. He turned his horse and loped back to the men standing and sitting around the bunkhouse. Bo relayed Henry's instructions, and he and his men were soon saddled and on their way to the north range.

CHAPTER 10

Sanchez led his platoon of riders south at a leisurely pace. There was a lot of riding to do in the next few days and too few horses for that kind of job. The MJ Ranch was not equipped to handle such a large quantity of men. Therefore, it was mandatory to conserve the strength of the horses as much as possible. The slow pace did allow the chuck wagon and the small remuda, with Denver and Cheyenne as its escort, to keep up with the main group.

About three quarters of the way to the ranch's southern boundary, Sanchez waved his arm, and Felipé, with five men, turned to the west toward the meadow with the hidden herd. Dusty parked the chuck wagon, passed the branding irons to Adams and Charles, saddled his horse and took over temporary control of the extra horses. Denver and Cheyenne, at the same time, each led a string of three cutting-out horses, the MJ's entire stock, and followed in Felipé's dust.

As soon as the group reached the meadow, Adams and Charles broke away, dismounted and began the search for firewood.

The rest of the riders, Felipé in the lead, made an inspection trip around and through the grazing cattle. Spencer and Sims, of course, had already spent considerable time and effort to separate the branded cattle from the unbranded animals. Felipé's inspection trip located two renegades among the branded group, and these were immediately cut out and driven over to their unbranded relatives. One rider then took up a position between the two groups to prevent any more animals from doing the same thing.

The remaining three riders returned to the branding area, dismounted and transferred their blankets and saddles to three of the cutting-out horses, which had just arrived with Denver. Cheyenne was right behind and picketed his three horses a short distance away before heading back to the main remuda to help Dusty.

Felipé and his two men pushed the unbranded herd a little closer to the branding fire and then began to cut out individual animals, force them toward the fire and then roped and hog-tied them for the application of the hot iron. At first the work went slowly. It took a little while for horses and riders, both new to each other, to begin functioning as a team. Once this problem was solved, the process picked up speed, and the two branders were kept busy, especially since each iron had to be somewhat reheated after each application. Denver collected wood and tended the fire as his contribution to the process.

After an hour or so the group took a little break, and the riders exchanged cutting-out horses. The process was repeated, and by late afternoon the branding was completed.

A total of 78 animals were nursing newly-applied hot bruises on their hips.

The tired men took another break, doused the fire and three men began to drive the newly-branded animals back to the main range. Felipé and the other two men then forced the remaining cattle to begin a short march, strung out in as thin a line as possible. Denver counted the animals as they drifted past him, as did Felipé, who had joined him as soon as the cattle started moving.

"One hundred and six," announced Denver, looking at Felipé for confirmation. Felipé nodded in agreement.

"Tex wants these animals left here," said Denver half to himself. "There's plenty of grass, and it shouldn't be too long before we figger out what to do with 'em. Let's get back to the wagon." He kicked his horse with his heels as he and the others raced to join their companions.

* * * * * * * * * * * *

Sanchez, in the meantime, had continued on to the southernmost boundary of the ranch, leaving Dusty, the chuck wagon, and the remaining remuda at the point where Felipé and his group had turned off.

The men spread out in a long, thin line and began the sweep north, using the bed of the stream as their right guide. Every arroyo, draw and depression in the land was inspected as was the brush surrounding each indentation. Individual steers and cows were driven out of their places of concealment and if a rider ran into a group too large for one man to handle, a yell and a wave soon brought reinforcements.

Most of the cattle had been grazing far back from the extreme boundaries of the ranch, however, and the location of such groups had been noted by the riders as they had moved south.

Thus, it was a relatively small number of cattle that had been driven back to the chuck wagon by nightfall to join their newly-branded brethren. Supper was eaten by the hungry men, the first shift of night riders joined the herd and the remaining men had a quick smoke, sought their blankets and were soon sound asleep.

* * * * * * * * * * * *

Lefty and his men followed the same process on the north range. After reaching the northern boundary, the men turned about, also spread out and began the sweep south. By dusk they were over halfway back to the ranch. Leaving Reno and Laredo with the cattle, Lefty and Blackie raced to the ranch to eat and then return to the herd. Kansas followed behind, pushing three unbranded steers as fast as he could. As soon as Lefty and Blackie returned to the small herd, Reno and Laredo left for the ranch to eat and to grab a few hours of sleep. Lefty and Blackie would night ride the herd until Reno and Laredo relieved them between one and two o'clock in the morning. Kansas would spend the entire night at the ranch.

Both night riders followed a half circle, meeting at each end. After a cigarette and a little conversation they would continue their patrol, sometimes singing or humming softly to reassure the cattle. This was a part of the life of a cattleman and puncher that Lefty enjoyed. Sometimes the solitude of night riding was just what he needed to clear his head and get back in step with his world. He, Charley, Kansas and Blackie had been trail mates for a long time, handling danger and pleasure alike. They had hunted wild horses together for several years and had sold a good-sized herd of horses to Slim Evers. Slim had been impressed with their skill in finding and breaking horses, so he offered them jobs at the Rambling R. The four had discussed the declining supply of wild horses, the time and distance required to find them and agreed that steady jobs might be a good idea. They accepted the offer, and it wasn't long before Slim discovered he had gotten a bonus in the deal. He soon found out that Lefty and Blackie were first-class gunmen, very close to being on a par with Tex Riley. Thus, incursions onto Rambling R property and raids on Rambling R cattle very quickly became a most painful, bloody and often deadly game for the perpetrators. The reputation of the Rambling R had risen accordingly, and Lefty was pleased about the contribution the four of them had made in this regard.

* * * * * * * * * * * *

Late afternoon found Tex behind the corral and away from the house. He had spent the past half hour practicing his draw with both hands, individually and together. He decided that the soreness in each hand did seem to interfere with the smoothness of his motions. Therefore, he decided to let Bronc and Trig baby him a bit longer, and he smiled at the thought. His reverie was cut short, however, as Cavalry approached at a trot.

"Reb signaled that two riders are comin'," he announced somewhat breathlessly. Western boots were not made for running.

"Okay," replied Tex. "You and Trig get to the bunkhouse and cover me from there. Tell Bronc to meet me on the porch and tell Apache to get in the house with Marty and Mary."

Cavalry dashed off as Tex checked his guns and then moved toward the house. Bronc was waiting for him on the porch.

Bronc looked at Tex's hands and reminded him, "If'n there's any gunplay, you let me lead. Your hands aren't well yet, and mine are itch'n for somethin' to do."

Tex nodded agreement. He felt sure he could cut in if necessary without any real danger to himself.

"We'll just see what's up and go from there," he said to Bronc.

After another couple of minutes he relaxed and announced, "Why, it's Doc Conklin, and he's got someone with him. A well-dressed hombre, too, if my eyes ain't failin' me."

Conklin's rig came clomping up to the hitching post, and Doc pulled the horse to a halt. Laboriously he stepped down and tied his horse to the post. His traveling companion had dismounted and was waiting to be introduced.

Conklin turned and faced Tex. His arm pointed to his companion.

"Riley," he said, "this is Ted Willis. He decided he wanted to talk to you in person."

Tex shook hands with the man.

"Doc, did you two leave town together?" Tex asked sharply with a frown on his face.

"No, of course not," retorted Doc. "I'm not that dumb. Ted left town heading east, and I left heading this way a half hour later. Ted circled around and met me two miles this side of town."

"Good thinkin'," acknowledged Tex. "Are you shore you weren't followed?"

"Yes, I'm sure not," interjected Willis. "I was very careful and checked my back trail several times. I think I understand your concern."

"Well, if'n you were followed, we'll soon find out about it. My men are checkin' it now."

"Your men are checking . . . ," began Conklin, raising his eyebrows. "You mean you knew we were coming?" More surprises, Mr. Riley, he thought to himself.

Tex didn't answer Conklin's inquiry. Instead he said, "C'mon inside and get out of the sun. I'm shore Mary has somethin' cold we can drink. By the way, this here is Bronc Evans, and the man comin' across the yard is Trig Mansfield. I want them both to hear what we talk about."

The men entered the MJ ranch house, and Tex noted that Apache had disappeared. He nodded his approval — the boy was learning fast. Willis glanced at the bandaged Spencer as he crossed the main room. Doc stopped and began to examine his patient while the others continued on to the big den, where Marty was waiting. In a few minutes, Doc rejoined the group. All had found comfortable chairs to relax in, and Conklin located a soft sofa to sink into.

Mary was informed that they just wanted water and soon had a pitcher and glasses handy.

Willis filled a glass, sipped his drink and looked at Tex. "Conklin tells me you've had some rustling problems. Also that you have two dead bodies laying around."

"Yes and no," replied Tex. "Yes to the rustlin' and, no, we don't have two bodies layin' around. We buried them this morning."

"There'll have to be some sort of official report regarding those two men," Willis reminded Tex. "Maybe an inquest."

"We'll do whatever is necessary at the right time," replied Tex. "But now ain't the right time. I guess the best thing to do is to tell you what happened and where we are in all of this."

Tex described the events of the previous day, and Willis listened intently.

"Your main witness is a Mexican, and so are all the others," he observed. "I'm afraid that won't do a whole lot of good up here. They aren't even citizens of the county. We need more than that, Riley."

"I have more, but before we can go too far down that trail, I have some questions that need answerin'," Tex stated. "First, what is the penalty for rustlin' in this state?"

"Well, we are quite a bit more civilized than most states. Probably a lot more so than where you come from. Ten years is the maximum here, and it has to be a very strong case to get that."

"And murder?" asked Tex as he rolled a cigarette.

Willis narrowed his eyes and looked closely at Tex. "That could be life or a rope, depending on the circumstances," he answered softly.

"Let's get back to rustlin'" said Tex. "Do you have any leeway on gettin' special consideration for a rustler that's willin' to testify for you?"

"Yes. If I can get a guilty plea from such a person, I can ask for a reduced sentence or even a suspended sentence if the testimony is good enough," Willis explained. "It also depends, somewhat, on their involvement in the scheme."

Tex scratched his chin and changed the subject again. "Where does the Henderson Ranch ship its cattle?" he asked.

The quick subject change surprised Willis. "Why, Canyon City, of course," he responded. "Everyone knows that. Why do you ask?"

Tex pulled a piece of paper from his shirt pocket. He read from the paper, "The Double H shipped 203 head out of Harding last August and 188 the September afore that. I can produce two witnesses who helped hide MJ mavericks and then drive them to Harding with Double H brands on their hides. They will identify Kip Kelso, Dan Sims and Salty Spencer from the Double H and Art French and Stan Cook from the MJ as helpin' with both the hidin' of the beef or being part of the drive. Them two witnesses did not see any of the brandin', though."

Tex paused for a moment and slipped the paper back into his shirt pocket.

"Those figgers came from the station agent at Harding after he was told he could give them to me by his regional office," Tex explained. "Can you get the actual shipping papers from the railroad?"

"Yes, I can get a court order and obtain affidavits regarding the records," responded Willis. "It will take a few days though."

Tex nodded his approval. "Unless I miss my guess, those papers will be signed by Donie Henderson," he said quietly.

Willis' jaw dropped, and he fell back in his chair in surprise.

"You can't be serious," he gasped. "Donie Henderson!"

Conklin rubbed his forehead and muttered, "I sort of thought you were getting around to that. Riley, are you sure Donie is involved?"

"Both of my witnesses will identify Donie as the one who made the shipping arrangements and sold the cattle. Both of these men are scared, of course, and I have promised them my protection in exchange for them testifyin'. I also said I would put in a good word for 'em at the right time if they earn it."

"Well, that would be strong testimony," Willis agreed, "provided the shipping papers do have Donie's name on them. Do you have anything more for me at this time?"

"Yes and no," acknowledged Tex. "I've talked to French and didn't get far. I haven't talked to Spencer yet. Been waitin' for him to get strong enough. Didn't want Doc to get mad at me either," he grinned. "Doc is a right tough hombre to tangle with."

Doc grunted in reaction to that statement but couldn't help smiling. "I reckon you can talk to him now, if you want to," Doc said slowly. "I'll have to be there to see how it goes, however. He's still a pretty sick man."

Tex held up a hand, and his gaze was fixed on Willis' face.

"Before we do that, I have a couple more questions. Willis, if'n what I've told you and what I believe is true, and the witnesses agree to testify, will you be willin' to take on the Hendersons?"

Willis thought for a few moments and then nodded in the affirmative.

"I know why you're asking that, and I understand your concern," he said. "Yes, I swore to uphold the law, and I will take on the Hendersons if I feel the evidence is strong enough to justify some action, but only I will make that decision."

Willis paused and again was lost in thought for a moment.

"Even if I have enough to issue a warrant for Donie's arrest, though, I don't know if Sheriff Hamilton would serve it. He owes his whole being to Henry Henderson," Willis explained.

"Can he refuse to serve a warrant?" snapped Tex, a grim look on his face.

"Not legally," responded Willis. "He could be held in contempt of court. If so, he could end up in his own jail. Of course, he could even resign as sheriff rather than face contempt charges."

"What would happen then?" asked Tex innocently.

"Why, the court could appoint a temporary sheriff until an election could be held," replied Willis. Suddenly his whole face lit up, backed by a large grin. "And wouldn't that be interesting, though, particularly since Judge Palmer and I know each other real well. I'm sure he would take my recommendation. How do I know if I might be recommending a wanted man?" he asked slyly.

"You don't," said Tex dryly. "You just might have to gamble on that."

Tex thought for a moment and then spoke again, "Supposin' Donie is tried and convicted. What kind of sentence do you think he'd get?"

"Ah, yes, an excellent question, Riley," replied Willis. "Henry is a powerful man in this county, and getting a jury to convict Donie is going to take some doing." Willis closed his eyes for a few moments and then continued, "If Donie said he was forced into the scheme by Kelso, he might even get off with a suspended sentence. Everyone around here was afraid of Kelso, and Donie could get a lot of sympathy, even if he isn't well liked."

"How about French?" pursued Tex.

"Well now, that's another story," retorted Willis. "Stealing from your own employer would not set well here. I'd surely go for the full 10 years."

"And Spencer?" pursued Tex again.

"Won't know about that until I talk to him," said Willis, "but I see what you're driving at. I could offer both of them a deal if they will help convict Donie. The more testimony we get, the less chance Donie will have to get off with a light sentence or none at all. Yes, it's a good idea, Riley, and I'll keep it in mind. Incidentally, where are your two witnesses, and when can I talk to them?"

"They're out on the range, helpin' with the roundup I have goin'," answered Tex. "They'll be back in two, three days. Don't worry. They'll be around when you want them. Also, Spencer and French will stay here until we want them for the trial. Spencer can't ride nohow, and I don't trust Hamilton and his jail after what you said about him."

"That's acceptable for now," agreed Willis. "But you better have them available when I want them. Now I want to talk to Spencer."

Willis rose and went back to the main room and walked over to the wounded man lying on the couch. He saw that Spencer was awake and alert.

"You're in big trouble, Salty," Willis began. "Rustling is a serious matter. You're looking at a long prison term."

"You've only got the word of a greaser!" retorted Spencer. "That won't go far around here."

"We've got a lot more than that," interrupted Tex. "We've got a herd of MJ cattle with a Double H burned on their hides. We've got your Double H brandin' iron, and after today, I'll have a half dozen or more men who will testify about the location of the herd, the new brands they have and the unbranded mavericks as well. And we got six Mexicans who can testify on what happened, not just one. And you and Sims had no business bein' in those parts to begin with. No, Spencer, like Willis said, you've got a big problem."

Spencer scowled but remained silent.

Willis leaned down closer to Salty and glared at the man.

"Salty, we know cattle was shipped out of Harding in each of the past two years and that you helped drive the herd to Harding. I'll even bet you some of the Harding residents will recognize you if we give them the chance. No jury will believe that was Double H cattle when it is hooked to the other evidence we have."

Spencer scowled again but still remained silent.

"Salty, we want the man behind all this," Willis went on. "You're looking at a 10 year prison term, but if you cooperate with me, I might be able to do you some good. No promises, but you'll find me reasonable. Think about it, Salty. That's a long time to spend in jail."

With that, Willis rose, announced he was going back to town and moved toward the front door, deep in thought.

"I'll get right to work on obtaining those railroad documents," he said when he reached the porch area. "From what you said, I don't think I need to talk to French just yet. Let's let him simmer for a while along with Salty. Maybe one of them will get smart."

Doc followed Willis out of the house and mounted his rig. Before Conklin could get it in motion, however, Willis walked his horse over to where Tex and Marty were standing and leaned down.

"Something else bothers me, Riley," he said. "You say almost 400 head were sold. Where is the money? As far as I know, none of the men you've named have shown any real evidence of sudden wealth. Donie plays poker a lot and buys fancy clothes. But he's always done that, and he wins more at poker than he loses. I'll nose around town about the others but don't expect to learn much. At $ 13 to $ 14 a head we're talking five to six thousand dollars here. Where is it? If we could locate some of that money, it would help our case plenty."

"I'll think on it," responded Tex, an idea suddenly popping into his head. "Find out what you can in town, and we'll talk ag'in. As soon as the roundup is over," he added.

Willis pulled his horse back and trotted out of the MJ yard, Doc close behind in his rig.

I hope they split up and return like they came, thought Tex. But I guess it don't matter much. It won't be long before the cat'll be out of the bag about us being here anyhow.

Trig left to go back to what he had been doing, and Marty went with him. But Tex motioned for Bronc to follow him back into the house, and Bronc was at his side when they reached Spencer's couch.

Salty looked up as Tex and Bronc approached.

"I didn't say anythin' in front of Willis," Tex started, "but those rustlin' charges are the least of your worries. The man I want is the man who killed Slim Evers. From what Felipé told me, you didn't do it, but you shore as hell know who did. Sooner or later we're goin' to get that man, and he's goin' to hang. If'n you know who did it and don't tell us, you're the same as pullin' the trigger as far as me and my men are concerned. If'n that's true, and we prove it's true, you'll hang right alongside the other fellar. You get my drift?"

Salty's eyes opened wide, real fear swept across his face and he turned pale. In a moment he regained his composure but continued to remain silent.

Tex waited for a few minutes but finally turned on his heel and left the room.

Bronc leaned over Salty and spoke quietly. "You ever see a man hang, Spencer?" he asked. "I have, and it shore ain't purty. It would be just plumb awful to hang someone who really didn't do nothin'. In jail for a spell, and you got a chance to git out. Once you're dead, you're always dead. Maybe Cook and Sims were the lucky ones. They didn't have time to think about dying. It looks like you might have a lot of time to think about it."

Bronc straightened up, smiled inwardly at the fear that had returned to Spencer's face and left the room.

Bronc joined Tex on the porch and grinned. "Spencer's got a lot to think about," he said. "If we work on him enough, he may break."

"Yes," agreed Tex. "We'll keep at it. I've already got an idear on what to hit him with tomorrow."

"Bronc," Tex continued, "tell Trig to take French on his usual mornin' walk and tell him to make it a long walk and away from the bunkhouse. While they're gone, you go through his bedroll and belongin's. Tear his bunk apart if you have to."

"What am I lookin' for?" asked a surprised Bronc.

"Money," answered Tex. "I want to know how much cash he has here. It stands to reason the gang must have split up the money they got when they sold the cattle. Maybe some of it is still around."

"It's been a year since the last bunch was sold," said Bronc reflectively, rubbing his chin. "Ain't likely much of it would still be around."

"That's true," replied Tex. "But I don't want to pass up any bets. Besides, from what Willis said, it doesn't look like much of it has shown up in or around Ridgeway and for good reason. Sudden riches might start some questions, even in Ridgeway."

Bronc nodded and began making his way to the bunkhouse. It was worth a try, he thought, but he really didn't expect to find much.

* * * * * * * * * * * *

Bo Franklin, Chick Snyder and the rest of the Double H punchers had completed the transfer of the herd to the grassy mesa shortly before dusk.

Bo sent the rest of the men back to the ranch but decided to keep Chick with him. He had decided to stay with the herd for a couple of hours to make sure it settled down, and he wanted Chick to keep him company. The two men walked their horses as they circled the cattle.

"Thanks for gettin' me away from Donie this morning," Chick volunteered. "I'm not sure I could have spent the whole day with him."

"I thought you might be happy I cut in," laughed Bo. Then he sobered and said, "The more I think about what you said last night, the less I like it. Donie is startin' to scare me."

Chick didn't reply, and the two men continued to walk their horses around the cattle.

Finally Bo spoke up again. "Another thing I don't like is have'n to do Dan and Salty's work ever so often. They seem to be gone more'n they should, especially in the last month or so. Wonder what they are doin'. Donie's answer to the old man this mornin' didn't really make sense to me. I didn't see any strays close to the MJ line the last time I was out there. What would make them drift that way now?"

"Don't ask me," retorted Chick. "I only do as I'm told. It's kind of funny we don't have a real foreman, though. Sometimes the old man gives all the orders, sometimes Donie gives some and even Kelso did, too, now and then. Why I sort of thought the old man was usin' you thataway the last couple of days. Has he said anythin' to you?"

"No, he didn't," replied Bo. "But, like you, I just do as I'm told. Well, let's make one more swing around these critters and then head for the ranch."

They made their circle and began the trip back to the ranch. About halfway home, however, Bo suddenly pulled up and raised his left hand. Instinctively, a surprised Chick pulled his horse to a stop as well.

"What the hell . . . ?" Chick began, but Bo waved him off.

"Chick, I've been thinkin'," Bo began. "Somethin's been botherin' me, and I just figgered out what it is. I'm missin' a bet. Remember last night I wondered if Donie is gunnin' for that MJ rider. Chick, I owe that MJ foreman a favor. If I hadn't lied about Donie, the old man and Kelso wouldn't have gone to the MJ. That foreman and I were lucky he was fast enough to take care of Kelso. It coulda been t'other way around. I'll bet he shore would like to know this gunslinger is lookin' for his man."

"Huh," grunted Chick. "You're right as rain, Bo, and you'd better include me in your thinkin'. I'm the only one, outside Donie, who knows what this jasper looks like!"

"Yes, of course," agreed Bo. "We've got to do it together. Chick, the first chance we get, we've got to get over to the MJ Ranch. And the sooner, the better. That gunman is due in Ridgeway in a day or two. In fact, he could be there already!"

Bo spurred his horse into motion, and Chick followed right behind. The rest of the trip was made in silence, both men thinking about how they would meet this new challenge.

* * * * * * * * * * * *

Art French had become a desperate man. The death of Kelso had been bad enough, but now the discovery of the stolen herd and the deaths of Cook and Sims, combined with the capture of Spencer, meant that the rustling scheme was history.

French had begun to think about escaping as soon as he had started to recover from the beating he had received from Tex. He knew his chances were slim, but he had to make an attempt.

French's main attention was directed to the ropes that bound him. He was now allowed to take short walks, three times a day, but was always accompanied by a Rambling R man, usually Bronc or Trig. Apache, as a rule, went along, too, and was in charge of securing the prisoner after each outing.

The Indian boy really knew how to tie ropes and truss up a person, French had to admit, grudgingly and profanely. It's a good thing the boy didn't use rawhide, he thought.

But when the Indian boy was otherwise occupied and Bronc or Trig was in charge of tying him, it was a different matter. If he tensed his muscles just right, he normally ended up with a little more slack than Apache tolerated.

On this particular night, he had done an even better job than usual and had ended up with a little extra slack. When he pulled himself up he could just reach the rope around his right wrist with his mouth. He began to attack the rope with his teeth. He could only hold himself upright for 10 or 15 seconds at a time before dropping his head back on his bunk. It was exhausting and backbreaking work, but he persisted. He was close to total exhaustion when he felt the rope give a bit. He fell back, took a longer rest than before, pulled himself up again and attacked the rope with renewed vigor.

Several more chews, and he felt the rope give even more. Covered with sweat, he rested again and returned to the attack. Finally he laid back, tensed himself and yanked his wrist with all the strength he could muster. The rope strands came apart, and his right hand was free!

He closed his eyes and smiled at his success. He rested a bit more and then began working on the knots on the rope holding his left hand to his bunk. It took a while, but eventually his left hand moved free. Again he closed his eyes and rested, listening to the snores and heavy breathing of the other men in the bunkhouse.

Now, he knew, he had to gamble. He sat up in his bunk and looked around to see if anyone had observed his movement. Satisfied that all was still, he leaned forward and began to work on the knots on the ropes holding both ankles. With both hands now employed, the work was much easier, and he was soon completely free. He slowly crawled out of his bunk and paused, wondering if he was being observed. But again there was no response to his movements, and he slipped out the bunkhouse door and breathed the cool night air with a great deal of pleasure and relief.

He had toyed with the idea of slipping into the main house and silencing Spencer for good, but he knew the porch was occupied with some sleeping men, even though many were out on the range engaged in the roundup. Further, he had listened to the bunkhouse conversations and was aware that other men usually spread their bedrolls in the main room of the ranch, where Salty was located, and that at least one was always awake and on guard duty. His chances of reaching Salty and killing him, therefore, were almost nil and not worth the risk. His best option, he thought, would be to get a horse, head for the Double H and Donie, secure a weapon and food and then put as much distance between him and the pursuit he was sure would follow.

Accordingly, he took a good deal of time reaching the corral by a circuitous route, using the shadows from the buildings and trees as cover. Finally reaching his destination, he grabbed the first bridle and reins he could find and crept among the horses, searching for the one he knew best. He located the animal and gently urged the horse toward the nearest fencing where he knew saddles would be hung. Locating one, he quickly saddled his horse and led him to the corral entrance. Removing the poles from the gate, he pulled his horse out, put one foot in a stirrup and froze when he heard a voice.

"Goin' somewhere, Mr. French?"

French turned, glanced over his right shoulder and saw Bronc Evans standing in a slight crouch about 15 feet away, both hands poised over his Colts.

French took a deep breath and pulled himself up into the saddle.

"I'm ridin' out of here Evans," he announced. "You're a tough hombre all right, but I don't think you'll shoot me in the back."

"Maybe not," drawled Bronc, "but I shore can fix it so you won't walk ag'in for a long time."

This disturbing comment made French pause for a moment. But again he took a deep breath.

"That's a chance I'll have to take, Evans," he said in a low voice and kneed his horse.

The horse had just taken its first step when a form came hurtling over the top pole of the corral fence. The form grabbed French around the neck, and both figures fell off the horse and landed with a thud on the ground.

A surprised groan escaped from French's lips as he rolled over and struggled to get to his feet. His progress was rudely stopped when a gun barrel in Bronc's right hand swung downward and landed on the back of his bare head. French slumped to the ground and lay still.

Apache picked himself up and brushed off his clothes as he and Bronc looked down on the unconscious prisoner.

"That was a nice flyin' leap," acknowledged Bronc. "Funny thing, too. He was right. Much as I wanted to, I couldn't have shot him. I must be gettin' soft in my old age."

Apache grunted in response to this comment.

"No, you're not getting soft, Bronc. You just remembered why we are here. Slim would be pleased. Besides, you would have shot the horse from under him to stop him, if you had to. C'mon, give me a hand. We gotta put this guy to bed before he wakes up. This time I'll tie him down. He won't get loose again."

CHAPTER 11

The second day of the roundup moved ahead as planned.

Sanchez began his portion of the operation by sending most of his men, and the remuda, across the stream whereupon they swung south, proceeded to the southern boundary line east of the stream, turned about and began the sweep north, employing the procedures of the previous day but using the stream as their left guide this time.

Four men pushed the first days' accumulation of cattle slowly north, picking up additional cattle along the way. About two miles from the main buildings the banks of the stream had widened somewhat, and here the water was at its shallowest and made an excellent ford. It was easy to force the cattle to cross at this point, and once across, they let the animals spread out and graze while they awaited the arrival of the riders from the south. By noon, these men, and the cattle they had gathered, began to appear.

In the meantime, Apache joined Lefty, Blackie and Kansas as they returned to the herd they had gathered on the north range. Reno and Laredo were waiting for them.

Leaving Kansas and Apache to watch the herd, the other four men spread out and continued to cull the range for hidden cattle. Only a few head were located, and after a couple of hours, Lefty called in his men, and the reunited group drove their herd south. They veered away from the main ranch, an eager Marty joined the group, and all continued south until they ran into Sanchez' men and their augmented herd. Since it was now past midday, the operation was halted for a rest and the noon meal. As soon as all had eaten, the next step in the process began.

Six riders exchanged their mounts for the cutting-out horses and began to infiltrate the grazing herd, seeking any unbranded mavericks. Cutting out these animals, they drove them to the outer edges of the herd where another rider would pick them up and force them toward the branding fires that had been started during the noon meal. Each animal was then roped, thrown, branded and released. Despite a thorough search, only about 20 unbranded animals were found, and within an hour the branding was completed.

The punchers then began to string out the cattle in a long, thin line as six horsemen formed a wedge, a large opening at the top and a much smaller opening at the bottom. Three riders, at about 15 yard intervals, formed each side of the wedge. When Sanchez and Marty took up positions on each side of the narrow end, the other men began forcing the cattle into the wedge and out the narrow opening, with Sanchez and Marty counting them as they passed through. Each man dropped a pebble in a hat for every 20 animals as they passed by.

The count was finally completed, and Marty and Sanchez compared their tallies. Sanchez had 873 and Marty one more.

"There was a little mixup there toward the end, and I may have counted one critter twice," Marty observed, a little disappointed with the total.

"Don't forget the 106 back down the trail," Denver reminded him.

"That's so!" responded Marty, brightening a little. "I had forgotten about them. That will help some. What a fool I've been!"

"Well, don't be too hard on yourself," said Denver in a low voice. "Besides, we've got two more ranges to comb."

Sanchez left Rusty and Curley to watch the herd and led the remaining men back to the ranch. It was getting late, the horses needed rest, and so he decided to quit a bit early and start fresh on the morrow.

* * * * * * * * * * *

As soon as Lefty and his three men had left to continue the roundup, Tex headed toward the bunkhouse for another talk with French.

Yesterday Bronc had made a thorough search of French's possessions and had only found about $ 70. No real wealth there, Tex admitted to himself. Surely some of that cash was earmarked for Adams and Charles. At $ 10 a month for each, it was likely only about $ 30 was really French's own money. Maybe I'm heading up a blind canyon, Tex reflected.

Tex entered the bunkhouse and moved to French's bunk. Apache's system of ropes and knots had French securely bound but still allowed the man some freedom of movement.

French looked up at Tex and sneered. "Someone went through my digs yesterday. You must be really hard up for things to do."

"Not really," replied Tex calmly. "But you'd better understand one thing, French. Me and my boys will do anythin' we want to do or have to do to get the answers I want. And, like I told you yesterday, we're goin' to stay here until we do get those answers. You thought any more on what I said yesterday?"

"Go to hell," answered French venomously.

"In due time, I suppose," Tex responded pleasantly. "But when I do, I shore expect to have a lot of company. By the way, how much of the herd money did you get?" he asked quietly.

"That's none of your business," retorted French, again with heat.

"Oh well, that's where you're wrong," Tex went on. "All of this is my business. I'm just curious to find out what 10 years in jail is worth in these parts. It shore sounds expensive to me, and, of course, there's still the rope that sounds even more expensive. You willin' to pay that kind of price for somethin' I don't think you did? Me and my boys figger that whoever was there is just as guilty as the one who pulled the trigger. It really makes no difference to us, though. We can hang two just as easy as one. That's no trouble a'tall."

Tex started to move away and then stopped and looked back. "Think about it, French. Look around you. You don't think I've got enough men to do what I want to? Who's goin' to stop me?"

For the first time Tex detected a trace of fear on French's face. It quickly disappeared, but Tex knew he had struck a hard blow. He felt satisfied as he left the bunkhouse. He would continue to work on French, but now it was Spencer's turn.

Tex entered the ranch house just as Mary was finishing feeding Spencer. It was his first solid food, and Spencer seemed very pleased. Bronc was sitting nearby, watching the proceedings.

"Your first real food in quite a spell," observed Tex.

"Yes, tasted good, too," admitted Salty. "Mrs. Johnson is a right good cook."

"Well, I'm glad you're feelin' better. It's time we had another talk. You remember what Willis and I told you yesterday?"

Salty nodded. "I'm thinkin' on it."

"While you're thinkin' on it, mebby I can give you somethin' else to think about. What was your share of the money from the cattle?" he asked.

Salty thought for a moment and shrugged his shoulders.

"Guess there's no harm in tellin'," he said. "I got $ 300 from the sale of each herd."

"What did you do with it?" asked Tex casually.

"I sent it to my brother, but don't ask me where he is 'cause I won't tell you," replied Salty with some vigor.

"Oh, I don't care about that," Tex assured him. "But I'm some curious. Why did you send it to him?"

Salty frowned. "Well, he and I wanted to buy a small spread and have a ranch of our own. Another couple of years, and we might have had enough to get started. Guess that's a dead idea now."

"Not necessarily," commented Tex. "Willis said he would be reasonable, and I told you who I was after. The rustlin' is only a side bet for me, and I intend to get that money back from Henderson. You meet me halfway, and you might have a chance for that ranch a lot sooner than you think."

Salty remained silent, so Tex went on. "Let's get back to the rustlin'. Was Sims' payoff the same as yours? What about Cook?"

"Yes, Sims got the same as me," responded Salty. "Don't know about Cook but always had the notion he was paid about the same. The others got the big money."

"French, Kelso and Donie Henderson," stated Tex softly, watching Spencer's face closely.

Salty couldn't conceal his surprise. "You know about Donie?" he asked.

"You'd be some surprised on how much I know," responded Tex coldly. "So be careful what you say. I catch you lyin' to me, and all bets are off. You remember that."

Tex leaned down and looked Spencer straight in the face.

"So you three boys only got your hands on $ 1,800. That leaves a lot of money for the other three. French paid Adams and Charles out of his share, and I'll bet Kelso and Donie took the biggest shares of all, well over a $ 1,000 apiece."

Tex paused, let this information sink in and straightened up.

"I don't think a miserable $ 600 is very good pay for 10 years in prison, Salty," he remarked. "In fact, it isn't very good pay for only five years in prison. Kelso is dead, but Donie might get off with as little as a suspended sentence, his father bein' who he is and all. Wouldn't that beat all? Donie gettin' the biggest share of the money and no prison time, while you get a lot less money and all that time in jail!"

Spencer's response was a deep frown. Tex figured he had scored a bullseye and thought it would be best to leave it there. He turned and headed for the front door. "Think about it, Salty," he said over his right shoulder as he left the room.

Bronc followed Tex out of the house, down the porch steps and out into the yard, a big grin on his face. Sure that they were well out of hearing distance, Bronc spoke up, "You shore hit him hard with that one. I'm bettin' he's goin' to spend the day with a lot on his mind."

"Let's hope so," Tex agreed. "He's the best line we got on who killed Slim. Even if'n we find out who it is, though, we'll still have to prove it, and it has to be good proof.

"I'll make any deal I have to to get that proof. I hope you and the boys understand what I'm doin' and why. I'm not goin' to rest easy until we get that killer. And I don't care who he is! But we got to do it legal and proper. Otherwise Slim's life and his ways won't mean a thing. We can't let that happen."

Bronc sobered and cast a wistful glance at the distant grave.

"Tex," he said, "you're the boss. Me and the boys will go along with whatever you do. We all know what Slim stood for and how he lived. I got a feelin' you were worried about Trig and me 'cause we were so close to him. But we can wait, and we'll back you all the way. It's hard, but we'll do it."

Tex put his hand on his friend's shoulder and squeezed it. The bond was complete, and nothing more had to be said. A few steps more and they separated, each going to his next task.

* * * * * * * * * * *

It was late afternoon when Dusty and Marty reached the ranch with the chuck wagon. Soon thereafter, the entire roundup crew came thundering in, dismounted and turned their tired horses loose. Denver, Cheyenne, and the small remuda followed right behind.

Marty and Sanchez met Tex and reported on their progress. Marty again expressed disappointment with the results. "And I know the other two sections won't have near that many cattle," he concluded bitterly.

"Well, if'n my figgers on the natural increases are anywhere near right, we should have about 1,800 head," muttered Tex. "Since we believe all the beef shipped out of Harding was ourn, we should now have about 1,400 left. We knew that goin' in, Marty, and if'n that's the way it comes out, at least we'll know where we stand."

"But I have so few cattle I can sell," retorted Marty. "I won't be able to pay the interest on that damn note let alone any principal. I sure didn't do a very good job of running this ranch. I really let Slim down!"

"We all make mistakes, Marty," countered Tex sharply. "Slim made a few himself over the years. I know where we can get the money, and if'n that don't work, the Rambling R will cover any money problems you got.

No one is goin' to get this ranch. You can bet on that! When is the next payment due on the note?"

"First of the year," Marty answered glumly.

"Oh, hell, that gives us plenty of time," Tex reassured him. We're goin' to have all this settled long afore then."

Marty sent Tex a grateful look. "I guess I should be thankful I have such good friends," he admitted. "I only wish Slim had called on you as soon as he thought something was wrong. He might be still alive today."

"Yes, he should have," agreed Tex. "Why he didn't, I'll never know. But we're here now, and we're goin' to stay 'til it's finished. And if'n that means takin' on the Hendersons and the whole damn county, that's what we'll do. People around here may have to hear about the Rambling R the hard way. But we'll cross that bridge when we come to it."

* * * * * * * * * * * *

After the evening meal Tex called all the men together.

"Tomorrow I want to finish the roundup," he announced. "Adams and Charles know these last two sections the best, and so we'll build on their knowledge. Sanchez, you'll take your men and Apache and go with Adams. Charley, I want you to leave the outpost and join up with Lefty, Kansas, Blackie, Reno and Laredo. You all go with Charles. Red, that means you and Cavalry will be by yoreselves. Can't help that, but I don't expect no trouble, leastways not yet. Curley and Rusty will stay with the herd in the south section. Bronc and Trig will stay with Reb and me at the ranch. Marty and Dusty will drive the chuck wagon, and Denver and Cheyenne will take care of the remuda. You're not goin' to have a lot of cattle to bring in, but every head is important so we don't want to miss any. Any questions?"

Hearing none, he said good night and returned to the ranch house. The men scattered, sought their bedrolls or bunks and turned in. The usual sentries were posted, and another day came to a peaceful close.

* * * * * * * * * * * *

Thunderclouds had begun to form in the atmosphere around the Henderson ranch house that morning. These thunderclouds, however, were man made, not the result of Mother Nature's unpredictable moods.

Henry Henderson had marched down to the bunkhouse shortly after dawn, noted the unslept status of two bunks in particular and demanded to know the whereabouts of one Salty Spencer and one Dan Sims. No one could give him a satisfactory answer, and so he stormed back to the main house and confronted Donie with the same question.

"I don't know," Donie had answered truthfully. "Maybe they ran into more strays than they expected. It was a long ride to that extreme edge of the Double H Ranch," he reminded his father. "Maybe they decided to hole up at a line camp and really do a thorough job of it."

His father had reluctantly accepted that explanation, but Donie knew he was rapidly running out of reasonable excuses. Besides, he was more than a little worried himself.

Donie had spent a restless night in his own right. While he had pretty much recovered from the injuries he had received at the hands of Lefty White, memories of the pain and suffering had lingered on.

Kelso's death had also been very unsettling. How could a foreman of such a small ranch be fast enough to handle an expert, as he knew the term, like Kip Kelso?

And speaking of that foreman, what had happened to Art French and, more importantly, where was he? Surely he would have gotten some word to Donie if he was able to. If he wasn't able to? Donie shuddered at the thought of what that might imply.

Now Salty and Dan were long overdue. Their task had been a simple one and, with French's and Cook's help, should have been concluded in a day or a day and a half at the most. Where were they?

They had agreed to speed up operations and get the small herd ready to drive to Harding. Donie had to make the shipping and sale arrangements and to do this he had to go to Canyon City. He also had to get word on when the herd could be moved and, here again, he would have to come up with a good reason to cover the extended absence of both Salty and Dan. Kelso had always figured out how to do this in the past, and now it was Donie's problem. Further, he figured French would have to lead this drive now that Kelso was dead.

But again, where was French?

All this uncertainty fairly made his head spin, and he had paced the floor a good bit of the night, seeking some answers. No useful ideas came to mind, however, and by morning he was in a vile mood.

The exchange with his father had not improved his state of mind one whit, and he soon began to find fault with any work he saw being done by the ranch hands. Fortunately, or unfortunately, depending on one's point of view, the elder Henderson had not made many work assignments that morning, and more than the usual number of punchers were on and about the premises of the main ranch. Thus, Donie's sharp tongue was directed at many bodies but, at the same time, nobody was missed. The tension in the air increased as the morning hours wore on.

Bo and Chick received their share of criticism but remained silent. Donie finally moved on to another location and out of hearing range.

"He's shore workin' himself up into a lather," observed Chick. "What's worse, he don't know what he's talkin' about a good share of the time."

"Yeah," agreed Bo. "But this gives me an idea. I'm goin' to see the old man. Maybe I can find us a way to get away from here for a spell."

Bo watched Donie disappear behind the blacksmith area and then headed for the main house. He entered and found Henry staring at a blank wall. Bo stopped at a respectful distance, held his hat in his hands and waited patiently. Sensing his presence, Henry finally turned and let out a deep sigh.

"What's wrong, Bo?" he asked softly. "I don't seem to know what's going on around here. Maybe I'm just getting old and losing my touch. Is that what's wrong, Bo?"

"Oh, I don't think so, sir," Bo answered. "This has been a bad week for all of us, what with Donie gettin' hurt like he did and then Kelso gettin' killed. I think we've all been on edge. Remember, Kelso was sort of a special friend to Donie, and maybe the boy is takin' it harder than you think."

Puzzled, Henderson stared at Bo.

"That was a strange word you just said, Bo," Henderson mused, again softly. "You called him a boy, and I've been looking at him as a man. I wonder if that's the problem. Is he still a boy? Have I pushed him along too fast? Is he ready to take over the biggest and best ranch in the whole territory? Is he ready to fill the shoes of Henry Henderson?"

"No one could fill those shoes," blurted out a surprised Bo. He was experiencing a view of Henderson he had never seen before. The man was close to tears. Bo couldn't help feeling very uncomfortable as he looked at Henderson.

"Well, they're going to have to someday," retorted Henry with some spirit. "No one lives forever. Donie will just have to grow into the job. I reckon I'm just going to have to give him more time."

Henderson shook his head, and that seemed to clear his mind a bit. He remembered that Bo had approached him.

"Well, you didn't come here to listen to an old man's lament," he said in a stronger voice. "What do you want, Bo?"

Bo had almost forgotten why he had sought out Henderson, but the question jolted him back to reality.

"Well, sir, I was thinkin'. Why don't Chick and I mosey down to the south range and see if we can find Dan and Salty? Maybe they need some help. Our work is caught up here, and we thought we might swing by town on the way back, if you don't mind. We haven't been to town in quite a spell, sir."

"That's a right good idea, Bo," eagerly replied Henry. But then his face fell. "No, it isn't a good idea," he amended. "If Donie wants to run this ranch, he has to make decisions and then follow through on 'em. I'll send him out tomorrow to check on Dan and Salty if they don't get back before then." He couldn't help noticing the sag in Bo's shoulders as he spoke.

"But Bo, there's no reason you and Chick can't go to town," Henry went on. "I've pushed you both hard lately, and you deserve a break. Go to town and have a good time and stay overnight if you wants to. I'll expect you back when I see you."

"Thank you, sir," said a relieved Bo. "Chick and I will be back tonight. And don't worry about Donie. Once he gets over losin' Kip, I think he will be all right."

Henry nodded and motioned with his hand.

Bo turned and began walking toward the door but stopped as Henry's voice reached him.

"Thanks for stopping by, Bo. I needed a chance to talk to someone. I appreciate it. Now go and have a good time."

CHAPTER 12

After a quick noon meal, Bo and Chick left the ranch and maintained a steady pace toward Ridgeway. Bo described the conversation with Henderson, and the two of them discussed this new and surprising side to Henderson's personality. After exhausting this subject, both riders remained silent until they reached the main trail leading into Ridgeway. Turning left meant heading into the town, while a right turn would send them toward the MJ Ranch.

Bo pulled up and pondered the situation for a few minutes.

"Chick, I'm not shore we're doin' the right thing here. I feel lower'n a snake's belly goin' around the old man. Maybe we should go back and talk to him."

"Hell's fire!" exploded Chick. "Why do that? He don't know what the kid has done, and he probably wouldn't believe us anyway. The old man ain't the problem, Donie is. Ain't you the one what told me you owed that MJ foreman a favor and that you'd been a part of one shootin' and didn't want to be part of another? Ain't them facts still true?"

"Yes, they're still true," sighed Bo. "I reckon we got to go to the MJ and at least warn them. If that keeps another shootin' from happenin', nobody needs to be the wiser. C'mon, let's go on to the MJ before I change my mind ag'in."

The two men picked up the pace, and it wasn't long before the MJ Ranch buildings came into sight. They slowed their speed somewhat and finally reduced it to a walk as they reached the ranch yard. Bo was relieved to see only the foreman and one other man on the ranch porch and no other punchers visible around the premises.

Bo and Chick pulled their horses to a stop and remained mounted while Tex and the other man approached them.

Bo touched his hat and said, "Howdy, I'm Bo Franklin, and this here is Chick Snyder. We ride for the Double H. I don't know if you remember me or not."

"Why, yes I do, Bo," Tex replied coldly. "Seem to me you're the one who had to change his story."

Bo reddened and nodded. "I thought you'd remember that. That's sort of why we're here. I feel I need to square things with you. May we step down?"

"Yeah, shore," replied Tex, his mind racing. "C'mon up on the porch and set a spell. This here is Bronc Evans. He's my right arm."

Bo dismounted, nodded his greeting to Bronc and nervously shifted his weight from one foot to another.

"What I want to tell you is kinda private, if you know what I mean," he said in a low voice, glancing at Bronc.

"I understand, Bo," said Tex, "but anythin' you tell me I'm going to pass on to him anyhow. He might as well hear it first hand, don't you think? What do you want to tell me?"

Bo sat down in a chair and just as quickly got up again and began pacing the porch. Tex waited patiently as Bo continued to pace. Bo finally took a deep breath, sat on a railing of the porch and looked at Tex.

"What I'm about to do ain't easy for me, mister. The old man is a tough man to work for, but I like him. He's treated me fair, and I don't like goin' around him. But he don't know what's goin' on, and I figger what he don't know won't hurt him."

Bo paused for a minute, moved a few paces away from the railing, threw up his hands in resignation and faced Tex again.

"Donie has hired himself a gunslinger, and, as far as I can tell, he's goin' to have this jasper go after that puncher of yourn that beat up Donie. I don't want any more killings done around here, and I figgered if I came to you, you might figger out some way to keep it from happenin'."

"How do you know Donie has hired this killer?" asked Tex quietly.

"Well, that's why Chick is here." Bo turned to Chick. "Tell him what you did for Donie."

Chick described his trip to Canyon City, his search for the gunman named Smiley and the cashing of the check.

As these latter words reached Tex's ears, it took all he had to keep his face from revealing his thoughts. Canyon City. Of course, he thought. Why didn't I think of that!

"You said his name was Smiley," Tex observed as calmly as possible. "What does he look like?"

Snyder described the man.

"That's Smiley, right enough." Bronc spoke for the first time. "He's shore a long way from home. I sort of thought he was dead a'ready."

"You know him?" said Bo in surprise.

"Yeah, I know him. Our paths crossed a couple of times. He don't like workin' for a livin'," responded Bronc, who glanced at Tex.

Tex got up from his chair, moved to the porch railing, took a long look at the distant foothills and turned to face Franklin.

"Bo, you said you like Henry Henderson. Do you think you could get along with him if you weren't workin' for him? In other words, do you think he trusts you?"

"Why, I guess so," Bo said slowly, taken somewhat aback by the questions. "What you got in mind?"

"Bo, I know your comin' here today was very hard to do, and I appreciate it a lot, a lot more than I can say. If'n this causes you any trouble at the Double H, I want you to know that I'll have a job for you here on the MJ. That goes for you, too, Chick. The MJ can always use good men, and you boys strike me as bein' just that."

Tex became thoughtful and motioned toward the courtyard and the open spaces beyond.

"Bo, there's no reason why these two ranches can't work together and be good neighbors. Maybe, if'n the MJ had someone Henry could talk to and trust, we could make this whole area a better place to live in. Certainly a peaceful setting would be good for both ranches.

"I'm goin' to tell you flat out that the MJ is here to stay. And that's somethin' Henry better understand right soon. Once we get that settled, we'll need someone to help keep things right between the ranches. Someone who knows Henry and is trusted by him would be a valuable man on the MJ. You just might be that man. Keep it in mind anyway. We can talk ag'in sometime. I really do thank you for comin' here today. You, too, Chick."

Bo and Chick rose, shook hands with Tex and moved to their horses. Soon after leaving the ranch, Bo pulled a red bandanna from his pants pocket and wiped his face and the back of his neck. He had been perspiring profusely.

"Well, Chick, I'm glad we came," he commented. "I guess we did the right thing. That foreman seemed glad we come, offerin' us jobs and everythin'. What he said is true, too. I kind of like him, Chick. He seems to act like a foreman should. Funny thing, though, I sort of had the feelin' he knew we were comin' before we got there. He shore didn't act surprised, did he?"

"No, he didn't," agreed Chick. "But did you notice those guns and holsters? Tied down they was, and those holsters looked greased to me. I'm beginnin' to think him gettin' Kelso was no accident. If trouble comes our way, I figger he might be the right guy to tie in with. And that Bronc fellar wears two guns, too. He knows Smiley and don't seem afraid of him a'tall. Wearin' two guns is like wavin' a red flag, and Riley shore wasn't bluffin' with Kelso. I'll tell you this, if things don't get better around our ranch purty damn soon, I just might take him up on that job offer."

"Yeah, I was thinkin' the same thing," said Bo. "And I just remembered that the MJ puncher who threw down on us when Donie got smart also wears two guns. Three two-gun men on a little ranch at the same time? It shore is a strange setup, and the more I think about it, the more I'm glad we came here. Some day we may need all the help we can get."

Bo was silent for a few minutes and then waved his hand in the direction of Ridgeway.

"I'm goin' on to town like we planned. I'm goin' to eat and only have one or two drinks, then go back to the ranch. From now on we gotta be careful what we say and who we say it to. C'mon, get that cayuse movin', I'm gettin' hungrier by the minute."

* * * * * * * * * * * *

Tex and Bronc watched Bo and Chick leave the MJ until they were out of sight.

"Well, I reckon I'd better tell Lefty to keep his eyes peeled for Smiley," Tex said grimly. "Smiley's shore in for a big surprise when he finds out who he wants to kill."

Bronc rubbed his jaw reflectively.

"I'm not shore you got things right about that, Tex," he commented.

"What do you mean by that?" asked a surprised Tex.

"Well, Lefty only beat up Donie, but some hombre named Riley killed his best friend. We know they were in on the rustlin' together, and Kelso was probably the brains behind the scheme. Kelso comes here and picks a fight with the new foreman. Why? 'Cause that was the best way to get the old foreman back runnin' things ag'in. Why wouldn't Donie want to do the same thing? He must be goin' loco wonderin' where French is and what's he doin'. No, Tex, it seems likely that Smiley will aim for you first and mebby Lefty next."

Tex looked at Bronc, admiration on his face. "You shore said a mouthful, my friend. You musta been doin' a lot of thinkin' while Bo was talkin', and damned if I don't think you're right on the money. We'll all have to keep our eyes peeled for Mr. Smiley, and the first man to run into him will have to take him."

"That's a job I figger me or Trig can do real easy," agreed Bronc. "And remember what I told you about your hands and our jobs. Don't forget it!"

Tex laughed and slapped Bronc on the back.

"I won't forget," he said and then sobered. "Bo and Chick may have done us a real favor, Bronc. So Donie has a bank account in Canyon City and big enough to handle a thousand dollars in checks. I wonder if French and Kelso have accounts there, too. I'll bet Ted Willis can find out for us. Let's go into Ridgeway tomorrow and get him started on that idear. Who knows, we might run into Smiley at the same time," he added and grinned at Bronc's reaction.

Their conversation was interrupted by the sound of the chuck wagon rattling its way on to the ranch courtyard with Dusty at the reins. Behind it, a short distance away, a large dust cloud signaled the arrival of the cavvy with Denver and Cheyenne driving the tired horses.

Dusty pulled the wagon to a halt and jumped down. Bronc joined him in unhitching the team and leading them into the corral.

Dusty turned to Tex and announced, "I've got to get a fire started and the brandin' irons heatin'. Juan and José are bringin' in about a dozen critters for brandin' to go with the three Lefty found in the north section. Marty and Sanchez are finishin' their count, and they and the rest of the boys should be along directly."

"Use the forge over in the blacksmith shop for your fire," directed Tex. "As soon as Juan and José get here, have Denver and Cheyenne give you a hand and get the brandin' done. Bronc, Trig and I will unload the wagon."

Each man did as he was told, and the two Mexicans soon arrived with their little herd. The branding immediately started and was being completed when the rest of the roundup crew arrived in a cloud of dust.

Marty and Sanchez dismounted and approached Tex with Lefty and Bronc following close behind. The entire group entered the ranch house and went into the big den.

Marty found a pen and some paper and began to do some figuring. Speaking out loud, half to himself, he mumbled, "873 on the south range, 106 hidden in the meadow, 457 we just counted, and 14 we just branded. 1,450 in all. Almost 400 short of what you thought we should have, Tex."

"Yes, the 391 they shipped out of Harding would make it 1,841. That's a little better than I expected and purty much proves they didn't include any Double H cattle in their drives," responded Tex.

Tex went on, "Figgering $ 13 a head two years ago and $ 14 a head last year, someone owes us well over $ 5,000. That would help out your finances aplenty, wouldn't it, Marty?"

"It sure would," replied Marty, shaking his head. "That would take care of the interest and take a fair bite out of the note's amount as well. And we'd have enough cash to meet our needs for the next year, too, especially if we could sell those cattle with Double H brands on their hides."

"Well, we'll sell some older critters first," commented Tex. "But maybe we could trade Henderson for some of his unbranded crop next spring. We'll keep that in mind after we take care of our rustler friends."

Tex spoke again, "Sanchez, tomorrow take your men and scatter that south herd farther from the ranch. Lefty, take a few of the boys and scatter today's herd farther west and north. Bronc, Trig and I are goin' in to Ridgeway in the morning to see what Willis is doin'. The rest of you can stay here, take it easy and keep an eye on our two guests. Tell all the boys they did a good roundup, and I thank them."

* * * * * * * * * * * *

Bo and Chick had almost reached town when they met Doc Conklin in his rig and headed in their direction. They pulled their horses to a stop and greeted Conklin.

"You're headed in the wrong direction, Doc," suggested Bo. "Your work ought to be done for the day."

"A doctor's work is never done, my boy," declared Conklin stentoriously. "However, I only have one more call to make, and then I will be able to enjoy the fruits of my labor. You boys spending the night in town?" he asked, hoping to change the subject.

"Aw, we're just going to eat and have a drink or two before headin' back to the ranch," replied Chick.

"Well, have fun, boys," Doc encouraged them as he clipped the back side of his horse with his whip. The buggy moved forward, and Bo and Chick watched as it made its way down the trail.

Nudging their horses with their spurs, the two men trotted into Ridgeway and pulled up in front of the Sweetwater.

"One drink before dinner, dinner, one drink after and then back to the ranch," muttered Bo as they dismounted.

They marched up to the bar and ordered their drinks before looking around to see if the patrons included anyone they knew.

Chick nudged Bo and spoke softly. "Don't look now, but that jasper over in the far corner is Smiley. He musta gotten here sooner than he expected."

Smiley must have recognized Chick, too, because as Chick eyed the room a second time, Smiley motioned for him to come over to his table.

Chick downed his drink and nudged Bo a second time.

"He wants me to come over," Chick again spoke in a low voice. "C'mon with me."

Bo, who had been sipping his drink, finished off the remaining liquid and followed in his friend's footsteps.

Chick reached the man's table, hooked his thumbs on his gun belt and waited.

Smiley looked at him and, in a cold voice, said, "You're the one what found me in Canyon City. Where's Henderson?"

"Out at the ranch, I reckon," answered Chick. "Leastways, that's where he was when we left there this afternoon."

"Good," Smiley muttered. "You go out to the ranch and give him a message. Tell him I want to see him pronto. I don't aim to stay in this flea bitten town any longer than I has to. Tell him I'll be here until tomorrow night. Then I'm goin' back to Canyon City. You tell him."

"Shore, be glad to," responded Chick in a friendly voice. "Me and Bo are goin' to get somethin' to eat and mebby another drink, and then we're headin' back to the ranch."

Smiley removed his hands from his drink and slid them under the table.

"You'll go now," snapped Smiley.

Chick's face started to flush in anger, and a retort was on the tip of his tongue when Bo's boot found his ankle. A flash of pain crossed his face, adding to the redness, but he managed to respond in an even voice.

"Me and Bo are goin' to have another drink, and then we'll go."

Smiley started to rise in his chair, thought better of it and relaxed. He motioned with his left hand. "Suit yourself," he said, "but don't take too long. I don't like bein' kept waitin'."

Chick and Bo returned to the bar, ordered their drinks and slowly sipped them. Finally they slid their empty glasses toward the bartender, dropped a few coins on the counter and sauntered out of the saloon. Smiley got up from his table and followed them out, stopping on the board sidewalk and leaning against a post.

Chick and Bo were very deliberate in grabbing their reins, examining their saddles and finally slowly mounting their horses. Their deliberateness was not lost on Smiley, who scowled but said nothing. Chick and Bo walked their horses out of town without looking back. Upon reaching open spaces,

Chick vented his fury with a long string of profanities. Bo was surprised and impressed with the completeness of Chick's oratory. Finally, out of breath, Chick fell silent.

Bo slapped him on the shoulder and tried to comfort him. "You shore covered the whole range with your feelin's," he said, admiringly. "Hey, those MJ jobs are lookin' better all the time, ain't they?"

* * * * * * * * * * * *

Reb Stuart notified Tex that two more riders were on their way to the ranch.

"It's Doc Conklin and another fellar," he explained. "Me and Cavalry worked out a special signal for him since he was comin' out here frequent."

"Good idear," agreed Tex. "You boys have done a right good job for me. It's best to know someone's comin' afore they get here. Spread the word we're havin' visitors."

Conklin and Ted Willis soon arrived.

"I'm glad your whole crew is here," observed Willis as soon as he had dismounted. "I want to talk to Adams and Charles. Also, I want to spend a lot of time with Felipé and Sanchez. Think you can scrape together some grub for us? This is going to take a while."

"I think we can round up a few beans and some bacon for both of you," Tex replied. He motioned for Bronc to locate the men named. "I've got some interestin' news for you too, but that can wait 'til later," he added, noting that Adams and Charles were already headed their way.

Willis herded the two men to a far corner of the porch and began talking with them and taking notes. Sanchez and Felipé soon arrived and remained with Bronc, Tex and Marty while Willis continued to question Adams and Charles.

When the two punchers left and headed for the bunkhouse, Willis motioned for Sanchez and Felipé to join him. He was pleasantly surprised that both could converse with reasonably good English, especially Felipé, who was the key witness.

Willis continued to take extensive notes. He double checked a few items and then wearily put down his pencil and gathered up his notes. Felipé left the porch, but Sanchez followed Willis back to Tex and his companions.

Wiping his face with a handkerchief, Willis sat down and faced the group.

"Felipé and Sanchez can provide good testimony," he announced. "Adams and Charles will give us good support." Then he looked at Tex and smiled. "Your hunch was ace high, Riley. I haven't got the affidavits from the railroad yet, but they sent me a letter saying Donie's name is on the shipping documents. It arrived today on the stage. Of course, they can't verify that Donie is the actual person who signed the papers, but no one but him or Henry would be shipping beef with a Double H brand. That should be very incriminating all by itself."

Tex related the details of Bo's and Chick's visit and saw Willis' eyes light up.

"Canyon City, huh! Well, we both missed that bet, Riley. I nosed around Ridgeway on the sly and couldn't find out anything. Now I see why."

Tex also explained what had happened to Spencer's money and how much Adams and Charles had been paid.

"That still leaves a lot of money without a trail," remarked Willis thoughtfully. "Canyon City may provide us with a lot of answers. I'm going there myself day after tomorrow, and I'll be ready to get my hands on the bank records. Let's hope we get lucky."

"I want you to issue a warrant for Donie's arrest," Tex said suddenly. "Another one for French and Spencer, too. We just finished the roundup and the MJ is short 400 animals. Me and my boys are tired of fiddlin' around. I want some action, and throwin' Donie in jail is a good place to start. Can you do it?"

Willis frowned, rubbed his chin and cogitated for a few moments.

"You're sure you're hell bent on starting this thing?" he inquired.

"Damn shore," snapped Tex. "If'n this weren't Donie Henderson, would you even hesitate?"

Willis thought again for a few moments and sighed. "No, I guess not," he admitted. "As I look around the ranch here, it's obvious you have enough men and guns to take on Henderson. And the rest of the county, too, I suppose," he added and fell silent for a third time.

"All right, we'll do it!" Willis finally declared. "You still want to be appointed temporary sheriff?"

"No," retorted Tex. "I got a better idear. If'n Hamilton gives you trouble, talk him into appointing Marty as a deputy. That might give him a good laugh, and he might go along with it. Me and my boys will go along and make shore it gets done."

Willis laughed. "I like it," he sputtered between chuckles. "And Ben is just dumb enough to fall for it, too."

"Can you have them warrants ready by late mornin'?" Tex asked grimly.

"Give me until noon," begged Willis, still grinning.

"All right, we'll be there by noon. Now here's what I want you to do."

Tex explained his plan, and the grin on Willis' face threatened his ears.

"By gum, I hope you can pull it off," he said as he sobered. "It sure would set the town on its collective ears."

Tex saw Mary motioning.

"Mary says it's time to eat," he explained. "While we eat, I'll tell you what we been doin' with French and Spencer."

After supper, Willis pulled Tex aside and spoke to him in a low voice. "I like the game you're playing with French and Spencer. And I'll put in a few digs, too. You didn't know it, but there is a provision in the law about being an accessory."

He looked at the pleased expression on Tex's face.

"Huh, maybe you did know about that," he said thoughtfully. "However, the warrant is only going to specify cattle stealing. Murder, assuming we can find out who did it, would be a separate charge. It's not likely I could get that mixed in with a trial for rustling."

"We'll only take one step at a time," said Tex. "But you give that some thought. The possibility of a murder charge has Spencer nervous already. Now that I'm shore of what I'm doin', let me work on him some more."

Tex went on. "I only told you to get warrants for French and Spencer. I'll let you figger out what to do with Adams and Charles, but I'd even be willin' to let them keep their jobs on the MJ if'n you thought that would give you an edge. I think I've got them so scared now they won't even breathe rustlin' for a long time."

"I sort of detected that," chuckled Willis. "But I agree with you. If they plead guilty and testify, I promised them I'd try for a suspended sentence. Giving them their jobs back would sell the deal, I would think. Judge Palmer is tough but fair. I think he'd go for your proposition. I'll mention it to him, and I'll tell Adams and Charles, too, if it's okay with you."

Tex nodded his approval.

As Conklin and Willis prepared for the trip back to town, Conklin indicated Spencer could be able to travel in a few days if his progress continued. Willis stopped at the bunkhouse as he left and had a few words with Adams and Charles. The two men glanced at Tex on the porch and then watched Conklin and Willis leave. They appeared to be more at ease than they had for some time.

* * * * * * * * * * * *

Bo and Chick had made a very leisurely trek back to the Henderson Ranch. On the way they had discussed their new situation from every angle. Since they now had the promise of jobs at the MJ, they decided to take a much more aggressive posture regarding their relationship with Donie. They then determined what course of action they would follow once they got back to the ranch.

They arrived at the ranch shortly before dusk and walked their horses to the corral. Donie, sitting on the porch, watched them arrive, and Chick motioned with his head that he wanted to meet Donie at the corral.

Donie arrived as Bo and Chick were stripping their saddles and blankets from the horses and hanging them on the corral fencing.

"Got a message for you from Ed Smiley," Chick announced as soon as Donie got close.

Donie stopped dead in his tracks, looked from Chick to Bo and back again and swore.

"You damn fool," he snarled. "Why'd you not wait until we were alone?"

"Figgered it would be healthier for me if two of us knew about Smiley, not just me," Chick replied.

Donie's anger rose several more degrees.

"You mean Bo knows everything?" he sputtered, not believing his ears. "You damn fool," he repeated. "I oughta fire you!"

"That means you'll have to fire me, too," interjected Bo. "How you going to explain that to your paw? I don't think you got the guts to fire anyone."

Donie's jaw sagged, and he was utterly speechless. None of the ranch hands had dared to defy him in the past, and he had no idea of how to handle this situation.

His confusion and silence was interrupted by Chick.

"You want Smiley's message or don't you?" he inquired sweetly. "Makes no difference to me."

Donie stammered a weak, "Yeah, I do. What is it?"

Chick repeated the message, word for word, and Donie's anger rose again, and he was again speechless.

He finally threw up his hands, turned around and headed for the main house, leaving two grinning punchers in his wake.

"I don't think his day is endin' any better than it started," mused Bo. "I'll bet he hot foots it to town tomorrow to see what his $ 500 bought. Wish I could be there to see it. C'mon, let's head for the cook house. He should have somethin' left over from supper, and I'm starved."

Suiting his actions to his words, he moved rapidly toward the cook house, and Chick hurried to catch up with him.

CHAPTER 13

Another hot and humid day dawned on the MJ. Tex called a meeting of his men and brought them up to date on recent events. He then made the work assignments.

Sanchez and his men would scatter the cattle on the south section, as previously planned. Red and Charley would man the signal outpost with Reb. Lefty, Kansas, Blackie, Reno, and Laredo would scatter the cattle back on the west and northwest ranges. Marty and Tex would head for Ridgeway accompanied by Bronc, Trig, Curley and Rusty, Tex having vowed that any such trips would be done in force. Denver, Cheyenne, Dusty, Cavalry and Apache would man the main house and watch their prisoners. It was nice to have enough men to do everything he wanted to and with a high degree of safety, Tex thought to himself, and smiled as he remembered Doc Conklin's comment about the general and his men. There was a lot of truth to it at that.

The men scattered, found their horses and were soon off on their assigned tasks. Tex and his ranch contingent worked on a variety of tasks in and around the main house and the ranch grounds until the height of the sun indicated it was time to head for town.

Tex and Marty rode at the head of the tiny column, Bronc and Trig followed, while Curley and Rusty brought up the rear. Just before reaching town the back four riders paused and let Tex and Marty gain a lead of several hundred yards. Tex did not want all of them to arrive in Ridgeway at the same time.

Bronc and Trig then moved forward, but Curley and Rusty held back until their two friends had also gained a lead of several hundred yards. Then they, too, urged their horses into a slow gait.

Marty and Tex walked their horses down the main street, passed the Sweetwater Saloon, crossed the intersection of the two streets and entered the second block of the business district. Halfway down this second block they turned to the right and dismounted before a large two-story building that contained the courtroom and offices of the county government, except for the sheriff's office. The sheriff's office and county jail were directly across the street from the courthouse.

Marty led Tex into the building, turned to his right and the two men climbed a stairway that led to the second story. They located the prosecutor's office, opened the door and went inside. Willis was waiting for them in his private office.

Ted greeted both men and picked up some papers from his desk.

"Here are the warrants we want," he said. "Judge Palmer is sure curious, to put it mildly. Let's go across the street and see what our great sheriff will do with them. Tex, I think it best if only Marty and I visit the sheriff. No sense in overplaying our hand."

Tex nodded his agreement, read the documents and extracted two that he put inside his shirt. "I'll keep these for now," he commented and added, "I'll stay here 'til you go into the building. I'll be on the street if'n you need me."

Willis and Marty left, and Tex watched from a window as they crossed the street and entered the sheriff's office. He hurriedly left the window and Willis' office, walked down the stairs and out on the sidewalk. He glanced around, noted the locations of his men and leaned against a post, his thumbs hooked inside his gun belt. He was ready for anything.

Willis and Marty entered the sheriff's office, nodded to the deputy on duty and made for a side office with a doorway but no door. Sheriff Hamilton was sitting at a desk reading some papers. He looked up as Willis and Marty entered the room.

"'Mornin', Ted," he said pleasantly but ignored Marty. "What brings you around here?"

"We have some official business for you to tend to, Ben. I want you to serve this warrant today," Willis said calmly, handing Hamilton the folded document.

"That so? Who does it involve?" he inquired, leaning back in his chair and not looking at the paper.

"Donie Henderson," answered Willis flatly and waited for the response. It was instantaneous.

Hamilton's upper body jumped forward, and the front legs of his chair hit the floor with a thud. His stunned face turned red.

"Donie Henderson!" he exploded. "Are you crazy or somethin'? What is the charge?"

"Cattle rustling," came the short reply.

"Cattle rustling!" Hamilton exploded again. "You must be plumb loco. Donie a cattle rustler and heir to the biggest ranch in these parts! Who had the gall to make a stupid charge like this?"

"I did," said Marty, speaking for the first time. "I'm short 400 head, and Donie helped take them. I want him jailed."

"You . . . want . . . him . . . jailed!" stammered Hamilton incredulously. "You want me to jail Donie Henderson?"

"Thats right," replied Marty calmly. "You're the sheriff, aren't you?"

Ignoring Marty, Hamilton turned to Willis, his face still crimson and going through many gyrations.

"You're not really serious, are you, Ted? You want me to serve a warrant on Donie Henderson? You know who he belongs to. You want both of us to lose our jobs?"

"You're an officer of the court, and that there is a court document," replied Willis, his voice rising. "I want it served, and I want it served today! You understand what I'm saying?"

"Well, just a darn minute here," exploded Hamilton again. "Serving any old warrant is one thing, but serving a warrant on Donie Henderson is a horse of another color. And on a stupid charge like this. No, I won't do it."

"You can be held in contempt of court," Willis reminded him.

"Contempt of court is nothing compared to old Henry going on the prod," muttered Hamilton.

"Send one of your deputies then," suggested Willis.

"What? And get him in trouble with Henry and the Double H? That's as good as gettin' fired, and they'll all know it. You're crazy, Willis. This is Henderson's town, remember."

"You got anyone with guts enough to be an officer of the law around here?" asked Marty sharply.

Hamilton turned to Marty with a sneer on his face.

"Don't get smart with me, Johnson," he snapped. "You and that rundown ranch of yours ain't got nothin' to say a'tall."

Marty leaned over the desk and looked Hamilton straight in the face.

"I repeat," he said coldly, "you got anyone with guts enough to be an official of the law around here, or are they all yellow tubs of lard like you!"

Hamilton couldn't believe his ears, and his face, a pale red before, turned a vivid crimson in anger. Speechless at first, he finally caught his breath and pointed a finger at Marty.

"You're so damn smart Johnson, maybe you'd like to try servin' this warrant on Donie Henderson." A malevolent look spread across Hamilton's face. "That shore would be funny. Maybe I could sell tickets so's people could watch that!" Hamilton laughed uproariously at his own joke.

Marty continued to lean over the desk and waited for Hamilton to finish his laughing. Hamilton finally got himself under control.

Marty again spoke coldly. "You make me a deputy, and I'll serve that warrant. Or ain't you got the guts to do that neither?"

Hamilton's jaw dropped, and his anger returned.

"All right," he snarled. "You're lookin' for trouble, and I'm goin' to make sure you get it. Raise your right hand!"

Marty did as he was told and repeated the words Hamilton threw at him.

"Now, gimme a badge and I'll go out to the Henderson Ranch and serve that warrant," he announced.

"You won't have to go to the ranch to find Donie," interrupted the deputy who had been standing in the doorway and listening to the exchange of words. "Donie's down at the Sweetwater right now," he went on. "I saw him go in there a little while ago."

"Well, sonny," Hamilton drawled with a leer on his face, "I guess we're goin' to find out how good a deputy you are right off. This I gotta see."

"You and your deputy stay here," snapped Marty. "I don't want you and that fat belly of yourn to get in the way. You didn't have the guts to serve the warrant on your own. You wait here, and let a man do it!"

Stung with anger again, Hamilton started to argue and then reconsidered. His satisfaction could wait for a little while. Let this upstart make a fool of himself on his own. He shrugged his shoulders, settled back in his chair and waved Marty and Willis out of his office, the malevolent look still on his face.

Marty and Willis left the office and made their way across the street where Tex was waiting. Marty's face wore a big grin.

"Hamilton went for it hook, line and sinker," he announced. "But we don't have to go to the Henderson Ranch to get Donie. He's at the Sweetwater right now."

Tex grunted his satisfaction.

"Let's get at it," he said. "Him bein' in town is goin' to make it easier than havin' to do it at the Double H. Willis, you better go back to your office. The fewer people I got to worry about right now, the better I'll like it."

As he and Marty started down the sidewalk, Willis' voice followed him. "Sure hate to miss this, but I guess you're right. Good luck!"

Tex motioned for his men to follow him. Bronc and Trig met them at the street intersection.

"Donie's at the saloon down the street here," explained Tex as he and Marty continued to walk in the direction of the Sweetwater. Curley and Rusty crossed the street and met them at the base of the two steps leading to the saloon. Tex repeated his information and added a few instructions. Both men nodded and didn't move until their four friends had moved up the steps and entered the saloon. Then they, too, climbed the steps, paused for a moment, pushed opened the doors, entered the building and immediately slid to the near far end of the bar where they could see the whole room. The bartender, his attention drawn to the four men who had walked past him, did not see either their entry or where they had stationed themselves.

* * * * * * * * * * * *

Donie Henderson, still enraged and frustrated by the events of the previous day, frittered away the early morning hours after convincing his father they should give Spencer and Sims another day to return to the ranch. Finally he felt he had better make the trip to Ridgeway and meet Smiley.

Arriving in town, he went straight to the Sweetwater, and his guess was right. Smiley occupied a rear table and was playing solitaire. His first drink of the day, untouched, was on the table next to the cards.

Donie expressed his anger at the tone of Smiley's message, and Smiley smiled thinly and let him ramble on.

"It got you here, didn't it?" came his laconic response. "Let's get down to cases. I'm not goin' to waste the whole day. What kind of job do you want done?"

An angry retort started to evolve, but Donie repressed it, with difficulty, and told Smiley what he wanted done. "I'm sure you've heard Kelso's name around Canyon City," he concluded.

"Well, yeah, a little," replied Smiley. "Never heard tell he was any great shakes with a gun, though."

"He was the fastest around here," Donie responded in loyalty to his dead friend.

"Mebby so, but that don't mean much," said Smiley nonchalantly. "How many gunmen you ever seen around here?"

A deflated Donie had to admit Kelso was the only one he had run into.

"This here foreman, what's his name?" asked Smiley, changing the subject and getting to the heart of the matter.

"Don't rightly know," replied Donie, feeling a little foolish. "Seems like I heard it once, but I don't recall it."

"Don't matter none," said Smiley complacently. "If he's only the foreman of a no- account ranch like you said, he can't be in my class. He musta got real lucky with Kelso."

"That's the way I figure it," agreed Donie. "He was probably shaking like a leaf when it was all over." Donie couldn't help laughing at that thought.

Smiley sipped his drink and thought for a moment.

"How you goin' to set it up?" he finally asked Donie.

"Ain't figured that out yet," admitted Donie. "Got to get him to town and make him have a run-in with you. Thought you could help me figure it out," he added hopefully. "That's part of the thousand dollars you want to be paid."

Smiley sipped his drink again, and neither man took particular notice of the four men who had entered the saloon. It wasn't until Donie looked up and saw Marty Johnson headed his way that he directed Smiley's attention in that direction.

"Don't look now," he whispered, "the owner of the MJ is headed our way. Maybe he could use a scare."

Smiley nodded his approval, stared at his drink for a couple of moments and looked up just in time to hear a cold voice speak.

"Well, if'n it ain't Ed Smiley," Tex drawled. "You're a long way from home, Ed. Are you shore you ain't in the wrong place?"

Utter and complete amazement swept across Smiley's face and then enveloped him completely. The appearance of this man was totally beyond anything Smiley could have contemplated. He was barely able to growl, "Riley?"

"You two know each other?" asked an astonished Donie. He looked at Tex. "Who are you?" he demanded. At the same time, he was baffled by the expression on Smiley's face.

"I'm Tex Riley, new foreman of the MJ," came the unexpected reply. Tex tensed for action and felt, rather than saw, Bronc and Trig do the same. Tex's eyes never left Smiley's face.

But nothing happened.

Smiley's system had received a second and third shock when he recognized Bronc and Trig. While he was dumbfounded at the sight of Tex, the appearance of Bronc and Trig sent his mind in another whirl, and he was speechless as well as incapable of taking any significant action.

Donie, too, remained speechless. What he had thought he wanted to happen had promptly occurred. But the suddenness of the event had left him totally incapable of responding.

The silence was broken by Tex, who had decided to push things harder. "Mr. Johnson has a message for you, Henderson. Marty, give it to him."

Marty produced the legal document and dropped it on the table.

"This is a warrant for your arrest, Henderson," he said simply.

Hearing those words shocked Donie and brought him back to the real world.

"My arrest?" he exclaimed. "On what charge?"

"Cattle rustling," answered Marty.

"Cattle rustling!" Donie repeated startled and angry. "You're loco. You ain't got no authority to serve a warrant on me!"

"Oh, but I do," responded Marty, producing his deputy's badge. "You're under arrest, and you're going to jail."

Fury engulfed Donie, and he sneered at Marty.

"You think you're going to arrest me?" he exclaimed again. "Why, you ain't even carrying a gun."

"No he ain't," interrupted Tex. "But I am. You've got a choice, Henderson. You can walk out of here, or you can be carried out. It's your call."

Donie lost all control of himself as he turned to Smiley and pointed at Tex.

"Gun him down, you fool! You said he wasn't in your class. I ain't goin' to no jail!"

But Smiley, still trying to get his thoughts under control, did not move.

Bronc, however, quickly penetrated the fog engulfing Smiley's mind by leaning over the table and speaking directly to him in a cold, harsh voice.

"Your class! Haw, haw, haw," he sneered. "You shore told this cub the truth there, Smiley. You and Tex ain't in the same class. What about me, Smiley? Am I in your class? Let's find out, you two-bit windbag!"

With that, Bronc's right hand flashed out, and the palm of his hand caught Smiley on the side of his face with a loud smack!

Smiley's head snapped back, and his left hand instinctively felt for his cheek where a red blotch began to form. He half rose out of his chair and reached for his gun. Bronc had moved back a step and had gone into a slight crouch, his right hand no more than an inch from his gun.

The fire in Bronc's eyes stopped any further movement on Smiley's part, and he slumped back into his chair.

"I pass," he said in a low voice.

"You pass! What do you mean, you pass!" shouted Donie. He, too, started to rise in his chair, and he, too, reached for his gun.

A blur of movement caught his eyes, and he looked into the hole at the end of the barrel of a Colt, held in the firm right hand of Trig Mansfield.

"You touch that hardware, and I'll blow you to kingdom come," a raspy voice informed him.

Donie froze. A funny prickly feeling began to move up the back of his neck. Perspiration suddenly broke out on his forehead, and, for the first time in his life, Donie had the sinking feeling that he might be looking at death, straight in the face.

Trig pushed the situation even harder.

"Get on your feet and don't touch that gun," he rasped.

Donie slowly rose, fear now consuming him.

Trig stepped back a few feet, gently slid the gun into its holster, and he, too, went into a slight crouch.

"*Now* you can go for that gun, sonny, any time you want to," he said, with an icy rasp. Then he waited.

The look on Trig's face and the nearness of death drained any vestige of courage still remaining in Donie's system. He threw up his hands and cried, "Don't shoot, don't shoot. I won't touch the gun."

"Unbuckle your belt with your left hand and drop it on the table," ordered Trig.

Donie quickly complied and raised his left hand again.

"You do the same, Smiley," echoed Bronc. "I'll just take it along with me and drop it off at the sheriff's office. You can have it back when you leave town. We wouldn't want you to make a mistake and get yourself killed, now would we?" he added in a sugary voice.

When Donie had first raised his voice at Marty, the Sweetwater bartender immediately assumed something was wrong. Keeping his eyes on the group of men at the end of the room, both his hands reached under the bar searching for the shotgun he knew was kept there. He had just located the desired weapon when he heard a hiss and the click of a hammer on a Colt revolver. He glanced over his left shoulder and looked into the barrel of the aforementioned Colt held by Curley Chance. His thumb was on the hammer.

Curley pointed the first finger on his left hand at the bartender and then moved it back and forth, as if to say, "That's a no-no." Then he flattened his left palm on the counter top and motioned with the gun for the bartender to do the same. The man quickly complied. Rusty, in the meantime, had the rest of the handful of patrons in his view, and his right hand held a Colt as well.

Trig grabbed Donie by the collar with one hand and picked up the gun belt on the table with his other. He pulled Donie toward the front door, and the others followed, Bronc carrying Smiley's gun belt, glancing back constantly to make sure Smiley didn't go for a hidden gun.

The five men passed the end of the bar and continued out of the building. Curley and Rusty slowly edged their way toward the door, their guns at the ready and their eyes never leaving the faces of those in the building, especially the bartender.

Once outside the building, Tex grabbed Donie's collar and gun belt from Trig and told his four men to cover them from across the street. They quickly crossed the street and took up positions as Marty and Tex marched down the center of the street, Donie in tow.

The four punchers kept pace with the threesome in the middle of the street by rotating their positions, one at a time. No interference came from the Sweetwater, however, and the few people on the sidewalks and in the street obviously didn't know what had taken place. The group, therefore, reached the sheriff's office without incident.

Marty walked into the building with Tex right behind him, still holding Donie in a tight grip.

"Here's your prisoner, sheriff," Marty said cheerfully. "Lock him up."

Tex pushed his prisoner forward, dropped Donie's gun belt on Hamilton's desk and waited.

A non-plussed Ben Hamilton looked from Marty to Donie and back to Marty again.

"You arrested him all by yourself?" he asked incredulously.

"Oh, no, I had a little help from some interested citizens," grinned Marty. "Sheriff, I want you to meet my foreman, Tex Riley."

Tex took a step forward and touched his hat.

"Howdy, sheriff," he said in a level voice. "Right purty day we got goin', don't you think?"

Hamilton took a long look at Tex, gulped and managed a weak, "You the fellar that done in Kelso?"

"Guilty as charged," smiled Tex. "He a friend of yourn?"

"Of course not," snapped Hamilton. "'Course I knew him," he amended, "but he weren't no friend."

Hamilton paused for a moment and then went on. "Kelso was the fastest man with a gun in these parts."

"He ain't no more," Tex corrected him.

Willis, who had watched the street procession from his office window, now entered the sheriff's office, closely followed by Bronc, who still carried Smiley's gun belt.

"I suggest you lock up your prisoner without further delay, sheriff," he said coldly. "Judge Palmer will hold a hearing tomorrow and probably set bail at that time. Until then, Donie stays in jail. You understand what I'm saying?"

Hamilton nodded helplessly and swore under his breath.

"I understand," he replied wearily. "The old man is goin' to have a fit over this. I wouldn't want to be in your boots, Ted. In fact, I don't even want to be in my boots. There's a storm comin'."

He motioned for his deputy to take Donie back to the cell block.

"One more thing, sheriff," Willis went on. "The judge is mighty unhappy about the way you handled serving that warrant. He'll be talking to you about that tomorrow morning. In the meantime, I'm going to insist that Mr. Johnson retain his deputy status and his badge. Henry has got to understand this arrest was legal and proper. I'll let you explain to him how Johnson came to having a badge."

Hamilton rubbed his forehead and shook his head in despair. He wasn't looking forward to meeting Henry Henderson.

Bronc interrupted his troubled thoughts by dumping Smiley's gun belt on the desk.

"This belongs to a fellar down at the Sweetwater," he said dryly. "I didn't want him to hurt hisself, so I took it away from him. He'll be along directly to pick it up."

With that, Tex and his companions left the building and walked to their horses.

"Well, you struck the first blow, Riley," Willis said in a low voice. "You'd better be prepared for some sort of comeback, although I don't know what Henry could or would do."

"We'll be ready for anythin'," Tex agreed. "But I don't think Henry will do anythin' until the trial. Besides, Donie's going to have to do a lot of explainin' to his old man. You go to Canyon City as soon as you can, Ted, and find out what we want to know. C'mon, boys. Let's head back to the ranch."

Tex, Marty and their companions mounted and rode out of town. A number of citizens had gathered on the sidewalks and watched them depart. Obviously the startling news had already spread through the town, and a great deal of curiosity had resulted therefrom. Strangely, many of these faces were hard put to control their owners' smiles and grins.

* * * * * * * * * * * *

As soon as Tex and his friends had left the Sweetwater, one of the few patrons rushed to the door and watched the procession head down the street.

"What happened," demanded the bartender, wiping his face with his apron. "I was busy and only heard a few words. Somethin' about cattle rustlin'?"

The man at the door answered him. "By gum, I never thought I'd see the day when Donie Henderson was arrested. For cattle rustling, too! Son of the biggest ranchman in these parts and cattle rustling? Old Henry will shore blow up over this. Yes sir, there they go in the sheriff's office. I gotta tell my friends about this."

With that, he pushed open the swinging doors and hurried out, stopping at the first business establishment he came to.

Not to be outdone, the handful of other patrons quickly left the saloon and began to spread the word, too. Only the bartender and Smiley remained.

Smiley was still shaken by the whole series of events, but calmness and reasoning were beginning to reassert themselves. Smiley had spent a little money and time cultivating the bartender's friendship before meeting with Donie and a gem of an idea was starting to form in his fertile mind. He sauntered to the doorway and watched Tex and his companions head out of town. As soon as they were out of sight, he left the saloon and went directly to the sheriff's office to claim his gun and belt.

Hamilton handed the items to him without a word, still preoccupied with thoughts about the storm he knew was coming his way.

Smiley buckled his belt and looked at the sheriff.

"Who's goin' to tell old man Henderson about Donie?" he inquired innocently.

"Oh, my God, that's got to be done," exclaimed Hamilton, even more concerned.

"I'm goin' that way," responded Smiley casually. "You want me to tell him?"

Hamilton leaped at the bait.

"That would be right kind of you, stranger. Shore it wouldn't be no trouble for you?"

"No trouble at all," answered Smiley. "Wouldn't mind seein' what that ranch looks like anyway. I'll get right at it."

Smiley left the sheriff and went to a nearby livery stable to get his horse. Saddled and mounted, he left Ridgeway and headed for the Double H.

Smiley maintained a leisurely pace on his way to the Henderson Ranch. He had much to think about. He was still stunned by the appearance of three of the most deadly representatives of the Rambling R Ranch. One such individual would be surprising enough, but three were inconceivable.

And to pass Tex Riley off as foreman of a tiny ranch here when he had much larger responsibilities on a ranch far away was laughable. But here he was and Bronc and Trig as well. The inconceivable had happened! Smiley shook his head in disbelief. Something was very wrong.

But Smiley had other problems as well. First and foremost was Donie Henderson. He had taken Donie's money figuring on some sort of easy job. Unfortunately he had spent the major portion of his $ 500 advance, and he already dismissed the possibility of getting his hands on the second $ 500. The problem now would be to figure out a way to keep the first amount.

Smiley also knew he had another problem with Donie. The man had come unglued in the saloon and had handled things very badly. Donie was a loose cannon with a quick temper, and the combination was deadly. Smiley wondered how Kelso had been able to keep him under control. Whatever Smiley had to do, it had to be done fast. He had to vacate this area of the county as soon as possible if he wanted to retain his good health. He figured he had one day to spare, and the plan that was taking shape in his mind was based on that fact.

He reached the ranch sooner than he expected. So absorbed in his mental gyrations, he had not been conscious of the passage of time. He trotted his horse down the courtyard leading to the main house and was pleased when he recognized the puncher crossing the yard in front of him as being the second man in the Sweetwater the previous night.

"Hey you," he yelled. "Where can I find Henry Henderson?"

Bo turned and was surprised to see it was Smiley who had called to him. Why was this man looking for Henry, he thought. Donie's not going to like this.

Bo pointed to the main house. "You'll find him up there. He may be eatin' though."

Smiley waved his hand and continued on, a puzzled Bo watching him. Bo shrugged his shoulders and continued on to the bunkhouse.

Smiley dismounted, tied his reins and climbed the three steps to the porch. He paused at the door, removed his hat and knocked.

After a short delay, the door opened and a hulk of a man looked at him.

"Well, what do you want? A job mebby?" asked a surly Henry.

"No sir," replied Smiley. "I'm lookin' for Henry Henderson. I've got a message for him."

"I'm Henry Henderson," scowled Henry. "What's the message?"

"Well, I got bad news for you," said Smiley, shifting his weight from one foot to the other. His nervousness wasn't faked. He cleared his throat and plunged ahead. "Yore son's in jail in Ridgeway."

Henry's jaw dropped, and his face showed complete surprise.

"In jail!" he roared. "What the hell for?"

"The warrant said cattle rustling," Smiley informed Henry.

"Cattle rustling!" again roared an astonished Henry. "Are you telling me that fool sheriff has arrested Donie for cattle stealing?"

"Well, yes and no," replied Smiley with a frown. "Your son was arrested, but it weren't done by the sheriff. A fellar named Johnson served the warrant. I guess he owns a ranch near here."

"Marty Johnson arrested my son!" exclaimed an incredulous Henry. "Is this some sort of joke you're trying to pull on me?"

"'Fraid not, Mr. Henderson," went on a more calmer Smiley. "I'm tellin' you what I seen. The sheriff asked me to come out here and tell you. Reckon you'd better ride into town and find out for yourself. I've done what I was told to do. I'll be movin' on."

"You're damn right, I'm heading for town." Henderson went down the steps in a flash, took a few steps, cupped his mouth and yelled, "Bo, come up here, pronto!" He then turned to Smiley.

"Where you headed, stranger?" he asked.

"Nowhere in particular," replied Smiley casually.

Bo was rapidly approaching the two men when Henderson yelled again, "Saddle two horses right away, Bo. You and I have to get to town fast."

Henderson faced Smiley again.

"I may be obliged to you, stranger. Won't know for sure 'til I get to town. Going nowhere in particular, huh? How about sticking around here for a few hours. I may want to talk to you ag'in."

"Guess I could do that," responded Smiley.

Bo arrived with the saddled horses. Henry leaped into the saddle, spurred his mount and was gone in a cloud of dust with Bo attempting to catch up with him.

Smiley grinned as he watched the two men grow smaller in the distance. His plan was working well.

CHAPTER 14

A grim Henry Henderson kept the lead all the way from the ranch with an increasingly puzzled Bo pounding along behind him. Not a word was spoken. There was no reduction in speed when they reached the edge of Ridgeway. Henry's eyes were riveted straight ahead as the two horses swept down the main street and, therefore, he did not see the knowing smiles and grins on the faces of the local citizenry.

Henry viciously pulled his horse to a stop outside the sheriff's office, quickly dismounted and plunged into the building, Bo at his heels.

Henry paused for a moment, located Hamilton in his office and barged right in.

"What's this I hear about Donie being in jail?" he thundered.

"I'm afraid it's true, Henry," responded Hamilton in a highly apologetic tone. "He's back in the cell block, if you want to see him."

"See him? I didn't come to see him," roared Henry. "I came to take him home. Open up, and let's get it done with!"

"I can't do that," whined Hamilton. "A warrant was served on him. Tomorrow morning Judge Palmer will hold a hearing, set bail and then you can take him home. I've got to hold him here 'til then."

"I heard tell of a warrant," said Henry in a slightly lower voice. "What for, and who issued it?"

"It's for cattle stealing, a ridiculous charge, I'm sure, and Ted Willis issued it as prosecuting attorney."

"On what grounds?" demanded Henry.

"Dunno that," answered Hamilton, again with a whine in his voice. "You'll have to ask Willis about that."

"I heard Marty Johnson served the warrant. How did he get mixed up in this thing?" again demanded Henry.

Hamilton's face took on a pained look.

"It was Johnson who said his cattle was stole, and as far as serving the warrant is concerned, I got tricked." Hamilton dropped his eyes and could not look at Henry.

"How was that managed?" asked Henry sarcastically, seething inside.

Hamilton tried to explain what had happened, and when he was finished, Henry was speechless with rage and Bo had all he could do to keep from snickering. Even the deputy who had witnessed the whole event and was still on duty had great difficulty in keeping a stern look on his face.

A disgusted Henry finally regained his voice.

"You damn fool," he snorted. "What do you use for brains?"

Henry thought for a moment and then raged again.

"You mean to tell me Johnson arrested Donie all by hisself?"

"I didn't figger he could do it neither," explained Hamilton helplessly. "He told me to stay put. I figgered he was headed for his own funeral, and so I stayed put."

"But he had help," Hamilton went on, after a brief pause. "His new fore-man, Riley, and a bunch of MJ riders went along with him. Donie never had a chance."

This added news forced Henry to pause again. Bo, for his part, again had all he could do to smother another grin. This Riley guy was some humdinger, he thought. Wait 'till Chick and the rest of the Double H riders hear about this state of affairs.

"Well, I'm shore wasting my time here," snapped Henry when his voice returned again. "I'm going across the street and see Willis. I'll get this mess straightened out right quick. You can bet on it. Bo, you wait for me at the Sweetwater. I won't be long."

Henry stamped out of the room and headed for the courthouse. Bo kept pace with him until they were outside, and then he headed for the saloon, eager to get more details on what happened earlier on this momentous day.

From the window in his office, Ted Willis watched Henry and Bo arrive and enter the sheriff's office. He waited patiently and eventually Henry emerged from the building, strode purposefully across the street and disappeared from his view. The thump, thump, thump of footsteps on the wooden stairs reached his ears. The door to his outer office slammed shut, and Henry's flushed face and bulky body quickly appeared in his office doorway.

Without waiting for a greeting, Henry began his tirade as he advanced into the room, repeating the questions he had asked Hamilton, interspersed with profanities.

Willis listened calmly and waited for the man to exhaust his repertoire of caustic comments. Henry finally stopped and tried to catch his breath.

"Sit down, Henry," said Willis evenly.

"See here, Willis . . . ," began Henderson.

"*Sit down, Henry*," Willis interrupted, again in an even voice but a bit louder.

Henderson raised one finger and opened his mouth to speak, but before he could get a word out, Willis spoke again, firmly.

"Either sit down, Henry, or this conversation is over!"

Henry Henderson stared a moment, closed his mouth and sat down.

"Henry, you've had a lot to say. Now it's my turn, and you'd better listen," Willis began. "I issued a warrant for Donie's arrest because I think he's guilty as hell. I wouldn't have done it if I didn't have sufficient evidence to justify it. There'll be a hearing tomorrow morning in Judge Palmer's court. The charges will be read, bail will be set and then you can get him out of jail. Then I suggest you take him home and have a heart-to-heart talk with that young man. You might try asking him what he's been doing with MJ cattle for a starter. Better yet, ask him what Kelso, Spencer and Sims have been helping him do with MJ cattle."

Willis sat back and let this stunning information set in.

"You'd better understand something, Henry," he went on. "This town and the people in it are fed up with being dominated by the Henderson family. Maybe it took Marty Johnson and his foreman to wake folks up around here, and today they sure enough did it. That Riley fellow is a whiz bang of a foreman and is not about to take any guff from you or anyone else. They've lost almost 400 head in the past two years, and they don't plan on losing anymore.

"Now, if I was you, the first thing I would do is go out and find myself a lawyer for Donie. He's sure going to need a good one. Now, get out of here and let me do my work!"

A non-plussed Henry Henderson sat in his chair, unable to believe his ears. He couldn't remember when someone had talked to him in that way and in that tone.

Henry finally got up and shook his head, as if to loosen some cobwebs. Finally he spoke, this time in a much milder tone.

"Do what you have to do, Willis, but I warn you. If you're playing loose with me or Donie, I'll nail your hide to a barn door, and you'll regret the day you ever came here. You understand me?"

"I understand, Henry," acknowledged Willis. "But I'm going to do the job that voters and residents of this area gave me to do. And as far as nailing someone's hide to a barn door, that can work two ways. Best you not forget that."

An angry retort began to form, but Henry repressed it and stamped out of the room.

* * * * * * * * * * * *

Bo bought a drink at the Sweetwater and sat back and listened to the talk of what had taken place earlier in the day. Each version became more interesting than the previous one, and he soon had difficulty separating fact from fiction. However, he did recognize the description of one of the men who had been heavily involved in what had taken place as being that of the man Riley called Bronc back at the MJ Ranch. Bo was surprised to learn that Riley seemed to have had little involvement in Donie's arrest. He ordered a second drink and was mulling over this apparent contradiction when Henry Henderson entered the saloon. All Donie talk in the room stopped immediately.

Henry trudged across the room to Bo's table, wearily sank into a chair and stared at his two clasped hands on top of the table. The bartender brought Bo's drink and stood by the table waiting for Henderson's order. Sensing the man's presence, Henry looked up, shook his head no and went back to staring at his hands again.

Bo watched him and realized that although the face was still flushed, the fire and brimstone had disappeared. Instead, Bo was looking at a bewildered, confused and very old man.

At last Henderson's mind returned to the present. He looked at Bo with a puzzled expression.

"Donie's in jail and has been accused of cattle rustling," he murmured, forgetting that Bo had been with him at the sheriff's office. "I don't understand what's going on, but I have a lot of things to do here before tomorrow morning when Donie will have a hearing. I'm going to stay in town overnight and get everything done. Don't know when I'll get back to the ranch."

Henry paused and thought for a moment.

"Bo, take my horse down to the livery stable and get it bedded down," he directed. "Then go back to the ranch and take care of things 'til I get there."

Henry paused again and stroked his jaw as he further contemplated his situation.

"As soon as Salty and Dan show up, you make shore they stay close to the ranch so I can find them," he finally drawled. "I got some questions I need to ask them."

Bo nodded.

"Anything else I can do for you, sir?" he asked.

Henderson slowly shook his head.

"I just don't understand it, Bo. Why would anyone think Donie would want to steal cattle? We got more'n we need now. It don't make no sense a'tall."

"Maybe someone has made a mistake," Bo observed.

"Well, if they have, someone is shore going to pay," snorted Henry, his voice rising and showing some spirit. "And I'll shore pay back that MJ outfit, especially Johnson and that high and mighty foreman of hisn, if this is a game they're playing. I shore enough will."

With that, Henderson looked up and signaled the bartender. The man came hurrying over, and Henry ordered a drink, directing a quizzical look at Bo at the same time.

Bo got the hint immediately, finished his drink, rose and left the saloon at a fast walk. He located their horses, still tied outside the sheriff's office, and mounted his own. Leading Henry's horse, he made his way to the livery stable and made the necessary arrangements for the care of the animal. He ignored the leer on the liveryman's face and soon was on his way to the Henderson Ranch. He traveled at a slow trot, remembering that his horse had to be tired from its previous run that day.

He arrived at the ranch and was surprised to see Smiley leaning on a corral post and watching the activity going on inside. A couple of Double H riders were trying to break in a new mount without much success.

Bo walked his horse to where Smiley was standing and stepped down. "Thought you'd be gone by now," he observed casually.

"I would have, too, except Mr. Henderson told me to stick around. Said he wanted to talk to me," explained Smiley.

"Well, the old man ain't comin' back 'till tomorrow sometime," Bo informed him. "Maybe he forgot you was here."

"Reckon so," said Smiley. "He must have a lot on his mind about now. Guess I'll hang around until tomorrow and see if I can find out what he wanted to talk to me about."

Bo shrugged and pointed to the bunkhouse.

"Throw your bedroll in there," he directed. "We still got a couple of unused bunks. But shut up about Donie," he warned. "I'll tell the boys tonight when they all get in from the range."

"Suit yourself," agreed Smiley. "It's none of my affair, nohow."

I wonder about that, thought Bo. Yes, I wonder about that. But he said nothing.

* * * * * * * * * * * *

Henderson spent some time at his bank, making arrangements for bail money without knowing exactly how much he would need. He also inquired about legal help. In recent years, Henry had little need for legal services and what little he had required involved civil rather than criminal matters. Further, the man he had hired in these instances was close to retirement. He would not be the right man for Henry.

His friends at the bank suggested a lawyer who had arrived in Ridgeway about two years earlier, Albert Thornton. They indicated the man was young and ambitious but admitted he had not handled many criminal cases. But they had been impressed with his energy and dedication.

Henry found Thornton in his office and told him what had taken place and how little he really knew.

"I have something I have to work on the rest of the afternoon," Thornton stated. "But I'll be free tonight. Why don't you talk with Donie and find out what you can. I could meet you at the hotel for dinner, say seven o'clock, and we could take as much time to discuss things as we want to. Would that be satisfactory?"

Henry nodded in agreement but was a little irked that Thornton didn't drop what he was doing and begin responding immediately to Henry's problem. I'll have to teach this youngster some respect, he thought to himself.

Henry left Thornton's office and headed back to the sheriff's office.

"I want to see Donie," he announced as soon as he entered the building.

The deputy grabbed his set of cell keys and led Henry back to the cell block.

"I'll have to have your gun," he said matter-of-factly.

"You think I'm going to bust him out of jail?" roared Henry.

"Don't think anything a'tall," responded the deputy calmly. "The rules say no guns. You don't get to talk to Donie 'til I get it." He held out his hand in expectation.

Henry swore in disgust but unbuckled his gun belt and handed it to the deputy.

"Shore you don't want to search me, too?" he asked sarcastically. "I might have a cannon concealed in my boot."

"Don't see none," said the deputy as he glanced down at Henry's boots. "Guess I can let you in."

He unlocked the cell and motioned Henry to enter.

"There's two cots; you can sit on one," he informed Henry, again in a bored tone. "Call me when you're through. I'll be outside in the office."

Henry's eyes followed the deputy's back, a dark scowl on his face. The world was full of smart young men, he mused. Didn't the Henderson name mean anything around this town anymore? He would have to give some attention to that problem, too, as soon as he got his current difficulties under control.

He turned and looked at Donie, who was sitting on the second cot in the room. Henry looked down to locate the edge of his cot, sat down heavily and looked at his son again.

"Well, what do you have to say for yourself?" he inquired, the scowl still on his face.

Donie had been thinking about this meeting and was prepared for the question.

"I don't know what this is all about, dad. Cattle stealing? Why in the world would I steal cattle when I'm the son of the owner of the biggest spread in these parts?"

"I don't know," said Henry wryly, watching Donie's face closely. "You tell me."

"There's nothing to tell," protested Donie. "How can I tell you something I know nothing about? This whole thing is ridiculous!"

"Ted Willis told me to ask you about Kelso, Salty Spencer and Dan Sims. Why did he say that?"

Donie's surprise at this question was not faked, and his face showed it, which made his words even more convincing.

"I don't know, dad," he said in exasperation. "Kelso's dead, you know that. Have Salty and Dan been arrested, too?" Donie's intense interest in the answer to this question also was not faked.

"Now that's something I don't know," replied Henry. "But they haven't come back to the ranch neither. Where do you think they are?"

"I don't know," answered Donie truthfully. "I sent them out to hunt strays on our southwest range, like I told you. I haven't seen them since."

"You shore don't know a lot of things," said Henry, half to himself. "There'll be a hearing tomorrow morning, and I've arranged for bail, although I don't know the exact amount yet. Then we'll go home to the ranch."

"Thanks a lot, dad," said a very contrite Donie. "I knew I could count on you. This whole thing's got to be a big mistake."

"If it is, I'm going to get to the bottom of it right soon," snapped Henry, laboriously rising from his cot. He took the two steps to the cell door and then looked back at Donie.

"You shore you've told me everything I should know?" he probed in desperation.

"I'm sure, dad," came the pious response. "I don't understand this any more than you do."

Strange, mused Henry to himself. Willis is too sure of himself to be playing games. Still, maybe that Riley fellar is calling the play, and Willis is going along for the ride. Well, if he is, he's made a big mistake. A deep scowl returned to Henry's face.

"Deputy!" he yelled. "Let me out of here."

The deputy quickly responded to the yell, unlocked the cell, let Henry out and handed Henry his gun belt.

Henry hooked the belt over his arm and left the building without a word.

* * * * * * * * * * * *

Donie heaved a big sigh of relief at the departure of his father. He had prepared himself well, he thought, and had handled Henry's questions perfectly, except one. But that one was a bad one and had brought back, in a rush, all the fears and concerns that Donie had barely managed to suppress.

How had Willis been able to hook him and Kelso up with Spencer and Sims, he wondered. And that thought caused him to shudder. Kelso was dead, so Willis could not have had anything to do with him. But where were Spencer and Sims? Had they been captured and talked? The sweat poured down Donie's face.

And what about French, and Cook, too, now that he thought about it. Cook also had not been heard from. Had French double crossed him, and with Cook, Spencer and Sims, taken the new herd to Harding? Had they tried to sell the cattle and got caught? The sweat continued to roll down Donie's face. He began to pace the floor of his cell. His nerves, already stretched thin, moved a little closer to the breaking point.

* * * * * * * * * * * *

Marty, Tex and their four friends left Ridgeway in the best of moods and traveled at a fast pace until they reached the MJ boundary line. There they slowed down somewhat.

A happy Marty tried to engage Tex in conversation during the ride, but Tex did not respond. Tex finally waved Marty off and continued in silence.

Upon reaching the ranch, Tex and Marty continued on to the main house while the others turned toward the temporary corral, dismounted and stripped their horses. They were soon engrossed in telling their friends about the events in town.

Tex stopped Marty on the porch and handed him the two other warrants.

"Hang on to these for a while," Tex told him. "I don't want to serve these yet. We might make better use of them later on. Marty, I'm goin' into the den, and I want to be left alone. Got some thinkin' to do. I'll see you later."

Marty, looking puzzled, nodded agreement and went to locate Mary. He knew she would be pleased with the day's events.

* * * * * * * * * * *

After the night meal, Tex called all the men together.

"I wanted you all to know that the fat's in the fire," he began. "We got Donie Henderson arrested today for cattle rustlin' and had him thrown in jail. He probably won't stay there long, and so we have to be ready for any comebacks either he or his father may have in mind.

"Sanchez, I want Juan to rejoin Red and Charley at the outpost with either Cavalry or Reb. We're also goin' to continue the three-man range patrols. You and your men will handle the south range; Reno and Laredo will ride with Charles on the west section; Denver and Cheyenne will ride with Adams on the northwest section; Lefty, Kansas and Blackie will handle the north range."

Tex paused for a moment and looked around at his men.

"The rest of you will stay around the main ranch house to make shore Marty and Mary are protected and to keep our two special guests safe and secure.

"One more thing. We ran into Ed Smiley in town today. Donie Henderson hired him to kill me." Growls interrupted him, and Tex grinned in response. "Well, he wasn't able to do his job, as you can plainly see. Bronc tried to get him to try, but he couldn't get up the nerve. So he's still around.

"But if I know Smiley, and I do, you can shore bet that Henry Henderson probably now knows why Bronc, Trig and I are here. But it ain't likely he has any idear how many more of you are along for the kill. We'll try to keep it that way for as long as we can.

"All we can do now is lay low, keep watch on the ranch and wait for Donie's trial to begin. Any questions?"

Hearing none, Tex waved to them and signaled Lefty to come over to him.

"Apache, Trig and Bronc have been doing a lot of the night watching," he told Lefty. "Have Dusty, Curley, Rusty and two of Sanchez' men spell them off some. Better keep them three man shifts, though. No sense in takin' any chances."

Lefty nodded his approval and said he would work out the manpower assignments with Sanchez.

Tex watched Lefty leave and sighed. Inaction was not Rambling R style, but nothing more could be done at the moment. However, they would need more supplies soon, and he would also need to see Willis and find out how the prosecutor had fared in Canyon City. Another trip to town in the near future would definitely be in order. He would just have to be patient and keep his men busy.

* * * * * * * * * * * *

Henry met Thornton at the hotel for dinner but could add very little to their limited store of knowledge.

Thornton was not pleased.

"It doesn't make any sense to me, Henry," he complained. "I've only been here about two years, but I know Willis well enough to know he wouldn't even think of issuing a warrant against anyone, let alone a Henderson, without having some pretty strong evidence. I'm going to have to talk to Kelso, Spencer and Sims as soon as possible."

"Kelso's dead," Henry reminded him, "and I ain't seen the other two for several days."

"You haven't seen Spencer and Sims for several days," repeated an astonished Thornton. "Why not?"

Henry shifted his weight uncomfortably in his chair, and his face became flushed.

"Well, Donie sent them out to check on strays along the MJ boundary a few days ago, and they ain't been seen since. I thought it was a good idea at the time."

"Why was that?" asked a curious Thornton.

"Well, we had a fracas with the MJ over strays about a week ago. Some of our animals strayed on to the MJ range, and one of their riders was driving them back when Donie and some of my boys ran into him. They had words, Donie lost his head and went after him with his quirt. Donie got purty well beat up. His face was a mess."

"Did Donie start the fight?" asked Thornton.

Henry sighed and nodded his head yes.

"Donie does have a quick temper," Henry admitted. "I hired Kelso to sort of keep him under control. Don't know now if that was a good idea or not," he added sheepishly. "I guess I maybe haven't held the reins tight enough with him. His maw died when he was five, and I've been purty well tied up with ranch affairs over the years. It don't seem possible so many years have gone by so fast."

"I can't see why that incident has any connection with our current problem, though," commented Thornton thoughtfully. "The disappearance of Spencer and Sims does bother me, however, especially since Willis made a specific reference to them. Has Donie been on or around the ranch the last few days?"

"Yes, of course," snorted Henry with some heat. "He and a couple of the boys hunted strays along another section of our range that butts ag'in the MJ one day, and he's been around the ranch house the rest of the time. He did come into town today, though," amended Henry.

"And this is the day the warrant was issued," mused Thornton thoughtfully. "That's a strange coincidence."

"But Donie didn't even tell me he was coming to town until this morning," protested Henry. "How could anyone know he was coming this way when he didn't know it hisself?" Henry emphatically shook his head. "Like you said, it don't make no sense. It fair makes my head spin, though."

"All right, Henry, take it easy," Thornton soothed him. "We'll go to the hearing tomorrow, hear the charges and go from there. But I want to see Spencer and Sims as soon as they show up. There has to be a connection there someplace."

Henry nodded, rose and shook hands with Thornton.

"I appreciate your taking an interest in Donie. I'll give you all the help I can, and I shore will bring Spencer and Sims to you the first chance I get."

* * * * * * * * * * *

The next morning, at 10:00, Judge Palmer opened the hearing, read the charges and asked for a plea.

"Not guilty," said Thornton, speaking for his client.

The judge accepted the plea, set bail and adjourned the hearing after setting a trial date for one week hence.

As the audience rose to leave, Judge Palmer added a comment.

"Sheriff Hamilton, I want you and Mr. Willis to stay. I have something to discuss with you both."

As soon as the room was cleared, Palmer turned to Hamilton.

"Mr. Willis informs me you refused to serve a warrant issued by this court yesterday and that a private citizen had to do it for you. Is that true, sheriff?"

Hamilton, who had suspected he would be questioned about the matter, decided to offer no excuses and nodded glumly.

"Very well," frowned Palmer. "This is a serious matter, sheriff, and this court takes a dim view of public officials who shirk their responsibility. This court, therefore, sentences you to a fine of $ 30 or 30 days in your own jail. Which will it be?"

Hamilton's jaw sagged in astonishment.

"Thirty dollars," he gasped, "or 30 days in jail. You can't be serious!"

"Oh, but I am serious, sheriff," replied the judge sternly. "And to make sure you understand that very fact, I will warn you in advance that a second such incident will result in a sentence that will be doubled over today's. Do I make myself clear to you, Mr. Sheriff?"

Hamilton gulped and nodded yes.

"I'll pay the fine, sir, just as soon as I can get the money," he stammered.

"You have until four o'clock this afternoon, sheriff," replied the Judge, "or your jail sentence starts tomorrow morning."

A bewildered Hamilton fled the courtroom while Palmer and Willis exchanged grins.

* * * * * * * * * * * *

Henry went to his bank, finalized the financial arrangements for bail and returned to the courthouse.

Shortly before noon, a silent and contrite Donie, playing his part for all it was worth, was released and accompanied his father back to the Henderson Ranch.

CHAPTER 15

Only a few words were exchanged between Henry and Donie as they rode back to the Double H. But Donie's mind was working overtime. His thoughts of the previous day had continued to gnaw at his mind. These thoughts, plus his first experience at trying to sleep in the confinement of a jail cell, combined to give him a night short on sleep and long on worry. He had spent a good share of the night either pacing the floor or staring out of his barred window.

Willis' reference to Spencer and Sims continued to be very disturbing. He could not understand how this could come about. While his father was anxious to confront these two, Donie was even more so, except that he didn't dare be too obvious about it.

In addition, the extended absence of French continued to plague him, and when he added Cook's name to the mix, as he had suddenly done yesterday, it was all the more confusing. Surely one of those two men would have made some sort of contact with him had they been able to do so. Maybe they weren't able to get to him. Why? What had happened on the MJ? Was Riley somehow at the bottom of all this?

The questions were endless, but his mind couldn't generate any answers. He was certain he would be in for another session with his father and as nerve-racking as that could be, he, at least, had some plausible answers. It was on this somewhat comforting note that Donie and his father reached the Henderson Ranch.

Both men dismounted in front of the main house, looped their reins around the tie rail and were about to mount the steps to the porch when a figure rose from a chair and stood at the top of the steps.

"Smiley!" a startled Donie exclaimed before he could contain himself. "What are you doing here?"

Smiley's presence had not immediately registered with Henry, who also had been deep in thought throughout the ride from town. His eyes finally settled on Smiley, but no sign of recognition crossed his face.

"Well, your father asked me to stick around when he went to town yesterday," replied Smiley. "When he didn't come back last night, I thought I'd better stay handy in case he wanted to talk with me ag'in."

His words finally got Henderson's attention, and Henry immediately recalled Smiley's part in the previous day's events.

"Why yes, son, I remember now. This is the man who came from town yesterday and told me about your trouble. I did ask him to stick around until I got back, not knowing I was going to end up staying in town overnight. You two know each other?" he asked curiously as the three men entered the ranch house.

"Yes we do," jumped in Smiley before Donie could think of an appropriate answer. "We met in Canyon City a few months back and had a few card games together. He sent word to me that if I ever needed a job, I should look him up. Even sent me some travelin' money, he did. I told one of yore riders, night before last, that I was in town and to let Donie know I was around. Donie met me at the Sweetwater, and we was having a friendly drink when all the trouble started. I figgered the least I could do was let you know what had happened, and that's why I come here yesterday."

At first Donie was puzzled at Smiley's mention of travel money, but as Smiley continued to talk, Donie had an inspiration.

"That's true, dad," he chimed in. "I even went so far as to offer him a job here."

"Why'd you do that?" snorted Henry. "We don't need any more punchers."

"Why, dad, I'm surprised at you," retorted Donie in any oily voice. "What with Kelso getting himself killed, I figgered you'd want to find someone to take his place. Mr. Smiley has a reputation even better'n Kelso's. I thought sure you'd be interested in talking to him. I even gave him some money as sort of a bonus for considering the idea."

"How much did you give him all told?" an annoyed Henry asked. "I like to do my own hiring."

"Of course, dad, I know that," responded Donie. "But you hadn't met Mr. Smiley, and I had, so I thought you wouldn't mind."

"How much did you give him?" repeated Henry.

"Five hundred dollars," answered Donie softly, holding his breath.

"Five hundred dollars!" exploded Henry. "Are you crazy? Where did you get that kind of money?"

"Oh, I'm pretty lucky at cards," explained Donie smoothly. "I've stored up my winnings over the past few months and thought this would be a good place to use them."

"Five hundred dollars in winnings?" mumbled Henry. "I didn't know you played for them kind of stakes. You better watch yourself and stay away from them sized games, son."

Donie smiled, assuming he had gotten around a very sticky situation.

"I'll be careful, dad. But what about a job for Mr. Smiley?"

Henry pondered the question for a few moments and then sighed.

"Son, I'm not sure hiring Kelso was a very good idea. It seemed so at the time, but I'm not so certain now. A ranch like ourn shouldn't need any kind of gunslinger on our payroll to get along with folks. I'm told Kelso wasn't liked around town, and that reflects on us Hendersons." Henry was thinking of his conversation with Doc Conklin as he spoke.

He looked at Smiley, rubbed his jaw and reflected for a few moments.

"No offense to you, mister," Henry finally drawled, "but I reckon I don't want to go that way right now. Donie shouldn't have offered you a job without talking to me first, but I understand why he done it."

Donie had expected his father to follow through on his so-called offer but that Smiley would turn it down, given what had happened in town. He concealed his surprise easily, since he still had accomplished his objective.

He looked at Smiley with a leer on his face.

"I reckon you'll just have to give me back my money then," he said sweetly.

Smiley smiled inwardly and shifted his feet nervously. The spoiled brat had taken the bait.

"Well now, that might be true," he admitted. "But I think I have some information that could be worth a lot more'n that to you Hendersons. But I'm not greedy. I'll trade you even up and be on my way, if you're interested."

"What kind of information would be worth $ 500?" demanded Henry, his voice rising. "You must be loco!"

A stunned Donie remained silent, his mind trying to absorb another surprise.

"Possibly," agreed Smiley. "But tell me, where does Donie stand with the law now?"

"He's out on bail and is scheduled for a trial next week," answered Henry. "Why do you ask?"

"Won't you want all the information you can get to be ready for that trial?" asked Smiley casually.

"Of course we do!" snapped Henry, starting to get irked at this cat-and-mouse game. "My patience is starting to wear thin, Smiley. Come out with it. What could you know that would be worth $ 500 to us?"

"I know who Tex Riley is," drawled Smiley, with a sly look. "I also know who Bronc Evans is and who Trig Mansfield is, too."

"Riley is the new foreman at the MJ, and I never heard of them other two. That news ain't worth a plugged nickel." Henry was now becoming quite agitated.

"Them last two fellars were the ones that helped Johnson and Riley arrest Donie," Smiley went on. "Ain't that of some interest to you? And Riley ain't no more the foreman of the MJ than I am. You got a big problem here and don't know nothing about it. I reckon that should be worth $ 500 to you all."

Smiley looked for and found a chair. Sitting down and twirling his hat with one hand, he looked up at the two Hendersons, a satisfied smirk on his face.

Henry's eyes followed Smiley, and a vexing feeling started to consume him as he thought for a moment.

"Nothing is worth $ 500 to me," began a nervous and perplexed Donie, but Henry cut him short.

"Shut up, Donie. This man is trying to tell us something, and I'm not getting the drift of it yet. You want to try a different trail for me?"

"We got a deal?" persisted Smiley.

"Damn you!" thundered Henry. "Quit playing games with me!" But Smiley's reference to the trial and the need for useful information caused Henry to pause.

"All right, we got a deal," he finally agreed. "But this information of yourn better be good, or I'm going to take the cost of it out of your hide!"

"Wait a minute, dad," began Donie again, seeing his $ 500 disappearing into thin air. But Henry waved him off.

"I want to hear what this man has to say," said Henry evenly. "And it better be good."

Donie grunted, slapped his knee in disgust and headed for the front entrance.

"Where you going?" demanded a surprised Henry.

"Outside, where I can get some fresh air," replied Donie, icily. "This is a waste of time. He ain't going to tell us nothing we don't already know." He slammed the door to emphasize his thoughts on the subject.

Donie's anger was flaring again, and his boiling point was rapidly coming within reach. All the frustrations he had contended with on the ride from town had returned, and to this number Smiley's name now had to be added. He had taken Donie's money, he hadn't done the job he had been paid to do and now he was trying to weasel out of giving it back. A four flusher, Donie thought bitterly, and he was in another of his vile moods by the time he got to the corral where Bo and two other men were doing some repair work on the fencing.

"Where are Salty and Dan?" he demanded of Bo.

"They ain't back yet, Donie," Bo replied carefully. "We ain't seen them since you sent them out to look for strays. Remember?"

"Of course I remember," retorted Donie savagely. "You mean they haven't come back yet?"

"No they ain't," said Bo, watching Donie carefully. Donie's tone and belligerence were beginning to scare Bo, and a wild look that had crept into Donie's eyes didn't help matters any.

Donie threw up his hands in disgust, mumbled something under his breath, turned and slowly headed back to the main house. Bo watched him go, more concerned than ever.

* * * * * * * * * * * *

Henry stared at the slammed door for a few moments and then turned his attention back to Smiley.

"Maybe Donie's right," he admitted grimly. "You'd better get this so-called information out on the table right quick, or you and I are going to tangle."

"All right, all right," snapped Smiley, raising his hands in protest.

"But first I got to ask one question. Somethin' just ain't right in all of this, and I can't put my finger on it."

Smiley sat up in his chair and looked straight into Henry's eyes.

"Has anythin' strange or unusual happened here or around Ridgeway recently?" he inquired.

"That's a damn fool question!" said Henry in exasperation. "What are you talking about?"

"I don't know, that's the hell of it," replied Smiley. "But somethin' had to have happened, or Riley wouldn't be here. Now stay on the trail with me and think carefully. Did anythin' strange or unusual happen here on the ranch or in Ridgeway in recent weeks?"

Henry concentrated for a minute, shook his head and then a thought came to him.

"Well, yeah," Henry said. "Kelso was killed by Riley on the MJ."

"No, no, no. Before that," said Smiley, his voice rising. "Hey, wait a minute. That gives me an idea. Did anythin' strange or unusual happen on the MJ?"

Henry rubbed his jaw and concentrated again.

"Well, now that you mention it, a stranger did come to visit Johnson more'n a month ago. Didn't stay around, though. As a matter of act, he went and got himself killed on their south range. Ambushed by parties unknown, I guess the sheriff called it."

"What was his name?" asked an eager Smiley as he hunched forward in his chair. "What was this stranger's name?"

"I don't rightly recall," replied Henry in a puzzled voice. "Is it important?"

"It might be, Mr. Henderson," soothed Smiley. "Think carefully. What was his name?"

Henry cogitated some more and slowly shook his head no. "I don't recall," was all he could say.

Smiley slumped back in his chair and closed his eyes. He felt he was on to something and the visitor was part of it. Suddenly the thought hit him, and he sat bolt upright.

"Mr. Henderson, by any chance was that man's name Evers?" he asked with a hopeful look.

"By golly, I believe it was," said Henry, the light of recollection brightening his face. "Yes, I'm shore it was."

Smiley jumped up in his excitement.

"That's it, Mr. Henderson! That's the connection," he said in a loud voice. "That's why Riley, Evans and Mansfield are here. I just knew it had to be somethin' like that. My God, Slim Evers dead. I can hardly believe it."

Henry's mouth sagged open as he was completely bewildered by Smiley's outburst. What was so important about Evers' name?

"Let me explain, Mr. Henderson," said Smiley, more calmly now.

"Slim Evers owns a big ranch, six or seven hundred miles south of here. It's bigger than yourn by far. Over the years he's collected a crew of hard bitten riders that don't back down to no one. A few of my friends found that out, and they either ended up in boot hill or prison. Believe me, this is a mean, tough outfit. And the meanest, deadliest man in that outfit is its foreman, Tex Riley! Your man Kelso was out of his class when he met Riley. And I have to admit it. I ain't in his class neither."

"A professional gunslinger?" questioned Henry with raised eyebrows.

"Well, yes and no," reflected Smiley thoughtfully. "He sort of sold his guns once, to Slim Evers. But let me tell you he's the fastest I've ever seen.

And I've seen a few. But don't kid yourself. Evans and Mansfield are only a whisker behind him. You and your whole crew wouldn't stand a chance ag'in the three of 'em."

Smiley paused for a moment to let this all sink in and saw that he had gained Henry's total attention.

"Them three are up here for one reason and one reason only," he went on. "They're here to get the man who killed Evers. And they'll stay around until they do just that!"

Smiley stopped and reflected again, his eyes fixed on Henderson's face.

"This rustlin' business must be a sideline with them," he continued. "They wouldn't have come all this way just for that. But they shore would know rustlin' if they saw it. You can bet on that."

Henry remained silent, digesting all that Smiley had said.

Smiley grimaced and lowered his voice, sure that his words were making a significant impact on Henry.

"I hate to tell you this, Mr. Henderson, but if Donie has had anythin' at all to do with rustlin' MJ cattle, he's in big, big trouble. Riley and his men won't let that pass neither, and if the rustlin' has somethin' to do with Evers gettin' killed, all hell won't stop those hombres from hangin' the man who done it! You can bet on that, too."

Smiley wiped the perspiration from his face. He had worked hard the past several minutes, and he was mentally and physically tired.

"The idear of my workin' for you had crossed my mind," he said softly. "But I can't stay now. Any one of them three men could kill me and never strain themselves. You reckon I've earned my $ 500?"

Henderson was still somewhat overwhelmed by this new information and for reasons he could not fathom at the moment, a sense of fear had made a small foothold in his mind. The series of events involving the MJ owner and his men were now beginning to make a little sense, but a lot of questions were still unanswered. But Smiley's information had proven to be useful, he had to admit.

Henry slowly nodded his head affirmatively to Smiley's question.

"You'd better ride on," he agreed. "In fact, it might be better if you left before Donie gets back. I don't think he was very happy with our arrangement."

Smiley nodded, put on his hat, exchanged a weak handshake with Henry and headed out the door.

* * * * * * * * * * * *

By the time Donie reached the main house from the corral, the rage and frustration he had been experiencing had become overwhelming. His hands trembled, his face had become contorted and his lips twitched and moved as he mumbled his trials and tribulations, half to himself and half to the world at large. His eyes looked so wild that they almost bugged out.

He had just reached the base of the steps to the porch when the latest source of his frustrations came out the front door.

Smiley instantly slowed his gait as soon as he saw Donie. Hesitantly he descended the steps, his right hand hovering very close to his Colt. As soon as he reached the level ground, Donie spoke.

"You took my money," he hissed through clenched teeth. "You didn't do the job I paid you for, and now you're weaseling out of our deal. You're nothing but a two-bit four flusher!"

Smiley's eyes glinted, but he held himself in check.

"I made a deal with your dad," he said evenly. "If you got any problems with that, you'd better talk to your old man. He seems satisfied. As for me, I'm movin' on to a new and healthier territory."

Smiley watched Donie carefully as he slowly mounted his horse. He touched his hat with a finger on his right hand and looked down at Donie.

"Good luck at your trial, kid," he said coolly. "You're shore goin' to need it." And with that he spurred his horse.

This last comment was more than Donie could bear.

"Damn you," Donie screamed. He yanked at his gun and pulled the trigger as fast as he could thumb the hammer.

Three shots went wild, a testimony to his shaking hand. But two found their mark. Smiley cried out, groaned, slid from his saddle and hit the ground face down.

The sound of shots brought Bo and his two companions running from the corral as Henry Henderson bolted from the front doorway. Henry stopped at the top of the steps, mesmerized by the sight of his son, gun in hand, with a wisp of smoke coming from the barrel of his Colt and Smiley's body lying in the dust.

Bo reached Smiley first and noticed two rapidly expanding pools of blood covering the back of Smiley's shirt. Gently he rolled the man partially over and felt for a pulse. Gently he returned the body to its face-down position.

He looked at Donie, then to a transfixed Henry and with a combination of wonder, anger and fear in his voice, uttered two words.

"He's dead."

* * * * * * * * * * * *

Tex didn't think it was necessary for anyone from the MJ to attend Donie's hearing. He knew it would be routine and relatively short and that Willis would capably handle that end of the process.

His men had dispersed and were carrying out his new standing orders. The men remaining at the ranch were busily engaged in a variety of tasks except Trig, who was taking French for his morning walk.

Tex asked Mary to make a list of the supplies they would be needing, and then he went in to the main room that Spencer still occupied.

The patient had taken a few steps that morning and now, while tired, looked pleased.

"It shore felt good to move around a bit," he admitted to Tex. "I figgered I was a goner there for a while."

"Sanchez wasn't tryin' to kill you, Salty," Tex informed him. "If'n he had, you'd be dead now. You must have moved a bit just as he fired, 'cause he hit you harder than he wanted to. Yes, you were some lucky."

"I didn't know that," said Salty reflectively. "He and his boys shore did surprise us. After that, things happened real fast."

Salty paused for a moment, and then he looked guiltily.

"Felipé can understand English, can't he?" he asked plaintively.

"Yes he can, Salty," answered Tex. "And he can speak it, too. He and Sanchez are goin' to be prime witnesses when it comes to a trial."

"You might as well know it," Tex went on. "We had Donie Henderson arrested and thrown in jail yesterday on a cattle rustlin' charge. You're startin' to run out of time, Salty. Your testimony will shore make our job easier, but I figger we got enough to convict Donie regardless of whether you testify or not."

"Donie won't stay in jail long," snorted Spencer. "In fact, he might not have to go to jail a'tall."

"You're dead right," responded Tex. "That's what I been tryin' to tell you. You ain't got no one but me to speak up for you. I've got a warrant for your arrest right now, but I ain't goin' to get it served until after Donie's trial. What we do with it after the trial is up to you. Like I told you before, it shore would be a shame if Donie got off without any prison time while you spent up to 10 years in the coop. Don't sound fair to me. I'll let you in on a little secret, Salty. I did jail time once, not long, but long enough. It ain't no fun a'tall. You won't like it one bit."

Tex watched Salty's face as he spoke and thought he saw a glint of reason begin to appear.

Tex thought he had pushed this topic hard enough and decided to change the subject.

"You got a bank account in Canyon City?" he asked, his voice calm and casual.

Salty's head jerked a bit, and he frowned.

"You know about that, too?" he grumbled.

"You'd be some surprised how much I know," Tex retorted.

"Well, you're dead wrong on this one," snapped Salty triumphantly. "I sent my money to my brother, like I told you. I don't have no such account in Canyon City."

"But others do." Tex made it a statement of fact rather than a question.

Salty sighed and nodded.

"I'm in so deep already, it can't get much worse," he muttered. "It was Kelso's idea. He didn't want us to show too much money around Ridgeway. Besides, most of us were plannin' on leavin' these parts once our stake was big enough. Donie could get the MJ. None of us wanted to work for him anyway."

"Donie was goin' to get the MJ?" asked a curious Tex.

"Shore. He figgered his dad would buy it cheap, once it went under, and then let Donie run it as his own. That's how Kelso talked Donie in on the rustlin' in the first place. The kid ain't too bright, you know."

"Let's get back to the bank accounts," laughed Tex. "Who do you know has one in Canyon City?"

Salty hesitated, not sure how far he should go in this matter.

"Lookey here, Salty," countered Tex. "Ted Willis is the prosecuting attorney, and he's going to Canyon City with a court order issued by Judge Palmer. This court order will allow him to look at any bank account he wants to. Now I'll ask you ag'in. Who has bank accounts in Canyon City?"

Salty heaved a deep sigh of resignation.

"Well, Donie and Kelso do for shore," he admitted. "I heard them talkin' about it. I think French does, too, but I ain't shore."

"How about Dan and Cook, too?" persisted Tex.

"Dan said he did," sighed Salty again. "I don't know about Cook."

"Well, you've been right helpful, Salty, even if I did have to pry it out of you," said Tex in a kinder tone. But then his voice turned icy cold.

"I'm gettin' mighty tired of havin' to pry it out of you, though," Tex went on. "If'n I have to do much more of that, I'm not goin' to have forgivin' thoughts when I want that warrant served. You get my drift?"

Salty didn't answer.

Tex rose and left the room. Salty had even more now to think about.

Tex decided a visit with French would be the next order of business. He found the man seemingly unconcerned regarding his fate.

When Tex told him about Donie's arrest, French just snickered. "So Donie got himself throw'd in jail. Bet he didn't stay there long."

"He was in there overnight," retorted Tex. "But I have to admit that you're right. He won't stay there long." Tex moved to the bunkhouse doorway and glanced at the height of the sun. "In fact, I wouldn't be surprised if'n he was out already. But his next stay will last a lot longer."

French snickered again.

"You're a fool, Riley, if you think old man Henderson will let Donie stay in jail long enough to say so. He owns this town and a lot of people in it. Before you worry about Donie's jail time, you're going to have to get him convicted. And I shore ain't goin' to help you none in gettin' that job done."

"Well, it's your call," said Tex, a little vexed. "Just remember what I told you. I may be the only one who can do you some good."

French didn't respond to this assertion. He simply closed his eyes and rearranged his position on the bunk, taking due notice of what little he could do in this regard, given his restrained state. It was obvious he felt the interview was over.

Tex waited a minute, shrugged his shoulders and left the bunkhouse.

French re-opened his eyes and smiled. You're dead wrong, Riley, he thought to himself. I know someone who can and will help me more'n you can. A lot more. You wait and see.

Tex walked back to the main house, half lost in thought.

Bronc saw Tex coming and waited until he had reached the porch.

"How'd you and French git along?" he asked pleasantly and was surprised at the response.

"Not worth a damn," snapped Tex. "Bronc, I had him goin' purty good the other day; you saw it, too. I figgered I had made some headway with him, but now I'm right back to where I started. And I'm tryin' to figger out why."

Tex remained silent for a minute and then frowned.

"It's almost like he knows somethin' I don't know," Tex explained, "but the only thing he knows that I don't know is who killed Slim. And if'n he helps us on that score, I'm really the only hope he has on the rustlin' charges. It don't make sense, but he says he won't testify ag'in Donie."

"Who else could do him more good than you?" asked Bronc, thoughtfully. "Willis?"

"Well, Willis is me as far as French is concerned," responded Tex. "I'm shore Willis will follow my lead as much as possible. No, that's not who could help him more'n me."

"Huh," grunted Bronc. "There's only one other fellar I can think of that might help him, and that's the killer hisself."

"That's it, Bronc!" exclaimed Tex brightly. "Of course that's it. Bronc, remind me to talk to you more often. Yes, the killer himself. Or . . . his . . . father!"

"His father?" grunted Bronc again.

"Shore, of course. French figgers Henry will get Donie off real easy; maybe even buyin' him off. If'n Henry can do that for Donie, why not French, too? Especially if French knows somethin' that Henry would do anythin' to keep quiet. Yes, it fits, but can we prove it?"

Tex went on. "Bronc, we gotta make dead certain that French and Salty don't get a chance to talk together. That's your job, along with Trig. I've got Salty purty worried, and I want it to stay that way. You make damn shore French doesn't get a chance to change it!"

* * * * * * * * * * * *

As the rest of the day went by, Tex became more thoughtful and preoccupied. He was anxious for the trial to begin and get over with. They had been away from the Rambling R for a long time, and while he was reasonably sure all was well back there, he didn't know it for certain. And that was cause for concern.

He was also troubled by the fact that Donie's trial would be for rustling only. If Donie was, in fact, the murderer, as Tex now felt sure, then the rustling charge was small potatoes. Further, if Henry somehow got Donie off with little or no prison time, all of this time and effort had been wasted. True, they had smashed the rustling scheme all to pieces, and three rustlers were dead, but that wasn't why they were here. Somehow, they had to get the fact of the murder out in the open and prove Donie's role in that murder. There had to be a way of doing this.

* * * * * * * * * * * *

The next morning Tex made one minor change in the work assignments. He pulled Red away from the outpost and sent him into Ridgeway with the ranch wagon, again for supplies. And, as before, Curley and Rusty went along with him.

The three men had been seen in Ridgeway earlier. There was no need to send different men this trip, as Tex wanted and needed to keep their numbers a secret for as long as possible.

About noon he saw lights flash from the outpost area, and Reb quickly informed him Doc Conklin was on his way in.

Tex was pleased. He had grown fond of the kindly gentleman and welcomed his company.

Conklin soon arrived, tethered his horse and greeted Tex with a big grin. "Riley, you sure set Ridgeway a buzzing when you had Donie thrown in jail. People can't stop talking about it. I think you really woke up this old town, and I doubt if Henry's influence will ever be the same again.

"Incidentally, Willis told me to tell you the trial's set for next Tuesday at ten o'clock in the morning. Says he expects the townspeople will fill the courtroom to the brim."

"Yes, that courtroom will be full," agreed Tex, but with a different concept of who some of those people would be.

Doc moved toward the door. "Let me look over my patient," he said over his shoulder, "and then we can talk."

Tex waited patiently while Conklin was in the house longer than usual. He finally emerged and sank heavily into a nearby chair. Bronc, who had seen Conklin arrive, had joined Tex on the porch and was sitting on a railing.

Conklin wiped his face with his big handkerchief and settled back in the chair.

"Well, I looked over Spencer real carefully, and he is making excellent progress," he announced. "That's the good news. But I don't think Salty can ride all the way to Ridgeway and still be able to give good testimony. It ain't likely he'll be strong enough to do all that."

"I've been thinkin' about that, too, Doc," said Tex. "If'n we use the ranch wagon and those springs we used to bring him in, could he handle that?"

"Why, sure, I don't see any reason why he couldn't," replied Conklin. "You'd have to take it real easy going into town, though. I'd allow an hour for that trip, if I were you."

Conklin suddenly grunted and shielded his eyes from a far-off flash of light that appeared and disappeared several times.

"That's a funny one," he growled. "The sun must be hitting something out in them hills. Does that happen often?"

"Yes it does, every once in a while," replied Tex, keeping a straight face.

Reb strolled over and waited for some guidance, looking at Tex, then Conklin and back to Tex again.

"It's okay, Reb. What's up?"

"Two riders comin'. You want me and Dusty in the bunkhouse?" asked Reb.

"Yes," answered Tex. "Bronc, wake up Apache and Trig. Tell them to stay in the house. Excuse me a minute, Doc."

Tex took several long strides toward the corral where two Mexicans were working.

"José, Federico," Tex yelled and motioned for them to come toward him. Tex met them halfway, talked briefly and the two men dashed back to the corral, grabbed rifles and took up positions behind some bales of straw.

Tex retraced his steps and rejoined Conklin on the porch. Bronc emerged from the house, leaned against a convenient support post and watched the incoming trail.

Conklin looked at Tex and shook his head.

"You always knew I was coming before I got here, didn't you? Those light flashes I saw. They were some sort of signal, weren't they?" he asked.

Tex nodded.

"I never did like unexpected visitors, Doc," he explained. "Figgered it would be best if'n we had time to get ready for anyone afore they got here."

"Riley, you continue to amaze me," remarked Conklin thoughtfully. "You're just full of surprises. And unless I miss my guess, I bet you're planning a few more for the trial. Are you sure you weren't a general in some prior life?"

Tex laughed. "Don't know about any prior life, Doc, but a lot of it is just plain horse sense. As long as folks don't know how many men I got with me, the more cards I got to play with. It won't last much longer, but any edge I got is all to the good."

Bronc interrupted the conversation. "They look like the same fellars that were here the other day," he muttered. "That Bo fellar and Chick, too. Shore didn't expect them back so soon."

"Bo Franklin and Chick Snyder?" an incredulous Conklin asked. "They've been here before?"

"Yes, but they didn't see anythin' they weren't supposed to see," replied Tex, "thanks to our warnin' system. But I didn't expect them back so soon, neither."

Tex got up and met the two Double H riders at the tie rail.

Bo and Chick remained mounted and looked down at Tex.

"Riley, things have gone plumb to hell back at the Double H," said Bo wearily. "A couple days ago you said you had jobs for me and Chick if we need 'em. Was your offer a good one? If that's so, me and Chick would like to take you up on it."

"Of course the offer's good, boys," agreed Tex. "Step down and set a spell. What's gone wrong at Henderson's?"

Bo and Chick dismounted, tied their reins and tramped up the steps to the porch. Bronc shoved a couple of chairs in their direction, and soon all hands were comfortably settled.

"Hello, Doc," acknowledged Bo. "Saw your rig as we rode up. What are you doin' here?"

"Making a social call," came the quick response. "What's happened at the Double H?"

Bo heaved a big sigh and spoke with exasperation.

"Donie's gone plumb loco. He killed that new fellar who's been around — Smiley. Shot him in the back, he did. He went clear out of his head. Took three of us to hold him down and drag him into the house."

Tex and Bronc exchanged knowing glances.

"Donie shot Smiley in the back," repeated Tex evenly. "What was that all about?"

"Don't rightly know," acknowledged Bo. "Smiley came to the ranch and told old Henry about Donie being arrested. Henry got me to saddle two horses, and we tore out of there and went to town. It seems Henry told Smiley to stick around, so Smiley stayed overnight while Henry stayed in Ridgeway, getting a lawyer, arranging for bail and such. When the two of 'em got back to the ranch yesterday, Smiley was there waitin' for 'em. The three of 'em went into the ranch house, but purty soon Donie came out and came down to the corral where me and a couple of the boys were workin'. He asked about Salty and Dan, who ain't been around for a spell, and when I couldn't tell him anythin', he got all het up and started to mumble all sorts of strange things. His eyes got real wild lookin', and then he headed back to the house. Smiley comes out of the house and meets Donie. They have a few words, and Smiley climbs aboard his horse. The horse takes a step or two, and Donie screams, yanks his gun and empties it at Smiley. Some of the shots miss, but two of 'em catch Smiley right in the back. He was dead by the time I got to him!"

For Bo this was a long narration, and he wiped his face with his kerchief at its conclusion.

"What did Henry do about all this?" asked Conklin.

"That's sort of strange, too, Doc," replied Bo. "He's got Donie hog-tied in his bed, and he took Donie's gun and smashed it all to pieces. After that, he's just sat in his den, starin' at the wall."

"Didn't he call the sheriff?" persisted Conklin.

"No, he didn't," answered Bo, "and that's what scares me and Chick. We stood up ag'in Donie a couple of times lately. Henry can't keep him hog-tied forever, and we figger Donie will be out to get us next. But he won't come at us straight on. It'll be an ambush or somethin' like that. I tell you, he has gone plumb loco."

"Your diagnosis may be more accurate than you think," reflected Conklin. "He got beat up, Kelso got killed and now the rustling charges. He's probably had a lot on his mind and being thrown in jail, him being a Henderson and all, may have triggered something."

"Well, old man Henderson has been pushin' him about Salty and Dan bein' missin', too," commented Bo. "Donie said he sent them to hunt strays a week ago and they ain't been seen since. It's shore puzzled the rest of us right enough."

"Bo, I shore appreciate you and Chick comin' here and tellin' us these things," Tex interrupted. "You and Chick have been more help than you can imagine. You both got jobs as long as you want them. In fact, I think it's time I did you a favor. C'mon inside, I want to show you somethin'. Doc, you'd better come, too."

The three men followed Tex into the house. It took a few seconds for their eyes to get used to the change in brightness. Bo and Chick were dumbfounded when their eyes finally got in focus and they saw Salty sitting on the sofa.

Chick finally recovered his voice. "What are you doin' here, Salty? How long you been here?"

"Almost a week, I guess," answered Salty, "but I don't remember much about the first couple of days."

"Salty has a lot to tell you fellars," interrupted Tex. "Tell them why you're here, Salty."

Salty started talking, and soon Bo and Chick sought chairs and pulled themselves up close to the sofa.

Bo sighed as Salty finished the tale of rustling activity and his wound.

"Dan's dead, and Donie and Kelso been stealin' cattle," Bo mused. "Donie thinks he'd be helpin' old Henry get a ranch for him. Hell, Donie couldn't run a ranch, and Kelso knew it. They used him, and Donie was too dumb to know better."

"True enough, Bo," Tex interrupted again. "Now I think it's only fair that you tell Salty about what's happened over at the Double H."

Bo nodded and began his own narrative. When he had finished, Salty shook his head.

"It was a bad game right from the start," Salty observed. "We needed Donie to get rid of the cattle, but he was the weak knot in the rope. Kelso was supposed to keep Donie in line, but even he was beginnin' to have some doubts about bein' able to do it. I think he wanted to get one more herd shipped, and then he was goin' to pull stakes."

The silence that followed was broken by Conklin as he motioned for the men to leave.

"All right, now," Doc said. "My patient has done enough talking for a while. He's still a sick man, and I don't want him to get too tired, so I'm going to shoo you hombres out of here."

Bo and Chick headed for the door and left the room. Tex started to follow, but Salty's voice stopped him.

"You win, Riley. I'll testify for you."

Salty paused and looked down for a moment, then cleared his throat.

"Donie killed Evers. I'll testify to that, too."

CHAPTER 16

The night meal was finished, and Conklin had long since departed for Ridgeway. Red, Curley, and Rusty had returned from the town with a full wagon of supplies. The range riders had drifted in, and the outpost crew had also arrived.

Bo and Chick had lounged around the ranch during the afternoon discussing the astonishing developments of the past two days. As Tex's men kept pouring in, their wonderment grew by leaps and bounds.

Tex joined the twosome for a few moments and made an encompassing wave of his arm in the direction of his men.

"As you can see, we're a bit crowded around here," he admitted. "I see you brought your bedrolls with you. I'll find a couple of bunks for you. My boys can sleep outdoors."

Bo objected at first, but Tex insisted they sleep in the bunkhouse, and Tex won the argument.

Bo smiled after Tex left them and headed for the main corral.

"I know why Riley wants us in the bunkhouse," he commented. "He's got so many men outside, we couldn't sneak out of here even if we wanted to. He and his men know right where we are, and that goes for Adams and Charles, too. My, wouldn't a lot of people like to know what we know now? Old Henry would be some surprised. Chick, I'm thinkin' that we're goin' to see a lot of changes hereabouts right soon. Henderson's law is goin' to be a thing of the past. Folks around here are goin' to be able to breathe deep ag'in."

Chick nodded and chewed on a long stem of grass.

"I feel it too, Bo, but at the same time, I feel a little sorry for the old man. A no-good son, who's a cattle thief and murderer. It must be tearin' the old man apart. That ranch has been his whole life. And now he won't have no one to pass it on to."

Bo didn't respond, but similar thoughts had gone through his mind, too. They'd wait to see how the trial turned out and go from there.

* * * * * * * * * * * *

The main room of the MJ Ranch was filled with people. Present were Marty and Mary Johnson, Tex, Bronc, Lefty, Blackie, Apache, Felipé and Sanchez. When all had settled comfortably, Tex looked at Salty and motioned toward the assembled group. "Well, we are all here, Salty," he said. "Take as much time as you need and tell us exactly what happened and how Slim Evers was killed."

Salty took a deep breath and began his story.

He related how French had been concerned about the questions Evers was asking and French's desire to stop the maverick operation until Slim had left. He told them how surprised the four rustlers had been when Slim threw down on them.

"I thought we were done for certain," he muttered when he described the scene.

He, Salty, had not even seen Donie until after the shot was fired.

"Believe me," he pleaded, "no one knew Donie was even around. He told French he had decided to come down on his own to see how we were gettin' along. He spotted Evers when Evers followed French and Cook up the draw. He left his horse and closed in through the woods. As soon as he saw Evers had the drop on us, he cut loose."

Salty paused and looked around the room.

"Believe me, fellars," he again pleaded, "no one *wanted* to kill Evers. It just happened. Shore, I rustled cattle. Can't deny that. I took my chances and took the money. Riley knows why. But I ain't a killer. I didn't want to kill Felipé! He can tell you that."

"I know that, Salty," said Tex softly. "Had it been any different, I wouldn't have played along with you."

Then Tex fixed a long hard gaze at Salty and locked in on Salty's eyes.

"You're dead certain you're ready to testify to all this?" he asked sternly. "'Cause if you are, I'll put in a good word for you. But if you double cross me, I'll go for the full sentence. You understand that?"

Salty nodded his head, really helpless to do anything else. The growls and looks from the other men, as they listened to the talk, were enough to frighten the devil himself, Salty thought.

Tex rose, suddenly very weary. They now knew who they were after, and the end was in sight. The other men also got to their feet, and all headed for the door and the coolness of the night air. Soon the room was empty except for Marty and Mary Johnson and Salty. Mary gave Salty a drink of water and helped him settle back on the sofa.

Tex put his arm around Apache's shoulders as they stood on the porch, looking at a full moon.

"It ain't right, and it ain't fair," Tex murmured. "Slim was at the wrong place at the wrong time. It just happened, as Salty said."

"I know, Tex," said Apache softly, tears flowing gently down his face. "An Indian isn't suppose to cry, but I can't help it. He was so good to me, and he looked forward to doing more things with me now that the ranch is going so well. If only he had sent for help, he might be alive today. That's what hurts the most, Tex."

"I don't understand it either, Apache," agreed Tex. "Maybe it was just meant to be. I'll tell you what. Let's get our horses and go for a ride. A little night air and some open spaces might do us both good."

* * * * * * * * * * * *

After a long ride, Apache said he was wide awake and that he would augment the number of night watchmen, at least for a few hours.

It was about midnight when flashes of lightning began to appear in the northwest, closely followed by rumbles of thunder. Black clouds began to appear and multiply. Apache watched the flashes begin to move in his direction, sniffed the air and decided that a storm would soon be upon them. The other sentries agreed, and they began to rouse the men sleeping outdoors and on the ranch porch. Apache went inside and woke Tex, who had barely gotten to sleep.

The two went out on the porch, and both noted that the wind velocity had picked up considerably and that the temperature was dropping steadily.

"This could be a gully washer," Tex mumbled, mostly to himself. "Apache, find Cavalry, Reb and Kansas and tell them to get out to the horses. In fact, we may need more than that."

Sanchez had joined them and heard the last comment.

"Sí," he shouted over the increasingly loud sweep of the wind. "I weel get my men an' help you."

By the time slickers were broken out and put on, rain had begun to fall. Tex led Sanchez and his men toward the corral as more men joined them.

Tex was pleased to see Bo and Chick race from the bunkhouse to help and nodded approvingly.

Now the rain was coming down in sheets, and visibility was poor. Further, the ground was getting soggy where there was no grass and slippery where there was. Men went down as their horses pulled and yanked their heads. The fallen men continued to hold the reins of their horses and struggled to regain their footing.

The flash of lightning and the crash of thunder was now almost continuous, and the horses reared and pulled on their reins in fear. Virtually everyone now was up and out in the rain, working with the horses. Bronc and Trig had started toward the corral, but remembering Tex's orders, Bronc turned and made for the bunkhouse after he nudged Trig and pointed back to the main house.

Cavalry, Reb and Kansas were the best men the Rambling R had, as far as horses were concerned, and on this night they performed yeomen's efforts. They constantly moved from horse to horse, talking to them, soothing them and giving them some sense of security.

About 45 minutes later, the rain slackened off and became a steady flow. But the lightning had moved on, the wind had decreased in velocity, and while a rumble or two of thunder was still heard, the horses had calmed down considerably. All the reins were checked and retied at the temporary corral, and most of the men headed for the main ranch house, a soaked and bedraggled lot indeed. Mary had lots of hot coffee waiting for them, which was most welcome.

The rain stopped shortly before dawn, although it was so overcast no one knew it had arrived. Most of the men had stayed up the rest of the night, wrapped in blankets to keep warm, as they waited for their clothes to dry. Those who could returned to the bunkhouse and tumbled into their bunks to get a few hours of sleep. The ranch's main courtyard was a quagmire.

Tex decided that rest and relaxation would be the order of the day and that the outpost would not be manned. Clothes were hung on lines stretched all through the ranch house as well as the bunkhouse. Even the pot-bellied stove in the bunkhouse was lit and going strong to aid in the drying out. Good humor had returned to the group, and laughter broke out frequently as someone would recall a fall in the mud, a near miss or sliding on the slippery grass.

Bo and Chick sat together and watched and listened, joining in the laughter and conversation when appropriate.

Red and his outpost crew had arrived late the previous evening, and Bo mentioned it to Chick.

"I don't know where that last bunch came from," he said, "but they all seem to know exactly what they're doin'. This is the most organized outfit I ever did see, and I suppose Riley is the man behind it all. If this bunch ever gets riled up, old man Henderson and the whole damn county won't know what hit 'em."

Chick rubbed his jaw reflectively.

"Yeah, I shore don't want to tangle with 'em," he agreed. "Us coming here with that warnin' was just blind luck, and I'm shore glad we did it."

Lefty White entered the bunkhouse, looked around until he spotted the two former Double H punchers and came over to join them. He shook hands with both of them.

"Tex says you want to join up with us," he remarked. "Thought I'd better come over and tell you there ain't any hard feelin's over what happened with Donie," he went on, looking at Bo.

Bo blushed and accepted the outstretched hand.

"I'm right sorry about that, Lefty," he murmured. "Kelso had us all runnin' scared, and I wasn't any better'n the rest of 'em. I was hopin' you'd understand."

"I do, seeing as how I work for a devil myself," laughed Lefty. "Besides, I managed to find a way to work it off. I don't think Donie thought much of it, though.

"Tex says you've both been a big help to us already," Lefty added. "We all appreciate it, knowin' how tough it must have been. Me and the boys are right pleased to have you ridin' with us."

* * * * * * * * * * * *

The wind continued to blow all day and helped to dry things out. Late in the day the sun finally broke through the clouds, and everyone's spirits rose accordingly. The day of rest and relaxation came to a close with the mood of the men both jovial and confident.

The next day began with a full sun and a clear blue sky, but Tex was facing a quandary. It was still several days until the start of the trial, and he was beginning to run out of things for his large crew to do. The MJ simply wasn't big enough to keep this large a body of men busy. And with Bo and Chick, he had two more men to keep busy. He also felt that the outpost crew needed a change in scenery, so he decided to make some different job assignments.

First, he reunited Charley Landers with his special friends, Lefty, Kansas and Blackie, and sent them to patrol the north range. Then he told Sanchez to take Bo and Chick with him, Juan and Felipé and show them the hidden herd with the Double H brands. Thirdly, he directed Rusty, Curley, José and Luis to man the outpost along with Reb. Finally, he used Red and Dusty to increase the two other range patrols to four men each. Tex further directed that each of these units sub-divide themselves into two-man groups to cover more ground and, in so doing, find out how much the cattle had scattered as a result of the storm. Bronc, Trig, Apache, Cavalry and Federico were to remain at the ranch house with Tex, a formidable force in case it was needed — an unlikely event.

Tex was relatively satisfied with all these arrangements. He was keeping them as occupied as he could under the circumstances. Unfortunately, it still left him with less activity than he wanted for himself.

He was pleasantly surprised when Conklin and Willis arrived about mid-afternoon. Regardless of whether Willis had good news or bad, at least it was something new that he could sink his teeth into, he thought.

Tex, Marty, Bronc and Apache moved into the big den with Willis while Conklin examined his patient. The men exchanged small talk until the doctor joined them.

Conklin lowered himself into a soft chair and issued a satisfied sigh of relief.

"Our patient is doing remarkably well," he assured the group. He looked at Marty with a twinkle in his eye. "Anytime that wife of yours gets tired of putting up with you rowdies, she can come into town and act as my nurse, Mr. Johnson," he went on. "She has followed my instructions to the letter and has done a very professional job of changing the bandages. I sure could use help like that."

A murmur of approval came from the group, and Marty smiled with pleasure.

"Thanks, Doc," he said, "but I'm sure we all realize that you had a lot to do with Salty making it, and we appreciate it. Keeping him alive has proven to be very important to all of us, as Tex will tell you."

"We'll get to that later," interrupted Tex. "First I want to hear how Ted made out in Canyon City."

"We hit the nail on the head," grinned Willis. "I was able to locate bank accounts for Donie, Kelso, French, Cook and Sims. Strangely enough, except for the deposits, all of which occurred at about the same time both years, none of the accounts have shown much activity."

Willis pulled out some papers from an inner coat pocket, spread them out on a table and arranged them in sequence.

"Donie only had one withdrawal, a five hundred dollar amount, about a week ago," he disclosed. "Kelso pulled out a fair amount every three months or so, but Cook and Sims didn't touch their accounts at all. What surprised me is that French only had a few withdrawals, even though he had to pay off Adams and Charles."

"French could pay off those two out of his foreman's pay," Bronc reminded Willis, "especially if'n he didn't have other needs of any size."

Willis nodded his agreement, scratched his jaw and motioned at the papers with one hand.

"When you add up all the initial deposits, the total is a little less than I had hoped for, but it's close enough to tie it to the sale of the cattle."

"Salty told us he kept his three hundred each year and sent it to a brother somewhere," Tex reminded Willis. "Won't that help take care of the difference?"

"Yes, that will bring it closer," admitted Willis. "But we have to assume each man may have held back some cash for his personal needs. I don't think I'll have any trouble convincing a jury this money all came from the sale of stolen cattle. Folks around here aren't that dumb!"

"Well, that will be good as far as the rustlin' is concerned," agreed Tex. "But I want to get Donie for murder!"

Willis' head jerked, and he stared hard at Tex.

"Yes, we finally got Salty to agree to testify, and he says Donie killed Slim," Tex went on. "We also know Donie committed a second murder! Any news in town on that?"

"What? A second murder? I haven't heard anything about that," snapped a surprised Willis. "What are you talking about? Doc, did you hear anything about another murder?"

Tex jumped in and explained what had happened at the Henderson Ranch with Smiley before Doc had a chance to reply.

"Bo saw the whole thing and is here with us now," Tex added. "I imagine you're goin' to want to talk to him and Salty, too."

"Yes," replied Willis thoughtfully. "But Doc didn't answer my question. Did you hear anything about Smiley?"

"No," replied Conklin quietly. "But it fits."

"It fits? What do you mean by that?" asked Willis, again surprised.

Conklin settled back in his chair and closed his eyes, deep in thought. Finally he opened his eyes, and his face took on a somber expression.

"Gentlemen, I'm only an old country doctor, and I don't have any way of proving what I'm about to say. But I strongly suspect that Donie has become mentally unbalanced, or at least he has periods where he becomes mentally unbalanced. Maybe his killing of Evers was too much for his system, and he hasn't been able to handle the impact of that event. I'm not exactly sure of what I'm saying, myself, but I'll bet old Henry doesn't know what to do about it. I can't believe Henry would try to handle it, even if he could at all, until after the trial."

"Well, unbalanced or not, I want to get Donie for killing Slim," growled Tex. "Is there any way we can do it now, Ted, or do we have to wait for another trial?"

"Let me talk to Salty," replied Willis, "and then let me think about it. Doc has to go back to town, but I intend to stay here for quite a while and go over what we're going to do at the trial. We can do that after I talk to Salty and Bo. By the way, where is Bo, and when can I see him?"

"Sanchez took Bo and Chick with him to the south range to show them the beef with the Double H brands," answered Tex. "They should be back before long."

"All right, then, let me talk with Salty. I made a list out of who all I want to testify and why. Look it over, Tex, and let me know how you feel about it. I want to meet with you and everyone on that list later today. I think it would be best if we met as a group and shared any ideas anyone may have. That okay with you, Tex?"

Tex nodded agreement, and as Willis and Conklin left the room, he and his companions began to study the list and talk through what was ahead.

* * * * * * * * * * * *

That night all the potential witnesses gathered in the main room of the ranch house, where Salty was still recuperating. Willis carefully explained what he was trying to do and how each person's testimony fit into the total scheme of things. Finally he discussed how he intended to bring Slim's murder into the picture and warned, "The judge could throw out all the testimony related to the murder on the grounds it is not relevant to the issue of cattle rustling."

"I accept that," said Tex. "I just want the whole world to know that Donie Henderson is a murderer, and I want you to have a murder warrant ready to serve at the end of the trial. I want to throw Donie back in jail and keep him there this time."

"Fair enough," responded Willis. "But I plan on having two murder warrants ready to serve in case I need them. Donie won't get out on bail this time. At the same time, we'll serve the warrants you're holding for French and Spencer. I've already talked to Salty about this," he explained as he looked at Spencer. "Salty knows it's only a formality if he testifies. But should he back out at the last minute, I'll be ready."

Willis paused, stared at Salty to emphasize his statement and then looked around the room.

"Anybody have any problems or questions?" he asked.

"Only one," responded Tex. "Tell Judge Palmer that me and the boys won't be givin' up our guns when we get there. We ain't takin' any chances. You know why."

Ted slowly nodded his agreement.

"Any more problems or questions?" Willis repeated.

Hearing none, he rose, thanked everyone for their attention and thoughts and headed for the door and his trip back to town.

Tex accompanied Willis to the tie rail and shook hands with him.

"You do good work, Ted," he said simply. "No matter how this all comes out, me and the boys are grateful for you being willin' to take on the Hendersons. You're goin' to have to live here after we leave, and if'n this turns out bad for us, you're goin' to be stuck with the result."

Willis smiled wryly and shrugged his shoulders.

"Well, I told you it would have to be a strong case. We have a strong case, and I want the rustling charge to stick so that I can ask the court to retrieve all that money sitting in those bank accounts and get it back for Mr. Johnson. And, of course, I need a conviction to survive around here, too. So, we both have a lot at stake, Tex. Just have your boys ready for court. It will be decided there."

Willis grabbed his reins and pulled himself up into his saddle. With a wave and a grin, he headed for Ridgeway.

* * * * * * * * * * *

Two nights later, the evening before the start of the trial, Tex called his key men together for a final review of the events scheduled for the next day. He arranged for Salty to be taken for a short walk and to be kept away from the house until the meeting was over.

"Well, tomorrow is the day we've been waitin' for," he began. "I don't honestly know how it will all turn out. Even though Willis and Conklin don't think the town will be hostile and we'll get a fair trial, we don't know how Henry will tolerate all this. For all we know, he may already have one or more of the jury members in his hip pocket. At any rate, we have to be ready for anythin'. I've played too much poker, like most of you, to be shore of anythin' until the last hand is laid down.

"Tomorrow we got to allow an hour to get to town so Salty can make the trip. We'll use the ranch wagon and springs for him ag'in. We're also goin' to take along French. I want both of them tied down and French gagged. That's your job, Bronc, along with Trig and Apache."

Bronc looked up and grunted his acceptance of that responsibility.

"Willis wants us to pack the courtroom," Tex went on, "and that we will do. But we're also goin' to do a couple of things he don't know about. And some of you are goin' to have to stay here at the ranch with Mary."

Growls and groans met this last remark, and Tex frowned.

"You didn't think I'd leave this place undefended, did you?" he growled. "Bronc, you, Trig, Reb, Cavalry and Dusty will stay here, just in case Henry tries somethin'. Lefty, I got a special job for you and Curley. Marty has made a sketch of the layout in Ridgeway, and I have it here. This is what I want you to do."

Tex spread the sketch out on the table and outlined his plan, using one finger to point out what he wanted done. Both men nodded agreement, asked a couple of questions and then left to make the necessary arrangements. The other men held a brief conversation and were soon on their way, leaving Tex and Marty alone in the room.

"We've done as much as we can, Marty," Tex said in a low voice. "Now we have to rely on Willis and the people of Ridgeway."

Marty said nothing but squeezed Tex's shoulder and went to find Mary.

The rest of the evening found many men cleaning and checking their revolvers and rifles, filling bandoleers with cartridges and preoccupied with thoughts of what they hoped would take place on the morrow.

CHAPTER 17

As dawn broke, the second shift of night sentries began to rouse the men, and the morning ritual, which looked like organized chaos, began.

Bo and Chick were fascinated with the activity, never having been involved with a crew of almost 30 men in the past. After breakfast they sat and watched the coming and going with no little admiration. By this time they were aware of the outpost crew and their function, and chuckled as they recalled their impressions from their earlier visit.

"That Riley fellar shore don't miss many bets," allowed Chick quietly. "Can't help wonderin' what surprises he has in store for old Henry and Donie afore this day is over."

"Can't answer that one," replied Bo. "But the folks in Ridgeway are in for a shock, too, I'm afiggerin'. I'm shore glad we're goin' to be part of it."

Shortly before nine o'clock, the ranch wagon was pushed back to the front steps of the main house. The springs were fit into the wagon bed, and a number of blankets were put down to cushion the ride. Spencer was half led and half carried out of the house and down the steps and was helped into the wagon. At the same time, French walked from the bunkhouse with Bronc and Trig alongside him.

Both men were to be lashed down; Spencer to prevent as much bouncing as possible and French to prevent him from getting at Spencer. As Tex ordered, French also was gagged.

Apache was preparing to climb into the wagon and supervise the security precautions when Tex touched his arm.

"Apache, make sure both men are tied facin' forward," Tex murmured.

Apache hesitated a moment, then nodded his understanding and leaped into the wagon to direct operations.

Finally all was in readiness, and the column of horsemen moved out, the eyes of their five friends and Mary Johnson watching their departure.

The trip to town was uneventful, but shortly before reaching the outskirts of Ridgeway the final eight riders slowed their pace until there was a good-sized gap between them and the rest of the column.

Tex, at the head of the column with Marty and Sanchez, turned in his saddle and looked down the length of the cavalcade. Curley, Rusty, Reno and Laredo immediately turned their horses and began to circle the town, moving to the east.

The rest of the column continued into town, lumbered down the main street, crossed the intersection into the second block and stopped in front of the courthouse, where a small crowd had gathered. It was obvious that most of the town's citizens had arrived early to get seats and were already inside the building.

The second set of four riders that had fallen back from the main body — Lefty, Charley, Kansas and Blackie — slowly walked their horses through town until they reached the end of the first block, whereupon Lefty and Charley turned their horses to the left, reached the tie rail and dismounted. Similarly, Kansas and Blackie had turned to the right and had also dismounted.

Curley and his men had now reached the north end of the second block. They, too, had split themselves into two sections and had followed the same pattern, two dismounted men on each side of the street.

Both of these movements were largely unnoticed as most of the towns-people were already in the courthouse and the small group of people outside the building were engrossed with the ranch wagon and its human cargo.

Inside the building, the courtroom was packed. Most of the people were already seated. At the head of the room, facing the audience, was a long table, that served as the judge's bench. At the left of the table were 12 chairs reserved for, and occupied by, the jury, which had already been selected. A witness chair was adjacent to the judge's table.

The defendant's table was located in front of the first row of chairs on the left side of the room facing the judge and was occupied by Henry Henderson, Donie Henderson and Albert Thornton, in that order, left to right. Seated directly behind Donie, in the first row of chairs, was Sheriff Hamilton.

The prosecutor's table was on the right side of the room, also in front of the first row of chairs. Ted Willis was its lone occupant. A single aisle separated the two sides of the courtroom in the middle, while additional aisle space was available between the end of each row of spectator chairs and the walls of the building. Directly behind Willis and in the first row of spectator chairs, in the seat closest to the center aisle, sat a sheriff's deputy who was left handed, and an empty chair was situated next to him, on his right, per instructions from Willis. If he had been right handed, the empty chair would have been on his other side.

The arrival of Marty and Sanchez with their men created a stir among the audience. Necks were craned, and the babble of sound increased significantly as the men filed into the room.

Marty led his squad of men, strung out in single file, into the room, turned left and followed the aisle space around the back of the room and down the left wall to the front row of chairs. Sanchez led his men to the right in a similar fashion. The small crowd that had been on the sidewalk filed in and stood in the back, or street side, of the room.

Tex led French down the center aisle until they reached the first row of chairs and the sitting deputy. Tex pointed to the empty chair, and French, no longer gagged but with his hands still bound, slid past the deputy and sat down, a scowl on his face. His entrance, with bound hands, had created further murmuring by the audience. Donie and Henry looked back over their shoulders at the missing foreman. Henry's response was a surprised look while Donie showed a flash of fear and shock in his eyes.

Tex turned toward Hamilton, took a couple of steps and leaned in toward the man.

"We have a warrant we want served on French as soon as this trial is over," he explained. "It's for cattle rustlin' too. Now are you willin' to serve it, or do we have to get Marty to do your job ag'in?"

"I'll serve the warrant," growled Hamilton. "Maybe it won't be necessary," he added hopefully.

"Don't count on it," warned Tex as he moved away.

If the room was buzzing with talk when Tex and his companions entered the room, the response was doubled when Denver and Cheyenne slowly led the bandaged Salty Spencer into the room, down the center aisle and over to a soft chair, located next to where Tex and Marty were standing. Willis had arranged for this as well.

Once Tex had left Hamilton and joined Marty to await Salty's arrival, he took a moment to look carefully at Henry and Donie Henderson. What he saw was disturbing to him.

Donie had a fixed grin on his face, but his eyes were constantly roving, casting furtive glances around the room. He seemed to be enjoying his notoriety and appeared to be oblivious to the potential outcome of the trial.

But it was Henry's face that disturbed Tex the most. The man looked like he had not slept in a week. His eyes were bloodshot, the bags under the eyes had doubled in size and his facial lines had deepened. He appeared to be defeated, dejected and exhausted.

Spencer's appearance affected Donie more than Henry. Henry simply looked up, nodded and then looked down again. Donie, on the other hand, was startled at first but then lapsed into shrill laughter and continued to glance around the room. Thornton, on the other hand, was mystified by Donie's behavior and by Spencer's appearance.

Judge Palmer gaveled the room into silence, and the trial began.

The charge was read, and both Willis and Thornton made very brief opening statements. Willis merely stated he intended to prove guilt and Thornton denying the same.

"Call your first witness, Mr. Willis," the judge ordered.

"I call Mr. Martin Johnson," answered Willis.

Marty was sworn in and identified himself.

He explained how he had been concerned about the lack in the anticipated natural increase in his cattle over the past two years and how he had written Slim Evers about the matter.

"Objection," interrupted Thornton. "I don't see the relevance of this information."

"My next question will show the relevance, your honor," replied Willis.

"I will delay a ruling on the objection, pending the next question and answer," ruled Palmer. "Proceed."

"Why did you write Mr. Evers?" asked Willis.

"I had two reasons," answered Marty. "First, Mr. Evers was the owner of the Rambling R Ranch and was an experienced cattle man. Secondly, and most important, he owned half of the MJ Ranch. He was my partner!"

Henry Henderson's head jerked up at these words, and he stared hard at Marty. A rumbling of sound exuded from the surprised audience.

Palmer gaveled the room back to silence and announced his ruling.

"Objection overruled. Please continue."

Willis and Tex exchanged knowing glances. Slim's name was now a part of the proceedings.

"Mr. Johnson, please explain to the court the basis for your statement," droned Willis.

"Be glad to," smiled Marty.

"I didn't have enough money to buy the MJ on my own. In fact, I only had about a quarter of the purchase price. Mr. Evers was kind enough to provide another quarter, and I signed a mortgage note for the remainder. However, I did not have enough assets to justify the loan, so my father and Mr. Evers joined the note as endorsers and pledged their personal assets as security. Mr. Evers was to remain as a full partner until I could buy him out."

"Did Mr. Evers respond to your letter?" continued Willis.

"Yes, he did. He came to visit me and brought along his adopted son, Paul Redstone."

Thornton started to object, but Henry reached past Donie and restrained him. Henry whispered to Thornton, and Thornton responded by frowning and shaking his head. Henry whispered again, this time emphatically, and Thornton spread his hands in frustration but nodded agreement.

"Did Mr. Evers provide any answers for you?" Willis went on.

"He didn't get a chance to," replied Marty, his voice rising. "He asked a lot of questions, but before he could come up with any answers he was shot and killed!"

Another undercurrent of sound burst forth from the audience, and again Palmer had to gavel the room back to silence.

Marty then described how French and Cook had testified at the inquest regarding the killing of Evers.

"What did you do next?" inquired Willis.

"Paul and I knew the situation was more than we could handle, and we decided we needed help. We composed a telegram for Paul to take to Canyon City and send. It was addressed to Tex Riley at the Rambling R Ranch and notified him of Mr. Evers' death and asked him for his help."

"No further questions. Your witness, Mr. Thornton."

Thornton rose, glanced at Henry and spoke. "I have no questions at this time, your honor, but reserve the right to recall this witness later on."

"Very well," said Palmer. "Call your next witness, Mr. Willis."

"I call Paul Redstone," responded Willis.

Apache surprised the room with his precise English and testified about his riding to Canyon City, sending the telegram and waiting for the replies that followed over the next few days.

When given the chance to cross examine, Thornton's reply was the same as before, "I have no questions at this time, but reserve the right to recall this witness later on."

Tex Riley was called next and described how the news of Slim's death had been received and how he had organized the response. He outlined how he had sent word of the tragedy to Sanchez, at his ranch in Mexico, and how Sanchez had insisted on being part of that response. He went on to describe their arrival in Harding. Hamilton's face lit up at this disclosure, as he was now able to solve a vexing mystery. Tex told of meeting Apache on the trail and having him guide them to the MJ Ranch.

"Describe your arrival at the ranch," queried Willis.

"I didn't trust anyone at the ranch outside of Marty," explained Tex. "So I had four of my men take over the ranch at gunpoint."

The crowd responded noisely to this statement and then quickly quieted down.

"Now, Mr. Riley, you have heard testimony regarding the financial arrangements made for the purchase of the MJ Ranch. Does the death of Mr. Evers change anything in this regard?"

"Not at all," replied Tex, looking straight at Henry Henderson.

"Slim allowed me, and any others who wanted to, to purchase shares in the Rambling R. Many of us did, and I speak for all of them. The entire financial resources of the Rambling R will be used, if necessary, to support Mr. Johnson in the purchase of the MJ. Mr. Johnson will never *have* to sell the MJ unless he wants to do so. That is our pledge to him."

Willis waited for this statement to sink in and then asked Tex another question. "Describe for the court how you managed the affairs of the ranch after you assumed the role of foreman."

Tex did so, outlining the system of patroling the ranges he had established. Based on the information he had received from Marty and Apache, he suspected that a maverick operation was going on and that it was probably centered in the south and southwest ranges, the areas closest to Harding.

"Did you have any other information that also supported your suspicions?" asked Willis.

"Yes," replied Tex. "The Rambling R ships a lot of cattle by rail, and I used this fact to get some information from the railroad that serves Harding. I found out that two small herds of beef had been shipped out of Harding by the Double H Ranch over the past two years. This seemed strange to me, since they usually ship out of Canyon City."

This statement jolted Henry, and he stared in disbelief. The audience also again erupted.

When order had again been restored, Willis picked up some papers from his table, moved to the judge's table and handed them to Palmer.

"We present to the Court two depositions, prepared by the legal department of the railroad, showing the shipment of cattle by the Double H Ranch on August twenty-seventh of last year and on September fifth of the year before that. Both shipping documents identify the shipper as being Donald F. Henderson."

Now the undercurrent of sound from the audience reached a noisier level. It took several bangs of the gavel before Palmer could restore order. Henry turned and stared hard at Donie, whose grin had now disappeared and who seemed to shrink in his chair. Thornton was shocked.

"Please continue, Mr. Riley," Willis went on when quiet had been established. "Tell the court what took place on the southern ranges."

Tex outlined how Sanchez and his men had been given that area to explore and how Sanchez and José had continued on their own after Cook and his escorts had gone on with their normal patroling.

He went on to describe how Sanchez and José had located the hidden herd of partially branded cattle and the need to establish who was involved. When Sanchez reported his discovery to Tex, they had devised a plan to see how Cook fitted into the puzzle. Felipé was to insist on following the draw to the meadow, using some sort of pretext. If Cook didn't eagerly support Felipé but turned on him instead, Sanchez and his other men would jump Cook at the first opportunity, capture him and see if they could learn who else was involved. The trap was set, but unexpected events created a dangerous situation.

Willis ended his questioning of Tex at this point, and again Thornton declined to cross examine and issued his one sentence statement.

Willis then called Felipé to the stand.

"If the court pleases," began Willis, "Felipé does speak fairly good English, but I will use questions that can be answered with either a yes or a no. I believe that by so doing we will be able to get good testimony."

"This is acceptable to the court," responded Palmer. "Does the defense have any objection?"

"Not at this time," said Thornton.

Using adroit questions, Willis was able to have Felipé describe his surprise at being able to use the telltale smoke as his excuse, his subsequent capture and of meeting Salty and Dan with the herd. He then told how he heard the names of other gang members mentioned while he was a prisoner — Donie Henderson, Kip Kelso and Art French.

Again the buzz of sound filled the room, but Palmer waited a few moments, and the talking quickly receded. The Ridgeway citizens were eager to hear more.

Willis terminated his questions at this point, and Thornton's response was the same.

Willis then called Sanchez to the stand.

With the same question and answer technique, Sanchez told of being surprised and dismayed by the arrival of Spencer and Sims. He decided that the plan was now useless and that they would have to improvise. He told of the attempt on Felipé's life and how he and his men had responded, killing

Cook and Sims and seriously wounding Spencer. He then outlined how they tried to treat Spencer's wound and how they got him back to the MJ.

Willis then presented the Double H branding iron found with the herd. Sanchez identified the iron, and it was added to the two previous exhibits as evidence.

This finished Willis' questioning of Sanchez and, as usual, Thornton followed with his one sentence response.

Willis then called Wes Adams to the stand.

Wes described his role in the scheme, how he had helped in one cattle drive to Harding and identified his drive companions as being Kelso, Cook, Spencer and Sims. He further indicated that French had paid him an additional $ 10 a month for his involvement.

Thornton's response to this testimony was the same as before.

Willis called Bud Charles to the stand. His testimony echoed that of Adams and identified the same four men as his drive companions. Thornton repeated his cross examination statement yet again.

Willis called Doc Conklin to the stand.

Conklin described his role in treating Spencer, being shown the bodies of Cook and Sims and then stated his concern about Spencer.

"My patient was wounded seriously and has not regained his full strength as yet. The trip to town from the MJ Ranch was arduous, and I respectfully request that the court allow him to testify from his present location instead of the usual chair."

"Unless the defense attorney has a reasonable objection, the court will grant the doctor's request," Palmer droned.

"The defense has no objection," replied Thornton, realizing he really had no choice.

Spencer was sworn in and described his part in the branding and the cattle drives and confirmed Felipé's testimony as well as that of Sanchez.

"How much were you paid for this special work?" asked Willis.

"I got $ 300 each year out of the money from the sale of the cattle. Kip Kelso gave it to me once and Donie did the other time."

"What did you do with the money?"

"I sent it to my brother in another state."

"Your honor, I wish to interrupt the testimony of this witness to provide several more exhibits regarding this situation," announced Willis.

"Very well," agreed Palmer. "What exhibits do you have?"

"I have signed depositions from the bank in Canyon City regarding bank accounts established by five members of this gang — Donie Henderson, Kip Kelso, Art French, Stan Cook and Dan Sims. As I read the dates of the original deposits and the amounts involved, the jury should recall the date of the first shipment of cattle out of Harding, as described in Exhibit 1. I will then read the dates and amounts of the second group of deposits, and again I request that the jury recall the date of the second shipment of cattle as described in Exhibit 2." He then repeated those dates for the benefit of the jury.

Willis then read the dates and amounts shown in the documents, and the faces of the jurors instantly showed their comprehension of what was being provided them.

"If we add the amounts Spencer sent to his brother each year and allow each man to hold back small amounts for his personal needs," Willis concluded, "the total dollars each year very closely approximate the amount that would be received from the sale of the cattle at $ 13 a head two years ago; and at $ 14 a head last year. Both of those prices are reasonable, as we all know."

Willis paused, and the babble heard around the room told him he had delivered a mighty blow, and a glance at the faces of the jurors confirmed his feeling. He was sure his rustling case was now beyond reproach. Now it was time to take the big gamble.

As soon as the noise in the room had again been subdued, Willis turned his attention back to Spencer.

"Mr. Spencer," he began, "you have described the rustling activities of you and your confederates. I must ask you, did any unusual events occur during the course of this activity?"

"Yes," Salty sighed. "Mr. Evers caught four of us startin' to brand MJ beef."

Thornton leaped to his feet and yelled, "Objection!" over the din that had erupted from the spectators in response to Spencer's words.

Palmer pounded his gavel relentlessly, while Thornton continued to scream, "Objection!" Finally order was restored.

"I object," repeated Thornton, his face red. "This trial is about cattle rustling, not a shooting. It is not relevant."

"Your honor," replied Willis soothingly, "we established Evers and his role as an integral part of the sequence of events at the very start of this trial. It is only reasonable that we try to find out the total impact of his presence and how it affected the events that followed."

Palmer looked at both Thornton and Willis, cogitated and finally reached his decision. "Objection overruled. The court is very interested in finding out how the rustling and Mr. Evers' death might be related. Proceed, Mr. Willis."

"All right, Mr. Spencer," Willis continued, a grim look on his face. "Tell the court exactly what happened when Mr. Evers discovered the four of you. Name the four and tell us what happened."

Salty did as he was told, speaking slowly and distinctly. He concluded his story by describing the killing of Slim Evers.

"Now, Mr. Spencer," said Willis in a loud voice, "is the person who pulled that trigger in the courtroom today?"

"Yes," answered Salty.

Willis paused for a moment, and as almost everyone leaned forward in his chair, including Judge Palmer, he spoke evenly. "Who is that person?"

"Donie Henderson!"

If the courtroom had been noisy before, it was sheer bedlam now. Donie leaped to his feet, screaming profanities at Spencer. Other spectators had risen to their feet and were shouting comments to neighboring friends and acquaintances, voicing their astonishment.

Donie began to crawl over the top of his table in an attempt to get to Spencer. Hamilton, despite his bulk, saw the danger, rose from his chair and quickly moved to stop Donie. Grabbing Donie's pants belt from the rear, he yanked Donie with all his strength. He was too successful, as Donie slid back off the table and rammed into Hamilton, knocking him back against his chair. The chair tilted, Hamilton lost his footing and both men tumbled to the floor, the chair falling with them.

The spectators around the two men were now all on their feet and watching the melee. The people nearest the two combatants surged forward and spread out, trying to see what was going on and blocked the view of Tex, Sanchez and their men.

Hamilton sensed, rather than felt, Donie's hand reach for the sheriff's gun, and his own hand reached for the same object. His quick reaction probably saved his life. There was a muffled explosion, and Hamilton screamed in pain, fell forward onto Donie, thereby inadvertently pinning Donie to the floor.

French's mind was racing. As soon as Spencer named Donie as the killer, French knew his plan to blackmail Henry into defending him and perhaps getting him off with a light sentence was now shattered. He had become as desperate as Donie.

The deputy next to French had risen when Donie tried to crawl over the table. As soon as Hamilton pulled Donie back, the deputy started to go to Hamilton's aid, completely forgetting about French.

French, too, had risen to his feet and as soon as the deputy moved, French moved with him. Even though his hands were awkwardly bound together,

French managed to grab the deputy's gun from its holster with his right hand and fired a shot into the room's ceiling. His left hand then clutched the deputy's shirt collar at the nape of the neck and pulled the man back and straight up. He placed the barrel of his gun at the base of the man's skull and pulled the hammer back.

The sound of the shot stopped the movement of bodies in the room and eliminated the accompanying babble as well.

"Listen to me," yelled French, "anyone shoots me, and the deputy will have his head blown off!"

"You pull that trigger, and me and my men will shoot you to pieces," yelled back Tex.

"It's a Mexican standoff, Riley," countered French. "Now, less'n you want to see this deputy killed and maybe some others as well, holster your guns."

Tex's gun did not waiver as he barked out some commands.

"Sanchez, Felipé, Red, keep him covered. Everyone else holster your guns. The rest of you sit down and don't move."

"That's the only deal you get, French," continued Tex grimly. "You pull that trigger, and you're a dead man."

French gritted his teeth and ignored the last remark.

"Donie," he shouted, "get out from under Hamilton. Get his gun and cover my back. We're gettin' out of here!"

Donie's mind had returned to some state of normalcy. Whether it was his struggle with Hamilton, the sound of the second shot, French's authoritative voice, or a combination of all three, he obeyed French's command. He finally pushed Hamilton aside, gripped the gun, rose to his feet and stood alongside French, facing the back of the room.

Slowly the three men inched their way toward the door, French's gun pressed against the neck of the deputy each step of the way.

As they approached the door, French gave Donie more instructions.

"Go outside kid, grab the first two horses you see, mount one and have the reins of the other one ready for me when I come out. I'll be comin' fast, so don't make no mistakes. Yell when you're ready for me. Now go!"

Donie did as he was told, slipped out the building and slid his gun inside his belt, as he needed both hands to handle the reins of the two horses. He quickly mounted and yelled to French.

As soon as he heard the yell, French tightened his grip on the deputy's shirt collar and spoke in his ear.

"You do as you're told, and you may live through this," he snarled. "We're goin' to back out the building, and you pull the door shut as we go past it.

As soon as we get outside, I'm going to shove you one way or t'other. You hit the sidewalk, face down and stay there. You understand?"

The deputy nodded.

The two men backed out the building, and the deputy pulled the door shut behind them. French shoved the man aside, took three quick steps into the street, clutched the reins that Donie handed him and vaulted into the saddle.

"Head south toward the mountains," he yelled at Donie. "It's our only chance."

Donie kicked his horse in action and headed down the street as French fired two shots into the courtroom door to delay pursuit and followed Donie. The horses had only taken a few strides as French swore and pulled his horse to a skidding stop. Four men, alerted by the shots, had stepped into the street and faced the two fugitives. Donie, also seeing the danger, had pulled his horse to a stop as well as he clawed for the gun in his belt.

Inside the courtroom, Tex fired a shot into the ceiling to get everyone's attention.

"Everybody stay right where they are," he yelled. "Those two won't get far."

He had barely gotten the words out of his mouth when a burst of gunfire was heard from outside the building.

"Everyone stay seated," Tex repeated. "Let Doc Conklin get through. The sheriff needs his attention."

Conklin pushed people aside as he slowly made his way to where Hamilton was sprawled. As the doctor bent down to begin his examination of the sheriff, Tex noticed that Henry Henderson still sat at his table, his head bent over, face down and cradled in his burly arms.

A few moments passed, followed by a loud knock on the front door. Guns appeared, automatically, in the hands of most of the Rambling R men.

Lefty White stuck his head around the partially opened door and raised his clenched right hand with his thumb extended.

"I got two dead bodies out there in the street," he announced to one and all. "Who wants 'em?"

EPILOGUE

It was nearly noon, two days later, when four riders — Marty, Tex, Bronc and Trig — slowly approached the courtyard of the Henderson Ranch. All four men could not help noticing a freshly dug grave in a tiny enclosed plot of well-kept ground under a large oak tree, away from ranch proper. The newly turned earth was adjacent to a headstone.

"Henry's wife," explained Marty, responding to an unasked question. "I understand she died a few years after Donie was born. The kid never really had a maw. Maybe that explains a lot of things."

"We'll never know, Marty," said Tex. "A lot of folks are born into tough circumstances but don't turn out bad. I don't think Donie would have lived long in any case what with his temper and all. If we hadn't done the job, someone else woulda."

Deuce Lawson had observed the riders as they made their way toward the ranch. He crossed the courtyard and entered the main house to tell Henry he had visitors. Henry and Deuce emerged from the house as the four men stopped at the tie rail. All four remained mounted.

Henry stepped off the porch, Deuce in his wake, and looked up at the four men. Despite the conflicting thoughts running through his mind, common cow country courtesy finally won out.

"Step down neighbors," he mumbled with an effort. "Come up on the porch and get out of the sun." He motioned for Deuce to continue on.

The four men dismounted, and Tex looked at his host with a critical eye. It was obvious that Henry had managed to get some sleep since the trial. His eyes were no longer bloodshot, and the lines in his face seemed to be a little softer and less dominant. The defeated and exhausted look had largely disappeared, but the anguish still remained.

Marty, Tex and Henry found chairs to settle in, while Bronc and Trig found the top rail of the porch fence to their liking.

"I just came over to let you know I'll be leavin' in the mornin' and takin' most of my men with me," Tex began. "I figger there is no need for us to stay around here any longer, and both Sanchez and I have ranches to get back to. Lefty and a few of the boys are goin' to stay for a spell until we can find good men to help Marty with the ranch.

"Lefty will be in charge, and, while you may think I'm tough to get along with, I got to tell you, next to Lefty I'm an angel."

Henry couldn't resist a thin smile at that jab.

"I find that hard to believe, Riley. You seem to know how to get your way, and I saw what you did to Kelso. Besides, Doc Conklin came out to visit me yesterday, and he and I had a long talk. I must tell you, you've made quite an impression on him. And Doc is hard to fool. I can vouch for that. By the way, he told me Hamilton will survive, although he'll be in bed for a spell. As soon as he gets back on his feet, he's going to quit the sheriffing business. Don't want a job, do you?"

"No," laughed Tex. "I told you I got a ranch to get back to and run. But I'm glad Hamilton is goin' to live. There's a couple of other things I need to talk to you about, though.

"I told Bo and Chick they have jobs on the MJ as long as they want them," Tex went on, "but I don't think that's where they really want to be. Both of them are good men, Henry, and Bo has the makin's of being a good foreman. He likes you, Henry, and it was awful hard for him and Chick to come to us. They had stood up to Donie and when he gunned down Smiley, they thought they might be next. Him bein' your son didn't give them much of a chance with you. They really didn't have any choice when they came to us."

Henry nodded slowly.

"I was angry with them for leaving me and the ranch," he admitted. "Looking at it from their point of view, as you say, they probably didn't have much choice. Your idea of Bo being a foreman is a good one. I've sort of used him thataway, off and on, and probably should have done more. Having Donie and Kelso around sort of blinded me, even knowing that Donie couldn't do the job. I just never gave up hope that he would come around, somehow."

"I can understand that," said Tex softly. "I got lucky when Slim took me on. Without him I would have been in bad trouble a long time ago. Do you have any words for me to take back to Bo and Chick?"

"Yes, I reckon I've got to move on and get this ranch back in shape ag'in.

I'll need Bo to help me and Chick, too. Tell Bo the foreman's job is hisn if he wants it, but have him stop by and we'll talk about it."

"I'll do better'n that," said Tex. "We've got a 106 critters with Double H brands on their hides. Lefty is drivin' them north right now and will have them close to your boundary line by tomorrow. Lefty'll have Bo and Chick tend to 'em. Why don't you and a few of your men ride out tomorrow, pick 'em up and you can talk to Bo then."

"I'll do just that," responded Henry with new enthusiasm. "That was right kind of you. What do you want in exchange?"

"I've talked to Marty," replied Tex, "and he's willin' to take an equal number from your calf crop next spring. I figger the year's difference might be worth about $ 10 a head. Is that fair?"

Henry thought for a moment and nodded agreement.

"Yes, that's about what they're worth at current prices. I'll have a check for Mr. Johnson tomorrow when I meet Bo. By the way, how are you coming out with the money in Canyon City?"

"Ted Willis says the court will issue an order and get the money back for me," answered Marty. "Salty has agreed to write his brother and have his share sent back. It'll be a condition of his gettin' a suspended sentence, according to Willis. That will ease my financial problems considerably."

"That will still make you some short of what you deserve," observed Henry. "Once you find out how much that is, let me know what it is, and I'll write you a check. I guess I was part of the problem, and I want to do what's right. Things shore got out of hand around here."

"I'm right glad you said that," exclaimed Tex. "That's the kind of friendliness these two ranches need. I told you that when I first met you. No one should have to hire a gunslinger like Kelso to get along with his neighbors. Shouldn't *want* to neither. It's a foolish policy, and both ranches now have graves to prove it. Those graves should serve as a reminder of that in case anyone gets funny ideas. The next time I come by this way, and I will, I want it to be as a visitor, not leading a bunch of Rambling R men on a killing expedition!"

"Well, you're shore right there, Riley," Henry agreed. "If Marty will shake hands with me now, I reckon we can start out fresh and do what we shoulda done right at the start."

The two men clasped hands in a strong grip as Tex rose and signaled Bronc and Trig to follow him. Marty and Henry exchanged a few more words before Marty joined the three mounted men.

As the four men left the ranch grounds, they again glanced at the new grave as they rode by.

"Funny thing," mused Marty. "I was going to ask Henry what he told Thornton at the trial and why Thornton did so little to defend Donie."

"Oh, I think I know the answer to that," responded Tex. "Henry wasn't thinkin' straight. After Donie killed Smiley, Henry probably figgered Donie was mixed up in the rustlin' as well, and now he had a murder problem on his hands, too. The penalty for rustlin' was a lot less than murder, and mebby Henry thought lettin' Donie get convicted for rustlin' might keep him from havin' to face the murder charge. Henry had no way of knowin' we were comin' in with two murder warrants and that the outcome of the trial really didn't solve Henry's problems. Besides, accordin' to Willis, there wasn't much for Thornton to object to. There was just too much evidence to back up the charges. Willis said he could see that in the faces of the jury."

* * * * * * * * * * * *

Shortly after dawn the next morning, a long column of men, complete with pack horses, were mounted and ready to head back to Harding and their waiting rail cars.

Tex swung into his saddle, leaned down and shook hands with Marty, standing in front of the porch with Mary at his side. Mary was dabbing at her eyes with a white handkerchief.

"You do what Lefty tells you to do, or I'll come back and fire you," he grinned. "Next time I come, it'll be for a visit, and I'll bring Apache along for the huntin' and fishin' he missed on this trip."

"We'll be looking for you, Tex, any time," smiled Marty, "and I'll have that headstone for Slim in place right quick. Thanks for everything. Mary and I will never forget what friends we have."

Tex waved his arm, and the column moved forward. However, as Tex, Apache and Sanchez, the first three riders, passed Slim's gravesite, they removed their hats and looked down at their friend's final resting place. The rest of the men did likewise.

The Rambling R men had finally come to the end of their trail of revenge.

Book 3
Catherine and Paul

To my wife, Patricia, for a lifetime of help, support, and understanding.

Prologue

The old steam driven locomotive chugged its way on the southbound tracks in a clear, star-bright night. In addition to the usual complement of smoking and auxiliary cars, it pulled an additional three cattle cars and two smoking cars. The three cattle cars were filled with picketed swaying horses that were kept busy adjusting their footing in response to the movement of the train.

Every so often a human would walk among them, patting their flanks, scratching their ears and manes, and comforting them as best he could. This was the third day of this kind of intermittent travel, however, and the horses had become somewhat accustomed to the routine. Furthermore, they had made a similar journey, in the opposite direction, about six weeks earlier, and the repeat of the experience seemed to be helpful in alleviating their natural fear of this mode of travel. Moreover, at two lengthy stops at sidings, awaiting connecting transportation, they had been unloaded, watered, allowed to graze, and had been able to recover their equilibrium.

The two smoking cars were filled with men, most of whom were stretched out in a variety of awkward positions, trying to find a way to be comfortable enough to get some sleep. Some used the seats, or a combination of seats, for a bed, while a few simply found the aisle between the rows of seats a convenient place of rest. These men, like their horses, were in the third day of this trip and, endured the discomfort with the same stoicism.

In the middle of the last smoking car a man sat slouched down in his seat, his eyes closed, but not asleep. Two or three inches over six feet tall, strongly built through his upper body, and with finely chiseled facial features, he would draw a second glance in any crowd of people.

Tex Riley, foreman of the Rambling R Ranch, was deep in thought, trying to determine how he was going to handle a variety of problems that were now going to be a permanent part of his life. In addition, he was reviewing the events of the past two months that had created these problems.

First and foremost, he was fed up with riding trains. The soot and cinders from the locomotive combined with the long delays, the clicking of the rails, and the swaying of the cars with every change in the road bed had almost exhausted his patience. Fortunately he and his men would reach their northern Arizona destination by mid-morning, and they would then be able to saddle their horses and enjoy a relatively short 50 mile ride in the clear air of an open range. The trip back from faraway Idaho had been boring, tedious, and longer, it seemed, to the whole group, in stark contrast to their journey north six weeks earlier.

That trip had been motivated by an intense anger over the murder of Slim Evers, owner of the Rambling R Ranch, their boss, the mentor to some of them, especially Tex, and a friend of all. Tex had organized the killing expedition. He and his men were determined to identify, locate, and hang the party or parties responsible for this deed. The extensive preparations inherently necessary for such an effort consumed a sufficient amount of time, however, so that the initial fiery demand for action and revenge had been replaced by a cold, calculating, unemotional plan to accomplish that goal. Furthermore, Tex had reminded his men that they must achieve this objective by staying within the rules of law, if it was humanly possible to do so. Failure to abide by this constraint, he had reminded his men, would make a farce out of the example Slim had made of his life and the philosophy he had tried to instill in his employees.

Tex smiled at the thought. In this regard, the expedition had been an unqualified success. Although it had taken longer than Tex had expected, the Rambling R men had identified the culprit, had apprehended the man, and had dispatched him in an appropriate manner, although not by the method they had intended. Best of all, this had been accomplished with only one casualty! Charley Landers had received a slight wound, a mere scratch, in the final gunfight—a small price to pay for accomplishing their objective. Tex permitted himself a second smile—this time reflecting his total satisfaction with the outcome.

But the death of Slim Evers had instantly created a number of new problems for one Tex Riley.

The first problem, of course, concerned the management of the huge Rambling R Ranch. Over the past several years Slim had concentrated his attention in the handling of the legal and bookkeeping affairs of the ranch, along with strategic planning for its future. Tex, as foreman, on the other hand, was primarily responsible for supervising the day-to-day operations of the ranch, especially the work assignments for the 20 or so ranch hands. Fortunately, Slim had shared his planning thoughts with Tex and, more importantly, had used his foreman as a sounding board and consultant in these matters. Slim knew, of course, that Tex would ultimately be in complete charge of the ranch, and Slim, therefore, wanted to train him toward that end. Furthermore, Slim encouraged all his employees to invest financially in the future of their ranch, and several, including Tex, had done so. Still, Tex thought ruefully, Slim never mentioned whether he had a will or not. Therefore, one of Tex's first tasks must be to meet with Dexter Boyd, the ranch's attorney, and find out what ownership and other legal papers would have to be filed with the proper territorial officials in Phoenix.

There was also a second legal problem. What about Apache? Paul Redstone had been a ward of the court in Hawthorne, Colorado. Paul, orphaned by the murder of his Apache father and white stepmother, had been allowed to make the Rambling R his foster home four years earlier at Slim's behest. Slim, in turn, simply treated Paul as if he were Slim's own son. Jurisdiction over the boy had been transferred to Judge Parks in Cravenville, and it was obvious that a new decision would have to be made regarding this situation. Tex frowned at that thought.

Tex Riley, in his younger days, had also been treated like a son by Slim Evers. Paul and Tex, therefore, had something special in common and, as a result, soon became fast friends. Tex suddenly had a younger brother who needed unusual attention, and Tex loved it. "Uncle" Bronc Evans had affectionately saddled the lad with the nickname of "Apache," and the boy had become a household fixture at the ranch. Would this now have to come to an end?

Tex, like Slim, had never married. Yet the Colorado court had seen fit to allow Slim to become a foster parent. Would it do the same for Tex should jurisdiction over the matter return to Colorado? Even if Judge Parks, in Cravenville, should retain jurisdiction over the boy, would Paul be forced to return to his native habitat at the San Carlos Reservation as had been requested by a delegation of Apaches four years earlier? Tex's frown deepened at that thought.

Paul, of course, had been the main reason Slim had reduced his involvement in the every day operations of the ranch the past several years. The presence of a young son had completely changed Slim's outlook on life and had provided him with a level of happiness that even surprised Tex and pleased him greatly. Slim had acted like a younger man, had felt like a younger man, and even looked like a younger man, or so it seemed. But, alas, he was now gone. Tex felt the heat of anger return to his body, his eyes opened, and his right boot stomped the edge of the opposite seat in disgust. He regained his composure, closed his eyes again, crossed his arms against his chest, and returned to his thoughts.

Obviously, the management of the ranch would now have to change. He would need to have a second-in-command. Two names instantly came to mind—Bronc Evans and Lefty White. Although neither man was a pure cattleman, both men had watched Slim, had asked questions, and had learned their lessons well. More to the point, both men were born leaders and top notch gunmen, a vital skill in time of trouble. Tex sighed. He had used Lefty in leadership roles in the past, and the little left-handed banty rooster had never disappointed him. Lefty, therefore, would get the job, and Bronc would not only understand this decision but probably would have refused the offer had it been made to him. Bronc had defined his job, and that of his friend, Trig Mansfield, several weeks earlier in Idaho, somewhat to Tex's chagrin, and he was not likely to deviate from that self-imposed assignment.

Unfortunately, however, Lefty and his three saddlemates, Charley Landers, Kansas, and Blackie Smith, were still back in Idaho. Tex had made Lefty acting foreman of the MJ Ranch. These four Rambling R men, together with the two surviving MJ punchers, would keep that situation under control until a more permanent arrangement could be found. Tex told Lefty it might take as long as 60 days to figure out what to do, and Lefty had agreed with this notion. Nevertheless, the name of an individual who might be a possible solution to this problem suddenly emerged from the recesses of Tex's brain. He would have to ponder it for a spell.

Tex again opened his eyes, this time with frustration. Marty Johnson had not done a good job in managing the MJ Ranch, at least as far as Tex was concerned. Marty's selection of a foreman to replace John Mason, the man Slim Evers had located, had turned out to be a disaster. It had given birth to a rustling scheme designed to bring the MJ and Marty Johnson to their financial knees. It almost succeeded and led to the murder of Slim Evers. It was only because of the timely arrival of Tex Riley and his avenging expedition that the plan was thwarted and the MJ was returned to financial solvency.

Lefty, therefore, had been assigned a second role. He was to insist that Marty spend a lot less time in and around the main ranch house and a great deal more time in the saddle and more involved in the range operations of his ranch. Lefty had been told to outline the fundamental processes of managing a cattle ranch and, if necessary, pound them into the easterner's skull. In addition, Tex reminded Marty that he should have learned all of this from

John Mason and since he had not, or had forgotten, this time he was to put it all down in writing, a sort of manual of procedures. While Tex expected to take Apache and visit the MJ frequently, he had no intention of dragging 20 more men along with him. Once was enough!

Tex again opened his eyes and looked at a swarthy Mexican in the seat across the aisle. Sanchez was stretched out, arms folded, sombrero over his face, and snoring peacefully. Tex smiled his gratitude at the man and, at the same time, wondered how the Mexican could sleep so well under these adverse conditions.

Sanchez, too, had been a beneficiary of Slim's kindness and financial generosity, and again Tex's eyes glinted at the thought of their great loss. Slim had helped Sanchez acquire his own ranch in Mexico and, in exchange, had gained the man's undying gratitude. Soon after hearing about Slim's demise, and the manner in which it had occurred, Sanchez arrived at the Rambling R, insisted on being part of the killing expedition, and brought along 10 men to support the effort. The additional manpower allowed a delighted foreman to use five Mexicans to augment the five men Tex would leave behind and thus provide the ranch with a skeleton crew that would assure reasonable security for the property. Moreover, Sanchez and his remaining five men were a welcome addition to the fighting strength of the group. A grateful Tex, therefore, appointed him second-in-command of the expedition, and the whole arrangement paid handsome dividends. Sanchez and his men played a critical role in identifying the rustlers and destroying the gang. Best of all, they did both without suffering any casualties, although it had been touch and go as far as the latter was concerned.

All in all, the entire avenging expedition had functioned extremely well, had produced more than the desired results, and had operated like a well planned military maneuver. Tex's face lit up at this thought, the thin smile turned into a big grin, and now he couldn't help remembering some conversations he had had with a certain country doctor in Idaho regarding this very subject.

These final thoughts now relaxed him. Tex closed his eyes, pulled his Stetson down over his face, folded his arms across his chest, and soon was matching the sounds coming from across the aisle.

****

The locomotive slowly backed its cars onto a siding, and as soon as its entire length was well away from the main track, gently brought it to a creaking stop. The siding itself was one of several laid out in a labyrinth of stock pens. A number of pens, at one end of the layout, were filled with cattle, obviously awaiting shipment to a far off market. Several small buildings, an office, and some sleeping quarters, located a short distance away from the pens, completed the shipping facilities. One of the small buildings served as a train station.

As soon as the train came to a complete stop, doors on the cattle cars were slid open, wooden ramps were lowered, and the Rambling R men began to lead, tug, and push saddled horses down the ramps. As soon as three or four horses had reached firm ground, reins were handed to one man, and the other men dashed back to the cars to help their friends. A few men led a number of pack horses and their loaded cargo out of the cars as well. A number of bystanders, primarily punchers responsible for handling the penned cattle, watched the activity with more than a little interest.

A small group of these bystanders, a white man and five Mexicans, were clustered together. As soon as Tex swung off his smoking car platform, he immediately headed for this group, a grin on his face.

The white man stepped forward, and his right hand met Tex's in a firm grasp. His grin was a duplicate of Tex's, but his face only showed a small fraction of the relief he felt within his whole body. Woody Meadows had been acting foreman of the Rambling R for six weeks, and he was now more than happy to relinquish this awesome responsibility.

"Shore glad to see you, Tex," he chortled. "Miguel and his boys and I got here yesterday, and I was beginin' to wonder if'n I had figgered out the days wrong. Guess it took you longer to get here than you figgered."

"Yes," responded Tex. "Our stops turned out to be longer than I thought they would be. But we got a chance to graze the horses and stretch our laigs, too, so it weren't too bad. How are things at the ranch?"

"Good, as far as I can tell," answered Woody. "I put one of Miguel's men and one of ourn in each line camp, as you said. Me and Miguel worked out of the main ranch. It's awful tough watchin' over the sized herds we got with so few men, but we done the best we could."

"I know I gave you an impossible job, Woody," acknowledged Tex. "We'll give the boys a week to take some time off and get their personal affairs in order. At the same time we'll get the chuck wagons ready, gather our horses, and then we'll do the fall roundup. We should find out right quick how we stand."

Sanchez had followed Tex from the smoking car, and he and his countrymen also exchanged warm greetings. Sanchez glanced back, noted that one cattle car was now completely empty, spoke to Miguel in Spanish, and motioned in the direction of the empty car. Miguel nodded his agreement, turned, and waved to his men. They responded by quickly walking to their nearby horses, grabbing their reins, and pulling their mounts in the direction of the empty car. Sanchez turned to Tex and embraced him with a bear hug.

"Eet was a muy bien ride my fren', and we deed wot had to be done," murmured Sanchez, tears in his eyes. "May God walk weeth you. I no want to do thes' again."

"I can't thank you enough, Sanchez," replied Tex, deeply moved, as he returned the hug. "We couldn't have done it without you and your men. If'n you ever need any help at your end, you let me know right quick, and I'll come arunnin'."

An impatient toot from the train engine interrupted the conversation, and both men turned toward the sound. Miguel, his men, and their horses were now safely on board. The ramps were pulled back on the cattle cars, and the doors were slammed shut.

Slowly the train moved forward. Sanchez hurried toward the track, grabbed the railing at the rear of the last smoking car, and pulled himself up the steps and onto the platform. The locomotive picked up a little more speed, swung out onto the main track, and headed south. Sanchez remained on the tiny platform, removed his big sombrero, and waved a final goodbye. Tex and his men responded with an enthusiastic wave of their own hats.

Tex motioned to his companions, most of whom were already mounted, accepted the reins of his saddled horse from Curley Chance, and swung into his saddle. Woody and the few remaining unmounted men did the same. Tex kicked his animal into motion and led his men back toward the north, the Rambling R, and home!

Chapter 1

About two weeks after the Rambling R men had disembarked from their train and headed for their home ranch, another locomotive chugged its way between Cleveland, Ohio, and Chicago, Illinois. A more modern engine, it pulled a number of sleek, new Pullman sleeping cars at a faster pace and with a smoother ride than that experienced by Tex and his friends. Seated in her compartment, a tall, full-bodied woman with long, light brown hair stared out the window at the passing countryside. One hand held a crumpled newspaper clipping. She glanced down at the newsprint, smoothed it out, and read it for the umpteenth time:

Ridgeway, Idaho. Sheriff Benjamin Hamilton announced the findings of an inquest held recently concerning the murder of Mr. Slim Evers. Evers' body, shot in the back, was found by the foreman and a ranch hand in a wooded area on the southwest range of the MJ Ranch. Evers was a visitor at the ranch, a friend of its owners, Martin and Mary Johnson.

The inquest concluded that Evers was killed by a party or parties unknown. Since he was a visitor to the area, there appears to be no motive and there are no suspects.

Catherine Cornell frowned and sighed her grief over this tragedy. Slim Evers and Tex Riley were like father and son. Tex must have been devastated by the news. Tex now needed her, assuming he had not married since she last saw him. Nevertheless, even if that possibility had occurred, it was mandatory that she seek him out and offer whatever help she could provide.

Her eyes shifted back to the window, and she again stared at the passing countryside. But her thoughts turned to the past.

****

More than four years earlier, Catherine had left her teaching position at Cravenville and returned to her Ohio home. It had been a most difficult decision. She had fallen in love with Tex Riley, the man, but at the same time was very uncomfortable with Tex Riley, the gunman, and his violent environment. She had tried to explain her feelings to Tex and knew she had hurt him deeply. She told him of her decision to go back east and asked him not to see her off. So they said their goodbyes on the steps of the schoolhouse, and the next day she was gone. But as the stagecoach left Cravenville, she saw him sitting on his horse, big against the horizon, some distance away from the road. The tears rolled down her cheeks, and she kept a white handkerchief busy for a long time. The other passenger in the coach, a man, was surprised and mystified by her emotions. He leaned forward, started to say something, but reconsidered, slumped back in his seat, and avoided looking at her.

Her reminiscing stopped for a moment. Even now, more than four years later, that vision of Tex remained with her, as clear as if it had happened yesterday. Her eyes glistened, and she dabbed at them with another soft handkerchief. But she soon regained her composure, and her thoughts again returned to the past.

Catherine had been very close to changing her mind during that interlude in the stagecoach. But facts were facts. Tex had resorted to violence three times in the nine months she had known him, and those were events she could not overlook.

First, Tex was furious over the physical abuse Paul Redstone had received at the hands of some of the other boys at her school. Although Paul was a full-blooded Apache, he had been raised as a Quaker. His parents, especially his white stepmother, had taught him that fighting was both evil and useless. Unfortunately, however, his small Apache stature made him an inviting target for older and bigger boys.

Tex, therefore, had assumed the role of big brother to Paul, and when the abuse was repeated, he responded in a forceful and dramatic manner. He caught the trio of abusers in the act and retaliated with a severe beating of the ringleader of the group. Tex, not content to let the matter end there, then dragged the lad to his father and proceeded to administer a savage beating to the boy's father as well. It was Tex's way of communicating his displeasure over the matter and his intention to stop the abuse in its tracks.

Catherine couldn't repress a shudder. The father had a broken jaw, a face that was a mess, and was virtually bedridden for over two weeks. Other Cravenville residents, even those who knew Tex well, were surprised at the extent of Tex's brutality. Yet, as Catherine later found out, Tex had valid reasons for his actions. Furthermore, the abuse directed toward Paul stopped immediately and did not return.

Then there was Shag Norton. The outlaw had abducted Catherine, raped her twice, and left her to die. Catherine witnessed the showdown when Tex caught up with Norton. Tex poured six slugs into the man, and again Catherine shuddered. Without a doubt the man was dead before the final two bullets hit him. Given Tex's deadly accuracy, Shag was probably dead, or close to it, before the third and fourth shots struck him. Catherine's system just wasn't conditioned toward that kind of violence, and she felt she had to protest against it in some way. Hence her decision to go back east and think through her future and what kind of life she really wanted.

Yet, as the stagecoach rolled on, Catherine's thoughts inevitably turned to the other side of the violence question. In all three instances, Tex's prime motives were to protect Paul and Catherine and, if necessary, to inflict enough punishment to deter further problems. And when Tex solved a problem, it stayed solved! And therein was the quandary that was so frustrating to Catherine.

Here she was, an educated person—a school teacher no less! And at the same time she was dealing with a man who had seemingly very little formal education and was a cattleman and a gunman. Yet, it seemed like every time she made a valid point against the use of violence, Tex made an equally valid counterpoint by using violence to right what he thought was a terrible wrong! Perhaps he was much wiser than she gave him credit for. He had asked her to trust him, and she did, but not enough. It was a most disturbing and perplexing dilemma.

These thoughts, and more like them, helped to pass the time for Catherine on the long and exhausting journey back to Ohio. She had wired her parents from St. Louis, and they met her at the Toledo train station. Tears of joy gushed from all eyes as Catherine and her mother embraced. Harold Cornell wiped his glasses several times before giving his daughter a big hug.

Lydia Cornell stepped back and examined Catherine carefully.

"You look a little peaked and pale, my dear," she observed. "Have you been eating and sleeping right?"

"No, mother," admitted Catherine. "I left Arizona almost two weeks ago. One does not eat or sleep well when the journey is that long. I can certainly use some rest, and I'm looking forward to your home cooking. I'll be just fine in a day or two."

Catherine's reply pleased Lydia, and she gave Catherine another hug and a kiss. Harold, in the meantime, collared Catherine's bags and placed them in the back of his carriage.

"We drove up from Bowling Green yesterday and stayed at a hotel last night," he explained as he assisted Catherine's climb into the back seat. He helped his wife get into the front seat, pulled himself up alongside her, and urged the team of black horses into motion. "We should be back home by supper time," he concluded. "Theresa decided to stay at home and not crowd our buggy too much, not knowing how much luggage you would have."

Harold Cornell's father had started the "Cornell Mercantile Company" in Bowling Green, but it was the son who was the better businessman, and it was he who had built the company into a thriving and prosperous operation. But with two daughters and no sons, he was becoming concerned about how this great tradition was to continue. Catherine's three year sojourn in far-away Arizona, combined with an apparent lack of interest in the business, only served to raise his anxiety level. The younger daughter, Theresa, was more interested in boys than his business and unless she picked an appropriate son-in-law, that, too, might be a dead end. He could only hope that Catherine's return might signal a change of heart on her part and a chance for him to get her involved in his business. Or, at the least, she might provide him with a second son-in-law who might be interested in participating in the business.

Theresa's welcome was even more joyous and demonstrative than her parents', and Catherine reveled in her sister's warm greeting. At the same time, Theresa was beside herself with curiosity about Catherine's experiences during her three years in Cravenville. The second night after Catherine's arrival, Theresa, unable to constrain herself any longer, slipped into her sister's bedroom, flopped on the bed, and insisted that Catherine provide her with more detailed information about her activities than the infrequent letters had contained. Reluctantly Catherine outlined her teaching duties, described the children in her charge, and talked about the residents of Cravenville. Something in her voice betrayed her, however.

"You mean you actually tried to teach an Indian boy, an Apache?" exclaimed Theresa. "Wasn't that hard to do?"

"No, not in the least," smiled Catherine. "He spoke and read English as well as you or I. He worked hard and, well . . . he was my favorite pupil. I loved him very much!"

"You loved an Indian?" gasped Theresa. "I don't believe it. For pity's sake, don't say that around here or in the neighborhood. But tell me about the men down there." Obviously this was a subject much dearer and nearer to Theresa's heart than that of an Indian boy.

"Well, there isn't much to tell," began Catherine carefully, but her voice betrayed her again.

"Don't give me that!" snapped Theresa. "You're pretty, and you know it! Surely you didn't stay in that town for three years without being noticed. C'mon, tell your sister the whole story."

"There really isn't that much to tell," repeated Catherine softly, but she couldn't avoid blushing at her thoughts. "Most of the men are ranch hands and don't spend much time in town. Oh, I went out a few times, but nothing came of it."

Theresa took a long look at her sister, a vexed expression on her own face. Catherine's blushing deepened, and she could not hold the eye contact with her sister.

"I knew it!" cried Theresa. "I know you too well, my sister. There was a man, wasn't there? What happened?"

Catherine got up from the bed the two of them had been sitting on and moved over to a window. It had begun to rain, and the pelting of the drops against the glass was the only sound in the room as Catherine stared out into the blackness.

"There was a man, wasn't there?" repeated Theresa breathlessly as she broke the silence.

"Yes, Theresa, there was a man," came the hushed reply as moisture gathered in Catherine's eyes.

"Was he tall, dark, and handsome?" asked Theresa excitedly.

"Well, he *was* tall," chuckled Catherine through her tears. "But the sun burns and tans everyone in the southwest, and so they are all dark, at least the part you can see is dark. Handsome? I think he would laugh at that. But he is strong, oh so strong. Unfortunately, he is also violent. I saw him kill one man, and he almost beat another man to death, although I didn't see that. It can be a violent world out there, Theresa."

"You mean what we read about in the papers is really true?" asked Theresa, with awe.

"Well, I don't know what you've read in the newspapers," answered Catherine. "But, yes, it can get violent at times but not *all* the time. All of the ranch hands wear guns, and when they get excited or drink too much, things can happen. It turned out to be too violent for me, and I don't think you would like it either."

"But, what about *your* man?" queried Theresa again, still not satisfied with what she had heard so far.

"He wasn't *my* man," responded Catherine, again rather hesitantly. "We liked each other, but it's all over now. That's all I'm going to say."

"Well, I think there is a lot more to the story," grunted Theresa as she bounced off the bed. "I won't press you now, but we'll talk again." She grinned and glanced back at her sister as she closed the bedroom door. Catherine remained standing at the window, tears still sliding down her cheeks.

****

Harold and Lydia Cornell enjoyed the fruits of their successful marriage. Both had been born and raised in an upper middle class household and had been childhood sweethearts. Lydia enhanced Harold's stature as a pillar of the community by joining numerous women's activities and organizations— her church circle of friends, a garden club, and a literary club. She enjoyed these relationships and sooner or later had a key role in these groups. It was natural, therefore, that she quickly volunteered Catherine as a speaker to each organization to relate her experiences in Arizona. Lydia also arranged a few teas and garden parties to give her daughter even more public exposure. Catherine was mildly upset at this news at first but decided to make the best of it and prepared some remarks accordingly. She decided to spice up the presentations a bit by including a description of the bank holdup in Cravenville, the killing of two bandits, and the tracking down of the two surviving outlaws by a civilian posse led by Sheriff Buck Buchanan. She deliberately built the sheriff into a folk hero and conveniently neglected to mention the roles that Tex and Paul had played in the process, certain she would be unable to control her emotions if she had not done so. The gasps of horror and other reactions from her audiences told her she had woven a credible and impressive tale, and this pleased her greatly.

Although Theresa worked at her father's store, she did manage to attend two of Catherine's presentations and came away from both of them somewhat puzzled. One night she again confronted her sister in Catherine's bedroom.

"I've listened to you twice," said Theresa, "and I haven't figured out who your man is in all of this. At first I thought he was the sheriff, but it doesn't quite fit. Are you sure you haven't left something out of your talks?"

"Of course I did," purred Catherine. "My relationship with him was personal, and I'm not going to share that with anyone, especially mother's neighbors and gossipy friends. Would you?"

"Well, everyone around here knows who I date and when," frowned Theresa, still not satisfied. "I think you're holding out on me, big sister, and I'm not giving up. Some day you'll have to tell me more about him."

Catherine only smiled and waved Theresa out of the room. As soon as Theresa closed the door, Catherine's smile turned to a frown. Theresa's curiosity was the least of her problems at the moment.

Catherine's pep and energy had not completely returned following her long trip home. At times she felt very tired and lethargic. Worse than that, on several mornings she had awakened in a nauseous state, she had recently missed her monthly period for a second time, and she had experienced an uncommon amount of tenderness with her breasts. As hard as she tried, Catherine could not conceal all these symptoms from her wise and experienced mother.

One afternoon, Catherine awakened from a short nap, and as she contemplated her situation, a soft knock on her bedroom door interrupted her meditation.

"Come on in," she called out. "I'm awake."

Lydia entered the room, softly closed the door, slowly strolled over to Catherine's bed, and sat down on the edge, facing her daughter. Catherine sat up, fluffed her pillows, stood them on edge, and leaned back in an upright position.

"Catherine, it's time we had a talk," said Lydia. "You haven't been yourself ever since you arrived home. Something is wrong, and it's high time we got to the bottom of it."

"Oh, mother, I'm just fine," protested Catherine.

"No, you are not fine," snapped the mother before Catherine could say anything more. "I stopped to see Doctor John today, and he wants to see you at two o'clock tomorrow. I told him you would be there, and I don't want to hear any arguments from you."

"But mother," began Catherine, but her mother waved off any further protestations. "You have your appointment, and you will be there," stated Lydia, sternly.

"Very well, mother, if you insist," agreed Catherine, knowing full well that any further objections would be useless. Besides, the same idea had occurred to her, and now she would not have to arrange for an appointment in an underhanded manner. Dutifully she kept the appointment, but not without a certain amount of apprehension.

Dr. John Carver, a general practitioner, had delivered both Catherine and Theresa and was an old family friend to the Cornells. He greeted Catherine warmly and chatted with her for a few minutes before beginning his examination. A half hour later, he put down his stethoscope, sat on his desk, folded his arms across his chest, and looked down at his patient.

"You're as healthy as a horse," he intoned, "and I think you know it. But if what Lydia told me is correct, you do have a problem. Do you want to tell me about it?"

Catherine sighed in resignation, looked down for a few moments, and then related the full extent of her difficulties. Carver listened intently and paused for a long time before responding to her tale of woe.

"I can't be 100 percent sure at this moment, of course, but I must tell you that all indications point to the fact that you are going to have a baby. I assume that possibility has also occurred to you. Most women do seem to know about such things long before we doctors do."

"Yes, of course," replied Catherine softly.

There was another long period of silence before the doctor cleared his throat and spoke again.

"Please forgive me, Catherine, but I must ask you a rather obvious question. Do you know who the potential father is?"

"Yes, Dr. John, I do. But that doesn't help the situation one bit."

"Why is that?" asked Carver, his bushy eyebrows raised in puzzlement.

"He's dead," replied Catherine, again in a low voice.

"Ah, I see. That does complicate matters considerably. Have you given any thought on how you want to proceed from here?"

"Yes, Dr. John, I have given a great deal of thought about this over the past two months. I am going to need your help."

"Well, of course I will help you all I can," replied Carver. "That goes without saying."

"You don't understand, Dr. John. I do not want to have the baby! And that's where I'm going to need your help."

"You can't be serious, Catherine. You don't expect me to . . . ."

"Of course not, Dr. John," interrupted Catherine. "I would not insult you with such a request. But you have lived and worked here for a long time. Surely you know someone who could help me."

A stunned Doctor John Carver stared at Catherine, unable at first to accept the suggestion he had just heard. He got up, walked around his desk, and sat down heavily in a nearby chair. He looked at Catherine again and shook his head in disbelief.

"I can't believe you are serious, Catherine," he finally muttered. "What will your folks say? Are you sure you have thought this through carefully?"

"My parents aren't pregnant! *I am!*" snapped Catherine, "and by a man I despise! And as far as being embarrassed is concerned, how are my parents going to feel about me walking around here with a big stomach for four or five months?"

"You could go somewhere else to have the baby," suggested Carver weakly.

"I will be going somewhere else as soon as I can," responded Catherine fiercely, "and the sooner the better. But first I have to take care of my problem. Will you help me?"

Carver rose from his chair and began to pace back and forth in his office, his hands clasped behind his back. Several times he stopped, looked at Catherine, and then resumed his pacing. Catherine remained silent, her eyes following the movements of the doctor. Finally Carver stopped his pacing, moved to the front of his desk, sat down on an edge, and looked down at his attractive but fearful, patient.

"Catherine, I want to think about what you have said, and I want you to think about it as well. Come back next Tuesday at the same time, and we'll talk about it again. Tell Lydia I want to do some followup work then. Fair enough?"

"Of course, Doctor John," answered Catherine, "I know I have shocked you. It's been a shock to me, too. I'll see you next Tuesday."

As soon as she returned home, Lydia cornered Catherine and demanded to know the outcome of the consultation.

"Doctor John says I'm healthy as a horse," Catherine truthfully informed her mother. "But he wants to do a little followup work next Tuesday to make sure."

Lydia Cornell bit her lip in vexation but said nothing. It was obvious that her concern had not been alleviated, but there was nothing more she could do for the moment.

Catherine spent the next several days impatiently waiting for Tuesday to arrive. Worse than that, she had two more sickness episodes, and she knew her mother had heard her discomfort. Finally Tuesday arrived, as it always does, and she again presented herself at Doctor Carver's office.

After a little chit chat, Carver got right to the point.

"Have you given any further thought to your problem, Catherine?" he inquired.

"Yes, Doctor John," answered Catherine in a firm voice. I . . . do not . . . want . . . to have . . . a baby!

Carver scowled and sighed in resignation. He picked up a piece of paper from his desk and handed it to Catherine.

"Here is the name of the man who can help you. He runs a pharmacy on tenth street, about a block from the school. As best as I can tell, he has had some medical training, but I have also heard that he is a victim of his own merchandise. If so, that is a very dangerous combination. I don't like doing this Catherine, but the decision is yours. I can appreciate how you feel, but I don't think you would be making the right decision if you go through with this."

"Thank you very much, Doctor John," whispered Catherine as she rose from her chair and planted a kiss on the older man's cheek. "You'll just have to trust me."

Catherine caught her breath as those words tumbled out. Tex Riley had uttered the same words to her less than a year earlier. She had trusted him but not enough. Then she had turned against him. Wasn't it ironic that she, now, must ask for the same kind of trust from Carver. She turned and quickly left the doctor's office.

✳✳✳✳✳✳✳✳✳✳✳✳

The name printed on the slip of paper was Ernest Crabb. The next day Catherine engaged the services of a carriage and driver and was transported to the location Dr. Carver had mentioned. Telling her driver to wait, Catherine entered the little shop. She slowly browsed the merchandise displays as two young people were waited on by a man behind a small counter. As soon as the two customers exited the store, she approached the counter and studied the man. He was of medium height, almost completely bald, with a blond moustache and goatee.

"Good morning miss," he murmured with a thin smile. "What can I do for you?"

Catherine took a deep breath and plunged ahead.

"I have a medical problem, and a friend of mine suggested that you could be of help."

"Well, I'm not a doctor, but I do have some knowledge about medicine. If you tell me what your symptoms are, perhaps I have some medication or ointment that will be of some assistance."

Catherine took another deep breath and began to speak.

"I have missed two monthly periods and have experienced a number of nauseous episodes over the past several weeks. My friend indicated you have a cure for the problem these symptoms might imply."

"I see," responded the man, stroking his goatee. "Does this friend of yours have a name?"

"Yes, but that is not relevant," snapped Catherine. "Can you help me?"

"It may not be relevant to you, miss, but it is to me," replied the man in an even voice. "Our local authorities take a dim view of anyone who solves the problem you have described in the manner you are hinting at. Therefore, the name of your friend is of the utmost importance."

"You won't get it from me," stated Catherine with vigor. "However, *my* name is Catherine Cornell, and my father is Harold Cornell. Do you think I would come here with a name like that unless I was serious?"

"Ah, yes," murmured the man, again stroking his goatee. "I did see your name in the paper. It seems you have been describing your Arizona experiences to a number of women's groups in the city. May I assume you have not been completely forthright in what you have told them?"

"Of course," smiled Catherine. "And for obvious reasons. Now can you help me?"

Crabb stared at Catherine for a few moments and continued to stroke his goatee.

"Very well, Miss Cornell. I can solve your problem. My fee is $ 30, $ 10 in advance. Should you fail to appear at the appointed hour, I will consider the $ 10 to be a consultation fee. I close this store at noon on Saturdays. Could you be here at two o'clock this Saturday?"

"Yes, I can," agreed Catherine as she removed a bill from her purse and handed it to the man. She watched him pocket the money.

"Come to the back door and knock three times, wait for a few moments, and knock three more times. I suggest you arrange for some transportation as you will have some discomfort and will not want to walk very far. But for heaven's sake, don't allow your vehicle to be parked anywhere near this store. If you fail to abide by these rules, we have no deal. Do you understand me?"

"Perfectly," acknowledged Catherine. "I'll be here. Thank you very much."

She left the store, returned home, and arranged for the same driver to pick her up at one thirty the following Saturday.

Chapter 2

The carriage driver pulled the rig to a stop a full block from the pharmacy. Catherine told the driver to wait for her and that she might be gone for more than an hour. She walked past her destination, turned left at a corner, walked a short distance further, found an alleyway, and back tracked to the rear of the store. She knocked three times, paused, and knocked three more times.

Catherine was surprised when the door opened, and she was ushered in by a woman who was much younger than Crabb.

"I am Mr. Crabb's assistant," the woman informed her. "I don't know your name, and there is no reason for you to know mine. Let's keep it that way. Do you have the money?"

Catherine nodded as she looked at her surroundings and handed the woman several bills. The room was obviously a storage area and contained numerous glass cabinets. A table in the center of the room drew her attention.

"Doctor Crabb will be here in a few minutes," the woman told her in a bored tone. "Let's get ready for him."

Catherine soon found herself flat on the table and half undressed. She couldn't help pondering why the woman had called Crabb "doctor".

Another door opened, and Crabb entered the room. Even though she knew what to expect, her face reddened in embarrassment as Crabb took a long, intensive look at the lower half of her body.

The man motioned to the woman and barked out, "Well, nurse, let's get started."

"Raise your knees and spread your legs," directed the "nurse," again in a bored voice. Catherine did as she was told and the blush in her face took on an even deeper color of red. She closed her eyes and waited.

It seemed to Catherine that Crabb did more poking and probing than should have been necessary, although obviously she had no experience in the matter. Her discomfort began to worsen as the man continued his work. Once he paused, took some deep breaths, glanced at his assistant, and wiped the beaded perspiration from his forehead with the back of his sleeve.

Catherine welcomed the temporary relief and took a quick peek at the man at the end of the table. She wasn't pleased at what she thought she saw.

Crabb's eyes seemed to be wider and the pupils more dilated than she remembered from her previous meeting with the man. Moreover, Crabb's face appeared to be flushed with excitement. Catherine closed her eyes again and gave herself a silent rebuke. I can't afford to start imagining things, she thought. It's too late now anyhow.

Crabb plunged back into his work, and Catherine's discomfort again increased significantly. Finally, the man issued a satisfied grunt and handed a tiny object to his assistant. The woman quickly left the room as Crabb drew in deep, heavy breaths.

"You can close your legs now," he informed Catherine.

Catherine did so and immediately felt something warm and wet on her inner right thigh.

"There's something wrong!" she cried. "I can feel it."

"It's just a little blood," Crabb calmly assured her. "It should coagulate in a minute or two. Your womb was distorted, which made the procedure more difficult than usual. Just rest for a few minutes, and you should be fine."

"Was it a boy or a girl," asked Catherine plaintively as a dull pain continued to consume her.

"Do you really want to know?" came the quick response.

"I guess not," answered Catherine, weakly. "What's done is done, and the quicker I accept that, the better off I'm going to be."

The assistant returned, and Crabb disappeared out the door. About 15 minutes later he came back and motioned to the assistant.

"You'll have to leave now," he told Catherine as he and the "nurse" pulled Catherine to an upright position. They helped Catherine slide off the table and stand on her feet. "We have another patient coming in a little while," he explained, "and we need to clean things up around here in order to get ready for her."

Catherine took a few gingerly steps with the assistant at her side. Satisfied she was mobile, Catherine left by the back door. Carefully, slowly, and painfully she made her way back to her carriage. As soon as she reached home, she staggered her way to the upstairs bedroom and threw herself into bed.

Fortunately, Saturdays were usually busy days at her father's store, and both Lydia and Theresa helped out in these circumstances. They had asked Catherine to go with them on this particular Saturday morning, but she begged off and complained of a headache. With this thought in mind, Catherine drifted off into a fitful sleep.

****

Catherine was awake but still in bed when footsteps announced the family arrival from the store. Lydia and Theresa burst into the room without knocking. Lydia moved to the side of the bed and looked down at her daughter while Theresa stopped at the foot of the bed.

"How are you feeling, Catherine?" inquired the mother, concern in her voice.

"Much better," lied Catherine as she forced a smile. "I even took a nice nap."

"That's good news," responded Lydia, greatly relieved. "Why don't you stay in bed. I'll bring you some hot soup and a sandwich in a little while."

"That sounds wonderful!" exclaimed Catherine as the smile expanded into a grin. "I'm sure that would make me feel even better."

Lydia swept out of the room as Theresa remained standing. The younger sister started to say something, paused, and then followed her mother and quietly closed the door.

****

A burst of intense pain woke Catherine in the middle of the night, and she sat up in surprise. Immediately she was almost overcome by intense dizziness and nausea. She fell back on her pillow only to realize that there was a significant amount of dampness in her bed and on the clothes below her waist. Slowly and carefully, she raised herself up and reached for the lamp on her bed stand. She managed to turn on the light and threw back her covers. She was astonished to see the large red stains and screamed in horror. Unable to hold herself erect any longer, she fell back on the pillows and fainted.

The next two or three hours were a blur in her memory. She could recall brief moments when Lydia and Theresa were bathing her face, the sound of excited voices, Dr. Carver's calming voice, being picked up and carried, being transported to another location, the smell of ether, and then complete oblivion.

Catherine's eyes fluttered open, and she groaned in pain. A shadow quickly moved to her side and felt her forehead.

Carver's calm voice penetrated her fog.

"You're going to be all right, Catherine. How do you feel?"

"Just dandy," muttered Catherine and promptly threw up.

The second awakening went a little better. Much of the pain was gone, but she was totally exhausted. Her eyes focused on a woman in a starched white uniform who was hovering over her.

"Where am I?" whispered Catherine weakly.

"In a hospital, my dear," answered the nurse. "Doctor Carver brought you in early yesterday morning. He had to operate on you, and I do believe he saved your life. You've lost a lot of blood, but I think you are now on the road to recovery. I'll tell Doctor Carver you are awake. He wants to see you." The nurse left the room.

Carver appeared in a few minutes, approached her bed, and shook his head enroute.

"We almost lost you, Catherine," he told her when he saw she was somewhat alert. "I never should have told you about that butcher. Was he sober when he worked on you?"

Catherine closed her eyes and tried to remember all that had taken place.

"I think so, Doctor John," she murmured. "Otherwise I wouldn't have let him touch me. It looks like I've just about spoiled everything. What all did you have to do?"

"Well now my dear, we can talk about that later. Go back to sleep and regain some strength. We've got to get you up and out of here. You're young and strong, and we've got the worst behind us."

Several hours later Catherine awoke again, and this time Carver allowed the rest of the family to have a brief visit with her. Lydia and Theresa displayed red eyes, and Harold could only wipe his glasses several times.

The greetings were warm but strained. After a minute or two of routine comments, questions, and answers, Carver shooed the family out of the room and motioned for a nurse to be stationed next to the bed. Catherine sipped some cold water and went back to sleep.

※※※※※※※※※※※※

Theresa returned early the next afternoon but all by herself. Catherine was awake, propped up in bed, and consuming some liquid refreshment when her sister peeked around the partially opened door. As soon as she saw Catherine was awake and alert, Theresa slipped into the room, pulled a chair up next to the bed, and sat down. Neither girl knew how to start the conversation, and so a lengthy silence ensued. Finally, Catherine decided to break the ice.

"I wasn't sure you'd want to come back, little sister, after the way I have dishonored the family," she began. "Aren't you afraid my sin might rub off on you? I assume you know all the gory details by now."

"Oh, shut up, Catherine!" retorted Theresa angrily. "You should know better than that. But now I know why you didn't want to talk about that man of yours. How could he do this to you and then send you back home?"

Catherine couldn't repress a thin smile at her sister's obvious indignation. She reached out and gently stroked Theresa's cheek with the back of her hand.

"You have it all wrong, little sister. My man, as you call him, didn't do anything to me. Quite the contrary. He knew there was a possibility I might be pregnant, and still he wanted to marry me. I turned him down for the reasons I've already told you."

"He wanted to marry you," mused Theresa, calmer now. "Catherine, I've had a fair number of boy friends, and I can't think of one of them who would tell me that if I got in trouble. In fact, I'm not sure any one of them would tell me that if he was the culprit. You said your man was violent and strong. If what you say is true, I see him as kind, forgiving, and very loving. Are we talking about the same man?"

Theresa's words struck home, and Catherine was unable to reply while she contemplated their significance.

"You are no more baffled and confused than I am," Catherine finally admitted. "It's almost like there are two Tex Riley's, and I don't know which one is the real one." Suddenly, she felt the blush steal across her face as she realized the name had slipped out.

Theresa sat straight up in her chair.

"Tex Riley! So that's his name. Rather colorful, I would say. Tell me about him, Catherine."

Catherine paused for a moment in confusion. Finally, she smiled at the eagerness showing in her sister's face.

"There really isn't much to tell, Theresa. He's the foreman of a large cattle ranch near Cravenville. We met because we both have a special interest in that Indian boy I told you about. Tex thinks of himself as being Paul's big brother."

"An Indian boy named Paul?" interrupted an astonished Theresa. "Is Tex an Indian, too?"

"No," laughed Catherine and instantly regretted having done so as a jolt of pain swept through her body and registered its presence on her face.

"Oh, I'm sorry," cried Theresa in dismay. "I didn't mean to cause you distress."

"Just give me a minute to catch my breath," said Catherine. She took the deep breath she wanted and waited for the pain to subside.

"Tex is white," she went on. "So is his boss, the owner of the ranch. The owner of the ranch is a man named Slim Evers. As best I can tell, he took Tex in some time ago and treated him like a son. Slim did the same for Paul and, naturally, Tex looked upon Paul as being his brother. It is really very simple."

"Simple indeed!" snorted Theresa. "Since when, Miss Cornell, is it simple when a white man takes on the job of being a father to an Indian boy and another white man assumes the role of being a brother to the boy? It sounds to me like we have two very unusual men here, Catherine, and your reasons for coming home are becoming more unbelievable by the minute!"

The vehemence of Theresa's words startled Catherine, and she closed her eyes and seemed to shrink back on her pillows.

"Oh, Catherine, I'm so sorry," exclaimed Theresa in anguish as she rose from her chair. "I've said too much, and you've overdone yourself! I'll go now and let you rest."

Catherine lifted her left arm as a sign of accepting Theresa's offer. Her sister bent over the bed, kissed Catherine on her forehead, and quickly left the room.

Catherine kept her eyes closed and continued to reflect on what Theresa had said. The debate that occupied her mind on the long trip from Cravenville now returned and with renewed vigor. Is it possible, she wondered, that I have misjudged Tex again? Could the achievements have been more important than the methods used to accomplish those achievements? These thoughts disturbed her, and she frowned. Her reverie, however, was cut short by the sound of soft footsteps. She opened her eyes and saw Doctor Carver looking at her intently.

"I didn't mean to waken you," offered the doctor, "but since I seem to have done so, I'll inquire as to how you are doing."

"Oh, I wasn't asleep, Dr. John," Catherine assured him. "I was just resting my eyes. And I'm feeling much better, thank you. I even think I could take on some solid food in the not too distant future."

"We'll start that tomorrow," smiled Carver. "In the meantime get as much sleep as you can. But we do have to talk. Is this a good time for you?"

Catherine carefully raised herself up a bit, rearranged her pillows, and settled back, looking satisfied.

"I'm wide awake. Proceed, my good man."

Carver again smiled, pleased at the joviality in her voice. But he quickly sobered because he knew what he was about to tell Catherine was not going to be funny.

"Catherine," he began, "I'm very angry about what Crabb did to you. He almost killed you. I want to bring charges against him, but I won't have a prayer unless you agree to testify against him. Will you be willing to do so?"

Catherine remained silent for a long time, and Carver patiently waited for an answer to his question.

"Doctor John, I know why you want to do this, and in a way I respect you for wanting to do it. But I figured you were going to ask me that question, and I'm sorry, but I cannot testify against the man. He didn't ask me to come to him. I did that on my own. And he *did* try to help me. I don't know what went wrong, but he did try. If a person like myself, regardless of the economic or social circumstances, cannot receive help from the medical profession and does not want to have the baby, that person has no other alternative. I realize there is a moral question here, too, but I made the decision, knowing that issue, and I alone will have to live with the consequences of that decision. I don't know why anyone would think that that is an easy decision to make." Catherine took a deep breath. "I'm sorry, Dr. John, but I won't testify against him."

"Harrumph!" snorted Carver, but he did not rebuke Catherine.

"Catherine," he said, "I'm afraid we have another problem here. The surgery was more extensive than I thought it would be. Well . . . I'm sorry to tell you this, my dear, but you will not be able to have any children."

A stunned Catherine slid down her pillows a bit and looked up at the ceiling. There was a long silence.

"I did everything I could," Carver continued, his eyes misting. "But he simply did too much damage to your uterus. It had to come out. That is why I am so angry with him. I'll ask you again. Knowing this, won't you testify against him?"

Catherine continued to remain silent and stared at the ceiling. Finally, she turned her head and looked straight at her doctor.

"Would my testimony repair the damage?" she asked softly.

Carver shook his head as he spoke, "Of course not. There is nothing we can do about that."

"Then I have nothing to gain by testifying, do I?" she asked.

"No, but other women might benefit, and you could very well save a life or two," he replied.

"But there is still no alternative," she reminded him. "We just don't have a solution, do we?"

Carver got up and leaned over the bed, his face very close to hers. "I think you're wrong, Catherine, but damned if I don't think you are a brave and thoughtful woman. I'll abide by your wishes even though they irk me."

Carver stood up and looked down at his patient.

"One more thing. I had to tell your folks the reason for the surgery and what the outcome was. They insisted on it, and as your parents, it is their right to know. Besides, Lydia was quite certain she knew what your problem was anyhow. As you might suspect, they are very upset and feel humiliated.

"I told you that you were a brave woman and you may need some more of that bravery as you have to deal with them. Somehow, I have the feeling that none of us here know the full story. I can't believe that the young lady I knew three years ago has changed that much. Perhaps I should pry until I get to the bottom of things. Do you want me to do that?"

Catherine smiled through her tears and reached for the doctor's hand.

"Thank you for trusting me that much, Doctor John. You have been my friend as well as my doctor. No, I do not want you to pry because I will not respond to it. Please, just continue to trust me."

Her hand dropped back to the bed. Carver turned and quietly left the room.

Catherine's tears continued to flow for a while. But strangely enough, a sense of relief began to come over her as the shock of the news wore off. The debate that had been going on so long in her mind was no longer a debate. The one unique gift that only a woman could bring to a loving marriage was no longer hers to give. She could not have Tex's children! Now she knew her decision was the right one. Going back to Cravenville was no longer an option. Instead of looking back, she could now concentrate on looking forward. Her relief grew even more, and she was sure she was now mentally prepared for the visit from her parents that would soon take place.

****

Harold and Lydia Cornell came to their daughter that evening and found Catherine again sitting up in bed. Their expressions of pleasure regarding her progress were heartfelt and genuine, but Catherine, at the same time, sensed a little reserve in their voices. After chatting for a few minutes, Lydia got right to the point.

"Catherine, your father and I are very disturbed by the recent events in our household. Your situation has brought great dishonor and humiliation upon us. We can't even look our neighbors and friends in the face and not be embarrassed. We have spent years building our reputation in this community, and in little more than a month you have made a shambles of it. You didn't even have the courtesy to bring the nature of your problem to our attention, and what little you did tell us, we now find out was a lie. We just don't understand you any more at all."

Catherine listened intently, hands folded in her lap.

"Father, mother, I am truly sorry to have caused you all this difficulty. First off, I didn't know for sure what my problem was. Secondly, I don't know how telling you about it would have changed anything. After all, I *am* a big girl, now. Lastly, it is my reputation that's been damaged here, not yours. I know that, and I will have to live with it."

Lydia bit her lip in vexation.

"Isn't there something you can tell us that might help us understand?"

"No, mother, I've had a great deal of difficulty understanding it myself. Besides, the damage is already done, as you are well aware of. It's much too late for explanations. I gambled on what I thought was a reasonable course of action that would have been a quiet and complete resolution of the problem. Unfortunately, I lost the gamble, and now I must pay the piper."

"You seem to be extremely calm and serene about all this," sniffed Lydia. "I should think you would be more distraught than we are."

"I suppose I should be," agreed Catherine. "But, somehow, I just don't see it that way. What's done is done, and I might as well get on with my life."

Lydia sighed in resignation as Harold stared at the floor.

"Well, my dear, since you brought up the subject we, too, want you to get on with your life. You are welcome in our house, of course, for as long as you need to recover from your surgery. But as soon as your recovery is complete, your father and I want you to leave. After all, we have Theresa to think about, too."

Catherine couldn't resist smiling inwardly. Obviously we can't have the sins of the older daughter infect the younger one. But she kept a straight face and replied in a calm, firm voice, "I agree completely, mother. I will seek employment elsewhere as soon as I am able. I'm grateful you will allow me to recuperate at home because I know I have hurt you and father very much. I also know this represents a real sacrifice on your part, and I thank you for it."

A greatly relieved Lydia Cornell kissed her daughter, and her husband followed suit.

"We'll be back to see you tomorrow night, my dear," she said. "You'd better get some sleep now and continue your improvement. Good night, Catherine."

****

Theresa came bouncing into the hospital room and was delighted to see Catherine sitting on the edge of the bed and wriggling her feet.

"That looks much better," she observed. "Doesn't it feel great to be somewhat vertical instead of horizontal?"

"Yes it does," agreed Catherine with a big grin. "I even had some breakfast today—toast and a soft broiled egg—and it stayed down. This afternoon I'm supposed to take a few steps. Dr. John says that if all goes well, he'll take out the stitches in a couple of days, and I'll be able to go home."

Theresa's face clouded as she heard the word "home." She moved close to Catherine and carefully hugged her.

"I want you to know I don't agree with father and mother's decision about your staying on with us," she whispered in Catherine's ear. "I know there's more to this than you've let on, and Doctor John agrees with me. I've tried to reason with them, but you hurt them real bad, and they can't understand why. Your silence isn't helping any, either. I don't know how to help you."

Catherine gently returned the hug and kissed her sister on the cheek.

"Thank you, little sister. Some day this may make some sense to you. But in the meantime, I have to go on with my life, and it's best if I don't do it here. I understand mom and dad and agree with them, for the most part. Everything is going to work out just fine."

****

Catherine's strength returned rapidly, the stitches were removed on schedule, she returned to her parents' home, and soon she was almost as active as she was before the surgery. Now decisions had to be made.

She contacted Ohio education officials and obtained a list of open teaching positions in the state. She wrote a number of letters and was rewarded with several favorable responses. She selected a rural school in a small community southeast of Cleveland, a contract was signed, and in early August she exchanged a tearful farewell with her family and began a new adventure. On the way to her new assignment she mailed a short letter to Tex. She provided no return address, mailed it at a neutral location, and, in effect, cut off any further communication with the man she loved.

Chapter 3

The first three years of Catherine's new teaching experience went well. She threw herself into the job, worked hard, and thoroughly enjoyed her interchange with the students. The memory of her departure from Arizona faded considerably as did the pain and frustration resulting from her difficulties in Bowling Green. Moreover, soon after her arrival at her new location, she was able to secure a summer position at the Cleveland Public Library. Although this required her to change her place of residence for three months, the extra pay was a welcome supplement to her meager teaching salary. In addition, this provided her with the appropriate reason not to return to Bowling Green and rekindle that emotional distress. Although Catherine did maintain a sporadic form of polite correspondence with her family, primarily Theresa, she did not feel any real desire to return to that area, even as a visitor. So, all in all, even though Tex and Paul remained in her thoughts, her life during these three years was quite good, almost too good to be true. Nevertheless, more than halfway through her fourth year, the situation changed dramatically.

Corey McCall was a big, well proportioned lad of 15. Unfortunately, he was also a very slow learner and had been held back a grade, once or twice, by the previous teacher. Despite her experience, Catherine was unable to decide whether the boy was just slow witted, very lazy, or if something was really mentally wrong with him. She gave him as much of her time as she dared and he seemed to be quite appreciative of her effort, even though that effort seemed to produce negligible results. Finally, in desperation, Catherine arranged for a conference with the boy's father.

Bruce McCall was a hulk of a man, barrel chested, and big boned. He was the owner of a manufacturing enterprise that employed 30 people and was well respected in his community.

"I'm glad you asked for this meeting, Miss Cornell," he began as the two sat facing each other in the classroom. "Corey tells me you have helped him a lot. I appreciate that very much."

"Well, he isn't making as much progress as I would like," responded Catherine carefully. "Tell me, does he spend much time at home on his school work?"

"That's hard for me to say," Bruce replied. "You see, he has chores to do around my shop. I want him to learn all he can about my business so he can take over some day. I work long hours, even after supper, and Corey likes to help me. Lots of times it's real late when we finish up, and then he heads right to bed. It don't give him much time to study."

"I see," said Catherine slowly. "I wish I could give the boy more of my time, but the other pupils need me, too."

"I say, now, that gives me an idea," smiled McCall. "If I was to tell Corey he could spend an extra hour at school a couple of afternoons a week and not work at my shop until after supper, would you be willing to help him? I would consider it a big favor if you could do that for him."

Catherine agreed that the idea had merit and began a special tutoring program with Corey. The boy seemed to be very happy with the after hours schedule, and his school work began to show discernable improvement. But Catherine began to experience some uneasiness with the program. Corey seemed to be exceptionally clumsy, especially in going to and coming from the blackboard. Somehow, when she least expected it, he would bump into her, stumble over a leg of a chair, or turn the wrong way. As a result his hands, arms, elbows, or torso would come in contact with parts of her anatomy. He would always laughingly apologize, and it wasn't a constant occurrence, but it happened frequently enough to concern Catherine.

One afternoon she was putting a problem on the blackboard when she heard him say, "Miss Cornell, do you like me?"

"Of course I do, Corey," she answered without looking around.

"I'm glad of that," came the response in a much stronger voice. A hand touched her shoulder, and she turned just in time to have his body squeeze against hers and his pelvis start to grind against her lower abdomen.

"What do you think you're doing!" cried Catherine as she pushed him back a step or so.

"I'm showing you I like you, too," replied Corey brightly. "Paw does this to maw all the time. She likes it a lot."

"Well, I'm not your mother," retorted Catherine as she tried to push him further away. But the boy was stronger than she thought, and he pressed forward again as he grabbed her shoulders for leverage. She couldn't help feeling the hardness of his body through her dress, and she used all the strength she could muster to push him away a second time. She didn't make much headway until, finally, she was able to drag the fingernails on her right hand down his left cheek.

Corey cursed, stepped back as if he had touched by a hot poker, and raised a hand to his cheek. It came back with a few spots of blood. His eyes turned dark with anger, but he did not resume his attack.

"Go home, Corey," gasped Catherine, breathing heavily from her exertions. "We won't be having any more after school sessions. You tell your father why, or I will."

Corey stepped back a pace or two, and the anger faded from his eyes. He shrugged his shoulders, turned, and slowly ambled his way out of the school house.

A shaken Catherine watched him until he disappeared out the door. She walked to her desk, sat down in her chair, leaned forward, and held her head in her hands as she tried to regain her composure. All the old memories came flooding back, and her eyes filled with moisture. It was so unfair! No matter where she went or what she did, trouble seemed to follow her like the plague. What did she do to deserve this? She straightened up, took a deep breath, and made a vow that this latest situation must be resolved quickly. She would question Corey on the morrow and, if necessary, seek out the father and bring the matter to a closure. She got up, smoothed her dress, and left the building, her head held high.

Corey did not appear in school the next day, somewhat to Catherine's relief. She was cleaning the blackboard after school let out when she heard the front door open and close, and she turned at the sound. Bruce McCall had entered the building and was striding rapidly in her direction, a dark countenance clearly evident. He stopped in front of her and began talking without the benefit of a greeting.

"Corey came home last night with his face scratched," McCall growled. "He told me what happened. Miss Cornell, when we made these special arrangements, I expected you to conduct yourself properly. Corey's nearly full grown now and has the same feelings as a man does. He says you been coming on to him ever since he began staying late. He said last night you gave him a lot of encouragement and he responded in a way any man would do. But you scratched him and told him to go home."

Catherine couldn't believe her ears.

"You think . . . I chased your son?" she stammered in amazement. "I assure you, Mr. McCall . . ."

"Maybe you don't think he's man enough to take care of you," interrupted McCall, his voice rising. "You holier than thou females lead on a man and then drop him like a hot potato if he ain't just what you think he should be. Well, Corey may not be man enough for you, but I sure as hell am."

With those words McCall clamped his huge hands on her shoulders, pulled her toward him, and held her tight as his lips crushed hers.

McCall's tirade had so astonished Catherine that she was slow to react. Again she was forced to struggle against the advances of a big and rough man. When Shag Norton had attacked her four years previously, she had been extremely sore and physically exhausted by the long ride and mentally worn out by the events of the day and the fear for her life. Her resistance at that time, she felt, was less than it should have been. None of that was true now, however. Furious at what was happening to her, she fought like a tigress. She managed to free herself from his grasp and finally disengaged her mouth from his. And for one of the few times in her life, she completely lost her temper and control of herself.

"You pig!" she hissed. "You miserable pig. You and that son of yours are two of . . ."

Whack!!

Catherine screamed in pain and staggered back from the force of the blow she had received from the flat of McCall's right hand. Blood began to trickle from the corner of her mouth. She used the desk to steady herself, drew herself up, clenched her fists, and glared at McCall.

"Oh, if I were a man . . . if only I were a man," she spit out, her eyes blazing. But the thought stopped her before she made a worse mistake. She once had such a man. Now all of a sudden she realized that violence, used in the right circumstances, was not as evil as she had previously assumed. If only Tex were standing beside her at this very moment . . . McCall saw her hesitation and leered at her. "Teacher, I don't believe you have ever known a man, leastways not a real man. You leave Corey alone. I'm the one you should be thinking about when you need something!" McCall turned and stomped his feet out of the building, a big grin on his face.

Catherine collapsed in her chair, half sick, and completely disgusted with the world she lived in. She put her head down on her folded arms and sobbed her heart out.

✳✳✳✳✳✳✳✳✳✳✳✳

A bitter and disillusioned Catherine Cornell managed to finish out the few remaining weeks of the school year. Corey McCall returned to school, and it was all she could do to give him what little help she was forced to provide. He functioned as if nothing had happened, however, which puzzled Catherine. But, at the same time, he neither said anything nor made any overt moves in her direction. The final day of school came and went, and Catherine breathed a deep sign of relief.

Catherine made her usual summer move to Cleveland and assumed her library job. It was here that she saw the newspaper article that reported the death of Slim Evers.

She immediately sent a letter of resignation to her school board and began the preparations for her journey back to Arizona.

✳✳✳✳✳✳✳✳✳✳✳✳✳

The train ground to a halt at the Phoenix station. A weary Catherine Cornell shook off her stiffness and descended the train steps to the station platform. Immediately behind her came a porter with her two stuffed pieces of luggage. The porter signaled for a drayman to assist Catherine as she pressed a tip into his hand.

The drayman transported her and her bags to the nearby Frontier Hotel, and she tipped him as well. Catherine was familiar with the hotel as she had stayed there on her trip back east. She paid for her room from a rapidly dwindling supply of money and was escorted to a second story room. She cleaned up as best she could and was first in line when the dining room doors opened at six o'clock. After she was seated at a small table, she ordered some coffee and began to peruse the menu.

A shadow moved across her view of the menu, and she looked up to see a man standing next to her table. He was extremely well dressed—silk shirt, fancy tie, and black suit. He spoke to her in a hesitant voice.

"Miss Cornell?" . . . "Catherine?"

"Yes, I'm Catherine Cornell," she responded in a puzzled voice.

Her answer brought a broad smile to his face. "I thought I recognized you as I stood in line. Permit me to introduce myself. My name is Dexter Boyd, I am an attorney, and I live in Cravenville."

"Of course, Mr. Boyd," said Catherine brightly. "Now I remember you. I'm happy to make your acquaintance.

Boyd bowed in response to her words. "Would you please join me at my table and allow me to buy you dinner?"

"I don't know," faltered Catherine, confused but pleased. "I've just met you."

"I would be honored to have you as my guest," he reassured her. "Please come and join me." He held out his hand as he spoke.

Catherine placed her hand in his, rose from her seat, and accompanied the man to his table. As soon as Boyd had seated her, he snapped his finger, and a waiter hurried to the table as Boyd, too, sat down. Catherine gave her order, Boyd seconded it, requested a refill of coffee, and looked at Catherine, his hands clasped in front of him.

"Does Tex know you are here?" Boyd asked quietly.

Catherine stared in surprise and could not prevent a blush from spreading over her face. "No," she replied softly. "How is he, Mr. Boyd?"

"He's fine," smiled Boyd, "except that he continues to pine for a certain young lady that he knew some years back. Are you on your way to Cravenville?"

Now the blush assumed a much deeper hue, and Catherine's confusion increased at a similar rate.

"Yes," she answered in a whisper, "I read about Mr. Evers being murdered. That must have been a terrible blow to Tex. I . . . well, I felt I had to come and see if I could help him in some way."

Boyd reached out and put his hand over Catherine's.

"I can't tell you how happy I am to hear you say that, Catherine," he said with a big grin. "Tex does need you, Catherine, now more than ever. His responsibilities have increased several fold since Slim died, and I would feel much better if I knew you were standing by his side."

Now Catherine's blush and confusion reached a zenith.

"Please, Mr. Boyd," she stammered. "You are assuming far too much. Tex may not want me to stay. Four years have gone by. Things have happened. Perhaps we are not the same two people we were before."

Boyd examined his guest closely, and her eyes fell. He decided to change the subject.

"There is a stagecoach tomorrow morning to Cravenville by way of Winslow. I assume you will be on it. So will I. Since we are going to be traveling companions, we can dispense with the formalities. First off, my name is Dexter, or Dex to my friends, and I sure enough expect to be your friend for a long time. Secondly, we will stay over in Windsor tomorrow night before going on to Cravenville. From this moment on you will be my guest, and I will not debate the matter with you."

"Oh, Mr. Boyd . . . Dexter, I can't let you do that. I hardly know you."

"I told you I would not debate the issue," laughed Boyd. "Besides, it's for my own protection. Tex would have my head on a platter if he found out I let you pay for anything. And he can be a mean cuss at times, as you well know."

Unfortunately, Boyd, in his attempt at humor, had not used a good choice of words, and as soon as he saw Catherine's reaction, he knew he had made a mistake.

"I'm sorry, my dear," came a quick apology. "I made an attempt at joviality, and I did it very badly. Tex would not harm a hair on my head, especially since they seem to be rapidly decreasing in number."

Catherine couldn't help smiling and thought to herself—he really is quick on his feet. She started to say something, but he raised his hand to stop her.

"I see our food coming, Catherine, and I suggest that we suspend this conversation until a more basic need has been satisfied. We'll have plenty of time to talk later."

The food arrived, Catherine attacked it with vigor, and Boyd did likewise. Fifteen minutes later, the dishes had been cleared, and fresh coffee had been poured. Boyd remained silent as Catherine stirred her coffee and stared at her cup. She looked up solemnly.

"Mr. Boyd . . . Dexter. I have to ask you a question," she murmured, with a trace of fear. "How did Tex react to Mr. Evers' death?"

Boyd nodded. "An excellent question, my dear. I was fairly certain that was on your mind." The man leaned forward, his hands again clasped in front of him, and he peered seriously at her.

"Catherine, listen very carefully to what I'm going to tell you," he began. "If you want to make your life with us out here, you must understand how we think and act. This is something most easterners don't understand."

"Tex, and most of the Rambling R men, went to Idaho to find Slim's killer and to hang him. A close friend, a Mexican, also brought some men up from Mexico and joined the expedition. All told, more than 20 men made the trip. But Tex didn't let this be a vigilante excursion. He insisted that they accomplish their objective by staying within the rules of the law. Some of his men didn't really feel that way, but Tex won out. They did find their killer, and he was indicted and brought to trial. During the course of the trial, he and an accomplice tried to escape and were gunned down by some of Tex's men. Tex was not involved in that gunfight!

"However, while Tex was in Idaho, he was forced to kill a man. But he did it in self defense. I should say, more accurately, that he did it in defense of someone else, who was unarmed and unable to defend himself at the time. Doesn't that sound familiar? Isn't that the Tex you knew?"

Catherine caught her breath at this disclosure.

"Was it Paul whom he was protecting?" she gasped.

"Paul? Oh, you mean Apache. No, it wasn't Paul, but he was there. In fact, he was visiting Idaho with Slim when Slim was killed. The lad responded to the crisis in a magnificent fashion, Catherine. You would be proud of him. Catherine, I must tell you something. It's been beautiful watching Tex and Paul act and function like brothers. I do believe that Paul saved Tex from himself after you left Cravenville. Slim and the other men helped, too, but Paul was the key. More to the point, Catherine, they both have missed you very much."

Catherine had listened intently to Boyd, and now her eyes were glistening. She reached into her purse, found the desired object, and dabbed at her eyes. Boyd glanced around the room and was pleased to see that the other diners were too busy with their own food and conversation to pay his table much heed. Patiently, he waited for Catherine to regain her composure. As soon as she had done so, he rose from his chair.

"I think we've done enough talking for one night," he observed. "You look tired. We'll meet for breakfast tomorrow morning and then be on our way."

Boyd paused to sign the food check, helped Catherine to her feet, and guided her out of dining room and into the hotel lobby. He changed direction a little bit and led her to the main counter. The man behind the counter nodded his greeting and waited.

"Mr. Avery, please be kind enough to refund Miss Cornell her room charge and put it on my bill. I have signed a ticket for dinner tonight and will do the same at breakfast tomorrow morning. Kindly have my bill ready when we check out. We will be catching the ten o'clock stage to Winslow."

"Very good, Mr. Boyd," replied the man. "I'll take care of everything."

****

A day and half later the stagecoach swung down the main street of Cravenville and pulled to a stop in front of the Regal Hotel. Tom Fleming, the hotel's owner, got up from a porch chair and approached the stagecoach, intending to greet any potential customers.

Dexter Boyd opened the stagecoach door, stepped down, spotted Fleming, and turned to assist the next person off the stage, Catherine Cornell.

"Get our best room ready, Tom," sang out Boyd over his right shoulder. "You got a special guest for a day or two, and she's got to be treated right."

"Who are you talking about, Dex?" asked a curious Fleming. He could only see the top of Catherine's head as she bent to get out of the coach. Quickly her face came into view, and Fleming grunted in surprise.

"Miss Cornell! As I live and breathe! What a pleasant surprise! Here, let me help you with your bags. Yes indeed, our best suite is yours for shore. What else can I do for you?"

Catherine was somewhat overwhelmed with the warmth of his greeting and rewarded him with a big smile. She moved up the hotel steps alongside the man with Dexter Boyd right behind them.

"Well, I know what I need most," she gaily replied. "A nice warm bath would be wonderful. I think I have half the dust from the whole territory on me."

"Take these bags up to the presidential suite," Fleming ordered an employee as they reached the lobby, "and get some bath water heating." He turned to Catherine. "We ain't never had a president come here, but we're ready if he ever does," he laughingly explained to a puzzled Catherine. "Besides, you'll do until one comes along. I'll register for you so you scoot upstairs and get ready for your bath. I'll get a maid right up there to help you."

Still overwhelmed by all the attention she was receiving, Catherine slowly followed the porter, climbed the stairs, turned to her left, and disappeared from view.

Fleming's eyes followed her back and as soon as she was out of sight turned to Boyd.

"Tex didn't tell me she was coming," Fleming fumed. "If I had known, we could have been all ready for her."

"Tex doesn't know!" Boyd informed him. "She showed up in Phoenix when I was there. My God, how are we going to handle this? It has to be a private meeting, that's for sure. I have to go out to the ranch tomorrow. Maybe that's the best way to do it. I'll take her along with me. My, won't Tex be surprised."

"Dex, that won't be private enough," objected Fleming. We've got to do better than that!"

"You're dead right," agreed Boyd, with a frown. He paused, deep in thought. "I've got it!" he exclaimed brightly. "I'll tell Tex we've got some legal problems regarding the ownership of the ranch and I've brought someone from Phoenix to advise us. Instead of me bringing her to him, I'll bring him to her. I'll tell him to come in for a conference over dinner. That should do the trick."

"Good idea," concurred Fleming. "I'll set things up in the little alcove off the main dining room. It has a curtain and will be just perfect."

"Excellent! But we can't have anyone let the cat out of the bag. We've got to organize things. We need to get the key people together tonight for dinner with Catherine. I'll bring my wife, and we'd better have Ollie and Elsa Woods there, too."

"We have to include the Leslies, too," added Fleming thoughtfully. We can't have anyone at the newspaper spilling the beans. That should be enough. We can all spread the word tomorrow before Tex hits town. Boy, is he going to be surprised."

Chapter 4

The return of the Rambling R men to their home ranch initiated a three week whirl of intense activity for Tex Riley. Simultaneously he had to take over the managerial activities that had been Slim Evers' domain and at the same direct the range operations necessary to prepare for the upcoming fall roundup. In addition, there was a significant accumulation of mail that had to be dealt with. During the ensuing time, Tex felt like he was meeting himself, coming and going.

His initial decision was to not move into Slim's living quarters. Slim had responded to Paul Redstone's arrival on the scene by immediately engaging in a major remodeling program for the main ranch. A two story wing was added to the house adjacent to the kitchen area. Antonio and Maria Martinez, his housekeepers, moved from their second story living quarters to the first floor of the addition. Maria was especially pleased with this new arrangement as it significantly reduced the number of trips she had to make up and down the stairs, and it also placed her in close proximity to her special domain, the kitchen. Antonio, therefore, assumed the primary responsibility for maintaining the upper level of the structure.

Paul, in turn, moved into the space vacated by the Martinezes, and Tex moved back from the bunkhouse and into his former quarters that Paul had been occupying. Slim was determined to have his entire "family" housed in one location. In addition, the second story of the new wing was transformed into a spacious guest room facility, and additional storage space, especially closets, was added to the upstairs area. Tex, therefore, decided to maintain these living arrangements and not touch the master bedroom, Slim's quarters, at least for the time being. Maria, however, bent his decision somewhat by having Antonio clean, pack, and store Slim's wardrobe and many personal items, not knowing at this point just what was going to be done with all these items.

Next, Tex made a quick trip to Cravenville to discuss the legal matters related to the ownership of the ranch with Dexter Boyd. He was surprised to find that Slim did have a will but that it was brief and provided no guidance in how the ranch was to be managed. Slim's will did not identify any living kinfolk and simply waived any claims against the value of his investment. He obviously trusted in his selection of employees, especially Tex, and gave his "adopted son" full authority and control over the future of his ranch.

Tex's visit to Cravenville included a conference with Bert Milner, president of the bank. It was primarily a courtesy call. Tex outlined the terms of Slim's will, and since Tex's name and signature were already on file for all the Rambling R accounts, Milner assured him that he had instant access to any funds he had need of. Tex responded by making a large cash withdrawal. His men had not been paid for two months, and most had personal needs that required attention.

Tex's third, and final, stop was the office of Judge Donald Parks. He explained his concern about Paul's status and sought the judge's advice.

"Tex, jurisdiction of Paul should remain in my hands," Parks informed him. "I see no need to involve Judge Pardee up there in Hawthorne. However, on second thought, I think I should notify him about what has happened as a matter of professional courtesy. Then he can suggest anything he wants to, and I will take it under advisement. I'll get off a letter to him right away and will contact you as soon as I get an answer."

Tex agreed with the plan, thanked Parks, and headed back to the Rambling R.

Tex distributed the payroll cash and began allowing four to six men at a time to have time off to visit Cravenville, to rest, or to do anything they had a mind to. At the same time, he began preparations for the massive fall roundup. The supply wagon made several trips to Cravenville. At the same time, both chuck wagons were inspected from top to bottom, and any necessary repairs were made. Riding gear for all the men was checked out for the same reason. The range riders began the task of bunching the cattle and scouring the farthest boundary lines of the ranch for hidden animals. Finally, the ranch's horse herd was gathered, and the new additions broken and domesticated. This latter process was complicated by the fact that the quartet, as Lefty and his three friends were affectionately called, was still in Idaho. Their primary responsibility had been the care and management of the Rambling R's horse herd. Reb Stuart and Cavalry stepped into the void and performed well, but the process was slow, and Tex became actively involved before the task was completed.

Time was of the essence because a herd of 2,500 animals had to be selected, branded when necessary, set apart, and then driven to the railhead 50 miles away for shipment. This was a third installment of a three year contract, and the proceeds from this sale provided much of the annual working capital needed by the ranch. The buyer had provided Tex with the shipping date, and the trip to Idaho had created a much tighter time schedule than had originally been contemplated.

On the other side of the ledger, when Tex waded his way through the pile of mail, he was pleased to find a letter from the Bureau of Indian Affairs. For three years Slim had submitted bids for supplying beef to the San Carlos Reservation. Now, at long last, the Rambling R had a contract to ship 300 head of cattle every other month for one year, beginning the next January. Tex grunted with satisfaction, as this would swell the operating revenue for the ranch and would also allow Apache to visit his former stamping ground and get reacquainted with his people. All in all, the future of the ranch looked bright, despite the loss of its former owner.

As soon as the preparations were completed, the roundup began. Tex divided his men into two groups. One group, under his command, rode to the eastern boundary of the ranch, turned about, and began to push the cattle west. The second group, led by Curley Chance, rode to the western extremes of the ranch and reversed the process. Each group was supported with a chuck wagon, one of the two ranch cooks, and a large remuda of horses. In addition, Tex had hired six temporary wranglers to augment his own crew, and each of the two ranches adjacent to the Rambling R property supplied two men to claim and herd any of their strays. Tex would reciprocate this arrangement when these ranches did their own roundups.

Two weeks later the roundup was completed, the branding was done, and the tallies made. Tex smiled as he compiled the totals. It had been a good summer. The natural increase in the herd had exceeded his expectations, and it was obvious that the ranch had survived the absence of most of its riders during the expedition to Idaho with no ill effects. Again, Tex gave Sanchez a silent expression of gratitude for his contribution to this result.

A few days later a weary Tex Riley was deep in thought as he watched Reb, Cavalry, Reno Lang, and Laredo Lee break and brand the last of the horse herd. In fact, he was so preoccupied that he wasn't conscious of the fact that Rusty Meyers had ridden up until Rusty swung from his saddle and tapped Tex on a shoulder.

Tex responded to the tap, turned, and was surprised to see Rusty standing next to him.

"Sorry to startle you, Tex," Rusty apologized. "You must have been miles away."

"Reckon I was at that," smiled Tex. "What brings you out here?"

"Well, Mr. Boyd stopped by the ranch a while ago. I told him I'd come and git you, but he said I didn't need to do that—just give you a message. He said he has run into a little snag on handlin' the change in the ownership of the ranch. Says he brung someone from Phoenix to explain things and git it fixed up. He told me to tell you to come to town tonight. You all will have dinner at the hotel and git it over with."

"Hell," snapped Tex in disgust as he frowned. "Boyd told me there weren't be no trouble a'tall. I wonder what went wrong?" The frown turned into a scowl. "Well, I reckon I'd better go in and get cleaned up and head for town." Tex swore again but headed for his horse.

✳✳✳✳✳✳✳✳✳✳✳

Tex swung from his saddle, tied his reins to the hitch rail in front of the hotel, and ascended the three steps to the boardwalk. Dexter Boyd vacated a chair and met Tex at the top of the steps.

"Hi, Tex," he murmured in as calm a voice as he could muster and shook hands with his client. "Glad you could make it."

"Damn it, Dex. I thought you said this would be easy as pie," said Tex, showing his irritation.

"Well, yes I did," admitted Boyd, having all he could do to keep his face straight. "But a slight complication came up, and only you can handle it. Come, I want you to meet the person who can help us."

An unhappy Tex Riley accompanied Boyd into the hotel and turned toward the dining room area only to have Boyd grab his arm.

"I thought it best if you met this person privately, before dinner," explained Boyd, his face now a blank. "Follow me upstairs."

Tex threw up his hands in resignation and followed his attorney up the stairs to the second story. Boyd turned to his left, headed down the hallway, and stopped in front of the door to the so called presidential suite. Slim and Tex had used the room on several occasions and knew its history.

"This fellar of yourn must be right important," Tex whispered as his companion knocked on the door. Boyd opened the door, stepped aside, and waved Tex into the room. Tex entered a gloomy room, gloomy because the curtains had been pulled over the windows and no lights had been lit. Before his eyes could get used to the change in brightness, Tex heard the door click shut behind him. He turned toward the sound, now puzzled as well as angry.

A woman rose from a chair near a window and took a few hesitant steps in his direction before stopping.

"Tex," come a soft, melodic, and somewhat strained voice, "I've come back."

An astonished Tex swung his head back at the sound of the voice and whispered hoarsely, "Catherine?"

Catherine could no longer contain herself. She rushed forward, threw herself into his waiting arms, and found his lips with hers. The embrace was an extended one, and many kisses were exchanged. Once Catherine whispered in his ear, "Tex, my darling," but no more words came as his mouth again covered hers. Finally, the passion ebbed a bit, and Tex held her at arms length, still unable to speak. Finally he released her for a moment, reached for the door, and flung it open. Still standing in the hallway was Dexter Boyd, a huge grin on his face.

"Dexter, you are a damned liar!" snorted Tex when he finally found his voice. "Come in here and tell me how you arranged all this." He drew Catherine close to him, his arm around her waist, as he spoke.

"I am not a liar," protested Boyd feebly as he laughed. "Well, maybe I circumvent the truth a bit, but I think in this case it was well worth it. However, that is not important. You two have a lot of catching up to do, and we have arranged for a private dinner downstairs."

"We?" asked a curious Tex.

"Catherine came in with me yesterday morning," explained Boyd, "and the whole town knows she's here. Some of us held a "welcome home" party for her last night, but I'll let her tell you all about it. Follow me. Tom and his crew are just waiting to take care of your dinner needs."

✳✳✳✳✳✳✳✳✳✳✳✳

It was a splendid dinner, but neither Tex nor Catherine ever remembered what they ate. Their eyes were only for each other, and their words were only for themselves to hear.

At Tex's insistence, Catherine briefly described her activities over the past four years but left out most of the pertinent events. She did tell him about reading about Slim's death and about her desire to return to Cravenville to help him deal with his tragedy.

"I wasn't even sure you weren't married and that I could be a terrible embarrassment to you if you were," she coyly confessed.

"You knew I loved you," he scolded her in return. "I couldn't have married anyone else. You will stay, won't you?"

Catherine leaned forward over their table and put the fingers of one hand on his lips.

"Darling, please hold that question for a little while. Four years have gone by. Times have changed, and maybe we have, too. Let's just enjoy tonight and not worry about tomorrow until tomorrow."

Tex nodded his agreement, and the conversation changed to his activities and the trip to Idaho. Catherine noticed that Tex did not mention the killing he was involved in. We both are holding back vital information, she thought to herself, not knowing how the other would react. That's fine. Tonight is for love, not confessions, and that's the way we'll keep it.

After dinner, Tex and Catherine strolled the town, hand in hand. They avoided the "Black Jack Saloon", but walked past the little bungalow where she had lived and where they had exchanged their first kisses. They did a reprise of that event, laughed at the sentiment, and continued on their walk. Eventually they found their way back to the hotel, and Tex walked her to her room.

"You mentioned tomorrow," Tex reminded her. "Well, tomorrow you are comin' out to the ranch, and you'll stay there for as long as you want. I figger we got a lot more talkin' to do." At these words, a shadow fell across his face. "Damn!" he muttered as Catherine looked at him in surprise.

"We've got a cattle drive to do, and it starts the day after tomorrow," he explained. "It'll only be for a week, but I gotta make it. But that will give you time to get rested up from your trip and get to know some of the people at the ranch. You'll love Maria and Antonio."

"Of course, I'll come," replied a relieved Catherine. "We have waited for four years. What is one more week? And I'm looking forward to seeing the famous Rambling R up close."

"Famous, I'm not so shore about," grinned a pleased Tex. "Notorious maybe but not famous. Tomorrow mornin' I'll send Red in with the supply wagon, and he can come by for you. You remember Red; he was part of the posse. I'll also send along someone that will be almost as happy to see you as I was."

"Paul?" asked Catherine as she kissed her man.

"Apache," Tex corrected her and returned the kiss.

They both laughed and shared one last embrace.

****

As soon as breakfast was over the next morning, Tex told Apache to locate Red Rollins and bring him to the den in the ranch house. Paul did as he was told and soon returned with Red at his heels. Tex handed Red a slip of paper.

"This is the last of the supplies we need," he told his redheaded rifleman. Hitch up the wagon right off and head for town. Apache, I want you to go with Red, but ride your horse, not the wagon."

Apache looked at Tex in surprise.

"There's so much work to do here, Tex," he allowed. "Red should be able to handle the supplies by himself."

"Well, yes and no," countered Tex. "I have another job for you two. After you get the wagon loaded, stop by the hotel. Mr. Boyd brought a special person back with him from Phoenix. I want this person to spend some time here at the ranch and learn about how we do things around here. That's your job, Apache. I just promoted you from ranch hand number one to teacher number one. Think you can do the job?"

"I guess I can," replied Paul slowly. Ever since Tex had gotten up this morning, he seemed different, but Paul couldn't put his finger on why. More banter than usual had been exchanged at the breakfast table. And Maria had seemed to be much more jolly than usual. It was all very puzzling to his young mind. Then he asked a question and was startled by the reply.

"I will be going on the drive, won't I?" he quietly inquired.

"I don't know, Apache. We'll talk about it when you get back from town."

Now the boy was really puzzled, as that commitment had been a longstanding promise. He had participated in each of the two previous drives, and these experiences with Tex had been especially enjoyable for both of them. Had Slim's death somehow changed things? But true to his Apache heritage and stoicism, he refrained from extending the conversation. Instead he quickly saddled his horse, mounted, and met Red at the corral. Red had already hitched up his team and, as usual, had placed his Winchester in the seat next to him. He cracked the team into motion, and they were on their way.

The trip to Cravenville was made in good time, the supplies were purchased and quickly loaded in the wagon, and the twosome swung down the town's main street and stopped in front of the hotel.

Tom Fleming came out of the hotel entrance lugging two heavy bags. He put one down and grunted as he swung the other one over one side of the wagon and on to some open space in its bed, just behind Red. Fleming repeated his exertions with the second bag and then returned to the entrance and extended his arm to the person just emerging from inside the building.

Both Paul and Red were flabbergasted when they saw who it was.

Paul found his voice first. "Miss Cornell!" Paul slipped out of his saddle and ran to her side as she reached the street level. He didn't know what else to say.

"Hello, Paul," smiled Catherine. "Tex said he wanted you to act as my host. I didn't think that was fair, but he said you would do it." She looked up at Red as Fleming and Paul helped her ascend to the seat next to him. "You're Red. Tex said I would remember you from our posse days."

"Yes, ma'am," acknowledged Red as he tipped his hat. "I'm right glad to see you ag'in." Red slid the Winchester behind his seat, in the bed of the wagon, and grabbed the reins. Paul quickly mounted, and the little cavalcade began the eight mile journey back to the Rambling R.

The noise of the wagon wheels and the bouncing of the seat made conversation between Catherine and Paul very difficult. Catherine suggested that the defer their talk until later, and Apache readily agreed.

While Tex had tried to make Catherine more comfortable by selecting someone she already knew, Red, as her driver, he had unwittingly triggered the rush of bad memories back into Catherine's mind when he referred to their posse days. Unknowingly, he had pushed to the surface the pain and grief related to her childless future. Catherine, in turn, began to feel the first pangs of guilt about whether or not she should have made her trip west. She hadn't slept well during the night until the warmth of her welcome from the citizens of Cravenville and the wonderful feeling of security she had felt within the confine of Tex's arms finally allowed her to drift off. Therefore, she had used the comment in her greeting to Red as a device to aid her in accepting a situation that neither she nor anyone else could ever change.

Tex was waiting for them when they arrived at the Rambling R, and Catherine was the recipient of another round of joyous greetings. Maria fussed over her, Antonio pressed her hand and gave her a big grin, and several of the men warmly welcomed her as well. Paul and Tex introduced the men, but she knew she was going to have trouble putting a name with a face, despite her teaching experience, at least for a while. Tex finally shooed the men away and let Maria guide Catherine to the guest room and help her get settled.

The lunch hour soon arrived, and Catherine gasped with pride. Eating together were Antonio, Maria, Paul, Tex, and Catherine—two Mexicans, an Apache, a white man, and a white woman. It was so simple, yet so beautiful, and Catherines's eyes glistened as she looked around the table. Paul, for his part, was just beaming with delight. The meal was finished, the dishes had been cleaned, and Paul, Catherine, and Tex were still sitting at the table when the sound of rapid boot steps was heard, and Bronc Evans came barging into the room. He stopped and held out his arms.

"There she is!" he barked, a big grin on his face. "I wonder if she remembers old Bronc. We rode the owl hoot trail together!"

"Of course I remember you," cried Catherine in return. She got up, took a few steps, and was immediately engulfed in a bear hug, and then, to her complete surprise and some consternation, was the recipient of a kiss, full on her lips.

Bronc stepped back, his eyes twinkling.

"I kissed your gal, Tex Riley, and I'm right glad I did it. I won't do it ag'in, but I shore enough was goin' to get one in afore the bars went up!"

Everyone laughed, and Catherine joined in. Bronc escorted her back to her seat, found another chair, and accepted a steaming cup of coffee from a smiling Maria. Some chit chat followed, but the meeting soon broke up as Tex signaled Paul and Bronc to follow him into the den. Catherine joined Maria in the kitchen and began to help her with the dishes.

"Apache," Tex began, "I know I promised to take you on the drive, but you are the only one around here that Catherine knows right well. I want her to be as comfortable as possible. Would you be willin' to stay here and see after her?"

"Of course I will, Tex," replied Paul earnestly. "You sure had me fooled this morning, but now I see why. I'll try to be as good a teacher for her as she was for me."

"I thank you, Mr. Redstone," grinned Tex, his eyes glowing with pride. "I doubt that she has done much ridin', so take the buckboard and drive her short distances around the ranch."

Tex then turned his attention to Bronc.

"Bronc, she told me why she has come back, and I shore enough believe her. But somethin' tells me I ain't heard the whole story yet. We ain't had time to talk much. She may be runnin' from somethin' or mebby someone. It's up to you and Trig to make damn shore that somethin', or that someone, don't catch up with her here. I want one of you close by at all times—and one of you go with Apache when he takes her for rides. You savvy?"

"If'n anyone tries to git her, they'll come to a quick and fatal end," a grim Bronc Evans assured Tex. "Don't you fret none. Me and Trig will handle our end."

Tex turned back to Paul.

"Not a word of this to Catherine, Apache. What she don't know won't hurt her. If'n I can do anythin' about it, she's here to stay."

Paul nodded his agreement, and his dark eyes, too, glistened with pride. He would do his best to make her happy and want to stay at the Rambling R, forever.

Chapter 5

More Rambling R men drifted in as the afternoon wore on, heard about their new arrival, and wandered up to the ranch house to meet their guest. Paul was kept busy introducing the men to Catherine and basking in the limelight he was garnering as the same time.

Tex had arranged for one chuck wagon, one cook, and the six temporary wranglers to stay with the drive herd while the Rambling R men returned to the ranch to complete any last minute preparations for the drive. The two representatives from each of the other ranches had long since departed, each twosome driving a few stray animals. The six temporary men and four Rambling R punchers, again led by Woody Meadows, would remain at the ranch and patrol the ranges until the drive crew returned.

After supper Tex and Catherine, hand in hand, strolled around the ranch's courtyard and ended up back on the veranda of the main house. Tex guided her to a swing that was hung from the porch beams. Gently and carefully, they sat down and Catherine immediately snuggled up close to Tex, her head on his shoulder, his arm around her shoulders.

"I don't cotton to the notion of leavin' you behind tomorrow when we start the drive," Tex murmured in her ear, "but it's gotta be did, and I gotta do it. Besides, a cattle drive is no place for a woman. I'll be back in a week, though, and I shore aim to spend a lot of time with you when I do get back."

"I understand," Catherine softly replied. "This is your job. I must admit I am very tired from the trip and can use the rest. Besides, Paul can't wait to show me around the ranch."

"Apache tells me he kept you right busy this afternoon, lettin' you meet all the boys," smiled Tex. I'm beginnin' to think he's gonna take his teachin' job right serious."

"I know he is," giggled Catherine. "He said something about giving me a test by the end of the week to find out what I've learned. I think he wants to get even with me for all the tests I've given him."

This thought made both of them chuckle in the gathering darkness.

"I know that if he gives me a test on matching the names with the faces of your men, I will surely fail," Catherine went on thoughtfully. "My goodness, I had no idea you employed this many men."

"It is a big crew," admitted Tex, "and remember, there are four more up in Idaho." Tex frowned. "I've got to get Lefty and his boys back here right soon, too. But I got an idear for that. It's somethin' I'll take care of as soon as I get back from the drive."

"I thought I was your top priority when you got back," pouted Catherine, a twinkle in her eye.

Tex grunted from the jab but didn't respond verbally. Instead, he bent down and sealed her lips for an extended period of time.

"Hmmm," breathed Catherine softly as he drew back. "I'm not sure I can wait a week for more of that."

His reply was a repeat performance.

The sound of a strumming guitar and a strong tenor voice, emanating from the bunkhouse, reached their ears and interrupted their reverie. Catherine quickly sat up.

"What a beautiful voice," she observed, awe in her own voice. Who is it?"

"That would be Cavalry, answered Tex softly.

"Cavalry! What a strange name. Your men have a lot of strange names, Tex. Why is that?"

Tex pulled her back down before replying, and again Catherine snuggled close to him.

"It's a good question, Catherine, and mebby when I tell you why you'll be able to understand us westerners a mite better.

"When me and some of the boys come here, we had some things in our past that we weren't right proud about. In fact, some of us were right ashamed of some of the things we had done. Slim told us that our pasts made no never mind to him. He told each of us that the Rambling R was a new start and as long as we played square with him, he would play square with us. He told us if changin' our names would help us forget our pasts and help us begin a new slate, he was all for it. A lot of the boys did, and Slim never asked why.

"Take Cavalry there. I'm bettin' he come from the military. And I'll bet he was a deserter. Mebby the Army discipline didn't agree with him, or mebby somethin' else happened. I dunno. But, if'n the deserter part is true, he shore wouldn't want anyone to know his real name. We just know he lit here, he does a good job, especially with horses, and that's all that counts."

"But what if he deserts you, too," asked a puzzled Catherine.

"No one around here has a ball and chain around his neck, Catherine. If'n Cavalry should decide to up and go, he'll draw his pay and go. It's happened afore. Not everyone likes it here. Some folks didn't even like Slim. You can't please everyone.

"Now, take Bronc and Trig. They was Texas Rangers at one time. Somethin' went wrong, and they drifted west. They took on the job of bein' Slim's travelin' companions, sorta like bein' bodyguards. But, Slim didn't take them to Idaho like he shoulda, and look what happened! Bronc and Trig were mad clean through. They figger Slim would be alive today, if'n they'd gone with him. So, you see, most of us have stories, some good and some bad."

Catherine mulled over this long explanation for a few moments. Then she poked Tex in the ribs and sat up again.

"Speaking of names, kind sir, do you realize I'm sitting here, letting you make love to me, and I don't even know your name! My parents would be horrified."

"You know my name," he retorted. "It's Tex, and quit pokin' me."

Catherine ignored his comment and poked him again.

"You know what I mean, silly. That isn't the name you were born with. C'mon now, it isn't fair. You know my name, but I don't yours."

"It ain't common knowledge," grunted Tex, "and I ain't aimin' to make it common knowledge, neither. My God, woman, you got sharp elbows."

Catherine would not be deterred and returned to the attack.

"Suppose my family should somehow come this way. How am I suppose to introduce you—Mr. What's his name Riley?"

"You'd just laugh," submitted Tex weakly.

"No I won't, just trust me!" retorted Catherine, in mock anger.

Tex looked at her in dismay and finally whispered, "Wilber."

"Wilber!" Catherine's hands flew to her mouth, but she could not completely stifle the shriek.

Tex held her at arm's length for a moment, his disgust showing.

"There, I told you you'd laugh!"

"I'm sorry," giggled Catherine as she slid in close to him and buried her face in his chest. His arm held her close, but she couldn't stop a snicker or two. She finally raised her head and maintained a straight face.

"All right, Mr. Riley. I surrender. We'll have to go with Tex. It's a terrible cross to bear, but I shall do my best to live with it."

"You're goin' to stay then?" asked Tex softly, remembering her words.

Catherine immediately sobered, sat up again, and her eyes locked into his.

"Darling, I want to, but I don't know if I should. Four years have gone by. We aren't the same people we were then. We need to think this through very carefully. We have a great deal to talk about."

"By God, I'll stay, and we can talk it out for as long as it takes," exploded Tex. "To hell with the drive!"

Catherine raised her hand and gently caressed his mouth with her fingers.

"No, Tex. You go on your drive. I'll be here when you get back. We've waited four years, and one more week won't change anything."

Tex's eyes bored into hers. "You *will* be here when I get back?"

"Yes, my love, I'll be here," Catherine assured him.

Tex pulled her in close, their lips met, and the bargain was sealed.

✳✳✳✳✳✳✳✳✳✳✳✳

The Rambling R erupted into a burst of activity at the crack of dawn. As soon as breakfast was finished, horses were saddled, bed rolls were packed in the second chuck wagon, and the exodus began. Cavalry, Reb, Denver, and Cheyenne raced out to the horse herd and got it into motion as the chuck wagon trailed behind.

The drive itself was uneventful and only took four days. For Tex, however, it seemed to be the longest trail drive he could ever remember.

Jack Keller, the cattle buyer, met them about four miles from their destination. Keller swung his horse in alongside Tex and stretched out his right hand in a friendly greeting.

"You're right on time, Riley," he observed. "I was sure sorry to hear about Slim. I assume you all took care of that matter."

"Yeah," replied Tex as he shook Keller's hand. "The slate was swept clean. Funny thing, though, it weren't as bad as it first sounded. Slim was just at the wrong place at the wrong time. He shoulda laid low for a spell and got a few of us up there to help him. But he didn't, and it shore cost him."

"Well, your herd looks to be in top shape," said Keller as he quickly changed the subject. "I'll give 'em a closer look as we count 'em. You ready to get at it?"

Tex didn't answer but rose in his stirrups and waved his right arm. He signaled Keller to follow him, and the two of them kicked their horses into motion and raced ahead of the herd. Six Rambling R men followed them and formed a rough funnel, three on each side of the trail, about 30 yards apart. Tex and Keller positioned themselves at the neck of the funnel and waited for the herd to arrive. The remaining riders forced the cattle to slow their pace and bunch together and at the same time directed the animals into the man made funnel.

Both Keller and Tex dropped pebbles into their hats for each group they counted.

"I get 2,514," announced Keller as he looked at Tex. Tex nodded his agreement.

"We threw in 15 extrees," he acknowledged, "and we lost one on the trail. Busted its leg, so we had to kill it. Gave us some fresh beef, though."

"I have enough cars to handle half your herd right now," Keller informed Tex. "The second set of cars will come day after tomorrow. We'll load the first half tomorrow and get them out of the way. That's the same way we did it last year."

"That's what I figgered," agreed Tex as he nodded his head. "We'll bed the herd down tonight and drive the first half into the pens at dawn. How did they look to you?"

"Good, as always," smiled Keller. "I expect the best from the Rambling R and always get it. I'm gonna want to write up a new three year contract with the Rambling R as soon as I get the paperwork done on this herd. With Slim gone, I assume I should direct it to you?"

"Yes, that's the way it's shapin' up," replied Tex, with a sad and worried expression. These arrangements had been Slim's bailiwick, and now they fell into Tex's lap. Tex again felt the loss of his mentor and wondered if he would be able to handle this end of the ranch's business as well as he should.

Keller reached out and slapped Tex on his back.

"Don't worry none, Tex. Slim was a good friend of mine, too, and I'll give you a fair deal. I couldn't live with myself if I did otherwise."

Tex sent a look of gratitude to the buyer and then turned his attention to the herd and the accompanying riders.

Although the stockyard facilities contained a small bunkhouse, all the Rambling R men stayed with the cattle and camped out during the night. Loading operations began the next morning and were completed by mid-afternoon.

Keller, Tex, and Curley were standing together and watched the train pull out. Tex turned and signaled to a nearby mounted Reb Stuart. Reb urged his horse to move closer and waited for instructions.

"Cut me out a fresh horse, Reb," Tex ordered, "and saddle it for me. I'm headin' back to the ranch."

"What's the matter," grinned Curley, "don't you like our company?"

"Yeah, I do," answered Tex, turning red under his tan, "but I like someone else's better. Jack, Curley will be in charge of the second loading. Give him your check when it's finished. I'll see you next year." Tex again shook hands with the surprised Keller.

The saddled horse arrived. Tex swung into the saddle and was off in a cloud of dust.

"I sure didn't expect him to leave so soon," snorted Keller, looking puzzled.

Curley quickly explained the situation: "His gal come back to the ranch a few days ago. They ain't seen each other for more'n four years. I reckon they got a heap of catchin' up to do."

Keller responded to the explanation with a big grin. "Don't blame him none. I sure hope things work out for him."

****

A weary horse and rider arrived at the ranch about midnight. Tex stiffly dismounted, unsaddled his horse, and turned the tired animal loose in the almost vacant corral. Quietly he entered the house, climbed the stairs, found his room, undressed, and tumbled into bed. When he awoke the sun was well above the eastern horizon.

A half hour later he entered the kitchen area and found Maria and Catherine busy at work. Both women turned at the sound of his steps, and Catherine squealed in delight. She rushed across the room and into his arms.

"You came back early," she cried between kisses. "What a wonderful surprise."

Maria's greeting was equally warm but not nearly as demonstrative. She pointed to a chair, told him to sit, and began to prepare his breakfast. Catherine poured two cups of coffee and sat down beside her man as her hand reached for his.

"Why are you back so soon?" she asked, showing some fear. "Did anything go wrong?"

"No, everything went as smooth as silk," responded Tex with a broad smile. "We got half the herd loaded yesterday, and the other half will be loaded today. It weren't necessary for me to sit around for an extry day.

Curley can handle the second loading. Now why do *you* suppose I decided to come back early?"

Catherine felt the blush spread over her face, and she squeezed his hand in answer to his question.

Maria placed a plate full of food in front of Tex and pushed him in the shoulder.

"I know why you returned so soon, Señor Tex," she said, with a hearty laugh. "Your heart brought you back. I will prepare a picnic lunch for you both. Take Señorita Catherine to the grove of cottonwoods west of here and spend the afternoon with her. You have worked mucho hard and need some rest. It's time you two had some private time together."

Tex looked up at Maria in amazement.

"You've read my mind, Maria. How did you know? I reckon I never will understand you women. Catherine, you get yourself ready. I'll finish eatin', and then I got a couple things I want to do. We'll leave in about an hour."

Tex made short work of breakfast, went to the den, spent some time going through the mail, and then did some work on his ledgers. Bronc Evans and Apache arrived while he was doing his book work and exchanged pleasant greetings with him. Tex outlined his plans for the rest of the day, and both men seconded the arrangements.

"That is one area I didn't take Catherine to," Paul informed him, his dark eyes sparkling. "I thought you would want to do that by yourself."

"It seems like everyone around here is doing my thinking for me," retorted Tex, both amused and exasperated. "You got any other plans I should know about?"

"No," smiled the lad. "The rest is up to you!" he shouted as he raced out of the room.

Tex shook his head in mock dismay as Bronc followed in Apache's footsteps. Bronc turned back to Tex as he reached the entrance and spoke softly and warmly. "Good luck, my friend. You both deserve each other. I'll get the buckboard ready."

✳✳✳✳✳✳✳✳✳✳✳✳

Tex, partly because of his late breakfast, used a circuitous route to arrive at his desired destination. At times he talked about the ranch, unknowingly repeating some of what Paul had already told Catherine. Catherine listened intently and responded appropriately, her left hand clutching his right arm as an anchor, and her right hand clasping a seat rail to reduce the amount of bouncing. But there were also periods of silence, and it was during these interludes that Tex would steal a glance at his attractive companion. It was at these times, it seemed to Tex, that Catherine was deep in thought and miles away. He smiled inwardly because she was reinforcing the suspicions that had already made an inroad in his mind.

They reached the grove of cottonwoods, and Tex parked the buckboard, tethered the horses, and helped Catherine to the ground. For a moment they clung together. Tex pulled her close, and the kiss was a long and deep one. Her moist, warm lips returned it with fervor before she reluctantly pulled away and reached for the food basket.

They finished eating and packed the utensils and the culinary remnants in the basket. Tex moved over in front of a cottonwood, sat down with his back up against the tree, and motioned for Catherine to join him. She quickly did so and, as before, snuggled up against him, her head on his shoulder and his arm around her.

Catherine broke a long period of silence. "I should be mad at you, Mr. Riley," she muttered.

"What for?" asked a surprised Tex. "What have I done now?"

"Well, Paul did as you told him to do, and we had some nice little trips over parts of the ranch. But no matter where we went, either Bronc or Trig seemed to have something to do nearby. At first, I thought it was a coincidence, but then I remembered that a man I know has some very devious traits. It wasn't a coincidence, was it?"

"No," admitted Tex. "They had orders to rope and hogtie you if'n you took off for parts unknown!"

"Tex Riley!" sputtered Catherine as she sat up and stared in disbelief at her tormentor. She saw a big smile spread across his face and laughed nervously. "You're pulling my leg, aren't you? I should know you better than that. But you did have a reason, didn't you?

"I thought so," replied Tex cautiously. "Catherine, you told me why you come back, and I believed you. But I also figgered you was leavin' somethin' out of your story. I figgered you might be runnin' from somethin' or somebody. I couldn't do anythin' about the somethin', but I shore as hell could do somethin' about the somebody. If'n anyone was to show up lookin' for you, Bronc and Trig was to handle things. Both of them boys are top notch gunmen and can be mean cusses when they want to be."

Catherine responded to this statement with a sarcastic snicker.

"Mr. Boyd said the same thing about you," she told him, unable to repress another chuckle.

"Well, I reckon that's true enough," admitted Tex, "and I guess that's somethin' we got to talk about. We sorta had the same kinda parley four years ago, if'n you remember."

Catherine nodded her head but didn't say anything.

"Catherine, I know you don't like the world I live in. I don't *like* killing and fighting, neither. But this is hard country out here, and this is where I grew up. But I look at it differently, now, than I did 10 or 12 years ago, thanks to Slim. Slim didn't like violence neither, but he had a ranch house, cattle, and land that needed protectin'. So he hired men to do it! There are always folks around that don't like workin' for a livin'. They think they can walk in and take anythin' of yourn that they have a mind to. Well, around here they don't get away with it. Some have tried, and most of 'em are pushing up daisies. The rest are in jail or a long way off. I regret a few things I did as a kid, but I don't regret nothin' I've had to do for the Rambling R and Slim."

Tex paused and took a deep breath.

"Now, I gotta tell you somethin' you ain't gonna like. But we gotta put all our cards on the table and be honest with each other. I had to kill a man up there in Idaho. It weren't what I wanted to do, but he wanted to kill Marty Johnson, and I couldn't let that happen. I'd be lyin' to you, though, if'n I told you I wasn't thinkin' of Slim when I done it. It turned out he weren't the killer, but he might have been. I ain't proud of it, but I ain't ashamed, neither."

Catherine slipped out of his arm, raised herself a bit, bent down, and gently kissed his mouth as her hands held his face.

"I'm glad you told me about it, Tex," she whispered. "I heard about it from Mr. Boyd, but I wanted to hear it from you. You are being completely honest with me, and I appreciate it. Now it's my turn."

Catherine got to her feet and began pacing back and forth, deep in thought. Finally she stopped and looked down at Tex.

"You are right on both counts, Mr. Riley. I hadn't thought of it quite that way, but I am running from someone *and* something. Unfortunately, that someone is me, and the something involves me, too."

She resumed her pacing, and now the tears began to come. She stopped in front of him a second time. "I don't know where to begin," she sniffed.

"Catherine, either you gotta begin by comin' down here," Tex admonished her in a stern voice, "or I gotta get up. Now I'm too full and too tired to get up, so why don't you come down here?"

Catherine couldn't help smiling through her tears and partly acquiesced by sliding to her knees directly in front of him. He reached out and placed his hands over hers, both to comfort her and to steady her.

But the tears didn't stop coming. "Oh, Tex," she blubbered, "I've lied to you, and I am so ashamed."

Gently he pulled her down, enveloped her with his arms, and carefully rocked her. She wept silently for several minutes, and he patiently waited for her to stop.

Finally she raised her head and brushed away the wetness around her eyes with the backs of the sleeves of her dress.

"I'm getting your shirt all wet," she said with a wry smile. "What do cowboys do with weeping females?"

"Let them weep, I reckon," replied Tex a little nervously, "I ain't had no experience at this sort of thing." Then he pulled her to him and kissed her long and hard.

"Hmmm, for a man of no experience, you seem to know what to do," observed Catherine impishly. "But this isn't getting us anywhere. I've got to be as honest with you as you were with me. Tex, I sent you a letter. I told you everything was all right. But it wasn't."

Catherine haltingly told her story as Tex continued to hold her. But when she told him of her decision to have an abortion, she had to stop and wait for his response.

"I wish you had told me, Catherine," came the mild rebuke. "I woulda come to you, and we coulda figgered out what to do."

"Tex, I couldn't bear the thought of trying to raise a child created by that brute. It wouldn't have been fair to the child either. Every time I looked at it, it would have to remind me of the father. I just couldn't do it, and I couldn't ask you to do it either!"

"You had a hard decision to make, Catherine, and you had to make it all alone, just like I've had to do. It ain't no fun killin' somethin', is it? Now you know how I have felt. Yes, it was a hard decision, but I'm proud of you for makin' it!"

"You really mean that, don't you? asked Catherine breathlessly. You really do mean what you said."

"Yes ma'am I do," said Tex simply. "But you're still not tellin' me somethin'."

Catherine heaved a big sigh and nodded her head.

"It does get worse," she admitted.

She related the aftereffects of the botched abortion and how Doctor Carver had saved her life.

"I'd like to meet that man some day," said Tex. "I owe him aplenty."

Catherine heaved another deep sigh.

"Yes, my dear, he did save my life. But in so doing, he was forced to take away any chance I had to ever have children. Oh, Tex, I can't give you that special gift that only a woman can bring to a marriage. I can't have your children. I can't be a whole wife to you. I'm so ashamed." And the tears came again.

Tex gently rocked her and couldn't resist a thin smile.

Finally the sobs stopped, and again he held her at arm's length.

"Catherine, the only thing I've ever wanted is you. Shore children would be a nice tally, but the most important part of the picture is you. I need you, and you need me. What better reason can two people have to live together?"

Catherine wiped away the last of her tears and sat looking at her man.

"I think you just asked me to marry you, Mr. What's his name Riley."

"You are plumb right, Miss Cornell. What is yore answer?"

Catherine leaned forward and gave him a long, silent answer.

****

Tex stopped the buckboard on a little knoll, and the two of them viewed the Rambling R buildings off in the distance.

"That's goin' to be our home, Catherine. You'd better send back east for any things you want. You're here to stay now."

Catherine leaned against Tex and stared at the floor of the buckboard.

"I brought everything I own with me, darling. It isn't much to show for seven years of teaching, is it?"

"Well, then, as soon as Curley gets back, I'll be sendin' you to town for some more duds. Most of all, you'll need some riding clothes and pants. We don't stand on formality out here, and if you're goin' to earn your keep, you're goin' to have to have some workin' clothes.

"Why, Mr. Riley. I do believe you asked me to marry you just to get some cheap labor. When do I start punching the cows?"

"Not right away," chuckled Tex, "but I do want you to learn how to ride. Apache's goin' to be your teacher for that, too. Besides, I got a couple of other jobs in mind for you."

"I did do some riding, if you recall, kind sir. And I was sore for a week. Paul is going to have a real greenhorn to work with. What jobs do you have in mind? Maybe I'll want to back out of our deal."

"Don't you even think such a thing," warned Tex sternly, before he saw the smile on her face. "Am I goin' to have to hogtie you at night to make shore you don't run out on me?"

Catherine leaned over, kissed him on the cheek, and whispered in his ear, "I'm quite certain you will be busy doing a number of things to me at night, Mr. Riley, but I assure you that hogtieing me won't be one of them. Now what *other* jobs do you have in mind for me?"

They both laughed softly before he attempted a reply.

"Catherine, I ain't no good at writin' letters, and I'm not right good at numbers neither. Them's the things Slim did so well. I need you to write letters for me. I'll tell you what to put in 'em, but I shore need you to write 'em. Apache has been helpin' me with the numbers, and it's been good for him, too. But we need someone lookin' over our shoulders to make shore we done 'em right. Think you can handle them jobs?"

"I'll be delighted, Tex," she answered brightly. She sensed, immediately, that he really did need her help and that maybe that's what Dexter Boyd had in mind back in Phoenix. She was trained to make just such a contribution, and it would be a perfect way for her to be a real partner in the ranch and its ongoing activities.

Tex nodded his approval of her answer, cracked the team into motion, and looked forward to the days of their future that they would enjoy together.

Chapter 6

Curley and the trail crew returned two days later, and Curley promptly reported to Tex in the den of the ranch house. He handed Tex a check as soon as he arrived.

"Never did see figgers that big afore," he observed. "A weaker man might be tempted to up and leave the country."

"He'd have me and the boys on his trail right quick," laughed Tex. "Was you tempted?"

"No," grinned Curley, "I like it around here."

Tex grunted and pointed to a chair.

"Set a spell, Curley. I got somethin' to talk to you about."

Curley did as he was told, removed his hat, and plopped it on the floor next to his chair. He looked at Tex, a combination of curiosity and anxiety evident in his expression.

"I've been watchin' you, Curley," Tex began, "and I know you're a good cattleman. You've done yore work around here right well, and you get along with the rest of the men."

Tex paused for a moment before going on.

"I had to leave Lefty and his boys up there in Idaho, as you know. I need Lefty back here right quick. I want you to go up there and be Marty's foreman. How does that set with you?"

"I'm right pleased you think that well of me, Tex," grinned Curley, both relieved and surprised. "I reckon I would like the job." But a frown crossed his face as soon as he voiced his acceptance.

"What's the matter?" asked Tex.

"Well, me and Dusty have been right good friends for a long time. I shore could use someone to talk to up there. Would it be too much to ask if'n you would let him go, too?"

"I shore hate to lose another good man," mused Tex. "But you're dead right. I'm sendin' you to a new place without no friends to help you. That ain't right. You shorely are gonna need someone to talk to. Besides, Charley can then come back with Lefty, and I need him, too. All right, you got Dusty. You and Dusty take a couple of days to take care of yore personal matters. I'll give you travelin' money. Go up by train and tell Lefty and Charley to come back the same way. They can leave their horses up there."

Tex paused for a few seconds and rubbed his chin deflectively.

"Curley, what's your real name?"

"Huh," came the startled response. "Aw, c'mon Tex, why do you need to know that? It's an old family name, and I shore hate it. I feel about it like mebby you feel like yourn."

"You're dead right again," laughed Tex, remembering his recent conversation with Catherine. "But I gotta reason for askin'. What is it?"

Curley screwed up his face, saw that Tex was serious, and whispered, "Cedric."

"Good," said Tex with a smile.

"Curley, you know I weren't happy with how Marty was runnin' the MJ. I told Lefty to get him out of the house and in the saddle and learn some things about cattle ranchin'. Lefty writ me once and said Marty was tryin'. Them's goin' to be yore orders, too. We gotta get Marty educated."

Tex paused again, letting all this sink in.

"Curley," he continued, "I want you to send me a report every two weeks or so. Tell me what you're doin' and what's goin' on. Sign them letters Curley. But, If'n someone is lookin' over yore shoulder or you can't tell me right out that you got a problem, sign the letter Cedric. I'll know somethin' is wrong, and I'll come arunnin'. You savvy?"

"Yes," replied Curley with a relieved smile. "That's smart thinkin', Tex. I'll shore call for help, if'n I need to. We can't let things git out of hand like they done afore."

"I agree," grunted Tex. "One more thing. Lefty said he ain't hired any new men yet. You need to hire two more right quick, so I can get Kansas and Blackie back here, too. Bo Franklin, over on the Double H, might be able to help you some on that score. You got any questions for me?"

"I reckon not," answered Curley. "I'm right glad you thought enough of me to give me this chance, Tex. I'll give it all I got. You won't regret what you done for me."

Both men rose and shook hands.

Curley reached to pick up his hat, turned, and began to leave the room, when Tex's voice stopped him.

"Curley, you ain't a gunslinger like me and some of the boys are. Don't do nothin' foolish. If'n you need help, you yell right quick. I don't expect any trouble, but I want to be ready if'n it comes."

Curley turned his head, grinned his approval, and waved his hand in response. He left the den and quickly set out to locate his friend, Dusty Rhodes.

****

A short while later, Catherine slipped into the room, pulled a chair up close to the desk, and sat down, using a prim and proper pose.

"Your private secretary is reporting for work, Mr. Riley," she announced in a haughty tone. "Where do I begin?"

"You might begin by giving Mr. Riley a proper greeting," Tex replied in the same tone of voice.

"I provided Mr. Riley with a proper greeting this morning at breakfast," she responded solemnly.

"Yeah, but it has plumb wore off," complained Tex, equally grave.

Catherine popped out of her chair, swept around the desk, and exchanged a long greeting with Mr. Riley. She returned to her chair and resumed her previous pose but with a frown on her face.

"If my kisses don't last very long, they can't be very good, Mr. Riley. If so, we've got a problem," she informed him. "What are you going to do when you have to travel?"

"Take you along," replied Tex with a straight face.

"Before or after we get married?" inquired Catherine, her eyebrows raised.

"Both," replied Tex, again with a straight face.

"Hmmm. You would take your private secretary on a trip without the benefit of a marriage ceremony? You could not introduce her as Mrs."

"I can call her my mistress," allowed Tex carefully.

"Hmmm. I think I prefer the Mrs."

"You could set a wedding date," suggested Tex.

"How about tomorrow?" retorted Catherine gaily as she was really enjoying this light-hearted banter.

"Whoa," protested Tex, his hands raised. "That's even too fast for me. Don't you women have a heap of things to do to get ready for such an occasion? I'm shore your folks will want to see you get married."

Catherine's eyes dropped at these words, and the gaiety left her voice.

"Oh, Tex," she sighed. "I still haven't been completely honest with you. I was so happy the other day, I didn't finish my story. It's time I did so."

Catherine described her difficulties with her parents and their reaction to her problem. She then completed the tale by outlining her teaching activities over the past four years but decided it wasn't relevant to mention Corey and Bruce McCall. She told Tex about her library job and repeated how she had read the story about Slim Evers.

"I resigned my teaching position and decided to come back here, not knowing what I would find," she concluded. "Thank goodness you were so understanding, and I love you for it. I really don't think my parents will want to make the trip all the way out here."

"We could go there," suggested Tex.

"Oh Tex, that is so kind of you. But no, your home is here, your job is here, and your friends are here. The people of Cravenville gave me such a wonderful welcome, I think of them as my friends now, too. And, to be truthful, I think I would rather have them as my friends than the people back home. Besides, if we went back to Ohio you would have to use your real name, and we can't have that." Catherine couldn't help chortling at that thought.

"But we do have to tell your parents and invite them here," Tex reminded her.

"Yes, I guess that's what I'll have to do," Catherine reluctantly agreed. "We can't set a date until we get this settled. Maybe Theresa would come even if my folks don't," added Catherine brightly.

"Who's Theresa?" Tex asked.

"My kid sister. She thinks Tex is a cute name."

"She knows about us?"

"Well, a little. She wanted to know about your good points. It was a very short conversation."

"I see. I'm some surprised you even told her my name."

"Well, it did come out rather accidentally, as I recall."

"I can see that this is goin' to be a right interestin' marriage," drawled Tex, hopelessly. "As soon as the men quit beatin' up on me, you're goin' to start in."

"Well, Mr. Riley, I seem to remember a few digs in my direction. I'm putting you on notice. If you can't take them, don't dish them out."

"How can I stop it?" pleaded Tex.

"You'll just have to make me keep my mouth closed," Catherine coyly suggested.

"That's the best idear I've heard in quite a spell," agreed Tex as he got up and moved around the desk. Catherine rose to meet him, and he did close her mouth for a long time.

"I guess I'd better get that letter off to mom and dad right soon," she whispered in his ear as they clung together. "Your private secretary didn't get much work done today," she confessed.

"We'll give it another try tomorrow," said Tex. "But, I think we accomplished a heap today. Run along. Maria might need some help in the kitchen. I've got to talk to some of the boys anyway."

****

Early the next day Tex sent Catherine to Cravenville as he promised he would. Apache drove the buckboard, and in his pocket was the check covering the sale of the trail herd. Bronc rode alongside the buckboard, much to Catherine's amusement.

Catherine spent a goodly amount of time shopping at Wood's store. She found a couple of checkered shirts that fit her, but the pants she liked all had to be altered. Elsa told Catherine that the alterations would be complete within a week and that she would order a couple more shirts for her.

"It sounds to me like you're planning on settling down here," observed Elsa, a twinkle in her eyes. "When is the wedding set for?"

Catherine blushed as she responded, "We haven't set a date yet, but you and Ollie will be the first to know when we do. I have some things to get settled before we can decide on a date."

"Just make sure you give me time enough to get you your wedding dress. It will have to come from St. Louie, and that takes time."

"I'm sure that can be arranged," agreed Catherine after a slight hesitation.

Paul deposited the check at the bank and patiently waited for Catherine to complete her shopping while Bronc Evans hovered in the background.

Paul tried to engage his former teacher in a light conversation on the way back to the Rambling R, but Catherine politely declined and remained unusually quiet during the entire return trip.

****

Tex was in bed and almost asleep when he heard his bedroom door gently squeak open and quickly close. Instantly wide awake, he reached for his gun belt, which was hanging from a bed post. His right hand found the butt of the nearest Colt as his eyes tried to pierce the darkness in his room.

A form floated across the room and stopped next to his bed. The sound of bed clothes hitting the floor reached his ears. The form pulled back the bed covers and slid in next to him. His right hand released his grip on his Colt while the left hand gently pulled the tousled head of his companion down close to his face.

"This *is* a surprise," he mumbled. "I kinda like the idear though."

"I was hoping you would approve," Catherine whispered as she laid her left arm and hand across his bare chest. "I fear that your private secretary has turned into a brazen hussy, Mr. Riley. I don't know who I'm shocking more, me or you."

"I kinda like getting shocked like this, Miss Cornell. In fact, I might get to like it a heap."

"Hmmm. I'm not sure I can take that as a compliment, Mr. Riley, seeing as how you were thinking of introducing me as your mistress."

They both chuckled at that comment.

"Tex, Elsa Woods asked me about a wedding dress today," Catherine murmured as her left hand toyed with the hair on his chest. "She said I had to allow time for it to be sent all the way from St. Louis."

"That's another right good idear, Catherine. You are just full of them tonight. You're gonna want a dress, ain't you?"

"Well, yes and no. Tex, a wedding dress is suppose to be white. The white color is suppose to tell the man, and everyone else, that his bride is coming to him clean and pure, or pure and clean, whatever. Unfortunately, my dear, I can't come to you pure and clean, and we both know it!"

"Whoa, wait a minute," Tex protested. "What happened to you weren't none of yore doin'. You couldn't help it. And it makes no never mind with me. You should know that by now."

"I do, my dear, but I want to come to you as pure and clean as I can. I've given this a great deal of thought, and crazy as it may sound, I have decided that the best way to do that is to be with you. Tex, tonight, right now, please make me pure and clean!"

Tex pulled her closer, cupped Catherine's chin with his hand, and lightly brushed her lips with his own. "Are you shore this is what you want?" he whispered softly.

"Yes, darling, I'm quite sure," Catherine whispered in return. "Just be gentle, my love. That's all I ask. Just be gentle."

Tex, quietly and gently, complied with her request, and sometime later Catherine fell asleep in his arms, a smile on her face. She was now pure and clean, based on how she had now defined those terms.

Shortly before dawn, however, Tex woke her by tickling her chin and suggested that a second treatment might be appropriate in order to be absolutely certain that they had accomplished their desired goal.

A contented Catherine Cornell readily nodded her approval.

****

Two carpet bags were flung into the bed of the ranch wagon, and two saddles, rifles, and sets of riding gear quickly followed. Curley Chance pulled himself up onto the seat alongside the driver, Rusty Meyers. Dusty Rhodes climbed up into the bed itself, assumed a standing position, and gripped the seat rail for support directly behind his two friends.

Rusty urged the team of horses into motion, and late in the afternoon delivered his passengers to the tiny rail station adjacent to the stockyards. Rusty remained with the two Rambling R men overnight and watched them board their train and depart before starting on his trip back to the ranch.

Two and a half days later, Curley and Dusty arrived in Harding, found a room at the little hotel, and arranged for passage to Ridgeway on the next day's stage. They were enjoying a leisurely supper in the hotel dining room when Curley nudged his companion's arm.

"Mebby I'm jumpy or somethin', but there are two rannies settin' at a table behind you in the corner, and one of them keeps lookin' our way. I've caught him at it two, three times. Take a look when you get a chance."

Dusty made a pretense of trying to signal a waiter for more coffee and took a long look at the two men. "Ain't never seed them afore," he reported. "Are you shore you ain't imaginin' things?"

Curley scowled and shook his head.

"No, I ain't imaginin' things. Oops, there he done it again! Don't that beat all. Hey, he's gotten up and is comin' our way."

The man approached their table and smiled a greeting.

"Howdy, gents," he began, "I reckon you been wonderin' why I been lookin' at you." He stared at Curley. "I reckon I know you. It goes back a long time, but I do believe yore name is Curley. Am I right?"

"Yeah, that's right," slowly responded Curley, his memory operating at top speed but without success. "You've got the best of me," he finally admitted. "I don't remember you."

"Don't blame you none," responded the stranger with a thin smile. "My name is Irish McLean, and I worked for Andy Tuttle over in Hawthorne, Colorado—five, six years ago. You're the fellar that plugged Tim with yore rifle. Yore friends gunned down Lem and Sam and threw the rest of us in jail."

"Now I remember," drawled Curley very cautiously. "I weren't around for yore trial, but I heard about it. I figgered you boys got a purty fair deal."

"I figgered that way, too," nodded Irish. "But Moe and Fargo didn't see it the same way. We had a big to do over it, and I seen I didn't belong with them. We split up, and I ain't seen them since. I'm right sorry about what happened, and I ain't never goin' to forget it. Well, I've talked enough. I'll get back to my partner."

"Have him come over and join us," suggested Curley. "Let me buy you both a drink. It took nerve to come over here, and I'd like to get to know you better. Meet Dusty, here."

Irish nodded in Dusty's direction, turned, and signaled for his friend to join them. He and Curley captured two chairs from another table, and the four crowded around one table as drinks were ordered.

"This here is Frisco," said Irish. "Frisco, this is Curley and Dusty. Curley is the gent I thought he was. What are you boys doin' this far north?"

"We're headed for Ridgeway," answered Curley. "We got us jobs at a ranch near there."

"That so?" said Irish in surprise. "Jobs is scarce in this neck of the woods. We come in from the east, and there weren't none out thataway. Me and Frisco figger on heading south and trying our luck down there."

"You're both lookin' for work, are you?" inquired Curley.

Both men nodded their heads as Irish spoke, "Yeah, we helped drive a herd from Colorado to Wyomin' but was let go at the end of the drive. We blew most of our money in Laramie and been lookin' for work ever since. Most of the spreads hereabouts seem to be cuttin' back instead of hirin'. You boys were some lucky to find spots."

Curley listened intently as Irish related his tale of woe. Curley liked the man, and his confession about the events of five years ago rang true. He had no reason to approach Curley if he wasn't sincere. Based on this and his own impressions, Curley made a quick decision, his first as the new foreman of the MJ.

"Me and Dusty are headed for the MJ Ranch, about 40 miles north of here. I happen to know they could use two more men. If'n you're interested, follow the stage road into Ridgeway. You can get directions to the ranch from there. I'll put in a good word for you, and that should help some.

"That's right kind of you," declared Irish, and Frisco nodded his head in agreement. "You goin' on the stage in the mornin'?" When Curley nodded, Irish continued, "We'll head out in the mornin', too. We'll take our time, and you'll likely pass us by noon. We should get to the ranch by nightfall."

"I'll guarantee you some grub and a bunk for the night," Curley assured the twosome as he downed his drink. "Right now, me and Dusty need some shuteye. We'll see you in the mornin'."

❋❋❋❋❋❋❋❋❋❋❋❋

Antonio slipped into the kitchen toward noon, glanced around to make sure Catherine was not present, and whispered to his wife in Spanish. "The Señorita's bed was not slept in last night, and Señor Tex's bed showed signs that two had slept there. That is shameful. What are we to do?"

"Hush up, my husband," replied Maria sternly, also in Spanish. "Are you getting so old that you forget your courtship of me? These people are young and so much in love. They have been apart far too long and have lost much too much time. Let them enjoy their happiness now. Who knows what tomorrow will bring? Look how quickly Señor Slim's life came to an end. Besides, I have seen the looks in their eyes. Mark my words, my husband. They will be married soon, perhaps much sooner than they now believe. Now, go about your work and do not speak again about what you know. Señor Tex will tell us when the time is right."

One part of Maria's prophecy came true much sooner than even she had expected. That night, as soon as the supper dishes were cleared and the coffee cups were filled, Tex asked Antonio, Maria, and Paul to remain at the table. He rose from his chair, extended his hand to Catherine, and pulled her to her feet. With his hand clasped to hers, Tex made his announcement.

"Me and Catherine are goin' to get married. We ain't sure just when yet 'cause Catherine has some things to settle first. But if'n we could, we'd get married tomorrow. Now I ain't right good at sayin' things, and what I got to say may not set right with you all, but I'm goin' to say it anyway. Tomorrow, me and Catherine would like to move into the master bedroom. Maria, you and Antonio have most of Slim's things put away. Can it be ready for us by tomorrow night?"

"Señor Tex," responded Maria, tears of joy in her eyes, "I have waited for a long time for someone to use that room for the purpose it was intended. Oh, how I have prayed for Señor Slim to bring home someone he could share it with and still his loneliness. The boy here, coming as he did, was a godsend," and Maria smiled at Paul as she spoke. "Do not wait for tomorrow. It is ready for you now. Antonio and I give you both our blessing. Walk with God!"

Tex and Catherine moved quickly to Maria's side and engulfed her with hugs. Antonio shook Tex's hand and received a hug and a kiss from Catherine in return. Now Tex and Catherine turned their attention to Paul, who was still sitting at the table, a big smile on his face.

Catherine broke the silence by walking over to Paul and putting her hands on his shoulders. "Paul, your feelings are important to us, too. Do we have your blessing?"

Paul got up, walked over to Tex and extended his hand. As soon as Tex released it, Paul took a side step and faced Catherine. "My big brother has chosen well, and my happiness goes out to both of you, but especially to you, Catherine. We have ridden together, you and I, and you have suffered much. I think I know why you left us four years ago. Now I hope that your life with Tex will be so good that your memory will contain nothing else."

Paul stepped sideways again and now faced Tex. "You have become more Apache than you realize. This is how an Apache takes his woman. But treat her well, my big brother, or I will have the entire Apache nation come down on you!" But his laughter negated his promise, and every one joined in. Catherine, for her part, could not remember a happier time in her life.

Chapter 7

The next afternoon Catherine began her secretarial work in earnest by reading the ranch's mail and then sorting each piece of correspondence in terms of the kind of reply required and its importance. The third letter made her pause, and she read it a second time. She set it aside and continued her work. About an hour later Tex arrived, and they exchanged the appropriate greeting before he sat down across from her. Catherine reached for the letter she had set aside.

"Darling, you've received a letter from Judge Parks. Who is Judge Pardee?"

"Pardee is a judge up in Hawthorne, Colorado," Tex answered. "He's the fellar that let Slim bring Apache here to the ranch. I told you about Apache's maw and paw gettin' killed up there. Pardee put Apache in Slim's custody and then transferred jurisdiction over Apache to Judge Parks here in Cravenville."

"I remember now," mused Catherine. "You did tell me that Paul's parents were murdered, but I didn't know any of the details. Didn't you say Paul's mother was white?"

"Yeah, but she was Apache's step-maw. She were a school teacher, too. Remember?"

"Yes, it's coming back to me now," replied Catherine thoughtfully. "But why does Judge Parks want to see you?"

"Well, I don't rightly know where we stand with Apache, legal like, now that Slim is gone. I went to Parks a few weeks ago to try to get a handle on things. He said he would write Pardee and let him know about Slim gettin' killed. Parks told me he figgered on keepin' jurisdiction over Apache. What I'm afeered of is that he will send Apache back to the San Carlos Reservation 'cause Slim ain't here no more."

"Oh Tex, that would be awful!" cried out Catherine, in horror. "We can't let that happen. Paul belongs here on the Rambling R. This is a real home for him."

"I agree," said Tex wearily. "I reckon I'd better mosey into town and see Parks right quick. Mebby he's figgered out a way to keep Paul here. In fact, I'll go see him in the mornin'. You got any more letters to go over?"

"Yes, here are a couple that need replies," answered Catherine. I'll read them to you, and you tell me how to respond. I'll write them up, and you can take them to town tomorrow."

****

Tex rode at a leisurely pace and reached Cravenville by mid-morning. He mailed his letters but found out that Parks was busy on some legal matters until noon and would see Tex after lunch. Tex visited the bank, had a short conference with Milner, and then killed some time visiting with Sheriff Buck Buchanan. He had lunch at the Steak House and returned to Park's office promptly at one o'clock.

Parks greeted Tex and motioned him toward a chair.

"I've heard from Judge Pardee, as I wrote you, and, as I suspected, he wants me to retain jurisdiction over Paul. Frankly, I'm not quite sure what I should do. That fact that the boy is almost of age makes it a rather unusual situation. You want him to stay on the Rambling R, don't you?"

"Of course I do," came the quick reply. "Me and Catherine talked about it yesterday. We both want him to stay there."

"Ah, yes. You and Catherine. Just where does that matter stand, Mr. Riley?" asked Parks, his face a mask.

"We'll, we ain't said nothin' yet, but we are goin' to get married. Not right away though, 'cause Catherine has to get some things settled back home first. I don't want it spread around 'till we're ready. Yore the first I've told."

"Very well, Tex. I'm pleased for both of you, and I will keep this information in the strictest confidence. In the meantime, I'll ponder Paul's situation a bit more and get back to you later." Again, his face did not reveal his real thoughts.

"Thanks a heap, judge," responded a pleased Tex. "Mebby I'll know more about me and Catherine by then, too."

Tex returned to the ranch and reported the judge's decision to an equally pleased Catherine. "The longer Paul stays with us, the better off we are," she told Tex. "Maybe that's what Judge Parks has in mind. It surely would strengthen our case for keeping him here permanently. This makes me very hopeful."

****

Two letters arrived on the same day at the Cornell residence in Bowling Green, Ohio. One was addressed to Mr. and Mrs. Harold Cornell, and the other was addressed to Miss Theresa Cornell. Both addresses were written precisely and clearly and both envelopes contained the same return address: Rambling R Ranch, Cravenville, Arizona.

Theresa was now a full-time employee at her father's store. She and her father picked up Lydia at the local library, the location of the mother's Literacy Club meetings, and drove her home in the early darkness of a late fall day. Theresa and Lydia entered the house as Harold parked the carriage and unhitched the horses.

Theresa immediately checked the mail, as was her custom, and squealed with delight as she found the letter addressed to her. She decided to clean up and change her clothes before opening the letter. She had discovered that adding a little suspense to the process seemed to make the infrequent letters from her sister more fun to read. Anxiously, she carefully opened the envelope and began to read.

"Whooppee!" came the cry from the upstairs as Harold was sorting through the mail, Lydia having ignored the correspondence and proceeded to the kitchen. Footsteps were heard pounding down the hallway and thence down the stairs as Lydia stuck her head through the open kitchen doorway, a surprised look on her face.

"Did you read your letter from Catherine?" shouted Theresa as she reached the bottom of the stairs.

"Land's sake, girl, control yourself," came the admonishment from Lydia. "I didn't know we had gotten a letter from Catherine."

"I just found it," Harold announced. "Open it, dear, and let's find out what Theresa is so excited about." He handed the letter to Lydia, who tore open the envelope and began to read.

"Catherine is getting married!" exclaimed an astonished Lydia. "And in Arizona, of all places. I didn't even know she was in Arizona."

"Isn't it exciting!" burst out Theresa. "She wants us all to come to her wedding."

"Good heavens, Theresa, control yourself," snapped Lydia as she continued to read. "Good Lord, the man doesn't seem to even have a Christian name. Tex!"

"What, you say his name is Tex?" queried a confused Harold Cornell.

"That's what she says," sneered Lydia. "It's probably the same ruffian that got her pregnant and sent her back to us."

"No, it isn't," Theresa contradicted her mother. "And I like the name Tex!"

"Now, how do you know that," retorted Lydia with exasperation.

"Because Catherine told me," replied her daughter. "Tex knew she might be pregnant and still he wanted to marry her four years ago. I know why she didn't, and I think she was all wrong."

Lydia pointed to a nearby couch and chair.

"Sit in that chair and explain yourself, Theresa. Harold, you sit with me on the couch. Now, Theresa, tell us what you know—you seem to be better informed than we are. Why is that?"

"Catherine and I had some sister talks," responded Theresa, now sorry she had gotten carried away in her enthusiasm over the news. "I felt that Catherine should be the one to tell you about what happened and not me. Besides, she really didn't tell me very much either."

"Why didn't she tell us more," probed Lydia, her anger now evident.

"I don't know, mother. Maybe she figured you wouldn't believe her any-way, especially after what happened."

"Harrumph," snorted the mother in disgust. "What do you know about this man?"

"Not very much," admitted Theresa again as she lowered her eyes. Catherine said he was foreman of a ranch out there and . . ." Theresa paused, now very uncomfortable.

"And what?" demanded Lydia.

"Catherine said she saw him . . . kill a man."

An astonished Lydia fell back in the couch and threw up her hands in exasperation.

"Our daughter is going to marry a murderer!" she groaned. "How could she do this to us? No wonder she doesn't want to come back here to get married. We would be the laughing stock of the whole city."

"Catherine didn't say he was a murderer," Theresa admonished her mother. "I think they do things differently out west than we do here."

"What else would you call it?" Lydia sternly chided Theresa. "Harold, I have no desire to witness my daughter marrying a murderer."

"Nor do I, my dear," agreed Harold. "I couldn't be away from the store for the time it would take to make a trip of that distance anyway. Catherine must have known that when she wrote the letter."

"Well, I want to go!" snapped Theresa, stamping her foot in anger. "She wrote us because she wanted us there. She is still my sister, and I'm going!"

"Well, we aren't going to pay your way!" retorted Lydia, also angry.

"Fine, I'll pay my own way," replied Theresa, somewhat lowering her voice.

"With what?" asked her father with a thin smile. "You haven't acquired a savings habit as far as I can see."

"I'm going to begin right now," Theresa assured him. "And as a starting point, I want a raise in pay at the store."

"You what?" Harold and Lydia spoke in chorus.

"I want a raise in pay," repeated Theresa calmly. "The main reason I haven't been able to save anything is that you haven't paid me very much. It's time we turned that around."

"I just told you we wouldn't pay for your trip, and now you want a raise so we will end up paying for it anyway?" asked an incredulous Lydia.

"What I do with the money *after* you pay me is my business," replied Theresa firmly. "Now, do I keep on working for you, or do I have to look elsewhere for a position?"

Lydia's mouth fell open, but she was completely speechless. She looked at her husband for support.

Harold Cornell had all he could do to repress a snicker. By golly, maybe he had misjudged Theresa and her business acumen. She was tougher than he thought.

Harold kept his face straight and coughed to clear his throat.

"Theresa has a good point, my dear. I haven't paid her very much, and she has become very helpful at the store. I do believe she has earned an increase in her remuneration. I'm sure that an accommodation can be found."

Lydia stared at her husband in astonishment, bounced up from the couch, again threw up her hand in exasperation, and stomped her way in the direction of the kitchen.

Harold Cornell looked at his daughter, smiled, and sent her a big wink.

****

Ty Matthews returned from Cravenville with the supply wagon and unloaded the portion allocated for Maria's kitchen. He saw Catherine in the kitchen and approached her as Catherine looked his way. "Elsa Woods told me to tell you your clothes are ready to be picked up. She also said your shirts are in."

"Thank you . . .?"

"Ty ma'am, Ty Matthews."

"Thank you, Ty. Aren't you rather young to be a ranch hand already?"

"I'm full grown, ma'am," said Ty proudly. "I joined up here just before the boys left for Idaho. I'm right proud to work here at the Rambling R. It's the best ranch in these parts."

"What a nice thing to say," smiled Catherine. "I'll have to tell Tex. I'm sure he will be pleased."

"Thank you, ma'am," stammered the embarrassed young man. He tipped his hat and raced back to the wagon.

Later Catherine told Tex what had transpired, and they both laughed about it.

"He's a good lad," Tex allowed. "He's got a lot to learn, but he'll come along." Tex then assumed a stern look. "I ain't shore I can allow the mistress of the house to flirt with all the young ranch hands, however. I may have to send her back to Ohio."

I am *not* your mistress, and I was *not* flirting with the help, Mr. Riley," exclaimed Catherine in mock anger. "Can I help it if I'm so beautiful that the men can't resist me?"

"I reckon I can't argue ag'in that," Tex ruefully admitted. "I reckon I'll just have to keep you here." Tex pulled her to him and closed her mouth before she could come up with an appropriate response.

"I'll have Apache drive you into town tomorrow," he told her as he released her. He moved to the kitchen door and looked back at her. "As soon as we get you into some proper duds, we'll get some real work out of you!" He quickly ducked out the entrance and slammed the door before she could generate a retort.

Catherine glared at the closed door, hands on her hips. Wait until you come to bed tonight, Mr. Riley, she mused. We'll continue this discussion, and I just might give you a chance to show me what you mean by "real work". And, with that thought, she couldn't resist breaking out in a big grin.

✳✳✳✳✳✳✳✳✳✳✳✳

Paul again drove the buckboard to Cravenville and Bronc Evans, as usual, rode alongside. Paul dropped Catherine off at Woods' store, parked the buckboard near the hotel, and did a couple of his own errands before returning to the buckboard to wait for Catherine. He sat on the edge of the rig, his feet dangling, and was deep in thought when the stagecoach from Windsor arrived. He absently noted its arrival and returned to his thoughts.

Tom Fleming opened the door of the coach, and the first passenger stepped out, asked Fleming a question, and Tom immediately guided the man up the steps and into his hotel.

A second man, portly and well dressed, slowly emerged from the coach, glanced around, and spotted the preoccupied Apache boy.

The man spoke in a loud voice, "Boy, I say boy, get my bags from the driver, carry them into the hotel, and I will give you a quarter." The man's face turned red when Apache did not respond. He took a few steps in Apache's direction and tapped the boy's leg with a walking stick that he carried.

Paul looked up in surprise.

"Well, I finally got your attention," the man sneered.

"Are you talking to me?" Paul asked, still a little surprised.

"Well, I declare," snorted the man. "The savage can speak English. So you understood me all the time, and you still didn't move. Pick up those bags!"

Paul looked at the man, then down at the bags alongside the coach, and back to the man again, noting the girth of the man's stomach.

Tom Fleming had returned to the sidewalk and was about to go down the steps when an arm restrained him.

"You didn't say please," Paul informed the stranger in a soft voice. "It appears to me you could use a little exercise. You might start by picking up your bags and carrying them yourself."

The man's mouth sagged open and for a moment he was speechless. Bristling at the words he had just heard, he finally found his voice and declared, "What an impertinent savage. I've a good mind to take you across my knee and . . ."

"And do what?" an oily voice interrupted him.

"Why give this scamp a good spanking and teach him some manners," barked the man as he turned in the direction of the voice. His eyes focused on a man slowly descending the steps. The newcomer's hands were hooked on a gun belt that held two Colts in holsters that were slung low and tied down.

Suddenly the portly man remembered some things he had read about the west in dime novels, and the hair on the nape of his neck became rigid and stood up. He now had an uneasy feeling that there was danger in the air.

"What did the boy do to deserve a spanking?" Bronc Evans inquired softly.

"I asked the boy to take my bags into the hotel," replied the man weakly. "I offered him a quarter as a reward."

"Did you *ask* him to carry the bags, or did you *tell* him to carry the bags," Bronc asked, again softly.

The portly man gulped and tried to moisten his mouth, which had suddenly become very dry. "I guess I may have told him," he admitted.

"I reckon that's the way I heard it, too," agreed Bronc. "What was his answer?"

The stranger recovered a little of his composure and answered with a somewhat stronger voice, "The impertinent cub told me to carry my own bags!"

"What else did he say?" came another question, this time in a harsher tone.

"Huh, I don't know what you are talking about," declared the man, his mind racing.

"What . . . else . . . did . . . he . . . say?"

"He told me I forgot to say please," whispered the man, fearfully.

"That's the part I heard, too," agreed Bronc, his eyes glinting. "You talked about manners a spell ago. I reckon yore manners are the ones that need attention, not the boy's. You said you wanted to spank the boy. I got me a better idear."

Bronc's right fist made a quick trip and found the pit of the man's stomach. The man doubled up in pain and surprise. Bronc spun him around, stepped to one side, and swung his right leg. The side of his boot made a direct hit on the man's abundant posterior and propelled him forward. The man stumbled for a few steps and collided with a watering trough. He lost his balance and plunged head first into the water.

A roar of laughter erupted from the crowd that had gathered, and Tom Fleming couldn't stop himself from joining in.

The portly man pulled himself to the surface and sputtered in indignation. Fleming, now barely holding his facial expression in check, helped him climb out of the trough and guided him into the hotel, leaving a trail of water in their wake.

Catherine hurried down the sidewalk and joined her two friends, her arms full of packages.

"I heard a big yell a minute ago," she informed them. "What happened?"

"The stage arrived, and one of its passengers wanted a bath so bad he couldn't wait to get in the hotel," explained Bronc, a grave look on his face. "Damned if'n he didn't up and plop right in the watering trough outside the hotel, clothes and all. The world shore has a heap of strange folks runnin' around in it."

Catherine listened intently at Bronc's explanation and was briefly distracted by a soft, gurgling sound that came from Paul. She glanced at the boy, but his head was down, he seemed to be staring at the dust in the street, and she could not see his face.

"Bronc Evans, I think you are pulling my leg," she declared.

"It's the gospel," Bronc assured her as he raised his hands in self defense. "C'mon let's head back to the ranch. I'm gettin' hungry as a bear."

Bronc and Paul helped Catherine stow her packages in the buckboard, and soon they were heading out of Cravenville. As soon as they got back to the ranch, Bronc headed for the bunkhouse, and Paul and Catherine joined Tex, Maria, and Antonio for a late lunch.

After the meal, Catherine showed Tex her purchases, and he assured her she had done a good job of shopping.

"Slip into some pants and come down to the den. You'll be so comfortable we oughta get twice as much work done today."

Catherine stuck out her tongue at him but hurried upstairs, did a quick change, and joined him in the den.

They exchanged the usual greeting, and Catherine picked up some mail to read. She started her perusal but plopped a letter down and looked at Tex.

"Darling, that friend of yours, one Bronc Evans, is getting to be as bad as you are," she informed him.

"Huh, what are you talkin' about?" asked a surprised Mr. Riley.

"I think he enjoys pulling my leg as much as you do," she complained. "But I can't get even with him like I can with you," she added, a impish look on her face.

"What brought all this on?" asked a perplexed Tex.

"Well, something happened in town today, and I think Bronc was in the middle of it. Maybe Paul, too. People were laughing, so it couldn't have been serious. Anyway, Bronc told me this ridiculous story about a grown man taking a bath in the watering trough in front of the hotel, clothes on and all. My goodness, does he really think I would believe all that?"

"Bronc is usually truthful," laughed Tex. "I would be more worried if'n the man didn't have any clothes on, though. But I'll talk to Bronc and find out what went on."

"Thank you, Mr. Riley. Now I can concentrate on my work."

Chapter 8

The surrey rambled down the courtyard of the Rambling R ranch, and its driver pulled it to a halt outside the main ranch house. The passenger, a well-dressed, stout individual laboriously lowered himself from the front seat and steadied himself with a walking stick when he reached the ground. He pointed his walking stick at the driver.

"You shall remain here and wait for me, my good man. As soon as I establish the appropriate rapport with the management of this establishment, I shall return, and you may assist in transporting that box to the inside of the house." His stick pointed to a long narrow container in the back of the surrey.

"Whatever you say, Mr. Digby," Abe Sinclair assured the man as he let loose a stream of tobacco juice in the opposite direction. He shifted the cud from one cheek to the other as Digby advanced toward the steps to the house. "Keep an eagle eye open for any waterin' troughs, Mr. Digby," Abe warned the man and couldn't hold back a snicker at the thought.

Digby paused and closed his eyes, a retort on the tip of his tongue. But he controlled himself and decided that the comment wasn't worthy of a reply. He moved forward and climbed the stairs.

Tex and Catherine were busy at work in the den when the door opened, and Maria stuck her head around the edge of the door.

"There's a señor here who wants to see the manager of our ranch. Do you want to talk to him?"

"I reckon so," answered Tex as he looked up from his work. "Send him in, Maria."

Maria had barely turned when Digby pushed past her and burst into the room.

"May I introduce myself, Mr. Evers. I am J. Laurence Digby, and I represent the Winchester Firearms Company. My card sir." Digby offered Tex a card as he spoke and glanced at the seated Catherine. "'Pon my word, who do we have here?" he continued before Tex could say anything. "What a lovely creature!"

Catherine stood up as Digby bowed and reached for her right hand. He brushed the back of the hand with his lips as a startled and amused Catherine looked on. She glanced at Tex to see what his reaction was, but his face was a blank.

Tex, too, had risen and was examining the business card as Digby paid his respect to Catherine. Digby turned back to Tex, and the two men shook hands.

"This is my . . . my secretary, Miss Cornell," offered Tex as Catherine could hardly keep her face straight at his hesitation.

"I am delighted to meet you, my dear," boomed Digby. He quickly examined her in greater detail. His displeasure with her lack of proper attire—a checkered shirt and Levi's—was more than offset by the admiration he had for the form that filled out the attire. For a moment he had difficulty turning his attention back to Tex.

Tex pointed to a nearby chair. "Make yourself to home Mr. Digby. Welcome to the Rambling R."

"Do you want me to stay, Mr. Riley?" asked Catherine demurely, still having trouble keeping her mirth to herself.

"Riley! I say now, there must be some mistake," barked Digby in surprise. "Our records show that a Mr. Evers is in charge here. Where may I find this gentlemen?"

"Up in Idaho," said Tex dryly. "Miss Cornell, you can stay, of course, but first would you please try to locate Paul and Mr. Evans and ask them to join us."

A puzzled Catherine hesitated for a moment. Tex seldom called Paul anything but Apache, and he *never* addressed Bronc as Mr. Evans. After a brief pause, she shrugged her shoulders, left the room, and softly closed the door.

"Mr. Evers is in Idaho," Tex said a second time as he turned his attention back to Digby. "He'll be there a right long time. I am authorized to act for the ranch in his absence. I have asked Miss Cornell to bring us two of the other owners as I may need their opinions. Why are you here, Mr. Digby?"

"Excellent idea, Mr. Riley," replied a pleased Digby. "Our records show that Mr. Evers purchased 10 of our rifles two years ago. I have brought with me two samples of our latest models and believe that Mr. Evers . . . I mean you, would want to upgrade your arsenal. After all, we both know that Winchester makes the best rifles in the world. You certainly would want the best equipment to protect the rather large investment you have here."

"I see," responded Tex thoughtfully. "I do remember the purchase you mentioned. I seem to recall that a different drummer made that sale to us."

"That is quite true, my good man," admitted Digby. "That gentleman has encountered some health problems and cannot now travel long distances. I have taken his place and assure you that Winchester will be well represented in the west. I fully expect to exceed all the existing sales records," he added proudly.

"I see," repeated Tex as he rubbed his chin. A knock on the door interrupted the conversation, and Tex responded, "Come in."

Catherine entered the room, followed by Paul and Bronc.

Digby rose from his chair and turned to greet the new arrivals.

Digby was thunderstruck when he recognized his two adversaries from the previous day. He gasped for breath, turned, and sank back into his chair, his eyes wide in amazement. He gulped for air.

"You say these are two owners of this ranch?" he finally inquired hoarsely. "Surely you jest?"

"Jest? If'n you are askin' if'n I'm tellin' the truth, you can copper it," Tex told the man, coldly. A totally confused Catherine looked at Tex, at Digby, and back to Tex again.

"You won't be makin' any of them sales you want so bad at this ranch, Digby," continued Tex as his voice took on an even harsher tone. "You don't seem to have any respect for the people who live out here and the way we live. And when I say the people, I mean *all* the people, includin' the Apaches. They was here long afore the rest of us come along. This is their land, and the white man took it from 'em. I ain't proud of that, but that's the way it is. Now, you go back home and tell yore people why you didn't make a sale here. You tell 'em the truth 'cause I'll be sendin' them a letter askin' for a new drummer in these here parts. Bronc, make shore Mr. Digby finds his way back to his buggy without fallin' into any waterin' troughs."

Glumly, Digby pulled himself upright and left the room, Bronc Evans at his elbow.

Catherine glared at Tex, her hands on her hips.

"What is going on here?" she demanded to know. "Tex, you were very rude to the man. Why? And what does he have to do with a watering trough?"

"Tell her, Apache," said Tex grimly.

Paul recited the event's of the previous day, and Bronc reentered the room before the tale was finished. Laughter erupted as Paul completed his narration, and Catherine was forced to use a handkerchief to dry her eyes. She moved beside Tex and kissed him on the cheek.

"Darling, don't ever let me talk you into going back to Ohio," she pleaded. "The people back there will never, never understand the man I'm going to marry. I'm so proud of you—and you, too, Paul. And Bronc, I'm proud of you, too. What a nice bunch of men I have around me. I'm so glad I came back to Arizona."

"We're all right glad you did, too, Catherine," Bronc told her. "Now, did my ears hear right—you two are goin' to get hitched, for shore?"

"Yes, for shore," smiled Tex as his arm swept around his intended. "I reckon we can't keep it quiet no more. It won't be for a while yet, Bronc. Catherine has some things to settle back home first."

"Can I tell the boys?" asked Bronc. "Most of us was bettin' that way anyhow. Will I get a chance to kiss the bride?"

"You already did that once," Catherine reminded him with a grin. "How many do you think you are entitled to?"

"As many as I can get," came the rejoiner. "Besides, who's countin'? I'm not. C'mon, Apache, let's leave these love birds alone. We got a heap of work to do." Bronc headed for the door as he spoke.

Paul did not follow him but instead walked over to Tex and shook his hand.

"Thank you for what you said, big brother," he murmured, his eyes gleaming. "I'm going to make an Apache out of you yet." He turned and raced after Bronc.

✳✳✳✳✳✳✳✳✳✳✳✳

The next day Toby Green rode in from Cravenville and delivered a telegram to Tex. It was from Lefty White, and Tex was surprised to learn that all four members of his "quartet" were returning instead of just Lefty and Charley. Lefty had included an estimated arrival date, and Rusty and the ranch wagon were again dispatched to meet them at the stockyards. Lefty and his men missed one train connection, due to bad weather, however, and arrived one day later than expected. Rusty, therefore, was forced to spend two nights at that location before returning to the Rambling R with his human cargo. They were late in getting back, and Lefty had supper before reporting to Tex.

Tex and Paul were playing checkers in the den with Catherine an interested spectator when Lefty arrived. Tex and Paul gave the man a warm welcome as Catherine looked on. Lefty removed his hat as he approached her with a big smile.

"I reckon I know who you are ma'am. I'm right pleased to make your acquaintance. We didn't meet when you was around afore. I reckon Tex hogged all your time back then, and now I can see why." He shook Catherine's hand as he spoke.

"Thank you, Lefty," smiled Catherine. "I've heard a lot about you."

"Don't you believe all that you hear!" retorted Lefty. "I ain't as bad as they say. Almost, but not quite. How come you two ain't married yet? You waitin' for ol' Lefty to get back afore tyin' the knot?"

"That's a long story," grinned Tex as he watched the blush come to Catherine's face. "But we'll cover that another time. Tell me, what's been goin' on in Idaho."

"Do you want me to stay, Tex?" asked Catherine.

"Shore, you're part of the ranch now. But how about you and Apache gettin' us some coffee? I shore could use some, and I'll bet Lefty could, too."

Lefty nodded his approval, and in a minute or two all four people had mugs of hot coffee to sip on.

"Curley picked up a couple of men when he come through Harding," Lefty began, "and that's why all of us come back at once. It seems that one of them knew him from his Hawthorne, Colorado, days."

"Who was that?" interrupted Paul, alarm in his voice.

"Said his name was Irish," responded Lefty. "Told Curley he was right sorry about what happened to your paw and maw, Apache. Said he split up with the other two fellars after the trial. Do you remember him, Apache?"

"A little bit," answered Paul slowly. "There were three that were thrown in jail and had a trial. Judge Pardee gave them probation and told them to leave town."

"I reckon he was one of 'em," drawled Lefty. "I had a little meetin' with them two, along with Bud and Wes. I spoke right plain to all of 'em. Told them to play square with Curley and Marty, or me and the boys would be back to square things permanent like." Lefty glanced at Catherine as he spoke those last words. "I think the new men got the message, but in case they missed it, I told 'em to have Bud and Wes tell 'em what happened the last time we had to come and how many we had to bury."

"We ran into a gang of rustlers when we went to Idaho, Catherine," Tex hurriedly explained. "Besides the one I killed, Sanchez and his men took care of two more, and Lefty and his men downed the last two when they tried to run off from the trial."

"Mr. Boyd told me about the two who tried to escape," responded Catherine. "I didn't know about the other two."

"There were three more members of the gang that we caught," Tex went on. "They was put on probation, and I let two of 'em keep on workin' at the MJ. That's why Lefty did what he done."

"You let two rustlers keep on working at the MJ," gasped Catherine in astonishment.

"Shore. They was small fish, and we scared the hell out of 'em. Did they give you any trouble, Lefty?"

"Hell, no," grunted Lefty. "They was too scared to spit sideways. I don't reckon Curley and Marty will have no trouble with 'em neither."

"Speakin' of Marty, how did you get along with him?" probed Tex.

"Right good, Tex. I think his brush with financial ruin sank in right deep. We spent a heap of time in the saddle together, and he writ down copious notes. Mary listened good, too, and I reckon the two of 'em will handle things better from now on. I talked to Curley, and he told me what you told him. I reckon we can quit worryin' about Idaho for a spell. How are things here? I kinda like the new addition you brung in," and he smiled at Catherine.

"I didn't bring her," grinned Tex. "She come on her own. And I'm mighty glad, too. All this paperwork was beginnin' to drive me crazy. She says she's my private secretary, and she was done right good in helpin' me get things cleaned up around here. I think I'll keep her."

Everyone laughed, including Catherine. Then a sober Tex looked at Lefty.

"Lefty, I need a second-in-command, now that Slim is gone. The job is yourn, if'n you want it. I'm goin' to be tied down here at the ranch more'n I like, so I want you to take over runnin' the range work. How does that set with you?"

"Right good, Tex," replied a beaming Lefty White. "I figgered you'd have to do somethin' like that, and I was hopin' you would pick me. I'm gettin' to old to break horses, anyhow," he grinned. "What do you want me to do right off."

"First off, you and yore boys deserve a few days off. Take 'em now and get yore personal things all took care of. Besides, you and the boys got four months wages comin'."

"Don't fret none about that," interrupted Lefty. "Marty paid us for all four months, gave us each a bonus, and travelin' money. I reckon he was right sorry to see us go. He told me to tell you he'd be makin' a payment on that note come January."

"That's right good news," said a pleased Tex as he eyed the little left-hander. "That takes care of Idaho for now. Hey, you head for the bunkhouse and get some shuteye. You look like you're about to drop. Meetin's over."

Before they went to sleep that night, Catherine, as usual, snuggled up against Tex. "You continue to amaze me, Mr. Riley," she whispered in his ear.

"What have I done now?" Tex whispered back.

"You allowed those two rustlers to keep on working at the MJ. You gave them a chance to rebuild their lives instead of going to jail. I never would have believed it if I hadn't heard it with my own ears. You are not the cold, ferocious beast I was led to believe you were."

"Thank you for them kind words, Miss Cornell. Perhaps I should be more of a ferocious beast with you!"

"No, that is a situation where gentleness counts much more. However, I do have a complaint."

"What now?" sighed Tex in dismay.

"Well, you said you were tied down here at the ranch. Am I tying you down?"

"Yup, you are," admitted Tex, "and that's the part I like best. It's the damned paperwork that I don't like. I'd druther be out on the range. But that's what I got Lefty for now, and that will take a big worry off'n my back once he takes over. That should allow me to spend more time with my private secretary. It's time we had another picnic!"

"Hmmm. I do believe that you're almost as fast on your feet as Dexter Boyd," declared Catherine as she kissed him on his cheek.

"I don't know what that means," allowed Tex, "but I do know that little peck weren't nearly good enough for all them kind words you just said to me. I reckon we could do a heap better than that."

They did.

Chapter 9

The next few days flew by. Tex and Catherine finally got all caught up on all the ranch's correspondence; Bronc, Trig, and Paul left on their annual three or four day campout; and Lefty and his three friends enjoyed their vacation. A week after the first meeting, Tex convened a second conference, and this time Bronc was included in the group. Tex had told Bronc about his decision to make Lefty his second-in-command, and Bronc fully supported his choice, as Tex had expected. However, Tex also felt that Bronc should be a part of the planning committee, and Lefty heartily agreed. Catherine and Paul were again in charge of the refreshments.

Tex read the letter Slim had received from the Bureau of Indian Affairs and told the group that an official contract had been signed.

"Lefty, I want you to be trail boss on these drives. But we gotta find the best trail to get there. That'll be yore first job. Take Charley, Kansas, and Blackie with you, figger it out, and draw us a route. Better yet, take Apache along and let him do the drawin'. Besides, he can speak Apache, and that might come in handy. You might have to buy some trail and water rights, too. Tomorrow, me and you and Bronc will ride into Cravenville, and we'll add yore names to our accounts at the bank. Milner will tell us what else we have to do."

Tex turned his attention to his private secretary.

"Catherine, 'till Lefty gets back I gotta spend more time out on the range and at the line camps, just so I know what's goin' on. You got a good handle now on how things should be done at this end. You keep goin' through the mail, write my letters for me, and write whatever checks you need to. I'll sign 'em whenever I show up."

Catherine's eyes glistened with pride. Tex had told her he needed her, and he certainly had provided ample proof that he was not pulling her leg and was not being condescending to her. She had an important role to play, and he wanted her to play it. In short, he wanted them to have a complete and fulfilling partnership. Her admiration for the man moved up another notch, if that was possible, and she wondered how she could have missed seeing all this in the man four years earlier.

****

Three weeks went by, and Tex did spend a significant amount of time away from the main ranch, as he told Catherine he would do. Catherine, for her part, performed her assigned duties well and helped Maria and Antonio with the maintenance of the main house. Already the two women had acquired a deep friendship for each other, as well as respect for each other's talents and the role each had to play within the household. Catherine suspected that this was another reason Tex decided to spend so much time away from the ranch house at this point in time and, again, she admired his practical wisdom.

Two letters arrived for her during one of his absences, however, and she eagerly opened them. One was from her mother, and one was from Theresa. Catherine was disappointed, but not surprised, at the contents of the former but was somewhat pleased at the words contained in the latter. She waited for Tex to return and then shared the contents of the two letters with him after supper, in the den.

"Darling, while I'm disappointed mother and father don't want to come to our wedding, I am more distressed at the harsh words mother has for you. During a weak moment, I did tell Theresa about you killing Norton, but I deliberately did not go into details about it. I fear that was a big mistake. It's obvious that mother and father have jumped to the wrong conclusions. I'm sorry, my dear, but I seem to have let you down again."

Tex pulled her into his arms and gave her a bear hug. He released her a bit, bent down, and closed her mouth for an extended period of time. Then he held her at arm's length.

"Don't fret none, honey, I reckon I'd look at it the same way as them," Tex assured her. "In a way, they're a heap like Digby. They don't know how we live out here. I'm just sorry we won't get a chance to show 'em we are civilized. Do you reckon they might change their minds?"

"I seriously doubt it," answered Catherine as she shook her head.

"But Theresa will be comin'," Tex reminded her.

"Yes, but that's a problem, too," frowned Catherine. "She doesn't say when she'll have enough money to pay for the trip. We don't know any more now than we did before. Oh, Tex, let's not wait. Let's get married right away. Theresa can visit us later on when she can afford the trip."

"Why don't we send her the money?" asked Tex.

"Darling, that's a wonderful idea," answered Catherine, her eyes glistening. "But I get the impression that Theresa wants to do this on her own, and I must admit I think that would be good for her. But thank you so much for offering."

"Catherine, I reckon we gotta set a spell then," Tex told her. "I want Apache to stand up for me, and it would be fittin' and proper for Theresa to stand up for you. We gotta give her time to work things out. We don't *have* to do nothin' right quick."

Catherine looked at Tex, her eyes filled with moisture.

"Mr. Riley," she whispered hoarsely, "have I ever told you I love you?"

"Not frequent enough," smiled Tex.

She was about to add another comment but was pleased to discover her mouth was again sealed shut.

****

At the conclusion of the same three week period, Lefty and his companions returned from their exploration trip. Lefty and Paul met with Tex, Bronc, and Catherine and reported on the results of their mission.

"I got us a trail all laid out in my mind," Lefty began, "and Apache has got it all down on paper. But we're shore gonna have a couple of dry stretches, especially during the summer season. I bought some water rights from one small rancher, but he ain't shore he'll have enough water when we'll need it most. It all depends on the weather. But I got me an idear.

"Tex, I'm gonna want to take both chuck wagons with us. The cook can drive one, and Woody can drive t'other. I'll put four water barrels in each wagon—puttin' 'em all in one would be too much for the horses to pull. That will give us an extry supply in case we need it. Apache's got it marked where we can fill 'em along the trail. If'n we has to, we can even hand water the cattle, if'n I can't figger a better way to do it."

"Sounds like a right good idea to me," agreed Tex. "How many men do you figger on needin' for the drive, besides the cook and Woody?"

"I've thought about that, too," muttered Lefty. "I'll want Charley, Kansas, and Blackie, of course, and Reb and Cavalry, too. I'm countin' on Apache comin' along and I reckon I'd like to give Ty Matthews a chance to work a drive. Besides, he's about Apache's age, and the two lads would be good company for each other. How does all this set with you, Tex?"

Tex glanced at Catherine and was pleased to see a big smile of approval on her face.

"Sounds first rate to me, Lefty," Tex replied. "Pick out the beef you want to take and herd 'em to the far southeast corner and start the drive in two weeks. Anybody got any more questions about the drive?"

Tex waited, but nothing was forthcoming. He reached for some papers lying on his desk.

"I've got more good news," he announced. "Jack Keller's sent me a new three year contract. He wants 2,800 head next year and 3,000 in each of the following two years. Do we all agree I should sign the contract?"

Tex smiled at the enthusiastic replies to his question and asked, "Is there any anythin' else we should talk about?"

"Yeah, there is," replied Lefty as he rubbed his chin reflectively. "Me and Apache got somethin' to bring up.

"Tex, this contract with San Carlos is kinda funny. It says they will pay us so much per head or so much per pound, whichever is higher. I've never seen a contract like that afore."

"I noticed that, too" admitted Tex. "Since we raise good beef, it tends to favor us. Does it bother you, Lefty?"

"Well, yes and no," grumbled Lefty. "I had us stay two days on the reservation and in the town of San Carlos and nosed around some. That also gave Apache a chance to spend more time with his people. Tex, I've seen some hell holes close up a few times in my life, but nothin' like that reservation. I don't rightly know how them Apaches manage to survive down there. It's just plumb awful.

"I never did meet up with the agent or his foreman," Lefty went on. The foreman's name is Zack Worthington. I did find out that what they do is weigh 10 to 15 of our critters, average the weight, and spread it over the whole herd. If'n it turns out in our favor, we get more money. Like I said, I ain't never seen it done that way afore."

"It is different," admitted Tex, "but we can't lose. We get the best price either way. It shore sounds fair to me."

"That's what bothers me, I reckon," mused Lefty. "It's almost too fair. It's almost like it might be rigged to be too fair."

"You've got a suspicious mind," smiled Tex.

"Reckon I do," agreed Lefty. "Me and the boys have broke and sold a heap of horses in our time, and we ain't never had a deal like this'n. Tell 'em what you found out, Apache."

"I share Lefty's concern," Paul confessed. "Tex, you should know that Eskiminzin died a year or so ago. I wish I could have talked to him before he died. But I did get to talk with Chato and told him about Slim's death. In addition, I had a chance to talk with some of the other chiefs. They all claim they aren't getting enough beef. Oh, they get enough to stay alive, but they have to ration it very carefully.

"There is also lots of trouble on the reservation. For some reason the agent has a policy of concentration. Too many Apaches are forced to occupy too little ground in some of the restricted areas. Worse than that, some groups of Apaches have been forced to occupy land either next to, or within, groups of other Apaches they hate, instead of groups they are friendly with. The Apache Nation has always had a number of tribes or sub-tribes. Some get along together, and some don't. I don't like it."

"Sounds like some white folks I've known," grunted Tex.

"But mixing them up together is bad, Tex," countered Paul. "It's almost like the white agent is just asking for trouble."

"I don't reckon we can solve that problem from here," sighed Tex. "Lefty, you play things close to yore vest when you make the drive, and Apache, you keep yore eyes and ears open after you get there. Anybody else have somethin' to say?"

None did, and Lefty, Bronc, and Paul left the room. Catherine went to the kitchen, refilled two mugs with coffee, returned to the den, and sat down next to Tex.

"Lefty and Paul are concerned, aren't they?" she inquired as she handed Tex his coffee.

"Yeah, it don't sound as good as I had hoped," admitted Tex. "Mebby I should go along on this first drive."

"I don't think so, Tex," Catherine disagreed. "You want Lefty to assume some responsibilities and get them off your back. You've said so, yourself. Isn't that why you gave him the job in the first place?"

Tex reached out and grasped Catherine's right hand. "I think I have gotten me a wise and thoughtful private secretary. Yore dead right, of course. How am I ever goin' to get along without you?" he asked plaintively.

Catherine leaned over and brushed his lips with hers. "You'd better not try," she whispered.

****

It was mid-morning as Catherine pushed open the screened front door of the ranch house and strolled out on the veranda, a coffee mug in her right hand. This was Catherine's most enjoyable time of each day. The breakfast dishes had been washed and dried, the beds had been made, and her other household chores had either been completed or put on hold for later in the day. Maria was in the kitchen and engaged in the preparation for the noon meal while Antonio was busy chopping wood for the big stove. It was a time to relax and enjoy life, and Catherine was determined to make the most of it and feel the warmth of the morning sun at the same time. Tex had been up early and had headed for one of the distant line camps with Paul. They would be gone for the better part of a week.

She found her favorite cane chair, sat down, sipped her coffee, and examined her surroundings. There were always a handful of Rambling R men about the ranch grounds. Maintenance work of one kind or another was constantly going on, and this morning Bronc Evans and Trig Mansfield were re-setting a few posts for the huge horse corral while Denver Pike was busily engaged in operating the forge in the blacksmith shop, probably doing repair work on shoes for some of the horses.

Bronc and Trig paused in their work, straightened their backs, and wiped their perspiring faces with their kerchiefs. Bronc glanced toward the ranch house, saw Catherine, and waved a greeting.

Catherine smiled, waved back, and sipped some more coffee. A few minutes later Trig roped a horse and began saddling the animal, while Bronc walked in her direction.

Bronc reached the veranda, clomped his way up the steps, and paused to grin another greeting at Catherine.

"Get some coffee and sit a while, Bronc," invited Catherine. "You and Trig had a hot job to do out there in the sun."

"You've read my mind," agreed Bronc. "I'll be back right quick." Bronc disappeared into the house and soon reappeared with a mug of steaming coffee. He found a veranda railing that suited his fancy, and he eased into a comfortable sitting position that faced Catherine. He took a moment to blow on his coffee, took a sip, and grimaced.

"It's hotter than I thought. Guess I'd better let it set a spell." He sat the mug down on the railing and looked at Catherine.

"Tex and Apache left for Number Two this mornin'," Bronc observed. "Me and Trig will head that way this afternoon. It'll be fun spendin' some time with the lad. Me and Trig are his uncles, you know."

"Yes, Tex told me that story," smiled Catherine. "Did I hear something about all of you doing some fishing while you are away?" she asked, an impish look on her face and her eyes filled with mirth.

"Aw, shucks, Catherine. You ain't suppose to know that!" exclaimed Bronc. "You're suppose to think we work all the time out here. Now the cat's out of the bag."

"You might be surprised at how much I know about your work habits, Mr. Evans," laughed Catherine. "We gals have ways of getting valuable information out of our intendeds."

"That may be true," grinned Bronc, "but I've known Tex a lot longer than you, and I know you're funnin' me. But speakin' about that man of yourn, you and I have got to talk about a problem we got."

"A problem with Tex?" asked Catherine in surprise. "I don't understand. What kind of problem?"

Bronc paused for a few moments, reached for the mug, sipped his coffee, and nodded approval of the milder temperature of the beverage. He turned his eyes back to Catherine as he returned his half empty mug to the porch railing.

"Catherine, it won't be easy explainin' what I got in mind, but I'll do the best I can. First off, I gotta tell you that me and all the boys are right happy you and Tex finally got together. Them four years were awful hard on Tex. If'n it hadn't been for Apache bein' around, I ain't shore Tex would have made it. But, I also gotta tell you . . ." and now Bronc paused and smiled at Catherine, "that havin' you come back here was the second best thing that ever happened to Tex."

"The second best thing!" sputtered Catherine, her brows raised in mock horror. "Well, I like that! Now, I think you're funnin' me, Mr. Bronc Evans."

Bronc raised both hands as if to ward off the verbal attack. He smiled his response but quickly sobered and replaced the smile with a serious look.

"No, I ain't funnin' you Catherine. The best thing that ever happened to Tex was him meetin' up with Slim. If'n that hadn't took place, you'd have never met Tex. More'n likely he'd be on the owl hoot trail somewhere, or worse yet, he'd be dead by now. You see, ma'am, Tex was purty wild and reckless in his younger days, and it took Slim a long time to get him under control."

Catherine, too, had assumed a more serious countenance, and she nodded her head in agreement.

"I think I know what you are saying, Bronc. After I first met Tex, I asked people in Cravenville about him and was disturbed to learn bits and pieces about the violence in his past. I felt like there were two Tex Rileys—the man and the gunman. I fell in love with the man, but the gunman frightened me. I just plain didn't understand him, especially how he determined what was right and what was wrong. That's why I left Cravenville when I did. It took me the better part of four years to acquire that understanding and the trust that goes along with it. I wouldn't be completely honest though, Bronc, if I said I completely understood it even now. I don't. But that is where the trust comes in. I have to rely on his judgment."

Both paused to drain their coffee mugs before continuing the conversation.

"Catherine," Bronc went on, "me and Trig are a lot like Tex. We ain't got family to speak of, we like guns, and we all spent a heap of time and money learnin' how to use them right good. And I ain't sorry one bit that I done it!"

Catherine responded by smiling ruefully. "I've heard a rumor or two that you and Trig are just as deadly as Tex. And that goes for Lefty and Blackie, too."

"Well now, I ain't shore you should believe all you hear about that," responded Bronc with a pleased look. "I guess that Tex told Sanchez, up there in Idaho that if'n me and him ever had it out, we would likely kill each other in an even break. I ain't so shore that's so, and I shore don't aim to try it out. But you gotta understand somethin' about gunslingers.

"Take me, for instance. If'n my right hand would ever throw down on my left hand, my right hand would win every time. I reckon the same is true with Trig and Blackie. Lefty only wears one gun, so we can't talk about him thataway.

"Tex, though, is different. He's greased lightnin' with both hands. Now I can't believe he practiced any more than me or Trig did. And I can't believe he practiced with both hands the same. He's just plain fast 'cause he was born with it. But he was born with somethin' else, too, that makes all the difference. Somehow his instinct, his brain, and his hands work so well together that not only does he move fast, he also moves *first*! I can't explain it, Catherine, but there it is.

"Now, when you put them skills together, you can end up with a very dangerous man. We was plumb lucky that Slim got to Tex when he did. I shore hate to think what might have happened if he hadn't."

"But where do we have a problem with Tex?" asked a puzzled Catherine.

"Well, you gotta understand somethin' about the makeup of a gunman. Most of us have one thing in common—we ain't afeared to die! We don't fear it 'cause we don't think about it. And that gives us an edge agin most everyone, common folk especially. We even believe that when we have to face one of our own kind! Like I said—me and Trig don't have no family to speak of—we been away too long. If'n anythin' would happen to us, there really wouldn't be anyone weepin' over our graves."

"But that isn't true, Bronc!" exclaimed Catherine, horrified at the thought. "You have all your friends here at the Rambling R."

"Shore, I know that," countered Bronc. "Me and Trig have a lot of friends here—good friends, too. But that's the point—they're friends, not family. Dyin' goes with this job, and we all know it. We've lost men afore, and, shore, we missed them at first. But life goes on, the job needs doin', and the memories fade. That's just the way it is, Catherine."

Bronc paused before continuing the conversation.

"But let's get back to Tex. What I just said don't fit him no more. Things are different for him now. You and Apache, especially you, are sort of like a family to him now. If'n he ever gets into a tight spot, and he hesitates one little bit, thinkin' about you and what might happen to you if'n he was gone, it could be plumb fatal. I ain't sayin' it right will, but I hope you can see it. No matter. We just can't let that happen. And that's why I need your help.

"Me and Trig were sort of Slim's bodyguards. One or both of us went with him on most all of his trips. But we didn't go with him to Idaho, and that's where he got himself killed! If'n me and Trig had been along, Slim Evers would be alive today! I ain't aimin' to make the same statement about one Tex Riley. I told Tex, up in Idaho, that where he goes, we go. And I ain't arguin' the point!"

"Even on our honeymoon, if we have one?" quizzed Catherine, her eyes sparkling.

Bronc blushed through his deep tan, and he stammered in confusion, "That ain't what I meant, and you know it!"

"I should certainly hope so!" laughed Catherine as she enjoyed Bronc's embarrassment. "I was just curious as to how far you intended to carry this idea of yours?"

"All right, you shore caught me there," admitted Bronc. "But while me and Bronc shore don't plan on bein' *with* you on such a trip, we damn well won't be far away, neither, if'n I can figger out a way on how to do it. And that's why I need you, Catherine. We can't have no secrets between us. Like I said, me and Trig made a big mistake with Slim, and we ain't aimin' to make it ag'in with Tex."

Catherine studied Bronc's face and was startled by the determination she saw in his features.

"Do you know what you are asking me to do?" she asked quietly.

"I shore enough do," replied Bronc carefully, "and I don't like it no better than you do. But it's got to be did."

Bronc picked up his coffee mug and walked into the ranch house while Catherine continued to stare at her empty container. Bronc returned to the porch and as he was about to start his trip down the steps, he paused and stared at Catherine. She felt his stare and looked up at the man.

"Think carefully about it, Catherine," came the soft voice. "We both got too much to lose. All it takes is one mistake."

Chapter 10

The Christmas season at the Rambling R came and went with relatively little fanfare. The only holiday that had any real significance for Slim Evers was the Fourth of July, and this was the one he celebrated religiously. Slim always gave his men two days off—the Fourth, so that they could participate in the picnics and social events in Cravenville, including the community dance, and the Fifth, so they could recuperate from their exertions of the Fourth. Many, but not all of his men, availed themselves of this opportunity. After Catherine left Cravenville, Tex was one of the men who did not.

But this Christmas was a special one for Tex, and he decided to make the most of it. A jewelry drummer from Phoenix made his semiannual stop in Cravenville, and Tex arranged for Catherine to meet him. They picked out a wedding ring style, but the drummer did not have a size that fit Catherine. So he measured her and promised to mail the ring within a couple of months. Catherine gently asked Tex if he wanted a matching ring, based on the eastern traditions she was familiar with. She was a little disappointed and hurt when Tex, politely but firmly, rejected the suggestion.

Catherine, in a moment of petulance, mentioned this to Bronc Evans one day.

"Catherine, Tex didn't mean to hurt you," Bronc responded, "but you gotta understand somethin'. A gunman's hands are his life. I don't rightly know if a ring would change anythin' for Tex or not, but, if'n I was him, I wouldn't take the chance. Besides, I reckon that's an eastern custom, and it don't quite fit a man's image out here."

"I guess I didn't understand Tex, again," Catherine sighed ruefully. "Bronc, I do need you as a friend—as someone I can talk to. Maybe, someday, I'll acquire the understanding I need to live out here. I have thought about what we talked about a while back, and I will help you all I can. But Tex must not find out about it. Do you agree?"

Bronc nodded his head, reached out, and squeezed her hand. "You and I are goin' to get along just fine," he assured her.

****

Tex was also very appreciative of the loyalty and devotion that the Rambling R men had displayed over the crisis in Idaho. He decided to show this appreciation this Christmas by giving each man a half month's pay as a holiday bonus, much to their surprise and delight.

When Catherine began her secretarial duties, Tex insisted on paying her a small weekly stipend, over her protests. He also included her in his holiday bonus arrangement, and she, too, was both surprised and pleased. Catherine, in turn, surprised him by insisting that a portion of her bonus be used to reimburse him for the clothes she had purchased earlier. Tex was not pleased by this turn of events, however, and it led to a discussion that was as close to an argument as they had experienced up to this point in time.

"Damn it, Catherine," he growled that night as they laid side by side in bed. "Yore my gal, we're goin' to get married, and if'n I want to buy you things, that's my right."

"That's true, my dear, but not clothes," whispered Catherine in response. "That smacks too much like it's a mistress arrangement. A girl has to keep her self respect, you know. After I'm your wife, you can spend as much money on me as you want . . . within reason, of course. I'll even help you," she giggled. "However, speaking about clothing, I don't know whether you've noticed it or not, Mr. Riley, but I have laid here next to you without a stitch on for quite a long time, and you have not made any effort to take advantage of the situation. Me thinketh you talk too much."

"I'll have to remember that," muttered Tex with a slight hesitation, but he was unable to extend his remarks any further as Catherine raised herself up, gently held his chin in place with her left hand, lowered her face, and covered his mouth with hers. Thus ended their first dispute.

****

Catherine, for her part, celebrated the holiday season in a quiet way as well. The Cornell household had been regular church-goers, as was expected, given their status in the community. Catherine continued this habit, to some extent, during her three year teaching tenure in Cravenville. But following her trip back to Ohio and the unfortunate events in Bowling Green, she had discontinued the practice. She did talk Tex into taking her to the Community Church in Cravenville one time, but they did not repeat the experience. While the greetings and words of welcome from the citizens of Cravenville were abundantly warm and genuine, the numerous inquiries regarding their wedding date made her uncomfortable, and she was sure Tex felt the same way, although he said nothing.

Catherine knew that Maria and Antonio held a short private service in their living quarters each Sunday, using a small alter. Accordingly, Catherine purchased a set of candles and gave them to Maria on Christmas Eve when she and Maria were alone in the kitchen.

Maria was astonished, very pleased, and a little embarrassed.

"I have nothing to give the señorita," she protested, tears in her eyes, as Catherine hugged her.

"You have already given me the best two gifts I could hope for," Catherine assured her.

"I have? I do not understand, Señorita Catherine," said a puzzled Maria.

"Well, first you welcomed me and allowed me to become a part of your household. You have been very kind to me, and I can't tell you how pleased I am to have you as a friend.

"Secondly, you have been most gracious and tolerant because you have not said anything about . . . well, about Tex and I sleeping together." Catherine couldn't conceal a blush as she spoke. "I fear that Tex and I may have offended you and Antonio."

"Many years ago it might have been as you say," replied Maria slowly, "but I saw how lonely Señor Slim was until the boy arrived, as I've told you. And I saw Señor Tex with even a deeper loneliness after you left so long ago. You both have lost four years that can never come back. You love each other. Make the most of the time you have.

"But I do have one concern," Maria continued, a twinkle in her eye. "I fear you two will have a little one before you have a marriage ceremony, if you don't watch out."

Catherine tried to cover her mouth and suppress the shriek that erupted from that last comment, she was only partially successful, and a baffled Maria stared at her, bewildered by Catherine's outburst.

"Oh, I'm so sorry, Maria," Catherine apologized. "Can we go to your quarters so we can be alone? I have something I must tell you—I have to talk to someone."

Maria, still puzzled, nodded her agreement and led Catherine to the Martinez apartment. Antonio was sitting in a chair, reading a book, when the two women entered.

"Antonio, Señorita Catherine and I have something to discuss that is for our ears only," Maria informed him. "Please take a walk, my husband, and give us some time together. I will leave the door open when I want you to return."

Antonio did as Maria directed and gently closed the door as he left the apartment. Maria and Catherine found two chairs, placed them close together, sat down, and faced each other. Catherine reached out and took both of Maria's hands in her own.

"Maria, what I am about to tell you must be our secret. No one else must know, not even Antonio."

"You *are* going to have a little one?" asked a confused Maria.

"No, Maria," smiled Catherine, but then the tears came. Haltingly, she described the whole series of events to Maria and, as she talked, the women's hands became even more entwined. Maria's eyes filled with tears as she listened, and the two women rose and fell into each others' arms as the tale was finished. A lengthy silence ensued before Maria gently lowered Catherine into her chair. Maria also sat down, still holding hands with Catherine.

"Señorita Catherine, I am pleased that you want to share, and have shared, your secret with me. Now I will share something with you. Antonio and I were never able to conceive a child. We tried very hard but were unsuccessful. Perhaps there was something wrong with one of us. We do not know. Our friends and neighbors could not understand our lack of success. Even our priest questioned if we were trying hard enough. Eventually we were ridiculed and shamed by those we called our friends. We left Mexico and came to Arizona. Señor Slim found us, gave us positions, and made us part of his household. We could not have been treated better by anyone, and given more respect. We became his family, and he became ours.

"Señorita Catherine, there is only one answer to a situation like this. When there are no children, a man and his wife must love each other twice as much. That is what God would want, and that is what you and Señor Tex must do. Give to each other what you cannot give to children. Again, I say to you, make the most of the time you have."

Catherine released Maria's hands and rose to her feet, her eyes glistening. "Thank you, Maria," she murmured. "I am blessed to have you as a friend."

※※※※※※※※※※※※

An angry and frustrated Theresa Cornell did not enjoy the passing of the holiday season. Her father had responded to her demand, had raised her pay, and in addition had given her a generous Christmas monetary gift. But at the same time, Lydia had decided to charge Theresa for the costs of room and board. Lydia was smart enough to keep the assessment low enough to make it economically unfeasible for Theresa to move elsewhere but large enough to consume much of her increased wages. In addition, Lydia insisted that Theresa actively participate in many of the holiday social events, and Theresa was forced to buy additional clothes appropriate for the occasions. This, of course, not only reduced Theresa's ability to save even more, but the younger daughter felt certain her mother was also attempting to remove the memory of Catherine's misguided social prominence from Lydia's mind. In any event, Theresa had made little progress toward the accumulation of enough funds to finance her trip to Arizona. By the end of January, her financial situation again showed very little improvement. In desperation, and with a good deal of embarrassment, she fired off a letter to Catherine.

****

Lefty, his trail crew, and the herd reached the San Carlos Reservation late one afternoon in mid-January. Two rainstorms had alleviated Lefty's immediate water concerns, but he also knew that the dry summer could still present significant problems for him and his cattle at that time. This dilemma gave birth to another idea—one that he would begin to implement on the way back to the Rambling R.

Worthington had been notified about the herd's arrival and rode out to meet Lefty a few miles from its destination. Lefty and his men thinned out the herd, and Worthington counted the animals as they plodded by. He had the trail crew cut out a dozen animals and showed Lefty and Blackie where a small holding pen and scale was located. Each animal was weighed, and then Blackie drove the little group back to the main herd, which now was controlled by Apache wranglers. Lefty accompanied Worthington to a small building adjacent to the holding pen and scale that served as the man's office. Both men dismounted and entered the building, which contained a desk, two chairs, and a file cabinet.

"If you will sign these weight slips, I'll get the paperwork finished tonight, and you can have your money in the morning," Worthington told Lefty. "Have your crew make camp back up the trail a mile or so. I'll see you tomorrow."

Lefty signed the forms, tipped his hat, left the office, mounted, and waved his crew into motion.

Lefty and his entourage reached their camp location, dismounted, unsaddled their horses, and began to put a campsite in order. Paul and Ty

Matthews didn't join in, however, and Paul motioned for Lefty to meet him off to one side of the site.

"I'm going to swing south and visit my people," Paul began. "Ty says he would like to go along, too. Is that all right with you?"

"I reckon so, if'n you say he'll be safe," cautioned Lefty.

"He'll be safe as long as he is with me," replied Paul. "I told him he would have to leave his gun behind, though. I don't want any accidents to happen. We'll stay overnight and catch up with you back up the trail late tomorrow. Are you planning to stop in San Carlos?"

"Reckon so, but it will be a short stop. We need some supplies, and I've got to buy me some shovels. If'n you don't join up with us by tomorrow night, we'll sit and wait 'til you do."

"We won't hold you up," smiled Paul. "We'll be there." He motioned to Ty, and the two boys met at their horses. Ty slowly unbuckled his gun belt and tossed it into the nearest chuck wagon. He had already fastened his bedroll behind his saddle. The two young men swung into their saddles, waved back at the group, urged their horses into motion, and were soon lost from sight.

****

The next morning Lefty let his crew sleep in and enjoy a leisurely breakfast. They packed their gear and headed north while Lefty and Blackie turned their horses and moved south.

As soon as the two men reached Worthington's office, Lefty dismounted, handed his reins to Blackie, and entered the building.

Worthington greeted Lefty and handed him an envelope filled with greenbacks. Lefty was unable to conceal his surprise.

"Wasn't expectin' cash," he muttered. "Figgered on gettin' a check," he continued, his face now under control.

"We always pay in cash around here," Worthington assured him, his own face a mask.

"You won't mind if'n I count it?" asked Lefty, not really caring whether the man minded it or not.

"Not at all," answered Worthington, a slight smirk on his face. "Go right ahead."

Slowly and carefully, Lefty fingered through the bills, his lips moving in silence. He finished his count, glanced at Worthington, and began a second count.

"There's about a thousand dollars more'n I was expectin'," he placidly announced as he completed the second tally. "How come?"

"Well, we were told the Rambling R produces good beef, and the weight slips proved it," replied Worthington, wearing a poker face.

"That's right good news," drawled Lefty as he slid the full envelope inside his shirt. "The boys back at the ranch will be plumb glad to hear that." He turned and took two steps toward the door.

"Where do you think you're going?" snapped Worthington as he rose from behind his desk.

"Back to the Rambling R where I come from," answered Lefty innocently as he turned back toward the speaker. His left hand rested on the butt of his Colt.

"I guess you don't know how we play the game around here," snarled Worthington, his face turning crimson.

"Reckon I don't," responded Lefty, his eyes narrowing as he spoke. "Just how do we play . . . the game?"

"Half of that extra thousand belongs to me," growled Worthington, his face now dark with anger. "That's how we do it!"

"I don't see why I have to give you nothin'," came the cold response. "You used yore scales, and the contract says we get paid extry if'n the weight comes out in our favor. Mebby you should read yore contract ag'in. Like I said, I don't owe you nothin'."

"You're real smart, aren't you?" snapped a very angry Worthington. "You know what the game is, and you're trying to hold out on me. You signed them weight slips, and you're part of the deal, whether you like it or not. Now, hand over my half!"

"So, I'm part of the deal," mused Lefty in a low voice. "Well, I just made a new deal—I get to keep it all!"

Worthington's mouth sagged open, and for a moment he was speechless.

"Damn you!" Worthington finally snarled through gritted teeth. "I ain't fooling around any longer. Hand over my share, get out of here, and *maybe* I'll forget what's happened."

"Why don't you try comin' and takin' it?" drawled Lefty, his voice now sweet and smooth. But his eyes glinted, and his left hand remained on the butt of his Colt.

Worthington took a step in Lefty's direction but stopped as Lefty's eyes bored into him.

"All right, smart guy, you've had your fun. I'll pass for now, but you got to come back this way again. You'd better think of that money as being a temporary loan. And you'll be paying interest on that loan—big interest, too. Now, I'll give you one last chance—hand over my money!"

Lefty shook his head and slowly backed to the door, reached back with his right hand, and pushed the door open, his eyes never leaving Worthington's contorted face. He slammed the door shut and yelled at Blackie, "Cover the door for me. If'n it opens, fill the room with lead!"

A Colt leaped into Blackie's right hand as he handed Lefty his reins. Lefty swung into his saddle, and now his left hand also held a gun, pointed at the door. "Let's ride," he cried, and both men kicked their horses into motion.

Worthington stepped out of his office and stared at the departing riders, scowling at the same time. He began a dialogue with himself, "All right Mr. Wise-assed Trail Boss, you've got to come back this way with another herd in a couple of months, and I'll be ready for you. I'll bet you won't have the guts to come back here again. No matter. I'll take it out of your hide or the hide of anyone who comes in your place. Nobody runs a blazer on Zack Worthington and gets away with it!" A grim smile replaced the scowl on his face. He turned, stomped back into his office building, sat down behind his desk, and reached for pen and paper.

****

Paul and Ty caught up with Lefty and his camped men at nightfall. Both boys filled tin plates with food, and Paul sat down beside Lefty as Ty joined Reb and Cavalry on the opposite side of the fire.

"Learn anythin?" inquired Lefty.

"Nothing new," replied Paul between mouthfuls. "Our beef was very welcome, but my people still feel they are being cheated."

"They are," came the short response.

"How do you know?" asked Paul in surprise. "Did something happen?"

Lefty nodded his head and told Paul about his encounter with Worthington. "I figger them scales of his are rigged to show about 20 percent more weight than there is. I'll know for shore the next time we come this way."

"He'll be waiting for you," observed the boy.

"I reckon so," agreed Lefty as the glint returned to his eyes. "In fact, I'm countin' on it. It's bad enough here as it is. Yore people don't need white skunks makin' it any worse. Yeah, I expect he'll be around when we come back ag'in. I figger on gettin' this problem fixed right quick!"

Paul examined the grim look on Lefty's face and was a little startled by what he saw. It was obvious that Lefty meant what he said.

****

The end of January was fast approaching before Tex was able to arrange his work schedule so he could spend three consecutive days in and around the main ranch house. The first day he and Catherine got all caught up on the ranch's paperwork, and he signed all the letters and checks Catherine had accumulated for him. The second morning Tex spoke to Maria after breakfast and received a big grin of approval. At mid-morning Maria shooed Catherine out of the kitchen and told her to relax on the veranda. Catherine did so and a little later was surprised to see Tex drive the buckboard up to the front of the house and park it. Tex bounded up the steps, removed his hat, and bowed in front of his private secretary.

"First and last call to board the picnic express, Miss Cornell," he announced gaily. "Go get your hat and do whatever you has to to get ready. We leave in 15 minutes."

Catherine rewarded him with a big grin, jumped to her feet, and raced back into the house and up the stairs to their room. She scrubbed her face, combed her hair, grabbed a soft, brimmed hat, and was back on the veranda well short of her allotted time span.

Tex helped her into the buckboard, deposited the picnic basket in her lap, moved around the vehicle, and pulled himself up into the seat beside her. He snapped the team of horses into motion, and they were off.

As usual, he took a circuitous route to their destination. He enjoyed glancing at his radiant companion, seeing the brightness of joy in her eyes, and hearing the melodic laughter in her voice. The tenseness, fear, and concern she had exhibited four months earlier was now completely gone and replaced by a relaxed, warm, and loving woman. He couldn't help feeling a little pride for the part he had played in that transformation.

They arrived at the grove of cottonwoods, tethered the horses, and ate their lunch. Tex found the appropriate tree, sat down and leaned his back against it, and motioned for Catherine to join him. Without a bit of hesitation, she lowered herself to her knees in front of him. He reached out and pulled her down to him so she laid across his chest, her head on his shoulder.

For a long time no words were spoken. Periodically he would bend down, raise her head a bit, and gently press his lips against hers.

"Darling," Catherine finally murmured, "I can only hope you are as happy as I am. I never dreamed it could be like this. When you hold me, I feel so secure . . . I can't express it in words. I love you so much."

"I know," Tex responded softly. "I feel the same way. Mebby we've been luckier than we thought, honey. Mebby having those bad things happen and being apart for so long has made us appreciate more what we now got. Mebby the other way would have been too easy."

"What a strange way of putting it," said Catherine, with surprise. "But I do believe you may be right. I wouldn't want to recommend that way of doing it for anyone else, but for us maybe it was necessary."

Catherine snuggled a little closer and let two fingers of her right hand toy with his lips.

"I think adversity helped Maria and Antonio, too," she went on. "I told you about our conversation on Christmas Eve. She is such a lovely person, Tex. I must confess there are times when I look at her and think she is like a mother to me. I think she would have been a wonderful mother."

"So would you, if'n you had the chance," allowed Tex.

"Well, I don't know about that, Mr. Riley, but thank you for those kind words. That's something we'll never know, will we?"

Tex didn't reply to the question and silently rebuked himself for making what appeared to be an unfortunate comment. There was a lengthy pause in their conversation.

"It's funny that you should say that," she mumbled, referring to the subject he was now trying to avoid. "It's been almost four weeks since Paul went with Lefty, and I miss him terribly. I'd better watch out. He'll think I'm some sort of motherly hen to him," and Catherine laughed at the thought.

Tex abruptly sat up, dumping Catherine off his lap in the process, and swore.

"Damnation, I had the answer to the puzzle right in front of my nose all the time, and I never saw it! I've been so busy on ranch matters, I missed the whole thing."

"What in the world are you talking about?" a somewhat shaken Catherine demanded as she brushed herself off and tried to recover from the physical jolt she had just received.

Tex grabbed both of her shoulders, straightened her up, and looked directly into her eyes.

"Miss Cornell, how would you like to have a son?"

"Tex Riley! That is *not* funny, and you know it! I can't have children— don't make fun of me!" An angry Catherine glared at her lover.

"Calm down, honey," smiled Tex. "I wasn't making fun of you. You can't have children, but you *can* have a son."

"What? I can have a son? Tex, this has gone far enough. What are you talking about?"

"Judge Pardee up there in Colorado weren't shore he should let Paul come to the Rambling R 'cause Slim weren't married. But he done it anyway. I was worried about the same thing—me not being married like Slim and not near as old as Slim, neither. But you comin' along has changed all that, and I was too dumb to see it. I'll ask you ag'in. Would you like to have a son?"

Catherine stared at him, unable for a moment to comprehend what he was asking. Then her eyes lit up, and both hands jumped to her mouth in an attempt to stifle a scream of sheer delight.

"Paul! Oh, Tex, that's a wonderful idea. Why didn't we think of it sooner?" She flung her arms around his neck and gave him an ardent kiss of agreement. He responded to her zeal with fervor of his own, and they exchanged many more kisses before she slumped back on her heels and looked at Tex as tears of joy started to roll down her cheeks.

"Darling, that would be the best wedding present anyone could hope for. When can we talk to Judge Parks about it?"

"Whoa, slow down," cautioned Tex. "Before we see Judge Parks, we gotta talk to Apache. I don't reckon Parks will tell us he can be a real son. Slim said somethin' about the Rambling R bein' his foster home and Slim being a foster parent to the lad. I don't rightly know what that all means, but we'll find out after we talk to Apache."

"Well, that's close enough for me," declared Catherine. "If Paul will approve of the idea, he'll be our son, and I fully intend to call him that. Oh, I can't wait now for him to get back. Tex, do you realize you asked me to marry you on our first picnic, and now you want to give me a son on this one. Do we dare come out here again?"

"I reckon I don't know," laughed Tex. "Them two things will be hard to beat. Mebby this is enough, and we shouldn't try for anything more and press our luck."

"I agree, Mr. Riley. Besides, we always have each other. That's reason enough to come here."

Tex's arms drew her to him, and her rationale was passionately endorsed.

Chapter 11

Tex took Catherine aside the next morning after breakfast.

"I'm thinkin' we need a change in plans. Help Maria in the kitchen, while I get a few things done around here. I'll hitch up the buckboard in about an hour, and then we're headin' for town."

"What change in what plans are you talking about?" asked a surprised Catherine.

"Our plans for Apache. I've been thinkin' about it all night."

"You were more restless than normal," admitted Catherine with a wry smile. "I'm glad you aren't always like that. What's bothering you?"

"I reckon we should talk to Judge Parks afore we say anythin' to the boy. He ain't had much luck with parents, real or otherwise, up to now, and I don't want him to get hurt ag'in. Let's make shore we can do what we want to afore we spring it on him."

"Mr. Riley, you continue to amaze me," smiled Catherine, admiringly. "I should have thought of that, too. I'll get my chores done and be ready when you are. I'll even let you buy me lunch," she added brightly.

****

Tex and Catherine arrived in Cravenville and found that Parks would be tied up in court until noon.

"Tex, I have some shopping to do, and I'm sure you don't want to get involved in that," said Catherine. "Why don't you wander around town, visit your friends, and I'll meet you at the Steak House at noon. I told you you could buy me lunch."

"Yes ma'am," responded Tex as he shook his head in simulated dismay. "Here you are orderin' me around like a henpecked husband, and I ain't even married yet."

"Better get used to it, my good man," retorted Catherine saucily. "You still have time to back out of our deal, you know."

"Fat chance I got of that," observed Tex with a straight face.

Catherine stuck out her tongue at him, giggled, and headed for Woods' Store, a big grin on her face.

Tex made a couple of stops to say hello to friends and finally ended up at the office of Sheriff Buck Buchanan.

The two men lit cigarettes, and Buchanan leaned back in his chair.

"I saw you and Catherine ride in," said Buchanan. "When are you goin' to marry that gal, Tex? The Rambling R has always moved faster than that as far back as I can remember."

"Not when it comes to marrying, you can't," laughed Tex. "That's one area the ranch has been more than a little shy on." He took a deep sigh before continuing. "It won't be too much longer, Buck, but we gotta wait for Catherine to clear up some things back in Ohio. We would like to have her folks and her sister come out here for the wedding, but that's a lot to ask of 'em. Her father runs a big business back there, and the rest of the family helps him. I reckon he figgers he can't be away for that long a trip."

"Have you thought about going to Ohio?" inquired the sheriff.

"Yeah, I even told Catherine I would do it. But she reckons her real friends are right here in Cravenville. The way you all welcomed her back and fussed over her made her feel right good. Besides, she taught school in another part of Ohio after she left here, and so she's really been away from home for over seven years. She's come to think of Cravenville as bein' her home and not Ohio."

"That's a good enough reason, right there," admitted Buchanan. "After what happened, I weren't sure she would ever want to come back here. I'm glad she didn't hold it against us, and I'm real glad she didn't get hurt worse than she did. That Norton fellar was a brute. If you hadn't killed him, I would have been tempted to myself."

Tex did not respond to the sheriff's remarks, as it was all he could do to maintain a calm expression on his face. No one but he knew how hurt she had been and what she had been forced to go through. It was their secret and would remain that way. And even Tex was not completely sure he knew the full extent of the pain and torment she had had to endure. He made a silent vow to himself—nothing like that was ever going to happen to her again, not as long as he was alive to stop it. He rose from his chair, shook hands with Buchanan, and ambled out of his office and down the street to the Steak House. Catherine was waiting for him, and they entered the restaurant.

"Where are all yore packages?" inquired Tex as they were seated. "I thought you were goin' shopping."

"Shopping doesn't mean buying, silly," responded Catherine gaily. "I'm afraid it's going to take me a lifetime to teach you all you should know about women."

"I reckon I just might sign on for that trip," grunted Tex.

"Good. Now that we got all that taken care of, let's eat. I'm hungry!"

****

Tex and Catherine arrived at the judge's office a little after one o'clock. After the appropriate greetings were exchanged and everyone was seated comfortably, Tex got right to the point.

"Judge, me and Catherine been doin' some talkin', and we got a proposition for you. Catherine will tell you all about it," he added, in accordance with a strategy they had agreed upon at lunch.

Catherine breathlessly outlined what they wanted to do, and at the end of her talk leaned forward in her chair and looked at Parks, somewhat apprehensively.

Parks crossed his arms, also leaned forward in his chair and returned Catherine's look, then switched his stare to Tex, and then turned back to Catherine.

"It's about time you two figured out what you should do," he informed them sternly. "Why do you think I've been dragging my feet all this time? I was about to give up on the both of you."

Catherine's mouth sagged open, and she looked at Tex in bewilderment. Tex was shaking his head as if to clear away some cobwebs.

"You mean you've been planning on this all along?" blurted out Catherine, still in a state of shock. "Why didn't you say something?"

"Because it had to be your idea," replied Parks in a matter-of-fact tone. "Why did it take you two so long to figure out what I considered to be a very simple solution."

"It was my fault, judge," confessed Tex with a grimace. "I've been so busy with ranch matters that I plumb forgot about Apache."

"No, it's *our* fault," interrupted Catherine as she searched for and found Tex's hand. Darling, we have been so wrapped up in our love for each other that we *both* forgot about Paul and what was best for him. If you give us another chance, judge, I assure you it won't happen again. Both of us very much want Paul to be part of our family, if that's his wish."

"I know that," smiled Parks. "I was giving you both a little test, and you both passed, if you will forgive me for using your educational format, Catherine. But we do have a slight complication," Parks added as a grave look returned to his face. "I can't do a thing until you two get married. Now, pray tell, when will that be?"

"I promise you, we'll get started on that problem . . . right quick, as my future husband would say," responded Catherine brightly. "First, I assume you want us to talk to Paul and get his approval."

"Yes, but I have to make one point very clear," replied Parks. "The Rambling R would be his foster home, and you two would be his foster parents. This would not be an adoption in the usual sense, especially since he is almost of age. I would, therefore, suggest that he retain his current name, unless both of you and he feel otherwise. Your jobs will be to nurture and sustain him and prepare him for the adult world. I am assuming, of course, that he will want to spend his adult world on the Rambling R, but that will be his decision at the appropriate time. Do you both understand all of this?"

Both Catherine and Tex nodded yes, and Catherine squeezed Tex's hand.

"There is one formality that I have to do," Parks continued, "but it should be just that, a formality. I'll have to question the lad about his wishes and whether he is in favor of this arrangement. Normally, I should also have a witness or two testify about the quality of life he would have on the Rambling R. However, I am obviously well informed about that issue, and we can dispense with it."

"What else do we have to do, besides bringing Paul to you so you can question him?" asked a thrilled Catherine.

"Set a wedding date and go through with it!" snapped Parks, but he couldn't keep his face straight after he said it. "I'll make the papers effective the day after you get married. Now, get out of here and get cracking!"

✳✳✳✳✳✳✳✳✳✳✳✳

Catherine nudged Tex as they began the trip back to the Rambling R.

"I'd marry you tomorrow, Mr. Riley, if that's what it would take to keep Paul with us. Do you feel the same way?"

"Yes, of course I do," Tex assured her, "but we gotta ask Apache first. Then he's gotta see Judge Parks. Now just calm down. We'll get it all done, and it'll be done right."

Catherine was silent for along time before she nudged Tex a second time.

"Darling, some time ago you offered to send Theresa the money to come out here. Is that offer still good?"

"Shore it is," replied Tex. "What are you thinkin'?"

"Well, as soon as we get back to the ranch, I'm going to write Theresa and tell her we want her out here . . . right quick. I would like to include a check so she can begin to plan the trip and let us know when she is coming. Then we can set a wedding date and get Paul taken care of. I'll tell her she should plan on staying here a month. Can I do that, Tex?"

"Course you can, honey," answered Tex with a grin. "But we better make shore that check is big enough to cover *all* her expenses, not just the train fare. Then she won't have no reason to hesitate."

Catherine's eyes filled with moisture, and she leaned against her driver.

"Have I told you lately that I love you," she murmured in his ear.

"Yup, but you can say it ag'in," drawled Tex. "I kinda like the sound of it."

****

Tex had picked up the ranch's mail as he wandered around Cravenville and noted that two had come from Idaho. As soon as he and Catherine arrived back at the Rambling R, the two of them went into the den, and Tex told Catherine to open the two from Idaho first.

"This first letter is from Curley," she announced as she quickly looked for the signature. "She handed it to Tex to read. She slit open the second envelope, flipped open the folded paper, and was surprised to have a check flutter out and fall to the floor. She glanced at the signature. This one is from Marty Johnson," she said and then grunted as she bent down to pick up the check. "My goodness, this is a check for $ 800. I wonder what it's for?"

Catherine began to read the letter, holding the paper in one hand and the check in the other.

"Marty says this check is to help cover your expenses on the trip to Idaho," she informed Tex. "My, wasn't that nice of him to do?"

Tex grunted his surprise. "Reckon we'd better send half of that on to Sanchez," he muttered, primarily to himself.

"Marty said he made a payment of a thousand dollars on the note," said Catherine as she continued to read from the letter. "I remember that Lefty said something about that when he got back from Idaho. What is that all about?"

Tex briefly described the arrangements that had been made when Slim had helped Marty finance the purchase of the MJ.

"Slim was quite a man, wasn't he?" breathed Catherine, sadly. "I had no idea he would do something like that."

"You said a mouthful there, honey," agreed Tex. "He done the same thing with Sanchez down there in Mexico. He wanted all of us to have a fair chance to do somethin' with our lives. He had no family or kinfolk, as far as I can tell, and so I reckon he just wanted to make himself a family of his own. I only hope we can do half as well, Catherine. Apache will be a good start along that trail."

Catherine moved around the desk, sat down in his lap, put her arms around his neck, bent down, and gave him a big kiss.

"I reckon you and I are looking forward to riding that trail together, pardner," she murmured.

****

Two days later, late in the afternoon, Lefty and his trail crew arrived back at the Rambling R. The chuck wagons were unloaded, the horse remuda was driven a mile or so out on the range to disperse and graze, and the men turned their own unsaddled horses loose in the corral and stowed their bedrolls in a separate area in anticipation of the laundering process.

Tex was late in riding in from the range, so it was after the night meal before the steering and planning committee met in the den of the ranch house.

Lefty dumped the greenback filled envelope on the desk in front of Tex as Paul and Catherine passed out mugs of coffee.

Tex thumbed through the pile of money and looked at Lefty, a frown on his face.

"I weren't expectin' cash," he confessed. "Is that the way they pay? . . . How come?" he continued as Lefty nodded his head in answer to the first question.

"Count it, and you'll see why," growled Lefty.

Tex did so and glanced at Lefty before repeating the procedure.

"There's almost a thousand dollars more here than I thought we'd get," he announced to the group, a combination of puzzlement and suspicion in his voice. "Was our weight that good?"

"Their scales said it was," sneered Lefty. "But that fellar Worthington told me that half of the thousand belonged to him. He didn't get it, though, and he was right upset about it. I figger them scales was rigged, and I'll shore find out how much when I go back next time."

"And Apache was told his people ain't gettin' enough beef," Tex mused, as he rubbed his chin reflectively. "Did Worthington try anythin' when you kept the money?"

"He had an idear of tryin' somethin' when I told him to come and get it, but he backed off," growled Lefty, his disappointment showing. "I was hopin' he'd try, but he didn't. I figger he'll have a surprise party waitin' for me when I take the next herd down there."

"I'm shore he will," agreed Tex, "and we'd better be ready for him. I figger we better have a few more guns along on the next drive, and mine will be two of 'em." He didn't see Catherine glance at Bronc Evans as he spoke.

"Will I still be trail boss?" asked a concerned Lefty White.

"You shore will!" responded Tex with a grim smile. "But you'll have three more men to boss around—me, Reno, and Laredo. I'll just be an extry hired hand along as far as you are concerned. I'll weigh myself on the scales at Crane's Feed Store in town just afore we leave. We'll check out Worthington's scales, and if'n it's like we think, you can have it out with him. If'n he's still alive and standin' after that, him and me will have a parley about how things are goin' to be done from now on."

"Do you really think the man is cheating all the Apaches?" interrupted a troubled Catherine.

"I shore enough do," replied Lefty, before Tex could answer. "That's why he wants half the money, Catherine. I'll bet it wouldn't bother him one bit if'n some Apaches starved because of him. I shore hope he has a surprise party all cooked up for me. He mebby will find himself dancin' to some Colt music at his own party."

Catherine could not repress a shudder as she felt the vehemence in Lefty's voice. Yet, she, too, felt an intense anger as she considered the possibility that Apache women and children, as well as the men, were not getting enough food because of the greed of a white man, especially a man involved in the administration of the reservation. Tex's voice penetrated her thoughts.

"Catherine, tomorrow you'll help me write a letter to the Bureau of Indian Affairs. We'll send them a check for a thousand dollars and tell them a mistake was made on our first delivery. I ain't ready to tell 'em they got a skunk at San Carlos 'til I can prove it. This way they can use the money to buy more food for them folks. I shore don't want dirty money here on the Rambling R. Does all this set well with you, Apache?"

Paul did not speak but nodded his head in agreement as he looked at Tex—pride, admiration, and gratitude in his eyes.

Sensing that subject had been pretty much exhausted, Tex spoke again to Lefty.

"How did yore water barrel idear work out, Mr. Trail Boss?" he inquired.

"Don't rightly know," grunted Lefty. "We got two rainstorms, and that helped aplenty. But I can see how we'll likely have a problem come summer and a real dry spell. So I did a little explorin' and come up with another idear. I found me a rocky spot and a little stream a few miles off our trail, not far from that rancher I told you about. I bought me some shovels in San Carlos, and me and the boys spent a couple of days doin' some diggin'. That's why we was so late in gettin' back. We dug ourselves a little sluice and a catch basin in them rocks. It's sorta like a . . . a . . . ."

"A reservoir?" supplied Catherine.

"Yeah, that's the word I was tryin' to corral," agreed Lefty as he shot an appreciative glance at Catherine. "We dumped four barrels in, and it seemed to hold the water. I'll look in on it the next trip down. It may not work, but I had to give it a try. But I'm not the most popular trail boss around these parts right now," he laughed. "Most of the blisters, includin' my own, ain't all healed up yet."

"You did right well," Tex told him. "It *was* worth a try."

"I still want to use the two chuck wagons and the water barrels ag'in," cautioned Lefty. "I'd druther have too much water instead of not enough."

"I agree," responded Tex. "Anybody got anythin' else to say?" inquired Tex as he looked around the room. Getting no response, he waved his hand and announced, "Meetin's over. Apache, you and Catherine stay a minute— we got somethin' to talk over." Lefty and Bronc left the room as Tex was speaking, closing the door behind them.

"Apache, you been away for quite a spell, and me and Catherine have missed you aplenty. Tomorrow we are all goin' on a picnic and get reacquainted. You reckon you can handle a day off from work?"

"I think I can," grinned Paul. "It sounds like fun, but won't I be in the way?"

"You certainly will not, young man!" declared Catherine sternly. "This will be a homecoming party for you, and you will be the most important participant of all. Now hop upstairs and get a good night's sleep. You must be exhausted from your long trip."

****

Late the next morning, Tex again hitched up the team of horses to the buckboard, helped Catherine and her bundle of goodies up onto the seat, climbed aboard himself, and urged the horses into motion. Apache mounted his own horse and rode alongside.

The little cavalcade reached its desired location, made a large dent in their food supplies, lolled around on the picnic blanket, and engaged in some idle conversation. Tex rolled a cigarette, lit it, and changed the nature of their talk.

"Apache, I was plumb serious when I said me and Catherine missed you aplenty. And I meant it when I said we needed to get reacquainted. I've told Catherine a little bit about you but not much. Slim told me about what happened up there in Hawthorne, but I never asked you to talk about it 'cause I figgered it mebby would hurt you a heap. Now that Catherine is here, we sorta got a family goin', and I reckon we both would like to hear more about how you grew up and such. Would it hurt you too much to tell us about Jacob and Ruth?"

"It's been a long time, and I guess I should talk about it," replied Paul slowly. "Your request surprises me somewhat, but it pleases me, too. And the fact that you think of me as being part of your family pleases me even more." Paul paused and stared at the ground a moment, trying to organize his thoughts. Therefore, he did not see the delighted looks that Tex and Catherine had exchanged.

"Jacob's Apache name was Turango," Paul began, "and my mother was Mourning Dove. She died when I was born." Slowly and carefully, Paul outlined what little he remembered about his first five years and the move to the San Carlos Reservation. But the memory of his years on the reservation was still fresh in his mind, and he eagerly described how Turango had trained him how to live in the desert, how to track, and how the two of them had met Ruth Tatum.

But the move to Hawthorne and the events that had taken place there were still painful to Paul, and his narration slowed considerably and became more difficult. Catherine slid over beside him and put an arm around him, tears in her own eyes.

"I never knew about the Holy Experiment, she admitted, "but it sounds like it was a beautiful idea. I did read a little bit about President Grant's Peace Policy, but I had no idea that it originated with the Quakers concept of the Holy Experiment. Jacob and Ruth were very brave to try to make it work, Paul. Take your time, my dear, and go on when you feel able to do so."

Paul did pause for a short time and then resumed his story. Now his voice became stronger and more vibrant when he told his audience about the role Slim Evers and his Rambling R men had played in the final outcome in Hawthorne.

"I even managed to acquire two uncles in the process," Paul laughingly concluded. "Best of all, I also found out I had a big brother, and he has been so good to me. The sheriff in Hawthorne told me I might find a good, new life on the Rambling R, and he was right. I have been very happy here."

Catherine wrapped both her arms around Paul and pulled him close to her bosom.

"Darling, I know Tex is very happy to have you as his little brother, and I happen to know that you were a tremendous help to him while I was gone.

"Paul, I have come back, and Tex and I are going to get married, as you know. We have something special to propose to you, but first I have to tell you something about me. You know I had some difficulty with Mr. Norton. I ended up with some medical problems, and now I cannot have any children. Even though he knew about that, your big brother asked me to marry him. He loves me very much, Paul. I sometimes wonder if I deserve all that love. But we both worry about how you think all of this will affect you.

"Darling, Tex and I also love *you* very much. When Tex told you that he thought of you as being family, he meant exactly that. We also think and hope you would like to stay on at the Rambling R and continue to make it your home. By chance, have you wondered about this now that Slim is gone?"

"Yes," admitted Paul. "I don't know what the white man's rules are when something like that happens. Will I have to go back to the San Carlos Reservation? Is that what you are trying to tell me?"

"Heaven forbid!" cried Catherine, tears in her eyes, as she again hugged him. "Quite the contrary. We have talked to Judge Parks, and he is willing to keep on designating the Rambling R as your foster home, provided you do one thing."

"What's that?" asked a puzzled Paul.

"Well, I know this may be a difficult decision for you to make," said Catherine softly, "but you'll have to let Tex and me be your foster parents. In other words, we want you to be our son, just like you were Slim Evers' son." Catherine drew back a bit and scanned Paul's face for some kind of reaction. She felt a twinge of fear when his face disclosed nothing.

Paul had been engrossed in listening to Catherine's words and remained silent for several minutes, while his mind processed what he had just heard.

"It is a difficult decision," he gravely admitted. "I see two big problems." And he paused again.

Catherine and Tex exchanged concerned glances.

Catherine leaned forward, placed her hands over Paul's, and maintained a steady look into his dark eyes. Tex dropped down beside her.

"What two problems concern you, Paul?" she anxiously asked.

"Well, first, I don't know how I will get used to calling Tex 'father' after calling him big brother all this time. And, secondly, I've just got to the point where I can call you Catherine instead of Miss Cornell. I don't know if I can handle 'mother' too."

"You rascal!" shrieked Catherine as she realized what he was saying. She reached out for him and, in her excitement, lost her balance, pulled Paul down with her, and the two of them rolled on the ground, Catherine giggling the entire time. Tex came to their aid, separated them, pulled them to their feet, and put his arm around each of them.

"I reckon we can solve them two problems right easy, Apache," he grinned. "But are you dead shore this is what you want?"

"Yes, big brother," came the impish response. "I shall do my best to put up with you two. If that means being your son, I shall just have to make the best of it."

A number of joyous hugs and kisses followed, and then Catherine grew serious.

"Paul, neither Tex nor I can take the place of Jacob and Ruth in your heart. That is not our intent. We simply want to give you the home they wanted you to have and the chance to live the Holy Experiment that they dreamed for you.

"Tex, I have a suggestion to make. I could feel the love Paul had in his voice when he talked about Jacob and Ruth. I know Paul was pulling our legs a bit when he mentioned his two problems, but he was making a valid point, whether he realized it or not.

"Paul, I think we could dispense with father and mother, if you agree. I would be honored if you would just call me Catherine, and I'll bet your big brother feels the same way about Tex." She looked at Tex for support.

"That would set right well with me, Apache," Tex assured the boy, "but it's yore call. We'll do it yore way, whatever you want to make it."

"I would like that, too," murmured Paul. "I think I would be more comfortable with Tex and Catherine. But I might forget and slip in a big brother now and then. Good habits are hard to break."

"I won't mind that a bit," laughed Tex. "I don't reckon many folks can have a son and a little brother all in the same package."

A happy Catherine rose to her feet and began to fold the picnic blanket.

"It's time my menfolk get back to the ranch and did a day's work," she declared loudly. "All this loafing has got to stop."

"Apache, we may have got ourselves hooked up with a slave driver," sighed Tex. "The Lord have mercy on our souls."

****

It was mid-February when Theresa received Catherine's letter. Her eyes widened in astonishment when she saw the amount shown on the enclosed check. It was obvious that their two letters had crossed in the mail; yet both sisters had written on the same subject. Theresa was both awed and thrilled by this coincidence and was barely able to contain herself during the evening meal. After the dishes were cleared and washed, she told her parents she had a matter to discuss with them. The three of them gathered in the living room.

"I now have enough money to go to Arizona," Theresa calmly announced.

"You what?" roared Lydia in disbelief.

"I said I now have enough money to go to Arizona," repeated Theresa in as calm as voice as she could muster.

"You can't have," snapped Lydia, anger replacing her surprise. "Harold, have you given your daughter some extra money?"

"No, I haven't, my dear. I'm as surprised as you are. Are you sure you have enough, Theresa?"

"Quite sure, father."

"Where did you get it?" Lydia demanded to know.

"Well, I won't lie to you, mother. Catherine sent it to me, and a bride has the right to pay for her bridesmaid expenses, if she desires, as you very well know."

"Where did she get it?" probed Lydia, only slightly less angry.

"She says she has become Tex's secretary and receives a weekly stipend," answered Theresa. "She writes his letters and helps him with his bookkeeping. She always was good with numbers, and she is an excellent writer."

"What else does he pay her for?" sniffed a bitter Lydia.

"Mother, that is uncalled for!" snapped Theresa. "I'm ashamed of you. She is *your* daughter."

"Yes, and I'm sorry I have to admit it," Lydia barked back.

"Well, I refuse to discuss it any further, if that's going to be your attitude, mother," replied Theresa calmly. "Father, I feel I have to give you as much time as possible to get some new help for the store. Will 30 days suffice?"

Harold Cornell had listened to the exchange between his wife and daughter and again was impressed by the maturity, the firmness, and the calmness exhibited by Theresa. His evaluation of her had again moved up several notches. His response to her question, therefore, was based on that evaluation.

"Thirty days will be fine, my dear, but I may not have a job for you when you return. How long do you expect to be gone?"

"Catherine wants me to stay a month, father. She says it will take 10 days or more to get there and a like amount of time to get back. I would think I would be gone all of seven or eight weeks. I don't expect or want you to hold my job open all that time. That isn't fair to you."

"Let me think about it, Theresa. We don't have to make that decision tonight."

"Very well, father. I've looked at the calendar and will plan to leave on March 17."

"I don't think you should go," said Lydia weakly, defeat now apparent. "You have no idea of what it's like way out there. Catherine told us about the ruffians that robbed the bank and the shooting and killing that followed. It doesn't sound safe to me."

"Catherine wouldn't want me to come if she didn't think it was safe, mother," responded Theresa. "Besides, she made it sound exciting. I'm looking forward to seeing what our west really does look like."

Lydia Cornell threw up her hands in frustration but made no further comments.

****

Catherine received her letter from Theresa and showed it to Tex.

"We did the right thing by sending her the money, kind sir, and I must thank you again for wanting to do it. How can I show my appreciation," she added, a devilish look on her face.

"I'll think of a way—by bedtime," answered Tex, a twinkle in his own eye.

"I can't imagine what you are talking about," came the response, amidst a hearty but melodic laugh.

Chapter 12

The United States mail service had also handled Zack Worthington's letter. A response to this correspondence came in the form of three riders who arrived on the San Carlos Reservation in late February. They sought out and found Worthington's office, dismounted, and the leader entered the building. He found Worthington at his desk.

"Something I can do for you, stranger?" asked Zack as he looked up at the sound of his visitor's entrance.

"Mebby. Are you Worthington?" drawled the stranger.

"Yes, I am," replied Zack as he leaned back in his chair. "You looking for me?"

"Yeah. Our mutual friend told me you have a job that needs done. Said you'd pay five hundred. My name is Matt Slade."

"Indeed I do," grinned Worthington as he happily bounced out of his chair and extended his right hand across the desk. "You come highly recommended. I didn't expect you quite so soon, though."

Slade met his grasp, pulled a chair closer to the desk, and sat down.

"Our friend said you needed help, and the five hundred sounded interestin'. So I came pronto. Am I too soon?"

Worthington pulled open a desk drawer, extracted a bottle and two glasses, and poured two drinks before answering.

"You're a mite early," he admitted as he handed one glass to Slade. "The herd ain't due for a couple of weeks. That will give you time to relax and enjoy the hospitality of San Carlos. You bring any men with you?"

"Yeah, I got two. But that ain't enough to run off no herd, if that's what you got in mind."

"No, no, no," protested Worthington, raising his hands. "But that ain't a bad idea as a followup. No, it's the trail boss I'm after. He run a blazer on me last month and took five hundred of my money. That's going to be your pay to take care of him."

"He'll be comin' back?" asked Slade in surprise.

"I don't rightly know," replied Worthington, "but it doesn't make any difference. He, and his ranch, got to be taught a lesson. Your target will be the trail boss, no matter who he is. That make any difference to you?"

"Reckon not," came the placid answer, "as long as the five hundred covers whoever it is. Why do you want him dead?"

Worthington described the confrontation, and Slade couldn't help chuckling.

"He caught you with bad scales," Slade observed and smiled at Worthington's reaction.

"My scales are none of your business," Zack growled, his face turning red. "Your only concern is that trail boss!"

"Hold your horses, Worthington," Slade cautioned. "I didn't mean to rile you. I just needed to get the lay of the land. Does this trial boss have a name?"

"Yes. He has a bad scrawl, but it's either White or Waite."

"Neither name means anythin' to me," shrugged Slade. "It ain't likely it would since I ain't been this far west before. A two-bit trail boss can't be anyone to fear, or he wouldn't be a trail boss." Slade laughed uproariously at his own statement. "By the way, me and the boys are goin' to need some expense money until this fellar shows up with his herd."

"I anticipated that," smiled Worthington. He reached into another drawer and tossed a bundle of greenbacks on the desk near Slade. "That's an advance of $ 100. You get the rest when the job is done."

Slade reached for the money, slid it inside his shirt, downed the remainder of his drink, rose from his chair, and headed for the door. He paused at the entrance and looked back.

"You'll get word to me in San Carlos when you need me?"

"Yes," answered Zack. "My Apaches will tell me when the herd is three days from here. That will give us plenty of time."

****

The preparations for the second drive were a duplication of those used for the first, except for the addition of three more men. Lefty had met with his crew during the eve of departure and announced that Tex would be his second-in-command, much to everyone's amusement. Earlier, he had talked to Tex.

"I aim to do some more explorin' on the way," he explained, "and I may be away from the herd for a couple of days at a time. Think you can handle things while I'm gone?" he asked, a serious expression on his face.

"I'll do my best, boss," responded Tex in a very grave voice. "How many lashes do I get if'n I get the herd turned in the wrong direction?"

"I'll have to think on that a mite," replied Lefty in an equally solemn tone. "That would be a right serious mistake, and the punishment would have to fit the crime. I just might have to send you off into exile and marry that gal myself!"

"I reckon I'd better not make no mistakes like that," admitted Tex. "I'll mind my P's and Q's, boss. Tell me, does the sun still come up in the east each mornin'?"

"I ain't heard tell of any changes along them lines," declared Lefty. "I'll check on that in the mornin'. Now, if'n I was you, I'd look in on that gal of yourn and spend some time with her tonight. I sorta get the idear that she ain't none too pleased about you being gone so long."

"Yore a plumb wise trail boss, Lefty," grunted Tex. "I reckon I'd better take your advice and get with the lady. I'll see you in the mornin'."

****

Catherine had cornered Bronc a few days after Tex had announced his intention to go on the drive. Her concern was obvious.

"Don't fret none, Catherine," Bronc told her. "Me and Trig won't be goin' along, but Lefty and Blackie will. I've already had a palaver with both of 'em, and they know the lay of the land. They're both right good gunmen, just as good as me and Trig. They won't let Tex do anythin' foolish. Now you gotta get used to this kind of thing and understand that it goes with the job. And you gotta make shore that Tex understands that *you* understand that fact of life. It ain't easy for any women to live out here. Trouble don't come as frequent as some folks think, but it does come ever so often. You gotta be strong, Catherine. Otherwise you might make Tex weak with worry, and that could be plumb fatal. Just trust me and the boys."

****

Catherine followed Bronc's advice and played her part well. But she couldn't completely contain the tears as she snuggled close to Tex the night before the drive.

"I'm going to miss you and Paul," she sniffed. "The last five months have been the happiest time of my life. I don't know how I'm going to stand not seeing you both for a whole month. It sounds like forever."

"I'll miss you, too, honey," replied Tex. "But I gotta go on the drive. It's my job, and I gotta help Apache's people all I can."

"I know," sniffed Catherine again, "and I love you for it. Just promise me you'll be careful and come back to me—and bring Paul, too."

"That's just what I'm aimin' to do," Tex assured her as he smiled in the dark. He, too, was more happy than he could ever remember, and he wasn't going to let anything or anyone change that.

Catherine raised herself up and gently kissed him.

"Darling, close your eyes, relax, settle back, and don't think about anything but us. Tonight I'm going to make love to you. If that doesn't bring you back to me, I don't know what will." She couldn't resist a giggle before she bent down and sealed his mouth for a second time.

****

Lefty waved his troop into motion as Tex and Paul rode up to the front of the ranch house, where Catherine, Maria, and Antonio were standing. Both Tex and Paul swung from their saddles as Catherine took a few steps and met them halfway. She gave Paul a big hug, kissed his forehead, and kept one arm around him as she turned her face toward Tex. She got the response she wanted and then released Paul.

"Tex, you take care of yourself and Paul, too. Bring our son home to me."

"I will, honey," grinned Tex as he and Paul swung back into their saddles. "Now you get our wedding all figgered out afore I get back. It won't be long afore Theresa gets here, and our day will come right quick after that. Maria and Antonio, you take care of my gal. So long."

****

Slade and his two men dismounted in front of Worthington's office as Zack came out the front door.

"The herd was only half a day away at dawn," Worthington informed them, with a satisfied smile. "It should be here by noon. You all ready to do your part?"

"Shore," came the complacent reply from Slade. "Concho, you ride out, meet the herd, and do what I told you. Blue, you stay here with me. Get goin', Concho."

****

Tex was riding the left point when a rider approached him from the south. "I'm lookin' for yore trail boss," drawled Concho.

Tex turned in his saddle and pointed. "He's the second man down, on this side of the herd."

"Thanks." Concho tipped his hat and urged his horse forward.

Tex signaled to the man behind him, pulled his horse around, and followed in Concho's tracks.

Concho reined his horse up alongside Lefty and asked, "You the trail boss?"

Lefty nodded as Tex and Blackie Smith pulled up next to Concho.

"I'm the trail boss," he admitted. "What can I do for you?"

"I got a message for you from Worthington," came the slow reply as Concho looked at the two new additions to the gathering. "He says he's got yore money and for you to come and git it. He says you're to come alone."

"He ain't counted the herd yet," countered Lefty coldly. "And I'll come when I get damn good and ready." He paused for a moment to let his words sink in.

"Besides, it's grub time, and I'm hungry. We'll mosey over to the chuck wagon, grab a bite, and then I'll go with you to Worthington's."

"I gave you the message," sneered Concho. "I ain't goin' to no chuck wagon. I'll tell Worthington what you said."

"You figger on walkin' back?" asked Blackie pleasantly. "Yore goin' to the chuck wagon, and if'n you eat or not is up to you."

Concho looked around and saw three sets of eyes boring in to him. "I reckon I could handle a little grub at that," he admitted weakly.

****

Worthington was pacing back and forth outside his office as Slade and Blue, sitting on chairs under an overhang, watched him.

He stopped in front of Slade, pulled out a watch, and swore. "They're almost two hours late," he groaned. "Something must have gone wrong!"

"Tighten yore cinch, Zack," drawled Slade. "Mebby the herd weren't as far along as you thought. No matter. He's gotta come here sooner or later to git paid. Concho will be along. Settle down."

Despite his words, Slade, too, was getting edgy.

He hadn't counted on this long of a delay and wondered why Concho hadn't returned with some information. He got up from his chair and examined the northern landscape, shielding his eyes with his hat. He was about to lower the hat when three riders came into view.

"Men comin'," he announced. He continued to peer at the horsemen as they drew nearer. "Don't see Concho," he muttered, half to himself. Worthington, too, was inspecting the advancing riders and suddenly he gasped, "One of them fellars is leading a horse, and it has someone slung over the saddle. Sure looks like Concho's horse, too."

Blue joined Slade, and both men watched the threesome get much closer.

"That shore enough is Concho's horse," growled Blue, "and that shore looks like him slung over the saddle. Wonder if he's dead."

Slade was wondering the same thing and getting more puzzled and angry by the minute. "Which one is the trail boss?" he asked Worthington.

"The one in the middle," replied Zack as he nervously wet his lips.

The three men reined their horses to a stop about 30 yards from the building, and Blackie pulled the fourth horse and its human cargo up alongside him. His left leg reached out and positioned itself underneath the two feet of the man doubled over the horse. Blackie yanked his leg upward, and Concho flipped over the horse and landed with a thud in the dust. Concho emitted a low groan but did not move.

Tex, Lefty, and Blackie dismounted and stepped forward a few paces.

"Yore messenger boy here didn't like our food, Worthington," said Lefty, "but he shore took a hankerin' to our whiskey. Course we had to pour it down him, but he didn't seem to mind much. He said you wanted to see me. What's on yore mind?"

Slade moved away from Worthington and Blue and faced Lefty. "Worthington didn't want to see you; I did. You took his money the last time you were here, and I aim to see you give it back, one way or t'other."

Slade's words lacked conviction, however. His professional eyes had quickly noted that the two men, one on each side of the trail boss, each wore two guns and that all the guns of the threesome, like his own, were slung low and tied down. This was not what he had expected and was more than a little disconcerting. The sound of Lefty's voice interrupted Slade's troubled thoughts.

"You must be Slade," observed Lefty. "Yore boy can't hold his liquor and did a lot of talkin'. Course he was prodded some, too. Mr. Cattle Buyer, here, figgered he had to hire a gunslick to help him with his stealin'.

Tex, you and Blackie make shore Worthington and Blue don't cut in. Slade, he ain't payin' you near enough."

With these words, Lefty slipped into a slight crouch and slid forward a few paces toward Slade. He continued his dialogue, but his eyes never left Slade's face.

"I'm gettin' closer, Slade—close enough so I can't miss. What's the matter, Mr. Gunslick—lost yore nerve?"

Slade was dumbfounded at the audacity exhibited by the trail boss he thought was going to be an easy prey.

For a few seconds he was mesmerized by Lefty's slow advance. "Damn you!" he yelled, and his right hand clawed for his gun.

A roar and a cloud of gunsmoke erupted from just above Lefty's holster.

Slade rose up on his toes, and his own gun spoke. But his gun barrel had barely cleared its holster and was pointed at an angle, downward. His slug kicked up some dust in front of his feet, and his body fell forward.

A stunned Worthington couldn't believe his eyes for a moment or two. Slade's demise finally registered with the man, and he took a step or two toward his office door. But he froze at the sound of a second shot, the whine of a bullet just above his head, and a shower of adobe dust. He turned and saw smoke drifting away from the Colt in the hands of the man farthest from him.

"Don't you move a muscle, Worthington," snapped Tex. "Blue, you drop your gun belt," he continued as he pointed at the man. Blue, too, was astonished by the outcome of the gunfight and did as he was told under the watchful eyes of Blackie Smith.

Tex sheathed his weapon and moved quickly to Worthington's side. Tex grabbed the man's shirt with both hands and propelled him in the direction of the scales.

"I'm goin' to try out yore scales, Worthington, and they had better be right," he growled as he continued to push the man toward his scales. The two men reached Tex's objective, and Tex shoved Worthington aside and stepped on the scales. Worthington looked around and found Lefty standing close by, gun in hand. Blue had moved up alongside Concho with Blackie close by, also gun in hand.

Tex fiddled with the weights and peered at the results. "I've gained almost 40 pounds since we started the drive," he muttered as he glared at Worthington. "You been cheatin' the Apaches for a long time, ain't you?"

"So what!" snarled Worthington. "Why should you care? No one gives a damn about what happens to a bunch of dirty, smelly Injuns!"

Whack!

Tex's right fist cut short the man's tirade and sent Worthington sprawling. Groggily, he half rose to his feet and caught the full impact of Tex's left fist. This blow spun him around, and he landed face down. Tex grabbed a handful of hair and yanked the man to his feet. Worthington swung weakly at Tex's face and received two vicious blows to his stomach in return. He started to sink when an uppercut straightened him up and drove him back against a rail of the holding pen. Tex moved in and launched two more blows directly into the center of the man's face. Tex stepped back, and Worthington slowly slid to the ground, bleeding profusely.

Tex used both hands to pull the almost unconscious man to his feet and drag him a few feet next to a small watering trough. He held Worthington upright for a moment, pushed him forward, and let go of the man.

Worthington toppled head first into the water and immediately began to thrash around in an attempt to raise himself. His head emerged, and he began to cough and sputter. Tex gripped the head, shoved it back below the surface, and held it in place for several moments. Finally, he pulled it back out of the water and let the half drowned Worthington collapse beside the trough, now coughing even more.

Tex gave the man a few moments to recover before he bent over, gripped the man's shirt behind his neck, and dragged him in the dust all the way back to the office building. He propped the mud-caked man against the wall of the building and looked around.

Blue, under Blackie's supervision, had dragged Concho's inert form over to the office building as well and had also propped his companion up against its wall. Lefty had holstered his gun and followed behind Tex in his journey from the trough. Lefty's face contained a grim smile of approval.

Tex waited for Worthington to quit coughing and then again gripped the front of the man's shirt with both hands and yanked him to his feet. Lefty opened the door, and Worthington found himself being propelled into the building. He collided with his desk, stumbled, and fell to the floor. Again, Tex yanked him to his feet, dragged him a few feet, turned him around, and slammed him into his chair.

"Now, you make out the right papers for our herd. There are 303 critters, and I want a check, not cash," Tex informed him.

"I can't!" protested Worthington as he gripped the desk with both hands to steady himself. "I haven't counted your herd, and we ain't weighed any of them."

"You had yore chance to count 'em, and you didn't do it," Tex grimly reminded him, "and yore scales ain't worth a damn. Now make out them papers!"

"I won't do it, and you can't make me," came a defiant response.

Tex made a quick movement, and the barrel of his gun came down on the back of Worthington's left hand.

Worthington screamed in anguish, and his defiant look was replaced with one showing intense pain.

"Who are you?" he managed to groan through gritted teeth. "Why are you doing this to me?"

"The name is Riley, and I run the Rambling R Ranch. You been cheatin' the Apaches, and you tried to get Lefty killed. Yore lucky I ain't killed you already. You started out with two hands, and now you got one. You got a mouth full of teeth. They're the next to go if'n you don't start that paper-work right quick."

Worthington's painfilled eyes moved from Tex Riley's livid face to Lefty White's grim countenance and back again. Zack now decided that discretion was the better part of valor. Besides, he had gotten this far in life because of his brains, not his brawn, and his brain was now working overtime since he was no longer the subject of physical abuse. He would outwit these bumbling cow punchers yet and get his satisfaction anyway.

Accordingly, he let loose a big sigh and nodded his head, a crafty look creeping into his eyes.

"All right, you win. I'll do the paperwork, but you'll have to hold the papers in place. I think my left hand is busted."

"It should be," agreed Tex calmly, "I hit it hard enough. Leastways, that's what I intended to do."

Anger replaced the crafty look in Worthington's eyes, and he was barely able to restrain himself from responding to this taunt. He managed to control himself, however, and began to do the necessary paperwork. Finally, he threw down the pen and said, "That's it. It's all done."

"Now the check," responded Tex as he read through what Worthington had prepared.

"I can't do that!" Worthington again protested. "There isn't enough money in the bank to cover the check."

"You got the cash here!" Tex made it a statement, not a question.

"Sure. It's in my desk. You can have all of it."

"I don't want it," snapped Tex. "But as soon as you put that cash in the bank, the check will be good. Lefty and Blackie will go with you to San Carlos just to make shore you don't forget how to make a deposit."

"I thought *I* was trail boss," grinned Lefty.

"You are," replied Tex. "That's why you're collectin' the money. As soon as the deposit is made, you trade Worthington's check for a bank draft.

That way he can't pull any tricks on us as soon as we head back to the ranch. Me and the boys will meet you back up the trail."

Worthington's mouth sagged open in astonishment. This so called bungling cattleman had seen through his plan and had checkmated him. Lefty interrupted Worthington's discomforting thoughts by pulling him out of his chair and directing him back out the door.

"Which one is yore horse, Worthington?" Tex inquired politely, "and which one is yore saddle?"

"The roan is mine," answered an irate Worthington. "My saddle is on the fence over there," Zack continued as he pointed out both objects.

"Saddle his horse for him, Lefty. Me and Worthington got one more thing to talk about."

"Worthington, I'll be comin' back with the herd in two months. When I do, I want to find them scales right or you gone. I was only playin' games with you this time around. If'n I find you here and them scales wrong, you'll wish you'd never been born. You savvy?"

✻✻✻✻✻✻✻✻✻✻✻✻

It was very late when a battered, angry, and pain racked Zack Worthington returned to his office. Blue and a partially recovered Concho were waiting for him. Slade's body was no longer in sight.

Worthington stiffly and slowly dismounted and spoke to Blue, "Unsaddle my horse and saddle your own. I got a job for you to do."

Worthington stomped into his office, located his pen and paper, and with great difficulty, composed a telegram.

Blue slipped into the room and waited for instructions.

"What happened to Slade?" Zack inquired.

"I buried him out back," replied Blue. "Didn't know what else to do with him."

Worthington nodded his approval and handed Blue a piece of paper. "Ride in to San Carlos and send that telegram. I suppose Concho better stay here for now."

Blue read the message and whistled. "Holy cow, you know Monk Allison?"

"We're related," answered Worthington. "His brother married my sister. I only met him a few times, but we liked each other. Now get going, stay overnight, and wait for a reply. Then come back here. Concho should be well by then. I'll want you boys to help me plan our next move. No one takes my job away from me."

✻✻✻✻✻✻✻✻✻✻✻✻

Tex returned to the herd, turned it over to the Apache handlers, and gathered the trail crew about him. He told them what had happened.

"We'll head back up the trail and camp where you did last time," he continued. "We'll wait there until Lefty and Blackie get back from San Carlos. Apache, I want you to ride south and meet up with yore people. Tell 'em about the scales and how they been cheated. Tell 'em from now on when the Rambling R delivers beef, they'll get what they pay for. Tell 'em about the trouble at the scales and how we took care of it. Tell 'em anythin' else you got a mind to."

Paul nodded his head and asked, "Can Ty come along again?"

"Reckon so, as long as you think it's safe," agreed Tex. "Tell him to leave his gun behind ag'in. Take as much time as you want to."

"Will you be going in to San Carlos to get supplies, like Lefty did last time?" inquired Paul as he waved at Ty.

"Yeah. I figger on laying over tonight and tomorrow afore heading back. We'll drive the wagons in to San Carlos tomorrow, fill 'em up, and go back to the campsite. Where do you want to meet us?"

"We'll catch up with you tomorrow night," said Paul. "That will give me plenty of time to do what I want to. I want to have a long talk with Chato about this whole mess. I'm going to remind him, too, about what Eskiminzin said to Slim almost five years ago."

"What was that?" asked a puzzled Tex.

"Eskiminizin told Slim he was a friend of the Apache Nation and that no harm would come to Slim and the ranch if he could help it. Chato must be told that you are a friend of the Apaches, too, and that no harm must come to you, either. I will prove that to Chato by telling him that you and Catherine want me to be your son. You want me to be part of your world, big brother, and I want you to be part of my world—the world that Turango and I knew. I told you I'm going to make an Apache out of you yet."

Tex silently stared at Paul, his eyes bright with pride.

"Yore one of a kind, Apache," he finally breathed. "Me and Catherine are right proud of you. Jacob and Ruth, somewhere out there, must be, too."

Paul grinned his appreciation and kicked his horse into motion. Ty Matthews did the same, and the two horseman rapidly disappeared from view.

****

Lefty White and Blackie Smith returned from San Carlos as the moon was rising. The two men dismounted, stripped their horses, grabbed tin plates, cups, and utensils, and heaped their plates with food. Lefty sat next to Tex and handed him a check after he balanced his plate in his lap.

"Worthington weren't none too happy about you changin' them checks," Lefty grinned. "I figger he was plannin' on crossin' us 'till you done him in. That was a good trick, Tex. I gotta remember that. I ain't too old to learn new tricks. I'm right glad you come along."

"I'm right glad of that, boss," laughed Tex. "I reckon I'd better come along ag'in next time, if'n you'll let me. I told Worthington them damn scales better be right or he'd better be gone."

"I can handle that end of things," drawled Lefty. "There's no need for you to have to make the trip ag'in. Besides, you got your weddin' to think about. I don't think Catherine would cotton to have'n you gone for another month about then."

"You do have a point, Mr. White," muttered Tex thoughtfully. "I will have to give that some thought."

"Speakin' of that lady," Lefty continued, "I'm plannin' on pullin' north and doin' some more work on our . . . res . . . catch basin. It may take a couple of days. Why don't you, Apache, Reno, and Laredo corral a pack horse and head straight for the Rambling R? You can save almost a week. Just don't go and get married afore me and the boys get there!"

"Lefty, I never thought of you bein' a romantic, but you shore enough are," said a delighted Mr. Riley. "Apache is due back here tomorrow night. We'll start out with you the next day and be on our way. I'll tell Catherine what you said. I reckon she'll have to figger out a way to thank you."

Chapter 13

Four weary horseman and their equally tired horses walked their way down the courtyard of the Rambling R Ranch in the gathering gloom of an early dusk. Reno and Laredo veered to the left, taking the pack horse with them, and headed for the cookhouse and its storage area. Tex and Paul continued on and slowly dismounted in front of the main ranch house.

Catherine flew out the front door, ran down the steps, and threw herself into the arms of her future husband. "I just spotted you from the kitchen," she gushed after a long kiss. She disengaged herself from Tex's embrace and hugged Paul. "My goodness, it is so good to see my menfolk again. You are back much earlier than I expected. Did everything go all right?"

"I reckon it did," replied Tex, "but we'll tell you all about it after we eat. Me and Apache are starved."

"I think we can take care of that problem," grinned Catherine as Maria and Antonio joined the happy group and added their own words of welcome.

The entire entourage made its way back into the house, and Tex and Paul headed upstairs to wash up. The two women marched back to the kitchen area, while Antonio untied the bedrolls from each horse and followed Tex and Paul upstairs, a bedroll under each arm.

Tex and Paul had just returned to the dining area when Bronc Evans burst into the room and added his greetings.

"Trig took yore horses back to the corral and will take care of 'em," Bronc added. "How did you make out at San Carlos?"

"All in good time, Bronc," replied Tex. "Grab a mug of coffee and set a spell. Me and Apache are right hungry."

"You gotta thank Lefty for us gettin' back so soon," Tex told Catherine between mouthfuls. "He said me and Apache weren't worth much on the trail and to skedaddle for home and get out of his hair. I told him to expect a reward from you."

Everyone laughed, and Catherine could not prevent a blush from sweeping across her face.

"Just what kind of a reward did you have in mind, Mr. Riley?" she demurely asked. "My favors do not come cheap, you know."

Everyone roared at her reply, and now it was Tex's turn to show a little embarrassment.

"I reckon we'll have to talk about that," he replied weakly.

After the meal was completed, fresh coffee was poured, and Tex, Paul, Bronc, and Catherine adjourned to the den. As soon as everyone was comfortable, Tex turned his attention to his private secretary.

"Catherine, we did run into some trouble down there, and we had to kill a man. It weren't what we wanted to do, but it had to be done."

"Were you the one who did the killing?" asked Catherine, plaintively.

"No, it were Lefty," replied Tex, and Catherine sighed with relief.

Tex went on to describe what had happened, and Bronc and Catherine listened intently.

"The man was deliberately stealing food from the Apaches and paying himself at the same time, wasn't he?" Catherine muttered, angrily. "You said you discussed the matter with him. May I assume the discussion was similar to the one you had with Mr. Stewart?"

"Yore assumption is correct, Miss Cornell."

"Do you think that will be the end of it?" Bronc broke in.

"I shore hope so," responded Tex. "I told him I'd be back in two months and them scales of hisn better be right or him gone."

Catherine caught her breath at these words and could not prevent a look of concern from making itself evident. Tex reached out and patted her hand.

"Don't worry none, honey. Lefty said I was such a bad trail hand that he didn't want me along next time. Said he would take care of our Mr. Worthington. He told me I had to stay here with you."

Catherine smiled her relief. "I reckon Mr. White does deserve a reward," she declared brightly. "We'll have to give that idea a great deal of thought, Mr. Riley."

Everyone again had a laugh at Tex's expense, and Bronc glowed inwardly. Lefty had certainly held up his end of their understanding perfectly. He looked at both Tex and Catherine and sighed his content.

****

Catherine snuggled close to Tex, and she, too, sighed her content. "You don't know how good it feels to be in your arms again, darling. I missed you terribly."

His right hand lifted her chin, and his mouth settled on hers in a silent agreement. They repeated the event several times before resuming the conversation.

"Lefty had no choice with Slade, honey," Tex murmured. "I hope you understand that. When trouble comes, you can't run away from it."

"I know, Tex," she whispered back. "It is very hard for me to get used to violence like this. I don't think I'll ever be able to accept it, but I do understand that at times it is a necessary evil. Besides, it could have been you, and not Lefty, involved. Why do men feel they have to kill over a few dollars?"

"I don't know, honey. I reckon pride and greed are right important to some folks. Pride is good if'n what you want is right—like runnin' a ranch and growin' good beef. But pride for the wrong thing, and mixed with greed, can be deadly."

A period of silence ensued before Tex changed the subject.

"How did you and the office work get along?"

"Only so-so," pouted Catherine in the dark. "You'll have to speak to your Mr. Evans about that. He caused me a great deal of pain and distress while you were gone."

"He what?" snorted Tex, in disbelief. "What in the world are you talkin' about?"

"Well, Mr. Evans decided to take Paul's place and supervise my riding lessons. He increased both the number and duration of these lessons. As a result, I was unable to perform my secretarial duties as well as I should have, simply because I could not sit down for as long as I should have."

"I thought . . . that Apache . . . had took . . . care of that," Tex blurted out between chortles.

"I sort of talked him out of a number of them," Catherine admitted. She raised herself up and looked down at her lover, who was still chuckling. "Well, I can see I'm not going to get much sympathy from you," she complained, in feigned dismay. "Maybe I should return to the guest room for the night."

"Don't you dare," replied Tex sternly, his face now under control. "You try sleepin' on hard, cold ground for three weeks after what we been doin'. I been thinkin' about you the entire time we were gone. You ain't goin' to no guest room, and that's final!"

"Your apology is accepted, Mr. Riley," Catherine responded coyly. "Your attitude seems to have gotten much better in the past few seconds." She snuggled back down beside him.

"I do have two pieces of important news for us, my dear," she whispered in his ear. "First, the ring came while you were gone, and it fits perfectly."

"Hey, that's right good, honey," came the pleased response. "I was gettin' a little worried about that. Where is it?"

"It's hidden away so you can't send it back if you get mad at me for shirking my secretarial duties. If you are a good boy and treat me right, I'll show it to you tomorrow."

"Hmmm," grunted Tex. "What's the other important news?"

"I heard from Theresa," replied Catherine brightly. "She was planning to leave Ohio on the seventeenth, but had to change it to the twenty-first for some reason. That was the day before yesterday. "She should be on her way here, now! Isn't that wonderful news, dear?"

"Yes ma'am," agreed Tex. "She should get here by about the end of the month. Have you got our wedding all figgered out and a date in mind?"

"Well, yes and no," answered Catherine slowly. "We need to talk about that. I know you'll have to do the spring roundup very soon, and we will have to fit the wedding in around that event. Theresa should be here by the first of the month, as you said. Do you have any suggestions?"

"The spring roundup is the big one, Catherine," said Tex slowly. "We gotta do a lot more branding, and that takes time." Tex paused and pondered the problem for a few minutes. "We could do half the roundup afore the wedding and half after," he drawled, half to himself and half to Catherine, "but that means we couldn't take no honeymoon trip for a spell."

"Darling, we've been on a honeymoon, right here on the Rambling R, for the past five months," Catherine reminded him. "I don't need any trip to enjoy our companionship. We have all we want right here. Why don't we give Theresa a chance to recover from her trip, let her get acquainted with the ranch, and you do half the roundup—all at the same time? As soon as she gets here and you figure out your time schedule, we'll set a firm date. Then you can finish the roundup. Does that sound all right to you?"

"I reckon that would work out right good," replied a pleased and relieved Mr. Riley. "It's the end result I'm after. I don't care how we get there," he laughed.

Catherine raised herself up and looked down at her lover. "You are very easy to please, Mr. Riley," she murmured before she bent down and covered his mouth with hers. "I hope you stay that way," she breathed after disengaging her mouth. He didn't reply but pulled her head back within range and caressed her lips with his.

"Who needs a honeymoon?" she whispered as he released her. She raised herself up on one elbow as her other hand slid across his chest, and her fingers started to play with the hair on his chest. "However, that subject does remind me of a problem we have, my dear."

"Huh? Now what?"

"Well, when Theresa does get here, I will have to move back into the guest room with her. I don't want to cause any more friction with mom and dad. Good Lord," she giggled, "I hope I don't talk in my sleep. You do understand, don't you?"

"I don't want to, but I do agree," replied Tex. "We'll just have to tough it out, Miss Cornell. But I reckon we should store up some lovin' to carry us through that difficult time. I suggest we quit talkin', get at it, and keep this honeymoon goin'!"

"I agree completely, Mr. Riley," came the contented reply.

****

After the noon meal, Tex sent Paul into Cravenville to deposit the check while he and Catherine met in the den and began to sort through the accumulated mail. Tex was a bit surprised at how little she had accomplished in his absence.

"It is obvious that you have thrown a wide loop as far as yore secretarial duties are concerned, Miss Cornell," came the mild rebuke.

"I realize that, Mr. Riley," admitted a contrite Catherine. "But Mr. Evans said it would be all right, and I have suffered severe pain as a result thereof, as I have told you. Isn't that punishment enough?"

"I reckon it will have to be . . . for now," concurred Mr. Riley. "But I intend to discuss this with Mr. Evans before I make a final decision. I want to know just how much progress you've made before I can properly judge whether that is enough punishment or not."

"Ugh!" exclaimed Catherine, with a frown. "I shall have to locate Mr. Evans and coach him before you speak with him. What kind of bribery works best with him?"

"You can ride, can't you?" exclaimed Tex, half in jest and half serious.

"Oh, yes. But not for a very long time nor for a very long distance. Mr. Evans says I am improving. But my behind is much softer than yours, kind sir, and it takes time for it to get acclimated to this new method of conveyance. Have you no appreciation for the sacrifices I have had to make for the good of this marriage to be?"

Both of them burst out laughing, and then she was in his arms, and a long period of silence ensured.

"Am I worth all those sacrifices?" he asked her softly.

"I shall have to ask Mr. Evans that question," she murmured in his ear, "especially since you have to get an opinion from him about my horsemanship. A turnabout is fair play, kind sir."

"Somehow, I don't reckon I'm goin' to win that one," Tex confessed as he released her. "Speakin' of that marriage, where are you on plannin' ours?"

Catherine reached for a chair, pulled it around the desk, placed it next to his, sat down, and motioned for Tex to do the same. He did so, and she reached for his hand.

"Darling, I have a big, big favor to ask of you. In fact, it really is two favors."

"Don't tell me yore goin' to ask for a raise in pay after shunnin' your secretary's work like you done?" exclaimed Tex in exasperation.

"No, no, no," laughed Catherine. "Hey, wait a minute. That's not a bad idea. A girl's parents are supposed to pay for a wedding or, failing in that, the girl is supposed to bring her man a dowry. I don't even have enough money to pay for my own dress. Perhaps a raise in pay is in order," said Catherine, an impish look on her face.

Tex squeezed her hand and became very serious.

"Honey, I ain't goin' to play no games with you on this one. This is goin' to be *our* wedding, and yore folks ain't goin' to pay for a thing. And the only dowry I want is you. You order what you want and don't worry none about money. I've waited too long for this, and money ain't goin' to be no problem!"

Catherine squeezed his hand in return as her eyes glistened. "I knew you would say that, my love, and I appreciate it. But the fact remains that we sent Theresa enough money to pay for several dresses. That was much more important to me than a silly old wedding dress. Besides, I should show you that I can be frugal. More than that, darling, I'm still not comfortable about ordering a big white dress despite what we have said and done. I'm sorry, Tex, but it simply does not sit well with me."

"What did have in mind?" asked a puzzled Tex.

"Well, I was thinking of using my new wardrobe," answered Catherine, the impish look back again. "You know—a checked shirt and Levi's."

A stunned Tex Riley paused before finding his voice. "You can't be serious," he began, but her laughter stopped him. He again shook his head in exasperation but couldn't resist a smile. "I said it afore, and I'll say it ag'in—this is goin' to be one interestin' marriage, Miss Cornell. If'n what you told me is true, don't you reckon you're tellin' folks somethin' they don't need to know? What do you have in mind?" he repeated.

"Two things, Tex.

"First, what you have just said might be true if we have a big wedding. I don't want a big wedding. Let's just have Theresa and Paul, Ollie and Elsa Woods, and us.

"Secondly, I'll compromise on the dress. I saw a lovely dress in Woods' store. It has flowers and other designs signifying the start of spring—a new beginning. That's what I want, Tex—a new life with you here on the Rambling R. Elsa said she could get a matching dress for Theresa, and the cost of both of them would be far less than a wedding dress. I told her to go ahead and order it.

"Darling, I've talked to Maria, and we could have the reception out here at the ranch—a barbecue, dancing, beer, the whole works. We can invite everyone for that but keep the wedding for ourselves.

"All of this will cost a lot, but if you give me a raise in pay, I should be able to pay you back by the time we celebrate our fiftieth anniversary. What do you say?"

"We can do all that *and* pay for a wedding dress," Tex assured her. "I can always give myself a raise in pay," he grinned.

"I know, darling, but I really don't want the dress, and I've told you why. I don't care what people think. It's what *you* think and know that matters."

Tex looked at the intense expression on her face and nodded his acquiescence.

"If'n that's what you want, that'll be the way it'll be. But you can change yore mind any time."

"Thank you, Mr. Riley," Catherine responded brightly. "Now, let's get to work. There's a lot to do. I had no idea running a ranch could be so involved. After we get our work done, I'll show you the ring."

✳✳✳✳✳✳✳✳✳✳✳

Four riders reined in their horses and dismounted in front of Worthington's office building. Several Apaches' ran up to the group, took the reins, and led the horses toward the little holding pen. Monk Allison had reluctantly relinquished his reins, and his eyes followed the equine procession toward the pen with surprise and uneasiness.

Worthington stepped out of his office and was followed by Concho and Blue.

"Glad to see you again, Monk!" came the booming greeting. "Don't worry about your horses. I keep a number of Apaches busy around here doing odd jobs, off and on. Even pay them 50 cents a day when they work. I get my money's worth." Worthington laughed at his own statement and shook hands with Allison.

"This here is Concho and Blue," Zack continued as he motioned toward his two companions. They came here with Matt Slade, and I told them to hang around 'til you got here. I figured you might have use for them. Slade is buried out back."

"Yore news about Slade plumb surprised me," Monk scowled. "You gotta tell me what happened. Meet my boys here—Keno, Jake, and Tulsa." Allison pointed to each man in turn and then glanced at Worthington's bandaged left hand. "What's the matter with yore hand?" he inquired.

"That's one of the reasons you're here," snarled Worthington. "C'mon inside, and I'll tell you about it. Concho, you and Blue show Monk's boys around and get acquainted. Monk and I have some serious talking to do."

Allison followed Worthington back into the building, drinks were poured, and Zack began his tale of woe.

"The trail boss beat Matt?" Allison blurted out in disbelief. "He must have been plumb lucky. Slade was good with a gun."

"Well, it sure wasn't lucky for Slade," replied Zack thoughtfully. "That trail boss sure looked like he knew what he was doin', though. It is a puzzlement."

"You want him took care of, is that it?" asked Monk as he filled his glass for a second time.

"At first I did, and if you can do that, too, I won't be unhappy. But it's the guy who called himself Riley that I want. Monk, he beat me up something fierce, and he busted my hand to boot. He says he's coming back and will do it again, only worse, if I don't get them scales fixed. I got a gold mine here, and I ain't giving it up. Riley's got to be took care of, and it would be best if it ain't done around here. I think I can keep the lid on as far as Slade is concerned, but another killing here would do me in."

"You say he runs the Rambling R Ranch?" asked Allison as he sipped his drink.

"Yeah. It's up near Cravenville," replied Worthington.

"Well now, why don't I take the boys and look over that town," mused Allison out loud. "Mebby, I can work out somethin' for you up there. That far enough away for you?"

"That would be perfect, Monk," said a pleased Worthington. "I would like to see it when you do it, but I can pass on that if I have to. Why don't you take Concho and Blue along with you? I don't need them here."

"I reckon I can do that," agreed Allison. He rose from his seat and ambled out the front door, Worthington in his wake. Monk almost stumbled over an Apache sitting by the doorway and swore.

"Damn injuns," he muttered in disgust. "Do you let them sit around like this and still pay 'em to boot?"

"He's just waiting for me to tell him what to do," said Worthington. Zack spoke in Apache, and the man got up and hurried toward Worthington's horse.

"They jump when I tell them to," laughed Worthington. "I told him to wash and scrub my saddle and trappings. They know who the boss is around here. They're nothing but dirt, and you gotta treat them that way."

"Yeah? Well I wouldn't turn my back on 'em, if I was you," cautioned Allison. "They said the same thing about Geronimo and Cochise, and a lot of folks didn't live to brag about it. Me and the boys will stay over in San Carlos and head for Cravenville in the mornin'." Allison motioned to his men as Zack spoke to Concho and Blue.

"Allison says he can use you boys. Concho, I'm sure you'd like to get back at them Rambling R punchers. Monk is heading for Cravenville, and you boys can go with him if you got a mind to."

Concho and Blue headed for the little corral and began to saddle their horses.

＊＊＊＊＊＊＊＊＊＊＊

The four Apaches squatted on their haunches and peered intently at Chato as he sat on his blankets and spoke to them. Their orders were explicit, their roles were defined, their mission was meticulously outlined, and their destination and its immediate environs were identified and described in no uncertain terms. Each Apache was to use his own horse and take one lead horse. Should trouble develop, they were to scatter and, if necessary, three would be sacrificed so that one would be sure to reach the agreed upon destination. Should scattering be necessary, they would reassemble at a designated rendezvous point, but under no circumstances would they wait more than three hours for their companions to arrive before proceeding to their ultimate destination. Chato and his men knew the area well, and several possible rendezvous points were identified in case of emergency. Chato had deliberately chosen men who could not speak even pagan English—a gamble he felt he to take. Three words were rehearsed over and over again—Tomad, Paul, Apache. The final questions were asked and answered, and Chato waved his hand. The four Apaches raced to their ponies, vaulted on to the backs of the horses, accepted the reins of the led animals from friends, and galloped into the night.

****

Lefty White and his trail crew returned, and Lefty immediately located Tex at his desk in the den and reported in.

"We had no trouble comin' back," he began, but before he could go any further, Catherine burst into the room, raced to his side, threw her arms around his neck, and gave him his reward.

"That's for sending my menfolk home early, Mr. White," she gaily informed him. "Tex said I should reward you, and I agreed."

"But I sent you *two* menfolk," Lefty reminded her with a straight face.

"So you did!" exclaimed Catherine with a big smile. "I must double the reward," and she proceeded to do so.

"Enough of this rewarding business," Tex complained. "Yore making me jealous. Besides, Lefty threatened to send me into exile and marry you himself. Don't encourage him!"

"Pooh on your jealousy," retorted Catherine, who was thoroughly enjoying herself. "However, you have been a good boy this morning, and I guess you deserve a reward, too." She swept around the desk, bent over, and gave Tex his due as Lefty found a chair and sat down.

Tex motioned for her to find a chair and do likewise as he turned his attention back to Lefty.

"You was sayin', afore you was rudely interrupted?" Tex glanced at Catherine and found her tongue pointed in his direction.

"We had no trouble comin' back," Lefty repeated. "We stopped at the catch basin and did some work on it. We gotta let the water run or it ain't gonna be no good to us. I reckon we'll be able to fill three or four barrels, if'n luck is with us. It will be a good ace-in-the-hole to have if'n we need it."

"Good work, Lefty," said a pleased Mr. Riley. "Catherine knows about you havin' to kill Slade, and she weren't near as upset as I thought she'd be. I reckon she's becomin' one of us."

"He brung it on himself," growled Lefty as he looked at Catherine. "But it's Worthington who's the real snake. He and I will shore tangle if'n those scales are still bad and he's around when I go back. I can cure that problem, right quick!"

"Let's hope he's gone and that won't be necessary," Tex murmured, as he, too, glanced at Catherine. Again, he was pleased at her calm reaction to Lefty's words. She really was becoming one of them.

Chapter 14

Each passing day brought Theresa closer to Arizona and heightened Catherine's level of anticipation and excitement. Her happiness was infectious, and all the residents of the main ranch house began to acquire the same fervor. Tex, in particular, watched her and glowed in the warmth Catherine exuded. She still had not identified a specific date, however, and Tex was about to bring up that subject at breakfast when Bronc Evans burst into the dining area.

"Tex, there are four Apaches down at the grove of trees!" he exclaimed. "They got a campsite set up, a fire goin', and they're cookin' their breakfast, big as all outdoors. They musta come in durin' the night. All the boy's are outside keepin' an eye on 'em."

Tex bounced out of his chair and issued some quick instructions. "Catherine, you, Maria, and Antonio stay here. Bronc, get Trig and stay with 'em. Apache, wait here a minute while I get my gun belt."

Tex raced upstairs, grabbed his gun belt, paused to swing it around his waist, buckled it, tied down both holsters, and returned to the dining area. Paul was nowhere in sight.

"Paul went out as soon as you went upstairs," said Catherine, fear in her voice.

Tex turned and raced out the front door, only to pause as soon as he reached the veranda. He quickly examined his surroundings as Bronc and Trig slid by him, going in the opposite direction.

The Rambling R men were scattered throughout the courtyard, and most of them were gazing at the distant campsite and Paul's form that had just reached that area.

Lefty White climbed the steps and stopped at Tex's side.

"Lefty, have the boys spread out and cover all four directions. Don't know what this is all about, but I'm goin' down and find out."

Lefty nodded his approval, descended the steps, and began to position the men. Tex slowly moved down the steps and began to walk toward his strange visitors when Paul turned, raised his arms, and waved Tex away.

Tex halted his advance immediately, and Lefty again joined him, with Blackie Smith at his side. They watched the discussion, which was calm at first, but the four Apaches became very animated for a brief period of time before calmness again returned.

After a long and tortuous 10 minutes, Paul turned and began to walk back toward Tex and his companions. The four Apaches resumed their cooking activities.

"Everything is fine, Tex," said Paul as soon as he got close to the three-some. "They are messengers from Chato and have important news. They need food and water for their return trip, and I promised them they would have all they could carry. Come, we must have a meeting immediately, Tex. I suggest that Blackie and Trig be included. You are in great danger, my big brother. I'm not sure you want Catherine to hear what I have to tell you."

Paul continued to walk toward the house as he spoke, and the three men were forced to keep up with him. Paul entered the building and headed for the den as Tex and Lefty paused to reassure their men. Despite Paul's words, Tex told Red, Rusty, Charley, and Kansas to position themselves with their rifles. The rest of the men were told to finish their breakfast and remain available for further orders. Tex, Lefty, and Blackie then followed in Paul's footsteps.

Catherine and her two male companions met Tex as soon as he entered the house. Tex motioned for Lefty and Blackie to continue on toward the den and told Bronc and Trig to do the same.

"What is wrong, darling?" asked Catherine, with concern. "Why are they here?"

"Apache says they are messengers from Chato, down there at San Carlos," replied Tex with mixed emotions. He paused, examined the face of the woman he loved, and made a silent decision. "Honey, tell Maria to make some travelin' food for them Apaches and then come in to the den. Apache says I might not want you to hear what he has to say, but I figger we're partners now and you got a right to hear what I hear. You and Antonio bring us all the coffee you can carry. We may be meetin' for a spell."

Catherine flashed him a look of appreciation and then dashed for the kitchen. Tex entered the den, sat down behind the desk, and looked around the room. "Coffee is on the way," he informed the group, "and Catherine will join us in a minute. Apache, I figger she has a right to hear what I hear, and so I told her to come."

Paul nodded his acceptance of Tex's explanation and patiently waited for her to arrive. After a short wait, Catherine and Antonio entered the room loaded down with cups, saucers, and a huge coffee pot.

"This will get you all started," she murmured. "Maria will have a new supply made in a little while."

Soon everyone was served, and all eyes were turned toward Paul.

"They are messengers from Chato," he began. "I guess my talks with him at San Carlos paid off, Tex. They have brought us important news. A few days ago, four more men arrived at San Carlos and met with Mr. Worthington. They stayed overnight in San Carlos, Concho and Blue joined them, and then all six men were supposed to head for Cravenville. Tex, their task is to find and kill you!"

Growls of anger erupted in the room as Catherine's hands flew to her face in horror.

"What about me?" snapped Lefty.

"They are to kill you, too, if it's convenient," replied Paul. "But Tex is the main target."

"It looks like Worthington ain't figgerin' on fixin' them scales," observed Tex softly. "That makes sense if'n he don't plan on seein' me ag'in."

"Chato said to tell you that if anything happens to you, Worthington will disappear and never be found," Paul informed Tex with a grim smile. "He said Worthington would die very, very slowly."

Catherine couldn't restrain a shudder at those words, but at the same time she did not feel the same degree of abhorrence toward the implied violence that was being described as she might have expected. Her man was now in danger, and she couldn't help remembering some of Tex's words from their discussions. Certain people had to be dealt with, and if violence was the only real and practical answer, so be it. She looked around the room, and the grim and determined looks on the faces she saw reassured her greatly. These loyal and true friends would not allow this to happen to Tex!

Tex had stolen a look at his beloved and was surprised at her serenity. She was handling the news extremely well. He glowed with pride and turned his attention back to the other occupants of the room.

"Anyone got any idears?" he muttered.

"I got one," stated Bronc quickly. "Me and Trig could mosey into Cravenville and tell Buchanan what's goin' on. He could be on the lookout for these skunks."

"Buck can't do nothin' but look," Tex reminded him. "Ridin' into town ain't agin the law."

"We ain't even shore they will try to take Tex head on," Lefty complained. "They might try to get at him by hittin' the line camps first or just the range riders, one by one."

"That would mean that we'd have to double the number of men at each camp and on the range, too," Blackie pointed out. "We ain't got enough men to do all that!"

"And we'd still be at risk," snorted Tex, disgustedly. "Look at what's happenin'. Six men plan on ridin' into Cravenville, and we think we are under siege. We think we gotta double our patrols, post guards, and quit sleepin' at night. The hell we will! That ain't the way the Rambling R has done things in the past, and it ain't the way we're goin' to do 'em now. Bronc, yore idea is a good one. You and Trig ride into town and tell Buchanan what's comin', but do it on the sly. Tell him to let us know when these hombres arrive. Once we know where they are, we can deal with 'em.

"Lefty, 'til we know when they get here and where they are, leave the line camps empty. If'n they decide to burn 'em down, let 'em do it. That'll be the excuse we need to do what we may have to do. Double yore range patrols for the time bein', though.

"Apache, see if'n our Apache friends might be willin' to do a little scoutin' for us. I'd feel a heap better if'n we had some extry eyes roamin' around the countryside to let us know if trouble is brewin'. If'n they agree, you go with 'em and be my messenger.

"Bronc, as soon as you and Trig get back from town, the ranch house, Catherine, Maria, and Antonio are in yore care. I ain't aimin' to be a sittin' duck for any longer than I has to. Once we get the lay of the land, *we'll* decide what comes next, not them. If'n they want a fight, they shore have come to the right place!"

Tex took a deep breath and looked around the room.

"Anyone got anythin' more to say?"

Silence prevailed, and Tex waved his men into motion.

Catherine remained as the other five left the room. This was the first council-of-war she had ever attended, and she was amazed at what had taken place. The nature of the required action to be taken was obvious to these men. Danger was to be met face-to-face with no thought of retreat. A threat to one man was a threat to all. The loyalty and devotion exhibited by these men was both profound and beautiful. She began to collect the dishes, her heart full of pride for the men of the Rambling R.

Tex remained silent as he watched Catherine do her work and leave for the kitchen. She promptly returned, and he motioned for her to sit on his lap. She responded, instead, by motioning for him to follow her. She walked out of the house, on to the veranda, and followed it around to the swing, sat down, and waited for Tex to join her.

Tex caught up with her, eased his body on to the swing, and put his arm around her. She snuggled up close to him and sighed her content.

"You heard some hard words this mornin', honey," Tex began. "I watched you, and I'm some surprised you ain't more upset. Are you shore you're all right?"

"I'm not happy with the news and what you and the men will, seemingly, have to do, of course," she murmured. "But I'm not as upset as I would have been four years ago or even two months ago. Maybe I'm beginning to better understand the world you live in out here. Tex, the time has come for me to tell you the rest of my story because it is related to what is happening now."

Catherine carefully and slowly described her experiences with Corey and Bruce McCall.

Tex growled in disgust at the conclusion of her tale.

Catherine quickly sat up and put the fingers of one hand on his mouth.

"Darling, I didn't tell you all this to upset you. Good Lord, you've got enough on your mind without me adding to it. I told you this so that you might understand me better. Evil can be anywhere. I found out violence can be back east just as it can be out here in Arizona. It's a different kind of violence for the most part, to be sure, but it is violence nevertheless. I didn't understand that at all five years ago, but I do now. As you have told me, we can't run away from it. You do what you have to do, and if something should go wrong, I do believe I can live with it. My only regret is that I didn't see this five years ago. We have lost so much time. But, as you told me, perhaps it was meant to be, and we are the better for it. These last six months have been wonderful, and I love you so much. Now, hold me tight for a few moments and then go about your business before I start bawling again!"

Tex did as he was told, their lips met in a long kiss, and then Catherine pushed him back.

"Enough of this dilly-dallying, kind sir. Your men will think you have gone soft. We'll continue this discussion in a more private setting tonight. Now, get cracking!" Catherine smiled as she repeated Judge Park's words.

Tex quickly bounced up, the swing reacted to the change in weight, and Tex looked down at his future wife as she gently swung to and fro.

"You are a thoroughbred!" he cried hoarsely and was gone.

****

The Rambling R had battened down the hatches and stripped for action. All of the men had been told what was going on, and the anger over Slim's death had returned at a fever's pitch. The line camps were left unattended, the range patrols were doubled, and each man rode with a rifle slung across the pommel of his saddle. Each man carried an extra supply of food and water in case he became stranded.

Paul found the four Apaches eager to be involved. Their food supply was replenished, and the group, now five in number, galloped off in a southeasterly direction to begin their scouting mission. Bronc and Trig were enroute to Cravenville.

Maria's kitchen had been the scene of intense activity all that mornin' as was the cooking facility adjacent to the bunkhouse. Sourdough Lampson and his assistant, like Maria, Catherine, and Antonio, had cooked large quantities of food for the immediate need of the Rambling R men and the Apaches and were preparing additional amounts as a precaution against an unknown emergency. In addition, a significant quantity of firewood was cut, gathered, and stored in support of all this activity.

Tex remained at the main ranch and began his personal preparations for the impending confrontation. He walked away from the house and past the little grove of trees that the Apaches had used as a campsite, thereby shielding him from view from the house itself.

He reached his desired location and immediately began to practice his draw. A few minutes after he began this ritual, he heard the sound of footsteps, whirled, and drew both Colts, all in one fluid motion.

"Not bad," grinned Blackie Smith, "but you can do better."

"What are you doin' here!" Tex demanded to know.

"Same as you," drawled Blackie. "Lefty said I weren't needed out on the range. You ain't figgerin' on goin' up agin that crowd alone, are you? Me and the boys will have somethin' to say about that."

"You and Lefty shore crowded me down there at San Carlos," Tex growled, his suspicions running rampant. "You boys are gettin' to be as bad as Bronc and Trig."

Blackie simply shrugged his shoulders, ignored Tex's comment, and began to imitate his boss's activity.

The two men would work for five minutes, rest, and then repeat the process. Right hand, left hand, both hands—the practice continued.

"This is all fine and good, but it ain't good enough," grumbled Blackie during one rest period. "We gotta do better. Hold up for a minute."

Smith headed for the grove of trees, examined several specimens in detail, pulled a clasp knife from a pocket, and carved a notch in each of two adjoining trunks. He motioned for Tex to move farther eastward and walked back to join him. He pointed back at the trees as he reached Tex's side.

"Them notches are the belt buckles of two of them hombres who are gunin' for you. You take the one on the right, I'll take the one on the left, and let's do it for real."

"They'll hear us, up at the house," objected Tex.

"Shore they will—what of it?" chided Blackie. "Tex, we ain't gettin' ready to go to no church social. As soon as the sun flickers agin your trunk, you pull and fire. I'll do the same."

****

Catherine finished her morning chores, filled a mug with coffee, ambled out on the veranda, found her favorite chair, and sat down to enjoy her usual mid-morning break. She had barely settled into the chair when she was startled by the roar of nearby gunfire. She jumped to her feet, spilling half the coffee in the process, and looked in the direction from which the sound had come. A whiff of gunsmoke caught her eye, and then she saw Tex and Blackie, standing but stiffly poised. Quick movements were followed by twin roars and more gunsmoke.

Mesmerized by what she was seeing, Catherine slowly slid back into her chair, forgot the spilled coffee for the moment, and continued to watch the two men. Three more volleys followed, and then both men spent some time ejecting the spent cartridge casings from their Colts and reloading. Those tasks completed, both men sheathed their weapons and headed back toward the house. Tex took several steps before he spotted Catherine sitting on the veranda. He hurried forward, bounded up the steps, and quickly moved to her side.

"Honey, I hope we didn't scare you . . . what happened to you?" His eyes had focused on the dark stains on the lower half of her shirt and on her Levi's.

Catherine's eyes dropped down, and she couldn't repress a gurgle. "I do look a mess, don't I?" she admitted with a wry smile. "Why don't you menfolk tell a girl when you're going to do some target practice?"

"I'm sorry, honey. Me and Blackie got carried away . . ." The look on her face was more than Tex could handle, however, and he couldn't hold back a burst of laughter.

At first Catherine glared at her man and then she, too, could not keep her face straight. Her laughter matched his, and then she slipped into his arms and exchanged a kiss with him.

"Go upstairs and change clothes," Tex told her and gave her a gentle whack on her behind to help her get started. "I'll get more coffee for both of us and set a spell with you." She disappeared from sight, and Tex leisurely headed in the direction of the kitchen.

Catherine sped upstairs, slipped off her shirt and Levi's and found that her underclothes had been victimized as well. She had almost completed her change of clothes when the thought struck her—he laughed and it was the first time he had done so since Paul had brought him the awful news. "I must remember that," she murmured to herself. "It was only an accident, but it reduced the tension. He has my love, but he needs my brain and any common sense I can generate as well. I can't help him much, but I must do everything I can. Mr. Riley, here I come, ready or not!"

****

Allison and his men camped a couple of miles southeast of Cravenville and discussed their strategy.

"We can't just ride into the town and start shootin'," complained Monk. "Besides I want this Riley fellar to know what's comin'. It'll make him sweat and suffer some for what he done to Zack. Me and Keno will ride into Cravenville and put up at the hotel, if they got one. Concho, you and Blue give us a couple of hours head start and then ride in, too. Jake, you and Tulsa stay here 'till I figger out what we do next.

"The first thing we gotta do is find out all we can about Riley and his ranch. Concho, you and Blue make out like yore lookin' for jobs and nose around. The saloons will be yore best bet, but don't drink to much." Monk's eyes bored into Concho when he spoke these last words, and Concho nodded in return.

"Me and Keno will act like we is cattle buyers and do the same. We'll meet, accidental-like, and go over things afore you boys head back to camp," he went on as he motioned to Concho and Blue. "Everybody got it straight? All right, hit yore blankets. It's been a long ride, and I'm tuckered."

****

The next morning Allison and his men began to implement his plan. Monk and Keno rode into Cravenville, registered at the Regal Hotel, and began to circulate in the town. Concho and Blue arrived two hours later and followed the same procedure. The four men "accidently" ran into each other at the Steak House and had adjoining tables. Concho and Blue returned to the campsite after the night meal while Monk and Keno wandered into the Black Jack Saloon, took possession of a corner table, ordered drinks, and reviewed their activities of the day.

"This is goin' to be a tougher job than I figgered on," muttered Monk in a low voice after their drinks had arrived. "This Rambling R is a bigger spread than I counted on. They must have more'n 20 punchers on their payroll."

"Yeah, and from what I found out, Slade gettin' himself killed may not have been no accident," added Keno. "I hear tell this White fellar is damn good with a gun, and there may be a couple more like him out at the ranch."

"And White ain't the foreman!" exclaimed Allison. "If he's that good, he oughter be foreman. It don't make no sense, Keno." Allison rubbed his chin, reflectively.

"Riley must be better'n him," suggested Keno.

"That's what I'm begginin' to wonder," drawled Monk, not at all pleased with Keno's remark. "It's a cinch we can't ride out to the ranch and cut loose. I gotta bad feelin' that most of us might not come out of that alive. No, we can't go to him and his gang. We gotta figger a way to get him to come to us here in town." Allison continued to rub his chin reflectively and poured himself another drink. A long period of silence ensued.

Monk and Keno were still mulling over their dilemma when a man approached their table, a bottle of whisky in one hand. He set the bottle down, pulled a chair close to the table, and sat down.

"We don't want no joiners," declared Allison, with a sneer.

"Even if he bears free drinks?" smiled the man. "My name is Stewart, and I own this place. I'll fill your glasses."

Stewart poured the drinks and raised his glass.

"To your good health, gentlemen," he intoned and sipped the beverage. "You boys are strangers in town," he continued. "Anything I can do to make you feel at home?"

"Don't rightly know," replied Allison cautiously as he, too, sipped his drink. "You do this for all the strangers who come acallin'?"

"No, not everyone," smiled Stewart. "You boys been asking some questions about the Rambling R and its foreman. I've lived here for over 20 years. Perhaps I can be of some help to you, Mr. . . ?"

"Allison. I buy cattle, and I'm just passin' through. Thought I'd find out some things about the ranches in this area as long as I'm here."

"No offense, Mr. Allison, but your inquires have only concerned the Rambling R. I don't think you're a cattle buyer at all!"

Monk raised up in his chair and glared at Stewart. "I don't like them words, and I don't need any more of yore whiskey."

"Simmer down, Mr. Allison. I told you I meant no offense," drawled Stewart and again smiled. "Like I said—I may be of help to you. What do you want to know?"

Allison stared at his host for a few moments and shrugged his shoulders. "You know this Riley fellar?"

"Unfortunately, I do," snapped Stewart as the smile faded from his face. "I hate the man. He gave me a terrible beating a number of years ago, and I do not possess the strength nor the skill to reciprocate. What do you want to know about him?"

"He seems to like beatin' up people," agreed Monk. "He did it to a friend of mine a while back—down at San Carlos. Is he good with a gun?"

"He's the best around here as far as I tell, Mr. Allison. If you've got any ideas along them lines, you'd better think twice. He's buried a number of good gunslingers—in Texas, around here, and in Idaho, if the gossip is accurate."

Allison frowned in response to these words and remained silent for a few moments. "I'm purty good, myself," he muttered.

"I suspect you are," agreed Stewart in an oily voice. "But if you got any plans along that line, don't do it out at the Rambling R. They are a tough crew, and there are a lot of them. You two wouldn't stand a chance."

"Keno here and me were figgerin' the same way," agreed Monk, now using a much friendlier tone of voice. "We need to get him to come to town and do it here. You got any idears?"

Stewart remained silent and toyed with his glass. Allison reached for the bottle and filled Keno's glass as well as his own. Stewart continued his meditation.

"There is a gal out at the ranch . . .," he began.

"Yeah," interrupted Allison, "Concho said somethin' about that. Who is she, and what is she doin' out there?"

"Those are very good questions," came the response. "She was a school teacher here a few years back," Stewart went on. "She was the main reason I got beat up by Riley. She left here sudden-like and popped up back here again about six months ago. Everyone around here thinks she's Riley's gal, but they ain't got married yet. Some folks are wonderin' just what she *is* doing out there."

Allison stared at Stewart as his companion picked up on the hint.

"Mebby Riley is smarter than we think," leered Keno. "He keeps a whore on the premises to take care of him and his men. Hell, I wouldn't mind that myself. Is she a good looker?"

"Good enough," replied Stewart as he studied Allison's face.

"I'm wonderin' if mebby we ain't found us a way of gettin' Riley to come to town," grunted Allison with a thin smile. "That gal may be the best bet we got. Tomorrow we'll play that card for all it's worth and see what happens. Where there's smoke, there should be some fire."

"You've been right helpful, Mr. Stewart," Monk continued. "What can I do for you?"

"You get Riley, and that will be plenty," growled Stewart. "I don't know what your friend may be paying you, but I'll add a thousand dollars when I see Riley dead—and I don't care how you do it! Will that make your trip worthwhile?"

"I reckon so," responded a surprised but pleased Allison. "Finish yore drink, Keno, and Lets get goin'. I'm thinkin' that tomorrow is goin' to be a right interestin' day."

Chapter 15

It was after dark when Sheriff Buck Buchanan trotted his horse down the Rambling R's courtyard and turned at the sound of hoofbeats behind him. A hard riding Paul Redstone swept by him, pulled his horse to a quick stop in front of the ranch house, and swung from the saddle.

"Hold on, Apache!" yelled Buchanan as he urged his horse into a faster gait.

Paul stopped and waited for Buck to reach him and dismount. Lefty White and Blackie Smith emerged from the bunkhouse and moved toward the twosome as Bronc Evans and Trig Mansfield rose from chairs in the veranda and waited for the enlarged group to mount the porch steps and reach him.

"Tex and Catherine are in the den," Bronc informed one and all as he held the screen door open. "Go on in. I reckon we got a lot to talk about."

The group jammed the den as additional chairs were brought in and mugs of coffee were passed around. Finally, when all were settled, Tex turned his attention toward the sheriff.

"You got any news for us, Buck?"

"I think so, Tex," replied Buchanan. "Four strangers were in town today, but they came in two at a time and a couple hours apart. All four of 'em wandered around town off and on all day and asked questions—mostly about you and the Rambling R. Two of my deputies and me left our badges behind and wandered around with them—not all the time, of course."

Buchanan described the four men, and Lefty's eyes lit up. "Don't know them first two, but them last two shore sound like Concho and Blue. It looks like our friends shore knew what they was talkin' about."

"The other two are camped about two miles southeast of Cravenville," spoke up Paul. "My friends and I found them easily, and we've been watching them since noon. The last two you described got back just before I left."

"Well, we know they're here and where they are," said Tex. He did not see Bronc and Trig exchange glances. "Anybody got any idear of what we do next?"

"I'll keep an eye on 'em, Tex," offered Buchanan. "As long as they don't break the law, though, that's all I can do."

"That's plenty, Buck," Tex assured the sheriff. "It's our problem for now, not yourn."

"One more thing, Tex. Them first two hombres are stayin' at the hotel. They spent some time in the Black Jack last night. Stewart brung them a bottle and spent a lot of time palavering with 'em."

"Stewart, huh! Ain't that interestin'," mused Tex. "I don't reckon Mr. Stewart has forgotten that little parley me and him had some time back."

"It weren't no parley, and you damn near killed the man!" retorted the sheriff. "You shore didn't intend for him to forget it!"

"No, I didn't," agreed Tex with a thin smile. "But mebby he needs some remindin'. That can come later, though. Buck, you got anythin' else to tell us?"

"No."

"All right. Why don't you head back to town. I don't reckon you want to hear what we talk about from now on anyway."

"I'm shore I don't," the sheriff confessed with a wry smile. "I'll come back tomorrow night or send Chuck Corwin. Good luck to all of you, especially you, Tex."

Buchanan left the room and was escorted to his horse by Bronc Evans.

"You boys don't miss a bet," he muttered as he pulled himself up and into his saddle. Bronc watched him depart before returning to the den.

"Buchanan's gone," he reported. "The parley can go on."

"Good. Anybody got any more idears?" Tex asked.

"Yeah, I got one," responded Bronc. "I think me and Trig should head for Cravenville tomorrow and look over them skunks. The more of us who know what they look like, the better off we'll be. You and Lefty and Blackie have seen two of 'em, but the rest of us ain't laid eyes on any of 'em."

"That is a good idear," said Tex, "pervided you don't start anythin'. We gotta lay low 'til we find out what they're up to. Then we'll do what we have to do."

"We won't start nothin'," replied Bronc, a little miffed at Tex's comment. "You know me better than that."

"I *do* know you, and that's why I said what I did," laughed Tex. "I also remember what you told me up there in Idaho, my good friend. Go to town, but play it tight and close."

A somewhat mollified Bronc Evans nodded his acceptance of those conditions and avoided looking at Catherine.

"I'll stay here overnight and rejoin my friends in the morning," said Paul, "unless you have something better for me to do?"

"No. I reckon that's the best job for you to handle," came the response as Tex looked at the boy with an intense feeling of pride. "Just try to hold a tight cinch on them Apaches. I don't want them gettin' in trouble over us. I owe Chato plenty already. Anybody else have somethin' to say?"

No response was forthcoming, and Tex waved his audience into motion. The Rambling R's second council-of-war had come to a close.

※※※※※※※※※※※※

Monk Allison had experienced a restless night, much to Keno's silent disgust. Matt Slade's death at the hand of a trail boss had been surprising enough, but to now find out that the Rambling R's foreman was probably an experienced gunman was even more so. Allison's plan to have Riley fret and stew about an impending confrontation was not likely to succeed. On the contrary, and even Allison wasn't really cognizant of this fact as yet, a small sliver of doubt had made a tiny inroad in his own brain.

Nevertheless, the thought of facing a top-notch gunman had also acted as a powerful stimulant, and his restlessness was partly the product of this prospect as well.

Allison finally fell into a deep sleep and had to be roused by Keno.

"First, you don't sleep at all," grumbled Keno, "and then I can't get you to wake up. C'mon, get dressed. I'm hungry as a hog."

"You always eat like a hog," retorted Allison, but he, too, now felt the pangs of hunger. He quickly dressed, strapped on his gun belt, tied down his holster, and followed his companion down to the hotel dining room. Both men were surprised to find Concho and Blue already eating and selected a table adjacent to that of their confederates.

Between giving and receiving breakfast orders, the four men exchanged a whispered conversation.

Concho and Blue had decided to eat at the hotel instead of at their camp and, therefore, had arrived early, seeking new instructions.

Allison told them what he and Keno had learned from Stewart and what the plan of action would now be. Concho and Blue listened attentively, nodded their agreement, paid their bill, and left the room. Monk and Keno ate at a leisurely pace before doing the same thing.

All four men slowly wandered around the town—sometimes in twos, sometimes individually. They would cautiously raise the subject of Catherine and her long sojourn out at the Rambling R, and if they received the least bit of encouragement or agreement, they would pursue this line of conversation even further. A few times two of the men would meet "accidently" in a public place and initiate the subject among themselves. While a number of their attempts fell on deaf ears, a like amount seemed to fall on fertile ground. By mid-afternoon, Allison decided they had done enough to get the ball rolling and told Concho and Blue to go back to camp. Keno declared he was going back to the hotel to take a nap, and so Allison decided to pay another visit to the Black Jack Saloon and enhance his relationship with its owner-gambler. He pushed open the swinging doors, waited for his eyes to adjust to the change in brightness, and was astonished to see a face he recognized sitting at a nearby table.

Still not sure his eyes hadn't deceived him, Allison walked over to the table and looked at the man more closely.

"Bronc Evans!" he breathed. "What in hell are you doin' here?"

"Just enjoyin' a drink and some relaxation," smiled Bronc. "Set down and let me buy you a drink." Bronc waved to the bartender.

Allison sat down and stared at Mr. Evans, still showing surprise.

"I lost track of you years ago," Monk admitted. "Seems like I remember you leavin' the Rangers about then. Whatever happened to yore pal, Mansfield?"

"Trig and I left the Rangers together and drifted west," replied Bronc, his face a mask. "What you been doin'?"

"Well, things got a little warm for me in Texas, as you know," Monk replied. "I drifted north and spent a few years in Kansas—around Abilene and Dodge City. I went back to Texas when things cooled off there. The last year or so I've split my time between New Mexico and Arizona."

"You seem to have done all right," Bronc observed.

"I've made a livin'," admitted Allison. "What have you and Trig been doin'?"

"Well, we decided Ranger life weren't for us," replied Bronc. "We figgered punchin' cows had to be a more peaceful way of life. It's shore worked out that way for us."

"You must be a foreman of a spread by now," suggested Monk.

"Nope. Never did like a foreman's job," grinned Bronc. "Too much responsibility and paperwork for me. I like the simple life—gettin' up, fillin' my own saddle, and mindin' my own business. I 'spect to live to be a hundred thataway."

Allison laughed at Bronc's words. "Speakin' of foremen, do you know a fellar named Riley?" he asked.

"Shore I do," boomed Bronc. "Right well, too, seein' as how I work for him."

"You work . . . at the Rambling R?" burst out a surprised Allison.

"Shore do," smiled Bronc. "So does Trig." Bronc leaned forward over the table and lowered his voice considerably. "That's the real reason I ain't no foreman," he confided to Monk. "You see, Riley is the foreman out there, and I saw him in action once when me and Trig first got here. I shore lost any idears I had about bein' foreman out there right quick. If'n it was to come to a showdown between him and me, I was a goner. You know how good I was, Monk, and I'm better now. But I ain't comin' on to that man." Bronc settled back in his chair and watched Allison through narrowed eyes.

A stunned Allison couldn't conceal his surprise. Bronc Evans afraid to take on Riley? It was a very disturbing turn of events. Allison knew how good Evans had been. Monk, himself, would have been hard pressed to face this man at that time. Evans said he was better now and still didn't feel confident about taking on Riley!

Bronc knew what was going on in Allison's mind and decided not to push it any further. He finished his drink, rose, dropped some coins on the table, and looked at Allison.

"Nice runnin' into you, Monk. It brought back some interestin' memories. See you around."

Allison gave him a half hearted nod in response, and Bronc left the saloon, a smirk on his face. He located Trig, and soon the two friends were headed back to the Rambling R. Bronc described a plan he had in mind, and Trig nodded his agreement.

Toby Green, on a galloping horse, passed them going in the opposite direction.

****

Catherine tore open the telegram Toby had delivered and squealed with delight. "Theresa will be here the day after tomorrow!" she cried.

Tex smiled at her excitement as Maria waddled into the den to seek the cause of Catherine's outcry.

"My sister, Theresa, will be arriving day after tomorrow," repeated Catherine for Maria's benefit. "Oh, I'm getting so excited." she looked at

Tex. "Darling, get your roundup schedule worked out. We'll want to talk to Reverend Price when we go in to pick up Theresa."

"Yes, my dear," grinned Tex. "Me and Lefty will figger it all out tomorrow mornin'. The boys have already started to bunch the cattle. As soon as we get our problem took care of, we'll get right back at it."

"Oh, Tex, I'm sorry," gasped Catherine in embarrassment. "I had forgotten all about that for a moment. Please forgive me, my dear. I didn't mean to be selfish." She rushed to him and threw her arms about his neck. He gave her a bear hug before releasing her.

"Don't fret none, honey. I'm as happy as you are, and I want you to set the date as much as you do. Let's go over them last two letters, and then it'll be time to get ready for supper."

****

Sheriff Buchanan again visited the Rambling R after dark, and again the den was crowded with human beings, although this time Paul was not among them.

"I reckon Apache ain't got nothin' new to report or he would be here," said Tex as he began the meeting. "Buck, what do you have to tell us?"

Buchanan sighed, shook his head, and glanced at Catherine.

"Human bein's are funny animals," the sheriff nervously began. "Most of the time the folks in town are good people and do the right thing. Once in a while, though, when they get confused or puzzled, some folks say things they don't really mean."

"What are you tryin' to say, Buck?" snorted a perplexed Tex Riley.

Buchanan sighed and glanced at Catherine a second time.

"Tex, them four strangers spent most of the day wandering through town, askin' questions, and sayin' things to get people riled up."

"About me?" grunted Tex.

"No. About Catherine."

"Catherine? What does she have to do with this?" snapped Tex. He looked at his intended, who was also astonished.

"It ain't pretty what they been saying, Tex, and I'm ashamed to have to tell you," said Buchanan, burning with embarrassment. "Some folks don't understand why she's been out here so long without you two gettin' married. It ain't none of their business, but that's how it is. What's worse, them strangers have been hintin' she's been paid to stay out here, and you know what they mean by that."

Growls erupted from all areas of the room as Catherine's mouth sagged open in amazement and her face turned red.

Tex had remained silent but reached out and took her hand.

"Oh, Tex, I should have married you months ago," blurted Catherine, tears in her eyes. "We shouldn't have waited for Theresa. Everywhere I go, trouble seems to follow me. Now I've brought it to you."

"Stop it, Catherine!" commanded Tex, but he quickly lowered his voice and squeezed her hand. "It ain't you, honey. Yore the excuse, not the reason. In fact, you've done us a big favor. We know what their game is now, and we can take care of it."

"Tex is right, Catherine," piped up Lefty. "Them coyotes are using you to get at Tex. They don't want to come out here—there are too many of us. But we gotta keep some men here to protect the ranch, and they know it. They want Tex to come to town. They figger they got a better chance at him there—more places to ambush him from, if'n they got a mind to."

Tex nodded his agreement with Lefty's assessment of the situation.

"We got another problem," he added. "Catherine's sister, Theresa, is due to arrive in Cravenville the day after tomorrow. I don't want her to see or hear any gunplay. Catherine's folks don't think we are civilized out here as it is. I don't want to make things worse for 'em. I reckon the answer is purty simple. Tomorrow I go to town."

"Me and Trig went to town today, like I told you we would," said Bronc. "We looked over them gents. The leader's name is Allison. The rest of them take orders from him."

"That's what I learned, too," echoed Buchanan. He and a fellow named Keno are stayin' at the hotel, but the other two ride in each mornin'." Buchanan was surprised that Bronc did not say anything about his meeting with Allison in the Black Jack, but decided not to mention it. Perhaps Bronc would bring that up later or wanted to talk to Tex privately about it.

"You ain't goin' into Cravenville alone, Tex," interrupted Lefty. "Me and the boys have cards in this game."

"Yore plumb right about that," agreed Tex. "I'll ride in alone, but you all will get there before me. Yore job will be to make shore none of Allison's men can cut in and bushwhack me. Lefty, I'll let you and Bronc figger that out. I don't want anythin' takin' my attention away from Allison."

Words of assurance came from around the room, and Catherine again squeezed his hand to tell him she would support him, too.

Tex paused and remained silent for a couple of minutes and then nodded, as if agreeing with himself.

"Buck, I got a job for you, if'n yore willin'."

"I'll do anything I can to help you, as long as it's legal," replied the sheriff.

"All right. About noon you look up Allison and tell him I'm right unhappy about the things he's been sayin' about Catherine. Tell him I'm comin' in to get him and shut him up for good. If'n he asks when, tell him you don't know. Tell him I'm comin' alone."

Bronc smiled inwardly, and his eyes glittered. Tex had made a perfect decision—one that fit perfectly into the plan Bronc had discussed with Trig.

"About five o'clock, look him up ag'in, Buck, and tell him I'll be there about six. Let's see how he likes waitin'."

Buchanan grinned his acceptance of his assignment and left the room.

As soon as Buchanan was gone, Tex continued the discussion. "I'll slip in around five thirty and look things over. Lefty, you and Bronc figger out what yore goin' to be doin' and let me know what you decide. I got a couple more ideas to think out, and we'll get our heads together in the mornin' to make shore we all know what we're about."

A few more questions were asked and answered, and then the meeting was adjourned.

****

Later that night, as Catherine snuggled close to Tex, he spoke to her in a quiet voice.

"Honey, tonight I don't want to say nothin'. Just let me hold you and feel you close to me. But I do want you to promise me one thing. You told me that if'n somethin' ever went wrong, you could live with it. I want you to do more than that. If'n somethin' does go wrong tomorrow, I want you to stay here on the Rambling R and help Apache become a man—not a fightin' man, but a man of peace, like Jacob and Ruth wanted him to be. The Rambling R is home to both of you now, and I want you both to stay here always. That's what Slim would want, and that's what I want. Promise me that's what you'll do."

"I promise you, my darling," replied Catherine softly. She fought back the tears and snuggled even closer.

****

Monk Allison had another restless night. The sliver of doubt that had made the tiny inroad into his brain the night before had returned and expanded somewhat. It was a very puzzling situation, and Allison was having a difficult time coping with it. A trail boss wiped out Slade. A foreman who is a first-rate gunman—so good that neither Bronc Evans nor Trig Mansfield would dare challenge him. Yet he, Allison, had never heard of the man. A man good enough to be a professional but with no professional reputation. Why? Allison tossed and turned as he tried to find an answer to that question. The psychological war he had intended to implant in Riley's mind had backfired and was now occupying his own mind. His tossing and turning continued.

✳✳✳✳✳✳✳✳✳✳✳✳

The next morning nothing happened that was out of the ordinary as far as breakfast in the main ranch house of the Rambling R was concerned. Tex gave no indication that anything unusual was scheduled for later in the day as his chatter was light and lively and his appetite was no different than normal.

Catherine felt a brief twinge of surprise at his behavior, but quickly realized what was happening. She had lain awake for a while after Tex had dropped off the previous night and had pondered the situation. Her conversation with Bronc Evans was recalled, and she decided Tex would find only strength, not weakness, in her on the morrow. This was the way she could help him, Bronc had said, and she was determined to maintain a normal facade for as long as it was necessary. There would be tears, but they come *after* he left for Cravenville and not before. She plunged into her morning chores and began a day that would turn out to be the longest in her life that she could remember. It seemed like the harder she worked the less she accomplished, and the hands on the clock in the main room seemed to be frozen in time. At mid-morning she heard gunfire, wandered out on the veranda, and watched Tex and Blackie for a moment or two before turning back into the house. Maria was waiting for her in the kitchen.

"Antonio and I know there is danger in the air," Maria began. "We have seen these situations before, but we know it is new for you, Señorita Catherine. Whenever we have had a problem like this in the past, Antonio and I have always looked to our God for strength and comfort. We are of different faiths, you and I, Señorita Catherine, but we both love this man, each in our own way. As soon as Señor Tex leaves for Cravenville, Antonio and I will light the candles and pray for his safety. If you would like to join us, we would be most pleased."

"Maria, that is a wonderful thought!" cried Catherine, having all she could do to hold back her tears. "I would be honored to worship with you and Antonio. Thank you so much for asking me."

The two women shared a long embrace before resuming their domestic activities.

****

Tex met Lefty and Bronc in the bunkhouse, away from Catherine's prying eyes, and finalized the plans for their activities later in the day. At the conclusion of the meeting, Tex motioned to Blackie, and the two of them strolled down to the grove of trees to polish their skills again.

Lefty and Bronc watched the twosome reach their destination, went to a corner of the bunkhouse, and became engaged in a heated debate. Lefty was very uneasy about violating Tex's instructions, but Bronc was adamant. He and Trig must be free to move about without regard to time and place. They must not be on a tether if they were to perform their self-appointed role. While it was true that Tex's ignorance about this part of the arrangement would provide some risk, it was a risk that had to be taken as far as Bronc was concerned. His arguments were long and profound, and, finally, Lefty reluctantly acquiesced. Laredo Lee and Reno Lang would replace Bronc and Trig in the agreed upon scheme of things. Both additions were more than adequate gunmen and could hold their own should a confrontation take place.

****

A little after noon Sheriff Buchanan entered the Steak House, located those whom he sought, and strolled over to the table where Monk and Keno were eating. Both men looked up as Buck stopped at their table.

"I got a message for you, Allison," he announced and then paused.

"You got nothin' to do with me," sneered Monk. "I ain't done nothin' in your town. Go away and let me eat."

"It ain't my message," replied Buchanan with a thin smile. "It's from Tex Riley. He told me to tell you that you got a dirty mouth, and he's comin' in to shut it permanently. He ain't shore you got the guts to fight a man, seeing as how women seem to fit yore style better!"

Allison swore and rose from his chair as his hand dropped to the butt of his Colt.

"Don't try nothin'," snapped Buchanan. "I've got two deputies with me, and they both got guns trained on you right now! You move, and they'll blow you apart and save Riley the trouble."

Allison and Keno looked around and saw that the sheriff wasn't bluffing. Monk sank back down in his chair.

"When's Riley comin'?" he muttered.

"He didn't say," smiled Buchanan. "He just told me to tell you he's comin', and he's comin' alone." Buchanan backed up, turned, and left the restaurant, his deputies following close behind.

"Riley fell for it," whispered Keno, "hook, line, and sinker. And he's comin' alone. It's just what you wanted, Monk."

"Yeah, I reckon so," mused Allison thoughtfully. "But why is he comin' in alone? He must know I have you and the boys with me."

"Mebby, he ain't as smart as you figgered," said Keno with a leer. Suddenly his face fell. "Unless . . ."

"Unless what?" growled Allison.

"Nothin'."

"What do you mean, nothin'?" retorted Monk. "Yore thinkin' the same as me—unless he's so good he's shore he can get me no matter what else happens." The thoughts that had plagued him over the past two nights now returned to Allison's mind and with increased emphasis. He threw down his napkin in disgust and rubbed his chin reflectively.

"Keno, ride out to the camp and get Jake and Tulsa. I need you all here just in case he don't come in alone. I'll round up Concho and Blue, and we'll meet at the Black Jack. I got a lot of thinkin' to do."

✻✻✻✻✻✻✻✻✻✻✻✻

It was mid-afternoon when Paul galloped down the courtyard of the ranch and swung from the saddle. He entered the ranch house and met an anxious Catherine. "Where's Tex?" he inquired.

"He rode out with Blackie a little while ago," replied Catherine. "He said he'd be back in a few minutes. Is there something wrong?"

"No, not really. Just wanted to report in," replied Paul.

"I have some news for you," said Catherine softly. "Come out on the porch with me. We need to talk."

Paul followed her out on to the veranda and continued on behind her until she came to the swing. Catherine sat down and motioned for him to sit beside her. He did so, and she began to describe what had happened and what was scheduled to happen.

Paul listened intently and reached out for her hand as she continued her narration.

"I was afraid it would come to this," he confessed as he squeezed her hand. "Worthington is a devil and must be dealt with. Catherine, you and I must help Tex all we can by being as strong as we can. You and I have seen much evil, and it cannot be allowed to possess us. Neither of us *like* fighting, and Tex doesn't either. But there are times when it must be done. We must pray for his safe return."

Paul's final comment startled Catherine, and she was unable to speak for a moment or two. She could only stare at the intense face of the boy she wanted to be her son.

"Darling, it is strange that you should say that. Maria has invited me to join Antonio and her in a prayer vigil in their apartment as soon as Tex leaves for Cravenville. I'm sure you would be welcome, too."

Paul nodded in agreement. "This is what Ruth would want me to do. Ah, here comes Tex. Not a word of this to him. We must show him we are strong and confident about the outcome."

Tex rode up, dismounted, and received a warm greeting from the rest of his "family." He put an arm around each one, and together they mounted the steps, entered the ranch house, and headed for the den. Tex released his companions, and each sought a chair while Tex moved around the desk and sat down.

"Apache, you got anythin' to report?"

"Not much, Tex. The man they call Keno rode out to the camp a while ago, and all three men rode back to Cravenville. We followed them until they reached town. I told the Apaches to return and watch the camp while I came here. They said they will wait until they hear from you."

"You did good, Apache. Has Catherine told you what is goin' on here?"

"Yes, big brother. What can we do to help you?"

"Just be here," answered Tex, calmly. "Apache, I want you to stay here at the ranch with Catherine, Maria, and Antonio. A number of the men will be around in case of trouble, but I'll feel better knowin' you're here, too."

Paul nodded his acceptance of that assignment.

****

A little less than two hours later, Tex emerged from the house and paused as he met Catherine and Paul standing on the porch. He pulled Catherine into his arms, and they shared a long embrace. But he was surprised and pleased at the absence of tears on her part.

Tex released Catherine and turned to Paul. "Son, look after Catherine for me."

He moved down the steps, pulled his reins from the tie rack, swung into the saddle, waved at Catherine and Paul, and urged his horse into motion.

Catherine put her arm around Paul's shoulders, and the two of them watched him get smaller in the distance. Finally, Catherine fit her hand around Paul's and began to move back into the house. "Let's find Maria and Antonio," she murmured softly.

The did, and soon a little church service was in progress.

Chapter 16

In the period of time following Buchanan's visit, Allison's mind had crossed the dividing line between puzzlement and concern. Although he did not possess a military mind, Monk was vaguely aware of the fact that although he had selected the general ground for the confrontation, Monk had bungled the rest of the process to the point where the initiative had passed from him to Riley. The foreman was now calling the shots as to where, when, and how the specific event would take place. This disturbed Monk as did the time element that was now part of the process. Concho and Blue accompanied him to the Black Jack and Stewart joined the gathering. Allison voiced his frustrations.

"This set up ain't workin' out the way I figgered it would," he grumbled. "Riley could come in anytime, and I wouldn't know it."

"I can help you out there," Stewart interrupted him. "I got a couple of night bartenders that wouldn't mind picking up a few extra dollars. I'll tell them to hang out at each end of town and let us know when Riley rides in."

"Good idea," agreed Allison. "You and me are goin' to get along just fine, Stewart. You got a good head on yore shoulders."

Stewart got up and left the saloon. He returned shortly and found that Keno, Jake, and Tulsa had joined the group. Stewart supplied a bottle of whiskey, but the men consumed little of the beverage and Allison none at all—which only increased his level of frustration even more. He wanted a drink very badly but dared not take the first one—he might not be able to stop with only one, and he had the uneasy feeling that a clear head might prove to be an absolute necessity.

"How come the sheriff is Riley's messenger boy," Monk growled as he looked at Stewart.

"They are good friends," responded Stewart, "especially since they were in a posse together a few years back. Shag Norton and his gang tried to rob our bank. Two of his gang were killed, but Norton and one other man got away. Buchanan and Riley tracked them down, and Riley killed Norton at the end. The other fellow, name of Sawtell, was captured and sent to prison. He's about due to get out again soon as a matter of fact."

"Sawtell?" asked Keno. "By any chance do you remember his first name?"

"Well now, I don't rightly recall," said Stewart slowly. "It weren't a common name, but I can't quite pull it up right now."

"Was it Slick?" probed Keno, his eyes bright with curiosity.

"Yes! That was it!" exclaimed Stewart. "Did you know him?"

"Yeah. I met up with him in Kansas some years back. Slick was right good with a gun, too," Keno added thoughtfully. "Funny he weren't the leader of this here gang."

"Norton was the leader all right," Stewart assured Keno. "Fact is, he took a hostage during the holdup and used her as a shield to make his escape." Stewart eyed Allison. "That hostage was Catherine Cornell," he continued. "She was Riley's gal then, just as she is now. Riley killed Norton just as soon as he caught up with him. The sheriff said it was a fair fight, but I don't know about that. Norton was shore enough dead, though. They buried him north of here."

"And I gotta believe Norton was better with a gun than Sawtell or he wouldn't have been boss," allowed Keno as he glanced at Allison. "Slick was right good with a gun."

"You already told us that!" snorted Allison in disgust. "You got some reason for sayin' it ag'in?"

Keno shrugged his shoulders and remained silent.

But Keno's remark was the straw that broke the camel's back as far as Allison was concerned. Monk had been involved in somewhat similar circumstances a couple of times in his past, and on each occasion he had used a gambit that had assured a successful conclusion to the event. Based on what he now knew or suspected, Allison decided it was time to use it again. He leaned forward and issued his instructions.

"As soon as we know that Riley is in town, Concho, you and Tulsa head up to the north end of town and position yourselves so you can watch the street. I'll do the same at the south end of town. If Riley is as smart as I think he is, he'll position himself in the center of the street—it'll give him the best view of the sidewalks and buildings. As soon as he moves out into the street, you boys do somethin' to get his attention—kick somethin', yell, I don't care what. As soon as he tries to see what's goin' on, I'll jump out and start shootin'. If he turns in my direction, you boys cut loose. He may be good, but he can't fire in two directions to once."

Keno smiled inwardly as he listened to Monk talking. He had read Allison's restlessness correctly. Stewart's mention of Sawtell was unexpected, but Keno couldn't resist the opportunity to turn the screw a little tighter. Twice in the past Allison had used a distraction to befuddle his intended victim, and he would now use this tactic again. Keno was hard pressed to prevent a sneer from appearing but was able to do so with some effort. Allison's voice broke into his train of thought.

"Keno, you, Blue, and Jake stay here until we find out if Riley is alone or not. As soon as we know what he's up to, I'll tell you boys what I want done."

"Supposin' some Rambling R riders come into town early," Keno asked, with a frown. "Supposin' they come here, knowin' we're here. What then?"

"A good question," mused Allison. "Stewart, is there a back way out of this place?"

"Yes, through my office," answered Stewart. "I know who all the Rambling R men are and will let you know if any of them come in here." Stewart paused for a moment before continuing. "Just to be on the safe side, Monk, when you want to leave, why don't you, Concho, and Tulsa mention out loud that you got something to see me about. We'll go into my office, and I'll let you out the back way. I'll stay put and keep the door closed for a while so no one will know you're gone."

"That's damn good thinkin', Stewart," grinned Allison, admiringly. "Like I said before, me and you are goin' to get along fine."

A critical decision had now been made, and the appropriate arrangements had been agreed upon. Allison, now much more at ease, reached for the bottle of whiskey and called for a deck of playing cards. One drink, but only one, would be just what his system needed.

✳✳✳✳✳✳✳✳✳✳✳✳

Lefty White led his contingent of Rambling R men into the Black Jack and was followed by Charley, Kansas, Blackie, Reno, and Laredo. They selected a table situated between the bar and the street entrance, ordered a round of beer, and settled in their chairs.

"Concho and Blue are in the crowd playing cards with Stewart," muttered Blackie. "The rest of them fit the descriptions that Buchanan and Apache gave us."

"Yeah, the whole gang is here," agreed Lefty with a thin smile. "Me and

Bronc figgered they would stay put 'till they find out what Tex is doin'. It won't be long afore Buchanan shows up, and then we'll see what happens." Lefty sipped his beer and continued to gaze at Stewart and his companions.

****

Stewart announced the arrival of the Rambling R men to Allison, and Concho confirmed it by leaning forward and spoke to Monk in a low voice, "That little fellar was the trail boss that done in Slade. The two-gun man next to him is the fellar that bounced me around."

Allison nodded in understanding and scratched his jaw reflectively.

"I figgered Riley might send some men in ahead of him. That's what I would do, for shore, knowin' that there were six of us. Keno, you and Blue and Jake stay put when me and the boys head for Stewart's office. You gotta make shore those Rambling R men don't drift outside after I'm gone."

"Yore loco, Monk!" protested an irritated Keno. "There's six of them agin three of us. How we gonna do that?"

"That's yore problem!" snapped Allison, his eyes ablaze. "I don't want none of them cuttin' in from the side."

"I don't think you got anything to worry about, Keno," piped up Stewart. "They'll think Monk and his men are in my office. As long as they believe that, they won't have any reason to do anything. By the time they know different, it'll be too late."

"Pervided they don't take it out on me, Blue and Jake," grumbled Keno. "They'll be fit to be tied when they find out somethin' has happened to Riley."

"Keno, I've never heard tell about Rambling R men throwing down on folks without giving them a chance," responded Stewart in a soothing voice. "You just keep your guns holstered, and you should be all right."

An unhappy Keno kept his thoughts to himself. He glanced at Blue and Jake and saw the same concern on their faces.

****

A little after five o'clock, Buchanan entered the saloon, looked around, located Allison and his men, and headed in their direction. He stopped when he reached their table.

"Riley told me to tell you he'll be here in an hour, Allison," Buck began. "He says that will give you and yore boys plenty of time to leave town.

Otherwise, he's got a spot all picked out for you in Boot Hill. I'd leave town if'n I were you!"

"You ain't me!" retorted an angry Allison. "That place in Boot Hill can fit him, too. You said yore piece—now git out of here afore I practice up on you!"

Buchanan turned and made his way back out of the saloon but smiled and winked at Lefty as he strode past the Rambling R table.

****

Jocko, one of the night bartenders, pushed open the swinging doors of the Black Jack and quickly made his way to Stewart's side. He whispered in the gambler's ear and then moved behind the bar with an idea of helping his friend, Clancy, in dispensing drinks. His efforts were not needed, however, as most of the remaining patrons suddenly rose from their seats and filed out of the establishment. A notable exception to this exodus was the group of Rambling R men.

"Riley arrived a few minutes ago and is at the hotel," Stewart announced to the group.

"The hell you say!" exclaimed Allison as he pulled a watch from a vest pocket. "He's half an hour early! That damn sheriff lied to me!"

"Calm down, Monk," Stewart cautioned the gunman. "I'm sure Riley is just trying to rile you. It don't make any difference. He's here, and that's all that counts. We'll wait a few minutes, and then we'll start the game."

The gambler's words pacified Allison, and he nodded his approval. However, Monk made a mental note to have a confrontation with the sheriff before he left town. Buchanan was obviously a willing participant in Riley's strategy and would pay for his involvement.

****

Fifteen minutes slowly went by. Allison rose from his chair.

"This has been a penny ante game gambler," he loudly announced. "How about a real game—private like."

"We can use my office," replied Stewart. "Clancy, bring me a fresh deck of cards. C'mon Allison, let's see how good you really are."

Monk motioned for Concho and Tulsa to accompany him, and the threesome followed Stewart into his office and closed the door.

Keno glanced across the room and was pleased to see no movement on the part of the Rambling R men. What he could not see, however, was the glint in Lefty's eyes and the sneer he was barely able to conceal.

∗∗∗∗∗∗∗∗∗∗∗∗

The back door to Stewart's office opened, and the owner exited the building, paused to light a cigar, and examined the surroundings as he did so.

"All clear," Stewart announced after he concluded his survey.

Monk, Concho, and Tulsa quickly slipped out of the building, paused for a moment, and then split up—Allison heading in one direction and his two confederates in the other. They stopped at their respective ends of the alleyway, cautiously peered around the corners of buildings, and slowly continued their advance toward their agreed upon locations. None of the three were aware of a pair of eyes that watched their every move.

∗∗∗∗∗∗∗∗∗∗∗∗

Tex examined the big clock in the lobby of the hotel, noted the time, shook his holsters, and stepped out of the building and onto the boardwalk. The walk and the street were deserted—Buchanan and his deputies having cleared the area in the time frame Tex had deliberately provided them.

Tex paused for a few moments to allow his eyes to become accustomed to the gathering dusk. Slowly he moved out into the street, his attention focused on the area in the vicinity of the Black Jack Saloon, where Allison had last positioned himself, as far as Tex knew.

∗∗∗∗∗∗∗∗∗∗∗∗

Concho carefully peered around the corner of a building, Tulsa at his heels. Both men had tin cans in their left hands and were prepared to toss them out in the street.

Concho watched Tex amble down the hotel steps and out into the street. He raised his left hand, and Tulsa did the same.

"Concho!"

Concho and Tulsa turned at the sound of the voice and were stunned to see a man, wearing two guns, poised to make a draw.

Each man dropped his cans and reached for his weapon, both at the same time.

Trig Mansfield's twin Colts roared their messages of death.

Tulsa staggered back from the force of one slug, his shoulders met the wall of the building, and he slowly slid down into a sitting position as his stiff legs straightened out in front of him.

Concho was spun around by the bullet that struck him. He stumbled forward a few steps, collided with a tie rack, pitched over this obstacle, and landed on his back.

****

Allison carefully made his way down the alley, turned, moved along the side of a building until he reached its front, and peered around it. He saw Tex stop, as the foreman stepped out of the hotel. Quickly Allison withdrew his head and braced for a quick movement. As soon as he heard the diversion created by Concho and Tulsa, he would go into action.

"I knew you wouldn't give Tex an even break, Allison, after what I told you, you yellow coyote," muttered Bronc Evans to himself as he watched Monk's movements. He saw Allison pull back and brace himself.

Bronc stepped out from the shadows and yelled, "Allison!"

Allison whirled, crouched, and froze.

"Yore a yellow dog," Bronc calmly informed the man. "You want Tex, but you gotta go through me first."

"I've always wondered if I could take you, Evans," hissed Allison, his surprise now under control.

A brief moment of silence ensued, and then both men moved. Their Colts roared in unison.

****

Tex whirled in response to the sound of gunfire behind him, crouched, and now both hands held Colts. He watched Concho stagger out from behind a building, but the roar of more gunfire behind him again made him whirl, but his eyes saw nothing.

Tex, now completely mystified by these events, remained poised until he heard Trig yell from behind him.

"Tex, I got both of these bushwhackers. Bronc is down at the other end of the street. You better check on him."

Cautiously Tex moved up the street, both hands still holding his Colts. He reached the end of the block and saw a huddled figure at the edge of a building. He quickly moved to the side of the man and saw it was Allison. Tex jammed his Colts back into their holsters and felt for a pulse. He found none and looked around. He saw what he was looking for about 30 feet away and dashed to the side of his friend.

Bronc was on his knees, his right shoulder was leaning against a wall, his right hand still clutched his gun, but his left hand was holding his stomach as tiny streams of blood oozed out between his fingers.

"He was . . . faster'n . . . I figgered," grunted Bronc through gritted teeth. He looked up at Tex through glazed eyes. "I missed . . . Slim's party . . . up in Idaho," he gasped. His mouth formed a crooked smile as he continued, "but . . . I shore enough . . . didn't miss yourn." His eyes closed, the gun slipped out of his hand, and he fell forward.

Tex caught him and gently lowered his frame to the ground.

Footsteps were heard, and Tex looked up as Trig arrived.

"Get Doc Hodges right fast," Tex cried. "Bronc is hurt bad."

"He's comin'," replied Trig, as he dropped to his knees and cradled the head of his best friend in his lap.

Tex reached for one of Bronc's hands, held it, and spoke in a low voice, "Hang on, Bronc, help's comin'. We got a heap of trails to ride together, my friend, and Catherine needs you, too. Hang on, pardner."

Doctor Fred Hodges pushed his way through the small crowd that had gathered and was followed by Buck Buchanan. Hodges knelt alongside Bronc and conducted a swift examination. Hodges looked at Tex and shook his head.

"He's gone, Tex. Nothin's working."

A terribly distraught Tex could only close his eyes and hang his head.

"Are you shore, Doc?" protested Trig as his voice quivered. "Say it ain't so!"

"Yes, I'm sure, Trig, I'm sorry, but Bronc has crossed the great divide. There is nothing I can do."

Tex reached out, squeezed Trig's shoulder, and brushed back some tears of his own. "Stay here with Bronc," he said, in a low voice. "I've got some unfinished business to tend to. Buck, will you please help Trig tend to things?"

"Of course I will, Tex," murmured the sheriff. "You do what you have to do."

※※※※※※※※※※※※

Lefty and his men bounced to their feet at the sound of gunfire and were poised for action. But Keno and his two companions did not move.

"Get on yore feet and don't make no false moves," directed Lefty, his face grim. "Just give me and my boys some excuse, and we'll blow you to kingdom come. Clancy, you and Jocko mind yore own business, and you won't get hurt."

Allison's men slowly got to their feet and moved away from the table.

"You got two choices," snarled Lefty. "You can either go for them guns or unbuckle them and drop them on the floor. You make the call."

"Some call," grunted Keno, "with you havin' six to our three." He unbuckled his belt with his left hand, and his two friends followed suit. The three belts, holsters, and guns hit the floor at about the same time.

"Back away from yore hardware and set down," commanded Lefty. "Keep yore hands on top of the table where I can see 'em. Kansas, collect them guns and hang on to 'em. Charley, keep an eye on them bartenders.

"Reno, you and Laredo cover the front door. Blackie, pry Stewart out of his office and don't be too gentle about it."

The Rambling R men responded to Lefty's instructions. Blackie didn't bother to knock. He simply kicked the door open and marched in. He yanked Stewart out of his chair, shoved the gambler through the doorway, and pointed at the table where Keno and his companions were located.

"Tex is comin'," announced Laredo with a big grin. "I reckon we can forget about Allison."

Tex pushed open the swinging doors and took stock of the situation as he marched to the table where Stewart and Allison's men were seated.

"Allison is dead, and so are yore other two friends," came the curt report. "It weren't my doin', but it should have been. Yo're damn lucky I don't clean the slate right here and now, but that ain't the way we do things around here.

"Lefty, Blackie, I got us some bad news. Bronc took the bullet meant for me. He's dead, and there's nothin' we can do about it."

Lefty and the other men winced at his announcement and glared at Keno and his friends as Tex pointed at Keno.

"You boys go back to yore camp and stay there 'til mornin'. Then you head back to San Carlos and tell Worthington what happened. Tell him the Rambling R will settle the score with him when we bring the next herd down."

"I'll do the settlin'," declared Lefty, seething with rage.

Keno nodded his understanding and headed toward the table where three gun belts were stacked.

"Yo're guns stay here!" snapped Tex. "And so do yore rifles!"

"What do you mean they stay here?" protested Keno, fearfully. "We can't ride all the way back to San Carlos without guns. That would be murder!"

"You can, and you will," replied Tex grimly. "Lefty, you and the boys grab their rifles. Stay here and help Trig all you can. I'm goin' back to the ranch. Catherine will be worried."

Before leaving the saloon, however, Tex walked over to a stunned, dejected, and apprehensive Melvin "Black Jack" Stewart.

"I ain't through with you, Stewart," he declared. "You backed the wrong hand in this game, and you're shore goin' to pay. As soon as I take care of Bronc, I'm goin' to come lookin' for you. If'n you think what I did to you afore was bad, you ain't seen nothin' yet."

Tex turned and with long strides walked out of the building and left Stewart to ponder his future.

✷✷✷✷✷✷✷✷✷✷✷✷

Tex used the ride from Cravenville to the ranch as an opportunity to get his emotions under partial control and to prepare himself for the ordeal he must now face—that of telling Catherine and Paul about Bronc. He had been impressed with the strength and courage Catherine had exhibited the previous day and night and all during this day as he had prepared for his own test. Now, as he continued his ride, he could almost feel her strength enter his body and reinforce his own. It was a strange feeling and one he could not explain, even to himself.

He also used his solitary ride to review what had happened and to plan the next move—for the game was not yet over. Tex was reasonably certain he knew why Bronc and Trig were not at their appointed stations and why, therefore, Reno and Laredo had become involved. He would confirm his suspicions at a more appropriate time. One more task did remain to be accomplished, though, and that would be Apache's job.

Tex guided his horse down the ranch's courtyard but veered off to left and approached the bunkhouse. Numerous men had been lounging outside their quarters, but all rose to their feet and directed a chorus of happy greetings as Tex swung from his saddle.

The expressions of pleasure and joy quickly faded from their faces, however, as Tex, quietly and crisply, told them what had taken place. Tex handed his reins to Red Rollins, as he finished his brief statement.

"Red, saddle me a fresh horse. I'll be goin' back to town as soon as I spend some time with Catherine and Apache."

Catherine and Paul were sitting on the porch swing, hands entwined, when Tex arrived. Catherine was both puzzled and surprised when Tex veered off and dismounted at the bunkhouse instead of coming directly to the ranch house. Both she and Paul and had risen to their feet when he appeared and remained standing during his stopover.

As soon as Tex began walking toward them, Catherine's puzzlement and surprise disappeared and was replaced by joy and gratitude for his safe return. She dropped her hold on Paul's hand, swept down the porch steps, and met her man at the edge of the courtyard with Paul at her side.

Tex's arms engulfed Catherine as her own arms swept around his neck, and their lips met in a long and passionate embrace.

"Darling, my prayers have been answered . . ." she began, but his mouth again found hers and prevented further talk.

Finally, he released her and shook hands with Paul. Then Tex's right arm circled Paul's back and gripped his shoulder while Tex's left arm was firmly in control of Catherine's waist. Together the threesome marched up the steps and met Maria and Antonio on the porch. Tex had to release both Catherine and Paul in order to receive a bear hug from Maria and a handshake from Antonio.

Catherine took a step toward the doorway, but Tex reached out and stopped her.

"Honey, I want to spend some time with you and Paul. Let's go and sit in the swing for a spell."

Catherine was happy to oblige, reached out to grasp one of his hands, and led the way down the veranda. They reached the swing and squeezed themselves into it with Tex in the middle. Tex put his arms around both of them and pulled them even closer. For a few minutes, the three of them gently swung to and fro, and not a word was spoken. Catherine, for her part, could not remember a more peaceful and contented moment in her life—her man was alive and safe! Tex cleared his throat.

"Apache, I got a job for you to do, but first I got somethin' I got to tell you and Catherine. There was trouble in town. Allison and two of his men are dead. They tried to ambush me, but Bronc and Trig stopped them . . ."

Tex paused for a few moments and took a deep breath.

"But we lost someone, too. Bronc took a bullet meant for me. He's dead."

Catherine sat up, saw the pain on Tex's face, and burst into tears. "No, Tex, no," she sobbed. "It can't be so! He was such a good friend."

Paul remained silent and stared off into space.

"I know, honey. I know," responded Tex in a strained voice. "You know what his last words were? He said he missed Slim's party up there in Idaho, but he didn't miss mine. And he said it with pride, too. I don't reckon anyone could have a better friend than that."

Catherine buried her face in Tex's chest and continued to quietly sob her grief. Paul, too, turned toward Tex, and Tex's arm pulled the boy close to his body as well.

"He loved you, Apache," Tex murmured. "About as much as I do. He was proud to call himself yore uncle."

Paul nodded but remained silent. After a few more minutes, Paul raised himself up and looked Tex straight in the face.

"You said you had a job for me to do. Tell me what it is, and I will get at it. I will grieve for Bronc in my own way—the Apache way."

Tex's eyes glowed with pride and admiration as he spoke to the boy.

"Find yore Apaches and give 'em a message. I sent Allison's other three men back to their camp, but I took all their guns away from 'em. I want yore Apaches to make shore they get back to San Carlos in one piece, but do it on the sly. No harm must come to them! I want Worthington to find out what happened and to sweat some and worry a heap. Make shore the Apaches understand what I want done. No harm must come to these men!"

"I understand," smiled Paul, "and my Apaches will understand, too. The return trip will be a long one and filled with worry. Perhaps they will decide to leave Arizona altogether. My big brother not only acts like an Apache, from time to time, but he thinks like one, too. I will leave now."

Paul got up, leaned down, and kissed Catherine's cheek.

"Honor Bronc with your grief," he whispered, "but then you must be strong again. That is what Bronc would want and what you must do. You and Tex comfort each other tonight, but tomorrow is a new day. The sun will rise, and Theresa will arrive in Cravenville. We must welcome her and make her comfortable. I will return and do my part."

Catherine pushed herself away from Tex and watched Paul head for the corral, her tears no longer falling.

"Darling," she muttered, "I think we have found ourselves a pretty nice son. I think we should keep him."

Tex responded by hugging her and then pulling her to a standing position.

"I've got to go back to town and help Trig, if'n I can. I'll get back as soon as I can."

"I'll wait up for you," promised Catherine.

They shared a kiss, and then Tex quickly left the porch and headed for a saddled horse being held by a patient Red Rollins.

※※※※※※※※※※※

Several hours later Tex and his men returned from Cravenville. Most of the horsemen veered right and headed for the corral, but two riders kept going until they reached the main ranch house. A weary and dejected Tex Riley dismounted and handed his reins to Lefty White. The latter pulled away and headed for the corral as Tex trudged up the steps to the porch. Catherine met him at the top of the steps, and they shared an embrace.

"Would you like some coffee?" she asked as she felt his arm envelop her waist.

"No. Let's just go to bed," came the soft reply as they entered the house. Arm in arm, they ascended the stairs, entered the master bedroom, quickly undressed, and crawled into the bed. Catherine immediately slid under his arm and laid her head on his shoulder.

For a while no words were spoken, each one of them occupied with his or her own thoughts. Finally Tex broke the silence.

"The boys took Bronc down to Willard's. Earl said he would have Bronc and a box ready by early afternoon tomorrow. We'll take the ranch wagon and pick him up at the same time we meet Theresa. Trig wants to drive the wagon, and I asked him if'n it would be all right if you rode along with him. He said he would like that. That way you won't have to do any ridin'." Tex couldn't resist a thin smile as he spoke.

"Thank you on both counts, kind sir," murmured a pleased Catherine. "I don't know how you could think about me and my poor behind at a time like this, but I thank you for that, too."

"You are always in my thoughts, Catherine," replied Tex softly.

"That's what Bronc was afraid of," said Catherine thoughtfully.

"Huh?"

"Yes. A long time ago Bronc told me that my presence now, and Paul's, too, could make you hesitate a tiny bit when you were in a tight spot and that could be fatal. He said it was his and Trig's job to make sure that didn't happen."

Tex digested this revelation and exuded a deep sigh.

"It fits. Trig told me that he and Bronc knew Allison from their Texas Ranger days. Allison always stayed one jump ahead of the law in them days and was right good with a gun. Bronc decided to face the man instead of me. I may owe him my life, Catherine."

The tears came, and Catherine quietly vented her grief. Tex squeezed her body even closer to his own and gently rocked her, his own eyes filled with moisture.

"Darling, he was a wonderful friend to both of us," Catherine finally sniffed. "He told me once that no one would weep over his grave. I'm going to prove him wrong about that. He will be buried here on the ranch won't he?"

"Yes. We have a little cemetery south of the house. He'll be the fourth man we put there. Slim should be there, too, and someday we'll have to take care of that."

"I've seen the spot," admitted Catherine, "but it needs flowers. That will be my job from now on. Theresa can help me get started, and, yes, I want Slim to be there, too. He doesn't belong up in Idaho. Let's talk to Mr. Willard about that. There must be a way we can get him down here."

Tex tilted her face and crushed her lips with his own—a silent concurrence with her wishes.

****

The next morning a solemn and subdued group of Rambling R men became engaged in a variety of tasks. Four men, led by Trig Mansfield, took turns digging a fresh grave in the tiny cemetery, while three more washed and scrubbed the ranch wagon and buckboard from stem to stern. Several more policed the ranch's courtyard, and Lefty assigned the remainder to range duty but told them all to report back by mid-afternoon at the latest.

Paul rode in during the morning and reported to Tex, "Allison's men broke camp shortly after dawn and headed south. The Apaches agree with your plan and will keep them in sight. In fact, they will deliberately show themselves from time to time. Keno and his friends should have a very interesting next few days." Paul could not help smiling at that thought. "What can I do here?" he asked.

"Whatever you want," replied Tex. "Why don't you start by helping Trig and his men dig the grave? I think Bronc would like that. This afternoon I want you to drive the buckboard and begin your job of bein' Theresa's host, like you done with Catherine. Think you can handle that?" Paul grinned his approval and dashed off to help Trig in his melancholy task.

Earlier in the day Catherine reluctantly transferred her belongings back to the guest room. As soon as they had awakened, she told Tex she wanted to stay with him, even with Theresa on the premises. But Tex assured her that while he would miss her terribly, he would be all right and probably needed some private time anyway. "We've got to talk about the wedding but not today," he concluded, and she agreed.

As soon as the noon meal was concluded, the wagon and buckboard were hitched up, Catherine joined Trig on the seat of the wagon, and Paul drove the buckboard. Tex and an honor guard of six riders accompanied the little caravan.

The entourage reached Cravenville and paused while Paul parked the buckboard near the hotel and helped Catherine down from the wagon. Trig urged his team into motion, and he and his escort proceeded down the street toward Willard's establishment. Tex remained with Paul and Catherine.

The stagecoach rumbled down the street as the seven men loaded the pine box in the back of the wagon and lashed it down. Trig climbed back into the driver's seat, the six men remounted, and the group waited for Tex to signal them to get in motion. Tex waved his arm, and the wagon began its deliberate journey back to the ranch.

A weary Theresa was overjoyed by her reunion with Catherine, was thrilled to meet Tex, but was even more intrigued by her introduction to Paul and the precise and clear words he used to welcome her. Her joy and excitement were quickly tempered, however, when Catherine took her aside and briefly explained what was happening as Tex was securing her luggage on the buckboard.

The wagon arrived, and Trig helped Catherine resume her seat, while Tex helped Theresa into the buckboard. The teams were cracked into movement, and Theresa was forced to reach for support as the buckboard rumbled down the street. Instinctively, she clutched Paul's arm with one hand, and he responded by glancing her way and smiling as he yelled, "Hang on!" She did as she was directed and had a great deal of difficulty taking her eyes off him as they made their way back to the ranch.

A goodly number of Cravenville citizens, led by Sheriff Buck Buchanan, followed the little procession to the Rambling R—some in buggies, some on horseback, and some in wagons.

As soon as the enlarged procession reached the ranch grounds, the Rambling R men assisted in parking the vehicles, helped the ladies exit their conveyances, and directed their guests toward the grave site.

Paul parked the buckboard, helped Theresa alight, and extended her his arm. It seemed so natural to accept his assistance, and Theresa did so without hesitation. Tex and Catherine joined them, and the foursome moved with the crowd toward Bronc's final resting place.

Trig had dropped off Catherine and then had driven the wagon about 10 yards past the pile of dirt. He and the honor guard carried the coffin to the site and placed it on top of several lengths of rope.

As soon as the crowd had completed its arrival, the Reverend Walter Price, pastor of the Cravenville Community Church, stepped forward and began the service.

"Bronc Evans was not a churchgoer," admitted Price, "but he was a member of our community. He fought for all of us and died for all of us. Therefore, it is fitting that we remember him with our prayers and the words from the good book."

Price read the appropriate scriptures and recited the twenty-third psalm. A moving prayer followed, and then Price stepped back and announced, "Mr. Riley has a few words to say."

Tex stepped forward, accompanied by Catherine and Paul. He kept one arm around each of them as he launched his eulogy.

"Bronc and Trig have been saddlemates for almost as long as they can remember. I won't try to speak for Trig—no one can do that. Trig don't want to say nothin', and we'll respect his wishes. But I can speak for Paul, Catherine, and myself. Bronc was a special friend to all three of us.

"Bronc was with Slim when they run into Paul and his folks, Jacob and Ruth, up there in Colorado. It was Bronc who saddled Paul with the name Apache, and he told Paul he was Paul's uncle. Each year he and Trig took Paul on camping trips. He really tried to be a good uncle to Paul.

"Bronc was in the posse that found Catherine and brung her back to us. He spent a heap of time talkin' to her about how we live out here and helpin' her get settled in her new home.

"Bronc and I hit it off right well when he and Trig joined up with Slim, almost 10 years ago. We all know Bronc loved to talk. But if'n you listened close, a heap of what he said was worth its weight in gold. As most of you know by now, Bronc took a bullet that was probably meant for me. What greater friend can one have than that?

"Goodbye, old friend. Me and Catherine and Paul are goin' to miss you aplenty!"

Pastor Price finished the service with the traditional "Dust to Dust" benediction while the honor guard carefully lowered the coffin into the grave with the ropes. As the Cravenville visitors began the retreat to their conveyances, Tex, Paul, and Trig threw several shovel's full of dirt into the grave as Catherine, unashamedly, let her tears flow. Theresa put her arm around her sister and was somewhat surprised at the depth of Catherine's grief. Tex and Paul handed their shovels to other Rambling R men and silently watched Trig and the other men continue to fill the grave.

Finally, Tex and Paul led Catherine and Theresa back to the house. They found that Antonio had already unloaded Theresa's luggage and Maria had prepared coffee and biscuits for refreshments.

A short time later, Catherine escorted Theresa upstairs and helped her get settled. Catherine also used this time to explain, in greater detail, what had taken place in recent days and why.

Chapter 17

The trip from Cravenville to San Carlos was a nightmare that Keno, Blue, and Jake would never forget. During the first day, they heard repeated animal cries, primarily the coyotes' howl, and bird calls but saw no such animals and no such birds. They suspected it was the work of Apaches but saw no Apaches. The second day their suspicions were confirmed when they sighted a pair of Indians far off—first on one side of the trail and later two more on the other side of the trail. The cries and the calls were repeated on the third day, and they again saw the Indians but as before, a long distance away.

However, it was the nights that were the worst. They felt they had to post a sentry and decided to use two four-hour shifts. But try as they might, the sentries could not keep from dozing off. As soon as the heads nodded, however, the screech of a bird or a howl of an animal, seemingly almost underfoot, would startle them back to attention. The threesome took turns cursing the night, Indians in general, and Allison in particular. Not only did they not have guns, they had no money to buy guns. Allison had retained control over the gang's funds except for a few dollars, and together these three could not boast of enough money to buy one gun, let alone three. They were tempted to leave the trail and try to steal what they needed, but each time they veered away from their route, the animal cries became louder and more insistent and drove them back to their original trail.

During the third night, about a day's ride from San Carlos, the four Apaches held a conference regarding the situation and decided on a new course of action. Their self-appointed leader slept for four hours, ate a midnight snack, jumped on his horse, and galloped away in the darkness.

****

At long last, Worthington's office building came into view as Keno and his two weary companions issued a huge collective sigh of relief. Keno dismounted and burst into the building without knocking.

Worthington looked up in surprise and rose to properly greet his visitor.

"You got a gun anywhere around here?" snarled Keno before Worthington could speak.

"Yeah, I've got one around here, somewhere," Worthington replied in a puzzled voice. His eyes widened as he glanced down at Keno's waist. "Where's yours?" he exclaimed.

"Back in Cravenville," snorted Keno. "Find that gun, right quick! I'm in no mood to discuss things 'til I get my hands on a gun!"

A very perplexed Zack Worthington opened two file cabinet drawers before he found the desired object and handed it to Keno. Keno spun the cylinder, saw that each chamber was filled, quickly walked back through the open door, and tossed the weapon to Blue.

"Keep yore eyes peeled," he told Blue. "I'm goin' to have a quick palaver with Worthington, and then we're gettin' out of here." Keno stamped back into the office, leaned over the desk and glared at Worthington, who had returned to his seat.

"Monk, Concho, and Tulsa are dead!" he boomed at a startled Worthington. "That Rambling R crowd jumped us and killed all three. Monk killed one, but it weren't Riley, and it weren't the trail boss. They took our guns and rifles away from us, kicked us out of town, and sent us back here with no guns! We're damn lucky to get back here alive—we been seein' and hearin' Apaches every step of the way."

"There aren't any Apaches on the warpath," protested a dumbfounded Worthington.

"The hell you say!" retorted Keno. "We've seen 'em, and we've heard 'em. That's shore good enough for me!"

"If you can see 'em and hear 'em, they ain't on the warpath," Worthington patiently explained. "If there's trouble, and you can't see 'em and can't hear 'em—that's when you gotta worry."

"Huh. Is that so! I'll trust my instincts—you can trust yourn. You got any cash around here?"

"Yes, I have *some*. Why do you ask?"

"Hand it over—all of it," Keno again snarled. "Me and the boys are gettin' out of here, and we need travelin' money."

"Now see here," protested Zack. "I gave Monk plenty of money."

"Monk's dead! I told you that afore. Either Riley and his crew got Monk's roll, or it's buried with him. Oh, yes. I got a message for you from Riley.

He says he has a score to settle with you, and from what I've seen of him and his outfit, that score will be plumb fatal. Me and the boys are leavin' this part of the country fast, and if I was you, I'd do the same. Now hand over the cash, or I'll start Riley's game right here and now!"

Worthington reached into a desk drawer and pulled out a small pile of greenbacks.

"That's all I got, Keno. You're welcome to it."

Keno counted the money and studied Worthington's face, his own suspicious running wild.

"I could tear this office apart," he suggested.

"Yes, you could," agreed Worthington, "but you wouldn't find any more, and you'd be wasting a lot of time. I thought you were in a hurry to get out of here."

Keno hesitated, studied Worthington's blank face again and swore. He stuffed the bills into a pants pocket, stamped out of the office, and Worthington heard the sound of hoofbeats fading in the distance. He smiled at the sound.

Worthington poured himself a drink and pondered the startling news that Keno had brought him. It was obvious that his tenure on the reservation was now about over. However, the Rambling R herd was not due for over a month, and the herd from the alternate supplier was due in less than a week. Zack's bank account in Tucson already contained a tidy sum, but another addition would be most welcome. The alternate supplier, unlike the Rambling R's Riley, was a cooperative man and did not mind sharing his extra money with Worthington. Zack sighed with satisfaction and sipped his drink. His departure could be delayed for a week. That would allow him plenty of time to plan his disappearance in such a way that neither Riley nor any member of his outfit could ever find him. He grinned his pleasure at that thought and idly noticed that darkness had fallen. Worthington finished his drink, blew out his lamp, and fished the keys to his office out of a pants pocket. He walked out into the night air, stared at the star filled sky for a moment, and turned to lock the door to his office. He reversed his direction, took one step, and was startled to see a dozen dusky forms rise up from the ground. One form moved closer, and Worthington peered at the dark face.

"Chato! What are you doing here?"

****

Tex knew that the best antidote to combat the gloom and grief that had resulted from Bronc's death would be work and more work. Fortunately, the need for a spring roundup provided him with a perfect solution. The morning following the funeral he issued his orders, and Lefty and the other men began the final preparations for this massive effort.

As soon as breakfast was consumed, Tex held a meeting with Catherine, Paul, and Theresa.

"Trig will be drivin' the ranch wagon to town to pick up the last load of supplies for the roundup," he told his audience. "Catherine, I want you to ride along with Trig, and, Apache, I want you to take the buckboard and drive Theresa. Catherine, have Theresa measured for that dress you mentioned and have her outfitted with new duds for around here. Also find out if Judge Parks can see you and Apache and get his questions answered. Honey, can you set a date for the wedding and reception, now that Theresa's here?"

"Will a week from Saturday give you enough time for the first phase of the roundup?" inquired Catherine.

"Yes," replied Tex. "We'll just make it come out right. That means you'd better see Pastor Price and talk to Leo Leslie about puttin' somethin' in the paper about the reception." Tex paused as Catherine exhaled a big sigh.

"Darling, I wonder if we should even have a reception after what has happened," she muttered. "Losing Bronc is bad enough, but after what some folks said about you and me, I'm not sure I even want them out here."

"Honey, them folks were all mixed up and don't need to come, if'n they don't want to," said Tex softly. "But I'm shore Bronc would tell you not to change a thing on his account. He wanted us to get married and have all the trimmin's almost as much as we did."

"It won't be the same without him," sniffed Catherine.

"Catherine, I agree with Tex," spoke up Paul. "Bronc will be here. We won't be able to see him, but he'll be here. My uncle was very proud of you, Catherine, and he would want you to be strong and not change a thing."

Theresa had listened carefully to the conversation, and Paul's words only increased the interest she had in the Indian boy that had begun the day before. She had difficulty taking her eyes off him. He was so different from what she had expected, despite what Catherine had told her. His oral English was virtually impeccable, much to her amazement. Tex's voice disrupted her train of thought.

"It's all set then," Tex drawled with a smile. "We'll have a wedding *and* a reception. That gives you even more to do in town, Catherine. If'n you run late, and Trig is all loaded up, you can have Theresa come back to the ranch with him. Take as much time in town as you need. Apache can bring you back with the buckboard."

****

Catherine's trip to Cravenville proved to be both enjoyable and successful. First she met with Reverend Price and finalized the wedding arrangements. The wedding ceremony would be at eleven o'clock in the morning, and the reception would begin at one.

Next, she, Paul, and Theresa marched into Wood's General Store, and she told Ollie and Elsa about the wedding plans and gave them their special invitation, much to the Woods' delight. While Theresa was being measured and fitted, Catherine and Paul visited Judge Parks. Parks questioned Paul privately in his chambers and received the answers he expected. He assured Catherine he would deliver the appropriate legal papers when he and his wife attended the reception.

Catherine and Paul returned to the General Store, and Catherine was pleased to find out that the information she had provided Elsa regarding Theresa's measurements had proven to be quite accurate. The dress only required minor alterations and would be ready in two days. Better yet, Elsa had shirts and Levi's that fit her sister perfectly, and Theresa had kept one set of new clothes on in preparation for the trip back to the ranch.

Trig arrived with a fully loaded wagon, and Catherine suggested that he drive Theresa back to the ranch. Trig shook his head no and said he would wait. Catherine wasn't surprised. Trig was obviously determined to carry on the role Bronc had established for the two of them and would not be deterred. Catherine smiled and sent a brief silent prayer of thanks skyward.

Catherine decided to limit her activities on this trip to one more stop, since they would return in two days to pick up Theresa's dress, and any additional arrangements could be made at that time. Therefore, she visited Leo Leslie, owner and editor of the Cravenville Clarion. The wording of the newspaper's announcement was agreed upon, and Leslie also gave her the names of the people she would have to talk to about the reception. Leslie concluded his comments by saying, "By the way, tell Tex that Mel Stewart and his family have left town. His house is up for sale, so I don't think he'll be back. Clancy Milliman is running the Black Jack now, but I don't know if he's buying it or not."

Catherine thanked him profusely for his help, returned to her companions, and soon they were on the road back to the ranch. Tex only grunted with satisfaction when he heard her news regarding Stewart.

✻✻✻✻✻✻✻✻✻✻✻✻

The next several days whirled by.

Catherine and her entourage made a second trip to Cravenville, Theresa picked up her dress, and the arrangements for the reception were finalized. Catherine was delighted to find that a local woman grew flowers—both as a hobby as well as for commercial purposes. In addition to arranging for her own small wedding bouquet, she bought a number of plants, and she and Theresa began a beautification project for the graves in the Rambling R's tiny cemetery.

Paul helped by assuming his duty as a host to Theresa and used the buckboard to take her on several rides to various parts of the ranch. On one such trip they approached the roundup activities, and from a distance spent an hour watching the activity as Paul explained what was happening. Instinctively, Theresa's hand found his arm while he was talking. She listened intently to his words and was again impressed by their clarity and comprehensiveness. Her admiration for the boy continued to grow.

The roundup itself was a duplication of the fall process but with one major exception. Lefty White was now on hand, and as the director of range operations was now in charge of the roundup. His first decree, therefore, was to tell Tex, in no uncertain terms, that he was not welcome at the moving campsites. Instead, he ordered Tex to return to the ranch for each evening meal and breakfast so that he could help Catherine in planning their wedding and be a proper host to his guest from Ohio.

Tex weakly protested, but Lefty was adamant. Tex did as he was ordered, much to Catherine's delight. She already liked Lefty very much, but now, unknown to him, she would be his friend for life.

Theresa, like Catherine, was somewhat awed and greatly inspired by the multicultural aspects of each meal. Paul, in particular, impressed her with his manners and the way he fit in. Someone has certainly trained this young man extremely well, she thought to herself.

The fourth night after her arrival Theresa sat on the guest room bed, Indian style. Her hand cradled her face, and her elbows were anchored by her knees as she watched Catherine brush her hair in preparation for going to bed.

"Big sister, if I asked you a straight question, would you give me a straight answer?" Theresa innocently inquired.

Catherine paused in her brushing and gazed as her sister's reflection in the mirror.

"That's a funny question," murmured Catherine. "I've always been straight with you. You know that."

"That was true when we were younger," admitted Theresa, "but it wasn't true the last time you were home. You didn't give anybody straight answers then—not me, not mom and dad, and not Doctor John. I'll ask you again, if I ask you a straight forward question, will you give me a straight forward answer?"

Catherine held the hairbrush, continued to look at her sister's reflection, and sighed. "That situation at home that you are referring to was very different and unusual, and I thought I was doing the right thing. It just didn't work out the way I wanted it to." She again gave a deep sigh.

"All right, little sister. Ask me your question, and I'll try to give you a straight answer." Catherine resumed her brushing and waited for the question.

"Catherine, what bed were you sleeping in before I arrived on the scene?" probed Theresa in a calm voice.

The brush stopped in mid-stroke, and Catherine felt a warm sensation spread across her face as she stared at her sister's image in the mirror.

"Theresa! How . . . could you . . . ask a question . . . like that?" stammered Catherine. "Do you have no shame?" she exploded as she turned toward her sister.

"Shame has nothing to do with it," retorted Theresa, with a big grin. "Good grief, Catherine, you've been here eight months. You love Tex. You're going to marry the man, and you can't get pregnant. I know exactly what I would do under those circumstances. Besides, I don't mind getting pawed at night, but I prefer to have a boy do it, not my own sister!"

"I didn't . . . I couldn't . . . oh, Lord," sputtered Catherine, her face now crimson.

"Catherine, either you hike your way down the hallway to Tex and show him you love him, or I will!" declared Theresa.

"You . . . wouldn't dare!" again stammered Catherine as she pointed the handle of her brush at Theresa. The look on her sister's face finally registered with her and Catherine burst out laughing. "On second thought, I don't think I will take any chances on that happening, however." She laid the hairbrush down on the dresser and moved to the door. She gripped the knob, paused, and looked at Theresa. "Not a word about this to mom and dad, little sister," she pleaded.

"My lips are sealed forever," Theresa assured her with a big grin.

As soon as the bedroom door closed, Theresa flopped back on the bed, kicked up her heels, and wildly shook her legs and feet in unabashed glee.

"Tee, hee, hee," she chortled. "I exaggerated things considerably, big sister, and did a lot of guessing, but I know you better than you think I do, Catherine, and my bluff hit pay dirt. Tee, hee, hee."

The laughter quickly faded, however, as Theresa muttered to herself, "I must admit that I do envy you, big sister." This thought elicited a deep sigh. "I wish I dared to try that with Paul," she mused thoughtfully. "He's so shy, though, I would probably scare him half to death." She pulled back the covers a bit and slid underneath them. "Maybe, later on . . ." she smiled impishly as she closed her eyes—a very contented young woman.

****

Tex sensed, rather than heard, his bedroom door open. No squeak was heard—Tex had corrected that problem after their first night together. His eyes followed the form as it approached his bed. The figure paused, the bedclothes dropped away from her body, and Catherine crawled in beside him.

"What are you doin' here?" he growled. "This ain't accordin' to our plan."

"Theresa kicked me out," Catherine giggled. "She said I was too active in bed and that I belonged with you. I don't remember doing anything, and I think she was pulling my leg, like everyone around here is prone to do. I decided not to debate the issue, however, as I'm finding out that all our preparation for this event has been inadequate for my needs. Are you sorry I'm here?"

"Not one bit," Tex assured her. "I was havin' the same problem you was. Do you think we can figger out a way of curin' our difficulty?"

"If we put our minds to it and concentrate hard, I wouldn't be surprised if we came up with an adequate solution," she happily murmured. "Now, quit talking and get on with it."

He complied with both of her requests.

****

More days flew by, and the ranch activities and wedding preparations continued unabated. Two days before the wedding, however, a worried Paul Redstone tapped Catherine on the shoulder and asked her if she would meet with him in the den. She agreed and followed him to that location. She entered the room, Paul gently closed the door behind her, and then the boy turned and faced her.

"Catherine, I have a problem," said Paul quietly, "and I need your help."

Catherine moved close to him and put her arms around him. "What is it, darling? Are the wedding activities bothering you in some way?"

"Not really," replied Paul, hesitantly. "Theresa says she is planning on doing a lot of dancing with me at the reception. Catherine, I don't know any of the white man's dances. In fact, I don't even know any Apache dances."

"Oh, my goodness!" shrieked Catherine as her hands flew to her mouth. "I never gave that a thought. The Cornell sisters are good dancers, but even I was surprised at some of the dances they do out here. Theresa will be surprised, too. *Well*, we can solve that problem, right quick, as Tex would say. Come with me."

Catherine took one of Paul's hands and almost dragged him out of the den. She stopped midway in the main room of the ranch and yelled at the top of her voice, "Theresa! Where are you?"

Theresa quickly appeared at the stop of the stairs.

I'm up here, Catherine," she yelled back. "I'm dusting the bedrooms. What do you want?"

"Well, drop what you're doing and come down here. We've got a problem that requires your immediate attention."

Theresa dashed down the stairs and raced to her sister's side. "What's wrong?" she asked, a bit out of breath.

Catherine explained their dilemma, and both girls laughed, which only added to Paul's discomfort.

"I'm sorry, Paul. We weren't laughing at you," explained Catherine. "It's such a simple little thing, but we both forgot about it, and we were laughing at ourselves. I've decided to resume my role of being a teacher, and both you and Theresa will be my pupils. It sounds like old times, doesn't it?"

Catherine showed both of them steps associated with one dance, and they practiced it for half an hour as Catherine hummed some music for them. They rested for a bit, and then the process was repeated for a second dance. Theresa picked up the steps quickly, as Catherine knew she would, but Paul was nervous, awkward, and a little clumsy. Theresa ignored his mistakes and awkwardness and quietly encouraged him. He began to make significant improvement, and Theresa rewarded him with a hug.

After more than an hour, Catherine called a halt, but her eyes glowed with pleasure as she watched her sister work with Paul.

"Enough for one day," Catherine announced brightly. "Paul, tomorrow morning take Theresa for a ride out to the roundup and see how they are doing. I'm going into town with Trig and make sure everything is set for Saturday. Tomorrow afternoon, however, we are all coming back here and have another dance lesson. Theresa needs some more work!" She winked at Theresa as she spoke, and her sister responded by sticking out her tongue at Catherine. Paul raced out of the ranch house and did not see the embrace shared by the two sisters.

****

The wedding ceremony went off as scheduled, and the wedding party spent a little time driving around Cravenville with Ollie and Elsa Woods, using their carriage. Paul drove the newlywed's vehicle with Theresa holding on to him in the front seat. They had a leisurely return trip to the Rambling R, and soon thereafter the guests began to arrive. Rambling R men helped park the vehicles and assisted the ladies, as they had done at Bronc's funeral. The wedding party greeted the guests, and Tex and Catherine were kept busy introducing Theresa.

The food was abundant and delicious, the beer flowed freely, and soon a three piece musical ensemble, consisting of a fiddle, an accordion, and a harmonica, was busy at work. Flat planks had been laid to provide a crude dance floor, and both Catherine and Theresa were kept busy dancing with the many guests, primarily their own Rambling R men. After about an hour, however, Theresa approached Paul and faced him, hands on her hips.

"Mr. Redstone, you have not asked me to dance with you yet, and I'm getting upset with you. I spent too much time practicing with you to get stood up. C'mon, it's time you got your feet wet."

"I need to get my feet wet?" asked a puzzled Apache boy.

"No, no, no," laughed Theresa. "It's a white man's expression that means you have to try something new, even when you don't want to." She took his hand and pulled him in the direction of the dancing area.

A very nervous Paul got a little mixed up during the first dance, but Theresa encouraged the boy instead of rebuking him and insisted that they do it again. This time he did better, and she let him sit out one dance. She then pounced on him a second time, and now he became her regular partner whenever the music covered steps he knew.

Tex was not much of a dancing fan, and he gladly let his new wife uphold the dancing reputation of the Riley family by passing from one guest to another and making sure every Rambling R man had one dance with her. In addition, as soon as she saw that Theresa was occupied with Paul, Catherine covered for her by dancing a second time with the men Theresa had missed.

About four o'clock, the musicians put away their instruments, and the Cravenville residents began to seek their vehicles and start their homeward trek.

Catherine corralled Tex, Paul, and Theresa and led them to the tiny cemetery. She knelt and placed her wedding bouquet on Bronc's grave. She rose, stepped back, and motioned for everyone to hold hands.

"Bronc, my dear friend," she began, "we had to finish the party with you. It is customary for a father to walk his daughter down the aisle and then give her away to her new husband. My father couldn't be with us today, my friend, but somehow I knew that you were here instead. I felt your presence beside me as I spoke my vows to Tex. Well, we're married now, and your job is done. Sleep in peace, my friend. You've earned it."

✽✽✽✽✽✽✽✽✽✽✽✽

That night, at Tex's request, Catherine, Paul, Theresa, Maria, and Antonio gathered in the den. When all were seated and settled, Tex picked up some papers from his desk and looked around the room.

"Judge Parks left us some papers today. I want Catherine to tell you what's in 'em."

Catherine got up and stood behind Paul.

"Tex and I approached Judge Parks some time ago and asked him to do something for us. The judge has seen fit to approve our request, and Paul has agreed to it as well. As of tomorrow morning, the Rambling R will again be Paul's official foster home, and Tex and I will be his foster parents. Tex and I have a son, and I couldn't be happier." Catherine bent down, and kissed Paul on the forehead.

A chorus of congratulations came from Maria, Antonio, and Theresa before Catherine raised her hand.

"Paul, Bronc and Trig called themselves your uncles. Well, people have aunts, too. Starting tomorrow morning, you will also acquire an aunt. Paul, meet your Aunt Theresa. Theresa, meet your nephew, Paul."

Everyone laughed, but Theresa got up, walked over to Paul, reached for his hands, and pulled him to a standing position. Still gripping his hands, she murmured, "Hi there, Nephew Paul," and before he could reply, she leaned forward and startled him by kissing him full on the lips.

"That's a lot better kiss than my sister gave you," she observed loudly. "Now, how about giving your aunt one in return."

Paul glanced at Catherine, saw her nod yes, and returned the favor, except that Theresa extended the duration of the embrace somewhat before Paul pulled back, still a little bewildered by the situation.

The two younger people received a small round of applause and were the recipients of verbal congratulations as well.

Thus ended one of the most memorable days in the history of the Rambling R Ranch.

****

After a day of rest and recuperation, the roundup was resumed, and the days flew by. Paul continued to act as Theresa's host but not on a constant basis. Since she was no longer engaged in preparing for the wedding, Catherine now found she had much more time to spend with her sister, and she used that time to tell Theresa more about the history of the Rambling R Ranch, especially Slim Evers, and most importantly, all she knew about Paul Redstone.

Catherine finished the story about Paul one morning as the two sisters were sitting in the porch swing and enjoying their coffee break. Theresa had been forced to use a handkerchief several times as she listened to Catherine.

"You like Paul, don't you, little sister?" commented Catherine at the conclusion of her narrative.

"Very much," responded Theresa, "I can't get over how shy he is. Has he always been that way?"

"Yes and no," answered Catherine slowly. "But, remember, I only had him in school for one year before being around him since I came back here. Paul is caught in the middle between two cultures, Theresa—the red man's and the white man's. Each culture has a different set of characteristics, customs, and mores. Mix all that up with the Quaker influence that Ruth provided Paul, and the world can be a very confusing place for him to live in. I'm sure Paul was very close to his father, and as a result he has no shyness when it comes to his Apache heritage and skills. I can personally vouch for that. Paul was very aggressive in tracking me down when I was abducted by Norton. He found me, Theresa, and probably saved my life in the process. Tex told me he was forced to take a back seat to Paul during most of that chase. That must have been awful hard for Tex to do," chuckled Catherine.

"It's the white man's world that puzzles Paul," continued Catherine, "and no wonder, after what has happened to him. It's going to take time for him to adjust to our way of life, and that's where I hope Tex and I can help him the most. So in reality he's mature beyond his years as an Apache, but at the same time he's very immature when it comes to living in the white man's world."

Catherine paused and reached out for Theresa's hand. "Little sister, please don't push Paul too hard and too fast. He's only 18 and has a lot of growing up to do in our world. Theresa, I think I know what's going through you mind. Right now Paul needs you as a friend, but not as a lover. You've already done more for him than you realize. You'll be going back to Ohio soon. Please don't do something that might end up hurting him—you won't be here to help pick up the pieces. He's been hurt enough already."

"You sound like a mother," smiled Theresa, her eyes filled with moisture. "I hear you, big sister, and I will control myself. If I could talk Paul into it, would you mind if we wrote each other?"

"Mind it!" exclaimed Catherine. "Of course not. In fact, I would encourage it. That would be a wonderful way for you two to remain as friends. Besides, it might be the best way to get you to come back and visit us again!"

"You aren't planning to go back to Ohio anytime soon?" asked Theresa, somberly.

"No, not in the foreseeable future," replied Catherine carefully. "My place is here with Tex, and I don't want to waste a minute of it. It's sort of strange, in a way, little sister, but Tex and I have become a business team as well as a matrimonial one. It's been very thrilling and rewarding for me to become involved in the management of the ranch, and I enjoy it immensely. Best of all, I've acquired a much better perspective of how people live out here. It is true that Tex and Bronc and Lefty and the other men have grown up in a violent environment and are violent at times, themselves. At other times, however, they can be extremely kind and gentle. They seem to have a kind of code of ethics and their loyalty to, and their love for, men like Slim and Tex is almost beyond belief. How else can you explain what Bronc did for Tex? I don't fully understand it, either, but I thank God for allowing me to become a part of it. I can't tell you how happy and secure I feel when Tex holds me in his arms. I can only hope you do as well, little sister."

"I'll try, Catherine," smiled Theresa as the tears of joy slid down her cheeks. "I'll also try to explain things to mom and dad, now that I know more of the facts. Mother will be the problem, of course. I think you made a big mistake in how you handled things, Catherine. You never gave the folks a chance to understand you and your situation five years ago. It's true that mother might have reacted the same way, regardless, but we'll never know that. I'll do what I can, and, yes, I will try to visit you again."

****

The time came for Theresa to return to Ohio. Paul drove her to Cravenville in the buckboard while Tex and Catherine rode alongside, Catherine insisting on going at least one way on horseback.

The stagecoach arrived, and Theresa's luggage was loaded while she shared a hug and a kiss with Catherine and Tex. Then she faced Paul, hands on hips.

"Paul Redstone," she began in a firm voice, "we've danced together, and we've kissed each other. I want a goodbye kiss from you, and it had better be a good one. A little peck on my cheek won't be good enough, and I don't care who sees it! I'm not ashamed to be kissed by an Apache boy, and I'm not ashamed to kiss that same boy back. C'mon, show me what you can do."

A nervous Paul Redstone complied with her request and did what he thought was a pretty adequate job. Theresa, however, was not satisfied, and when he drew back a bit, she moved with him, gripped his shoulders with both hands, and returned his effort with a significant increase in vim, vigor, and fervor. Paul's eyes widened in surprise.

She released the boy, turned, and winked at her sister. She walked to the coach, took one step, paused, and looked back at Catherine. "I want him to be much more worldly when I come back again," she said, with an impish look. "You'd better include some of that in your motherly training!"

Theresa pulled herself up, settled back in her seat, and waved as the coach rumbled down the street, a satisfied smile on her face.

Chapter 18

The roundup was over, and Tex was again pleased with the preliminary results as best as he could ascertain them. He pored over the tally books, made an enormous number of calculations, and finally threw down a well-worn pencil in disgust.

Two days later, Lefty, Paul, and the Trail Crew were dispatched with a third herd bound for San Carlos, and Tex asked Catherine to join him in the den.

"Honey, numbers give me fits," he began, "and I shore enough need yore help." Tex showed Catherine the tally books and told her what he was trying to accomplish. She listened carefully, made some notes, asked some questions, and made some more notes. Finally, she shooed him out of the room and told him she would spend the next several afternoons reviewing the records and trying to understand the process and, further, told him to leave her alone while she was so engaged. Tex gratefully agreed and reminded her he wanted to spend a much greater proportion of his time range riding, in Lefty's absence, anyway.

Catherine went back five years in the records, waded her way through Slim's entries, and acquired a pretty good idea about how the system worked. Slim wanted his records to show a goodly amount of detailed information, much to Catherine's surprise. In particular, he wanted to know the ages and sexes of his animal inventory. This, in turn, determined what cattle he would sell and when as well as the expectations he had regarding what his annual natural increase should be. Catherine was fascinated by what she found. In addition, she was able to find several clerical errors and adjusted the books accordingly. She kept Tex informed about what she was doing and was rewarded with an abundance of enthusiastic praise from Mr. Riley. Catherine also found out she now had a new role to play and was thrilled to know she had become an even more important member of the management team.

✳✳✳✳✳✳✳✳✳✳✳✳

Lefty, Paul, and the Trail Crew returned from the last drive, and Tex chaired a meeting of the Planning Committee. Tex felt he had to find someone to fill Bronc's empty spot on the committee, and out of courtesy first approached Trig Mansfield. Trig respectfully declined, as Tex was reasonably certain he would. Blackie Smith, on the other hand, was eager to participate and was included in the group that gathered in the den.

"How'd you get along with Worthington?" was Tex's first comment as Lefty handed him a check.

"Didn't run into him," smiled Lefty. "Apache, here, will tell you why."

"Chato sends you greetings, Tex," spoke up Paul. "He told me to tell you that if Worthington is doing any more cheating, he is doing it with his ancestors. He left this world in a very slow and painful manner."

Catherine couldn't help shuddering at Paul's words but at the same time felt no sympathy for the man.

"I'm some surprised," admitted Tex with a frown. "I didn't figger on anythin' like that seein' as how nothin' happened to me."

"Yes, but you were the target, big brother," and Paul grinned at the slip of his tongue. "Chato said that Bronc was your brother and he was hit with a bullet meant for you. It amounts to the same thing as far as the Apaches are concerned."

Catherine reached for Tex's hand, squeezed it, bent down, and kissed the back of his hand. "Bronc had the last word again," she murmured.

"I reckon Worthington tried to buy his way out of the game afore he cashed in," Lefty broke in. "I hear tell them Apaches asked the agent to go over Worthington's records and damned if they didn't find a good sized cache of money in a Tucson bank. The agent hopes to get that money back and use it to help Chato and his people."

Catherine again squeezed her husband's hand and glowed with pride over the role Tex and the Rambling R men, especially Bronc Evans, had played in the whole matter.

✳✳✳✳✳✳✳✳✳✳✳✳

A weary Theresa grunted with pleasure as her train pulled into the Toledo station. Harold Cornell had dispatched a carriage and driver to meet her, and Theresa was mildly amused by the apparent snub, although she suspected that her mother was the real culprit.

Theresa arrived home, trudged her way upstairs to her room, and was partially unpacked when she heard the sounds that indicated her parents had entered the house. She quickly left her room, descended the stairs, and exchanged warm greetings with her parents. A gusher of questions followed, but Theresa threw up her hands in protest.

"Mother, father, I'm dead tired, dirty, and hungry," she explained. "I'm going to finish unpacking, soak in a hot bath, and take a quick nap while you all relax and mother can prepare supper. Wake me when it's time to eat. We'll have supper, and then I'll answer all your questions and tell you about my trip and the wedding."

The schedule Theresa had outlined was adhered to, and as soon as the supper dishes had been cleared and stacked, she told her parents to sit in the parlor—that she had to go upstairs for a few minutes and would be back shortly. Lydia frowned at this additional delay, but Harold smiled inwardly and moved a step closer to a decision he had been debating over the past several weeks. He looked at his daughter carefully as she entered the parlor and thought he detected a higher level of maturity and confidence in the way she walked and carried herself.

"My, that's a pretty dress," observed a fashion-conscious Lydia. "I don't remember seeing you wear that before, my dear."

"This is my bridesmaid dress, mother," Theresa informed her. "Catherine bought it for me. Mr. and Mrs. Woods own a store in Cravenville, and they ordered it for me. They told me it came all the way from St. Louis."

"Harrumph," snorted a surprised Lydia. "I assume Catherine got her wedding dress from the same place. I imagine it was long, billowy, and white." Lydia couldn't completely conceal a sneer.

"No, mother, it was not," replied Theresa, calmly. "In fact, it was a duplicate of this one—we were a perfect match."

Again Lydia was surprised, and she decided to try a different tack. "That must have made a big impression on all her wedding guests."

"It was a very small wedding, mother, but they did have a big reception at the ranch. Besides the minister and his wife, there were only six of us at the wedding—Tex and Catherine, of course, Mr. and Mrs. Woods, Paul and myself."

"Paul? Who's Paul?" Lydia demanded to know.

"Paul Redstone is an Apache Indian boy who lives with Tex and Catherine," responded Theresa with a smile.

"Good heavens," exclaimed Lydia, in horror. "Harold, did you hear that— a savage living with our daughter! Has she completely lost her senses?"

"Calm down, mother!" Theresa replied sternly, before her father could respond. "Before you look down your nose at this so-called savage, you'd better know more about him. But before I get into that, I have to tell you something about Catherine. Do you remember Catherine's story about the bank holdup in Cravenville?"

"Somewhat," came the curt answer. "What about it?"

"Well, Catherine left a few important items out of her story. First of all, she didn't tell us she was *in* the bank when the robbery took place. Worse than that, when the bandits were cornered, the leader abducted her and used her as a shield in order to make his escape. He forced her to ride with him deep into the wilderness where he beat her, raped her, and left her to die. Remember that, mother—Catherine was many miles from civilization, was beaten up, her clothes were torn, and she had been raped! Not only that, she didn't know where she was, she was on foot, and she had no food and no water. Her chances of survival, under those conditions, were almost nil."

"Good heavens," Lydia gasped, again in horror. "How did she manage to get out alive?"

"Well, if you remember, Catherine told us that Sheriff Buchanan led a posse in pursuit of the outlaw and one other survivor of the gang. That was only partially true, however. Tex Riley and Paul Redstone took out after the outlaws and left the trail for the posse to follow. Paul's Apache father taught him how to follow a trail, even when someone is trying everything they can not to leave a trail. Out west they call it tracking, and Tex says Paul has a marvelous talent for tracking, and, to make a long story short, it was Paul who found Catherine and led the posse to her. Make no mistake about it, mother, Paul Redstone is the main reason Catherine is alive today!"

Theresa let this startling information sink in for a few minutes before she continued her story.

"After finding Catherine, the posse continued the chase after the outlaw and his companion. That same night they caught up with the two men. Tex tricked the leader into coming out of his hiding place, confronted the man, and killed him. Tex was furious over what the man had done to Catherine and gunned him down in what the people out there call a fair fight. That certainly doesn't make Tex a murderer. In fact, I say hooray for Tex—the outlaw was a beast and didn't deserve to live. We were all wrong about Tex, and I can understand why—we didn't know all the facts, and we jumped to the wrong conclusion.

602   *Apache, My Son*

"I have to blame Catherine for part of that," admitted Theresa, "and I told her so. But she was shocked by the violence she had encountered, the pregnancy that resulted from that violence, and even the violence that Tex had used to correct the situation. She tried to solve her own problem as quietly as she could and without hurting you and father. She failed in her attempt and only made the situation worse. But I cannot judge her too harshly. I don't know what I would have done in the same circumstances. I only ask that you look into your heart, mother, and find some compassion for your own daughter."

Theresa paused again to let her words sink in and saw her mother bite her lip in vexation.

"Mother, you did turn out to be right in one aspect of my trip, however. There was a gunfight in Cravenville the night before I arrived. Four men were killed, including a man that was an extremely close friend to both Tex and Catherine. Listen carefully, mother, and you, too, father, because it is important that you understand what happened and why.

"Tex's ranch has a contract to deliver beef to the Apache San Carlos Reservation, which just happens to be one of Paul's former homes. Tex found out that one of our government officials was cheating the Apaches in his purchases of beef, and Tex not only refused to cooperate with the man but threatened to expose him if the cheating didn't stop. As a result of Tex's action, this official hired a gunman named Allison to kill Tex. Allison brought five men with him to help him accomplish his task. Tex and his Rambling R men were warned about Allison, and without Tex knowing about it, his men intervened, thwarted the attempt on his life, and killed Allison and two of his men in the process. Unfortunately, one of the men who actively intervened in Tex's behalf, Bronc Evans, was also killed in the battle. As I said, Bronc was a special friend to Tex and Catherine, and both of them took his death very hard. Mother and father, can you imagine love and loyalty like that? It's difficult for me to comprehend it, but I saw the results of it with my own eyes. And there is nothing these men wouldn't do for Catherine, too!

"Remember, now, I told you Tex and his men had been warned in time to prevent a tragedy. You won't believe where that warning came from. Paul's Apache friends on the San Carlos Reservation heard about the plan to kill Tex, and four of them rode day and night to warn him. Isn't that amazing? Apaches risking their lives to protect a white man! I hope you both realize that Paul Redstone had a hand in saving Tex's life just as he did for Catherine.

"Mother, father, let me assure you that you have a fine son-in-law. Tex is strong and, apparently, has earned the loyalty and devotion of the men who work for him, as evidenced by the man who gave his life for him. More importantly, Tex adores Catherine and wanted to marry her five years ago, even knowing she might be pregnant by another man. Furthermore, I have never seen Catherine more happy than she is right now. She loves Tex, she loves the ranch, and she is right where she wants to be. I can only hope I do as well as she has."

Lydia, more than a little overwhelmed by all that she had heard, remained silent for several moments. Finally, one final concern penetrated her confused brain, and she felt obliged to voice it.

"I never thought I would see the day when Catherine would be happy working on a farm with a few cows."

"Mother! The Rambling R is *not* a dairy farm! It's a cattle ranch, like I told you. I know you and father like to have a steak dinner once in a while, and you love to have roast beef on Sundays. It is very possible that your steak or your beef may have come from the Rambling R Ranch! Catherine told me they are planning to ship almost 5,000 head of cattle this year."

"Wait a minute," interrupted Harold. "You must be mistaken, Theresa. I've done a little dabbling in the agricultural markets from time to time, and the sale of that many animals would amount to about a hundred thousand dollars. That's a huge sum of money, my dear."

"I don't know about that, father," replied Theresa earnestly, "but that is what Catherine told me. It's pretty obvious that it must take a lot of money to run the ranch. Catherine said that over 20 men are on their payroll, not counting two cooks, Paul, and Maria and Antonio Martinez."

"Who are Maria and Antonio Martinez?" inquired Harold, who was rapidly becoming overwhelmed himself.

"They are two older Mexicans who functioned as housekeepers for the former owner, Mr. Evers. They've been fixtures at the ranch for a long time. Mr. Evers died in Idaho last year, and Tex insisted that Maria and Antonio stay and continue to be part of his family. Maria is a dear and a joy to be around. The six of us always ate together, and it was great fun. Think of it, mother and father, there were six of us at each meal—two Mexicans, an Apache boy, a white man, and two white women eating together as equals. It was beautiful, and I enjoyed it immensely."

"Catherine has *two* housekeepers?" muttered Lydia weakly, still unable to comprehend what she was hearing. "Where do you all sleep?"

"Well, the main ranch house is probably three times as big as our house," continued Theresa. "The Martinez living quarters are on the ground floor adjacent to the kitchen. There is a big den, a large main room, and numerous closets and storage areas downstairs and four bedrooms and more storage areas upstairs. There is also a pantry area off from the kitchen. It's a lot to take care of, to be sure. Catherine pitches in and does her share of the work, and, of course, I helped, too. Catherine made me earn my keep, mother.

"Catherine needs Maria's and Antonio's help, too, because she functions as Tex's private secretary and his bookkeeper. She told me it is much more complicated running a ranch that size than she ever dreamed.

"Mother, I am getting very tired and I have much more to tell you and father, especially about Mr. Evers, but that will have to wait for another time. However, I do have one more piece of good news I must share with you both before I turn in. I'm glad you are both sitting down because you are going to be very surprised. Ready? All right, I'm pleased to tell you that you have a grandson."

"What?" cried Lydia in disbelief. "That's impossible—Doctor John said Catherine couldn't have any children. Theresa, I've tried to believe everything you have told us tonight, but this it too much. I think you are making fun of us, and I don't like it!"

"Mother, I'm telling you the truth. His name is Paul Redstone, and he is 18 years old. Tex and Catherine became his foster parents the day after they were married. I'm his aunt and you two are his grandparents. Mother, that should give you plenty to talk about at your club meetings. I'm sure no one else in town, or probably in the whole state, has an Apache grandson."

Lydia Cornell fell back in her chair and closed her eyes, now in a complete state of shock. Harold Cornell was also stunned but could not resist looking at his daughter with a great deal of pride. She had handled the discussion extremely well, and he was now sure, more than ever, that what he had in mind had an excellent chance of being successful.

Theresa rose from her chair, stretched, and made no attempt to stifle a huge yawn.

"Mother, father, I *am* very tired, and I believe I have given you more than enough to think about for one evening. I have a great deal more to tell you, but it will have to wait for another night. So I will say goodnight and see you in the morning."

Harold and Lydia watched Theresa leave the room, heard her slowly ascend the stairs, and tramp down the hallway to her room.

Harold looked at his wife, who was still in a state of shock, and spoke in a low voice, "Lydia, my dear, I do believe our daughter has really grown up and matured in the past six months. This trip west may have been just the right experience for her. More than that, I have a strong feeling that she and Catherine are now as close as they have ever been. Maybe we have a lot to be thankful for and don't really know it. C'mon, grandma, it's time for bed."

Lydia Cornell threw up her hands in resignation and followed her husband upstairs.

****

Theresa woke out of a deep slumber, stretched, and enjoyed the luxury of relaxing and recalling the pleasure of her trip west and of meeting Paul. She emitted a deep sigh at that last thought, threw back her covers, slipped out of bed, walked to the nearest window, pulled back the curtains, and was surprised at the height of the morning sun. She put on a robe and paddled downstairs in her bare feet.

A note from her mother indicated that her parents had decided to let her sleep in, that they would be at the store, and that they would be back for supper.

Theresa made herself a late breakfast, skipped lunch, and spent the rest of the day doing laundry and organizing her clothes. She was still in her robe when her parents returned late in the afternoon. Theresa apologized and raced upstairs. When she returned to the downstairs, she startled her parents yet another time.

"What are you wearing?" inquired an astonished Lydia.

"These are the clothes I wore while I was in Arizona, mother," explained Theresa, with a laugh. "This is what the ranch people wear all the time out west, and Tex told Catherine to buy them for me. These are what they call their work clothes. The Rambling R is not a fashion emporium, mother and, believe me, these Levi's are really comfortable. Tex teases Catherine about getting twice as much work out of her since she quit wearing dresses."

"Theresa, I hope you don't intend to go outside with that on," pleaded Lydia. "I can't imagine what our friends and neighbors would think if they saw you parading around in men's clothes."

"Mother, I'll compromise with you. If you let me wear these in the house, I'll promise not to wear them outside the house. Is it a deal?"

"I suppose so," replied Lydia helplessly. "I swear you two girls are going to be the death of me yet."

"Thank you, mother," gushed a happy Theresa as she kissed her on the cheek. Theresa had already noted that Harold didn't seem to mind her new look at all.

After supper the threesome again gathered in the parlor, and Harold cleared his throat.

"Theresa, your words last night were eloquent and quite persuasive. However, your mother and I were taken aback by your news. Could you tell us some more about our grandson? You must admit that this is a bit difficult for us to handle."

"Father, I shall be happy to tell you as much as I can. But in order to tell you more about Paul, I must first tell you about Mr. Evers. I can't talk about one without talking about the other—the two are inseparable parts of the same puzzle. Let me explain."

Theresa began to talk, and part way through her narrative, she noticed that Harold's hand found Lydia's and by the time Theresa had finished her story, Lydia had found it necessary to use a handkerchief several times.

"Father, mother," she concluded, "I'm sure I haven't done an adequate job in telling you about Mr. Evers. I never met the man, of course, and Catherine only knew him for a short time. But the way he defied convention and did what he could to raise Tex and Paul speaks volumes. Maria worships the man, and Bronc's grief over what happened in Idaho was deeper than even Tex surmised.

"As for Paul, he is a very nice young man. Ruth did a wonderful job in bringing him up—he has excellent manners, he is neat and clean, and he speaks English as well as you and I. He is painfully shy, which is understandable, but I can think of much more worse traits in a boy. In fact, if he was five or six years older, I wouldn't mind marrying him, myself!"

"Theresa, you can't be serious!" cried Lydia, aghast at the thought.

"Oh, mother, I was only joking. Well, maybe half joking. I could do a lot worse than that. But, he *is* five or six years too young," sighed Theresa. "Nevertheless, I love having him as a nephew, and I intend to write him and continue to be his friend.

"Father, mother, I will tell you again that Paul is a fine young man. Life has not been kind to him—Tex and Catherine will be his third set of parents, if you pair up Mourning Dove and Mr. Evers. That could have driven a weaker person to Lord knows what. You would love him, too, if you could only meet him and get to know him. It's wonderful what Tex and Catherine have decided to do for Paul. I know Catherine would be thrilled if you two would give her your moral support. It's time this family forgot the past and looked to the future. We are a bigger family now. I believe it's time we became a whole family as well. All I can ask you to do is think about it and pray about it."

Theresa paused and leaned back in her chair. She was exhausted, now mentally as well as physically.

There was a long period of silence, and Harold Cornell took the opportunity to study his daughter again as his eyes glowed with admiration. She really had matured right before his eyes, and now she needed a new challenge.

"You've had a pretty exciting two months, haven't you," he commented with a wry smile. "I think you had better stay around here for a while and give your mother and me time to recover from this trip before you go on another."

"I'll have to," laughed Theresa. "I'm broke again, and couldn't go anywhere even if I wanted to. I'll rest up for a day or so and then start looking for a job."

"Maybe you won't have to look very far," observed Harold. "Theresa, I have a proposition for you. I hired some part-time people to work while you were gone and, therefore, your position is still open. However, I have been mulling over some changes I would like to make at the store, and you have been in my thoughts in this regard. If you are willing and interested, I would like to put you through an intensive training program for six months. At the end of that time, if we are successful in what we do, I will promote you to a manager's position, and you can help me run the store. Hopefully, that will allow me to have some time away from the store and give your mother and me more time to spend together and even do some traveling. Perhaps we could even visit Catherine in Arizona.

"I will give you a small increase in pay while you are in the training program," he continued, "and a much bigger one as soon as you complete the program. I think it is about time you had a place of your own and the freedom that goes with it. You don't need your mother and I hovering over you all of the time. Your salary would be more than adequate to allow you to find the appropriate living quarters and set up housekeeping. I'm not trying to kick you out of here, mind you, but I believe it is high time you struck out on your own and handled your own affairs. Would you be interested in doing what I have suggested?"

Now it was Theresa's turn to be stunned and somewhat overwhelmed. She glanced at her mother and saw that Lydia was as astonished as she was. Theresa bounced out of her chair, ran to her father, threw her arms around him, and gave him a big kiss.

"I would like that a lot," she gushed and kissed her father a second time. "I know I can do the job, and I won't disappoint you. If one Cornell can help run a cattle ranch, the other Cornell can help run a store. Oh, father, this is a wonderful welcome home present. Wait until Catherine hears about this. I am so excited, I can hardly breathe. But I am also very tired. If you both will excuse me, I'm going to run up to bed and get some sleep. I'll be ready to go to the store with you in the morning, father." Theresa raced out of the room and up the stairs.

"Harold, I hope you know what you are doing?" sighed a bewildered Lydia.

"I do, my dear. I'm sure I do. Our daughter has grown up, Lydia, and we should treat her like the adult she is. She's right, my dear. We do need to be a whole family again. From what we now know, I think we have raised two pretty nice young ladies. Give yourself some credit, Lydia—you've done a good job, perhaps even better than you realize."

"Are you serious about going to Arizona?" breathed Lydia.

"Indeed I am, my dear. I would very much like to meet both our son-in-law and our grandson and see that ranch. It must be a monster. We only travel this road of life once, Lydia. Let's not spoil any more of it with bad thoughts and misunderstandings. C'mon, grandma, it's up to bed for us old fogies. I've got a feeling that tomorrow will be the dawn of a new era for the Cornell family."

Chapter 19

The matrimonial preparations and actual event were now history, the spring roundup was finished, a third herd had been delivered to the San Carlos Reservation, and the Rambling R men settled into a daily and somewhat boring routine that would continue for the rest of the summer, except for the bi-monthly drives to San Carlos. This interlude was neither boring nor routine as far as Catherine Riley was concerned, however. Being part of the management team of a cattle ranch was still a new world for Catherine, and it seemed to her that something significant was going on all the time. She looked forward to the weekly pickup of mail in Cravenville as she now knew Tex and his decision making style and she could match wits with him and rough out responses to correspondence before he even read the letters. Tex expressed his approval and appreciation for her aggressiveness and when she erred in her interpretation of a matter, he painstakingly explained what was wrong and needed correcting. This, in turn, expanded her knowledge of how to manage the ranch. She laughingly accepted the role reversal she now found herself in—Tex being the teacher and Catherine the pupil. She learned her lessons well, however, had an excellent memory, and the misinterpretations soon became few and far between.

In addition, Tex made a slight managerial adjustment that surprised her at first but soon proved to be most pleasing and helpful to her.

Years before, when Slim made Tex foreman, he had asked Tex to leave the bunkhouse and reside in the main ranch house. Slim felt that a foreman should not be too close to the men he supervised and he also wanted Tex to be readily accessible for detailed conferences and discussions as well as spur-of-the-moment talks. Tex had been very reluctant to make this change and fought against it for some time. Slim's logic and wishes eventually prevailed, and Tex soon discovered it was a good physical move, once he was able to make the mental transition.

While Tex was not now the owner of the Rambling R, like Slim had been, he was functioning as the general manager of the operation, and Lefty White, in turn, had become the ranch's de facto foreman. It was, therefore, logical and desirable for Tex to ask Lefty to make the same physical move that Slim had asked Tex to do.

Lefty, like Tex before him, found this decision to be a very painful one. Unlike Tex, who had pretty much been a loner, Lefty had three extremely close friends—Charley, Kansas, and Blackie—with whom he had been a saddlemate for a very long time. The physical separation from his friends, therefore, was much more acute for Lefty than it had been for Tex.

Nevertheless, Lefty knew this would be a likely event when he accepted the job, and in addition he had seen the logic and benefits of the move in the person of his new boss. Thus, he responded favorably to Tex's request and move in to Tex's old quarters when he returned from the May drive to San Carlos.

Catherine found Lefty almost as fascinating to talk to as had been Bronc Evans. He wasn't as verbose as Bronc, but he wasn't reticent either and was able to describe his experiences in finding, breaking, and selling horses in such a way that Catherine found them to be as informative and entertaining as was Bronc's descriptions of his Texas Ranger activities. Moreover, she was already impressed by Lefty's sensibility to her needs prior to the wedding and her friendship with the little left-hander deepened as the summer wore on.

The summer contained several more pleasant experiences for Catherine as well. She received a letter from Theresa, and her sister's ecstasy over Harold's business proposal was clearly evident. Catherine smiled her own delight and silently wished her sister well. Theresa also mentioned that she had given their parents a detailed description of her visit and thought she had cultivated some fertile ground but that only time would tell.

Paul, too, received a letter from Theresa, somewhat to his consternation. He hesitantly approached Catherine and voiced his concern.

"Catherine, I've done very little letter writing in my life and never to a girl. How do you write a letter like that? What do you say?"

"Paul, it's about time you got your feet wet," laughed Catherine. "You don't want Ruth and me to think we wasted all that school time with you, do you? Just tell Theresa what you are doing here at the ranch. Remember, you were her host during most of the time she was here, and depending on what you told her, she may not really know what you do, day in and day out.

I'll bet she would like to know about your growing up at San Carlos, too. You can tell her how Bronc and Curley got you started with ropes and making knots. You can also tell her what happens on the cattle drive to San Carlos. See, there are lots of things you can talk about. Don't try to do it all in one letter, though. Make a list of all the things you haven't already told her and discuss one in each letter. You shouldn't do really long letters, anyway. That should give you plenty to talk about for a long time."

Paul's eyes lit up as Catherine spoke, and that night he took the first step in maintaining his friendship with Theresa and beginning a new adventure for himself.

Catherine's pleasure at receiving Theresa's letter was nothing compared to the delight she felt when a long letter arrived from her mother.

"It look's like Theresa accomplished far more than I ever dreamed possible, darling," she murmured in Tex's ear that night. "Mother is very conciliatory in her letter, and I must respond in a like manner. Theresa pointed out to me that I might have handled things a bit badly before, and she is probably right. I was upset over walking out on you after what happened and all the violence that had suddenly become a part of my life. Looking back, I might have done a better job of coping, but finding myself pregnant just did me in. Worse than that, I inadvertently gave them the wrong impression about you. Somehow, Theresa has brought us all back together again, and I must not lose this opportunity."

"I agree, honey," responded Tex. "You write yore folks back right quick and leave some room for me to say somethin' too. It's time for me to be a part of this family as well as you."

Catherine raised herself up and looked down at her husband. "You keep this up, and I just might marry you, Mr. Riley," she murmured.

"You done that once already," Tex reminded her.

"Hmmm, so I did," she acknowledged. "It goes to show you, I must be a pretty smart girl."

"I won't argue agin' that," laughed Tex.

Catherine joined in and then bent down and sealed his lips before he could comment further.

****

The letters from home did not signal the end of Catherine's pleasurable experiences for that summer. As the end of July approached, following the fourth cattle drive to San Carlos, Tex suggested that she, Paul, and himself take a trip to Idaho, visit the MJ Ranch, and get back before the September drive to San Carlos would take place. It wouldn't be a honeymoon trip, as such, but it would be a trip that combined business with pleasure and give them all a breather from their Rambling R responsibilities. Catherine readily agreed, preparations were made, and soon they were on their way with Trig Mansfield joining the expedition as their chaperon and a companion for Paul.

The train connections had improved somewhat over the past year, and the trip wasn't quite as long and tiresome as had been the previous excursions as far as Tex was concerned. Perhaps the fact that this was a pleasure trip instead of a mission of revenge made it less tiresome. Nevertheless, Tex routed the group through Harding as he explained to Catherine how the past year's expedition had been planned and carried out as well as the deceit that was an essential ingredient in the process. He also described Paul's contribution to the success of the operation in greater detail and again Catherine glowed with pride and admiration as she looked at their son.

The three week visit at the MJ Ranch was both relaxing and fun for all concerned with one exception. That exception, of course, was the mandatory visit to Slim's grave. Nevertheless, even that sad event contained a small silver lining. Tex and Catherine had discussed their wishes regarding Slim's body with Earl Willard in Cravenville before they made their trip north. Willard, in turn, wrote his counterpart in Ridgeway, and arrangements were made to exhume Slim's coffin and ship it by train to Cravenville, together with his headstone. The Ridgeway undertaker suggested that Canyon City represented a better departure point than Harding, and Tex rearranged his group's travel connections so that they could accompany the coffin and headstone on its journey south.

As far as the visit itself was concerned, Catherine found both Marty and Mary Johnson to be delightful hosts and their eastern backgrounds easy to relate to. She and Mary did a considerable amount of riding together with the ever present Trig Mansfield hovering nearby.

It was a satisfying visit for Tex as well. It became obvious that Marty was doing a far better job of managing the ranch's affairs, and this impression was confirmed by a lengthy discussion with Curley. Tex met Irish and Frisco, approved Curley's decision to hire both men, and got reacquainted with Wes and Bud. In addition, he found time to visit Henry Henderson and Bo Franklin at the Double H and had an especially enjoyable talk with Doctor James Conklin. Conklin was recovering from a serious illness, and Tex's visit proved to be a strong tonic for the kindly gentleman.

The highlight of the trip, however, was when Tex took Paul on a three day fishing trip deep into the surrounding countryside. This had been Slim's plan a year earlier, and Tex was determined to follow through on this desire in memory of Slim. He invited Catherine to come along, but she declined, instinctively knowing that this should be a men-only adventure and that Tex and Paul needed this time together.

This arrangement, however, created a difficult and painful dilemma for one Trig Mansfield. He could not be in two locations at the same time, and now Bronc's absence was acutely felt—both from a physical and a mental standpoint. Trig approached Tex and voiced his concern.

"You and Apache goin' on this here fishin' trip and Catherine stayin' behind gives me a problem," he complained. "If'n Bronc were here, we could split up and cover all of you. But he ain't, and I can't be in two places to once. I don't know what to do."

Tex grinned and slapped his friend on the back.

"Trig, me and Apache gotta do this by ourselves. 'Tain't likely any trouble will come up here at the MJ, but I would feel a heap better if'n I knew you were close by Catherine. Me and Apache can take care of ourselves. You see to it that my bride don't get into any kind of trouble."

Trig reluctantly agreed but was very happy when Tex and Paul returned three days later, and all his charges were now in one location again.

The three week vacation visit came to an end, the visitors escorted Slim's coffin and headstone to Canyon City, the train connections were met on schedule, and the return trip to the railhead, south of the Rambling R, was uneventful. The travelers were met by Red Rollins in the ranch wagon and an escort of six Rambling R men, led by Blackie Smith. Blackie and his men brought along horses for Tex, Trig, and Paul, while Catherine sat with Red on the wagon seat.

As soon as the group reached the ranch, Slim's coffin was lowered into the prepared grave site as the entire complement of Rambling R men, Maria, and Antonio silently watched under an appropriately dark sky. Some additional tears were shed and not exclusively by Maria and Catherine.

The Reverend Walter Price had conducted a memorial service for Slim in the Community Church prior to the avenging expedition trip to Idaho the previous year. Tex thus decided that any additional ceremony was neither desirable nor necessary and that a simple announcement regarding the burial would be made in the next issue of the Cravenville Clarion. Catherine agreed with his decision as did Maria. Both women were especially pleased to have Slim back where he belonged—on his beloved Rambling R Ranch.

****

As soon as they returned from Idaho, Tex and Catherine found themselves totally immersed in the affairs of the ranch, especially since Lefty
and his trail crew were soon convoying another herd of cattle to San Carlos.

As soon as Lefty and his men returned from San Carlos, the massive
drive to the rail head was made, and then it was time for the fall roundup,
Tex deciding it was far easier and economical to do this after the big drive
than before. Catherine continued to be amazed at the never ending round of
activity that was inherent in the life of the ranch.

"There seems to be something going on all the time," she commented to
Tex one afternoon as they worked in the den.

"Well, it has been a busy year," admitted Tex. "All these drives to San
Carlos have kept us jumpin'. The money shore comes in handy, and we've
begun to cut the size of our own herd down to where I want it to be, but it
shore eats up a lot of time and manpower to make the drives. It's time to bid
on a new contract, and I ain't shore just what to do."

"I saw that, too," said Catherine. "Darling, they want us to bid on about
2,000 head. Would it be possible to increase the size of each drive and make
fewer drives?"

"Yeah, that's a good thought, honey," mused Tex. "It really wouldn't
take any more men to handle a bigger herd. If'n we could drive 500 head
once every three months, it shore would make things easier around here. I
reckon that's what we'll do. We'll bid it thataway and see what happens."

"What if they reject the bid?" asked a concerned Catherine. "Won't that
hurt us financially?"

"It won't help none, that's for shore," replied Tex thoughtfully. "But
remember, this is extry business we didn't useta have. I'll shave the price a
dollar a head, and I'll bet they jump at it. Asides, we saved them a heap of
dollars this year and got rid of a bad apple they had on the reservation to
boot. On second thought, I'll remind them of them facts and not shave the
price. Let's put that letter together and get the bid in the mail. I can always
shave the price a year from now if'n I have to."

✶✶✶✶✶✶✶✶✶✶✶✶

The remainder of the year flew by rapidly. Tex and Catherine were pleased
to have the contract with San Carlos renewed with deliveries scheduled for
the following February, May, August, and November. Lefty and his crew
made the sixth and final drive to San Carlos. His catch basin idea had proved
to be helpful, especially in July and September, as had the inclusion of water barrels on each trip. Both Tex and Lefty were pleased with these results

from his innovations, and Tex rewarded his trail boss with a substantial raise in pay. In addition, Tex decided to share the ranch's prosperity with all his men and gave each man a month's pay as a Christmas bonus. Also there was an exchange of small gifts among all the residents of the main ranch house, Catherine almost forgetting to tell Lefty about this new custom. The year 1896 thus passed into history on a warm and happy note despite the tragedy it had contained.

✳✳✳✳✳✳✳✳✳✳✳✳

The new year began on a high note as far as Catherine was concerned. During the middle of January, two letters were received from Theresa, one of them addressed to Paul. Putting the latter aside with a smile, Catherine opened the second letter, and the smile expanded to a big grin as she read the contents.

"Darling, Theresa says she has completed her training period with father and has been promoted to manager at the store. Isn't that exciting!"

"Shore is," agreed Tex. "Is she still livin' at home?"

"No, she's found an apartment and moved in right after the first of the year," replied Catherine. "Tex, my little sister has really grown up in the past year. I'm so happy for her."

Catherine continued to read and grunted in disappointment. "Theresa says her new responsibilities will prevent her from visiting us again this year. She says she wants to devote all her time and energy to proving to father she can do the job. I can't blame her for that, even though I would love to see her again."

"Sorta sounds like what her big sister is doin' right here on the Rambling R," Tex reminded Catherine. "You shore have been a big help to me, honey. If'n Theresa can do the same for yore father, he won't regret givin' her this chance."

"Thank you for those kind words, Mr. Riley," murmured a pleased Catherine. "I must admit this past year has been a real education for me. They don't cover matters like this in books, you know."

Catherine paused and couldn't prevent a tear from sliding down her cheek.

"Bronc told me once that this real world was something Ruth couldn't teach Paul either. He said book learning was a necessary good start but that it had to be merged with the real world that Paul had to live in. It's strange— I didn't understand that about you either when I first met you. Book learn-ing has its place, but so do real life experiences that temper the educational process. You taught me that, my love, but it took me a long time to figure it out. Almost too long, as a matter of fact."

"But you did, you came back, and now you're here for good," Tex reminded her.

Catherine rose from her chair, took two quick steps, sat down on his lap, cupped his face in her hands, and covered his mouth with hers. Finally she drew back and whispered, "That's the best decision I ever made, my dear. Thank you for understanding me. I love you so much."

They exchanged another kiss before she slid off his lap, went back to her chair, and resumed reading the letter as Tex watched her, his face aglow with happiness.

"Theresa says father is eager to come to Arizona, but mother is holding back. It's not that Lydia doesn't want to come, but the length of the trip seems to be quite daunting for her. I shall have to write her immediately and support father all I can."

"Honey, we don't have much to do today, and what we have can wait," observed Tex. "Why don't you get at that letter, and if'n you get it done, we'll ride into Cravenville tonight for dinner, and we can mail it then."

"Are you proposing a dinner date with your wife?" gaily asked Catherine.

"I shore am," laughed Tex. "It's time we had a night out. Asides, a buggy ride back in the moonlight would be good for both of us."

"That sounds very interesting and suggestive, Mr. Riley," came the coy response. "We'll dine and have a romantic buggy ride back to the ranch. And after that?"

"We'll think of somethin'," Tex assured her.

****

Catherine carefully worded the letter to her mother while Tex fiddled away the rest of the afternoon with a number of routine tasks. They cleaned up, Catherine slipped into a dress, and soon the twosome was on its way to Cravenville, the letter resting in Catherine's lap.

They mailed the letter, had a leisurely dinner in the hotel, wandered around the town on a lengthy walk, and finally enjoyed their moonlit journey back to the ranch. They were so consumed with their own companionship that not once did they spot their uninvited chaperon, who maintained a constant vigil but at a discreet distance. Bronc Evans must have smiled his approval and satisfaction.

****

Catherine's letter dutifully arrived in Bowling Green and became the basis for a quiet but intense debate within the Cornell household.

"Harold, I really do want to go to Arizona," Lydia admitted to her husband, "but the magnitude and duration of a trip like that overwhelms me at the moment. I need to get used to this traveling idea of yours. Let's take a couple of short trips at first and let me get acclimated to this new life style before we take on a massive journey to Arizona. That would give Theresa some experience at managing the store in your absence. You'll be away but not so far nor so long that you can't get back in time to help her if she needs it. She is still very young in terms of her managerial experience, Harold, and we don't want anything to happen that would ruin her confidence. After all, neither the ranch, nor Paul, is going anywhere as far as we know. Let's wait on that trip for a little while and get ourselves in shape to really enjoy it."

"Very well, my dear," sighed Harold. "There is a trade convention in New York in June that I would like to attend. We'll make that our first trip, add a few days after the convention for sightseeing, and see how Theresa gets along in the store. A fall trip to Chicago could be next on the agenda. I just hope we aren't making a mistake about not going to Arizona."

"I don't see how a delay can be a mistake, Harold," sighed Lydia, who was very pleased at her husband's response. "I'll write Catherine and tell her what our plans are, and I'm sure she'll understand. If the trips to New York and Chicago work out well, I'm sure I'll be ready for a trip to Arizona, a year from now."

****

Catherine continued to help Paul with his letter writing to Theresa. She was a little uncomfortable in being involved in his private correspondence, but Paul insisted he needed her help because he, too, was a little uncomfortable with the arrangement. Catherine decided to use the opportunity as an educational experience for the boy. While she helped him with his literary mechanics, Catherine also described how romantic feelings were a normal part of the white man's world and how this affected boy and girl relationships—first as friends and sometimes as lovers. She illustrated the latter situation by telling him about her feelings for Tex. Then she brought Theresa back into the picture.

"Theresa loves you as a friend, Paul," she assured the boy. "The two of you haven't known each other long enough yet to become emerged in a deeper relationship, and that's best for both of you. Theresa has many friends back in Ohio, and she should continue to associate with them and live her life there. You have your life here on the Rambling R, and you have many friends, too."

"Yes, but I don't have any girls as friends here," stated Paul in a puzzled voice. "It is fun to know Theresa, though."

"I know," sighed Catherine. "This is something Tex and I are going to have to give some thought to. In the meantime, continue to write to Theresa. It's obvious she loves to hear from you."

Catherine voiced this concern to Tex that night in bed.

"Poor Paul," Catherine murmured. "The only other person his age around here is Ty Matthews. I get the impression that the other children in school didn't associate much with him after what happened and after I left."

"I reckon that's true enough," said Tex thoughtfully. "Slim kept him in school one more year after you went back east and then told him to stay put here. Mebby I did the lad more harm than good when I stood up for him."

"No, I don't think so," said Catherine. "The beatings had to stop, and you stopped them the best way you knew how. It's a very difficult situation, and I just don't have a ready answer. It's almost like we're going to have to do some sort of Holy Experiment right here on the ranch. I wish I had Ruth's faith and knowledge. Maybe there's an obvious answer here, and I can't see it."

"If'n you can't see it, it shore ain't obvious," complained Tex. "We got time, though. He's still only a boy."

"Yes, but he'll be a man before we know it," commented Catherine, still not satisfied with the outcome of their discussion. "Tex, we'll have to give more thought to this. He's such a nice boy. We've got to help him all we can."

****

The remainder of 1897 flew by and was a duplicate of the previous year as far as the ranch activities were concerned. The deliveries to San Carlos were made on schedule, the spring and fall roundups were completed, and the big drive to the railhead was accomplished.

However, toward the end of the year, the Cravenville Clarion contained several articles about the plight of Cuban natives under an oppressive Spanish regime, and a wave of indignation began to sweep across the Cravenville community as well as the entire United States.

Chapter 20

The Cravenville Clarion used a double sized headline to trumpet its message:

U.S.S. MAINE BLOWN UP IN HAVANA HARBOR

The indignation that had consumed the United States about the Cuban problem was now replaced by fury and a demand for vengeance. Despite Spanish claims that the explosion must have been an accident and an offer to provide a public apology if it was not, Congress was in no mood to accept the Spanish point of view and after two months of negotiations and debates finally declared war on Spain. President William McKinley, in the meantime, issued a call for volunteers to augment the nation's tiny standing Army of only 25,000 men and authorized his assistant secretary of the navy, Theodore Roosevelt, to spearhead this effort by recruiting men for a volunteer cavalry regiment. Roosevelt immediately resigned his political position to begin the recruitment. The response was so overwhelming that Congress soon authorized the raising of three cavalry regiments and quickly thereafter increased the strength of each regiment from 780 men to 1,000 men.

While men from every state and territory would eventually be members of this famed and unique fighting force, Roosevelt concentrated his recruiting efforts in the sections of the country he knew best—the west and southwest. He wanted the cowboys and hard riding plainsmen from these areas to be the core of his particular regiment and, therefore, mustering locations were set up in Arizona, New Mexico, Oklahoma, and the Indian Territory. Strangely enough, Roosevelt felt he should not be the commander of his regiment and persuaded the War Department to name Colonel Leonard Wood as its commanding officer while Roosevelt, himself accepted the rank of Lieutenant Colonel, the regiment's second-in-command.

Roosevelt's recruitment efforts, supported by his popular name, soon reached every community in Arizona, and Cravenville was no exception. The war fever ran high and quickly invaded the hearts and minds of the men of the Rambling R.

Tex pulled in the men from his line camps and arranged for a mass meeting in the main room of the ranch house one evening to discuss the situation. All of his men were present as were Catherine, Paul, Maria, and Antonio.

"I can't tell each of you what you should do," he began. "If'n you feel you should answer the call for fightin' men, I will tell you this: All of you will have jobs here when you come back. As for me, I have a ranch to run, and I'm goin' to stay here and do it. I owe Slim that much. But I also know that our Army will need food, as well as guns and ammunition, so it can do what has to be done. The Rambling R grows good beef, and we'll have that beef ready for the Army, if and when it needs it. That's all I'm gonna say, except that whoever leaves will get a full month's pay and my best wishes for a safe return."

"Campaignin' is a young man's game," grunted Lefty, "and I ain't young no more. I'm stayin' and helpin' Tex with the ranch."

"Tex, me and Cheyenne had some tussles with explosives in our younger days," piped up Denver Pike. "I reckon the Army might have some use for what we know. Leastways, I reckon we'd better give 'em a chance to tell us, one way or t'other."

Tex nodded his agreement as a chorus of other voices was heard. Tex held up both hands and got the meeting back under control.

"All right now. You all sleep on it and let me know what you decide to do in the mornin'. I reckon those of you who want to go should be in Cravenville by noon. As soon as I know who you are, Catherine will write checks for each of you to take to town."

The men filed out of the room, Lefty followed his three friends to the bunkhouse to discuss their situation, Maria and Antonio went to their apartment, and the room fell silent as Tex, Catherine, and Paul watched their friends and employees depart, not knowing who, for sure, would be gone on the morrow. Finally Paul broke the silence.

"Tex, Catherine—Ruth told me that the purpose of the Holy Experiment was to bring the white man and the red man together into one society and have them live together in peace. Is that not so?"

"Yes, that *is* true, as best I understand it," replied Catherine slowly. "Darling, is there something bothering you?"

"Well, Sheriff Edwards up in Colorado told me that coming to the Rambling R might give me a chance to be part of a better world than I might have had with Jacob and Ruth. I can't be sure about that, of course; but, because of Slim and you and Tex, I have had a wonderful world to live in—much better than my people have on the San Carlos reservation. My life here on the Rambling R has been very good, and I feel I am part of your world. You have made it so. But if your nation is now my nation, and if I have enjoyed all the good things that go with that, do I not also have some responsibilities that go along with it? If that is true, I must act accordingly. My new nation has been attacked by another nation. Do I not have the responsibility to defend my right to be here—just like the others? Lefty said war must be fought by the young. I am young and must do my share. Tomorrow, I must leave with the others."

Catherine caught her breath, her hands flew to her face, and tears immediately welled up in her eyes. But after a brief moment, she fought them back and watched Tex grab Paul, wrap his arms around the boy, and draw him to his chest.

"You have to do what you think best, son," Tex murmured softly, "I can't argue agin what you just said. I think Catherine wants you," he continued as he released Paul.

Catherine, too, enveloped the boy and stared at Tex, both pride and fear in her eyes. Gently, Paul pushed himself loose from her grasp, turned, and walked upstairs to his room. Tex and Catherine watched him until he disappeared from view, and then Catherine threw herself into Tex's arms as the tears now flowed unchecked. Tex held her for awhile, then guided her out of the house and around to the porch swing. They sat down, and Catherine buried her face in his chest as her gentle sobbing continued.

Catherine finally raised her head. "I'm getting your shirt all wet again," she sniffed. "Tex, I don't want him to go—he shouldn't feel he has to after all that has happened to him. But at the same time, I'm so darn proud of the boy I don't know what to do or say. I never dreamed he would want to do this."

"I never figgered on this, neither," admitted Tex ruefully. "Years ago, I told you that some day he would have to fight his own battles and make his own decisions—that I couldn't be his big brother forever. But this way and at this time? No, I never figgered it thataway. Like you, though, I'm proud of him, too."

"We'll have to pray for his safety every night, darling," declared Catherine as she rose to her feet. She took his hand and led him back to the entrance of the house. "We'll begin that habit tonight," she continued, in a firm voice. "I'll bet Jacob and Ruth will be doing the same thing."

****

Eight men—Woody Meadows, Cheyenne Walters, Denver Pike, Jud Ramsey, Ty Matthews, Cliff Reynolds, Sandy McAllister, and Paul Redstone—gathered in the main room of the ranch house, accepted the checks Catherine provided each and shook hands with Tex and Catherine. The group tramped out of the room and found the Rambling R men congregated on the ranch's courtyard. A general milling around followed as Tex, Catherine, Maria, and Antonio watched from the veranda. Midway during this congregating, Tex motioned to Woody Meadows and met him at the top of the steps.

"Woody, you and the boys will keep an eye on Paul for me, won't you?" Tex muttered hoarsely.

"Shore we will," grinned Woody. "Don't fret none. This war will be over, and we'll all be back afore you know it."

"I shore hope so," sighed Tex as Catherine joined him. He put his arm around her waist, and both waved vigorously as the little troop trotted off in the direction of Cravenville. Lefty and several other men accompanied the volunteers and would bring back their horses.

"I'm glad Ty Matthews is with them," observed Catherine as the group began to disappear from sight. "He and Paul are good friends and about the same age. That should help them both."

"Outside of Denver and Cheyenne, they're all purty young," growled Tex. "Even Woody ain't all that full grown."

"I told Paul he would be getting plenty of letters from us," said Catherine with a wan smile. She poked Tex in the ribs. "I expect you to do your share of that effort, kind sir. It will be important for him to hear from you as well as from me. Besides, I told him he had to practice his penmanship." Catherine couldn't resist a little chuckle. "I'll have to write Theresa as soon as we know where he goes for training. Oh, Tex, we will have such an empty house now!" The tears started to fall again, but Catherine brushed them back and stamped her foot in disgust. "I can be strong, and I will be strong," she muttered to herself. "Tex needs me that way, and so does Paul." She glanced skyward, said a quick prayer of "thank you" and waved briefly in the direction of the little Rambling R cemetery.

****

Tex's assumptions about the Army needing beef proved to be correct when he received a telegram from Jack Keller. Keller proposed to amend their contract by adding 1,600 head and calling for half to be delivered in April and the other half in September.

"Our bid to renew the contract to San Carlos was turned down," Tex reminded Catherine as they discussed Keller's wire. "I cut the price a dollar a head, too, and still we didn't get it. It makes me some suspicious that someone may be pullin' some shenanigans down there ag'in."

"Well, you can't do anything about that now, and you only have your suspicions anyway," retorted Catherine. "Besides, prices have jumped because of the war, and we'll be a lot better off dealing with Mr. Keller."

"Yeah, that's so," agreed Tex. "We'll be better off, but what about them Apaches? It don't seem fair somehow. Well, like you said, we can't do nothin' about it. I'll send a wire to Jack and agree with his proposal. He'll send us the full papers later on."

****

"Paul is in San Antonio, Texas," Catherine announced to Tex as she read the first letter they had received from their son. "He says he has been assigned to L Troop and that his commanding officer is a Captain Allyn Capron. He says Capron is a former Captain of Indian Scouts, is an expert in Indian sign language, and a great hunter. He asked Paul to be a member of his staff!" Catherine paused and continued her reading.

"Paul says the newspapers are calling his regiment "The Rough Riders," and he has seen Colonel Wood and Colonel Roosevelt from a distance." Catherine paused again.

"Listen to this, Tex," said an excited Catherine. "He says he feels right at home. Not only does his troop include a lot of cowboys, but they also have a Pawnee as well as some Cherokees, Chickasaws, Choctaws, and Creeks." Again came a pause. "Jud and Sandy are in his troop, and Woody, Cliff, and Ty are in the troop next to his. He doesn't know where Denver and Cheyenne went to."

Catherine continued to read and then groaned. "He says he's had some target practice. Oh, Tex, I wonder if this is what he should be doing. Ruth must be turning over in her grave."

"Bronc told me he tried to get Apache to do some shootin' on their campin' trips," replied Tex. "He said Apache weren't half bad with a rifle but that he didn't like a Colt at all. That ain't surprisin'—a rifle is some easier to get used to. Honey, he knew he would have to do this when he joined up. But shootin' at a target in one thing; shootin' at a man is somethin' else. I ain't shore how he'll handle that, if'n he has to, after bein' with Ruth as long as he was. What else does he say?"

"He sends us his love, darling. I miss that boy so much, Tex. Whenever he made the trip to San Carlos I was reasonably certain he would come back. I don't have that assurance, now and can only hope and pray."

"I know," sighed Tex. "Hey, we ain't got nothin' that has to be done right off. Let's both of us write him a letter and go into town to mail 'em."

"A splendid idea, Mr. Riley," declared Catherine brightly. "I'll find the paper, you get the pens and ink. I'll send a quick note to Theresa, too."

****

The correspondence between Arizona and Texas continued during the spring until there was a disturbingly long gap in time without a letter from Texas. Catherine was almost frantic with worry when a long awaited letter finally arrived.

Nervously she tore open the envelope and began to read while Tex waited for her to relay some information.

"Paul is in Tampa, Florida," announced Catherine breathlessly. "All three regiments left San Antonio by train on May 29 and took all their horses and mules with them. Huh, that must have been fun for everyone." She paused, gasped, and glanced back to the top of the page.

"This was dated June 6, and Paul says they are going to board ships the next day. That's strange—he says that they are leaving all their horses and mules behind except for a few horses for the officers."

"I don't reckon horses and mules would take kindly to boats any more than they do to train cars," grunted Tex with a wry smile. "I shore found that out on our trip to Idaho."

"Darling, this letter was dated almost two weeks ago! Good Lord, they must be in Cuba by now. Tex, I am so worried. He shouldn't be there!"

Tex pulled Catherine into his arms, held her tight, and gently rocked her, as the tears flowed. His own eyes contained moisture as he knew that the fun and games had now ended, and the real crisis was at hand.

****

Catherine's assumption as to when her son had landed in Cuba was not accurate, however. After the troops embarked on June 7, they remained stationary in Tampa Bay for almost a week for some unknown reason. The crowded conditions on board were not eased by numerous cases of seasickness, but on June 13, the troopships finally got underway and began steaming for Cuba. The convoy bypassed Guantanamo Bay and landed the troops at the tiny port of Daiquiri. The absence of appropriate landing craft made the disembarkation very difficult, and several men were drowned as well as one of the two horses Roosevelt had brought along.

Once the landing was completed, the troops were organized and began the march inland. A few days later they fought their first engagement at Las Guasimas, drove the Spaniards back, and pressed onward. Following this encounter, Colonel Wood was promoted and left his regiment to replace an ailing General Young. Theodore Roosevelt, in turn, was promoted to a full Colonel and assumed command of the Rough Riders.

****

Major General Joseph "Fighting Joe" Wheeler, a former Confederate cavalry leader, put down his field glasses and stared at the obstacle in front of him.

The San Juan Hills protected the approach to Santiago and formed an excellent defensive position. The three main hills—El Caney on the left, El Poso in the middle, and Kettle on the right—were well fortified by the Spanish soldiers. Trenches dug at the crest of all the hills were protected by barbed wire—a familiar obstacle to the men of the west. Moreover, a significant portion of each hill was densely covered with young timber undergrowth, interlaced with thorny vines, or studded with a natural abattis of cacti, palmetto, and brambles. Wheeler knew it was probably against all the rules of modern warfare to attack so strong a position without the aid of heavy artillery, which he did not have. The potential loss in human life made the general pause and call a meeting of his regimental commanders to discuss the situation.

Roosevelt was adamant. A delay in the attack would only give the Spaniards more time to make the positions more difficult to take and would cost even more lives. "If you will let me, I will lead the way!" he cried.

Wheeler slowly nodded his head in agreement and issued his orders. All three hills would be assaulted simultaneously by his Army. Roosevelt and the Rough Riders would lead the attack on the right flank, up Kettle Hill, and be supported by the first and ninth cavalry, the latter a Negro unit commanded by John J. Pershing.

Shortly after noon, on June 1, 1898, Roosevelt rode to the front of his men, flashed his sword, and cried, "Forward! Charge the hill!" The dismounted Rough Riders leaped to their feet, issued a tremendous series of cheers, and followed their commander forward. Within the cheers could be heard the wild "rebel yell" and the cries from American Indians.

Forty yards from the crest of the hill, Roosevelt dismounted and released his wounded horse, Texas. Again he flashed his sword and yelled "Follow me!" The surviving Rough Riders, now sprawled on the ground and behind any kind of cover they could find, again rose to their feet, poured a deadly volley of fire at the entrenched Spaniards, and rushed forward, behind their impetuous leader.

****

The nation's newspapers announced the great victory at the San Juan Hills in resounding fashion and exalted over the bravery and tenacity of the American troops that had made the attack, especially Roosevelt and his Rough Riders. The Cravenville Clarion was no different and spent half of one issue printing the stories it had received from the major newspapers. Far down in the Clarion story, however, as Catherine quickly noticed, it was admitted that the cost of the victory had been high. That night she and Tex prayed more fervently than ever before.

****

Several days went by, and Catherine began to lose some of her concern. She and Tex were working in the den when Maria entered the room.

"Toby Green just delivered a telegram," Maria announced, fear on her face. She handed the envelope to Catherine.

Catherine looked at Tex, also fearful, and tried to tear open the envelope. Her shaking fingers made the task difficult, but she finally succeeded. She glanced at the contents, screamed in agony, dropped the telegram, and fell back in her chair.

Tex bounced out of his own seat, reached her side in an instant, bent down, and picked up the telegram.

It began, "We regret to inform you . . ."

****

The rest of the day was a nightmare for Tex and Catherine as well as for all the residents of the ranch. Sympathetic words were expressed, over and over again, until Lefty shooed all the men out of the house and accompanied them to the bunkhouse. Maria prepared a splendid night meal, but Catherine only picked at her food, and Tex didn't do much better. As dusk turned into nightfall, Catherine took Tex's hand and guided him out to the veranda and around to their swing. She put her head on his shoulder, as soon as they sat down, as his arm cradled her body.

"We didn't have our son very long, did we?" she murmured softly. "Last year I began to get worried about him finding the right girl, and now he won't have to!" She burst into tears and buried her face in his chest.

Tex held her tight, rocked her, and ran his fingers through her long hair. The sobbing began to ebb and finally stopped altogether.

"I'm so sorry mom and dad didn't get a chance to meet Paul," Catherine whispered. "They'll never know what a wonderful boy he was—what a fine grandson he would have been. We had better send a telegram to Theresa to tell her about Paul, and she can tell the folks," Catherine paused, but no more tears fell.

"Darling, it just isn't fair. We didn't have Paul nearly long enough!"

"But we *did* have him," Tex reminded her. "Honey, you gotta remember that—we did have him! He was good to be with and have around us. I reckon we're better, too, for knowin' him. This is what he wanted to do, honey, and we know a heap of others died with him. Those other men had mothers and fathers, too, and a bunch of them musta had wives and sons and daughters to boot. We ain't alone, Catherine, but it shore is hard. Let's take a little walk and tell Slim and Bronc what's happened. They'll want to know."

＊＊＊＊＊＊＊＊＊＊＊

The next three days were very difficult for both Tex and Catherine but especially Catherine. She did her work mechanically and ate little. She refused to shed more tears, however, and made a trip to the little cemetery each day to have a talk with her friend, Bronc Evans.

"Be brave, be brave," she could almost hear him saying.

The third afternoon, as she returned from her visit with Bronc, she saw Red Rollins drive up in the ranch wagon and hurried in his direction, wondering if the mail would contain any more information about Paul. Red saw her coming, waved her on, and pointed to the stack of mail he held in one hand. She ran forward and soon reached his side, partly out of breath.

"There are three letters here that you and Tex need to look at right quick," Red informed her. "I saw Tex down past the corral. I'll get him for you."

Catherine thumbed through the mail and barely could suppress a scream. One stained envelope was addressed in Paul's handwriting.

Tex approached her at a fast gait, grabbed her arm, and guided her up the steps.

"Tex, one letter is from Paul," she gasped as she tried to keep pace with her husband. "Tex, could he still be alive?"

"I dunno, honey," replied Tex as they reached the den. "Sit down in my big chair, and let's see what's goin' on."

Catherine tried to open the letter, but her hands were shaking so much she could not do so. She passed it up to Tex, who was looking over her shoulder. "Open it for me, darling, please. I can't do it," she bowed her head and held it with one hand.

Tex managed to get the envelope open, unfolded the sheet of paper, and could not avoid seeing the two dark stains. He began to read it silently and soon paused. He dropped to his knees, took one of Catherine's hands in his own, and faced his wife.

"Honey, it's dated June 30—the day before the battle. He musta had it on him when he was hit. I'm shore these are blood stains. I'm sorry, but it don't look good for us."

Catherine nodded, pressed forward, and threw her arms around his neck. Her weight pushed him off balance, and the two of them fell to the floor. They laid together, arms entwined, as she softly cried for a few moments. Catherine pulled back, brushed away her tears, and scrambled to her feet as Tex rose with her.

"I'm all right now, Mr. Riley," she assured him as she heaved a deep sigh. "Read the whole letter to me. I won't fall apart again."

It was a relatively short letter. Paul knew that an engagement was likely the next day and wanted them to know his thoughts were with them and about them. He mentioned that Captain Capron had been killed earlier and that Cliff Reynolds had been wounded but that all the rest of the Rambling R men were well as far as he knew. He closed his letter in his usual manner—sending them his love.

"Red said there were three letters that we should see," commented Catherine. "What else came?"

"There is one from Woody Meadows and one . . . is from the War Department," replied Tex carefully. "Which one do you want me to open first?"

"Do Woody's," said Catherine.

Tex did as he was told, began to read, and winced.

"Woody and Ty searched the battlefield after it was over and found Paul," Tex quietly informed her. "He says he'll do what he can to help us with Paul, but I don't know what that means. Woody says Sandy McAllister is shot up real bad and most likely won't make it. Lordy, this damn war is hittin' the Rambling R mighty hard!"

"What does the letter from the War Department say?" inquired Catherine, wearily.

"Just that they have Paul's body and will wait for instructions from us," Tex answered after opening the letter. "I reckon that's what Woody was talkin' about."

Catherine rose from her seat, motioned to Tex to follow her, and strolled out on the veranda and around to the swing. Tex followed her and sat down beside her. She snuggled close to him and let the swing gently move to and fro. A long period of silence ensued.

Catherine heaved a big sigh.

"Darling, the letter said they need some instructions on what to do with Paul's body. Do you have any thoughts about that?"

"I reckon he belongs with Jacob and Ruth," answered Tex slowly, "but I don't cotton to havin' him that far away from us."

"I don't either," agreed Catherine. "Tex, didn't you tell me that Jacob and Ruth had to be buried away from Hawthorne; that the people there didn't want the Redstones in their cemetery?"

"That's what Slim told me," replied Tex. "Seems like one man wanted it thataway, and the rest of the folks up there didn't bother to argue about it."

"Paul will *not* be buried up there!" declared Catherine, firmly. "Darling, if I understand it right, the Holy Experiment was an attempt to bring our two cultures together and in harmony with each other. I look around and see that the Indians are confined to reservations and are virtual wards of our government. That can't be what the Quakers had in mind, and if so, I have to believe that their concept has been a failure. Yet, it was a good idea and should have succeeded.

"Tex, I don't know why it hasn't worked anywhere else, but *we* can make it work here on the Rambling R! Let's have Paul's body brought back here— and we'll get him a headstone, too. We'll let him sleep alongside Slim and Bronc—his white foster father and his white uncle. We'll show the world that here, at least in one spot of this earth, these two cultures have in fact lived together, loved together, and now, in death, will sleep together, forever! I'm sure Jacob and Ruth would want it that way, too."

Epilogue

Catherine's perception that the Holy Experiment seemed to be a failure was essentially correct. Born from a deep feeling of love for fellow humans and a concern for the rights of a diverse culture, it was doomed to failure from the very start.

The Quakers themselves began this process by trying to convert the Indians to their religion and to an agricultural economy. They never stopped to examine the culture they were invading and the nature of the people they were trying to help. The Plains Indian was a horseman—a nomad, warrior, and hunter. His diet consisted primarily of meat, not vegetables. Farming, or gardening, was women's work and beneath his dignity. Even aside from this, the land on the reservations to which the Indians were assigned was virtually untillable. It would have taken a massive influx of federal funds to build the appropriate irrigation systems to support an agricultural effort—something no Congress had any intention of doing.

The Holy Experiment was also the victim of the government's two-headed, incompatible policies. In accordance with President Grant's Peace Policy, the Department of Interior/Bureau of Indian Affairs attempted to find ways to make the Indians self-sufficient and/or mesh in with the white man's society. The military, on the other hand, wanted to exterminate these people. The Indians were caught in the middle and didn't know from one day to the next which government unit was really in charge. John P. Clum discerned this problem immediately and tried to do something about it. Unfortunately, his efforts were undermined by the merchants and business people of Arizona who did not want the Apaches to become self-sufficient because they, in turn, would lose lucrative contracts to supply the Army and the reservation with food and materials.

Eskiminzin, like Jacob and Ruth, thought he was doing the right thing when he left the San Carlos Reservation with his large family and began his own ranch on the banks of the Rio San Pedro. For a time he was very successful—it is said that he had a five thousand dollar line of credit, a huge sum in those days, anywhere in Tucson. But when Geronimo went on one of his many escapades, an angry Tucson mob took out their frustrations on Eskiminzin, killed his animals, and burned his buildings to the ground. A cavalry detachment rescued Eskiminzin and his family but did nothing to prevent the destruction of his property. Eskiminzin returned to the reservation—a bitter and beaten man. Worse than that, he was eventually put in chains and exiled to Florida and Alabama. His old friend, John P. Clum, finally secured Eskiminzin's release, and the elderly chief returned to San Carlos and died soon thereafter.

In 1887 Congress passed the General Allotment (Dawes) Act which was designed to provide the Indians with individual allotments of farm land (80 acres) or grazing land (160 acres). While designed to assimilate the Indians into the white man's society, this act probably was the most destructive legislation ever devised for the welfare of Indians. Here again the government was trying to make farmers out of non-farmers but, even worse, did not understand that a part of the Indians' religion was not to divide the land. The Indians felt that private ownership of land was immoral and, therefore, that tribal property was, in fact, community property.

Nevertheless, under these provisions of the Dawes Act, the government retained title to the land for 25 years, after which the allottee would receive title to the land and become a citizen. Land-hungry whites used the ignorance of the Indians regarding land ownership and weaknesses in the law to quickly relieve the Indians of their land once the leases began to expire. When the Dawes Act was passed, Indian reservations comprised 138 million acres. Forty-seven years later, only 22 years after the first leases expired, these same reservations retained only 48 million acres, mostly eroded, desert, or otherwise useless land. At least 90,000 thousand Indians were now landless.

The Apaches in Arizona did not suffer as badly as many of their brethren did under the Dawes Act, but they had other, similar troubles. Whenever anything of value was discovered on the San Carlos Reservation that might help make the Apaches become self-sufficient, the land containing this value, sooner or later, disappeared from control of the Apache Nation. Today this reservation is only half its original size, and much of this remainder lacks fertile soil and water.

Although Congress had promised to provide schools for the various tribes, they kept this promise, primarily, by letting various church groups establish mission schools on the reservations. Many dedicated teachers like Ruth Tatum made a valiant effort to educate the Indians, but other missionaries seemed to be more interested in converting their charges instead of educating them.

One special effort involved the establishment of the Indian Industrial School at Carlisle, Pennsylvania. Over the years hundreds of frightened and homesick children from the western reservations did attend the school only to find out, after graduation, there were few jobs open to them in the white man's world. Many returned to their reservations, where their educational training was virtually useless and, even worse, most of these graduates were even ridiculed by their own people.

Given this sequence of events, it is little wonder that alcoholism became a major problem on many reservations.

Early in the 20th century a number of reformers began to take a serious look at the conditions of all Indians, and by the 1950's virtually all of the tribes, including the Apaches, had achieved a level of political independence similar to that envisioned by John P. Clum decades earlier. It was a hollow victory at best, however, as by then there was virtually nothing of value left for the white man to steal. Economic independence, therefore, had not kept pace with the improvements in the political environment.

Late in this same century a new phenomenon appeared on the scene as an answer to the economic issue. It would be ironic if casino gambling on Indian reservations becomes the mechanism by which the Quakers notion of a Holy Experiment finally becomes a reality after all these years.

THE END